Praise for Bradley Beaulieu

'Çeda and Emre share a relationship seldom explored in fantasy, one that will be tried to the utmost as similar ideals provoke them to explore different paths. Wise readers will hop on this train now, as the journey promises to be breathtaking'   Robin Hobb, bestselling author of *Fool's Assassin*

'I am impressed . . . An exceedingly inventive story in a lushly realized dark setting that is not your uncle's Medieval Europe. I'll be looking forward to the next installment'   Glen Cook, author of *The Black Company*

'Beaulieu has crafted a rich, fascinating world, filled it with compelling characters, and blended them into an epic tale that grabbed my attention on the first page and refused to let go. I look forward to more stories of Sharakhai'   D.B. Jackson, author of the *Thieftaker Chronicles*

'Sumptuous and incredibly entertaining, Beaulieu has created memorable characters in a richly imagined world'
Michael J. Sullivan, author of *The Riyria Chronicles*

'Beaulieu's new fantasy epic is filled with memorable characters, enticing mysteries, and a world so rich in sensory detail that you can feel the desert breeze in your hair as you read'   C.S. Friedman, author of *Dreamwalker*

'A memorable heroine, a poetically told tale of revenge, and superb world-building make *Twelve Kings in Sharakhai* a splendid read'
John Marco, author of *The Eyes of God*

'*Twelve Kings in Sharakhai* isn't the same as the last epic fantasy you read. Like the desert sands of Sharakhai, this first volume of Beaulieu's new series is a constantly shifting narrative of betrayal and friendship, loyalty and vengeance. Leave the farm boys to their chickens and the scullions to their pots, because Çeda's bringing a knife to this fight. It's vivid and diverse, full of complex relationships, eye-opening magic, and world building for this new age of fantasy that's brok⸻   Dribble of Ink

By Bradley Beaulieu from Gollancz

THE SONG OF THE SHATTERED SANDS

Twelve Kings
Blood Upon the Sand
A Veil of Spears
Beneath the Twisted Trees
When Jackals Storm the Walls

Novellas:
Of Sand and Malice Made

WHEN JACKALS STORM THE WALLS

BRADLEY BEAULIEU

Book Five of
The Song of the Shattered Sands

GOLLANCZ

LONDON

First published in Great Britain in 2020 by Gollancz
an imprint of The Orion Publishing Group Ltd
Carmelite House, 50 Victoria Embankment
London EC4Y 0DZ

An Hachette UK Company

1 3 5 7 9 10 8 6 4 2

Copyright © Bradley Beaulieu 2020

A CIP catalogue record for this book is
available from the British Library.

ISBN (Trade Paperback) 978 1 473 22363 9
ISBN (eBook) 978 1 473 22365 3

Printed in Great Britain by Clays Ltd, Elcograf S.p.A.

www.gollancz.co.uk

The Story so Far

The Song of the Shattered Sands is a vast and complex tale. I consider that a good thing, and if you're reading this, you likely do too, but it can present a problem. It's easy to forget what happened in the earlier volumes. I do my best to catch readers up with little reminders along the way, but even so, I recognize the need for a refresher.

It is with this in mind that I provide the following synopses.

As always, thank you for joining me in this grand tale. I hope you enjoy your return to the Great Shangazi.

—Bradley P. Beaulieu

* * *

The Song of the Shattered Sands

The Song of the Shattered Sands is an epic fantasy series in the vein of *One Thousand and One Nights*. The story centers on Çeda, a young woman who lives in the slums of the great desert city of Sharakhai and fights in the pits for money. In the eyes of the city's wealthy, she is nothing. She is one step above slavery, a fate that constantly nips at her heels. Through clues in a book left to her by her mother, Çeda realizes she is one of the thirteenth tribe, a legendary group of nomads who were nearly eradicated by the Twelve Kings of Sharakhai four hundred years before. In the decades that followed those dark days, Sharakhai became the single, unquestioned power in the desert. In more recent years, however, the city's iron grip has weakened.

The asirim, strange and powerful creatures of the desert, once members of the thirteenth tribe, have always protected Sharakhai, but they have become fewer, their power enfeebled. Sensing weakness, the kingdoms bordering the Great Shangazi close in like jackals, hoping to snatch Sharakhai, a jewel they've long coveted. But it may be the wandering people of the desert, insulted by the very presence of Sharakhai, who prove more of a threat.

After a grand bargain with the gods of the desert, the thirteenth tribe were betrayed by the Twelve Kings of Sharakhai and transformed into the cursed creatures they are now. Fearing retribution, the Kings sent the asirim to hunt their own kinsmen, to kill every man, woman, and child who had blood of the thirteenth tribe running through their veins. The asirim wept, but they had no choice. They were bound as surely as the sun shines on the desert. Çeda's book is one of the last remaining clues to their secret history.

Twelve Kings in Sharakhai

Çeda uncovers secret poems hidden in a book left to her by her mother. Through clues in the poems, she learns more about Beht Ihman, the fateful night when the people of the thirteenth tribe were enslaved and turned into the asirim. She also learns that she, herself, is a descendant of the thirteenth tribe, which gives her a clue to why her mother was in Sharakhai. She later discovers, to her shock and revulsion, that she may be the daughter of one of the Kings, and that this too was part of her mother's plan.

Refusing to let the mystery go unresolved, Çeda goes into the desert to the blooming fields, where the adichara trees shelter the asirim when they sleep. The Kings are immune to the adichara's poison, and their children are resistant. To all others the poison is deadly. To prove to herself once and for all that she is the daughter of one of the Kings, Çeda poisons herself and is later brought to the house of the Blade Maidens, where the warrior-daughters of the Kings live and train. There, with the help of an ally to the thirteenth tribe, Çeda survives and is allowed to train as a Blade Maiden.

As she recuperates, Çeda investigates the clues left in her mother's book. Her mother died trying to unlock the secrets of a fabled poem that promises to show Çeda the keys to the Kings' power and the ways they can be defeated.

Meanwhile, the Moonless Host, a resistance group made up of *scarabs* who hope to end the reign of the Twelve Kings, hatch a plan to break into the palace of King Külaşan, the Wandering King. Hidden in its depths is his son Hamzakiir, a blood mage and a man the Moonless Host hopes to use for their own purposes. It won't be so simple, however. The Kings stand ready to stop them, and their resources are vast.

There are also Ramahd Amansir, a lord from the neighboring kingdom of Qaimir, and Princess Meryam, who travels with him. They have different plans for Hamzakiir. Ramahd came to Sharakhai in hopes of gaining revenge for the loss of his wife and child at the hands of Macide, the leader of the Moonless Host. He stumbles across Çeda in the fighting pits, and the two of them come to know one another.

They might even have become involved romantically, but Çeda has more to worry about than love, and Meryam has other plans for Ramahd. Meryam knows that allowing Hamzakiir to fall into the hands of the Moonless Host would be terrible for her cause, so she makes plans to steal Hamzakiir from under their very noses.

At the end of the book, Çeda manages to unlock the first of the poem's riddles. Along with her best friend, Emre—who against Çeda's wishes has joined the ranks of the Moonless Host—she infiltrates King Külaşan's desert palace and kills him. Emre and the Moonless Host manage to raise Hamzakiir from his near-dead state and steal him away from the palace. Before they can reach safety, however, Meryam and Ramahd intercept them and take Hamzakiir.

Of Sand and Malice Made

Roughly five years before the events depicted in *Twelve Kings in Sharakhai*, Çeda is the youngest pit fighter in the history of Sharakhai. She's made her name in the arena as the fearsome White Wolf. None but her closest friends and allies know her true identity, but that changes when she crosses the path of Hidi and Makuo, twin demigods who were summoned by a vengeful woman named Kesaea.

Kesaea wishes to bring about the downfall of her own sister, who has taken Kesaea's place as the favored plaything of Rümayesh, one of the ehrekh, sadistic creatures forged aeons ago by Goezhen, the god of chaos. The ehrekh are desert dwellers, often hiding from the view of man, but Rümayesh lurks in the dark corners of Sharakhai, toying with and preying on humans. For centuries, Rümayesh has combed the populace of Sharakhai, looking for baubles among them, bright jewels that might interest her for a time. She chooses some few to stand by her side until she tires of them. Others she abducts to examine more closely, leaving them ruined, worn-out husks.

At Kesaea's bidding, the twins manipulate Çeda into meeting Rümayesh in hopes that the ehrekh would become entranced with her and toss Ashwandi aside. To Çeda's horror, it works.

Çeda tries to hide, but Rümayesh is not so easily deterred; the chase makes her covet the vibrant young pit fighter all the more. She uses her many resources to discover Çeda's secret identity. She learns who Çeda holds dearest. And the more restless Rümayesh is, the more violent she becomes. But the danger grows infinitely worse when Rümayesh turns her attention to Çeda's friends. Çeda is horrified that the people she loves have been placed in harm's way. She's seen firsthand the blood and suffering left in Rümayesh's wake.

Çeda is captured but manages to escape, and in so doing delivers Rümayesh into the hands of Hidi and Makuo, who torture her endlessly. But the ehrekh is still able to reach out to Çeda, forcing her to experience the torture as well. Knowing that she can never be free unless she liberates Rümayesh from the godling twins, Çeda recruits one of her childhood friends, a gifted young thief named Brama, to aid her in her quest. With Brama's help, Çeda steals into Rümayesh's hidden desert fortress in hopes of freeing her through the use of a sacred ritual.

Çeda succeeds, but at the cost of Brama becoming enslaved instead of her. Knowing she can't leave Brama to the cruelties of an ehrekh, Çeda searches for and finds a different, more ancient ritual that prepares a magical gemstone, a sapphire, to capture Rümayesh. In a climactic battle, Çeda manages to trap Rümayesh within the stone and free Brama. In the end, Çeda knows that Brama is perhaps the one person who would be most careful with the sapphire, and so leaves it with him.

With Blood Upon the Sand

Months after the events depicted in *Twelve Kings in Sharakhai*, Çeda has become a Blade Maiden, an elite warrior in service to the Kings of Sharakhai. She's learning their secrets even as they send her on covert missions to further their rule. She's already uncovered the dark history of the asirim, but it's only when she bonds with them that she feels their pain as her own. They hunger for release, they demand it, but their chains were forged by the gods themselves and are proving unbreakable.

Çeda could become the champion the enslaved asirim have been waiting for, but the need to tread carefully has never been greater. The Kings, eager to avenge the death of King Külaşan, scour the city for members of the Moonless Host. Emre and his new allies in the Host, meanwhile, lay plans to take advantage of the unrest caused by Yusam's death. They hope to strike a major blow against the Kings and their gods-given powers.

Hamzakiir escaped Queen Meryam and Ramahd and insinuated himself into the ranks of the Moonless Host. Through manipulation and sometimes force, he is slowly taking the reins of power from Macide, leader of the Moonless Host, and Macide's father, Ishaq. Hamzakiir's plan for Sharakhai is bold. The many scarabs of the Moonless Host, who itch for progress, buy into Hamzakiir's plans, which are nearly upended when Davud, a young collegia scholar, is captured along with many others from his graduating class. Hamzakiir's spells trigger Davud's awakening as a blood mage, nearly stopping Hamzakiir and his dark agenda. Davud fails, however, and burns his fellow classmate, Anila, in a cold fire, almost killing her.

The Moonless Host fractures in two, many following Hamzakiir, others following Macide, who is revealed to be Çeda's uncle. In a devastating betrayal, Hamzakiir kills many of the old guard in the Moonless Host, giving him near-complete control of the group. With them at his beck and call, he attacks Sharakhai, planning to take for himself the fabled elixirs that grant the Kings long life.

Emre and Macide, however, want the elixirs destroyed so that neither Hamzakiir nor the Kings can have them. Meryam, recognizing that depriving Hamzakiir and the Kings of their ability to heal themselves will only help her cause, commands Ramahd to help Emre.

An attack on Sharakhai unfolds, where the abducted collegia students, now grotesque monsters, are used to clear the way to King's Harbor. As the battle rages, both Hamzakiir and his faction, and Macide and his, infiltrate the palaces in search of the caches where the fabled elixirs are stored. Two of the three primary caches are destroyed. The third falls into Hamzakiir's hands.

Çeda, meanwhile, caught up in the battle in the harbor, tries to kill Cahil the Confessor King and King Mesut. The Kings are not so easily destroyed, however. They discover Çeda's purpose and turn the tables, nearly killing her. Sehid-Alaz, the King of the Thirteenth Tribe, is so fearful Çeda will be killed that he manages to throw off the shackles of his curse and protects her long enough for her to free the wights, the trapped souls of the asirim, from King Mesut's legendary bracelet. Once free, the wights come for their revenge and kill King Mesut.

Çeda, having been revealed as a traitor to the Kings' cause, flees into the desert.

A Veil of Spears

The Night of Endless Swords was a bloody battle that nearly saw Sharakhai's destruction. The Kings know they won a narrow victory that night, and since then, their elite Blade Maidens and the soldiers of the Silver Spears have been pressing relentlessly on the Moonless Host. Hundreds have been murdered or given to Cahil the Confessor King for questioning. Knowing that to stay would be to risk destruction at the hands of the Kings, the scarabs of the Moonless Host flee the city.

Çeda is captured by Onur, the King of Sloth. Onur has returned to the desert and is raising an army of his own to challenge the other Kings' right to rule. After escaping Onur, Çeda finds the scattered remnants of the Moonless Host, who are now calling themselves the thirteenth tribe. Her people are gathering once more, but the nascent tribe is caught in a struggle between Onur's growing influence and the considerable might of the Kings who, with Sharakhai now firmly back under their rule, are turning their attention to the desert once more.

In Sharakhai, meanwhile, a deadly game is being played. Davud and Anila are being kept by Sukru the Reaping King. They're being groomed for their powers, Davud as a budding blood mage, Anila as a rare necromancer. A mysterious mage known as the Sparrow, however, is trying to lure Davud away from King Sukru for his own dark purposes. As Davud and Anila both grow in power, they fight for their very lives against the machinations of the Sparrow.

In the desert, Emre comes into his own as a prominent member of the thirteenth tribe. More are looking to him as a leader, including Macide. Emre helps to navigate the tribe toward safety, but the threat of King Onur grows by the day. Even with Emre's help in securing allies among the other tribes, it may not be enough. Things grow worse when the Kings of Sharakhai sail to the desert to confront Onur. They hatch a deal with him: crush the thirteenth tribe first, and they can deal with one another later.

Çeda knows that the thirteenth tribe will be destroyed unless she can free the powerful asirim from their bondage. She vows to lift the curse the gods placed on them, and soon returns to Sharakhai and its deadly blooming fields to do just that.

The Kings have not been idle, however. Nor are they fools. They know the asirim are the key to maintaining power. Making matters worse, their greatest tactician, the King of Swords himself, has made it his personal mission to bring Çeda to justice for her many crimes. Queen Meryam has also decided to throw in her lot with the Kings. She's even managed to steal away the sapphire that contains the soul of the ehrekh, Rümayesh.

The night before the final confrontation, Çeda manages to liberate the wights still trapped inside Mesut's bracelet. The tribes and the Kings clash, and as the battle unfolds, Ramahd, Emre, and the young thief, Brama, stage an ingenious attack on Queen Meryam's ship. There, they free Rümayesh, adding a powerful ally to their fight.

Near the end of the battle, it is revealed that Queen Meryam has long been dominating the mind of the blood mage, Hamzakiir. She has designs on more than just Macide or the Moonless Host. She wants the city for herself. In order to secure it, she forces Hamzakiir to take on the guise of Kiral the King of Kings. Kiral himself, meanwhile, is sent into the battle and is killed.

In the battle's closing moments, Çeda is nearly killed by the fearsome ehrekh, Guhldrathen. Guhldrathen, however, is swept up by Rümayesh and destroyed. This frees the path for Çeda to kill King Onur, which she does in single combat.

Beneath the Twisted Trees

Sharakhai was sorely weakened after the Battle of Blackspear, the intense conflict that saw King Onur die and the thirteenth tribe narrowly escape the royal navy and the Sharakhani Kings. Sensing that Sharakhai is ripe for conquest, the kingdoms of Malasan and Mirea sail hard across the Shangazi Desert, each planning to take the city for their own.

Unbeknownst to all, Queen Meryam sent Kiral, King of Kings, to die in the Battle of Blackspear, while putting Hamzakiir, disguised with her blood magic, in his place. To further secure her power, she forces Hamzakiir, in his guise as Kiral, to marry her, thus cementing her place as a queen of Sharakhai. Their nuptials are interrupted by the goddess, Yerinde, who demands that the Kings kill Nalamae, her sister goddess, who has remained in the shadows for centuries but who Yerinde fears may interfere with her plans. Knowing Yerinde could undo all they've worked for, the Kings agree and a hunt for Nalamae begins.

Çeda, meanwhile, searches for a way to liberate the asirim from the curse placed on them by the desert gods. She frees a family of asirim that, against all odds, has remained together since Beht Ihman four centuries earlier. Çeda discovers a way for the asirim to bond with her handpicked warriors, the Shieldwives, which helps them to resist their compulsion to obey the Kings.

Using a legendary bird known as a sickletail, the Kings find Çeda in the desert and attack, but she and those with her are saved when Nalamae suddenly returns. While escaping, they take a lone prisoner, none other than Husamettín, King of Swords. Nalamae was wounded in the battle, however, and is in desperate need of a safe haven, so Çeda sends her to a valley where the bulk of the thirteenth tribe hides.

Çeda, meanwhile, along with Sümeya, Melis, and the asirim, sneak into Sharakhai and corner her former sister in the Blade Maidens, the famed Kameyl. Çeda explains to Kameyl the Kings' betrayal of the thirteenth tribe on Beht Ihman, the enslavement of the asirim, their deceptions to hide their crimes. Kameyl is unconvinced until Çeda tricks Husamettín into revealing many of his long-held secrets. Realizing it's all true, Kameyl helps Çeda, Sümeya, and Melis to steal into Sharakhai's uppermost palace, Eventide, and free Sehid-Alaz, King of the thirteenth tribe, from imprisonment.

In the process, they're nearly captured, but King Ihsan has been working behind the scenes to forestall the gods' plans. After reading a prophetic entry in the Blue Journals—of Çeda's freeing Sehid-Alaz—Ihsan helps her and the others to escape but is captured by King Emir of Malasan, who has begun his invasion of Sharakhai. King Emir's father, Surrahdi the Mad King, was long thought dead but is revealed when Ihsan arrives in the Malasani war camp. Surrahdi created hundreds of golems for the assault on Sharakhai but was driven mad in the process. On seeing Ihsan, Surrahdi cuts out Ihsan's tongue, robbing him of his magical voice and its power to command others.

Emre has been traveling to the southern tribes on a mission for Macide. He hopes to form an alliance among all thirteen tribes to act as a unified force not only against Sharakhai, but Mirea and Malasan as well. Emre hopes to secure peace with the Malasani King, but when King Emir makes it clear that any accord will entail the desert tribes' bowing to the will of Malasan, Emre is certain he's failed.

Queen Meryam, forced to deal directly with the looming threat of Mirea, goes with Sharakhai's navy and confronts them on the sand. The Mireans have managed to entice an ehrekh, Rümayesh, to work with them. Rümayesh has a servant, Brama, who eventually sympathizes with the Mireans when a plague is introduced into their ranks. The plague is voracious, but Brama finds a way to nullify it with the help of Rümayesh, thus saving a good portion of the Mirean fleet.

After her near capture in Eventide, Çeda returns to the desert and works to free King Sehid-Alaz, finally succeeding when she realizes that Husamettín's own sword, Night's Kiss, can be used to kill and rejuvenate. Sehid-Alaz, his chains broken at last, frees the rest of the asirim. This momentous event occurs just as Meryam is throwing the might of Sharakhai's royal navy against the weakened Mirean fleet. Things look to be going Meryam's way, but when the asirim all flee at Sehid-Alaz's bidding, the tide turns and the royal navy is forced to retreat toward Sharakhai. The Mirean fleet, badly weakened, remains to lick its wounds in the desert.

During the battle, Brama learns that Rümayesh has been trying to steal his soul. He stops her using a powerful artifact, the bone of Raamajit the Exalted, but Rümayesh manages to save herself by fusing her soul to Brama's. Brama and Rümayesh are now inextricably linked, their souls sharing the same scarred body.

King Emir, meanwhile, renews his assault on Sharakhai using the Malasani golems, an unstoppable force. But Ihsan, even though imprisoned and mute, is not powerless. He's learned the reason for Surrahdi's madness: the golems themselves, each of which required a splinter of Surrahdi's soul, weigh on him, putting him on the very brink of insanity. Ihsan, using his gift of manipulation, convinces Haddad, a woman Surrahdi loves and respects, to force Surrahdi to face his misdeeds. Surrahdi becomes distraught and slips entirely into madness. The golems do too, and the entire Malasani assault is thrown into chaos.

Davud the blood mage, Anila the necromancer, and Lord Ramahd Amansir of Qaimir are all in similar circumstances: they're on the run from the powers of the city. They join forces for mutual protection but are split up when King Sukru captures Anila and takes her back to his palace in the House of Kings. King Sukru wants the return of his brother, the blood magi known as the Sparrow, and he hopes Anila can help him using her power over the dead and the wondrous crystal beneath the city, which acts as a gateway to the farther fields. When her family is threatened, Anila agrees to help, but tricks Sukru in the end and then kills him when her brother is summoned from the dead.

As the battle for Sharakhai reaches a fever pitch, Davud and Ramahd work to free Hamzakiir from Meryam's imprisonment. They manage to do so in grand fashion, breaking the chains Meryam has placed on him and, in the process, revealing Meryam as a traitor to her own throne and to Sharakhai. Meryam, however, has allied with the children of the Sharakhani Kings to start a new order. With them, she overthrows the old power structure and takes a position of leadership among the new.

Never abandoning the quest for Nalamae, King Beşir goes with a sizable force to conquer the thirteenth tribe in their mountain fastness. Çeda kills King Beşir and returns to the fort where she finds Yerinde standing over her wounded sister goddess, Nalamae. Çeda sneaks up on Yerinde and slays her with Night's Kiss, a sword forged by the dark god, Goezhen. Nalamae, having been given a mortal wound by Yerinde, dies moments later.

As the story closes, Emre frees King Ihsan in repayment for his help in saving the city. When Emre returns to the tribe, however, he's intercepted by Hamid, a childhood friend of Emre's and once a rising star in the Moonless Host. Hamid, both jealous of Emre and incensed by his actions, attacks Emre and buries him alive in the sand.

King Ihsan, meanwhile, gets the Blue Journals from Queen Nayyan, planning to read them all to find a path to save Sharakhai.

And in the valley, Çeda plants the acacia seed her mother left for her. The acacia tree begins to grow at an incredible rate. Knowing Nalamae would have been reborn, Çeda vows to find her in her new incarnation—Çeda is determined to learn the plans of the gods and stop them once and for all.

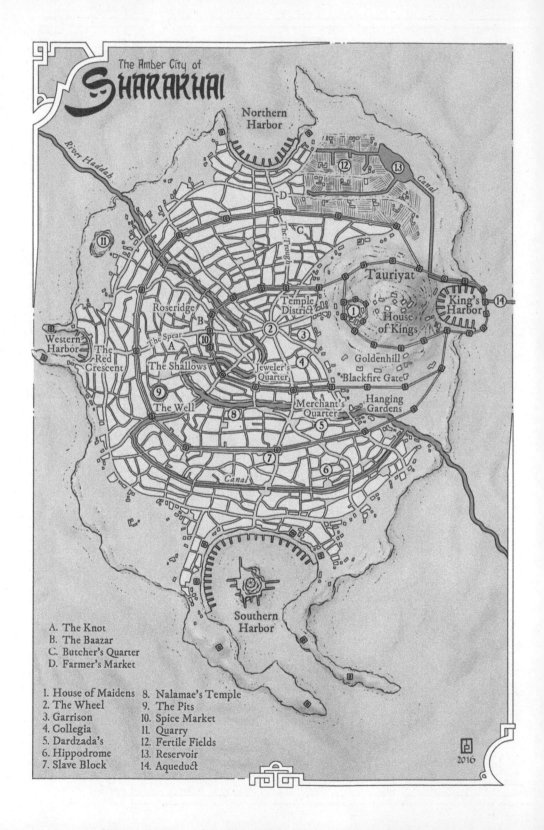

The Amber City of
Sharakhai

Northern Harbor

River Haddah

The Trough

Tauriyat

King's Harbor

Roseridge

Temple District

Western Harbor

The Red Crescent

The Spear

The Shallows

Goldenhill

Blackfire Gate

Jeweler's Quarter

Hanging Gardens

Merchant's Quarter

The Well

Canal

Southern Harbor

A. The Knot
B. The Baazar
C. Butcher's Quarter
D. Farmer's Market

1. House of Maidens
2. The Wheel
3. Garrison
4. Collegia
5. Dardzada's
6. Hippodrome
7. Slave Block
8. Nalamae's Temple
9. The Pits
10. Spice Market
11. Quarry
12. Fertile Fields
13. Reservoir
14. Aqueduct

2016

Prologue

THERE WAS A PARTICULAR VAULT below the Sun Palace that had once belonged to the royal vivisectionist but that Meryam shan Aldouan, queen of two kingdoms, had found convenient for her own purposes. The vault was cool and humid. It had a ramp leading down from the palace proper that could accommodate large, rolling tables for the delivery and removal of corpses, even those as massive as the Malasani golems Meryam had been studying. It was stocked with a hundred instruments for cutting, and sawing, and chiseling, all useful tools for the sorts of operations Meryam had been conducting on the golems since the terrible battle with Malasan three weeks earlier.

As Meryam walked along the easily sloping ramp, braziers lit the passageway and the room ahead in a sunset glow. When she reached the vault itself, an open space the size of a small temple, a broad marble table was revealed, and on it, the latest subject of her experiments, a massive clay golem wearing the face of Surrahdi the Mad King.

The golem was awe-inspiring, as were all the Malasani golems. More importantly, it was impressively pristine, so much so that Meryam was actually starting to believe that the opinion King Yavuz had shared with her a little over an hour ago was true: that the golem, or, more accurately, the crystal heart inside its chest, might provide her the opportunity to rid herself of one of her most powerful enemies, King Emir of Malasan, who had yet to give up his quest for Sharakhai.

On the table's far side stood Yavuz himself, son of the departed Kiral, King of Kings. He waited patiently, studying Meryam's approach over the golem's rounded belly. He wore a rich khalat of white and silver. Pinned to the fabric of his white silk turban was a diamond and pearl broach. He was a tidy man, his dark beard sculpted, his nails impeccably clean. He'd taken his father's throne on the discovery that Kiral had not survived the Battle of Blackspear, as everyone had thought, but had died, a victim of the terrible blood mage, Hamzakiir. Or so Meryam had made them all believe—in truth *she* had killed Kiral; Hamzakiir had merely been a convenient scapegoat.

Kiral's death had been one of many sweeping changes that had unfolded in the past few years. Eight of the original twelve Kings had been taken by the lord of all things. Azad, the first King to die, had fallen to the blade of Ahyanesh, Çedamihn's mother. Çeda herself had assassinated Külaşan, Mesut, Onur, and Beşir. No one was certain how Yusam had died, but signs pointed to a supposed ally of his, King Ihsan, as having done the deed. Sukru had grown overly ambitious and had been murdered by the necromancer, Anila, in some strange scheme to bring his brother back from the dead. With Meryam herself having arranged for Kiral's death, it left only four: Ihsan, Husamettín, Zeheb, and Cahil, all of whom had fled the city, leaving their houses in disarray. The other eight thrones, meanwhile, had been filled by the Kings' sons and daughters—the *lesser* Kings and Queens, as many referred to them. It made for a greatly altered landscape in Sharakhai, but one infinitely more favorable to Meryam and her goal of ruling the city alone.

Across from her, Yavuz motioned to the golem, his pride plain to see. "We found it in the southern harbor, buried beneath the sand."

Ignoring his overly eager look, Meryam inspected the golem with care. She ran her hands over it, felt the grit of the clay, which had bronze-filings worked into it. There were nicks here and there, and one great, gaping hole that went clean through its abdomen—all signs of the pitched battle Malasan had waged for control over the city—but the golem's upper chest, the area Meryam cared about most, was free of wounds.

"It's in surprisingly good condition," she said.

His relief plain, King Yavuz pointed to the golem's chest. "No doubt we'll find the heart intact."

At this, Meryam frowned. "Let's not get ahead of ourselves."

Yavuz's pride, so bright and clear moments ago, dimmed, then went out altogether. *And well it should.* A month before, in hopes of currying her favor, he'd attempted to liberate, on his own, the heart of the only other pristine golem they'd found. He'd bungled the operation badly and cracked the precious artifact.

Meryam, holding the broken pieces in her hands, had barely been able to hold her rage in check. "Why didn't you send word?"

Yavuz might have been Kiral's son, but you wouldn't know it from the way he'd fidgeted and avoided her gaze. "I'd hoped to save you the trouble," he said, like a boy admitting he'd broken his mother's prized vase. "It's still *mostly* intact."

"Mostly intact does me no good." She lifted the broken pieces of the heart. "This is useless to me now."

When the intense battle for the city had ended, Meryam had examined dozens of golems. Formed of a special clay and infused with a fragment of a mortal soul, the Malasani golems had historically been crafted as protectors. Not the ones that had swept like a storm through Sharakhai, though. Those had been violent machines of war, set upon the city by King Emir.

Emir's father, King Surrahdi the Mad, had made them over the course of decades by shearing off splinters of his soul and trapping them in crystals, which were then placed inside the golems' chests. Each golem was autonomous, but Surrahdi had stood among them all, creating a grand, mind-bogglingly complex web. By the end there were a thousand of them, each placing an incremental strain on Surrahdi's delicate sanity.

It was hardly a surprise the golems had gone insane; their madness was an echo of Surrahdi's own. He'd taken a knife to his own throat in the end, but Meryam could still use him. In fact, his being dead only *helped* her. Surrahdi wouldn't be able to fight her for his soul. By the time he was summoned, he would already be beholden to her.

Meryam hoped to use the heart to peer into Surrahdi's mind and learn more of Malasan's secrets, or animate his body and use it to sow chaos on whatever ship had been given the unfortunate duty of bearing it home. She'd taken great care with the rituals but had always fallen short of her goal, and she knew perfectly well why. The golems' hearts had all been broken, cracked, imperfect, leading to imperfect connections to Surrahdi himself.

This time, Meryam vowed, *it will work.*

She regarded the tools laid out on the slab above the golem's head: a variety of hammers made of iron and wood, a few iron spikes, several picks and saws, and a set of gleaming steel chisels of various sizes. She chose a wooden hammer and one of the smaller chisels—she'd learned from experience it took a delicate hand.

Using the chisel's edge, she scored several lines to guide her—indicators of where the golem's heart would be buried—then placed the spike against the skin and tapped just so. A chunk of it splintered away. When Yavuz cleared the debris, she laid the spike, tapped again, and broke more of the clay free. Like this, the two of them continued, Meryam tapping, Yavuz sweeping away the flakes with a horsehair brush, until something new was revealed: a brilliant, chromatic gleam amongst the dullness of the clay. It looked like the tip of a massive diamond, but it wasn't. It was a crystal, its nature and the secrets of its making known only to the Malasani priests.

Meryam slowed her pace, taking all the care of an archeologist liberating a fossil from stone. Well over an hour passed until she had it: a pear-shaped crystal with facets that glittered green, gold, azure, and coral. She could hardly take her eyes from it. It was perfect, and miraculously whole.

"Summon Erol," she said. When King Yavuz paused, Meryam let out her breath slowly. "What is it now?" Meryam would never have spoken in such a brusque way to his father, but Yavuz was not cut from the same cloth as the King of Kings.

Yavuz took a deep breath. "Allow me to take Erol's place."

Meryam gave him a flat stare. "You?"

Yavuz nodded. "Erol is a fine man, and brave"—he waved at the golem between them—"but he fears this. He fears *you*. I saw it in him every time we tried this. I think his fear is as much to blame as the broken crystals." He motioned to the golem's heart in her hands. "Let me try. I have no such fear."

Meryam was surprised at his sudden fit of bravery until she noticed the

redness in his eyes and the way his hands quavered. Yavuz was one of a growing number of royals who'd become disaffected by his lot in life. Only a year
ago, the order of succession was an all-but-meaningless distinction for the
sons and daughters of the Sharakhani Kings; those waiting to sit the thrones
of their fathers had as much hope as any in the last four hundred years,
which was to say none at all. So many frittered their fathers' money away—
on black lotus, on brightwine, on the many other narcotics that flowed into
Sharakhai from the four kingdoms and lands beyond—and Yavuz was one
of the worst offenders.

He was constantly on the lookout for new highs, and what would becoming the focus of her spell be if not a wild rush of emotion and fear that he
could later share with his friends? Who among them, after all, could claim
to have melded minds with the Mad King of Malasan?

Putting a Sharakhani King in danger was nothing to take lightly—it
would create no end of complications if something happened to him. Even
so, Yavuz wasn't wrong. The willingness of the participant was a factor. And
the intact heart might be her last, best chance at using Surrahdi's soul.

Her decision made, Meryam walked around the slab and twisted the
blooding ring on her right hand into position. "Give me your wrist." Her
words echoed in the harshness of the stone-walled room.

Yavuz complied, nostrils flaring as she pierced his skin. She sucked on the
wound, swallowed his blood. Power flowed through her, giving her the same
heady rush as always. She held it in check, a reservoir ready and waiting for
her to call upon.

After smearing the crystal heart with more of his blood, she held it out
for him to take. "Hold it to your chest, near your heart."

He did so, gripping it in both hands like an offering to the gods.

In the air before her, Meryam drew a complex sigil. She immediately felt
a difference from the other attempts—her connection to Yavuz and to the
soul still attached to the crystal was strong, and *through* Yavuz, she felt the
stirrings of Surrahdi's soul. He was drawn toward the land of the living.
Drawn toward his own body, which lay in a distant ship, wrapped in a fune-
real shroud within a wooden coffin. She could feel how cold his lifeless
corpse was, how tight its desiccated frame.

"Come, Surrahdi," Meryam intoned, "I have need of you."

She felt his soul inhabit his dead body, felt his eyes open. He tore away the shroud that confined him, then pushed on the coffin's lid. With a great crack, the lid was rent, the pieces thrown aside. He sat up. Around him lay a dozen more coffins—surely more men and women of royal blood who'd died during the ongoing war between Malasan, Mirea, and Sharakhai.

A dim light from the far side of the ship's hold caught his attention. There, a ladder led up a short set of stairs to a door. Part of Surrahdi wanted to lay back down, to find his final rest, but Meryam's will overwhelmed him, forced him on. On creaking limbs he climbed from his coffin. The ship swayed as he lurched up the stairs. Meryam felt a desire in him to seek out his son, King Emir. She fanned that desire, allowed it to guide his steps toward the rear of the ship, then up another flight of stairs and along a short passage that led to Emir's cabin.

Meryam's heart pounded like a kettledrum on hearing Emir's voice. When it went silent, another voice, too soft to make out clearly, replied. She thought of waiting, of listening, but the chance of being spotted by a crewman was too great.

Months ago both Malasan and Mirea had sent fleets racing across the desert so that they could be the first to take Sharakhai. Meryam had been working with the Kings ever since to stymie them, to push them back beyond the desert's borders. Now, at last, she'd found a way to deal with Malasan. She would force Surrahdi to enter Emir's cabin and kill him, sending Malasan a clear message: that the desert's Amber Jewel was hers, and any attempt to take it would end with her feeding their bones to the Great Mother. When Malasan had fled east with its tail tucked between its legs, she would turn her attention to Mirea, who would buckle in short order. Then, with Sharakhai secure at last, she could focus on her deepest desire: to see Macide Ishaq'ava and every single one of the Moonless Host dead.

Surrahdi drew a ceremonial dagger from a sheath on his golden belt. He trudged closer to the intricately carved cabin door. His leaden steps thudded against the wooden planks, so much so that Meryam feared he'd be discovered, but the volume at which Emir was recounting the invasion of Sharakhai to the cabin's mysterious second occupant was loud enough that it masked the Mad King's approach.

Surrahdi gripped the door's curving brass handle. The latch clicked. The door swung wide, revealing an opulent cabin. King Emir sat in a padded chair with a small table nearby, bathed in the glow of the hanging lanterns. Across the table from him was an empty seat. Emir turned toward the opening door—he might have thought it was the ship's captain coming in unannounced, or a crewman—but soon recognition dawned and his expression became one of abject terror.

"Father?"

Knowing the time was ripe, Meryam filled the Mad King with purpose. Knife raised, Surrahdi launched himself at his defenseless son, but managed only one vicious swipe of the ceremonial blade before a form sped in from the right and powered his frail form against the hull. Surrahdi's head crashed hard against it. Something glinted below his vision while a terrible pain, bright as a forge fire, exploded over his heart. Staring down, he saw a long steel hairpin inexplicably sticking out of his chest.

King Yavuz, who should have been nothing more than a conduit with no free will of his own, recoiled in surprise, fear, and pain. His hands grasped ineffectually at his chest—he clearly thought the pin was sticking out of his *own* chest.

Suddenly a woman wearing an orange silk dress cut in the angular Mirean style stepped into Surrahdi's field of vision. Her appearance was of a woman who'd seen some fifty summers, but Meryam knew she'd seen many, many more. It was Queen Alansal, a woman centuries older than she looked who'd spent her entire life collecting artifacts like the miraculous hairpin.

When she took its mate, the second pin, from the half-unfurled bun atop her head, her raven black hair flowed down over her delicate shoulders. "Did I not tell you?" Queen Alansal said in halting Malasani. "Soon enough, I said, she will come."

Understanding dawned on King Emir as he stared into Surrahdi's eyes. "Queen *Meryam* is behind this?"

Alansal twirled the second pin in her fingers with absent ease. "Undoubtedly."

Meryam commanded Surrahdi to attack, but he didn't move so much as a muscle. Worse, the spell that had seized Surrahdi had Yavuz and Meryam in its grip as well. It was as if the pin had pierced all three of their souls, binding them together.

Emir's eyes flitted nervously between the animated corpse of his own father and Queen Alansal. "Is she still there?"

"Yes." Alansal gave a pleasant smile. "She's trapped."

Indeed, Meryam was trying everything to free herself, but there was nothing she could do. For the first time in a long while, she was fully and unwillingly in the grip of someone else's power.

She did the only thing she could. It was hardly ideal, but it was precisely the reason she used men like Erol and Yavuz, and Ramahd before them, as her conduits. They protected her. All she need do was eliminate the conduit and she would be freed, steel pin or no.

Using the power from Yavuz's own blood, she pressed down on him, smothering him. He fought her when he realized what was happening, but he was like a toddler trying to fend off a lioness. It didn't take long for her to still his heart. Still his breath. She felt the life leaving him and her own will returning.

Alansal, who had just pulled a honey-colored gemstone from inside her dress, turned suddenly toward Surrahdi, her eyes wide as a frightened oryx. She knew. She lifted her right arm and brought the steel pin down against Surrahdi's skull in a movement so fast it blurred. Meryam felt the crunch of bone. Felt the thump of Alansal's fist against her forehead. Pain exploded as the vision of the distant cabin went dark.

Meryam woke lying on the cold stone floor of the vault below the Sun Palace with a headache so intense she was certain Alansal's bloody pin was stuck through her skull. She rubbed her forehead, wondering how much time had passed. The braziers, bright earlier, glowed dully, bathing all in red, leading her to believe it could be no more than an hour.

Nearby, King Yavuz lay still, unmoving, dead.

She pushed herself to her feet, knowing she should be more worried than she was over Yavuz's death. It would cause problems, to be sure. Explanations would need to be made, perhaps an apology or two. But much worse than a lesser King's untimely death was the discovery that King Emir and Queen

Alansal had decided to throw in their lot together. The Malasani and Mirean fleets had been deeply wounded during their clashes against the Kings, but Sharakhai was worse—few knew it, but the city couldn't stand against their combined might, not with Qaimir's help, not with Kundhun's.

From the neck of her dress Meryam pulled out a red beaded necklace. As the realization she might lose everything began to squeeze the breath from her, she kissed it and spoke to her dead sister. *What am I going to do now, Yasmine?* Her fears were beginning to cascade when she noticed a glow coming from the tunnel she'd taken to the vault. She thought a servant might have come, but the glow was too perfect—and lanterns didn't cast that sort of pure, blue-white light.

Understanding dawned a moment later, and a nearly irrepressible urge to bolt away through the room's other passageway threatened to overwhelm her, but really, what good would that do? If she was right about the identity of the one approaching, running wouldn't help. With no small amount of effort, she managed to press the fear deep down inside her, smothering it temporarily, and wait as calmly as she could manage.

The silver light brightened. A female form, a full head taller than any man or woman Meryam had ever seen, strode through the archway and into the room. It was the goddess, Tulathan, the sister of golden Rhia. She was naked, her breasts bared, her skin radiant. Silver hair flowed over her lithe shoulders, rippling as if she were underwater.

Goosebumps rose along Meryam's arms. The pain in her forehead suddenly felt as if it were days old, a faint memory. The urge to kneel was great, but Meryam denied that as well—the goddess had come for a reason, after all; she *wanted* something from Meryam—so instead Meryam gave her the slightest bow of her head, a sign that they were equals, at least for the purposes of this meeting.

Tulathan, her metallic eyes taking Meryam in from head to toe, seemed amused. She wandered the room. Where she walked, the dull red light of the braziers was drowned in silver. She stared at the table, at the golem, at Yavuz on the floor with the crystal heart still in his hands. Her hair trailed behind her languidly, as if it refused to obey the laws of the mundane, material world. Then the goddess spoke.

Much has happened in the Great Shangazi.

Meryam's mouth had turned suddenly dry, so she waited to speak until she could do so clearly, strongly. "And much is yet to come."

Of this there can be no doubt.

As Tulathan continued her circuit of the room, Meryam's skin prickled. She shivered as if *she* were the naked one. *Steel yourself, Meryam. What follows means everything.*

The goddess leaned in and whispered into Meryam's ear, "So many possible outcomes." How ephemeral her voice. How her breath tickled.

"Not so many if one applies oneself," Meryam said. "The fates reward the brave."

Tulathan stood before Meryam once more, her look of amusement vanished. *The fates reward no one.*

"Why have you come, goddess?"

To offer thee thy heart's desire.

"Sharakhai?"

Thy desire is for a city? Tulathan's silver gaze drifted down to Meryam's neck, to her beaded necklace. *If it is so, but speak it, and it will be thine.*

For the first time in a long while Meryam felt exposed. She felt beholden to the goddess, and if there was one thing Meryam hated, it was to have her fate resting in the hands of others. But what was there to do? The goddess was offering her a way to get what she wanted. What sort of fool would turn her down?

"No," Meryam said, "that isn't what I desire the most."

Tulathan, her amused smile returning, waited.

"I want Macide Ishaq'ava delivered to me," Meryam went on. "I want to see him suffer."

As he made thy sister suffer?

"Yes. And I want the Moonless Host to suffer as well."

If that is so, it is as simple as making a wish.

A wind rose and swirled about the room. Drifts of silver sand were borne upon it. They circled Meryam, making her feel trapped by the goddess. Tulathan, meanwhile, held her hand out flat, her palm facing upward. When it was clear she meant for Meryam to do the same, Meryam did, and a portion of the sand pooled within her palm.

Tulathan meant for her to whisper to the sand as it fell between her fingers, as the people of the desert did when begging the gods for favors, but it made her wonder . . .

"What do you want in return?" she asked the goddess.

Tulathan's smile revealed perfect teeth. *So very little.*

"Name it."

The goddess stepped closer, and whispered the terms of their bargain to Meryam. When she was done, the goddess strode away, her light fading with her. The room plunged into shadow, the walls returned to their former bloody, muddy red.

Staring at her closed fist, Meryam swallowed hard.

Nothing she'd done on her road to power had been more dangerous than this. Not dealing with Guhldrathen. Not dominating Hamzakiir. Not forcing King Kiral to change places and to walk into the desert to his death. Not even killing her own father, King Aldouan, had been more risky.

Reaching up, she touched the worn beads of her sister's necklace. Then lifted her fist to her lips. Allowing the silver sand to sift slowly between her fingers, she whispered, "I pray for your help, Tulathan. I pray you deliver me all that you've promised."

As the sand fell and pooled near her toes, it did so in a pattern that looked familiar. It was shaped very much like a particular crystal hidden deep beneath the city.

Chapter 1

ÇEDA FOLLOWED THE FLOW of traffic through the bazaar. All around her, the aisles were choked, the myriad patrons shoving past her, trading and chatting as if war hadn't nearly torn the city apart five months ago.

The meeting she was about to have was nothing if not dangerous. Nevertheless, Çeda found herself smiling beneath her veil. She wore a threadbare dress. A dusty, eggplant-colored turban wrapped her head. A beaten old shamshir hung from her belt. It was tatty attire at best, yet she felt like a queen. She hadn't realized how much she'd needed this homecoming until she'd arrived in Sharakhai.

Sümeya, the former First Warden of the Blade Maidens, walked alongside Çeda. She wore a head scarf as well, its veil covering her face. The skirt of her midnight blue dress was uncharacteristically long, frayed along the hem, hopelessly dusty from walking the streets of the city. "Where are we meeting the girl?"

Ahead of Çeda and Sümeya was Kameyl, the vanguard of their small contingent. Çeda pointed beyond her towering form to the horseshoe archway into the spice market. "Just inside the arch."

The last of their number, Jenise, one of Çeda's Shieldwives, trailed a few stalls behind. She wore a belted kaftan. Her brown, shoulder-length hair was unbound and flowed freely on the gentle wind. She'd never been to Sharakhai, and it showed in the way her striking green-and-gold eyes flitted around, the way she flinched when others brushed past her.

As the four of them entered the spice market, the din of business and barter became intense, and Çeda found herself looking for signs that they were being followed—by Silver Spears, by Blade Maidens in disguise, by one of the Kings' elite Kestrels. Sümeya had assured her that Nayyan—*Queen* Nayyan, the woman they were about to meet—would abide by her word and listen to what they had to say. She'd further agreed to bring three and only three Blade Maidens, and promised that, no matter how the conversation went, neither Sümeya nor any of those accompanying her would be taken into custody. It was risky, but Sümeya trusted Nayyan, and Çeda trusted Sümeya. The closer they came to the meeting, though, the more Çeda's doubts were starting to resurface.

For years Nayyan had posed as her father, King Azad, but those days were behind her. She'd stepped out of her father's shadow at last, unveiling herself as the rightful heir to his throne, which was precisely why Çeda was worried. With all the other young monarchs in the House of Kings, and a dominating force like Queen Meryam leading them, Nayyan needed notoriety. What better way to get it than by delivering the White Wolf and Sümeya, the former First Warden turned traitor?

A few stalls in, Çeda spotted Mala, an eleven-year-old girl with curly brown hair pulled into a long, scraggly tail. Several strands hung down her face, adding to her angry, distrustful look.

"Hello, Mala," Çeda said.

Mala glanced at the milling patrons. "Don't use my *name*," she spat. "You know better than that."

Çeda gave her a second look. Then caught an older girl staring at the two of them from across the way. Further down the aisle stood more gutter wrens, all of them girls, watching this exchange carefully.

In Sharakhai's west end, children were often pressed into gangs, either by choice or by the tough hand that life in the city's poorest quarter often dealt them. When inducted formally, they were forced to stand up to a random person and cut them after some forced argument. It was a ritual called *taking up the knife.* Mala was only eleven, but it was clear she'd taken up hers. She looked harder than she once had, more prepared to protect herself and those she'd come to call family. Çeda wanted to ask about her swordcraft, wanted to trade a few blows as they used to, but she couldn't. She'd become an outsider in Mala's eyes.

"Did you follow her?"

Mala's chin jutted out. "Money first."

Çeda considered challenging her, but she saw how fixedly Mala was staring at her. Mala needed this. She had to show that she could handle herself. So Çeda took out the handful of six-pieces she and Mala had agreed upon but held them just short of Mala's waiting palm—this was deadly serious; the other wrens could easily have sold their identities to the Silver Spears.

"Do they know who I am?" Çeda asked in a low voice.

Mala shook her head.

"You're sure?"

"They don't know."

"Do they know you were sent to watch Queen Nayyan?"

She shook her head again. "I told them you were an heiress feuding with her sister over an inheritance."

Çeda stared at her, weighing her words, and found no reason to disbelieve her. "Here," Çeda said, handing over the money. "Now tell me what you've found."

"She came in through the east entrance and went straight to the tea stall. Three women joined her. She's been there for half a turn. There's no one else watching her."

"No more Spears than normal? No enforcers wandering the aisles?"

"None, and we've been watching all morning."

"Good," Çeda said, and lowered her voice even further. "Take care of yourself, Mala."

A quick smile, a bit of the old Mala returning. "You too," she said, and then she was gone.

It was as Mala had said. Near the center of the spice market was a tea shop with several small tables and chairs. Within it, sitting by herself at a table with two empty chairs, was a woman in a rust-orange dress that was rich but not too rich. Standing at the corners of the shop were three women in tribal niqabs, the veils covering their faces a cascade of beaten coins and coral beads. Each wore a voluminous skirt that had been bunched beneath the belt at one hip. No doubt there were ebon blades beneath those skirts, ready to be drawn.

As Jenise and Kameyl took up positions near a counter dominated by open bags of aromatic teas, Çeda followed Sümeya, who was just rounding Nayyan's table. Sümeya suddenly stopped in her tracks. Çeda had no idea why until she reached Sümeya's side and saw that Nayyan was cradling a newborn.

"You have a child," Sümeya said in a voice that was distant as the Austral Sea.

Nayyan was a woman of some forty summers who stunned with her beauty. Thin eyebrows arched above expressive eyes as she took Sümeya in. She had full lips, a dimpled chin, and rounded cheeks that accented the unbound waves of her hair. The folds of her dress were pulled wide at the chest, allowing the babe to suckle while her mother patted her swaddled bottom.

Nayyan's eyes might have been locked with those of her child, as if the baby were her sole concern, but her words gave lie to that impression. "When you asked me here, you said nothing about inviting the daughter of my father's killer to sit across the table from me."

Sümeya pulled out a chair and sat. "Nayyan, this is as much about Çeda—"

"I should have her throat slit here and now."

"I told you we'd be discussing the asirim and the thirteenth tribe and all the things Çeda discovered in the desert and in the mountains. Who better to tell it than Çeda herself?"

"Don't bandy words with me, Sümeya." Nayyan stroked the peach fuzz on top of her baby's head. "It doesn't suit you."

"It isn't Sümeya's fault," Çeda said. "I insisted."

"The Sümeya *I* knew wouldn't let *anyone* insist on *anything*."

"Then maybe you don't know her as well as you thought."

Nayyan regarded Çeda at last, her gaze turning razor sharp. "I know her better than you ever will, scarab."

Just then the baby squirmed, fell off the teat, and began to fuss. Only then did Çeda realized the babe had mismatched eyes: one brown, one hazel.

Nayyan pinched her nipple and used it to rub the baby's lips, at which point she latched back on, gave one last squirm, and continued feeding. Çeda actually felt bad. It was clear Nayyan had brought the baby away from the safety of the palace specifically so that Sümeya could meet her, and Çeda had ruined the moment.

When it became clear Nayyan *wasn't* going have Çeda's throat slit—not yet, at least—Sümeya waved to the tea merchant and signaled for two more cups. "What's her name?" Sümeya asked when tea had been poured. She'd asked almost casually, which told Çeda just how much she cared.

Nayyan surprised Çeda when she let down her guard and gave an unabashed smile. "Her name is Ransaneh Nayyan'ala, heir to the Throne of Thorns."

Sümeya shared a look with Çeda as the sound of the market washed over them. Nayyan had given the matrilineal version of her daughter's name, which meant she considered herself the child's sole provider, or enough that it made no difference.

"Will her father be pleased to hear it?" Sümeya asked.

"Her father wasn't there to witness her birth"—the fire in Nayyan's eyes was plain to see—"nor has he been attentive enough to warrant his name's precedence over mine." She kissed the crown of Ransaneh's head. "Now tell me why you've come. I have no wish to sit in this traitor's presence for a moment longer than I need to."

Sümeya, apparently oblivious to the seriousness of Nayyan's words, stared at Ransaneh with a forlorn expression, as if with her presence one of the hopes Sümeya had secretly harbored had been dashed. Çeda had known of Sümeya's feelings for Nayyan—she just hadn't realized how strong they were.

"She's beautiful," Sümeya said with a melancholy smile.

Wary at first, as if unsure whether Sümeya had some ulterior motive for paying her daughter the compliment, Nayyan's look eventually softened. "Why did you ask me here, Meya?"

"Because Sharakhai is in trouble."

Nayyan snorted. "Do tell."

"It's the gods," Sümeya went on. "They're playing a game, and have been for four hundred years. How can we win that game if we refuse to acknowledge we're even playing it? How can we make a move when the rules have been hidden from us?"

"And how do you think *I* can aid you?"

"In the mountains, something happened that few outside the thirteenth tribe have heard about. You know King Beşir led a battle against the thirteenth tribe. You know he failed. You know that the goddess Yerinde arranged for that battle. She *wanted* Nalamae to die." Sümeya leaned closer. "Yerinde succeeded, but was slain in the process."

Nayyan scoffed. "Yerinde cannot *die.*"

"She fell to Night's Kiss, a sword of Goezhen's making."

At this, Nayyan sobered. "Who killed her?"

"Çeda."

Up to this point, Nayyan had seen fit to ignore Çeda, but now she took her in as she might a west end trollop brought in for questioning. "*This* one killed the goddess?"

"Yes," Çeda replied, "*this* one did."

"Yerinde was slain," Sümeya went on quickly. "I saw her body with my own eyes. Nalamae fell too, but she will return, or has already, as she has done since the days of Beht Ihman."

"Well, which is it? *Has* returned, or *will?*"

"We don't know," Çeda interjected. "We've been searching the desert since the battle in the mountains."

Nayyan's nostril's flared. "Your betters are *speaking*, child."

"The wise would not silence me. What we search for is nothing less than a way to stop the gods."

"From doing *what?*"

"I don't know," Çeda said, "but I know this much. Ihsan is searching for the same information. He wants a solution to this riddle of the gods' desires and what they mean to do with the crystal. He told me as much in the desert."

"Yes, well"—Nayyan pulled Ransaneh from her breast and tugged the rich fabric of her dress back into place—"the more time passes, the more I think Ihsan is a fool."

"He isn't, though," Çeda said. "He was right about the gods hunting Nalamae. And he was right not to kill me when he had the chance. Nalamae will return, and when she does, we must be there to meet her. Only then do we have a chance of learning what the gods mean to do."

Nayyan laid the baby's head against her neck and patted her back. "Then why aren't you off finding her?"

"We've tried."

Ransaneh squirmed, then whined, the sound barely audible above the roar of the market. Nayyan, meanwhile, was about to speak, but Sümeya cut her off. "Before he died, King Yusam told Çeda he'd seen her, Çeda, kneeling beside his mere, peering into its depths. He said she was caught in a vision, rapt."

Nayyan waited for more. "And?"

"Çeda has never done so." Sümeya shared a look with Çeda. "We think that time is now. We think she uses it to search for Nalamae."

"We . . ." Nayyan was looking at Sümeya in a new way.

Nayyan still loves her, Çeda realized.

Sümeya stepped into the silence. "We need this, Nayyan. For the good of the city, we must find Nalamae."

Nayyan responded, "I've spent years getting to where I am, Sümeya. And I'll be fighting until the day I die to remain there. I've made many mistakes along the way. I've learned hard lessons." Nayyan held her baby close and stood. "*I* decide what's good for the city, not you." She turned to Çeda. "And certainly not you."

She turned, ready to walk away, but before she could Çeda stood and snatched her wrist. Nayyan's eyes went wide, and the veiled women who'd accompanied her began to close in. They stopped when Çeda released her and Nayyan signaled them to back away.

"This isn't for me," Çeda said, "It isn't for Sümeya, either. It's not even for you. We've lived our lives and could be content with them." Çeda's gaze drifted to the soft bundle in Nayyan's arms. "This is for her."

Nayyan stared into Çeda's eyes as if she'd never heard anything so foolish in her life. She looked ready to slap Çeda for it. Holding Ransaneh close, she turned and strode away. As one of her Maidens led the way through the crowd, the other two watched Çeda and Sümeya carefully, then followed in their queen's wake.

"You were right," Çeda said, her head hanging low, "I never should have come."

"Well?" Kameyl grunted as she and Jenise joined them.

Sümeya shook her head.

Kameyl suddenly put one hand on the hilt of her shamshir. One of Queen Nayyan's escorts was striding quickly toward them. "Return here tomorrow," the Maiden said, "at the same time. I'll have instructions for you then."

As she turned and lost herself in the crowd, a wave of relief washed over Çeda.

Chapter 2

As KING IHSAN guided his golden akhala over the dunes, the wind pressed against him like a drunk lover. His eyes were reduced to slits. The veil of his turban, now hopelessly soiled with amber dust, was pulled tight across his face. It left only a slit through which to see, yet time and time again the tireless, biting sand found its way in. He turned away from it, blinked the grit from his eyes, then scanned the amber-streaked horizon ahead, praying he was near his destination.

His golden akhala and stalwart companion, Barkhan, plodded ever onward, as much a victim as Ihsan was to the unrelenting storm. No, it was *worse* for the horse, Ihsan reasoned. The poor creature had no say in it; Ihsan certainly did.

He would have apologized for it had he not lost his tongue to Surrahdi the Mad King. *With my own bloody knife, too.* In place of words, he patted Barkhan's neck, flaking away some of the sand caked into his coat. *I am sorry, Barkhan. Truly.*

The horse threw his head back and nickered, sending a baleful look Ihsan's way.

It couldn't be helped! Ihsan thought. *And besides, if you want someone to blame, blame Yusam. Or the gods. Or even the fates, but don't blame me! We are both but puppets in their schemes.*

Barkhan plodded on, cresting a dune and taking to the shifting surface of its windward side.

In the months since Nayyan had delivered Barkhan to him in the blooming fields, he'd considered selling the horse. Barkhan was purebred, and many, upon realizing this, would inevitably think of Sharakhai, purebreds being somewhat rare anywhere but in the city. It was the sort of association Ihsan needed like he needed his eyes put out. But Barkhan was an amazing animal. Nayyan had personally chosen him for Ihsan from her own stock—he was a horse sired from two of the finest beasts ever to gallop across the Great Mother. No one could pay him what Barkhan was worth. And the simple truth was that Ihsan had come to trust the horse more than anyone he'd ever known. He'd part with the grapes between his legs before he'd sell Barkhan.

The wind suddenly changed direction, and Ihsan was caught in a powerful squall. Sand scoured him from the left, threatening to throw him from the saddle. Barkhan, accustomed to such things, stopped, lowered his head and, when the squall had passed, resumed his stoic pace.

Ihsan hoped they were still headed toward the caravanserai known as Çalabin but was no longer sure. Earlier that day, when he'd left from the slopes of the nearby hills, the caravanserai had been distant, a smudge along the horizon. The wind had been meager then, but had picked up shortly after they'd embarked and hadn't let up since. He'd decided to let Barkhan find their path on his own.

But gods, the wind. It was so fierce it was hard to breathe. He was just about to rein Barkhan over, lay him down, and use him for shelter when a dark shape loomed ahead. A ship, Ihsan realized—a ketch, perhaps one of the fleet he'd seen anchored near Çalabin that morning. He might have considered it bad luck had he not read about this meeting in the Blue Journals, left behind by Yusam after his death, where Yusam had recorded his visions.

In a small caravanserai, Yusam's entry had read, *to the north, I reason, Qarthüm or Çalabin. A King of Sharakhai wanders through a haze, surrounded by ships, searching for hints of his past. He is looking for a key, or perhaps many keys. Keys to saving Sharakhai. He enters a dark pit, a place one goes to forget. There he meets two others: one who preens, another with the mark of a traitor.*

In the margins, written beside the primary entry, was a note:

The vision seen again, but this time the three of them speak in a small room with two beds. The sound of an oud warbles. The air is heavy with fragrant smoke. A parlor?

Ihsan urged Barkhan on. He was confident in his purpose, confident he wouldn't be stopped even when a squad of Kundhuni guardsmen with dark clothes and bright blue turbans appeared before him and one of them, a leggy tree of a man, raised his hand. He shouted at Ihsan, though his words were swallowed by the wind.

Ihsan snapped Barkhan's reins, refusing to slow. When the tall soldier grabbed the reins roughly, Barkhan threw his head back, but the man held tight. Ihsan nearly put his fingers to his lips, ready to whistle an order for Barkhan to rear up and club the man for his presumption, but he thought better of it and instead pulled his veil down to allow the man to see his face. He set his lips to quavering and put on a look of raw, honest intensity, as if he counted himself fortunate to be alive.

The soldier glared at him from behind his bright blue veil, took a good look at Barkhan, then released his hold on the reins as if the horse had offended him. He jutted his chin toward what Ihsan assumed was the caravanserai itself, and in a thick Kundhuni accent shouted, "Go!" as if he were lord of the Great Shangazi itself.

Ihsan spurred Barkhan on. He passed several ships. There was a prize hidden somewhere inside those ships, Ihsan knew, a man who might very well be scared off if he learned of Ihsan's presence. It was a worry for another time, though. There was something he needed first, and it lay in the caravanserai ahead.

When he reached the caravanserai's outskirts, he guided Barkhan between walled-off gardens and clutches of mudbrick homes, all barely discernible through the roaring amber wind. He finally reached the heart of the caravanserai: a blocky expanse of sandstone where the wells were kept and a dozen ships were moored. In the far corner of this structure was an oud parlor known simply as *The Abandon.*

After giving Barkhan over to a stable girl, Ihsan stepped inside the parlor and shook himself off. The sound of the wind dropped, mixing with the hubbub of the tight crowd and the mournful melody of the oud being played in one corner. Many eyes shifted to him. He let them look—they'd only been drawn by the sound of the wind—but how strange it felt to be on display; indeed, to be back among humanity after a full five months in the desert with only a horse and a set of cryptic journals for company.

One by one, the patrons returned to their conversations. Hookahs, liquor bottles, and glasses complicated the surfaces of the low tables. The people surrounding them sat on dusty, mismatched pillows, the bright colors muted by the clouds of pungent tabbaq smoke. Ihsan wove his way to the bar, where a dozen patrons leaned or sat on stools, and ordered a glass of araq, not in the customary way, but by pointing at the drink of a burly man sitting on a stool nearby.

The barkeep, a goggle-eyed fellow with deep wrinkles webbing his face, leaned in and shouted, "You sure, friend? It's expensive."

With a nod, Ihsan dropped two silver six-pieces onto the bar. The barkeep smiled, grabbed a bottle of liquor from the highest shelf behind him, and poured a glass. Ihsan, meanwhile, swept his gaze over the crowded room to a corner table he'd noticed on his way in.

At the table were two men. Both wore weathered khalats and turbans with their veils hanging loose. The lighting was dim enough that their faces were shadowed, but he recognized them from their postures alone.

One was imposing, the sort of man you'd think twice about offending, then once again for good measure. He was Husamettín, the King of Swords. He had his turban pulled down over his forehead, so low it practically swallowed his eyebrows. *One with the mark of a traitor*, Yusam's vision had read. Was that what he was hiding?

The shorter of the two, King Cahil, looked cockier. He had the same look he'd worn for four hundred years, like he was ready to challenge anyone in the room for looking at him the wrong way.

His drink poured, Ihsan took a sip and shrugged. It was expensive all right, but it was nothing compared to the blends that could be found in Sharakhai. Even so, he savored it. He'd long run out of Tulogal in the desert.

When the front door opened again, Husamettín and Cahil looked up expectantly. The stable girl entered, ran up to the bar, and waved to the barkeep. When the barkeep bent close, the girl cupped her hand over his ear and spoke, too low for Ihsan to hear.

"When?"

"Just now," the girl said. "They're still leaving."

The door opened again, and a Kundhuni, the very same man who'd stopped Ihsan earlier, waved sharply to a table of his countrymen, who immediately stood and left with him.

"Take care of the drinks," the barkeep said to the girl. With a worried expression on his lined face, he ducked through a gap below the bartop and headed into the howling wind.

In the corner, the pair of mislaid Kings had watched the exchange carefully. When Cahil nodded, Husamettín stood and slipped through a nearby archway. A woman bearing a shamshir, who'd blended well into the crowd, stood from her stool and followed Husamettín. The sheath was of poor workmanship, but Ihsan would bet that the sword inside was made of ebon steel. It was Yndris, Ihsan realized, Cahil's bloodthirsty daughter and one-time warden of the Blade Maidens.

When they'd gone, Ihsan took up his drink and wove through the crowd toward Cahil. Of the two men, he would vastly have preferred speaking to Husamettín who, though rigid as sandstone at times, had always listened to reason. Cahil, on the other hand, often acted like a child who'd missed his last meal.

Cahil dropped some coins onto the table and was just heading for the front door when he noticed Ihsan. His eyes widened in surprise and he scanned the crowd anew, perhaps wondering if a storm of Silver Spears were about to sweep into the parlor and attack, or a hand of Blade Maidens in black battle dresses.

When neither materialized, Cahil grabbed Ihsan by the ruff of his thawb and dragged him into the dark passageway after Husamettín. Cahil passed several doors, dragging Ihsan along with him until they reached the end of the hall. There he shoved Ihsan through the doorway and threw him onto one of the nearby beds.

He loomed over Ihsan, his knife held up, plain for Ihsan to see. "If I think you're about to use your power on me, I'll slit your throat, understand?"

Ihsan's reply was to open his mouth, thereby revealing the ruin Surrahdi the Mad King had made of it. Cahil stared and smiled as if he were picturing himself doing the cutting. Then he sobered, the momentary fantasy dissolved.

"Why the fuck are you here, Ihsan?"

Ihsan made several hand signs, the sort the Blade Maidens used. *For the same reason as you,* he said to Cahil through the signs, *to find Zeheb, our lost King.*

He'd never bothered much with the non-verbal language before his self-imposed exile, but Nayyan had included a detailed dictionary of them, a resource that included illustrations and a wider vocabulary than the one the Maidens were typically taught. He'd mastered the entire book in the months since leaving Sharakhai.

As the meaning of Ihsan's words sunk in, Cahil's demeanor went dark. "And you think to *help* us?"

Why else? Ihsan signed.

"No." Cahil coughed. His free hand went to his chest. "No, yours is the last sort of help we need."

You're wrong. Without my help, you will fail.

Cahil gave a scoffing laugh, but there was doubt in his eyes.

Yusam saw it, Ihsan went on. *He wrote about it in his journals.*

Cahil blinked. He'd gone completely still, as if working through the implications of Ihsan's words. The hand against his chest pressed harder while his cheeks and forehead turned a splotchy red. He blinked and shook his head like a drunk trying to wake himself, then fell to one knee. The only thing keeping him from collapsing to the floor was a hand against the edge of the opposite bed. By the gods who breathe, he looked like he was going to perish on the spot.

Ihsan helped him onto the bed, then poured a glass of water from a nearby pitcher and held it out. Cahil glanced at it, then focused on the ceiling, as if the dusty slats were the only things keeping him alive. After a moment, however, he accepted the glass, took several sips, then set the glass on the bedside table with a healthy clack.

Ihsan sat on the opposite bed, elbows on his knees, and waited for the spell to pass.

Breathing steadily, Cahil's eyes flicked Ihsan's way. "If we fail it's likely because you arrived"—he waved along his body—"and caused *this.*"

Ihsan echoed Cahil's motion. *I hardly think* I'm *responsible for your condition, whatever it is.* When Cahil's face went dark, Ihsan went on. *It was Meryam, wasn't it? There was a vision, a woman in red stabbing you in the heart.*

Cahil's face screwed up in annoyance. "That was always the problem with Yusam. He got things wrong as often as he got them right. It was your bloody Nayyan who nearly killed me, and with a crossbow bolt, not a knife."

Nayyan, Ihsan mused. She hadn't shared that when she'd told him the story of the confrontation between Cahil and the lesser Kings who'd deposed their elders. *It's still rather close, don't you think?*

For a time, Cahil simply breathed. "You said we'd fail without you. What did the vision show?"

Just then the door flew open and Yndris rushed in. Her torn dress was filthy with amber dust, and now the veil of her turban was down. More importantly, she held a naked shamshir in one hand, an ebon blade, which she appeared all-too-ready to use.

The old Cahil, the one in Sharakhai with all the power he could handle, might have allowed his daughter to lop off Ihsan's head, as she clearly wanted to. *This* Cahil, however, the broken one, forestalled her with a simple lift of his hand. Yndris didn't seem pleased but stayed her sword anyway while, behind her, Husamettín watched their odd exchange with his piercing, hawklike gaze.

Ihsan could see several thin scars on Husamettín's forehead. Were Ihsan to lift the dark head cloth, he had no doubt he'd find a scar, the mark of a traitor, rendered in the old tongue.

"Zeheb?" Cahil asked.

"Gone," Husamettín replied, "along with his Kundhuni caretakers and all seven of their ships." His gaze swung to Ihsan. "They were unnerved by a wanderer entering the caravanserai on a golden akhala."

Cahil's head rolled toward Ihsan. "*You* caused them to flee." He stared deeper into Ihsan's eyes. "You *knew* it would happen!"

Ihsan thought of lying, but what would be the point? *I had to secure my services somehow, didn't I?*

Cahil's face went purple. Yndris drew back her sword, looking as if she was ready to take Ihsan's life no matter what her father said, but she held back when Cahil, with great effort, lifted himself off the bed. "Enough, Yndris," he said with clear reluctance. "Ihsan's with us now."

Chapter 3

Young princess Meryam smiled and laughed as she traipsed across Santrión's perfect green lawn after her sister, Yasmine, who was headed toward the palace's vast hedge maze. Behind them loomed the broad wings of the palace, the angular chapel beyond, and the height of Redhawk Tower with its banners flapping lazily in the breeze. The banners were emblazoned with Qaimir's royal seal, a wave crashing against stone.

The day was bright, with perfect white clouds flung across a deep blue sky. Near the palace, preparations for Meryam's twelfth birthday celebration were underway. A pavilion had been erected. Floral wreaths hung from the palace's many sconces and the statues in the rock garden. Many had been left in place after Yasmine's celebration the day before, a thing that might have annoyed Meryam years ago. In the past, the celebration of their birthdays had always been combined into one grand affair. There was no denying the celebrations were festive, but Meryam always felt like an afterthought, due in no small part to Yasmine herself, who lorded the fact that her actual birthday came one day before Meryam's.

"It's *my* birthday, you know," Yasmine would tell Meryam every year. "They just *tell* you it's yours too so you won't be upset."

"No," Meryam would say. "I get presents too."

"Well of *course* you do," Yasmine would reply easily. "They could hardly give you nothing. But look at what gifts we receive, and you'll see *your* birthday is just tacked on like the sorry postscript of a beautiful letter they've written to me."

"You take that back!"

But Yasmine never would, and then Meryam *did* compare their presents. No matter how grand the gifts she received were, the gifts they chose for Yasmine always seemed grander. One year Meryam had fawned over Yasmine's latest, a wolfhound pup. Yasmine hardly seemed to care about it, but oh, whenever *Meryam* wanted to pet it, she would scoop it up and coo and refuse to let Meryam so much as touch it. Only when Meryam was in tears would Yasmine allow her to pet the pup, even then controlling the proceedings, as if each rub of the hound's coat was the loan of a gold coin and she was the most miserly moneylender in all the kingdom.

"I've a surprise for you," Yasmine had told her months before. "I've convinced Mummy to let you have your own birthday this year."

Meryam had sneered, but the longer Yasmine stared back with those pretty green eyes of hers, the more Meryam's certainty that it was a cruel joke began to crack. "You *haven't*."

"I have. I said you ought to have *one* birthday of your own before you're married off to some stupid lord and have babies with birthdays of their own to celebrate."

Yasmine had said it to rankle, but Meryam didn't care. She was to have her very own birthday! Visions of a day filled with wonders sprouted, becoming ever more grand in her mind. She was imagining a bevy of wolfhound pups to call her own when she wondered, "When will it be?"

Yasmine replied, as if it were of no consequence. "The day after mine, of course."

Meryam's face had fallen. "The day *after*?"

"Well, when else would you expect it to be?"

Of course she was right, but Meryam was crestfallen. She hated the idea of her birthday being *attached* to Yasmine's. Mighty Alu, better it was delayed by a month than have it the day after, but what was there to do?

All throughout Yasmine's celebration the day before, Meryam had sulked.

Yasmine's cruel proclamation from years ago had never felt truer: Meryam's celebration *was* the sorry postscript to Yasmine's. But when the morning of her birthday arrived at last, all such thoughts vanished. Yasmine's celebration was behind them, and *hers* had begun.

Father woke her early and led her down to the stables for her first present, a brand-new saddle for her horse. And when she returned to the palace Mother unveiled a new dress she'd had made for Meryam, especially for the day. Yasmine pretended to be happy for her but spent breakfast detailing every extravagance from the day before, knowing that each small comparison in Meryam's mind would tarnish her day just a little bit more. Yasmine made much of the necklace she wore, a gift from their father, the King, and made by a renowned artist. Each of the ceramic beads was hand-painted, each a small work of art. Unlike most of the other things she'd so far mentioned, Yasmine seemed genuinely impressed by it. "See the red? The artist's blood was mixed with the pigment. It's meant to protect me when I'm queen."

The comment only served to remind Meryam of their brother, Indio, who had died two months earlier after succumbing to an infection that had confounded physics and blood magi alike. And because of something so stupid: two of the most powerful houses in Qaimir were warring, and Indio, who'd always fancied himself a leader of men but had never been very good at it, had hoped to defuse the situation. He invited the eldest sons of the warring houses to best him in a game of pin finger with a dirty old knife. Indio had gone first, promptly cut the webbing between his thumb and forefinger, and in his embarrassment hidden the infection until it was too late.

Yasmine, knowing she'd misstepped, took the necklace off and put it around Meryam's neck, but only until her frown had vanished and she could take it off again, calm in the knowledge that she'd replaced Meryam's sadness with jealousy over the necklace.

"Does it really protect you?" Meryam asked as they reached the hedge maze at the far end of the lawn.

"Well, of *course* it does. There's *blood* mixed with the paint."

But having blood mixed in with the paint didn't mean anything at all. "She was a mage, then, the artist?"

"Undoubtedly," Yasmine said, though she did so with a tilt of her head and a twitch of her shoulders, which was her way of admitting she had no idea whether the artist was a blood mage or not. "Now count. And *don't* be scared. You *won't* get lost in the maze. And there *certainly* won't be any *ghuls* lurking around the corners waiting for you."

Yasmine made claws of her hands and pawed at Meryam's new dress, her eyes spread so wide it was grotesque. When Meryam laughed and shied away, Yasmine stifled a smile and ducked into the maze.

As her sprinting footsteps crunched over gravel, Meryam did as she'd been told. She counted while, near the palace, the royal servants busied themselves around the pavilion like a host of riled ants. Meryam's smile was wide as the seas. Mighty Alu but it was going to be a grand day.

Her count complete, Meryam crept into the maze, moving on tiptoes so she might better hear Yasmine's movements. She *did* hear them, but they were distant, and then they went silent. Yasmine might have stopped moving, but Meryam doubted it. Lately she'd taken to making lots of noise, then removing her shoes and creeping around the maze in her stockings to trick Meryam, who knew the maze well and had grown better and better at anticipating Yasmine's moves.

Listening carefully, Meryam found she was right. She heard the careful patter of feet a few rows over. She took off her own shoes, ignoring the prickle of the gravel against the soles of her feet as she took silent, exaggerated strides toward the opening to the next row.

Yasmine's dress rustled as her movements quickened. Crouching low, Meryam caught a glimpse of her legs, then ran giggling down the row to catch up. She heard a squeal as Yasmine, knowing Meryam was near, sprinted away.

By the time Meryam reached the next row, she caught only the barest glimpse of Yasmine's dress as she turned a corner. Meryam was running hard toward the turn, imagining her victory, when she heard a small grunt, a gasp of surprise or pain. Then rustling, sounds of a struggle.

Meryam dropped her shoes and ran.

When she reached the turn in the maze she found Yasmine, her eyes wide as the moons, caught in the arms of a brute of a man. He stood behind Yasmine with one meaty hand clamped over her mouth while his opposite arm snaked around her waist, lifting her off the ground.

Yasmine twisted and fought, her arms and legs swinging wildly. Her desperate screams were muffled. She gripped the man's wrist, the tendons along her arms going harp-string tight, but the man was an ox and hardly seemed to notice. With a calm assurance that made Meryam's blood run cold, he backed slowly into the hedge maze, taking Yasmine with him.

Meryam jolted awake in the morning light. *A dream,* she told herself. *Only a dream.* And yet it was a long, long while before the look on Yasmine's face faded from her mind.

For a moment Meryam couldn't think where she was—the arched, gold-leaf ceiling was different than what she was used to—but then she remembered. It was the faint smell of smoke that reminded her. She was in Sharakhai, in the Sun Palace, the palace she'd claimed as her own, the lingering smell of smoke evidence of the fire that had raged through the palace during the battle with Malasan five months earlier.

The journal she'd been reading the night before, thoughts on the crystal deep beneath the city penned by King Sukru himself, lay across her stomach. Eyes itching from the dry desert air, she slid the leatherbound journal aside, propped herself onto her elbows, and stared through the nearby window, where a brilliant view of the southern reaches of Sharakhai and the desert beyond was revealed.

From the table at her bedside, she opened a small chest and took out a vial. Uncorking it revealed a measure of softly glowing liquid. She downed the contents and felt her aches and pains and, most importantly, her fears fade away. They were amazing, the elixirs, but they were fewer and fewer in number. She replaced the empty vial and stared at the others inside the chest. Less than a dozen remained. She'd been using them to counteract the debilitating effects of the blood she needed to consume daily to maintain her control over Sharakhai. And in this respect they were working, but . . .

You're using them too often, Meryam. They won't last forever.

She knew she needed another solution. Her stock of vials was going to run out soon, and she might have the last few cases of them in all the desert. But that was a problem for another day.

She closed the lid and ran her fingertips over the embossed surface. *You'll see me through until I have what I want.*

After dressing, she left her apartments and summoned Basilio, Qaimir's primary ambassador in Sharakhai and Meryam's closest advisor. He joined her at the staircase that led to the palace's lower levels.

"I bring news of our offer of peace to the desert tribes," Basilio said. "Shaikh Neylana of Tribe Halarijan has sent a reply."

"Has she accepted?"

"I'm afraid not, but she hasn't declined either. She's considering the offer, as are the two other tribes aligned with her."

Rumors of an alliance forming between the desert tribes was an alarming possibility, which was precisely why Meryam had sent offers of peace to twelve of them. Despite all advice to the contrary, she'd refused to send one to the thirteenth, to their shaikh, Macide, even though he was apparently the lynchpin to the entire alliance. Macide had been the one responsible for the Bloody Passage, a slaughter in the desert that had seen the deaths of Meryam's sister, Yasmine, and her beautiful daughter, Rehann. Instead, she'd offered much to the other tribes, more than most considered wise, so that they would band together *against* the thirteenth tribe, or at the very least form an alliance with *her*.

"I suppose such things take time," Meryam conceded. "And what of the cavern? Is everything prepared below?"

"Yes, although . . ." He paused before striking the lantern. There was color in his round nose and heavy jowls, which happened when he was nervous to broach a subject.

"Spit it out, Basilio."

"It's only . . . there's been talk among the other vizirs and viziras."

"About the cavern."

Basilio nodded. "Yes, about the cavern. It seems there's some worry over whether we should be meddling with it."

"They're afraid."

"They're concerned, and with good reason." He motioned to the dark stairwell below them. "The goddess, Yerinde herself, visited that cavern and made demands of the Kings."

"They're worried she'll return."

"They're worried the rumors of the goddess's death are true. They're worried that the other gods will come to meddle in the affairs of the Kings once more."

"Do they suppose that merely stepping foot in that place will summon the gods' attention?"

"That is precisely their thinking, yes."

"Yours as well?"

Basilio looked embarrassed. "Sometimes it's best to let sleeping dogs lie."

Meryam scoffed. "As if the gods need an excuse to visit misery upon mortals." She had yet to tell Basilio, or anyone else, for that matter, about Tulathan's sudden appearance in the cold vault beneath the palace with the golem on its slab. She saw no reason to change that now.

She headed down the stairs, forcing Basilio to light the lantern and rush to catch up. "Inform the other Kings that I've come to see things their way," she told him, "and that we'll leave the cavern alone for now."

"Of course, my queen." He looked at her strangely. "But . . . despite that message, we'll be continuing?"

"How very astute of you, Basilio." At his chagrined look, she went on. "This palace is mine, now. What I do within its walls is no one else's business."

"Yes, Your Excellence."

They reached a hallway that transitioned to more natural stone. Soon after, roots appeared, a few at first, covering wall, ceiling, or floor, forcing them to step more carefully. More and more funneled in from various cracks, tunnels, and chutes, to the point that the natural stone was completely obscured. The floor was so thick with them it felt as if she were walking on layers of coarse blankets.

Ahead, a violet light lit the tunnel. It became so bright Basilio extinguished the lantern. Soon, they arrived at a massive cavern whose every surface was covered by a mesh of interlaced roots. At the center of the cavern stood the now-legendary crystal. It was immense, easily three times Meryam's height, and it glowed brightly, violet at its outer edges, white at the center. Beside it was a wooden scaffold with stairs leading up to a viewing platform. The air was laced with a mineral scent, but it was overpowered by the smell of fresh wood as Meryam climbed the stairs.

By the time she reached the viewing platform, her breath was on her. From her new vantage, the roots looked like scar tissue, the crystal itself the head of a spear piercing the brindled flesh. Above the crystal, a lone strand, the terminus of a root, hung down from the cavern's roof, which was lost to the gloom.

As Basilio joined her at the rail, Meryam waved to the cavern around them. "Imagine it, Basilio. Four hundred years ago, this was all bare. The adichara had yet to grow. No tributes had yet been given to them, no blood had been drunk. Their roots had yet to filter the distilled essence of the tributes"—she pointed to the crystal's top—"onto that very spot."

"Ghastly," Basilio said.

He'd said it with a note of disgust, but Meryam was filled with wonder. She leaned over the rail and stared into the crystal's light, marveling at all that had gone into its making. "It is a thing of vast power, a thing crafted by the gods themselves."

"Perhaps another reason it should be left alone."

"All the more reason it should be *used*," Meryam countered. "This is a gift, granted to the people of the desert."

"Gifts can sometimes be poorly chosen."

Not this one, Meryam thought.

She flicked her hand at Basilio's wrist, at which point he held it out. She pierced his skin with her blooding ring, sucked the blood that welled from it, then closed the wound with a sizzling swipe of her thumb. She drew a sigil in the air, a sigil of knowing, of searching, then held her hand over the crystal's smooth surface. Within, she felt a deep well of power.

"There's more power here," she said absently, "than I have ever felt in one place before." Even more than Tulathan, though she chose not to share that with Basilio. "It's like the oil in that lantern. It has *potential*, Basilio. The question is: how do we use it?"

She could feel the objections forming on Basilio's lips, but he remained silent. He was right to be nervous. Part of Meryam was nervous too. She knew she had to tread carefully, but Tulathan herself had pointed Meryam here. What had she meant if not to use the power in this crystal to get what she wanted?

She'd learned from King Sukru's writings that since the days of Beht

Ihman the tributes from Sharakhai had been taken by the asirim and fed to the adichara, and that their essence was eventually delivered to the lone tendril suspended above the crystal. *The crystal is fed by the drip of the root*, Sukru had written. *That essence has accreted over time into the crystal, the purpose of which is still unknown to me.*

However reliably the root had fed the crystal in the past, it was now dry, as was the surface of the crystal beneath it. The reason was obvious, of course. No tributes had been taken for months, not since the asirim, freed by Çedamihn and Sehid-Alaz, had entered the service of the thirteenth tribe. The water that fed this well had run dry, but if the blood could flow once more, the crystal could grow and Meryam could unlock its potential. As blood could be used to control the one who'd given it, so could the adichara trees' purified essence be used to control the crystal.

That was what Tulathan had meant. That was how Meryam could use the crystal to get what she wanted most. *I must feed the trees and collect the essence. But it isn't a matter of tossing random people into the twisted trees. They must be chosen with great care.*

"Does the House of Kings keep records on lineage?" she asked.

"Extensive records are kept for the royal houses."

"And for the rest of the city?"

He shook his head. "There are none that I'm aware of."

Meryam considered. "In Almadan, we conduct a census. Does Sharakhai do the same?"

Basilio's face pinched in thought. "Yes, I believe the collegia conduct a census every five years."

"And the prisoners in the internment camps, the ones that held the scarabs from the Moonless Host, were there records kept of their names, their lineage?"

After the Night of Endless Swords, the terrible battle in King's Harbor that had seen the deaths of two Kings, Mesut and Yusam, the Kings had waged a months-long campaign to capture as many scarabs and sympathizers to the Moonless Host as they could. They'd been placed in camps to await trial and punishment, but when the Malasani had broken through the walls, they'd been freed with the understanding that if they fought for Sharakhai they would be absolved of their crimes. They had, and the Kings had followed through on their promise. Those who'd fought had been let go after the battle, many being allowed to fill the depleted ranks of the Silver Spears.

Meryam had been incensed by their release, but all hope was not lost. If there was one thing the House of Kings was good at, it was in documenting such things. They'd likely recorded each of the prisoner's names, relations, and places of birth as they were taken into custody. It could help Meryam find the subjects she needed for the next stage of her experiment.

"I don't know," Basilio said, "but I can find out."

The plan that had already begun to form expanded in Meryam's mind. "Does Nebahat of the Enclave still reside below the collegia?"

"As far as I'm aware, yes."

"Have him brought to me. I wish to speak to him about the collegia's chancellor and their hall of records."

"Yes, my queen."

"Now return to the palace." She turned to the crystal once more. "I'll find my own way back."

"Of course, Your Excellence."

She hardly heard his footsteps on the scaffolding stairs, and was only vaguely aware of his diminishing form as he left the cavern. She was too fixated on the light emanating from the crystal and the thoughts swirling in her mind. One move followed another followed another until her plan, while not complete, felt mature enough to start acting on.

"Enjoy your days, Macide Ishaq'ava." She placed her hand on the crystal and felt its latent power that much more keenly. "Enjoy them, for they are numbered."

Chapter 4

WHEN QUEEN NAYYAN first told Çeda that her *disguise* would consist of little more than a flowing turquoise abaya and a bit of cosmetics, Çeda thought she'd gone mad. But by the time Nayyan had shown her the dress and applied the makeup, she was having second thoughts. Her hair, unbound and lightly curled, fell about her shoulders. Her eyebrows had been plucked mercilessly. Kohl lined her eyes and shaded her lids, making her look decidedly sultry. The most distracting thing—well, other than the fact that Çeda's nipples could be discerned clearly through the sheer fabric—was the balm Nayyan applied to her lips. Made from beeswax and crushed mother of pearl, it had a faint blue tint and made her lips *glitter*.

"This will attract too much attention," Çeda said.

"It isn't the *amount* of attention you'll attract, but the *sort*. Believe me, the more time men spend looking at your chest and lips, the less they'll spend on *you*." Nayyan pinched Çeda's chin, turned her this way and that, appraising her like a jeweler might her biggest buy of the year. There was something in her eyes that told Çeda she was pleased with her efforts, and yet the longer she looked, the more annoyed she seemed to become.

Having had quite enough of her scrutiny, Çeda slapped Nayyan's hand away, a thing that, infuriatingly, seemed to have no effect on Nayyan whatsoever, as if Çeda's feelings meant nothing to her.

"She'll do," Nayyan said to Sümeya, "so long as she doesn't go opening that fool mouth of hers any more than is absolutely necessary."

They left for Yusam's palace immediately after, where they were met by King Umay, Yusam's son, one of the lesser Kings. Umay stared intently at Çeda when they were introduced. Nayyan had been right. He kept admiring her shape, or staring at her lips, and when he seemed to linger over her for too long, Nayyan would distract him with stories of Ransaneh or question him about his many children—the latter seemed to annoy Umay, and he would answer in only clipped replies.

As they neared their destination, Umay gathered himself and interrupted Nayyan's prattling. "Tell me again why you wish to use the mere?"

"I've had strange dreams since childbirth. I believe they're visions of my future, or rather, *Ransaneh's* future."

"And?" he asked.

Nayyan smiled pleasantly. "Surely you're aware that in addition to the visions in the mere, your father had prophetic dreams." He'd had no such dreams to Çeda's knowledge, but Yusam, while alive, was famously distanced from his children. Nayyan was certain Umay would have no idea if the claim was true or not and would be too embarrassed to admit it. "He would go to the mere to clarify them," Nayyan continued. "The gods willing, so it will be for me."

Umay's gaze slid to Çeda. "And your servant? Perhaps I could entertain her while you sit beside the mere."

"Normally I would agree, of course, but I need her. She's gifted at interpreting my dreams."

Umay seemed displeased, but said no more about it.

They passed through a scalloped bronze archway and entered a lush garden with sculpted trees and manicured bushes. Overhead, the sky was bright blue. The sun shone against the uppermost leaves and the bare brown rock face on the garden's opposite side, while the grass and the trickling stream beneath the trees lay in shadow.

After giving Çeda a light shove, Nayyan turned and faced Umay, preventing him from following the two of them into the garden. In the awkward silence that followed, Umay glanced over Nayyan's shoulder at Çeda, and his sad face turned even sadder. Here was a man unaccustomed to being told no, but Queen Nayyan refused to budge.

"You'll share what you find with me?" Umay finally said.

It was a command, not a request, but Nayyan shook her head. "I'm afraid that's impossible. The visions are of a rather *personal* nature."

"I see." He looked over his shoulder, as if he'd heard someone calling to him. "I'll leave you to it then, shall I?"

Nayyan merely waited.

"Yes, well," Umay said. "Good day to you, then."

As the sounds of his boot heels striking the tiled floor faded, Nayyan joined Çeda in the shade beneath a pair of strange trees with spiraling boughs. "Are all the young Kings like that?" Çeda asked

Nayyan shrugged. "Let's just say they're unaccustomed to holding the reins of power and handle it in different ways." She waved to the mere, which was little more than a stream-fed well with emerald green coping around its edges. "You may begin," she said, "and you will share with me *everything* you see."

Çeda nodded, wondering just what it was Nayyan hoped to find. Çeda suspected it was half the reason Nayyan had agreed to this caper at all.

As Çeda settled herself onto the manicured grass, she noticed movement behind Nayyan. An animal's tail hung down from the trees, swaying this way and that. Peering into the branches, she spotted one of the mountain leopards Yusam had kept as pets. The leopard stared back, blinking languidly, tail flicking.

Nayyan glanced over her shoulder at it, then motioned for Çeda to continue. "It's well fed," she said, as if that were enough to allay Çeda's fears.

Çeda had never been comfortable with the big cats, but she ignored it as best she could and stared into the depths of the pool. Beneath the water's surface, the stone was coated in a sea-green moss that faded to black at the center. It looked like a round, lidless eye that was beckoning her toward it, so much so that she was forced to kneel lest she plunge in, a thing that seemed a very bad idea indeed.

Nayyan stood across from her, looking as though she were about to say something snide. "Yusam used to say he could find the thread of someone's future by recalling his last memory of them. Resonance, he called it. He wasn't able to do it reliably, but when it worked, it worked well enough to follow it to other events, both future and past."

With that she strode further along the stream, sat on a bench, and proceeded to ignore Çeda entirely.

Çeda wasn't sure what to think of Yusam's *resonance*, but without anything better to try, she gripped the coping, stared into the clear depths of the bottomless mere, and summoned her last memories of Nalamae: the goddess lying in the hold of Leorah's yacht in a bunk too small for her, her chest wrapped in bloody bandages; Nalamae holding the acacia seed Çeda's mother, Ahya, had left for Çeda in an engraved box; Nalamae lying on a broken courtyard with thousands of black moths storming through the air while Yerinde stood over her, holding the adamantine spear that had pierced Nalamae's chest and killed her.

Suddenly Çeda felt herself being drawn forward. Felt herself tipping forward. Her entire body tensed, the tendons along her forearms tightening to the point of pain. Just when she thought she was going to fall into the water, she blinked and saw before her a navy ship, a galleon. The decks were pristine, the sails a perfect ivory. The ship rested on the sand of King's Harbor. The great doors creaked and groaned as they were swung wide. The ship was towed outside the harbor. Its sails were set by the crew. A woman stood on the deck. She had a pinched face and small, hard eyes. Her graying hair was pulled back into a tail, but wisps fluttered in the stiff wind. In one hand, she had a board with a piece of paper attached to it. She was walking about the ship, taking notes as she went: the set of the sails, the tightness of the standing rigging, the sway of the mainmast as the wind changed and as the ship heeled over the dunes.

She was the shipwright, Çeda realized, and the ship was on its maiden voyage. It must be one of the ships being built, or that *would* be built, after the terrible clash with the Mirean fleet and the smaller battles since.

The shipwright went belowdecks and had just started to inspect the infirmary when a sound like thunder rocked the ship. She looked up as footsteps boomed across the deck above. The sound of cracking timber was followed by the ceiling above her being ripped away—crossbeams, joists, deck boards and all. Sunlight and sawdust flooded the space. Through the hole just made, a creature with skin as black as night could be seen. Great ram horns swept over its head. A crown of thorns wrapped around them, covering the top of its skull. A pair of tails lashed and snapped as it bent low and stared at the woman.

It was Goezhen, Çeda knew. She'd seen him before.

The god smiled, revealing a rending of teeth. With a wave of his clawed hand, more deck boards broke and flew like wounded birds into the vivid blue sky.

Just as Goezhen's great, clawed hand was reaching down for the stunned woman, the world shifted. Time passed. The desert moved beneath Çeda's feet. She saw a man being hung from a gibbet, much as Çeda's mother had been hung: feet first. Çeda gasped when she realized who it was. Macide, with a sigil drawn on his chest. His face was a bloody mess.

Below his swinging form, a crowd conversed easily. They milled about, talking, drinking from goblets, as if they were attending some grand social affair. Some wore crowns—the lesser Kings and Queens of Sharakhai, perhaps? Many ignored Macide entirely while others spoke in hushed tones and stared up with eager eyes, as if participating in a macabre art auction, Macide the next sculpture up for bid.

The crowd turned at a scream. Some backed away, though what might have frightened them Çeda had no idea. Before she could wonder over it, she was whisked away again, and now she stood before Emre. He was ignoring her, staring into a blindingly bright light. Not far away, walking toward him, obscuring the light as he approached, was his brother, Rafa.

The scene felt wrong. Rafa was dead, but Emre was pacing toward him as if he didn't realize, or didn't care. Çeda's worry felt like a weight upon her chest. It grew so bad she could barely breathe.

"Don't, Emre!" she managed to shout. "Leave him be!"

But Emre just kept walking.

"Emre, stop!" She tried to run toward him, to tear him away, but the vision faded, and Çeda was once more staring into the depths of the mere.

"No!" she screamed at it.

Her breath came in ragged gasps. Her body was tight as a bow string. Her hands ached from the death grip she had on the mere's emerald coping. Gods, the look of acceptance on Emre's face . . . He'd wanted to join Rafa, but there was only one way that could happen.

Queen Nayyan still sat on the nearby bench. Aloof earlier, she stared at Çeda with an intensity that made it clear how invested she was in this endeavor. "Well?"

Çeda, still disorientated, crawled away, sat on the grass, and held her head tight until the suffocating feeling passed. "I found Nalamae. She was a woman, fully grown, a shipwright, I think, sailing on a royal clipper." Hoping Nayyan might have some clue as to where Nalamae might be found or when the attack might take place, she told her the rest, but withheld the visions of Macide and Emre.

"Who can tell where or when she'll appear?" Nayyan said when Çeda was done. "It could be today, it could be a year from now."

"Could I speak to someone in King's Harbor? They might know her. They could tell me which ships she's building and how close they are to completion."

Nayyan nodded. "I'll make enquiries." And with that it became clear that Nayyan *wanted* to remain involved. She had believed the effort worth pursuing, worth conspiring to get Çeda into Yusam's palace, and now she wanted to know more.

It was then that Çeda realized how vulnerable Nayyan seemed. She understood why a moment later when Nayyan asked, "Did you see me or Ransaneh?"

"No," Çeda said while shaking her head.

"Ihsan? Any of the other Kings?"

Çeda shook her head again, reckoning that Nayyan didn't need to know of the other visions until Çeda had had time to consider them. She was sure of one thing, though: as soon as she was able, she would return to the thirteenth tribe. She needed to see Emre and Macide safe.

"Come," Nayyan said as she stood and made for the archway into the palace. "It's time we head back."

Çeda pulled herself up, dizzy for a moment. She caught the leopard staring at her. It was lounging on the same bough as before, looking pleased with itself. Ignoring it, Çeda brushed her skirt clean and followed Nayyan into the palace.

Many knew that the garden of King Yusam's famous mere hugged the mountainside. It gave a stunning view of a sheer rock face, even a bit of the mountain's bare, rocky peak. What few knew, however, was that there was a flat shelf of rock that could be reached after a short climb.

Gerta, a girl of ten, knew. She'd found it years ago when she was sent to pull the weeds and clip the decorative hedges. She'd gone there sometimes to hide from her mother, the palace's master gardener, or from her brother, who was always bossing her around, or from the Silver Spears who were often sent to fetch her.

Gerta also had very sharp hearing. It was a secret she'd shared only with her brother, and even then she'd only told him while playing clobber sock, after he'd built up enough points to give her a good thumping unless she told him something really important.

One day, after she'd splattered warm porridge in his face, he'd thrown her to the jackals: he told everyone she'd been listening in on the King's conversations, which he should never, ever have done. According to the un-spoken rules of clobber sock, *no* secrets divulged during the game would ever be told, but her brother . . . Well, he'd always been a bit of an ass.

On the wings of gossip, the secret was carried to the King's ear—Umay, not Yusam, and for that she was glad. King Yusam had always terrified her. She was sure that if *he* had been the one to find out, he'd have given Gerta to the Confessor King for questioning. King Umay, however, found another purpose for her. He hid her in his grand audience chamber and asked her to listen to a businessman and his son confer after what was sure to be a heated bargaining session. Gerta had listened to their positions and reported it to Umay. He'd surely used their words to leverage a better deal for himself.

Again and again Umay asked her to eavesdrop, usually inside his palace, but sometimes without. Once she was delivered to the city and secreted away in the very top of Bakhi's temple so she could listen to the high priest, who gave up a trove of information about one of his most generous donors, a man who was in trouble for having slain a woman in an attempt at covering up their affair.

So it was that Gerta had been asked to listen to Queen Nayyan and her pretty servant. Umay hadn't believed Nayyan's story, and Gerta could see why. It hadn't been *Nayyan* who peered into the mere, but her *servant*, and it had had nothing to do with Nayyan's baby, but with the goddess, Nalamae, who some said had been killed near Mount Arasal when the Malasani had invaded Sharakhai with their golems. Gerta wondered vaguely whether it was Nalamae's death that made the golems go mad during the Battle for the Mount.

Whatever the case, the vision had apparently shown the goddess reborn as some shipwright on a royal clipper. Who Nayyan's supposed servant was in truth, Gerta had no idea, but she was nearly certain the woman was no servant at all. Perhaps Gerta would be able to wheedle it out of King Umay. He wasn't nearly as sly as he thought he was, and she'd grown quite good at getting him to talk about the reasons behind her missions. Either way, Umay would be pleased. She might even get the brass akhala she'd been after.

Enough time had passed that Gerta felt it safe to climb down from her perch. She rolled over, ready to do just that, but froze when she spotted movement beneath the treetops. One of King Yusam's bloody leopards was prowling along, heading toward the mere. As it went, however, it began to change. By the Kings who rule, it was growing, lengthening, its fur drawing into its body, revealing black skin. It became taller and taller, rearing onto hind legs shaped more like a goat's than a mountain cat's. Horns sprouted from its forehead and curled back. A crown of thorns pressed up and outward from its skull. Bloodshot eyes stared fixedly at the mere, a pleased expression on the beast's demonic face.

Gerta felt herself quivering all over. She lay flat on the stone and tried to control her breathing. She truly did. But she was gasping like a fish. She wouldn't in a thousand years have thought to witness a god, yet here was Goezhen come to eavesdrop on Queen Nayyan, just as Gerta had. Her mind went mad trying to figure out why, but after a moment her thoughts rearranged themselves and she realized she need look no further than the vision of Nayyan's supposed servant. In it, Goezhen had found Nalamae. But why would a vision like that matter to Goezhen? Surely he knew of it already. The gods knew everything.

She went still as stone, telling herself not to look anywhere but up at the blue sky. But every moment that passed felt as if Goezhen was preparing to leap up and rend her limb from limb. Shivering badly, she rolled and peered over the edge.

Goezhen was there, his baleful eyes staring straight at her. She swallowed hard. Something warm trickled between her legs. The smile on the dark god, as though he'd be pleased to take a measure of her flesh, made her heart falter.

"Climb down, child." Goezhen spoke in a low rumble.

She did as he bade her, and soon stood before him. She nearly fell to pieces as one great hand reached out and slipped around her waist. He picked her up and with a blackened claw traced a glowing sigil in the air.

That done, he set her back down. She stared numbly at the moss-laden trail of water that trickled down the face of the stone. Beside her was a looming shape. A moment later, however, it seemed to vanish. Wind rushed past her and a noxious black smoke filled the air. She thought she should run from it, but it dissipated before she could decide whether to head for the trees or the palace.

She looked around and found herself in an empty garden. She wondered why she'd come here in the first place. Oh yes. Queen Nayyan and her servant. Realizing her britches felt cool, she stared down and saw the patch of wet cloth between her legs. Gods, she'd pissed herself. She must have fallen asleep on the rock. King Umay wouldn't be pleased. He wouldn't be pleased at all.

Unless she told him a story . . .

Perhaps they *did* have a vision about Nayyan's daughter. That was the key: tell him something useless about Nayyan and her daughter, and all would be well.

As the pieces of the story began ordering themselves in her mind, she headed into the palace toward her rooms. Her britches needed changing.

Chapter 5

HUSAMETTÍN, AFTER FINALLY RESIGNING himself to endure Ihsan's presence in their alliance for the good of Sharakhai, told Ihsan how some in Zeheb's family had feared for their King's life before the Malasani invasion; how during the Battle for the Mount they'd forced their way into Eventide and freed Zeheb the Whisper King from imprisonment; how they'd used the battle itself as a way to steal down to the caves to the southeast of Sharakhai, where many royal families kept yachts that were well maintained and ready to sail on a moment's notice. They'd secreted Zeheb in one of those ships and sailed west, hoping they might heal their King of his malady and ride out the storm of the Malasani occupation.

Little had they known that the Malasani horde and their golems would be rebuffed. Even so, it had allowed them to save Zeheb, a man they felt had been unjustly accused, perhaps even set up for a fall by the other Kings. They'd been right, of course. Ihsan had framed him and manipulated the other Kings just enough to prevent any of the blame falling on him.

To Zeheb's family, the war had surely seemed like the perfect opportunity to spirit their patriarch away, to heal him if possible, and plan to return after the war and take up what power they could. But the battle's strange end, with the golems going mad, had soured their plans. The other Kings had won the day, leaving them on the outside, looking in. By then it was Meryam and the lesser Kings who held the reins of power in Sharakhai. And with Temel, one of Zeheb's many sons, sitting on Zeheb's throne, there were many in his own family who didn't wish to see his return.

Several days later, Ihsan found himself crawling, flat on his stomach, toward the edge of a rocky slope. Hidden by a clutch of wiry bushes, he peered through his spyglass toward the pan of flat sand below where six ketches and a tumbledown dhow were clustered. Sitting in the shade of a distant cliff, they looked like a pack of maned wolves taking their rest. Zeheb was hidden inside one of those ships. Ihsan hadn't seen the man himself, but he'd spotted several of his family members walking among the ships: a pair of women with the bearings of his two eldest living daughters, and Zeheb's grandson, a man of forty summers who bore his weight as Zeheb once had: like an overweight dune lizard readying for a long winter sleep.

"What do your precious journals say about those ships?"

Ihsan turned to see Cahil's daughter, Yndris, standing in full view of the ships below. Even when Ihsan waved for her to get down, she remained there, cloaked in her own impudence, forcing Ihsan to shift closer to her and tug hard on her sleeve.

Rolling her eyes, she dropped down and crawled next to him. *Please,* Ihsan prayed to the fates, *if you grant me anything, grant me this: have my daughter grow up to be nothing like Yndris.* Nayyan had surely given birth weeks ago. In his absence she would be raising their child alone, which weighed more on his heart every day.

Ihsan signed to Yndris, *As I've told you many times, my precious journals do not detail every step we need to take.*

With a sour expression, she snatched the spyglass from him and trained it on the arc of ships. "Well surely they told you *something.*"

He was forced to wait until she looked at him to give his answer. *Yusam's visions are nearly inscrutable. They're like trying to follow a trail from a description of pebbles along the road.*

"By the gods who breathe, Ihsan"—she waved to where her father and Husamettín were huddled, talking in low tones—"why should *we* trust them at all when you hardly believe in them yourself?"

I didn't say I don't believe in them. He sent a pointed glance toward the other two Kings. *See how far they've taken* me, *and consider how far they may take us all.*

Yndris's pert face made it clear she was skeptical. "Well, then, what does the next pebble look like?"

Ihsan glanced toward the Kundhuni ships. *It shows us with Zeheb.*

"Zeheb." Yndris spat onto the dirt. "The King who spouts useless nonsense."

No, Ihsan signed vehemently. *Yusam's vision was clear in this much. It's Zeheb who points us to the* next *pebble. That's why we need him.*

Yndris resumed her inspection of the small Kundhuni fleet. Ihsan was disappointed she hadn't the forethought to ask the next logical question. He would have lied, but part of him still wanted her to ask what designs Ihsan had of his own on Zeheb. Cahil and Husamettín wanted to use him to listen to the whispers in Sharakhai, to gain an edge over Meryam. Yndris was apparently dim enough that she thought Ihsan wanted the same.

But there was something much bigger in play, which made Ihsan's fingers tingle just to think about. Four centuries ago, the gods had set a grand game of aban into motion. Everyone, including Ihsan, had been certain they knew the players: the Twelve Kings of Sharakhai pitted against the desert tribes, especially the thirteenth. But it wasn't so, and never had been—it had always been the gods against mortal man. *That* was the importance of Yusam's journals. Their dizzying visions had lifted Ihsan up high enough that he could see the board in full, or enough of it that he could start making real moves of his own. And just in time. The endgame had arrived, the closing moves were being planned, and Ihsan himself was preparing some that would shake the foundations of the desert.

Beside him, Yndris went stiff. Ihsan waited for her to say something, but she was silent, transfixed. Tugging on her sleeve like a lost gutter wren had no effect either, and suddenly it returned in full force: the sense that he was no player at all, but a powerless imbecile being swept along the river of fate just like everyone else.

Finally Yndris relinquished the spyglass. "There"—she pointed to the fourth ship in the line—"on the quarterdeck."

He trained the spyglass on the ketch she'd indicated. There, at long last, was Zeheb. He was being helped into a chair by one of his daughters while the other adjusted a silk sun shade over him. They'd needed this—the knowledge that Zeheb was still alive, that they weren't chasing a ghost. They also knew for certain which ship he'd been hiding in.

Ihsan pulled the spyglass down, then immediately brought it back to his eye. A flock of sparrows took flight inside his chest as he spotted it again: a dark, angular shape on the horizon, a trail of dust lifting behind.

"What?" Yndris asked.

Ihsan handed the spyglass to her and pointed. She raised it up and stared for a long while. "That's a royal galleon."

Indeed, Ihsan thought, and there were only two reasons it might have come. The first was that Meryam or the new King of Zeheb's house, Temel, was sending a peace offering, a way for Zeheb to return to Sharakhai and avoid punishment for having fled. The second and more likely by far was that the ship had been sent to kill him.

We have to move, Ihsan said. *Now.*

Yndris remained where she was, a pensive expression on her face. She jutted her chin toward the Kundhuni ships. "You said Yusam saw many possibilities in his mere."

Ihsan nodded, curious where she was headed.

"That implies you've chosen one of them. I wonder, at the end of it all, where did those visions see *you?*"

Well, well, so Yndris wasn't stupid after all. *They saw me,* he signed, *in a Sharakhai that was still intact.*

"I assumed that much. Where were you? Where was my father? Where was Husamettín?"

The visions were unclear in this respect.

"Might I read some of them, these visions? Perhaps you've overlooked something."

I left the journals in a safe place—he waved toward the ships—*far from here, as we head into danger.*

Yndris put on a look of calm acceptance. "Then I'm sure when the danger has passed you'll allow me to read them?"

Ihsan smiled easily. *Your wish is my command.*

Yndris snorted, and the two of them crawled back, away from the drop-off.

That night, when the light of dusk had failed save for a dying ember in the western sky, Ihsan crouched beside Yndris, only a hundred paces from the campfire shedding light on the Kundhuni ships. A handful of lanterns glowed golden on the decks. The rest was naught but shadows and starlight.

When a cry lifted up from the far side of the camp, several guardsmen broke away from the fire and ran toward the shouting. The clash of steel on steel followed. Battle cries rang out. Several men began barking orders in percussive Kundhunese.

A pair of guardsmen lingered near Zeheb's ketch, apparently unwilling to abandon their posts. Ihsan was just thinking he and Yndris might have to deal with the guards themselves when an agonized scream rent the air and the guards rushed toward it.

As the sounds of battle rang out—smithy-anvil peals, the grunts of soldiers fighting for their lives—Yndris and Ihsan ran low and fast toward the ship's unguarded stern. Soon they reached the rear hatch, the one that could be lowered to take on cargo directly from the sand. While Yndris drew her sword and watched for signs that they'd been spotted, Ihsan wedged a stout iron bar into the gap. He was no physical specimen like Husamettín, but he still had the inhuman strength the gods had granted all the Kings, so it took little time for the hatch restraints to give.

As soon as it fell to the sand, Yndris stormed into the hold. Ihsan followed, and together they climbed up to the ship's middle deck, where the crew's quarters would be. Earlier, Ihsan had seen one of the rear cabins' shutters being opened from inside. They rushed toward that cabin. When Yndris crashed the door in with a sharp kick, they found Zeheb sitting up in the lone bunk, staring at them with wide eyes and messy, pepper-gray hair.

A small lantern hanging from a ceiling beam lit Zeheb in ghostly relief. His lips moved soundlessly. He was listening to the whispers all around. Suddenly, with a surprisingly lucid look on his face, Zeheb whistled like a Blade Maiden, a command that meant, simply, *halt.* "See there," he said softly, "they're being attacked." His voice changed to a slightly lower pitch. "Do we still go for the ketch?" Then in the soft voice once more, "Yes, but keep your eyes peeled. They'll spirit him away if they think the sands are shifting beneath them."

Yndris seemed confused, but Ihsan had seen this sort of behavior from Zeheb before. He was repeating the whispers of others, perhaps those who'd been sent from the royal galleon. To ensure their mission's success, a full hand of Blade Maidens, five deadly swordswomen, would likely have been dispatched, maybe more.

Before Ihsan could consider the implications further, a clicking sound came from his right. He'd no more turned toward it than the door of the cabin's armoire burst open and a body flew toward him. It was a woman, a knife gripped in her upraised hands, her curly brown hair trailing behind her like a pennant on the wind.

Ihsan was caught completely flat-footed. Yndris, however, was already on the move. She swung her ebon blade in a deadly arc, cutting the woman down. The wound was mortal—that much was plain—and yet as the woman crumpled to the dry wooden planks, the only sound she uttered was a single, sharp yelp. She lay on the floor, breathing in short, sharp gasps, while blood spread across the bodice of her simple linen dress.

Zeheb stared in shock. His eyes turned red and began to water, but his lips, ever bound to listen to the whispers, kept moving.

The woman was one of his daughters, Ihsan realized. It was in that moment that he felt the first twinge of regret for what he'd done to Zeheb, a man he'd once counted as a friend. It had been necessary, and Zeheb had deserved it after threatening Nayyan and Ihsan's unborn child. Even so, to be rendered unable to whisper a word of prayer for your own dying daughter . . .

Yndris snapped her fingers before Ihsan's eyes. "What, you expected no bloodshed?"

Ignoring her, Ihsan went to Zeheb's bedside and helped him to stand. Ihsan thought he might resist, but Zeheb came willingly, docile as a lamb, tears falling as whispers flew.

They fled through the ship, chased by the sound of footsteps thudding down a set of stairs behind them. "Anann?" Just as Ihsan, Zeheb, and Yndris reached the hold, a surprised shout came from above, followed by a wail of anguish. "They've taken him!" a woman's voice rang out. "They've killed Anann and taken my father!"

They ran down the ramp and onto open sand.

"Halt!" called a voice in sharp Kundhunese.

They pressed on, both Yndris and Ihsan staying close to Zeheb, which was likely the only reason arrows weren't raining down on them.

"What are you waiting for?" the Kundhunese captain snapped from the deck. "Let fly!"

Most of the arrows were off target. Yndris blocked several more with her small shield. Darkness cloaked them, but by the light of the ships' lanterns Ihsan saw a small host of forms sprinting over the sand—a dozen warriors bearing spears and shields and khopeshes with their distinctive, crescent-moon blades.

As slow as Zeheb was moving, it was impossible to outdistance their attackers. Ihsan was just preparing to turn and fight when a lithe male form slashed into the soldiers. By the light of the campfire, Ihsan saw Cahil using his war hammer and shield to battle the Kundhuni soldiers. He was a dervish, a devil with a blest hammer, and his daughter was nearly as fast. Together the two of them fought off the soldiers, leaving only one for Ihsan to deal with, which he did with a deep thrust to the man's chest. Zeheb, meanwhile, watched everything while mumbling into the wind.

Suddenly a woman in dark armor flew in, delivering a terrible strike to Cahil. It rang off his scale armor, which blunted the blow, but the strength behind it sent Cahil staggering. Suddenly he and Yndris were locked in combat with three Blade Maidens.

As Ihsan turned away, another resolved from the darkness ahead of him. He immediately retreated, knowing his only real hope was to delay—he hadn't the skill of even the worst of the Blade Maidens, especially if they'd taken a petal, which these women surely had.

The Maiden wasted no time. She pressed him hard, her shamshir blurring through the night. He wore fine mail armor, but it couldn't withstand an ebon blade, not when driven by the powerful sword arm of a Blade Maiden. He took a cut to the leg, then a terrible blow to his right shoulder. He managed one feeble slash to her arm, but at the cost of a cut to his ribs that felt like it went all the way to the bone.

Beyond the Maiden, Cahil stumbled. He fell to one knee, his off-hand grasping at his chest just as he had at the caravanserai. Seeing him falter,

Yndris gave a cry of desperation and sent a storm of blows against the Maidens.

Does it end here? Ihsan wondered. *Were Yusam's visions wrong?*

The Maiden fighting Ihsan sent a stunning blow against his feeble defenses and followed it with a ruinous back kick that knocked the wind from him and sent him flying. As he crashed onto the sand, he saw that Yndris had felled one Maiden to reach her father's side. She fought like a cornered cat, perhaps hoping that her father would recover enough to help, but Cahil could hardly move. He held perfectly still, eyes blinking fiercely, while the spell passed, leaving Yndris to fight alone against three Blade Maidens.

While Zeheb watched with a vaguely pleased expression, Ihsan whipped sand into the face of the Maiden coming for him. It sent her momentarily reeling. Yndris, meanwhile, took a blow to the back of one thigh. She stumbled, then ducked beneath a killing stroke from another Maiden.

The Maidens were surrounding her, hemming her in. She was blocking furiously, expending all her energy on her defense. Just when Ihsan thought surely she would fall, a tall swordsman rushed in from the darkness. It was Husamettín, and he was like a raging river, fluid, powerful, and relentless as he sent a series of blurring strikes against his enemies. He'd lost Night's Kiss to Çedamihn and now wielded a mundane, two-handed shamshir, but he seemed no less deadly. His turban was gone, leaving his long hair swaying as he moved and revealing the mark of the traitor that had been carved into his forehead. Deadly as he was, eyes wide like a demon in the night, he seemed to wear it like a badge of honor.

The Maiden attacking Ihsan thought better of it and rushed to help the others in her hand. It did little good, though. Husamettín, with Yndris's aid, dispatched them all.

Then they were off, while the calls of the Kundhuni crew and Zeheb's surviving daughter chased them into the night.

Chapter 6

Hamid, now second in command of the thirteenth tribe, answering only to Shaikh Macide, stood on the foredeck of a fleet galleon named the *Amaranth*. Astern, sailing in arrowhead formation, were three light frigates, each armed with more than the normal share of ballistae, catapults, and soldiers. The *Amaranth*'s armaments had been expanded as well. They sailed southwest toward a meeting of tribes, after all, and Hamid was sure things were going to get dicey—having crews ready to draw blood was only prudent.

Scanning ahead with his spyglass, Hamid spotted a cluster of ships, barely visible in a heat that made the horizon waver.

"Wind's favorable," Sirendra called beside him. "Another hour of sailing and we'll be there."

He glanced over at Sirendra, the leader of the ten Shieldwives who'd accompanied him on the journey. Her ivory turban, with its hanging beads and the medallion set at the center of her brow, accented her turquoise eyes and round face. She was a good woman, dependable, yet Hamid always found himself annoyed with her. He knew why. It was her battle dress. It was cut in the style of the Blade Maidens, yet another reminder of Çeda's growing influence over the thirteenth tribe. The very fact that there were a group of women who'd trained under Çeda—a woman who'd wielded a blade in service to the Kings of Sharakhai—showed how bloody incestuous the desert had become, a thing Hamid hated more with each passing day.

"If you want to fight, fine," Hamid had told Sirendra at the start of their journey two months ago. "Just wear armor like any other soldier."

But Sirendra had been adamant. "You know the Blade Maidens stole the design from the tribes, don't you? I lay claim to it, as do my sisters, and there's no King, no Blade Maiden"—she'd looked him up and down with a sneer—"nor captain of a bloody ship who's going to tell me otherwise."

The story was probably horse shit, but Hamid had let it go.

"You think the tribes will agree to join the Alliance without a fight?" Sirendra was staring at him in that judging way of hers.

"In truth," Hamid said, "I don't much care if they put up a fight or not. Shaikh Neylana is the one counseling the last three tribes not to join, but that changes now. Fight or no fight, she's going to agree to our demands."

Sirendra frowned. "But you'll do your best to avoid bloodshed as Macide asked, yes?"

"You're afraid of a bit of bloodshed now?"

"I want the tribes united."

"As do I, but it isn't up to me." He waved to the ships ahead. "It's up to them."

A deep voice called from the deck behind him. "It's time they learned, right, Hamid?"

Hamid turned to find Frail Lemi taking the stairs leading up to the foredeck in a single bound. The wind tugged at his scruffy beard, made his sirwal pants flap, but it was his dark leather vest that drew the eye. It might have looked comically small if it weren't for the sheer amount of muscle it revealed. The gods had seen fit to grant Frail Lemi the rare combination of height, brawn, and the grace of an acrobat. He even had rugged good looks. *If only they'd let him keep his wits*, Hamid mused, *he might have become a power in the desert.* "Didn't I tell you to stop talking like that?" Hamid asked him.

With an incredulous look, Frail Lemi spread his arms wide. "What? We're among friends."

"Yes, but you talk like that around everyone."

Lemi stared at the ships in the distance and rubbed his bald head, which he'd recently started shaving. He'd seen another crewman doing it, and had become fixated with sharpening his straight razor every morning and cutting it close. "You're smart, Hamid, but sometimes you can't see the dunes for the sand. Tell your enemies how badly you're going to beat them into a pulp and they start to wonder if it's true. Their doubt grows. They start making mistakes. What you call bravado, I call fate."

The buzzing at the back of Hamid's head was coming back again. He might have believed those words had they come from another man. He might even have believed them from Frail Lemi if he wasn't constantly fucking things up. "We went over this," Hamid said with all the patience he could muster. "There's a time and a place for intimidation. This isn't a fight in a shisha den."

Frail Lemi cracked his knuckles, sending the muscles along his arms and chest to rippling. "You're still taking me with you, though, right?"

"So long as you keep that big trap of yours shut."

Frail Lemi sniffed. "You know I will."

Hamid knew no such thing. But he reckoned that having the big man there for the intimidation factor alone was worth it. An hour later, after anchoring, Hamid, Frail Lemi, and Sirendra disembarked and headed toward the Halarijan ships, which were set in a defensive circle. A herald came to meet them, a short, potbellied man with a pompous look Hamid wanted to slap from his face the moment he appeared.

The herald bowed. "If you'll but follow me."

They were led inside the ring of ships, where the wind dropped precipitously. On the way to a striped, orange-and-yellow pavilion they passed a group of men and women standing around a fire, tending to a large soup pot and several racks of spitted goat. The air was thick with the smell of it.

"Smells good," Frail Lemi said.

Hamid glared at him. "Will you concentrate?"

Frail Lemi shrugged while sending a longing look over his shoulder. "Man's gotta eat."

They were led into the pavilion, where Shaikh Neylana waited with a half-dozen elders with dour looks on their faces. They sat in an arc on a circle of carpets. Neylana, a stone-faced woman of some fifty summers, wore a simple brown dress with white stitching that somehow accentuated her vulturous looks.

After waving Hamid and the others to the empty carpets across from her, her eyes lingered on Frail Lemi. "This one I remember."

Which was her way of saying she *didn't* remember Hamid.

"This looks like a tribunal," Hamid said as he sat cross-legged.

To which Neylana replied, "In a way, it is."

Which only served to intensify the buzzing at the back of Hamid's skull.

Introductions were made—the effeminate son of Tribe Okan's shaikh had come, the vizir of Tribe Narazid as well—but Hamid paid them little mind. He knew good and well Shaikh Neylana was the lynchpin. Convince *her* that the Alliance was in her tribe's best interests and Okan and Narazid would follow like the lemmings they were.

Araq was poured, but the buzzing in Hamid's head had become so marked he could hardly taste it. "We've come to convince you to join the Alliance," he said when it had become too much.

Neylana pursed her lips. "Direct . . ."

"There's no point waiting until our bellies are full to start talking. I've come at Macide's behest with our final offer."

Neylana plucked an olive from a small bowl. "Final offer," she repeated in a singsong voice, then popped the olive into her mouth and chewed with a leisurely smile. "One might think you're trying to threaten us before you've even *shared* Macide's offer."

"Take it however you wish." Hamid drew a scroll case from his khalat. Inside was the offer Macide and the other shaikhs of the Alliance had drawn up, including a map with new territorial lines—drawn more than generously, in Hamid's opinion—for all three tribes represented in the pavilion.

Neylana accepted the scroll case, removed the paper within, and unrolled it. Time passed slowly as she read. The pavilion walls bent inward from the wind. The cook fire crackled. Somewhere in the distance, children played. Neylana made a show of considering the conditions and trade agreements written below the map itself, passed it over to Tribe Narazid's vizir, then rubbed her fingers as if she'd picked up a bit of grease from the paper.

"Macide has hardly shifted from his previous offer."

"It isn't Macide alone," Hamid countered while motioning toward the map. "Nine other tribes have backed us, the thirteenth, in making this offer."

Neylana's infuriating smile deepened, which intensified the buzzing in his skull, nearly to the point of pain. Hamid felt like Frail Lemi, unable to control his emotions or his actions. He was so eager to see the smile wiped from Neylana's face he nearly drew his knife to ensure it. He managed to keep the urge in check, but even so, he shifted on the carpet, itching for this farce of a negotiation to be over so he could deliver their final incentive.

He blinked. Calmed himself. *Not yet, Hamid. Not yet.* Macide had made him swear that he would give Neylana a chance.

Neylana's expression turned serious, as if she sensed his black urges. "Don't mistake us. There is a desire in us all to see the desert united. But we have the welfare of our tribes to consider. The Malasani have been raiding the caravanserais we depend on for trade. They've taken or destroyed a dozen of our ships."

"Which is precisely why an alliance would benefit you," Sirendra said.

Hamid glared at her for speaking out of turn. "Sirendra speaks the truth," he said. "The threat of reprisals from the thirteen tribes would ensure that Malasan touches *nothing* of ours, nor threatens a single caravanserai. And when *that's* done, we can get to the real business of the Alliance."

Neylana's eyebrows rose in surprise. "You speak of war."

Hamid saw right through her. Her look and her words were all a preamble to her rejection of Macide's offer. "War is inevitable."

Neylana gave a small, tittering laugh. "Men *always* think war is inevitable"—she motioned to the map, which the son of Tribe Okan's shaikh was looking over in great detail—"and little wonder when you think terms such as these are acceptable."

"Do you think the Malasani are here to bargain with us? Do you think once they'd taken Sharakhai, they would allow us to sail the Great Mother as we please out of the goodness of their hearts?"

"No, but they are hardly the only powers in the desert one can make arrangements with."

It took Hamid a moment to understand, and when he did, the buzz became a rattle that nearly overwhelmed him. "You mean Sharakhai."

"You speak it like the gravest insult, which makes me wonder if you've heard. There's a new power sitting atop the mount."

"*Meryam?* Who is she but a King in queen's raiment?"

"You fear an enemy that no longer exists. The old Kings are all gone, dead or fled or mad. Queen Meryam, meanwhile, has sent us an offer of peace, an offer backed by the young Kings and Queens of Sharakhai."

"Any offer from Queen Meryam is an offer filled with lies. Our offer is real."

"Queen Meryam's is real. She has already sent ships. She sent money to fill our coffers even before we've given our answer. What have you ever brought besides demands that we cede to you what *we* have bought with our own blood, sweat, and tears?"

"If her offer is so sweet, why haven't you taken it?"

"Because to join her, we must give you up. She wants the thirteenth tribe delivered to her."

She was thinking about it, Hamid realized. She was considering giving them up. If she hadn't, she would already have told Meryam no. She'd held off to see how the thirteenth tribe would counter Meryam's offer.

Hamid's rage built. He could hardly think. He could hardly see. Around him, he saw only enemies, men and women who would gut him as soon as release him from the pavilion. How he'd love to see the sand stained red with Halarijan blood. *Then we'll see what becomes of you, Shaikh Neylana, you and your snide little smile.*

"We bring the promise of a brighter future," Sirendra offered, perhaps seeing no other choice than to take over from Hamid.

Neylana swung her displeased gaze to Sirendra. "My children cannot eat brightness. And they don't live in the future but in the harshness of the here and now."

Hamid stood in a rush, refusing to sit with this woman any longer. "You're going to accept Queen Meryam's offer," he said with certainty.

"In truth, I wished to speak to you first. She's offering much that we might join her to fight the desert's invaders. She's desperate. Together, the tribes might convince her to call off her quest against you."

"You would have *us*, the thirteenth tribe, join forces with Sharakhai?"

"A *new* Sharakhai. I'm certain we can convince her to drop her demand that we give you up, particularly if we speak as one."

"A *new* Sharakhai?" Hamid spat. "There's nothing new about it. Those who took the vacant thrones are the sons and daughters of the Sharakhani Kings, men who taught them how to control, how to manipulate, how to absolve themselves of their fathers' treasonous past that they might keep their place on the mount. Oh, they will smile, they will hold out their hand in friendship, but only so they can draw you near enough to stick a knife through your ribs, or cast you down to writhe with the masses, those they've stood upon even as they claim it is they and they alone who lifted themselves high."

Neylana seemed unimpressed. "I would still ask that you take my offer to Macide."

Hamid spat on the sand between them. "Never."

"Then we'll send an envoy of our own, as we've done to the other tribes."

Hamid stared, aghast as understanding dawned. Neylana was a cancer. She would infect the other tribes. She would ruin everything the thirteenth tribe had worked for, everything *Hamid* had worked for. With that realization, the buzzing in Hamid's brain ceased. He became calm itself, knowing with a certainty that what he was about to do was right.

"Macide did give me leave to make one last offer." Macide had done no such thing, but Hamid knew this was the right way to proceed.

"Oh?" Neylana asked. "And what's that?"

Hamid strode toward the exit. "Better to be shown than told."

Sirendra and Frail Lemi rushed to catch up with Hamid. "What are you doing?" Sirendra asked under her breath.

Hamid kept moving, striding beyond the circle of ships and heading toward the *Amaranth* and her complement of three frigates. Neylana, the vizir, and the shaikh's son followed behind. As did the other elders, plus a dozen warriors in turbans and veils.

When they'd gone far enough, Hamid stopped. "Call them," he said to Sirendra.

Sirendra hesitated, her eyes shifting toward Neylana and the gathering crowd behind her.

"Now, Sirendra."

With a flinty look, she pulled her veil across her face. "I hope you know what you're doing."

Turning to the frigates, she gave a piercing whistle. On the three frigates, three more Shieldwives whistled back, then stepped down into the holds of their ships. Moments later, loading ramps built into the hulls of the ships fell open with heavy thuds. Sand and dust sprayed, momentarily occluding the figures inside the hold, who were now moving forward along the ramps. A score of Shieldwives, all veiled, came first. Following them were forms that hunkered low, that walked strangely. Some crawled on all fours like insects.

A collective gasp rose up from behind Hamid. He turned to look at them, the members of Tribe Halarijan. Dozens had gathered to watch, and more were joining them by the moment. Some stared with mouths open. Some drew shamshirs or readied their bows. Soon nearly two hundred had gathered outside the ring of ships, staring as the Shieldwives led fifty asirim forward over the sand. Behind Hamid, Sirendra, and Frail Lemi, the Shieldwives arrayed themselves in a line, and behind *them*, the asirim clustered in ragged groups.

Hamid waited several breaths, then turned and faced the asirim. "They," he said, pointing to Tribe Halarijan behind him, "would align themselves with Sharakhai. They would have *us* do the same. But we cannot. We *will* not. I will die before I join hands with any of the Kings, their sons, or their daughters."

Hamid had no ability to sense the asirim's feelings as Sirendra and the Shieldwives could, but he saw the anger in their faces, he saw the way their necks craned and their limbs twitched, as if they had a storehouse of pent-up rage they were eager to let loose.

That they had been sent with Hamid showed how important this mission was to Macide. The asirim were meant to protect them from the Malasani or the Mireans or even the holdout tribes if things went poorly. They hadn't been sent to intimidate, but even before they'd embarked Hamid thought what a waste it would be not to use the asirim.

Sirendra had pressed Hamid hard when he told her of his plans. She said Macide would never have agreed to it had he known. But Hamid had stood firm and eventually she'd relented. Whether Macide would have agreed or not wasn't the point—when the last three tribes agreed to join the Alliance, Macide would see that it was the right decision.

Hamid turned to face Neylana and her tribe. "Here," he shouted, spreading his arms wide, "is Macide's final offer."

Neylana broke from the crowd and strode toward Hamid, incensed. She raised one crooked finger and jabbed it at the asirim. "You would draw the blood of a sister tribe?"

Sirendra drew her shamshir. "Wouldn't joining hands with Queen Meryam, with *Sharakhai*, amount to the same thing? Would you abandon us, the thirteenth tribe, to the fates once more?"

Hamid could see Sirendra was wasting her breath. A man like Emre might have taken this time to explain that it was in Halarijan's best interests, that they would still have a say in all decisions once they joined the Alliance. Hamid didn't see it that way. Sometimes people needed to be *shown* the consequences of their actions. And, he admitted, part of him didn't *want* Neylana to agree. The past five months had seen his urge to draw blood grow and grow and grow to the point that he ached for it.

"We'll have your answer now," Sirendra said.

Hamid tried to read Neylana—he was usually pretty good at it—but found her inscrutable. As it turned out, he would never learn which way she leaned, for just then a crossbow bolt twanged. It sped past and fell short of an asir—one of a pair of twins, Huuri or Imwe, Hamid could never tell them apart.

Both of the twins, smaller than any of the other asirim, bolted forward, straight toward the one who'd shot the crossbow. The man looked shocked and confused. It had been nerves, Hamid realized.

Hamid could have given an order for the Shieldwives to rein the two asirim in. But he didn't, and the twins closed the distance like hungry wolves. The man retreated, but Huuri and Imwe both fell on him and tore into his flesh with abandon. Blood flew. Others rushed to the man's aid, but they were taken down as well. A loose group of Halarijan warriors closed in. Howling, more of the asirim began to break away to help the young twins.

"Enough!" Hamid called. "Enough! Call them away!"

The Shieldwives came forward, summoning the asirim to them. Huuri and Imwe, both inhumanly fast, had escaped with hardly a cut to their shriveled black skin. Tribe Halarijan, on the other hand, had two dead and five more wounded.

The twins smiled as they backed away. Hamid wanted to smile, too, but there was business to finish. He'd save his smiles for a bottle of araq later while lying in bed with Darius.

"You see what comes of defying us?" Hamid said to Neylana, who watched in shock. "Their might and anger should be directed against the Kings. Against the Mireans. Against the dirty Malasani and their ragtag fleet. Join us, Shaikh Neylana. Join us, or suffer the consequences."

Her gaze shifted from him to the dead and wounded who were being carried away. She blinked several times, her mouth working, but no words came out. "I will need to speak with the other shaikhs," she finally managed.

"We both know Tribes Okan and Narazid will follow your lead." Before she could say another word, Hamid spun and strode away. "You have one day."

Chapter 7

WILLEM KNEW THE COLLEGIA in Sharakhai well. He knew it better than the architects who'd designed it, better than the builders who'd built it, better than any of the masters, scholars, or students who'd walked its halls. He'd traversed every path through the grounds. He'd walked every hall, both above ground and below. He'd circumnavigated every room and hidden inside every closet, even the chancellor's while he slept at night.

He traveled its byways regularly, cataloguing changes like an accountant at his ledger: the desert's sudden windstorms working untold damage, coats of paint being added to disguise the passage of time, new wings of the collegia being planned then excavated then built, or in some cases *re*built. He took note of each new statue, each new piece of artwork, most commissioned from alumni, that graced the plinths, shelves, and walls. (The art was meant to add grandeur, Willem supposed, though each new crop of artists seemed to bring a greater fondness for gaudiness than the last.)

One night, on one of his many forays, Willem saw a student heading across the esplanade toward the sciences building. Even from this distance Willem knew it was Altan. He'd spied on him many times, watching him sleep from outside his window, watching him go from place to place, watching while he ate in the student cafeteria. More than the cut of his collegia robes or the awkward, somewhat self-conscious way in which he walked, it was the light he shed that defined him. Altan glowed brighter than the other students, with a slowly altering hue that was pleasant beyond description.

Altan took the steps up the stone building's arched entryway. When the wooden door had boomed shut, Willem scrambled up a tree, sprinted along a particular bough, and used the spring at its end to launch himself toward a balcony. Scrabbling up to the third floor, he entered through a shuttered window, one that was never kept locked, and slunk into the building's central hall. Looking down over the railing to the cavernous interior, he caught Altan's sparkling form as he headed toward the far corner.

Now that he had a better look at him, Willem could see that Altan's light was more subdued than normal, which made Willem wonder where he might be going at this late hour. He was taken for a moment by thoughts of Altan coming to him in the depths of the lower levels, the secret archives that only a handful were aware of. Altan might ask Willem questions about, well, anything, and Willem would answer. He had a gift for reading quickly, reading endlessly, and retaining it all. There was hardly a passage in the thousands of books he'd read he couldn't summon on demand.

Gods, the secrets Willem could share. He hadn't read *every* text in the collegia, but he'd read most, including those squirreled away by the blood mage, Nebahat, Willem's master, a high-ranking member of the secret society known as the Enclave. Nebahat's carefully culled archive held texts of deeper knowledge—*dangerous* texts, Nebahat had called them once. Nebahat wouldn't be pleased if Willem shared them with anyone, but *Altan* certainly would be. How could he not?

They'd become fast friends. They'd talk long into the night, laughing, debating topics that challenged them both, making them each glow the brighter.

Except . . .

Except Altan didn't know Willem existed. Willem made sure of it, exactly as the spells Nebahat had placed on him prescribed. (There had been another before Nebahat—he'd been the first to cast a spell of binding on Willem—but what matter was that now? Willem couldn't even remember his name!) And besides, even if Altan *did* learn of Willem's existence, Willem couldn't talk to him. His voice had been taken from him long ago.

So why *had* Altan come to the science building? Why was he taking the hallway that would lead, assuming the right route was followed, to Nebahat's hidden lair? Willem shimmied down a sandstone pillar to the second floor. He supposed it was possible that Altan *wasn't* headed toward Nebahat's secret archives, but Altan's glimmering had a resigned shade to it, the sort that combined purpose, secrecy, and no small amount of worry.

So it came as no surprise when Altan entered the alchemycal lab, continued into the storeroom, and pulled the hidden latch on the trick shelf. The shelf creaked open. Altan's footsteps resumed, then faded. Only then did Willem ease into the room filled with shelf upon shelf of glass beakers, labeled wooden boxes, and bottles filled with a kaleidoscope of chemical agents and reagents.

Quiet as an owl on the hunt, Willem slipped into the passage beyond the half-open shelf, wound downward along the spiraling stairs, and sped through the catacombs in the deepest part of the collegia grounds. He heard distant voices, which hid the sound of his padding footsteps as he sprinted along a side passage to a narrow ventilation shaft. Arms and legs pressing the sides of the shaft, Willem climbed down and eventually reached the lair's uppermost level, where he spent much of his days. Creeping along the aisle between the towering bookshelves, he reached an iron railing that overlooked a circular space with a hearth, a carpet-lined floor, and seven tables; the surface of each was filled with stack upon stack of disordered books, scrolls, and ancient tablets, both copper and clay. In the hearth, a black cone of porous, volcanic rock burned, the wavering emerald flames shedding an eerie light that mixed with the golden lanterns spaced throughout the room.

Nebahat's large frame blocked much of Willem's view, but he could see Altan's lean build, his clean-shaven face with its lighter skin. Altan was a young man—Willem's age more or less—with brown hair cut tight to his well-shaped head. He wore the simple, wheat-colored robes of a collegia student. Nebahat, on the other hand, though not old, had clearly passed the summer of his life. His skin was deep bronze, and his peppery beard was so bristly it looked like a snow mink had sunk its teeth into his chin and died there. His clothing was rich, from his khalat of patina green to the turquoise blue kaftan beneath to the pristine ivory silk turban that peaked above the bright stripe of orange and yellow pigment covering his forehead.

"You spoke to no one of your findings?" Nebahat asked Altan.

"Only Cassandra and the chancellor."

"Cassandra and the chancellor," Nebahat echoed, to which Altan nodded. "You questioned the chancellor as to the purpose behind our little project. Why?"

"Because I—" The light around Altan shifted toward mauve, a sign of anguish and indecision.

"Come, Altan," Nebahat said. "There's no use fighting me."

Altan's face burned red, then a deep shade of purple. "Because *I* am descended from the thirteenth tribe."

"Oh?" Nebahat paused. "On which side?"

"My mother's." The pain on Altan's face made Willem burn with anger and frustration and impotence over what was happening to him.

Nebahat nodded as if, with his question satisfactorily answered, he could continue on his prior course. "How many more names have you found?"

"Ten."

Altan was normally so loquacious, his voice lively, yet he was responding to Nebahat's questions with tight, curt answers, his voice lacking all semblance of life. *Like a man who's lost all hope.*

The very thought made Willem want to cry.

As Nebahat stepped away from Altan, Willem gasped. Nebahat had been partially blocking his view, but now he could see that Altan had a hand out, palm facing up, as if he were offering almonds to Nebahat. Except his hand *wasn't* filled with almonds. It was filled with blood.

Nebahat paced back and forth, a thing he often did when he was bothered. Willem had no idea what Altan had done, nor what it meant to Nebahat, but he was certain Nebahat was about to make a momentous decision.

Nebahat's face suddenly hardened and he returned to Altan in a rush. Willem nearly shouted for him to stop as he dipped a finger into Altan's blood and proceeded to wipe a long, crimson stroke on Altan's forehead. Willem had always known Nebahat was a blood mage, but by the gods, he'd never seen Nebahat use it on another person. Stroke by stroke Nebahat was drawing a sigil—in effect casting a spell over Altan that would compel him to do as Nebahat wished. The combined knowledge that something irreversible was about to happen to Altan and that Willem could do nothing about it was terrifying, doubly so because it was happening before his very eyes.

When Nebahat finished the final, curving stroke, he wet a rag and wiped his finger clean. After doing the same to Altan's palm and forehead, he waved to the yawning passageway behind Altan.

No, no, no, Willem wanted to scream. *Please don't go!*

But he was silent as ever, bound to work in Nebahat's interests, never his own. Willem's silent plea unanswered, Altan turned and strode away as if what had just transpired was little more than a polite chat.

Heart beating like a kettle drum, Willem rushed back to the ventilation shaft, climbed it, and followed Altan up the winding stairs. He maintained his distance, but when Altan left the science building and returned to the pathways of the esplanade, he grew bold and closed the distance between them.

Altan was going to do something terrible. The glimmering told him so. It was dim, like a distant, dying funeral pyre. Willem paced just behind him, repeatedly trying and failing to summon the courage to tug on Altan's sleeve. The cage that Nebahat had placed around his mind—the one that forbade both touch and conversation—was almost impossible to ignore.

Is impossible, Willem corrected himself.

No. If he wanted, he could override Nebahat's spell. Wasn't that what he'd always told himself? He could. He could reach out and he could touch Altan, and Altan would wake from this spell and everything would be well again. The two of them would return to Altan's dorm room and hold one another until the sun rose, and then they'd figure out what to do about Nebahat. And Willem wouldn't have to say a word. Who needed to talk when saving someone's life was the most personal form of communication of all?

As they neared the edge of the collegia grounds, Willem's face screwed up with purpose. He swallowed hard, stretched one arm out, his fingers close to Altan's elbow.

Grip his arm, Willem screamed from within. *With one touch he'll be freed!*

And yet his hand remained a whisper away from the simple flaxen fabric of Altan's robe. Then Altan was beyond the grounds and onto the lizard-skin cobbles of the old city streets, while Willem's footsteps slowed and halted on the esplanade's fine gravel border.

He stood there a long, long while, tears streaming down his face. *Please come back.*

What were his thoughts, though, but dust on the wind? Altan strode onward, into the night, unaware that Willem had ever existed, the glimmering around him dimming, dimming, until it was lost altogether.

Chapter 8

AT THE PEAK of a crescent-shaped dune, Brama sat cross-legged, in plain view of Sharakhai's northern harbor a half-league distant. The city's western face was awash in the glow of sunset. The rest lay in shadow, a mismatched collection of gray and onyx blocks. In the east, Rhia hung low, a coin of beaten, weathered brass. Tulathan would soon follow her sister, and together they would begin their trek across the heavens. Beht Zha'ir had returned to Sharakhai, and it made Brama wonder what it would be like without the asirim.

Across his lap lay a short spear, the very one Mae had given him, the one he'd used to slay the ehrekh, Behlosh. It was a mundane weapon, and yet somehow it had always acted as a focus for Brama, allowing him to harness the bone of Raamajit's power, trapped below the scarred skin of his forehead.

"I wish you lying down," Mae said beside him. She lay on her stomach on the dune's leeward side, a spyglass held to one eye.

"I told you. They can't see me."

"I know you say. But it's making me nervous."

A sudden gust of wind sent a scouring of sand over Mae, forcing her to duck her face. The sand didn't touch Brama. It worked its way around him, as was his will.

"I don't like touching the sand sometimes," he said. "I feel too much."

It nearly overwhelmed him at times. It was Rümayesh's presence, he knew. She'd found a way to become a part of him, or make him a part of her—he wasn't sure which. It infuriated him, the loss of control. It made him feel desperate. In the weeks after it had happened he would be taken by violent urges that became so intense he wanted to rend, to kill, just so he could sate it. He'd never given in, but several times it had been a near thing. He'd resorted to hiding himself in the desert until the urges passed. Thankfully they'd diminished since then.

Brama was nothing if not a realist. As much as Rümayesh still haunted his dreams, the wish to be parted from her had been reduced to a passing fancy.

In the distance, a figure approached, little more than a wavering black flame.

"She come," Mae said.

"I know." Brama had sensed the woman's departure from Sharakhai. He'd not told Mae, though. He liked experiencing her excitement when she spotted such things.

I feel you growing tired of her, spoke the voice inside his head.

Be quiet, replied Brama.

The feeling will only grow. Soon you won't be able to stomach it.

I said be quiet.

By the time the woman—one of Queen Alansal's spies in the city—arrived, night had fallen. The moons cast the city in ghostly relief. In months past, the asirim's cries would have filled the night. The asirim would have already been on their way to Sharakhai to collect the tributes marked by Sukru's whip. But Sukru was dead and the asirim had been freed by Çeda and the thirteenth tribe.

Sharakhai is changing, Brama. We could do so much more than this. We could be a part of that change.

Brama glanced toward Mae, who just then was approaching her queen's spy, a wisp of a woman. Mae spoke with her in rapid Mirean. After what looked like a particularly sharp exchange, the spy handed Mae a wooden scroll case—maps of the city's caverns, made in anticipation of Alansal's coming offensive on the city.

Brama wanted to deny Rümayesh's words. More and more he wondered why he remained with Queen Alansal, but then Mae glanced back at him. *It's because of her,* Brama told himself. *Who else would have remained a steadfast friend to the likes of you?*

I would, cooed Rümayesh. *What need have you of some simple villager from Mirea?*

Brama scoffed. Mae might have been a simple villager once, but she was a qirin warrior now, a protector of her queen. And then Brama realized. Rümayesh was *jealous* of Mae.

He was about to comment on it when he sensed another approaching: a man, moving vaguely toward them. It was strange, though. Despite passing only a few dozen yards from their position, the newcomer never once looked their way. He wore the robes of a collegia student, Brama could see now. Whether it meant anything or not, he wasn't sure.

Mae and the spy finally spotted him, and both ducked down behind a dune. Brama, meanwhile, picked up his spear and trailed after him. Mae immediately caught up to Brama and tugged on his arm. The flare of anger that rose up inside him was so strong he found himself ripping his arm away and summoning power through the spear. Mae stared back, fearless, while Brama breathed deeply, slowly calming himself.

He was horrified at how close he'd come to using his power on her, at how quickly it had happened. It was happening more and more of late, any small annoyance or impatience leading to instant rage or hatred or a simple will to inflict pain. Each of those moments was like the blow of a battering ram against the walls he'd built against Rümayesh. When those walls fell, and they would eventually, she would gain dominance over him once more.

Before the dark urges intensified, Brama touched the lump on his forehead. There, beneath a meshwork of scars, lay the bone of Raamajit the Exalted, a thing of immense power. In a fever dream following the death of the ehrekh, Behlosh, he'd cut a slit along his own forehead and held the blackened bone to the wound, at which point his skin had regrown, subsuming the artifact whole. Or so Mae had told him; Brama didn't remember any of it. He touched upon that power now, separating himself from Rümayesh so that *his* will would reign supreme.

Recognizing how dangerous things had just become, Mae sent the spy away, urging her to move with haste with several flicks of her hand, an order the spy seemed only too happy to obey. As the sound of her retreat dwindled, Mae stared at Brama, watching his movements carefully. She was aware of Rümayesh's growing influence, but chose to remain silent about it. Instead, she motioned to the desert. "Come, Brama. We go now. We return to Alansal."

"Go if you wish," Brama said, and resumed his steps in the wake of the collegia student, who continued his steady march toward the blooming fields.

Mae followed Brama with a look suggesting she was angry with herself for doing so. "Whoever he is, he is of no matter to our queen."

"*Your* queen," Brama corrected.

Much may have changed about Beht Zha'ir, but one thing hadn't. The adichara trees were still aglow, their blooms full, blue diamonds spilled over a glooming streak of kohl. With the buzz of the rattlewings sounding in the distance, the man lost himself within the nearest of the groves.

Brama and Mae followed. The branches around them clattered and clacked, not from the wind but from some arcane animus woven into them by Tulathan when she'd planted them four centuries earlier. Eventually they reached a misshaped clearing. Curiously, the student had come to a stop before a tree that stood out from the rest. Its boughs drooped. Few leaves adorned the branches. Its blooms were dimmer than those of its neighbors. It looked diseased. Dying.

The young man, transfixed, took slow steps toward it, offering himself to the tree. Had Brama been in his right mind, he might have tried to stop him, but Rümayesh's influence was on him now, his will to experience death strong, so he merely stared.

"No!" screamed Mae, coming to the same realization a heartbeat too late.

She dashed forward, but the man was already stepping into the tree, the tortured limbs curling around him like a child finding a toy thought lost forever.

Despite Brama's growing numbness to the frailties of mortal man, there was something about Mae that always reminded him of who he really was. Just as Mae had sensed the danger to the student, Brama now sensed the danger to her.

"Stop, Mae!" When she continued, he pointed his spear and sent a powerful gust of wind against her. Blown by the wind, she stumbled backward, which gave Brama the time he needed to grab her arm. "The thorns," he told her. "Their poison is deadly."

But Mae wasn't having it. One moment, she was staring in impotence as the branches tightened and the young man screamed, and the next, she was drawing her sword and hacking at the branches. But the adichara groves held many hidden dangers. The branches of other, nearby trees curled down, stretching, reaching for Mae as if trying to protect their sister.

"The thorns, Mae!"

He grabbed her again, and this time Mae relented and let herself be led toward safety. It was in that moment that the diseased tree wrapped a branch around the student's throat. His screams became wet gasps, then stopped altogether. He thrashed a while longer, making the tree rattle all the more, then he and the tree both went still. The man's blood, dark under the light of the blooms, stained his flaxen robes, dripped down along the branches, guiding it toward the adichara's trunk. The blood glistened as runnels formed, more and more of it coursing down toward the sand, toward the tree's roots.

As the sand drank the blood, Brama's eyes fluttered closed at the heady feeling of the student's soul crossing to the land beyond. He felt the touch of the farther fields, however briefly, and it filled both him and Rümayesh with light. For once, Rümayesh was silent. She basked in it.

And then a wondrous thing happened. One by one, the tree's blooms, already dimmer than those on the neighboring trees, winked out. When the last one had been extinguished, the tree's branches went lax, and the blooms of the nearby trees dimmed, as if in its death the diseased tree had somehow infected the others. Brama was just beginning to wonder if the effect would be permanent, if the other trees would die the same death as this one had, when Mae rounded on him.

"You let him die!" she shouted.

Brama didn't know what to say. He felt as if he were just waking from a spell.

Mae poked him in the chest. "You *let* him die!"

"You and your queen are preparing an assault on Sharakhai. Why would you care about a lone collegia student?"

"I fight for my queen. Together we fight for the greater glory of our land. But I do not revel in death, Brama. I do not revel in seeing innocents die." She looked him up and down. "That what you are now. You *her*, not the Brama I knew."

She wanted him to defend himself, but what could he say? She wasn't completely right, but she wasn't far off the mark, either.

Mae stalked off, and Brama let her go. The thought of Mae leaving him, of his being alone with Rümayesh, made him feel as if he were tipping over a precipice he'd never return from, but for the moment he was too intrigued by the mystery of the student.

He was a tribute, Brama thought. *With the asirim gone, someone is sending fresh tributes to the blooming fields.*

As he stepped toward the dimmed adichara, the soft clatter of the nearby branches enveloped him. He crouched and touched one finger to the blood along the base of the trunk. He opened himself to the blood's journey. He felt the adichara's roots sink down, felt them join with others, then combine and recombine as they led inexorably toward the city.

"You coming?" Mae asked from beyond the edge of the grove.

"Mae, I need to show you something."

Silence.

"Please, Mae. Your queen will want to know about this."

After a long pause, she returned to the clearing. Brama pointed the tip of his spear at the base of the adichara, and a strong wind blew. Both sand and stone were blasted away, exposing more and more of the adichara's trunk. Roots were revealed, then something smooth and rounded buried *beneath* the roots. More earth lifted. A skull was revealed. Then the jagged vertebrae of a spine. Rows of ribs and the axehead shapes of two shoulder blades followed. Soon half the body had been excavated, along with the cocoon-like mesh of tree roots that encased it.

As Mae stared at the body, understanding dawned. "The trees. They eat the people."

"In a way, yes. The branches kill them if they're not already dead, but either way the roots draw them down into the earth and feast upon their remains."

Mae stared warily at the adichara. Her eyes shifted to the collegia student and the shriveled branches of the tree that had killed him. "It fail to pull him down because it die. That's what you thinking."

"I suspect so. But why?"

"And who send him to a tree full of disease?"

"Precisely. It may have to do with the offensive your queen is planning. I want to look into it, Mae. I want to find out who's doing it and why."

"Speak it plainly. What do you wish to do?"

"I want to search the blooming fields for more clues. Look for more offerings. Let's you and I circle the city and find the truth of it."

Mae considered the adichara, then stared deeply into Brama's eyes. Her gaze slipped briefly to his forehead, and her look softened. "Very well, Brama," she said. "We look, we find more, then return to our queen, yes?"

Brama smiled. "Yes, I promise."

Over the course of the following days, they wandered from grove to grove, cataloguing the trees' many horrors. Again and again they found corpses, each having been recently killed, squeezed to death by an adichara, and in each case the tree appeared to be dead and the surrounding trees unhealthy.

To his surprise, Brama sensed a handful of asirim beneath the adichara. They were shriveled, curled up like lost children, too weak to heed whatever call had drawn the rest away.

On the third night, they made camp as usual. Brama had fallen asleep near Mae beside a small fire but woke standing, mere paces from one of the dead trees.

Brama blinked, unable to comprehend what had happened or how he'd suddenly found himself standing before the horrific tableau arrayed before him. The tribute, an old man with dark hair and a trim beard, had been slit open at the belly. His entrails, as if displayed in a depraved sausage maker's shop, hung not only from the dead tree but from others nearby. Ancient runes were carved in the man's skin. Covering the stone near his naked feet were more dark signs, sigils of power that granted insight to those who could read them.

Brama shivered as he took in the grisly scene.

He was already dead, Rümayesh purred.

Of course Rümayesh had used his dead body. She'd wanted answers. She wanted to understand what was happening to the trees and who was sending the tributes to the blooming fields. It wasn't the fact that she'd used a dead man's viscera to scry into the future that so unnerved Brama—he was just as curious as she was to find answers. What unnerved him was realizing that, having seen all this, he knew how to do it. The *meaning* of it, the results of Rümayesh's divination, lay just out of reach, but he was certain that if he'd been awake during the ritual, he *would* know. Day by day, moment by moment, he was becoming more like her.

This is who we are now, Rümayesh said.

"No!" Brama touched the lump on his forehead. "This *isn't* who *I* am!"

Viciously angry that she'd managed to gain dominance over their shared form, he pushed her down harder than he had in months. When he was done, he was shaking, sweating. He turned to find Mae standing at the gap between the trees that led to open sand.

"Brama?" She stared at the grisly scene with horror-filled eyes. She had a bow in her hands, a diamond-tipped arrow nocked.

He didn't know what to say. Neither, apparently, did Mae. She studied him with a stunned expression, her arrow still trained on him, but said nothing as he walked past her into the desert, well beyond their camp. He lay on the cold sand that night, shivering, welcoming the strangely grounding touch of the sand against his skin. He didn't sleep at all. He was too afraid of what would happen if he did. He was too afraid of what Rümayesh had found in the entrails.

You have but to ask, Brama.

Brama's spear lay by his side, both a symbol of, and a talisman against, his worst fears. He thought again of taking it up, of using the power of the bone to try to cut his soul from Rümayesh's. But found that he couldn't. In the days after waking to his new reality, he'd tried and failed many times. In all likelihood he'd fail again. When he did, it might give Rümayesh dominance over him forever.

No, a voice whispered to him. And this time it wasn't Rümayesh's voice that spoke, but his own. *You won't do it because you're afraid it will work. You're afraid you'll die if we're parted. It's a coward's choice you make.*

Turning away from the spear, Brama pulled himself into a ball, much as the asirim did deep beneath the adichara. The wind, meanwhile, whistled over the dunes, *Coward, coward, coward.*

Chapter 9

ERYAM'S HEART SEEMED to stop when she saw Yasmine's abductor back calmly through a hedge and out of the maze, dragging Yasmine with him. Crushed gravel bit into the soles of Meryam's feet as she sprinted after them. She reached the hedge and forced her way through, heedless of the branches scraping her skin.

By the time she reached the opposite side, the abductor, a stocky fellow in woodman's clothes, was lumbering toward the old oak forest. She couldn't see Yasmine's face, didn't know if she was unconscious or worse. A skinny man waited at the forest's edge, holding the reins of two horses. On seeing Meryam, he dropped the reins and ran straight toward her. In an instant, all of Meryam's naive courage turned to terror. She hadn't the sense to scream earlier, but she did now.

Even so, the man was on her in four long strides. With a hand over her mouth, he picked her up and carried her into the trees as easily as he might a sack of neeps.

Meryam flailed, hoping to free herself, hoping to make a mad sprint for the pavilion, but it did no good. Soon a gag was being forced into her mouth. The foul taste was just registering when Meryam was lifted roughly and thrown over the back of one of the horses. The skinny man's face leered. "Stop struggling, girl." He held up a knife for her to see. "It'll go easier on you."

Meryam felt her bones turn to jelly. She was reduced to a shivering, blubbering mess. A blindfold was forced over her eyes just as she was beginning to cry.

"*Quiet!*" the skinny one hissed, so close she could smell his foul breath. "I hear a peep from either of you and you're not going to like what happens next."

She couldn't help it, though. She cried as they rode through the forest and kept crying until the horses slowed and she was tossed into some sort of enclosed wagon—she could tell it was enclosed for how the sound of her own, rapid breathing intensified. Her blindfold and gag were still on, her wrists and ankles still bound. She was terrified they were separating her from Yasmine, but a moment later there came a grunt of pain as Yasmine was thrown in beside her. Meryam shouldn't have been relieved that Yasmine was trapped alongside her, but she was. She didn't know what she would do if she'd found herself alone with those men.

The wagon door clattered shut, and then they were off, trundling down the road at a leisurely pace. Meryam tried to speak, but the gag made her words unintelligible. Yasmine tried to respond, but as soon as she did, there came a knocking from the front of the wagon.

"What did I say?" yelled the skinny one.

They remained silent after that.

That they could do this, steal the king's daughters and ride away at their ease, felt wrong—even more so than being abducted in the first place. It spoke of their certainty that they wouldn't get caught, which only intensified Meryam's fears.

Where were they going? What would they do when they got there? Were they to be ransomed? Murdered? Raped? A thousand scenarios played through Meryam's mind as the wagon rattled on, all of them involving that leering face and stinking breath.

Hours later, they were dragged out of the wagon and laid down in a place that felt dry but smelled dank. A moment later hinges squeaked and a metallic door clanged shut. A clinking followed, as of a lock being closed. Meryam pushed herself up and scooted along the dirty floor until she found Yasmine.

Yasmine shoved her hard with her shoulder, and for a moment Meryam was hurt by it. She thought Yasmine was angry with her, but when she felt Yasmine's fingers fumbling at the rope around her wrists, Meryam realized she was trying to undo the knot. It took a while, but Yasmine did it, at which point Meryam was able to untie the ropes around her ankles, then free Yasmine.

The moment Yasmine's gag was off, she rasped at Meryam, "You complete idiot! Why didn't you *run?*"

Meryam stared in shock. "I wanted to save you!"

"And how would you, a *princess,* stop men such as these?"

"Well, I don't *know.*" Tears were gathering in her eyes again. "I just—" She broke down, her breath coming in great, uncontrollable gasps. "Oh gods, they're going to kill us, aren't they? They're going to slit our throats and leave us for the crows."

"Oh, stop it, Meryam. If they'd wanted to do that, they would have done so already."

Meryam blinked tears from her eyes and tried to control the suffocating feeling overtaking her. Only when Yasmine's words finally began to sink in did the tightness in her chest begin to ease. The men wanted something. Meryam and Yasmine being princesses, it surely meant they wanted something from their father, King Aldouan.

For the first time, Meryam took in their surroundings. They were inside a circular grain silo. The dirt floor had been cleared, but there was still some old grain piled against the wall. Above was their only light source, a small, misshapen hole in the stone walls.

"It's big enough to get through," Yasmine said.

Meryam stared up at it. "If you're a bloody owl, perhaps."

Yasmine didn't have a chance to respond, for just then a clanking sound came from the granary door and it flew open. The big man with the bearded jowls stood in the doorway holding a jug and a cloth sack. Meryam thought he might be angry that they'd untied themselves. He seemed only gruff, though, as if he'd expected it.

"No one will hear you if you scream," he said, "but I'll still come in and slap the one who *didn't* scream. Understand?" He dropped the sack and the jug onto the floor. "Now I know what you might be thinking. What if we both scream?"

Meryam knew the question was a trap, but couldn't help herself. "What happens then?" she asked in a tiny voice that made her feel all the tinier.

"Then I bring my knife."

Meryam was terrified but his words only seemed to embolden Yasmine. She walked straight up to him, raised one finger, and held it inches from his nose. "Do you know what my father's going to do when he gets hold of you?"

He stared down at her finger. "I don't rightly know," he said, then walked over to Meryam and backhanded her across the cheek so hard she spun to the ground. "But I can promise you this," Meryam heard over the ringing in her ears. "The next time you raise your finger to my face, I'll do more than slap your pretty little sister."

Meryam's world was bright pain. The right side of her face felt as if it were on fire, and the point of her elbow, which had struck the ground hard, hurt so much she was sure it was broken. The man left and slammed the door shut. The metallic clank of a lock was followed by the fade of his footfalls.

Meryam tasted blood. As the pain slowly began to ebb, she touched the tip of her tongue to the inside of her cheek and cringed from the pain. Moaning, she swallowed the blood and probed more gently, finding several places where her teeth had cut her.

Yasmine knelt beside her, her lips set in a grim line. She held Meryam's chin and checked the damage, then turned away and began unwrapping the sack, which contained one small loaf of crusty bread and a pair of oddly shaped sausages. After ripping the loaf into two rough pieces, she handed the smaller to Meryam.

Yasmine sat facing the door, staring at it as if she could open it through sheer will alone. She bit off a hunk of bread and chewed it like a stablehand. "Mighty Alu's grace," she said around the bread, "why didn't you run and get help?"

"My queen?" came a voice.

It was Basilio, calling from the next room. Somehow his voice mingled with Yasmine's, an echo of her fear tinging Basilio's resonant tenor.

"Come," Meryam said.

The crisp ring of leather heels over marble tile was interspersed by muffled thumps as he walked over the carpets. He stepped briskly through the high, horseshoe archway into her bed chamber but, upon realizing she was only wearing her sheer night dress, immediately averted his gaze and retreated.

Meryam rolled her eyes. "I said come."

"Would you like me to fetch your night coat?"

"I'm too hot." Meryam levered herself up on one elbow, hung her legs over the side of the bed, and wriggled her feet, willing the nagging remnants of her dream to fade. When they didn't, she removed her necklace—Yasmine's necklace—and tossed it to the other side of the bed. Sometimes the weight of it was just too much. "Just get in here and fetch me some water."

He complied, pouring a fresh glass from an ewer and bringing it to her, eyes cast down. The morning sun twinkled off the green glass as she lifted it to her chapped lips and downed half of it in one go. "You come with news, I presume?" She finished the glass and held it out for more.

"I do." He poured her a fresh glass, then handed it to her, eyes facing the corner.

"Oh, stop it." It was only serving to make her more conscious of how skinny she'd become. Not since she'd had feelings for Ramahd had she been so aware of it. "Am I *that* difficult to look upon?"

"It isn't that, my queen." His bald pate went red as he stared down into the ewer. "It wouldn't be proper."

"Then stare into my eyes if you must. I don't like talking to a craning stork."

He did, and looked like a stunned owl while doing it. "I've brought good news from the warfront. The navy has retaken Ishmantep."

"Well, that *is* good news."

After finding Queen Alansal and King Emir together on his ship, Meryam had worried they would rush to attack the city. It was the very reason she'd ordered the navy to press harder. Ishmantep, the largest of the caravanserais on the eastern trade route toward Malasan, had been held for months by King Emir, and was an important part of Meryam's plans to seal the Malasani off from Sharakhai.

"And Samandar?"

Samandar was a large caravanserai along the northern passage toward Mirea and a key resource to control if one wanted to supply water to a fleet of invading ships.

"The effort continues, but the losses there have been harder. Mirea will not give it up easily."

"Nor did I expect them to. Lose Samandar and they'll be forced to retreat to Aldiir." The two forces would likely become one at some point, but that was easier said than done. After Ishmantep and Samandar, the only other caravanserais of any size were Aldiir and Ashdankaat, and neither was big enough for their combined forces. There were simply too many soldiers to feed and water. Both forces had supply trains, but the Kundhuni fleet had been sent to harry one of them, and her own Qaimiri fleet the other. Caravan after caravan had been caught and burned, preventing tons of food, water, and feed grain from reaching the fleets.

For the time being it looked like she'd successfully delayed a second invasion of Sharakhai, which should give her the time she needed to deal with her other main concern.

"What of our efforts on Beht Zha'ir?"

At this, Basilio's enthusiasm drained. "The Maidens followed several of the tributes. They witnessed each tribute walk to the blooming fields and give themselves to the trees."

Meryam couldn't help but allow herself a small smile. "Very good."

So much was falling into place. The collegia's chancellor had agreed to join her with hardly a fuss. Years ago, his brother, wife, and their three-year-old child had been murdered by the Moonless Host when they'd refused to give them money from the simple hostelry they'd run in the Red Crescent.

Nonetheless, in order to ensure his loyalty, Meryam had taken the chancellor's blood, suspecting she would never have use for it. For his own reasons, he would remain hers. The Enclave was a different story. Take *their* blood and she invited ruin. So she'd played to their desires instead. The leader of their inner circle, Prayna, pretended to be divorced from politics, but behind that facade lay something deeper, something she herself hardly knew she wanted. Prayna was well aware of the contentious relationship the magi of the city had had with the Sharakhani Kings, but what if the Enclave were given free rein at last?

"Free rein?" Prayna had asked Meryam when the offer was made. They'd been sitting in Meryam's anteroom.

"Within reason," Meryam clarified.

One of Prayna's elegant eyebrows lifted. "The new Kings and Queens have agreed to this?"

"I've not given them that choice, nor will I," Meryam replied. "They don't get to decide who's free and who isn't."

"And in return you're asking us to send some few to the blooming fields?"

"Just so."

Prayna's dark eyes probed Meryam's. "You're asking us to murder for you."

Meryam's eyebrows rose. "I'm asking you to see us through to a day when the magi of this city no longer need to cower in fear! What are a few lives, of the worst elements in Sharakhai, when weighed against that?"

"And what happens when this is all done, Meryam shan Aldouan? What happens when the city is yours?"

Meryam knew in that moment that she'd been right about Prayna. She'd been hiding in the shadows for so long there was a pent-up desire in her, not simply for freedom, but for *control*, for *power*. She was a woman after Meryam's own heart.

"You can do what you will, but if you stand by my side, as I hope you will, we move on to Malasan. Then Mirea. Even Kundhun. You are witnessing the birth of an empire, Prayna, and much of that empire could be yours."

Prayna's wide, almond eyes had softened. "I note that you fail to mention Qaimir."

Meryam took the comment in stride, but she felt her heart racing. She should have known Prayna would dig deeper before coming to see her. She would know that there was trouble in the courts of Almadan. "There are rumblings in my own country, yes, but those threats will be dealt with."

Ramahd had escaped with Mateo and Duke Hektor II. Meryam had ordered Hektor's father, Duke Hektor I, Meryam's uncle, hung after she'd learned he'd conspired with Ramahd and Mateo to depose her. The elder Hektor was dead, but the younger lived on, and so did their conspiracy. If the last report she'd heard of them was true, the three of them, Hektor II, Mateo, and Ramahd, were hiding in the desert. Or they might have returned to the city since. Meryam had tried to search for them, but Ramahd had become more skilled at preventing her spells of finding. With so much else to attend to, she'd given up. She knew it was only a matter of time before they returned and caused problems, either here or in their homeland, but it was a matter for another day.

Prayna took a while to consider. "With your own magi occupied in the battles to the east, you're going to need more help than just me."

"You have someone in mind?"

"Several people, yes. I'm certain I can convince Nebahat to join us. From there, a half dozen more will follow."

Meryam smiled. Surely this was Tulathan paving the way for Meryam to get what she wanted. The people Prayna was referring to were other members of the Enclave. Nebahat himself was another of the Enclave's inner circle. With seven or eight powerful magi at her beck and call, her goals were that much closer.

Meryam's thoughts returned to the present. Gods but the day was hot. With Basilio still standing there like a possum playing dead, she dribbled a stream of water from her glass onto her hand, then wiped her face and the back of her neck. "What of the trees themselves?"

"It was as you said. The trees enveloped the tributes—"

"Not *tributes*, Basilio. *Scarabs*. Scarabs of the Moonless Host."

Basilio nodded, if reluctantly. "The scarabs were enveloped and the blooms on the trees went dim. The surrounding trees seemed to dim as well." He set the ewer back into its cradle. When he turned to face her, all hints of his earlier embarrassment had vanished. His look was now deadly serious. "My queen, let me speak plainly. Your hope is to punish those who killed your sister and niece, and I don't blame you for that, but don't you think it might be better if we found those we were *certain* had been scarabs in the Moonless Host?"

Meryam took off her slip and threw it onto the bed. Basilio, more intense and focused on his point than she would have guessed, refused to avert his gaze. After pulling on the vermillion silk dress her maid had laid out the night before, she said, "I'm surprised at you, Basilio. You make it sound as though one must wield a knife to be a scarab, but wars are fought in many ways. There are those who gave money to support their cause. Those who provided shelter, hiding the wicked from the hand of justice. There are those who hid truths that would otherwise expose those who've committed evil, preventing us from moving toward peace."

"Surely there are some who fit that description—"

"Did you not have members of your own family caught in the Bloody Passage? Did three of your cousins not feed the Great Mother that day? Three widows made? Seven children who grew up without their father?"

"Yes, but that doesn't justify wanton slaughter. There are already people in the city comparing you to Cahil the Confessor. The sentiments built now will—"

"Enough!" Meryam shouted. "I came to the desert for a reason, Basilio. If you're not willing to help me then tell me now and I'll send you home. But if you stay, accept that I will do whatever it takes to bring the Moonless Host to justice."

Basilio held her gaze, shocked, then all the energy seemed to drain from him and he lowered his eyes. "I would stay, Meryam. I am loyal to you, as always. It is part of my duty to guide you, to bring up concerns you haven't thought of. Having done that, I will do as my queen commands."

She weighed his words, his sincerity. She actually respected him for what he'd said. As obsequious as he usually was, she knew it had taken a lot for him to say a word against her. "I *do* want your counsel, Basilio, but in this case we will stay the course and continue as planned." She exposed her back to him. "Tie me."

The bodice tightened around her chest as he tugged on the laces. "You'll return to the cavern today?"

"Of course. And every day until I'm sure it's working."

He finished tying her dress. "I'll leave you to it, then."

As his footsteps faded, Meryam retrieved the beaded red necklace from her bed, slipped it on, and left. She wound her way through the Sun Palace, down through the tunnels, and to the cavern with the crystal. There she climbed the scaffold stairs and reached the top of the crystal, hoping, praying. Despite her prayers, the crystal's surface was dry. She looked up at the tendril snaking its way down from the cavern's high ceiling, willing it to give her what she needed, but it too was dry.

She did her best to bury her disappointment. "You said yourself it would take time." The cavern all but swallowed her words, making her feel alone and forgotten. She stayed a long while, hoping for a change, but eventually she gave up. She was just walking back over the roots when she heard a sound, a soft tap.

She spun and stared up, then ran back up the stairs, using the support beams to pull herself faster along the steps. When she reached the top, she saw it, a drop of glistening liquid at the very tip of the tendril. As she watched, it fell like a shooting star and *tapped* against the crystal's glowing surface. It had worked! The scarabs fed to the trees had given their blood to the adich-ara, and the adichara in turn had delivered their essence here. This tool, this grand engine made by the gods themselves, was working again.

Meryam touched one finger to the crystal's damp surface and held it to her tongue. A rush of power like she'd never experienced ran through her. It felt like she'd drunk moonlight, an elixir crafted by Tulathan herself.

This, Meryam said to herself, *this is what I need*. "I know you've been waiting a long time, Yasmine"—she gave her necklace a gentle squeeze—"but the wait is almost over."

Chapter 10

*T*HE NIGHT FOLLOWING the ultimatum to Shaikh Neylana, Hamid lay awake in the captain's cabin with Darius. He couldn't sleep. His mind was afire, replaying the skirmish with Tribe Halarijan over and over again. It had been no fault of *his* that blood had been shed. The crossbowman had sparked everything. Huuri and Imwe had merely been reacting to the threat. Even still, commanding such power had been a rush unlike anything Hamid had ever felt. The time would soon come when he could unleash even more on the thirteenth tribe's enemies. He could hardly wait.

Tread carefully, though. Move too quickly and Macide will grow nervous over the optics. He'll demote you, force you into the role of lackey once more to appease Shaikh Neylana. But bide your time and you'll prove what might be done with the power of the asirim standing behind you, and then no one—not Macide, Leorah, Shal'alara, nor any of the other elders—will try to stop you from using it. You might even rise to become shaikh if you play this right.

Eventually he grew tired, but by then the wailing and mewling and growling of the asirim kept him from sleep. Darius couldn't sleep either. He lay with his head on Hamid's chest, absently rubbing the hair along his stomach. Hamid felt Darius cringe as a warbling howl broke the temporary silence.

"How it gnaws at my soul," Darius said.

Hamid didn't mind the asirim's wailing so much. It served as a reminder of what would happen to Neylana and her entire tribe if she refused him. "I wish they would obey *me* and not the Shieldwives."

Darius chuckled.

"What?"

"Always looking to control."

"Not *always*." Hamid shrugged. "Well, all right, almost always, but why not? I've paid my dues. At long last I'm rising up in the tribe. I'm *entitled* to a bit of control."

A vision came to Hamid. Of him and Darius throwing shovelfuls of sand over Emre. Tied and helpless, he lay in the grave they'd dug for him. From the moment Emre had joined the Host—a thing *Hamid* had arranged for—Macide had looked on him like a favored son. Assignments that would once have gone to Hamid were instead given to Emre. When Macide went to treat with the eastern tribes to fight the rising threat of King Onur, Emre had been chosen to stand by his side. And when a delegation had been sent to treat with the Malasani, Macide had chosen *Emre* to lead it. He'd even had the gall to order Hamid join Emre and *report* to him, as if Emre were the one who'd dedicated his life to the cause. What had Emre ever been but a man looking to steal glory and hoard it for himself? As kids, Emre had always been the show-off, outshining even Tariq in this respect, which the gods knew was no mean feat.

Hamid blinked. He focused on the wooden planks of the cabin's ceiling, on how Darius felt in his arms, and his anger slowly subsided. These spells of jealousy were happening more and more of late, and it was getting worse, but he was sure that if he returned to the tribe victorious, all would be well.

"The other elders are giving me my due as well," Hamid went on, "but Macide doesn't trust me fully. Not yet. I have to show him I can bend Neylana to my will."

"You have to prove that you can *lead*."

"Exactly, which is why I need the asirim to follow my orders." Part of Hamid wished they were beholden to the thirteenth tribe as they'd been to the Kings. He wished he could simply command them, but he couldn't. Sadly, that power had vanished the moment the King of the asirim, Sehid-Alaz, had broken their curse.

Darius had fallen silent.

"What?" Hamid asked.

When Darius looked up, he had trouble meeting Hamid's eyes, a thing he often did when he was circling a subject he knew Hamid wasn't going to like.

"I hate it when you do this," Hamid said. "Just say it."

"I know you want to be strong," Darius said carefully. "Being a leader sometimes means giving orders and having others follow them, but sometimes it means leading by example, showing them the way."

"Well, of course"—Hamid motioned to the hull, beyond which lay the frigates and the asirim—"but how do you show *them* the way?"

"I don't know, but you can hardly blame them for disobedience." As if they'd heard Darius's words, a low growl rose up from the asirim, followed by a yap, then a scuffle. After several heavy thuds, the asirim fell silent. "They're newly freed. They're their own people now."

Darius had a point. If *Hamid* had been cursed to obey the Kings for four hundred years, the last thing on his mind would be following someone else's orders.

There was at least a silver lining. While some of the asirim, tired of dealing death, had refused to fight any longer, others had grown protective of their descendants and saw themselves as soldiers of the thirteenth tribe, willing to do whatever their undying King, Sehid-Alaz, and their shaikh, Macide, asked of them. And then there were those like Huuri and Imwe, who missed the bloodshed, who yearned for its return, and relished any chance to relive their darker days.

Even so, what if they'd been dealing with a true ally to the thirteenth tribe and Huuri and Imwe had attacked? What if they'd been facing an enemy too powerful to cow? He couldn't allow their disobedience to continue. He *had* to find a way to get them under control. He was just wondering if they'd respond to the whip when a knock came at the cabin door.

"Hamid?" called a deep voice.

Hamid rolled his eyes. It was Frail Lemi. "Go back to sleep, Lemi."

As the asirim wails grew louder, there was silence beyond the cabin door.

"Lemi, I said go back to sleep."

"Oh, stop it," Darius broke in. "You know how he gets. Are you afraid, Lemi?" he said, louder.

Frail Lemi's fear of the asirim was famous. Strangely, it had grown even worse after he'd killed one that had bounded toward Emir, the Malasani king. Most nights they anchored the *Amaranth* far enough away that he could find sleep, but this close it was likely impossible for him.

"Lemi," Darius tried again, "you can sleep in here if you want."

A pause. The latch clicked and the cabin door creaked slowly open. There stood Lemi, occupying the threshold like a fully grown man stuffed into a child's coffin. He wore his night clothes and carried the balled-up nest of cotton rags he used as a pillow. He looked profoundly embarrassed.

"Just get in here, will you?" Hamid said, which earned him a slap on the chest from Darius.

"Lie down," Darius said. "I'll sing you a song."

And Darius did. Soon he heard Frail Lemi's thunderous snoring, which managed to put Hamid to sleep as well.

The following day, when the sun reached its zenith, Hamid headed toward the Halarijan camp with five of the Shieldwives. "I'll have your shaikh's answer," he called to the men who stood aboard the ships staring down at him.

"You gave our shaikh one day," one of them said back. "We were all there to hear it."

Hamid was about to bark back that he would see Neylana now when he noticed dust lifting in a long, low cloud beyond the circle of ships, a telltale sign of ships on the move. He stepped back until he could see the horizon clearly, and saw three ships were sailing toward their camp.

The buzzing in Hamid's head had returned. "What's going on?" he bellowed.

The warrior merely backed away until he was lost from sight.

With a growing urge to punch a knife into someone's gut, Hamid stalked beyond the line of ships, ready to head to the pavilion, but the pavilion was gone, as were the cook fires. He had no idea which ship Neylana was on, and he didn't wish to look foolish by calling for her, which she would no doubt ignore, so he stalked back toward the *Amaranth*.

"Find her!" he shouted over his shoulder.

But they didn't. And the ships kept coming. Through his spyglass he saw that one flew the white tree pennant of Halarijan, another the flowing red horse of Narazid. The third flew the black wings of Okan. They sailed close and anchored, and a small delegation spilled forth from each. All were led to a large clipper in the Halarijan circle.

"You will have your answer," their potbellied herald told Hamid nearly an hour later.

Hamid went with Frail Lemi, Darius, and all the Shieldwives. He ordered the asirim kept in the frigates' holds, but the crew was prepared for his signal. Should anything strange occur—anything at all—Hamid would order them to storm from the ships and attack.

Neylana came, looking old and frail. Her people arrayed behind her in dresses and thawbs and simple cloth vests. There were more from Tribes Narazid and Okan, their origins recognizable from the style of tattoos on their faces and hands. Two were dressed in rich khalats with jewelry on their turbans. These, no doubt, were their shaikhs. They were younger than Neylana, and more plump, but to Hamid they looked just as weak.

"You came to ask us to join your alliance," Shaikh Neylana said, without introducing Hamid. She spoke loudly, her gaze taking in those nearby and those who stood on the ships. "You came with false offers of riches and shared glory while holding a hammer behind your back, ready to strike should our answer displease you. Your actions have made me wary of the thirteenth tribe, and wary of Macide."

In the silence that followed, Hamid curled his lip. "I should warn you, long speeches bore me." He had half a mind to call the asirim now, but this was strange. Neylana's mood had changed since yesterday. What had caused it?

"I'm impatient as well, Hamid Malahin'ava, so let us get to the point. I could have lied to you yesterday. I could have hidden the fact that Queen Meryam sent us an offer, but I didn't. I wanted to see what the messenger of the thirteenth tribe was about so that I might better know the man who chose him."

Hamid's face was turning red. He refused to look at anyone—not Siren-dra, not Darius, no one—for fear of what he'd see in their eyes.

"I was promised an answer."

"And you will have it, though perhaps not in the way you envisioned. Though your actions shame you, there is one who has convinced me that all are not the same in Tribe Khiyanat. One who thinks you might be acting of your *own* accord, not Macide's, and that, if you were removed, we might find a place of more equal footing with our fellow tribes."

Hamid laughed. It sounded pitiful in the emptiness of this space. It made him want to hurt something. "And who might that be?"

Neylana smiled and stepped aside. Those behind her did likewise, dividing the crowd neatly in two and creating an aisle that traveled from Hamid to the sandworn hull of the galleon. There, standing alone, was a man wearing sirwal trousers and a simple linen shirt. Leather bracers adorned his forearms. A braided beard waggled from the end of his sharp chin. His dark hair was braided, too, pulled into a style of overlapping plaits that started just above his temples.

Hamid knew this man. He'd grown up with him. They'd run the streets of Sharakhai together, two gutter wrens flying in and out of various flocks until Hamid had grown tired of it all and joined the Moonless Host. It took long moments for him to understand, to put a name to the ghost who stood before him, and even then Hamid stood dumbly, unable to find words.

It was Frail Lemi who broke the silence. "By the gods who breathe," he cried, both hands raised in joy, "it's Emre!"

Chapter 11

ÇEDA SNAPPED THE REINS of the wagon and turned it onto the stone quay that hugged King's Harbor's impressive inner edge. Tauriyat loomed above. Eventide could be seen clearly, as could Cahil's palace. The others were hidden beyond the shoulders of the mountain.

The harbor itself was abuzz. Dozens of Silver Spears patrolled the walls and the watch towers. Work gangs scoured the hulls of partially repaired ships, readying them for their return to battle. Along the far side of the harbor lay the ship yard, where some fifty ships lay in three ordered rows. There were galleons, clippers, and a smattering of barques, all of them in various states of construction. Çeda was already watching the shipwrights as they moved over the ships' skeletons calling orders, inspecting the lay of the keel, and supervising the work gangs as they swung the ships' hulking ribs, suspended by ropes on tall wooden cranes, into place.

Çeda wore the threadbare garb of a field worker: trousers, shirt, sandals, and a conical reed hat like one would find in the distant rice paddies of Mirea. Sümeya and Jenise sat at the back of the wagon, their legs swinging as the wagon rattled along. They were dressed similarly to Çeda, whereas Kameyl, sitting on the driver's bench beside Çeda, wore a simple khalat and turban. With her tall frame and bold features, they'd all agreed that casting her as the leader of their work gang would be best.

The traffic shifted as they arced around the harbor. They were nearing the barracks, where hundreds of Silver Spears moved to and fro. Cavalry units conducted mock battles in a paddock. Infantry trained in a dusty yard, some moving in ordered ranks with spears set for the enemy while others drilled with sword and shield. The metallic clash of their drills mixed with the sound of industry as many loaded ships, effected repairs, or worked on the sand, applying wax to the skis on ships that had been lifted using special hoists.

Çeda did her best to cast a bored look over it all as she guided the plow horse toward the stables, which were conveniently situated beside the shipyard. The shipyard itself was the most likely destination for Nalamae, who according to the vision in Yusam's mere had been reborn as a shipwright. She might be anywhere, though. She could be working in one of the completed ships. She could have been called away to deal with repairs on one of the older ships. Sand and stone, she might have been summoned to the palaces to speak with the son of King Beşir, who after the death of his father was overseeing the rebuilding of Sharakhai's navy.

"Stop it," Kameyl said under her breath, keeping her eyes on the road ahead.

"What?" Çeda asked.

"Looking about like that. You're like a bloody sand tit fresh from its den."

Çeda took a deep breath and calmed herself. Kameyl was right. It was just that there were people everywhere, and they had no idea where they might find Nalamae. And there was the gnawing feeling that Goezhen lay in wait just beyond the harbor walls, ready to break through the moment Çeda *did* find her. The vision from the mere had shown him attacking the goddess on a clipper taking its maiden voyage, but Çeda's actions since might already have altered the flow of time, forcing Goezhen to find some other path to Nalamae. Or worse, Çeda's very presence in the harbor might put him on Nalamae's scent.

All too soon they'd reached the stables. As Çeda pulled the wagon to a stop, Kameyl hopped off and barked at a boy standing inside the stable's open doors. "Where's your master?"

He pointed nervously to the stable's far end, where the silhouette of a diminutive man could be seen speaking with two older boys.

Kameyl strutted toward him with a look that was not merely self-assured, but bordering on displeased, as if she had many important things to do and this was the least of them. In short order she reached the stable master and began bellowing orders. They were here for manure, and she would only have it from purebred akhalas. The stable master would of course laugh in her face, at which point Kameyl would reveal the fertilizer was bound for the vineyards that supplied Bhylek House, a distillery that made the araq favored by many of the Kings. The argument would unroll deliberately, Kameyl adding more and more demands, slowly revealing tiny nuggets of information about the Kings' direct interest in this agrarian oddity.

"It's too much," Jenise had argued the night before, "too complex. It's a bunch of shit about a bunch of shit."

"Exactly," Kameyl replied confidently. "The more details we give, the more he'll see the trail leading from that manure all the way to the halls of the Kings. He won't dare deny us." Kameyl had shrugged and laughed that bellowing laugh of hers. "Who would lie about a pile of horse shit?"

It was all designed to take time, to let Çeda and Sümeya search for Nalamae. And indeed, it was playing out just as Kameyl had predicted. As the conversation between her and the stable master grew heated, Çeda left the stables for the shipyard. Sümeya, meanwhile, wandered the nearby piers, where many of the most damaged ships were being repaired. Jenise remained by the wagon so their search wouldn't look too suspicious.

A few of the work crews gave Çeda looks. One of the gang leaders, a scarred cuss of a man, even pointed back toward the stables and shouted at her to keep the yard free of trespassers. Çeda complied, but only until he returned to his work laying the decking on the far side of a half-completed galleon.

The shipwrights were easy to spot. They were the ones others came to, the ones who gave orders, the ones using instruments to measure how true the masts had been set. She spotted ten shipwrights in all, six of them women, but none looked like the one from Çeda's vision in the mere.

"Oy!" Çeda turned to find the gang leader stalking toward her. "I thought I told you to get back to whatever shit work the gods cursed you with." He stared at her clothes, then looked back at the stables, where Kameyl was leading the wagon into the stable's cavernous interior while Jenise took up a shovel from the bed. The gang leader laughed. "The gods are just! Your shit work *is* shit!" All trace of humor faded in an instant. "Now get back to it before I spank your backside for the trouble."

Çeda sneered. "Try it and I'll cut off your sausage and stuff it down your throat. I'd keep my lunch handy if I were you, though." She glanced at his crotch while trudging past him. "That thing looks more mouthful than meal."

The gang leader stared, mouth agape, then barked a jackal's laugh. "I like you, girl. You coming back tomorrow?"

She kept walking, giving the ship yard one last scan as she went.

"I'll look for you!" he bellowed behind her.

She was just nearing the front of the stable when a great bell began to toll, calling for the harbor doors to be opened. The mechanisms clanked. The doors groaned inward.

"Çeda?" Sümeya called in a worried voice.

Çeda turned to find her walking purposefully from the piers. She motioned to the far side of the harbor, where a brightly painted clipper was being towed from its berth by a train of black mules. It looked very much like the ship Çeda had seen in Yusam's mere. Sümeya knew the vision well, as did Kameyl and Jenise. Çeda had shared it in great detail, and that clipper could very well be the one she'd seen. If so, Nalamae might be on it in her new form, the shipwright who'd managed the clipper's construction. She would be taking the ship through its paces before declaring it sandworthy for the royal navy.

"All could be lost if it sails beyond those doors," Çeda said, more to herself than Sümeya.

Without a word spoken between them, Çeda and Sümeya swung their gazes to the horses in the stables. There were many swift akhalas in the stalls. Çeda could ride one out to the ship. She could find Nalamae. They could flee through the open harbor doors. It would be like lighting a beacon fire, a warning to the entire harbor that something strange was afoot, but it was preferable to letting Goezhen find Nalamae.

Çeda and Sümeya nodded to one another. Çeda whistled, and when Kameyl and Jenise glanced back at them, she made a series of hand signals. *Advance to the enemy's rear.*

Neither made an outward sign that she'd understood, but they took her meaning. To the complete and utter consternation of the stable master, Kameyl headed toward the rear of the stables, stopping and looking in each stall in turn, apparently judging the worthiness of the manure inside. Jenise, meanwhile, guided their plow horse so that his view of Çeda and Sümeya was blocked.

"Bloody gods, just take whatever you want," the stable master said, and stalked through a nearby door to the training yard.

Çeda couldn't believe her luck. A few stable hands were all that remained. She and Sümeya moved quickly toward a nearby stall, where an akhala with a copper coat and iron fetlocks stood waiting. It gouged the dirt with a fore-hoof as Sümeya swung the gate open and Çeda mounted it bareback.

The horse was nervous but accepted the bit and bridle with little more than a shake of its dark mane, and when Çeda snapped the reins, it skipped sideways out of its stall, then calmed.

In the center of the harbor, meanwhile, the mule train had been unhooked from the clipper. The ship's sails were set, and it was starting to gain speed.

"Hiyah!" Çeda called, and kicked the akhala into motion.

The sun beat down as they cleared the stable doors. She was just heading for a ramp that led to the sand, ready to give the akhala free rein, when she noticed a group of four riders on akhalas of their own heading easily along the quay.

The noise of the harbor, so dull a moment ago, was suddenly deafening. Three of the riders were Silver Spears. The fourth was a woman wearing a sensible gray dress. She had piercing eyes, a flinty look, and graying hair pulled into a bun.

She was the shipwright from Çeda's vision.

When Çeda had first learned how the goddess returned to life, over and over, each time as someone new, it had seemed so fanciful, a tale like those spun about Bahri Al'sir or Fatima the Untouchable. There, staring at the woman riding with the Silver Spears, it seemed doubly so, an impossibility. This woman was plain. She was *ordinary*. She *couldn't* be Nalamae.

As the woman rode past, she noticed Çeda's stare and gave a sour look back. When she noticed Sümeya staring too, she reined in her horse. "You've nothing better to do than to gawk at your betters?"

Çeda didn't know what she'd been expecting. For Nalamae to recognize her, she supposed. But how could she? The goddess may have been reborn as this woman, but she had no memory of her past life. *When I am reborn,*

Nalamae had told her, *I find myself somewhere in the desert, naked and alone. I am blind. I know so little.*

"Well?" the woman said.

Çeda cast her gaze downward. "Apologies, my lady."

The three Silver Spears accompanying her had reined their horses to a stop. "Is all well, Lady Varal?" their captain called.

The woman glanced back at the other riders and in that moment seemed to remember her purpose. "Yes, all is well." Sending a final withering stare in Çeda's direction, she flicked the reins and headed into the stables with them.

Çeda guided her horse to the side of the stables so that Varal wouldn't find her any more suspicious than she already did. Sümeya met her there with two shovels in hand. "You're sure it's her?"

"I'm sure," Çeda said as she took one of the shovels.

Sümeya nodded. "Kameyl and Jenise are loading the wagon. It's up to us."

Çeda nodded back, and they headed into the stables together. Two of the Silver Spears, who seemed to be in a hurry, were handing over their horses to Jenise. The stable boys were nowhere in sight. Çeda had heard Kameyl ordering them about; she'd surely sent them on errands that would keep them out of the immediate vicinity. Varal was conversing in low tones with the captain of the Spears, who nodded every so often. When he left the stables, following his brothers-in-arms through the side door, Varal headed toward the front, toward the shipyard.

Steeling herself, Çeda stepped into her path. For a moment time slowed. The two of them looked into one another's eyes, Çeda hoping again for some glimmer of recognition.

"Do you know me?" Çeda asked her.

Varal stared with a confused look, but then her flinty gaze returned. "Get out of my way," she said, and was just starting to bull past when Sümeya rushed up behind her and slipped a wet cloth over her nose and mouth.

Her eyes went wide. She struggled hard, arms flailing, legs kicking ineffectually at Sümeya, but all too soon her eyes rolled back into her head and she went limp.

By then Kameyl was steering their wagon toward them. Jenise, kneeling on the bed, pulled the tarp back. As soon as the wagon came to a stop,

Sümeya and Çeda hoisted Varal up and set her onto the warped boards of the wagon bed.

"Oy!"

Çeda spun to find the gang leader from before, striding toward her like a cock in a hen yard. He was leering at Çeda with that nasty grin of his. The closer he came, however, the more his grin faded. He'd been so busy trying to make eye contact with Çeda, the scene before him hadn't fully registered. It did now, though. He had an utterly perplexed look on his face as Jenise covered Varal with the tarp.

"What are you bloody doing with her?"

Sümeya leapt up to the driver's bench. Kameyl snapped the reins. Çeda, meanwhile, pasted a pleasant smile on her face and approached him. Releasing her breath slowly, she reached outward, feeling for the gang leader's heart.

The man's confusion lasted only a moment longer. He drew the small knife at his belt and opened his mouth to speak or perhaps yell out a warning, but when Çeda *pressed* on his heart, he bent over and coughed. By then Çeda was on the move. He swiped once—a clumsy thing. Çeda let it swing past her before darting forward again. She hooked his neck, then transferred her forward momentum to him while lowering her center of gravity in a controlled crouch. She followed his movement, keeping hold of his neck.

As his ponderous weight was wrenched hard onto the stable floor, his breath exploded from him. Çeda immediately hooked one leg around his knife arm, pinning it in place, then tightened her arms around his neck as he struggled. It took only until the count of eight before he went slack. After dragging him into a stall and covering him with hay, she took a flying leap onto the back of the wagon. She'd felt so bloody tense before, but gods it had felt good to work some of it out on that vulgar man.

Their wagon trundled along the quay, heading with speed, though not *too* much speed, toward King's Road. With luck, the man would go undiscovered until they made it past the House of Maidens and returned to the city.

Çeda cast a backward glance at the tarp, where the body of Varal the shipwright was outlined. The farther they went, the more she started to doubt her vision.

The fates grant me this favor, she prayed. *Let this woman be Nalamae.*

Chapter 12

As the blazing sun settled in the west, Davud and Esmeray stood side by side in the shadow of a portico. Amongst members of the Enclave, Esmeray was once the mage known as "the crazed one." She and Davud had fallen in with one another, then fallen in love, after finding common cause in trying to bring King Sukru to justice for his many crimes, particularly against blood magi. Esmeray had since lost her ability to use magic—it had been burned from her by the Enclave's inner circle—but the two of them had remained together. They were both still wanted by the powers of the city, the Enclave and Queen Meryam foremost among them, and they needed protection.

The portico they stood beneath was the entrance to the only reputable moneylender in the quarter of the city known as the Well. The fluted columns out front were chipped. Graffiti was everywhere, though it was interesting to note that more recent gang symbols had started to eclipse the sign of the spread-winged scarabs of the Moonless Host.

"Times change," Davud mused.

Esmeray, her thick braids wrapped in a head scarf so that they spread toward the sky like a potted fern, gave the wall a passing glance and shrugged. "Even mountains crumble, Davud."

Beyond the columns, an arrowhead-shaped plaza unfurled. The shadows of sunset were long. Only the ancient mudbrick building at the plaza's opposite end, Sharakhai's famed fighting pits, rose above it. The upper two floors stood brightly in the sunlight, a golden ship on a dark sea of iron.

When a roar rose up from the pits, Davud knew the final bout had just been decided. Soon hundreds were spilling out onto the plaza. The sound of their conversations rolled like a wave through the neighborhood. Young gutter wrens flocked, hands cupped for handouts. Some few of the spectators— those addled by drink or naiveté or the high of winning a large purse—actually handed out a few copper khet, only to be rewarded with dozens more children swarming toward them calling for the same. Most, however, ignored the wrens and took to the oud parlors or shisha dens or brothels that bordered the pits, living off its riches like parasites.

A group of boys climbed the base of the portico steps, perhaps wanting the space for their own, but stopped in their tracks when they noticed Davud and Esmeray already standing there.

"Fuck off," Esmeray said.

Had it been any other woman, the boys might have used it as an invitation to start something, but Esmeray was not just any woman. The tribal tattoos along her cheeks and forehead gave her an angry look. And her eyes had a wild look about them, a look made all the more jarring for the fact that they were the color of ivory, evidence of her magic having been burnt from her by the Enclave.

The boys slunk away, leaving Davud and Esmeray alone once more. As the crowd began to thin, a handsome young man with long, light-colored hair pulled into a tail stepped onto the plaza in front of the pits. His name was Tariq, and he was flanked by two massive guards with cudgels in their meaty hands. Many waved to Tariq or called in greeting, but Tariq passed them by with hardly a look.

As they neared, Davud stepped out from under the portico. "A moment of your time, Tariq?"

One of the guards moved to intercept, but stopped when Tariq raised a hand. "Davud?"

Davud smiled easily. "How've you been?"

Tariq stared at him quizzically, then glanced at Esmeray, who leaned against one of the nicked columns like a street tough. Tariq's look turned calculating, as if he were already trying to figure out what their angle was. "I thought you were dead," he said to Davud.

Davud waggled his head. "A common misconception."

"I've got business to attend to," Tariq ventured, though he didn't seem overly insistent about it. He was curious.

Davud flourished to the crowded street ahead of them. "And I don't want to keep you from it. We can walk while we talk."

Once, when they were young, Davud had come across Tariq in the choked aisles of the bazaar. He'd been running the streets with Hamid and Emre and was in a right foul mood. Davud had been heading back to his sister's bakery stall with a bag of fresh mint, but Tariq stopped him.

"You're smart," Tariq said. "Settle an argument for us. Emre says the gods control what we do. Hamid says it's the fates. I say they're both beetle-brained fools. *We're* the ones who control what we do."

Davud remembered thinking how enlightened a question it was. "Actually," he'd replied, "one of the books Master Amalos gave me says it's none of those things." He'd said it more to spark conversation than anything else. He'd thought Tariq genuinely curious about the answer, when what he really wanted was for Davud to agree with him. "The philosopher, Kosmet, says that our every action is determined by all previous actions, and that we have no free will at all."

Tariq's face had turned red. "Then it isn't really me doing this," he said, and slapped Davud across the face so hard he fell to the ground, spilling the mint from the bag.

Tariq stormed away, being sure to grind the leaves into the dirt as he went. Hamid followed in his wake, sparing an unsympathetic look that said Davud should have known better. Only Emre stopped and pulled Davud to his feet, then helped to collect the mint. "You're not in the collegia now, Davud," Emre said under his breath. "You've got to learn to read your audience."

Tariq may have forgotten that day, but Davud never had. Tariq had always been full of bluster, acting like everyone was out to get him. It had only grown worse as he'd risen through the ranks of Osman's organization—an enterprise that combined a number of legal and illegal ventures, including the fighting pits themselves—eventually becoming Osman's right-hand man. Davud thought Tariq would look him up and down and tell *him* to fuck off, just like Esmeray had with the gutter wrens. He didn't, though. For several long heartbeats he weighed Davud, then gave an even-handed nod, the sort Osman might have given years ago when he'd been running the pits. Was Tariq, dare Davud say it, growing up?

"Tell me what you need," Tariq said as Davud fell into step alongside him.

Esmeray followed. The two towers of meat Tariq used for protection came last.

"I need to speak to someone," Davud said.

A flash of annoyance passed over Tariq's face. "You badgered *me* into a conversation easily enough. You can do the same to them."

"Yes, well, they're in your employ, and could use a bit of convincing."

They passed an intersection where a group of boys and girls were kicking around a ball made of old, patched leather. "Who?"

"Your physic, Hayal."

"And what might you need from Hayal?"

Davud had debated how forthright to be. Esmeray had argued against honesty, saying there was no way they could trust Tariq. In fact, she'd argued for ensorcelling him and *taking* the information. But Davud didn't want to risk using magic, not only because it risked the Enclave's finding them, but also because it was imperative he reach the blood mage, Undosu, an associate of Hayal's, on peaceable terms. Force Tariq or Hayal to do what they wanted and Undosu might hear of it, and if *that* happened Davud's chances of gaining him as an ally dwindled to practically nothing.

"Hayal sells alchemycal ingredients to a man named Undosu," Davud went on. "I'd like a meeting with him."

Tariq stopped dead in his tracks, ignoring the people staring from the tea house down the street. "Undosu . . ."

"Yes."

His eyes drifted down to Davud's left hand. He glared at the blooding ring Davud wore on his thumb, a ring with a sharp thorn, which he could use to gather blood when needed. "It's true, then?" he asked in a low voice. "You're a blood mage?"

Davud nodded.

"And you want Undosu for what?"

"A bit of protection."

Tariq nodded sagely, then began walking again, forcing Davud to keep up. They turned a corner and headed down a section of street with a veritable jungle of thawbs and shawls and veils hanging to dry on lines between the buildings. Tariq said, "You know, I could use a man like you. And in return, *I* could provide you the protection you need."

Davud glanced back at the two toughs trailing behind them. "That's not the kind of thing I do."

"You might be surprised how vast Osman's network is, Davud. There's a lot we could do for you."

"I can't."

"Not even if I get you your meeting?"

Davud paused as a gaggle of laughing children swept past the five of them like a school of fish through cattails. "There's a reason you thought I was dead, Tariq. Queen Meryam herself is after me. The Enclave is as well. That's why I need to speak to Undosu. I need safety for me and for Esmeray."

"Queen Meryam is after you . . . ."

"Yes."

Tariq seemed to reconsider. "Well, maybe once it's all done, then."

"No, not even then."

For a moment the old Tariq returned—his face became cross; he looked like he wanted to make something of it—but then the dark cloud seemed to dissipate and he shrugged. "Can't blame me for trying."

"I don't." They turned a corner onto a street that ran between two rows of old, crumbling tenements. "I need that meeting, Tariq."

"I'm a businessman, Davud. I need *something* for it."

"What do you have in mind?"

"Something simple for you, I imagine. I want you to find someone for me." They passed the mouth of an ancient well—*the* well, the very one the neighborhood had been named for—and came to a boulevard, the most affluent street in the entire quarter. "You may have heard of him," Tariq went on, "my little cousin, Altan. Like you, he found his way into the collegia after impressing one of the masters enough to sponsor him. He was in his second year. He was a studious little runt, impressing everyone. He was halfway to making a name for himself. Then five days ago he went missing."

"Missing how?"

"When he didn't show up for his classes, his mother came to me, worried, so I had the boys ask around. The night before, Altan was seen heading north along the Trough by a few girls who were out drinking. Altan refused to so much as turn and wave to them."

"Maybe he didn't like them. Maybe he was drunk."

"Maybe." Tariq stopped before a set of stairs leading up to an elegantly carved door. "But he was never much of a drinker, and the girls entered the collegia with him. They were close friends."

"So you want *me* to find him?"

"Yes. It would put his mother's mind at ease, even if it's only to know he's dead."

"I wouldn't even know where to begin!"

"You've always been smart, Davud. You'll figure it out." He walked up the steps, his guards following. "Find out what happened to Altan and I'll get you your meeting."

Before Davud could say another word, Tariq and his men went inside, the door clattering shut behind them.

"We don't need him," Esmeray said.

But Davud's mind was already working. This might all turn out to be something perfectly innocent. The collegia put a lot of pressure on their students. Altan might have decided to take a break without telling anyone—it wouldn't be the first time it had happened to a student—but this smacked of something more nefarious. Davud couldn't help but think of what Hamzakiir had done to him and the other scholars: he'd abducted Davud's entire graduating class and turned them into foul creations, shamblers, that he'd used against the Kings on the Night of Endless Swords.

"Davud?"

He met Esmeray's ivory eyes. "I'm going to find out what happened to Altan."

"Don't be an idiot," Esmeray said. "We don't need Altan. And we don't need Tariq."

"I'm not doing this for Tariq."

Esmeray knew of his history at the collegia and what had happened with Hamzakiir—the abduction, the strange experiments, the shamblers he'd turned them into. "This isn't your fight, Davud. You've got enough to worry about."

"I'd never forgive myself if I didn't look into it." He took her hand and led her away. "I'm going to find out what happened to Altan."

Chapter 13

As *THE WAYWARD MILLER* sailed east, Ihsan was confident of two things. The first was that if anyone could get Zeheb to listen, it was Husamettín and his famously dogged persistence. The second, far more important to Ihsan's cause, was that Husamettín would fail spectacularly in his task—Zeheb hadn't been named the Mad Bull of Sharakhai for no reason. They were on the deck of their cutter, *The Wayward Miller*. Husamettín leaned against the gunwales while Zeheb sat on a chair before him, babbling incoherently. The sun shone brightly, casting stark shadows of lines and sails across the *Miller*'s deck.

Cahil manned the wheel—poorly, it seemed to Ihsan. He caught every dune wrong, setting the ship rolling constantly, to the point that Ihsan felt like he'd swallowed a bag of snakes. He might have gone to the edge of the deck and tossed his breakfast over the gunwales if he thought it wouldn't hurt his standing with his fellow Kings, but it would. In this respect, Cahil and Husamettín were cut from the same cloth: to show weakness of any sort was a sign of inferiority.

"Baük," Husamettín was saying to Zeheb. "Find the Blade Maidens in Baük and tell us what you hear."

Zeheb, his lips working like a burbling stream, swiveled his head and stared southeast toward Baük, a moderately sized caravanserai along the trade route from Sharakhai to the rolling grasslands of Kundhun. Husamettín was bidding him to listen for certain whispers: those of the serai's master, or the Blade Maidens assigned to the garrison, or the captains of the ships in dock. But nothing he, Cahil, or Yndris had done had so far managed to snap him from his spell of muttering madness.

"Come here," Zeheb was saying. "Let *me* do it!"

"Who is it you're hearing?" Husamettín asked in a patient but forceful tone. "What are they doing?"

"Stop it! Stop! You're ruining it!"

"Who is it, Zeheb?"

Zeheb pulled his gaze away from the horizon and stared into Husamettín's dark eyes. His eyes drifted to the scar on Husamettín's forehead, the mark of the traitor. These moments when Zeheb seemed to be present, able to talk, were rare. He suddenly seemed so lucid Ihsan thought he might actually say something rational.

But then Zeheb's face soured. "Days like these I'm sad to call you my son. Give me those."

Husamettín, his monumental patience finally run out, stood and walked away, shaking his head as he went. As was often the case, the spell of lucidity had been a mirage, Zeheb's reactions not his own, but those of the person he'd latched onto from afar.

A little over a week had passed since they'd stolen him from the Kundhuni fleet. They'd steered clear of the two primary sailing lanes from the caravanserai, Çalabin, and anchored a full day's sail from Baük. It was risky, their being anywhere near a caravanserai, a risk that grew by the day. The royal galleon would be hunting them, and likely its captain would have sent a skiff to Çalabin with orders for the caravanserai's master to send more ships to hunt for their cutter.

Husamettín had reckoned the delay worth it, though. They had Zeheb, and they still hoped to use him for their own purposes. They needed a place like Baük where he could hear the whispers, a place to test how they could use him against Meryam in Sharakhai.

Suddenly, Zeheb's demeanor changed. His mouth worked. He looked up at Yndris, then swiveled his head toward Ihsan. There was a spark of recognition, a flare of anger. Ihsan worried he would speak of Ihsan's many betrayals, that he might reveal just enough to ruin Ihsan's plans, but the look soon faded and his face became calm as a desert morning.

He glanced at Yndris in a distracted way. His hands ran back and forth, as if he were running a plane across a wooden beam. "Don't forget the pot of grease from Abdul." His voice had softened. "We need it for the wagon."

"Who's speaking?" Yndris asked, taking Husamettín's place in the questioning. "Who are they?"

But nothing she did—no amount of coercion, bargaining, browbeating, or simple acts of patience—would get through to him. Zeheb was immune to it all. Ihsan could have told them as much, but none of them had asked him, and Ihsan hadn't volunteered it. He needed them to become frustrated by their inability to reach Zeheb. Only then could he reveal his true purpose.

Or so he thought. He'd no more voiced the notion in his head than Cahil spoke from the pilot's wheel, "Give it to him."

"Not yet," Husamettín replied.

"Why not?" Cahil pressed. "Nothing has changed, and nothing is *going* to change." He flung a hand toward Zeheb. "We risked our lives for a reason, and it wasn't to listen to his blathering until the end of days has come."

What's he talking about? Ihsan signed to Husamettín.

Husamettín, clearly unwilling to share, stared at Ihsan, his pinched brow making the scar on his forehead wrinkle in strange ways.

It was Yndris who answered. "We have a brew my good father's alchemyst made in Sharakhai," she said. "It coerces. It forces the one who drinks it to obey."

"But," Husamettín added, "it wears on the mind, and quickly. We might be able to use it for a time. A few weeks. A month, perhaps. After that"—he looked to Zeheb with something resembling sympathy—"he will become but a mindless husk."

"He's that already," Cahil said.

"He's that already," Zeheb said softly.

They all stared in surprise. It might have seemed at first like Zeheb had snapped out of his spell. But he hadn't. Not completely. He'd still been *listening* with his god-given power; it was just that he'd used it on Cahil. He'd somehow drawn his attention here, which was a potentially devastating development for Ihsan. If they thought that Zeheb could train his power on certain individuals, that it wasn't entirely random, it would give Cahil added leverage to apply the serum.

Indeed, Cahil gave a bright, ringing laugh. "You see? There's more to him than idle wandering. He can do what we want, but not if we leave him to his own devices."

"Leave him to his own devices," Zeheb echoed. It felt like a desperate appeal from a man who knew he was doomed and was communicating in the only way he knew how. The look on his face was one of complete and utter terror.

There may be another way, Ihsan signed quickly. He couldn't let Husamettín think on Cahil's course for too long.

"To do what?" Husamettín asked.

To free his mind . . .

Husamettín waited expectantly. Cahil and Yndris did as well. Even Zeheb seemed eager for his answer, but gods, Ihsan wasn't ready. He'd wanted them at the end of their rope. He should have known they'd have something else in mind for Zeheb.

"Well, out with it!" Cahil shouted.

I've been thinking on it, Ihsan signed. *If my powers were returned to me, I might order him to do what you wanted.*

Husamettín's dark eyes narrowed. His long, pepper-gray hair blew in the wind. "If your powers were returned to you . . ."

Yes.

"And how might *that* happen? You said you'd tried the healing elixirs, to no effect."

Ihsan turned toward Cahil and signed to him. *Years ago, your son, Gallan, lost his leg. You healed it for him.*

Cahil's eyes had turned hard and distrustful. He was staring at Ihsan, not as though he were remembering his son whom he had healed, as Ihsan had said, but as if he were close to unraveling the mystery behind Ihsan's offer. Suddenly his eyes went wide and he turned away from the wheel. He pulled at the rope that secured the rake to the transom, then shoved it hard.

The rake struck the sand and left deep furrows. It threw everything and everyone aboard the ship forward. Zeheb slid away, still in his chair. Husamettín lowered himself into a half-crouch and spread his arms, balancing himself like the expert swordsman he was. Yndris arrested her fall by grabbing a nearby shroud. Ihsan, meanwhile, was thrown to the deck, where he slid along the deck boards until coming to an ignominious crash against the short stairs leading up to the foredeck.

When the ship had come to a halt, Cahil stormed forward and thrust a finger toward Ihsan's chest as though he wished it were a spear. "*This* is why you came all this way. *This* is why you intercepted us. Not because of *Sharakhai*, as you claim, not because you want to see us back on the mount and in our palaces, but because you lost your precious tongue and you want it back!"

Cahil's breath came loudly. His nostrils flared, and his eyes gained a certain brightness. Ihsan had seen this sort of change overcome Cahil before. Like a dog slavering before food is laid in his bowl, the look came when he was set to inflict torture, Cahil imagining the acts in detail before things truly began.

There were a hundred different ways Ihsan could take his reply, and he wasn't sure which he should choose. The wrong step here would see his throat slit, his body given back to the desert, the Kings moving on without him now that they had another option, however feeble and temporary it might prove in the end.

But then he saw something he hadn't noticed before. Cahil was *afraid*. He'd lost his place in the world, and he wanted it back. He wanted all to be as it had been for centuries, since the days of Beht Ihman, and suddenly it was plain as day how to deal with him. It wasn't to profess his loyalty to Sharakhai, nor the desert, nor its people. It was to appeal to Cahil's underlying sense of fear.

Wouldn't you have done the same in my place? Ihsan signed.

Cahil's jaw worked. He swallowed several times. For a moment Ihsan thought he'd erred.

In the end, it was Yndris who saved him. "He might last longer under Ihsan's power than the serum," she said.

It was a reasonable point, but sometimes reason only made Cahil grow more petulant, more eager to demonstrate his power over others.

"And there's little doubt," Husamettín stepped in, "that his having his power returned might get us what we all want in the end."

Cahil turned to him, red-faced. "Get him what *he* wants, you mean."

Husamettín was unfazed. "Might the two not align?"

Cahil stared at him as if he were mad. "You've had four hundred years to find an answer to that question. If you can't figure it out by now—"

He stopped at movement from Ihsan, who had chosen that moment to pull a piece of papyrus from his khalat. He held it out for Cahil to take, which he did with a quick snatch of his hand. As he read it over, his expression calmed, and much of the redness in his cheeks and forehead faded. He stared at Ihsan warily. "We'll find her?"

Husamettín took the note from Cahil's stilled hand, read it over with a look of wonder, then handed it absently to Yndris.

Yndris read it as if her life depended on it. "Well," she said when she finished, "will we?"

From everything I've read, yes. It's one of the strongest threads in the journals.

"Then why didn't Yusam ever mention it?" Cahil pressed.

Don't you remember how he was? Flighty. Scared. He had trouble remembering his way to the privy—Ihsan motioned to the slip of papyrus—*much less piecing together a dizzyingly complex puzzle like those I've found in his entries. He was good at connecting visions, I'll give him that, but by the end he was terrible at following them to their logical conclusions.*

They all looked at one another—Cahil, Husamettín, and Yndris. Husamettín nodded. He would give Ihsan his chance, especially to gain a prize like the one mentioned in Yusam's vision, Nalamae herself. Yndris gave her father a tentative nod, the sort that implied: *we can always kill him later.*

Cahil, clearly frustrated by his own inability to read minds or see the future, took the papyrus from Yndris, crumpled it up, and threw it hard at Ihsan. It hit Ihsan in the chest and rolled down to the deck. "We'll try it your way. But if we go to Sharakhai and we don't find her, it's your head."

Very well, Ihsan said, not bothering to pretend to be affronted at the threat. Why should he? If the vision didn't come true, he'd know that all his efforts had been for naught anyway, and that Sharakhai and the desert truly were doomed.

He stuffed the papyrus back into his khalat's inside pocket. It relayed how three Kings went to Sharakhai to find a woman. How they convinced her to join them. How they used her to challenge those who stood against the city. The woman, Yusam's vision made clear, was the goddess Nalamae reborn. She was malleable. She could become a weapon if groomed properly.

They would return to Sharakhai. They would find Nalamae. And they would use her to stop what was happening—not the invasion by Malasan and Mirea, but the grand designs of the desert gods.

Chapter 14

WILLEM COULDN'T SLEEP the night Altan walked away. He was too haunted by the dimming of Altan's light. The resulting darkness had created a terrible hole inside of him, and the more he thought about it, the wider it became. He felt consumed by it.

He tried to occupy his mind by reading the myths of the elder gods. There were dozens of such accounts in the hidden archives. He pored over them in his small, carpet-lined cubbyhole. He often read by lamplight because it helped him to read faster. But when he really wanted to immerse himself in a story, he read in complete darkness. The ink glimmered for him, even in the eldest of texts, some faint remnant of the one who'd penned the pages. It made for slower reading—he could only manage several books per hour instead of his usual dozen—but there was something about reading stories like this, as if it were only him and the world the words created, everything else having moved on to the farther fields just as the elder gods had done. It never failed to relax him, except this time it wasn't working. He couldn't stop thinking about Altan.

When Nebahat had questioned him, Altan had spoken a name: Cassandra, another student at the collegia. She was a charming young woman with straight black hair, a pert chin, and a nose slightly too big for her face. Her glow was bright. Not so bright as some, certainly nothing like Altan's, but it was pretty enough. Willem took to watching her as she walked along the halls of her dormitory. He watched her eating dates and cheese on the esplanade with the other students. He watched her sneaking out to visit the oud parlors along the Trough. He watched her studying the texts of history in the halls of records and jotting notes into a small book with a finger on the page of whatever massive tome happened to be laid in front of her.

Nebahat had asked Altan who he'd spoken with about his findings.

What findings? Willem wondered.

Those were the key. Altan's *findings* had led Nebahat to summon him. They were the reason Nebahat had sent Altan away. They were the reason the glimmer around Altan had dimmed, a clear sign of impending death. And Cassandra had been part of it. Watch her long enough, Willem thought, and he would find out what it was.

"Today," Cassandra was saying to her study mate, who sat across the table from her inside the collegia's largest library.

Willem watched them from a dark passageway behind one of the floor-to-ceiling shelves. The tiny door through which he peered was built just high enough that he could see over the books to their table.

"What?" the other said absently. She was a dull woman who hardly glowed at all, but basked in the glow of others.

Like you, a voice whispered in Willem's ear.

No, Willem thought. *I would glow if I could. It's just, I'm not* allowed *to shine.*

"The battle of the books," Cassandra explained. "It starts again today."

Willem sat perfectly still. This was precisely what he'd been waiting for. Why else would the glow around Cassandra have changed so much? With those words the light around her had become scintillant, shifting toward green. And it fractured more, like a gemstone under firelight.

"Have they found Altan?" the other student asked.

"No. I think he's chasing after that boy he met."

"And you don't think he'd tell anyone about it?"

Cassandra shrugged. "Boys do strange things for love. All I know is Altan's gone and *I'm* the one left to pick up the pieces. He started two months before I did. He had all the house names in his head, who married whom, which children came from which mothers."

"How dull."

"You've no idea. It's like following trails in a dung beetle's nest," Cassandra said. "It's enough to drive a woman to drink."

The other woman laughed. "As if you didn't drink already."

Cassandra's lips curled in a lascivious smile. "I didn't realize you were watching me so closely. Perhaps you want to come by my room tonight and watch me some more."

"You're such a whore," the other whispered, then added, "What time?"

Both of them laughed, which elicited a thorough shushing from the harridan sitting behind the central desk.

"I don't see why the chancellor cares," the dull one said a while later.

To which Cassandra shrugged. "He said the records were incomplete." Cassandra stiffened her back and made her voice go mockingly low. "Lineage is important. We should know who the members of the thirteenth tribe are, particularly among the highborn." She relaxed and leaned over her book. "But *I* think the orders are coming from the Kings."

"Why do you say that?"

"Who was it that ordered the thirteenth tribe to be murdered in the first place? Who fears their return to Sharakhai with the rest of the tribes at their back? Likely whoever it is wants to know who they can use as bargaining chips when the day comes. Or perhaps they plan to massacre the people of the thirteenth tribe, like they did after Beht Ihman. Who knows?" Cassandra, whose face had shown more and more annoyance, slapped several large books closed. "I can't concentrate. I might as well head over there now."

Cassandra left, the glimmering around her brighter than ever. Willem didn't bother scrabbling up to the roof to watch where she was going. He knew perfectly well she was headed to the hall of records. After closing the tiny door in the shelves, he paced seventeen steps to his left, took the spiraling stairs down to the longest of the collegia's underground tunnels, and flew along it until he felt the telltale curving that indicated he was close to the hall of records.

He climbed the seven flights to the hall's uppermost floor, the one set aside for records of marriage and birth, and reached his usual hiding spot behind an iron grate. Eventually Cassandra walked into the hall, approached a rolling cart, and began sorting through a massive stack of books that Altan had compiled before his abrupt departure.

For several hours, Willem watched Cassandra read through the books, tracing the roots of lineage from the days of Beht Ihman to modern-day Sharakhai, trying to identify the descendants of the thirteenth tribe. Willem could tell her at least forty of them. He adored tales of lineage, not because he thought there was power inherent in blood, as so many others did, but because it held so much sway over life in the desert. He'd spent several months in this very hall, poring over the same tomes Cassandra had stacked before her now.

But he'd spit at Bakhi's feet before he gave Cassandra anything. This was what had got Altan killed.

Willem felt a tug inside him. It was a summons from Nebahat, a summons he couldn't refuse. He could delay it, though. And delay he would. His anger over all that had happened, for what might still happen—more bright lights of gifted students being snuffed out—gave him the strength he needed to deny Nebahat's call.

Even so, Nebahat was impatient today. After only a short pause, the summons came again. Willem was about to leave when he noticed something most strange. Another light. A bright one. Bright like Altan's. Brighter maybe.

It floated through the room, wavering ever closer to the table where Cassandra sat. It hovered in the air behind her, as if someone were reading over her shoulder.

And then Willem realized he *knew* that light, though he hadn't seen it in over two years. The last time was during the graduation ceremony just before the massacre, the one led by the Moonless Host and orchestrated by the blood mage, Hamzakiir. How Willem had wept that day. How he'd grieved for those lost souls, taken before their time.

He'd thought Davud had been taken just like the rest, but he hadn't. Here he was even though Willem couldn't see him. The question of how he'd survived flared in Willem's mind, but it was dimmed by the sheer joy of seeing his light shine once more. More important than how he'd lived was the question of what he was doing here. How was it that he'd come to watch

Cassandra just as Willem was? Did he know about the list of descendants? Did he know about Altan?

Willem wanted to wait and find out, but just then Nebahat called again, and this time it was painful. Willem gave one last look at the hovering light, picturing Davud bending down over the pages of Cassandra's book, then left, moving silently, returning to the darkness of the collegia's hidden arteries.

When Willem reached the hidden archives, Nebahat asked, "Where were you?" in that way of his, a calm manner that made it perfectly clear he expected the truth, and quickly, or Willem would be punished.

Nebahat had always taken solace from the fact that Willem was forbidden from lying. He'd never guessed Willem had learned ways of telling the truth without telling the *whole* truth. Using his most typical reply, Willem put his palms together and unfolded them, like the covers of a book falling open, a thing that might be interpreted as him reading or going to the hall of records or any number of other activities. Most often, Nebahat didn't much care what Willem had been doing, only that he'd been inconvenienced by Willem's late arrival.

Scratching his chin absently, Nebahat sat behind his desk near the hearth, unfolded a wrap of cloth, and took out half of a massive sandwich of meat and cheese and what looked to be dried tomatoes. After taking a large bite, he spoke, the words muffled by the food. "Did you get the texts I asked for?"

Willem's mouth watered. He wanted desperately to return to the room where Davud was but he could hardly take his eyes off the airy crumb of the bread, the creamy golden hue of the cheese.

"Yes, yes, I brought some for you as well," Nebahat said, and held out the other half of the sandwich.

Willem shook his head. He felt his face go red a moment later as his stomach rumbled. Luckily Nebahat seemed more preoccupied than normal and took no note of it.

"Did you get the texts?"

Bowing, Willem motioned to the nearest of the tables that complicated the archive's central, open space.

"Very well." Nebahat chewed, and proceeded, as he often did after one of his forays into the city, to rattle off a series of alchemycal agents that he required, including the amounts for each. This time the list included copper filings, sand drake scales, and lye, three of the primary ingredients used to create a potion that could lure and pacify an efrit, at least long enough to extract a favor from it. Dealing in such things was a specialty of Undosu, another blood mage and a member of the Enclave, a group of magi who'd formed primarily for mutual protection against the Kings, to share in knowledge, but also to do precisely what Nebahat was asking of Willem: gather and distribute the rare ingredients necessary for the creation of certain serums, potions, and elixirs.

Though Nebahat had never volunteered it, Willem knew *he* was a member of the Enclave as well—a high ranking member, in fact, one of the inner circle. Only three others held that title, one of them being Undosu. Even with all Nebahat had done to him, Willem had taken pride in Nebahat's achievement. Willem might be a lowly servant (some might call him a slave) but he was working for one of the most powerful men in Sharakhai—no, in the entire Shangazi Desert.

Since Altan had left, however, Nebahat's light had taken on a different hue. His light still shone strongly, but it was now ominous. Dangerous. Willem had despaired in the days after Altan's departure, thinking he'd failed to recognize the signs of Nebahat's evil nature, but after pondering it, he reckoned it must be due to the recent changes, the chancellor's sudden interest in the descendants of the thirteenth tribe.

The notion that he hadn't been serving a murderer his entire life made Willem feel better, but it did nothing to ease the sting of Altan's death.

"Well, if you're not going to eat," Nebahat said, "you might as well get to it."

With a nod and a bow, and one last longing look toward the half sandwich he was leaving behind, Willem stepped backward until he reached the darkened tunnel outside the secret archives. Then he was sprinting headlong for the hall of records. Gods help him, he considered taking a shortcut over the lawns of the collegia grounds, but one of his many compulsions forced him to remain hidden, to keep his life in the collegia secret from everyone, so he kept to the dark, winding ways and eventually returned to the space behind the iron grate.

He was breathing heavily, something he always made sure to let subside before approaching a peep hole. Not this time, though, and his heavy breathing made Cassandra look up. It was a terrible, terrible mistake. But for once he didn't care, because Davud was gone, and he'd taken his light with him.

Chapter 15

DEEP IN THE DESERT, Emre stared as the crowd parted before him, revealing Hamid, Frail Lemi, and a woman in a wheat-colored battle dress who it took Emre a moment to recognize as Sirendra.

Hamid, clearly confused and angry, addressed Shaikh Neylana, "What do you think you're doing?"

Neylana waved to Emre. "This man, Emre Aykan'ava, has filed a grievance against you. He came to me on a skiff, but he was wounded, nearly dead of exhaustion, exposure, and malnutrition. He claims to have been attacked while on his way to rendezvous with a ship named the *Amaranth*"—she pointed over Hamid's shoulder—"the very ship you now sail."

Hamid stared with those sleepy eyes of his. He looked heavier than when Emre had last seen him. Or maybe it was just that Emre's memories had distorted, turning the man who'd tried to kill him into a mad, twisted creature like the asirim. *Except the asirim, even the worst among them, have more humanity than you, Hamid.*

Hamid was still staring at Emre, his mouth working, no words coming out. "Perhaps we should retire to our ships to discuss this," he finally managed.

He was looking at Emre, but the words were meant for Neylana.

"No," she said flatly. "Emre has leveled dire claims against you. They will be settled here, now."

"Any grievance Emre has should be brought before *our* shaikh."

"The alleged crime was not committed in Tribe Khiyanat's territory, but on *Halarijan's*. Therefore, you will be tried here, by us." She waved to the other shaikhs.

"What does he claim?" Hamid asked.

Neylana had requested that Emre remain silent, but he couldn't. "That you attacked me without provocation." He strode forward as he spoke. "That you dug a hole and threw me into it. That you buried me alive." He stopped beside Neylana, hoping Hamid wouldn't see how terrified he was. Not a day passed that he didn't relive those harrowing moments when he thought he was going to die, and now the fear buried deep within his psyche was storming up, blowing like a foul wind, threatening to send him into a panic. He calmed his breathing, stilled his quavering hands. "You sought to murder me in cold blood for actions that saved Sharakhai from the Malasani threat."

"A lie!" Hamid took in all those watching with a look of shock. "I don't know what happened to you, Emre, but that isn't true. After leaving camp on that skiff with King bloody Ihsan, you never came back. We waited, but the Malasani fleet was on the hunt for us and we were forced to leave. We thought Ihsan must have killed you, or you were taken by the Silver Spears!"

"No," Emre said. "Darius was there. Frail Lemi was, too."

Hamid turned to Frail Lemi, who was staring at Emre in naked wonder, his jaw hanging open like a winded jackal. "Do you remember us looking for Emre?"

Frail Lemi nodded. "We looked, Emre. I swear we did."

"I know, Lem. It wasn't you. I heard them rushing to keep you from reaching from the grotto where I landed my skiff. You couldn't have known."

Hamid, seeing how hard Frail Lemi was trying to piece together the past, turned to him. "Don't believe a word he says, Lemi. You remember how he was. Wrong about Haddad. Wrong about King Emir. Wrong about King Ihsan."

Frail Lemi's brow creased even more. He looked like a child who'd taken a wrong turn and become lost in a bad neighborhood and was desperately trying to retrace his steps.

Sirendra looked warily between Hamid and Emre. "If it went as you said," she said to Emre, "how did you escape?"

"By the grace of the gods."

Emre had been in a state of panic as Hamid and Darius threw shovelfuls of sand on top of him. Emre had felt it pressing down on him, but the layer of sand must not have been very thick by the time Frail Lemi interrupted them. Emre had fallen unconscious shortly after. The air seeping in from the surface above must have been enough for him to breathe. He'd awoken some time later in darkness, and his panic had risen to new heights. No longer stunned from the blow to the back of his head, he'd been able to twist and writhe and work enough of the sand around him that he could take proper breaths. Finally he'd been able to squirm like a rattlewing grub, up from his sandy grave, and untie his bonds.

Hamid spread his arms like some magnanimous lord to the masses. "We'll call Darius here. You can question him yourself. He'll confirm he has no memory of this."

"He is your lover, is he not?" Neylana asked.

"He is, but no one is more trustworthy than Darius."

"It matters not," Neylana said. "Emre has asked for, and been granted, trial by combat."

Hamid was staring hard at Neylana. Emre was certain he was about to deny her—why should Hamid fight? He had the upper hand—when his gaze shifted to Emre. Pain was building at the back of Emre's skull, where Darius had struck him with the shovel. Despite Emre's attempts to hide it, the pain was starting to show through. One eye pinched shut as a particularly sharp wave of pain passed along the left side of his head. It set his hands to shaking. Hamid was surely oblivious to Emre's condition—he couldn't know that Emre had suffered from debilitating headaches since freeing himself—but he guessed some of it. His smug expression was proof of that.

"I accept," he said.

Neylana, perhaps expecting more pushback, paused, then said, "Very well."

Within the circle of ships, the warriors of Tribe Halarijan created a clearing ten paces across and stood with spears at the ready, a makeshift arena in which Emre and Hamid would fight.

Hamid stepped into the clearing and drew his shamshir. As Emre followed, Darius rushed between a ketch and a ramshackle galleon. When he saw what was happening, he raised his arms, his good one going higher than his injured one, and yelled, "Hamid, no!"

But Hamid merely raised one hand. "Don't worry, Darius." He smiled and flourished his blade. "This will all be over in a minute."

As Emre was stepping between two of the warriors to enter the makeshift arena, his eyes met Darius's. Darius betrayed himself in that moment, a look of shame overcoming him, but a moment later it was gone and his fearful eyes swung back to Hamid.

Frail Lemi, meanwhile, had gone stone still, his gaze distant, as if he were still trying to piece together the facts.

Hamid unstrapped the buckler from his belt and fitted it over his left hand. Emre did the same, and the two of them met at the center of the circle. The crowd closed in. Hundreds gathered on the ships, watching from the gunwales. There were men, women, and children of every age; some held young ones to their chests as they waited.

Shaikh Neylana raised her arms and turned slowly, taking in the entire assemblage. "Two enter the arena. One leaves, the other will be given back to the desert." She faced Emre and Hamid. "May the gods have mercy on your souls." With that she clapped three times. Around them, the warriors began to thump the butt of their spears onto the sand, creating a strange, rolling rhythm.

"Better if you'd gone back to Sharakhai," Hamid said, soft enough that only Emre could hear.

"I couldn't live with myself, knowing the man who attempted to murder me was still free," Emre replied as he gripped his own buckler.

"It was *conquest*, Emre."

"It was cowardice."

"Well, we'll see who's a coward now."

Hamid rushed in, sword flashing. Emre blocked him, backing away, hoping Hamid might use up a bit of his nervous energy. But Hamid was relentless. He pushed Emre to the edge of the arena, and when the warriors crossed their spears and shoved Emre back, he kept up the pressure, raining his sword down against Emre's shamshir or his shield.

It was all Emre could do to keep from losing a limb. He'd tried to practice, hoping the debilitating headaches would fade in time. And they had, somewhat, just not enough.

Even now Emre could feel it, a weakness in his limbs, a creeping pain at the back of his skull. *Calm*, Emre thought. *Calm*. It was the only thing that had helped. But with his heart beating so madly, all his attempts at finding a place of peace were failing.

Hamid hammered his sword against Emre's buckler, then backed away. "You're not yourself, Emre."

Hamid bulled forward, forcing Emre to retreat. When he tried the same move, Emre sidestepped and drove Hamid's sword to one side. When Hamid did it a third time, he discovered it was all a setup. When Emre parried and riposted with a sharp flick of his blade, Hamid blocked it easily and brought his sword against Emre's shield like a battering ram. The blow was so fierce it made his arm go numb.

Emre rushed forward before Hamid could get another blow in, and the two of them locked swords.

"You've lost a step," Hamid said, then crashed his forehead against Emre's.

Emre's skull flared with bright white pain, a perfect echo to the blow Darius had delivered to the back of his head with the shovel. Dazed, he staggered backward. He tried to keep his sword and shield at the ready, but he was shaking so badly it felt comical. Hamid stared for a moment, wary, as if it were all some ruse. Emre, meanwhile, couldn't seem to keep his balance and fell backward onto the sand with a heavy thud.

As the spears thumped in a rhythm that made Emre nauseous, Hamid strode calmly forward, his look half confusion, half disgust. "I don't know what you were thinking," he said, "but I'll thank Bakhi for it later."

He raised his sword to strike, but just then a soul-wrenching roar rose up along the edge of the circle. Men shouted. Hamid turned. Then a massive form came flying in and caught Hamid around the middle.

Down they went, Hamid and Frail Lemi. Hamid tried to fight him off, but he stood no chance against Frail Lemi. In moments Frail Lemi was straddling him, bringing his pair of ham-hock fists crashing down against Hamid's face over and over and over again.

"You tried to kill him!" Lemi cried. "You tried to *kill* him!"

Emre had never seen Frail Lemi so angry. His face was splotched with red. And his eyes. Gods, his eyes made him look like he'd been crafted of flesh and fury by the hand of Thaash himself. The sun shone off his corded muscles as his long, powerful arms rose and fell.

Warriors swarmed, trying to pull him off, but Lemi shoved them away. Only with half a dozen working together were they finally able to drag him back.

"I'll kill you, Hamid! You hear me? I'll fucking kill you!"

Hamid had long since fallen unconscious.

Emre managed to push himself up so that he could sit and breathe and wait for the shaking to subside. Despite himself, despite all his anger at Hamid, he recoiled at the state of him. His face looked like the leavings from a butcher's block. There was blood everywhere, pooling in cuts, even pooling in the hollows of his eyes. One of the cuts, a ragged fissure along his cheekbone, was so deep Emre swore he saw bone.

Emre realized Shaikh Neylana was standing near him, staring at Hamid with a grave expression. "That was unfortunate."

"Don't harm Lemi," Emre said. "Please. He was only trying to protect me."

Neylana was silent for a time. "I suspect, if we gave him time to calm, he would tell us that he's remembered how things went that day. He realized you were right."

Emre nodded.

"Furthermore, I suspect that, were we to put Hamid's companion to the question, he would reveal the same version of events."

Emre nodded again. "I've no doubt that's true."

"Well, then," she said with a look over to where Hamid lay on the sand, "I don't imagine anyone in Tribe Halarijan would squawk if you considered the trial still in effect and took his life where he lay."

A chill ran down Emre's frame, which only added to the dizziness and trembling that still plagued him. She would look the other way if Emre wished to kill Hamid in cold blood.

Emre nearly agreed. It would be as simple as kneeling beside him and putting his hand over Hamid's nose and mouth, choking the life from him as Hamid had tried to do to him.

But he found that he couldn't. He refused to let it end like that. He refused to become the sort of person who could do that to a man he'd once considered a friend.

Emre stared at the sun, which was lowering in the western sky. "We'll resume this tomorrow." Hamid would hardly be in a state to fight, but then neither would Emre. The two would be evenly matched, each haunted and hobbled by Hamid's past actions.

Neylana stared at Emre's shaking hands with a disappointed look. "Very well," she said, and glanced over at Frail Lemi, who was still growling and struggling against the men trying to hold him down. She held out a hand to Emre. "You'd better help with your friend before we're forced to kill him."

Emre nodded and stood with her help.

It took him nearly an hour to calm Frail Lemi down. Hamid had betrayed Emre and, in so doing, betrayed Frail Lemi as well. It had taken him a while to figure that out, and was taking even longer to process. Lemi was simple in the head, and took betrayals like a child would, which is to say he took them very, very hard. He fixated on them, working them over and over in his mind, reliving the hurt. Hamid would never recover from this in Frail Lemi's eyes. Emre doubted the two of them could ever be near one another again without Lemi trying to kill him.

Eventually, Frail Lemi calmed enough that they could lead him to the *Amaranth*. Emre stayed with him long into the night in the captain's cabin, telling stories about Sharakhai, about their childhood, about Frail Lemi's tiny mother who always babied him, even after he'd grown to outweigh her by ten stone.

Darius and Hamid were taken to one of the frigates and watched. The asirim were uncharacteristically quiet. Eventually Frail Lemi fell asleep, and Emre slept too.

In the morning, Sirendra rushed into the cabin. "They're gone."

"Who?" Emre said.

"Hamid and Darius. They snuck off the ship last night and stole away on a skiff."

Chapter 16

THE HIPPODROME WAS ONE of Sharakhai's most famed attractions. Thousands flocked daily to watch chariot races, tests of skill on horseback, even jousting as they did in the lists of Qaimir far to the south of the Great Shangazi. The hippodrome's front entrance spilled onto a broad plaza, at the center of which was a fountain with a statue of a rearing horse. Water flowed from the horse's mouth. Its mane and tail blew wildly in the wind.

On reaching the plaza, Ramahd headed toward the fountain. Beside it, one foot resting on the tiled enclosure, stood Cicio, Ramahd's most trusted servant. He had a distant look as he stared at a pair of young children playing, a wild-haired boy and a girl in pig-tails who toddled as she ran. They chased one another in dizzying circles over the plaza's broad stones. When Cicio noticed Ramahd coming, he looked momentarily surprised, maybe even a bit embarrassed. Recovering, he pointed toward the mother, who was speaking with an old, bent man.

"What you think of her, ah?" Cicio asked as the fountain splashed.

Ramahd didn't bother to look. Cicio had only said it so that Ramahd wouldn't guess his true thoughts, but Ramahd had being seeing the signs for months, his bouts of sadness, his longing stares at the families they happened to pass in the streets of Sharakhai. "You know, it's okay for you to miss your son, Cicio."

For a moment Cicio looked lost. He ached for Qaimir, their homeland. He ached to see his son, who had grown two years since Cicio had been away in Sharakhai. He looked like he was going challenge Ramahd, perhaps brag about how he was going to bed the mother, but instead he jutted his stubbly chin toward the hippodrome's grand, arched entrance. "He there. Same place he always take."

"No one with him?"

"No one I could see."

Ramahd was eager to speak with the man in the hippodrome, but he tarried a moment. "This is the first step," he said to Cicio. "This is going to lead us home."

"Bullshit," Cicio said chidingly. "This city is a fucking maze, ah? Once you enter, you never get out."

Despite his words, Ramahd could see the hope in him, and for that he was glad. If he did nothing else after all this business with Meryam was done, he wanted to see Cicio returned to his home in Qaimir.

As Ramahd and Cicio entered the hippodrome, a gong rang and the crowd roared. The sound of galloping horses and rattling wheels rose above it. Below the cavernous space of the arcade, where one placed bets and collected winnings, dozens of people milled. Hearing the race starting, many of them rushed along the tunnels, tickets in hand after placing bets with the hippodrome's bet takers. It was there that they met Renzo, a honey-haired youth assigned to them by Vice Admiral Mateo.

"He's still there," said Renzo in their native tongue. He couldn't speak a lick of Sharakhan.

When Ramahd nodded, Cicio and Renzo took one of the tunnels leading to the arena proper. Ramahd took a different tunnel, and soon the hippodrome opened up before him. It sprawled in a grand oval. Eight chariots, each led by a pair of akhalas, were just entering the first curve. They jockeyed for the lead, some of the chariots' wheels coming dangerously close to one another as they fought for inside position. Others steered wide, hoping to take advantage if their opponents' chariots happened to crash into one another or scraped the stone wall at the track's inner edge.

Ramahd peered up at one of the sections farthest from the main entrance. It was shaded by orange fabric strung between long poles that reached out from the top of the hippodrome. Sitting there by himself was an older man in a white turban, a belted kaftan, and a hooded, sleeveless cloak that hung loose about his shoulders. There was little remarkable about the man—you might find a hundred more just like him in the stands—but he was the lynchpin to all Ramahd's plans.

Ramahd walked along the stone seats toward him, climbing row after row, wary of spells being cast or power being gathered. Spells could be made to act like snares as well, with tripwires of sorts that caused them to trigger when an enemy came near. Ramahd sensed nothing, however, and was soon nearing the vacant area where the man in the white turban sat alone.

In the shaded arcade above, Cicio and Renzo leaned against the simple sandstone columns, watching. Each had their hands behind their backs, hiding small crossbows with poison-tipped bolts. When Ramahd came within several paces of the old man, he sensed something at last, a subtle spell of hiding. It had transformed the man's face, as Meryam had done to Ramahd and his men on the Night of Endless Swords. Ramahd recognized a few of his former features—his long nose and the set of his jaw—but unless one knew him well, one would fail to recognize him as Hamzakiir the blood mage, son of Külaşan the Wandering King.

He was the rightful heir to a throne of Sharakhai and yet here he sat, watching the chariot races as he'd done for most of the past two weeks. Ramahd had been walking along the streets of the southern harbor when he'd come across Hamzakiir by pure chance. He'd been casting his senses outward, searching for any spells Meryam might be using to find him, and had sensed the arcane mask Hamzakiir was using to hide his identity. Ramahd hadn't recognized him immediately. It was only after he'd followed him to the hippodrome and watched as he'd paid his way in and sat among the stands and watched the horses race that he'd been able to pierce his disguise.

"You may as well come and sit," Hamzakiir said.

Ramahd snorted softly and sat beside him, a blood mage who'd been raised from a crypt beneath his father's hidden desert palace, a man who'd lived an abnormally long life due to the bargain he'd struck with the ehrekh,

Guhldrathen, a man who'd been captured and tortured by Meryam, then dominated for months on end for her own ends. It felt strange to sit beside a man who by every right should be his sworn enemy—Hamzakiir had done much to harm Qaimir, not the least of which was summoning the ehrekh, Guhldrathen, and leaving Ramahd, Meryam, and King Aldouan for dead—but sit he did, while the chariots charged around the track.

"Your men don't need those crossbows. I won't harm you or them." He swung his gaze to Ramahd. "The question is whether *you* mean to harm *me*."

In his eyes Ramahd saw sadness and a deep loneliness, but no fear.

"I wish you no harm," Ramahd said.

"Good." Hamzakiir returned his attention to the track, where a chariot had just overturned in a spinning gyre of wheels and reins and dirt thrown high. The crowd roared.

"Why do you come here?" Ramahd asked.

Hamzakiir chuckled, a low rumble. "That's what you wish to know? Why I come to watch the horses?"

"Well, yes." Below, a chariot racer wearing sandals laced to his knees and light armor over his white kaftan was straining to right his chariot. With a great heave, it thumped back onto two wheels, and he leapt onto the bed and cracked his whip above the horses' heads. "You had designs on the city. You thought to rule Sharakhai alone."

Hamzakiir's gaze swung to where the heights of Tauriyat and the palace of Eventide could be seen over the hippodrome's stony expanse. "I did, yes."

"You've given up on that dream?"

More and more in the crowd were coming to a stand, pumping their fists as the two leaders neared the finish line.

"I suppose I have."

It felt strange to see a man once as ruthlessly ambitious as Hamzakiir become so deflated. "And if I said I know why you've lost heart?"

"It hardly takes a man of great insight to determine *that*."

"It's because of what Meryam did to you," Ramahd continued. "Losing control over your own actions and thoughts for that long would unnerve anyone."

Below, the two lead chariots crossed the finish line so evenly with one another that the crowd stood as one, cheering for their pick to be declared the winner. Groans and louder cheers followed as the lineman twirled a yellow flag, indicating which of the two chariots had won.

Hamzakiir licked his chapped lips. Stared at the sun through the orange fabric above them. "You were hardly innocent in what happened to me, Lord Amansir. You stood by and watched as she broke me. So why don't you spare me your false concern and come to your point?"

"My point is this city isn't safe. Whatever gains the royal navy has made in taking back a few of their lost caravanserais, the Malasani and Mireans will soon recover, and then they will move to take the city once more."

Hamzakiir was unmoved. "So now you care about Sharakhai?"

"I do, but I care more about my homeland. I want Meryam in chains. I want her taken back to Qaimir and tried, so everyone can see that her rule was founded on betrayal and murder and we can transfer power peacefully to the rightful ruler, the son of Duke Hektor, King Aldouan's brother."

"And what would you have *me* do?" He glanced up at Tauriyat. "Go to Eventide and attack her?"

"Could you?"

Hamzakiir sneered. "Meryam has dozens of safeguards in place to prevent it."

"That's all that's stopping you? Her\safeguards? Because I can—"

"You will recall from our time together in Qaimir," Hamzakiir said, "what it feels like to be dominated. To be so for a day or two leaves one mentally and physically exhausted. Meryam did it to me for months. When that happens, cracks begin to form in your mind, cracks that grow wider the more you fight them." He swallowed hard, and seemed to bear down, as if something pained him. "And believe me, I fought her. You begin to question your very existence. You become like a Malasani golem, a splinter of a soul whose only purpose is to serve another, so that when you're freed"—he motioned to the people in the stands, who were sitting, or filing out to place new bets—"you wonder if it's real at all, and if it is, whether you truly have free will."

"You do," Ramahd assured him, "and you can use it to set things aright."

Hamzakiir waggled his head in a lip-raising sneer. "Things will find their new equilibrium once the war has ended. So it has always been."

"At what cost, though?"

"Blood and lives," Hamzakiir said. "Pain and anguish. But there's little you or I can do about that."

"But there *is*—"

Hamzakiir stood, cutting off Ramahd's next words. "Tell it to someone who cares, Ramahd Amansir. Tell it to the lords and knights who've come from your country. Tell it to your blood magi."

"Some few knights *have* joined me. But all the blood magi are beholden to Meryam."

"Then the knights will have to be enough." He sidled over to the stairs and began taking them up, his worn leather sandals scraping the steps as he went. "I've no interest in your war. Not any longer."

Both Cicio and Renzo cast questioning glances at Ramahd, asking if he wanted them to prevent Hamzakiir from leaving. But Ramahd waved them away, and soon Hamzakiir was gone.

Chapter 17

WILLEM SPARED NO EFFORT in his search for Davud. He broke his habit of sleeping during the day so he could return to the hall of records as often as possible. For several days he hid behind the grate in the hall of records and watched Cassandra. He wisped from hall to hall: sciences, architecture, medicine, alchemy, history, literature, and the long, curving building where trivium and quadrivium were taught. He perched in the dark recesses of the dormitories' eating halls. He crept through the kitchens, peeked into larders, secreted himself within the student shisha parlors, all in the hopes of catching a glimpse of Davud's light. He even haunted the administration building, his least favorite place, hoping Davud might want to follow the trail from Cassandra to the chancellor. But there was no sign of Davud.

Cassandra's research continued apace. Every so often she would write down a name. Willem was intensely curious to learn those names—the hope that he might be able to save them was patently ridiculous, what with the restrictions Nebahat had placed on him, but it was a hope to which he subscribed wholeheartedly. He might not have been able to save Altan, but by the gods, perhaps he could save others. He never learned those names, though. Cassandra always took them away with her at the end of her session.

She received a new partner to help in her research efforts, a dull boy with an unappealing halo named Manu, who did everything Cassandra told him with one eye on the hourglass.

You'll never replace Altan, Willem thought sourly.

Not that Manu was trying to. The argument didn't even make sense, really, but Willem couldn't shake the thought and always hoped that Manu would leave early, which he did quite often.

Willem's continued lack of sleep wasn't helping things. Several times he woke leaning against the gap in the walls, snoring softly. Dull Manu even heard him and began casting his gaze about the room to locate the source. Angry with himself over his own weakness, Willem fled and found a place to nap.

Compounding the lack of sleep (and the fear that he'd never see Davud again) was the fact that Nebahat's tasks for him seemed to be multiplying. Sometimes he demanded more alchemycal agents. More and more, though, he asked Willem to locate specific texts from the collegia's many libraries.

Despite the lethargy that hung over him like a pall, Willem read them all before delivering them to Nebahat. Largely they were memoirs, apparently unconnected to one another, but taken together they painted a picture. Each of them had some mention, even if only in passing, of Beht Ihman. There were stories told of Suad, the Scourge of Sharakhai, the shaikh who'd rallied the tribes against the Sharakhani Kings. There were tales of the Kings' contentious early decades leading up to Suad's grand offensive. There were even hints of visits from the gods to the various desert tribes, visits that were clearly meant to enflame their hatred of Sharakhai and the power that had concentrated there over the centuries.

Though he sensed some connection, Willem couldn't quite piece together what Nebahat was looking for. He was nearly there, but he was just so tired. One day, he was watching Cassandra and Manu in the hall of records, and beginning to think that getting sleep was what he should be doing, when something strange happened.

"I need to see Master Luwanga about my scholar's thesis," Manu said.

Cassandra rolled her eyes. "You mean you're going to the oud parlor early."

"No, this time I really *do* need to see her."

"Your graduating is contingent on this project too, you know."

"Yes, but you're doing such a good job of it." He buckled several books together with a leather strap, swung them over his shoulder, then leaned over and kissed Cassandra. "I'll put in extra time tomorrow."

Cassandra rolled her eyes. "I never should have recommended you for this."

"Have I ever told you how much I love you?"

When he tried to lean in and kiss her again, Cassandra shoved him away. It was then, as Manu was strutting away like a cock in a hen yard, that Cassandra began toying with the blue topaz pendant hanging from her necklace. It sparkled. Not like gemstones sparkled, but like *people*. Willem thought it was somehow refracting a bit of Cassandra's glow, but the color was all wrong, as was the way it kept changing, like gears made of crystal turning under sunlight.

It was Davud's color, he realized. Davud had ensorcelled it.

A spell then. Gods, this was why Davud hadn't been coming to see Cassandra. He didn't *need* to come. He was using the pendant to watch her, to check on her progress. Willem found himself admiring Davud—it was an ingenious solution to his problem—but it was also frustrating as it left Willem without a way to find him.

Unless . . .

He stared closely at the pendant as Cassandra released it and returned to her reading. There was only one way he might find more answers. If he was going to do it, though, he needed his wits about him.

Sleep, Willem thought. *I need sleep.*

He left Cassandra and returned to his small alcove near the top of the hidden archives. He'd already delivered Nebahat a dozen more books, books which Willem would read and ponder another time. Tonight was for Davud. Tonight, Willem would find him.

Settling himself in, he smiled and fell fast asleep.

Willem crawled silently along the slate roof of the collegia's oldest dormitory. The stars were out and the night was cool, but he'd already seen from his hiding place in the courtyard's trees below that Cassandra's window was cracked open. Lowering himself over the roof's edge, he dropped down to the small balcony and slipped inside her room, which was small and narrow, its floor cluttered with cast-aside clothes. Taking care to avoid them, he tiptoed to Cassandra's bedside and the small table beside it where she kept her jewelry.

From her heart-shaped jewelry box, he lifted the blue pendant, careful that it didn't snag any of the bulky earrings or bangles around it while also ensuring that the face of the pendant always pointed away from him. The topaz sparkled, sending shards of light playing across the far wall.

Cassandra's breathing suddenly hitched. Willem waited, controlling his own breathing, nervous to so much as move a muscle. The greatest danger wasn't that Cassandra would wake and see him, but that Davud was watching even now. In a flurry of movement, Cassandra rolled over and yanked the blankets more tightly over her shoulders. Thankfully she fell right back into the easy rhythms of sleep.

With exaggerated care, Willem spun the pendant toward him. The light played wildly. His nerves screamed for him to set it back in the box, to leave before he was found out after all his careful sneaking these many years. In all his time at the collegia, no one had seen so much as his shadow, and now he risked being discovered, his secrets laid bare, over what? Davud and *his* purposes? Willem didn't even know what those were!

I'm merely curious, Willem told himself.

That's hardly a reason, a doubting voice whispered a moment later. *You're curious about a great many things, like the answers Nebahat is after. Why don't you search for those?*

It was the sensible plan, yet there he remained, the pendant stilled in the air before him.

Altan, another voice whispered. *This is for Altan and others like him.*

Holding his breath, Willem turned the pendant just a bit more. He stared into the facets of the blue gemstone, squinting from the glow. Davud's glow. Seeing nothing of note, he swallowed hard and rotated it just a little bit more, and saw a reflection in those tiny facets. No, not a reflection. The facet was acting as a tiny window, revealing a small portion of a different room entirely.

Willem twisted the pendant further, brought his eye closer to the large, central facet. Twisting it this way and that, he saw more: the seams between large sandstone blocks; a closed wooden door with a coat hook nailed on the inside; shoes set with care beside one another and pressed against the wall; and at the very edges of the vision, varnished wood, a desktop.

It wasn't much, but for Willem, it was more than enough. Davud was hidden inside faculty housing. Except, Willem had been to that room only two days before, late at night. He'd stepped through it, examining it for clues.

Or had he?

Now that he thought about it, he remembered approaching the room. He remembered holding his set of lock picks in his right hand. He remembered kneeling, preparing to defeat the lock, a thing he was particularly gifted at. And then he remembered creeping along the hall and moving on to the next room, satisfied. The memory of being *inside* the room was fuzzy and gray, as if he'd drummed up one of his visits from months ago and placed it there haphazardly, imperfectly.

Suddenly everything was clear, and Willem knew exactly where to go. After placing the pendant back inside the jewelry box just as he'd found it, he left and clambered up to the dormitory roof. He fairly sprinted along it as he headed toward the faculty building.

A short while later, Willem crept out of the janitor's closet on the second floor of the faculty quarters and made his way quietly and carefully to a long corridor filled with many doors. A lone lantern on a small table near the stairwell somehow made the hallway look a league long. Snores emanated from several of the doorways he passed on his way to the third on the left—a nondescript door leading to a nondescript room.

He'd not noticed when he'd been there last, but he could see it now that he knew what to look for: the faintest of shimmers around the edge of the door, evidence of a spell. It was meant to force one to move on, to bypass the room—maids, carpenters, the housing secretary, anyone who might have an interest in the room would simply go on as if they'd never had a purpose there in the first place, or had entered and completed whatever it was they'd meant to do.

Even knowing the spell's effect, Willem felt a strong urge to return to his cubbyhole and go to sleep, safe in the knowledge that he'd searched this room and found nothing, but he concentrated hard on the light glimmering through the keyhole.

There are answers in there, Willem told himself, *and I mean to get them.*

Crouching, he readied his lock picks, holding them just before the keyhole. As he moved them forward, he willed the slim instruments to slip through the light as if they were made of a special alloy of iron, shadow, and silence. As he worked the lock, his excitement rose to the point that the mechanism rattled. *Careful, Willem. Careful now.* After a deep breath to calm his nerves, he lifted the handle the precise amount that would prevent it from clicking audibly, then swung the door inward.

It revealed the outer edge of Davud's spell, which shimmered like a waterfall across the threshold. As he'd done with the lock picks, Willem forced the spell to slip around him as he stepped inside the room and closed the door.

There, sleeping on a bed, were two people: Davud and a woman Willem had never seen before. Davud looked just as Willem remembered him from his time attending the collegia as a promising young student: a moderate frame, a shapely neck, his hair cut short so that it framed his handsome face. He looked older, of course, and there were faint scars on his cheeks and forehead, another small one across his upper lip. The woman, sleeping on her side, one arm across Davud's chest, had a strange glow about her. It was dim but colorful, and there were flashes of radiance, as if she wasn't as bright as she'd once been but while she dreamed some small amount of her former brilliance shone through.

Willem moved to the desk, where another large, topaz pendant hung facing the door—the twin to Cassandra's. Spread about the desktop and another table toward the corner of the room were various scrolls and books. Most important was a leatherbound journal. It glowed as the pendant had glowed, as the threshold glowed, which was how Willem knew it was Davud's personal journal.

With care, he opened it and found that there was a glamour over the pages. It obfuscated the writing, but Willem had dealt with such things before. He was able to dim the glamour to see through to the real words beneath. He read it from start to finish, using the faint shimmer of the revealed ink to read by. He finished and read it again, his fingers starting to tingle. A thought had occurred to him about halfway through his first read, and he had trouble shaking it. By the time he'd finished his second reading, it felt like a directive, something the gods themselves were demanding.

Contained in the journal was a series of meticulous notes, the same as Davud had always taken during his time in the collegia, except they weren't notes about language or history or rhetoric—Davud's areas of focus during his time at the collegia—but an account of Davud's attempt to uncover what had happened to Altan. It wasn't mentioned much in his notes, but Willem could tell Davud was frightened. He wanted to protect himself and Esmeray, who was surely the woman lying beside him in his bed. They'd both fled from King Sukru, hoping to find solace in the Enclave. The Enclave had declined their proposal, but Davud still hoped to come to an accord. In order to do that, he needed to speak to one of the Enclave's inner circle.

He'd wanted Undosu, but after speaking with a man named Tariq, he'd come to the collegia instead to learn of Tariq's cousin, Altan. Since arriving, Davud had found evidence of many people gone missing, Altan among them. The trail had led to Cassandra, which had led him to more names. Many more.

Willem set the journal down exactly as he'd found it and turned to face the bed. How he wanted to wake Davud. *I can lead you to Nebahat,* Willem would say to him. *You need but follow me.* And then he would take Davud down to the hidden archives, where he would confront Nebahat and make him pay for his crimes.

But Willem couldn't. He was forbidden. He was bound to do Nebahat's will. More than that, Nebahat was a dangerous man. Admitting *anything* to Davud could put him in danger.

He left the room heartbroken. He'd been so consumed with finding Davud. Now that he had, he had no idea what to do. He might come to watch him sleep. He might follow Davud now that he knew where he was keeping himself and learn more. But either plan felt perfectly hollow.

He returned to his cubbyhole in the hidden archives. Part of him wished the stone above him would collapse, burying both him and Nebahat. The world would never see either of them again, which was perhaps for the best, because Nebahat was evil and Willem was useless. As he lay himself down to sleep, he touched the books piled around him, ran his fingers over their bindings, felt the scruff at the edges of one fraying leather cover.

He considered reading that particular volume to help soothe his fears, but couldn't bring himself to do it. He lay away from the books instead, wondering what sort of stories would be written about him. *None*, Willem told himself. *No one even knows you exist.*

Suddenly Willem sat up, his eyes wide, his heart beating like a drum.

The books. The stories within them! What better way to convey the answers to Davud's questions?

He was so excited he yelped, then immediately clapped his hand over his mouth. He waited, praying Nebahat hadn't heard. As the silence lengthened, his fears quelled, and he began collecting the books he would need.

Chapter 18

"DAVUD, WHAT'S THIS?" Esmeray asked one night.

She and Davud were sequestered in their room in the collegia's faculty quarters, the one they'd been hiding in for several weeks as they looked into Altan's disappearance. Davud was jotting thoughts in his journal, but when he heard the note of concern in Esmeray's voice he turned and found Esmeray with a stack of nine or ten books in her hand.

"Where did you find those?"

"Just inside the door." She opened the door, peered into the hall, then closed it with a frown and set the books onto the desk.

As she thumbed through the topmost book, Davud spread his hands wide, closed his eyes, and carefully checked the spells of detection and concealment he'd placed over the room. They were intact, untouched, and yet someone had managed to breach them and leave them a stack of books.

Esmeray flipped open more of the books, scanning them quickly. "They're children's tales." She flipped through the rest. "All of them."

Satisfied his spells hadn't been altered in some way, Davud took up the topmost book and paged through it, skimming the fables. He paused when he came to one of Fatima, the desert's most infamous thief. It told the tale of how she'd stolen the entirety of an ehrekh's hoard and left in its place a lone copper coin with a note that read, *To begin your hoard anew.* The ehrekh had found it so amusing he'd not only allowed Fatima to live, he'd gifted her with slippers that made no sound and left no footprints upon the sand. Fatima, incensed the ehrekh thought she would need such things, had burned the slippers and stolen back the copper coin.

He went through more of the books, hoping to find a hidden message or some commonality among the tales. He found no hidden notes, though, and the tales were as varied as could be. They ranged from nursery rhymes to epic poems to morality tales from the Al'Ambra, the oldest of the desert's religious texts. Perhaps there was some common thread running through them, but if so it was too well hidden for him to detect.

"Who would have done it?" Esmeray thumped the book she'd been reading onto the top of the pile. "Who *could* have done it?"

"I don't know," Davud said.

"We have to leave," Esmeray said. "Tonight. It isn't safe here anymore."

She was worried. Davud was too, but even so, he wondered over how someone could have managed to defeat his spells and, more importantly, why. "Maybe we should try to contact them."

Esmeray looked completely shocked. "You can't be so thick, Davud. This is a trap. The Enclave are trying to catch us."

"If that were so, don't you think they would have sprung the trap already?"

"Davud, we're leaving, and those fucking books are staying here."

Davud, knowing hers was the safer path to tread, reluctantly agreed. That night, they moved to a cellar outside the collegia grounds, one of several places Davud had scouted should the need to move arise. The chandler who lived upstairs had recently moved his operations to a small shop, leaving the old workspace in his cellar unused. It wouldn't be pleasant to sleep in—it reeked of the cheap perfumes the chandler used in his candles—but it was close to the collegia, which was all Davud really cared about.

Davud used Esmeray's blood to lay spells over the cellar. They were the same ones he'd used before, the sort that masked sounds and scents and confounded any who came near, making them think of something more important than entering the small, subterranean space.

When he was done, Esmeray said, "Let's add one more."

Her ability to use magic had been burned from her by the Enclave, but she could help Davud weave spells by creating the framework for them. She did so now, creating a spell that would alert them if magic was cast anywhere near the workshop. They hadn't cast it before because it took energy to maintain and so required more of Esmeray's blood, but Davud agreed the step was necessary.

It seemed to work. The two of them took turns watching the workshop door throughout the night, but days passed and they saw no one, and not a single book showed up on their doorstep.

During the day, Davud watched Cassandra through the topaz pendants. Her strange project of collecting the names of the descendants of the thirteenth tribe continued. She copied the names into a small leather journal, presumably so she could deliver them all at once to the chancellor, who had apparently authorized the project.

Davud always made sure to copy them into his own journal. He wasn't always fast enough to catch them all—Cassandra's topaz wasn't always positioned properly—but he got most of them.

One day, while Davud was copying more of the names in his journal, Esmeray leaned over him and stabbed her finger at one of them: Damla Kuram'ava. "I know her."

Davud paused, thoroughly confused. "For some reason, I assumed the people she was finding were all dead."

"So did I, but Damla is a jewelry maker. She has a stall in the bazaar."

"How do you know it's the same Damla?"

"I don't," Esmeray said. "There's one way to find out, though." Davud cringed as she ripped out a piece of paper from the back of his journal. After writing down a list of the names he'd taken down so far—over a hundred in all—she kissed the crown of his head and made for the cellar door. "I'll be back."

She didn't return until two days later. Davud was worried sick. Beht Zha'ir came and went, which he assumed was the reason she didn't come back the first night. Even so, she should have sent word. When she finally *did* return, she whisked into the abandoned workshop and said nothing about her strange disappearance. Breathing hard, she handed him the piece of paper with the names, many of which had been marked with small stars, circles, or diamonds.

"The ones with the stars are all missing," she said.

"What?"

She flicked the paper with one finger, making it snap. "The names Cassandra's been collecting. Many of them have been reported as missing."

Davud scanned the list of names. "You've checked everyone on this list?"

"No. The ones with the circles are people I've verified are alive and well. The diamonds are deceased. Those with no marks, I've yet to confirm."

Davud stared at all the circles. There were more than thirty of them. "All missing?"

"All of them. And the others are in danger."

Davud couldn't help but agree. There was only one conclusion to draw: the Kings were targeting the thirteenth tribe again.

"But why?" he asked.

"Why else?" Esmeray said. "The lesser Kings and Queens are resuming their fathers' ancient campaign."

"Perhaps." The new Kings and Queens of Sharakhai hadn't been rounding up the Moonless Host much in recent months, but that only made sense; the Host were but a pale shadow of what they once were. So why the sudden interest in their bloodline?

"You've a better idea?" Esmeray asked.

"Not yet." He handed the paper back to her. "Have you warned them?"

"Not yet."

"We have to, right? We have to find any others who are alive and warn them too."

Esmeray seemed surprised, and more than a little happy at his reaction. "You're sure?"

"I'm sure." Contact with the outside world had the chance of revealing their location, but there really was no choice.

Esmeray's smile broadened, then suddenly she was leaning in and kissing him. It felt good and warm—a *proper* kiss, he and his collegia mates used to call it.

"What was that for?" he asked when she broke away.

"I wasn't sure if you'd agree." She pressed her forehead to his. "And a good heart deserves rewards lest it become shriveled and blackened like my own."

The following day, Esmeray prowled the city, delivering warnings to those she'd found through Cassandra's research. Some seemed confused or even angry over the reason Esmeray gave them for invading their lives, but most took the warnings seriously—there wasn't a soul in the west end who wasn't familiar with how cruel the rulers of the city could be. That done, she continued to search for more on the list who'd yet to be identified.

Davud, meanwhile, watched Cassandra through the link he'd created between the topaz pendants. One night, while Esmeray slept, he was scribbling notes in his journal, collecting his thoughts. His topaz pendant hung nearby, twinkling under the light of the nearby candle. No, he realized with a start. It wasn't twinkling. There was something *moving* in the facets. Cassandra was awake, which wasn't so odd in and of itself, but it was late and he wondered where she was going.

He picked up the pendant and held it to his eye like a jeweler's loupe. The view was swaying, as if Cassandra's pendant were swinging back and forth, but the movements began to still. A bronze statue dominated the view, lit by a small brass lamp on the gravel near its base. Davud recognized the statue immediately. Any collegia scholar would. It was a statue of the collegia's founder, Abdul-Assim, a heavyset man with a potbelly and a laurel wreath adorning his partially bald head.

More interesting by far was the stack of books sitting near the lamp, the very same stack as had been left inside Davud and Esmeray's room in the faculty quarters. The chill over being discovered once again traveled down Davud's arms and the back of his neck, but his curiosity was nearly overwhelming. Why books? Why those particular stories? There must be a reason.

Davud glanced over at Esmeray where she slept. He knew there was risk in going to get those books, but whoever had left them had proven he could track Davud and Esmeray wherever they went, and so, knowing she would be angry with him for going, he left Esmeray asleep and returned to the collegia grounds.

The grounds were almost completely empty. He passed only a patrol of four Silver Spears along the way. Eventually he came to the plaza he'd seen through the pendant. Wary of being seen, he peered into the shadows of the arcade that connected the halls of science and history. Seeing no one, he approached the statue, the books stacked near its base, and the small lamp. Several paces from the books, a stick had been driven into the gravel. From it, Cassandra's pendant hung.

The spell of masking Davud had cast over himself was still intact, but he still felt terribly exposed as he crept forward, blew out the lamp, and picked up the stack of books. Leaving the pendant hanging from the stick, he returned to the cellar and stayed up the entire night, devouring story after story. One could argue that many different threads bound the tales together, but there was one that stood out from the rest: each book had at least one story that alluded to an intrigue of some sort. Mysteries. There were stories of diabolical plots against kings and queens and emperors. Crucially, there was at least one tale in each book that described how monarchs, unjust rulers, had conspired against their own people.

The most important story, Davud was now certain, was found in the bottommost book. It told the tale of an ancient sage who taught the children of a forest when they came to him for learning. The sage was preyed upon by a woodland warlock and tricked into leading the children in a dance that ended in them all, sage and children alike, tipping from the end of a plank into a great roiling pot set over a blazing fire, a gruesome stew which the warlock used on a night of terror to feed the demonic hordes that lay deep in the center of the forest.

"What are you doing?" Esmeray, naked, sat up in bed, rubbing her eyes. She yawned, then stared at the stack of books, recognition dawning. "Davud, what in the name of *fuck* are you doing?"

Davud's mind worked feverishly. "It's someone from the Enclave, Esma."

"What is?"

"The people from the lists. The people who are going missing. Someone from the Enclave is causing it."

Chapter 19

THE DAY AFTER having his offer declined by Hamzakiir in the hippo-drome, Ramahd arrived at a small orphanage to the southwest of Sharakhai. He stepped through the gates set in the surrounding stone wall to reach the interior, where a host of small children played. When an old matron with rheumy eyes approached him, Ramahd pressed a sylval into her palm, as he had several times before. The matron turned the other way, focusing all her attention on the children while Ramahd stepped inside the orphanage and headed down a narrow hallway.

As he neared the orphanage's small, central courtyard, he felt the borders of a spell of detection. He searched for its edges, then carefully untied the threads that held it together, slipped within its bounds, and retied them as they had been.

From the shadows he watched as a girl batted at something in the air. It looked like a butterfly, but wasn't. It flapped too strangely, and sounded like a ruffling sheaf of papers.

Taking one step closer, Ramahd found Hamzakiir sitting at his favorite bench. He was folding a piece of paper into a shape, like the Mireans do. Finishing it, he held it in his hands and waited as the girl, who'd seen no more than three summers, tottered closer, her eyes wide. She approached carefully, one pudgy hand reaching out toward the origami crane that rested in Hamzakiir's palm. When she came too close, the crane flapped its paper wings and lifted high into the air, narrowly avoiding her hand. The thing she'd been batting at earlier was also a crane, both having been animated through Hamzakiir's magic.

Giggling, then screaming, the girl followed the origami birds, hoping to catch either, failing miserably in her quest. Ramahd, meanwhile, stepped into the sun. Unlike the hippodrome, Hamzakiir shivered in fright when he realized he wasn't alone.

Sensing something amiss, the girl turned, spotted Ramahd, and backed slowly away. The paper cranes fell to the stones in two soft *ticks*.

When Hamzakiir said to the girl, "Take them," she picked them up and ran from the courtyard toward where the other children were playing. When she was gone, Hamzakiir turned to Ramahd and said in his low, somber voice, "I already gave you my answer."

"An answer I refuse to accept."

"Well, I'm sorry, but that's just the way it is."

Ramahd motioned to the place where the girl had just been playing. "Suppose Meryam were to learn about this place. About that little girl, whom you seem to care about."

Hamzakiir's eyes narrowed, and for a moment the old Hamzakiir returned. The man who calculated. The man who schemed. But then they softened. "You would never tell Meryam. You aren't nearly that ruthless, Ramahd."

"That isn't what I'm getting at. The point is that Meryam *will* learn of it. I think deep down you know that. And she'll learn about any *other* place you decide to hide. Or the Enclave will. She has them in her pocket. I'm surprised they haven't found you already."

"Yes, well, this old mage has spells they know nothing about."

"This is precisely my point," Ramahd said. "Meryam brings only rot. Leave her for too long and you'll hardly recognize the city she leaves behind."

Hamzakiir looked scared sitting on that bench. Defeated. "I was once a supremely confident man. I was convinced I would have Sharakhai for my own. And I nearly did. Several times. But the mind works in strange ways.

As confident as I was then, I'm certain I'll fail if I stand against her again."
He looked positively terrified in that moment. "I'll die."

Ramahd understood then why he'd been hiding in an orphanage all this
time. The children gave him some semblance of life, of purpose. This place
likely felt like a sanctuary to him. "You have allies," Ramahd said. "Powerful
allies."

Hamzakiir laughed. "And Meryam doesn't?"

"You have no choice but to fight."

"We all have choices to make, Lord Amansir. Always."

Ramahd was certain Hamzakiir was about to say he couldn't help, but
then his eyes slid to the shadows. The girl had returned, holding one of the
cranes in her open palm. Behind her, a boy the same age was holding the
other between pinched fingers. They wanted a show. They wanted to play.
Hamzakiir stared at them, then began to cry. He did so for long moments,
moments in which the children backed away, perhaps feeling they'd done
something wrong.

Hamzakiir, meanwhile, wiped away his tears. He took a long, deep breath.
Then he stared at Ramahd with a dawning clarity of purpose in his eyes. "Go
on, then. Tell me this fool plan of yours."

Ramahd did just that, taking his time, explaining everything so that
Hamzakiir could see it was no half-baked scheme. Over the course of the
story, Hamzakiir stared into the middle distance. He composed himself,
became still, serene as a windless oasis. Then a change took place in him that
was as surprising as it was encouraging. His jaw worked. His brows pinched.
A wicked gleam came to his eyes. Ramahd had worried that Hamzakiir's
appetite for revenge had been beaten from him during the months of torture
at Meryam's hands, but here he was, purposeful once more, a fire pot lit,
ready to explode.

When Ramahd finished, Hamzakiir stroked his beard, separating the
wiry strands. "It isn't a bad start"—his eyes were alive, as if his mind could
hardly contain his thoughts—"though I have a few humble suggestions, if
I may."

Ramahd stopped himself from smiling, but only barely. "Go on."

Chapter 20

IHSAN AND THE OTHER Kings reasoned that to remain anywhere near Baük risked being discovered, so they set sail for a line of rocky hills three days north and made camp near a clear spring that trickled into the desert. The following morning, Cahil led Ihsan into the cutter's hold, where there was a table with straps on it. It was a surgeon's table but reminded Ihsan more of the fiendish confessional slabs Cahil had kept in his palace on Mount Tauriyat.

Cahil went to a foot locker. "Sit," he said as he opened the lid with a rough flick of his foot. Ihsan did, while Cahil took a bottle of araq from the locker and held it out. "Drink."

Ihsan accepted it and pulled the cork, which released with a reverberating *thoomp*. Cahil, meanwhile, reached back into the locker and retrieved a gleaming steel clamp and a leather-wrapped bundle. After setting the clamp down on a work table with a clank, he undid the buckle on the leather bundle and unrolled it to reveal a set of scalpels, saws, pliers, and an unnerving collection of gleaming steel needles. Seeing it all, Ihsan took a good, long swig of the araq, then another.

When he tried downing a third, Cahil took the bottle from him. "Sand

and stone, we don't have *that* much araq. This is going to take some time."
He set the bottle on the table. "You have the elixirs?"

Ihsan handed him five metal vials, each filled to the brim with the fabled
elixirs King Azad had created before he died. They were the last of the ones
Nayyan had given to him in the blooming fields, shortly before he'd ridden
into the desert with the Blue Journals.

Cahil stared at them. "This is all you have?"

No, I have a galleon filled with more, Ihsan signed. *It should be here any
day now.*

Cahil sneered. "Five won't be enough."

It will have to be.

"Well, that's not up to you, now is it?" Cahil stared at the vials in disbelief, as if he were reliving all that had happened since their fellow King, Azad,
had brewed the elixirs. Feeling Ihsan's eyes on him, he glanced up, then
jutted his chin toward the table with a sneer. "Lie down."

Do you really need to strap my hands down? Ihsan had come to view his
hands as his gateway to the world. Losing the use of them, even for a short
while, would make him feel infinitely more powerless than he already did.

Cahil stared at him in disbelief. "Assuming you really want me to do this,
yes! I won't have you fouling things up because you can't control yourself, and
believe me, you won't be able to."

Resolved to do whatever it took to get his tongue back, Ihsan lay down,
and Cahil proceeded to tighten the straps—forehead, neck, wrists, waist,
and finally his ankles. To this point Cahil had seemed bored, but the more
tightly Ihsan was strapped down the more his eyes seemed to brighten, particularly as he inserted the metal clamp into Ihsan's mouth to hold his jaws
wide.

The preparations complete, Cahil took up a pair of long-nosed pliers and
a bright, shining steel scalpel. "I cut the scar open. I apply the elixir. We wait
and then we do it a second time. That's one session." He spoke with dispassion, as if he were inured to the pain he was about to inflict, but it was belied
by the boyish grin tugging at the corners of his mouth. "If you know how I
healed Gallan, you know it took five months and hundreds of applications
before his leg was regrown. With your tongue, I'm guessing we'll need three
weeks, two sessions a day."

Ihsan's breath came raw and ragged through his nostrils. The feeling that he was about to be choked kept gnawing at him. Spit gathered in torrents, forcing him to swallow over and over.

"Ready?" Cahil asked.

Ihsan made a noise that any sane man would have trouble interpreting as affirmation, but Cahil, taking it as such, immediately pinched the remains of Ihsan's severed tongue with his pliers and dipped the scalpel into the gaping maw of Ihsan's mouth.

Ihsan felt something tug at his tongue. It felt like a thread buried within it had just been tugged free. Then a bright white line of searing pain flared to life. Cahil had been right. Ihsan struggled. His whole body spasmed. Tears slid down his face to his temples. Sweat tickled his scalp. The pain rose higher and higher, and Ihsan moaned, tasting blood at the back of his throat, smelling it.

"Still yourself or I'll spill the elixir."

It took a mighty force of will, but Ihsan managed it. As soon as he had, Cahil stuffed cotton gauze inside his mouth, pressing hard to stanch the flow. After removing the cotton, he used a bulbed pipette to drip some of the softly glowing elixir into Ihsan's mouth. Ihsan felt all five drops. Cahil paused, waiting for the elixir to take effect. And it did. Ihsan could feel it numbing the incision already. The pain fell steadily until it felt like he'd taken a swallow of hot tea and mildly burnt his tongue on it.

"Ready for the second?" Cahil asked.

Ihsan wasn't, but he made the same useless noise he'd made earlier and Cahil set to. The pain was more intense this time. Even so, Ihsan stilled himself, knowing that the sooner he did, the sooner Cahil would apply the elixir. But Cahil still waited. Ihsan had known Cahil would revel in his pain, but he hadn't imagined how impotent it would make him feel. Being strapped to a table already made him feel powerless; having Cahil wallow in his misery made him feel doubly so.

Finally Cahil pressed the gauze to the wound and applied the elixir. The slow dwindling of his pain felt like the sun setting as it faded to a dull ache that flared to life any time Ihsan was foolish enough to move his tongue. It was disheartening knowing this was but the first step up the mountain of pain to come. *But at least it's started. If this works, it will all have been worth it.*

Cahil unstrapped him, then set about a meticulous cleaning of his instruments. "I hope this works," Cahil said as Ihsan headed toward the stairs leading up.

Ihsan stopped halfway up. *You do?*

"For your sake, not mine." Using a bit of clean cotton dipped in alcohol, he rubbed the scalpel. "I meant what I said. If this doesn't work, I don't see why we would have any need of you."

You've become less subtle in your old age, Cahil.

Cahil actually laughed. "The time for subtlety has passed, Ihsan. Husamettín may be upset with me for it, but I tell you this. If you can't wake Zeheb from his stupor"—he held up the scalpel—"the next thing this goes over is your throat."

I'm rather attached to the smile I have, Ihsan replied. *I hardly need another.*

Cahil laughed again, and Ihsan headed up to the deck.

The days melded into one another, Cahil applying his *cure*, Ihsan recovering. Even with the elixirs Ihsan was exhausted each night. It felt as if he slept right up until the next session. He could hardly eat for the pain and started to lose weight. After a week of consuming little more than broth, water, and the araq he was allowed before each session, it felt as if he were competing with Zeheb to look most like a bag of bones.

But the cure was working. The morning after the first session, Ihsan could already tell the stump of his tongue had grown slightly. After a week, nearly half of its missing length had been restored.

Cahil had been right, though. He was going through the elixirs at an alarming rate. They'd used four of them already. The fifth wasn't going to be enough.

Do you have more? Ihsan signed to Cahil as they entered the second week of his treatment.

Cahil had barked a laugh. "No, Ihsan, and I wouldn't give you any if I did."

Husamettín said he didn't have any either, and Ihsan believed him. If he'd had any and didn't want to give them up, he'd just say so and be done with it. The man was inflexible, but he was never one to bother lying in order to spare feelings.

It left Ihsan in a bind. He had more elixirs, but not of the sort Cahil and Husamettín would be expecting him to have. They weren't the ones Azad had made before his death at the hands of Çeda's mother, Ahyanesh, but the ones Nayyan had concocted at his direction, elixirs that mimicked them, elixirs he and Nayyan had hidden from everyone while planning their conquest of Sharakhai.

It would be dangerous admitting that he had them, but he had no choice. It was either that or leave and try the treatment on his own, and the moment he did *that*, he'd lose his chance at lifting Zeheb's curse, at finding Nalamae and of saving Sharakhai. Leave, and there would be no getting back into Cahil's good graces.

"What are these?" Cahil asked when Ihsan gave him six new vials.

Elixirs I gave up the last of my wealth for, a concoction from the hill witches of Kundhun.

Cahil opened one and smelled it, then wrinkled his nose at the pungent odor. "And you want me to use them on your tongue?"

Ihsan nodded. The less said the better.

But there was no hiding their true nature when they worked. As they entered the third week, and the new elixirs worked as well as the old, Cahil grew suspicious.

"We come all this way," he said by the fire one night, "hundreds of leagues from Sharakhai, and you find elixirs we would all have killed for."

Zeheb sat cross-legged near the fire, burbling softly. Yndris was silent but, judging from the look on her face, was prepared to doubt anything that came from Ihsan's rapidly flashing hands.

Husamettín's dour expression looked all the more dour for the mark of the traitor on his forehead. "Well," he said, "what of it? How did you manage to come by this miraculous cure?"

Like each of us, Ihsan signed, *I'd been searching for replacements to Azad's elixirs since the day he died.*

"And you waited until you were exiled into the desert to look into it?"

The rumor came to me only recently, and led to Ganahil. For obvious reasons, I trusted no one to find the truth of it for me. I had to go myself, but there were always things to attend to in Sharakhai.

Husamettín used a stick to poke at the fire, sending sparks flying like constellations in the moonless sky. "Why didn't you share the rumor with us?"

I daresay none of you bothered to share every rumor you heard with me. And thank the gods! We'd never have got anywhere. It made no sense to share it until I'd learned whether it could truly heal.

"And what good fortune," Yndris said. "Just when you need it most, a cure has arrived."

Just so, Ihsan replied evenly, refusing to rise to the bait.

"And now that you've found them," she pressed, "I'm sure you're willing to share whatever remains."

Ihsan bowed his head theatrically. *Two will likely remain once Cahil is done. I gladly offer them to this happy coalition.*

Husamettín leaned back from the fire to look at Ihsan squarely in the face. "And your tongue?"

What of it?

Husamettín made a sour face. "Can you use it? Has your power returned?"

Over the past several days, he'd tried to speak. It was painful, but the sounds were coming closer and closer to real words. He signed, *It's coming slowly,* while at the same time speaking the words. All that came out was a tangle of vowels and sibilants.

Cahil gave Ihsan that hangman's stare of his. He'd suspected from the beginning that this wasn't about Zeheb or saving the city, but about Ihsan's most basic desire: to restore his power. He'd be only too glad to see Ihsan fail—indeed, he'd be glad to follow through on the promise he'd made to Ihsan in the hold: "If this doesn't work, I don't see why we would have any need of you." But just then, Ihsan kept his silence.

What Ihsan refused to admit was that he'd tried several times already to command Zeheb. "*Wake,*" he'd tried to say when the others were away, but it had come out like *walk,* and nothing had happened.

As the days passed, Ihsan's tongue healed more, and his words came more clearly. His tongue still felt leaden, though, with no power to speak of, and Ihsan started to wonder if his ability to command had been lost for good when Surrahdi had cut out his tongue.

Three weeks into the grueling process of healing, Cahil declared his efforts complete. And Ihsan agreed. His tongue was as healed as it was going to get. "The rest is up to the fates," Cahil said.

That night, Ihsan sat on the sand beside the campfire and faced Zeheb. The others were there, watching. "Wake," Ihsan said to him. It sounded wrong, as if he were a mute trying to speak, but it was intelligible enough.

More important was Ihsan's intent. In the past, he'd always been able to tell when his power flowed. Sitting there by the campfire, he tried, he really did, but he couldn't tell if it was working or not. In a pure miracle, he felt the well of power inside him again, but it felt inaccessible. None of it was flowing through to Zeheb.

"*Wake*, Zeheb," Ihsan repeated slowly. "Control the whispers. Suppress them as you once did."

Zeheb stared intently into the flames, giving no indication he'd heard Ihsan's words. Ihsan tried for nearly an hour, but when Zeheb began mumbling softly to himself, Ihsan knew he'd lost him.

We'll try again tomorrow, Ihsan signed, refusing to speak. His tongue hurt terribly.

Husamettín's face was unreadable. Yndris had already given up and gone to sleep. Cahil was standing nearby, cleaning his fingernails with a gleaming knife, staring at Ihsan with an expression of naked eagerness.

Ihsan woke early the next morning. Zeheb, as he often did, had slept beside the fire. He was sitting up, staring into the dead coals as if he might scry his way out of madness.

"Wake, Zeheb. Suppress the whispers."

Again the tickle of power. Again the cold assurance that it wasn't working, that the walls of Zeheb's insanity were still impenetrable.

"Follow the path," Zeheb suddenly said. "Sail deeper, deeper into the desert."

He was echoing the words of another. Ihsan didn't really care who. The fact that he was doing it meant he was lost in them and likely wouldn't be able to hear Ihsan's words. And even if Zeheb *could* hear him, there was the possibility that he'd sunk so deeply into madness he would never properly recover from it, silenced whispers or not.

"Shut them out, Zeheb. Return to us. Return to yourself."

"Sail north," Zeheb replied. "Sail north, north, north."

Soon the others were up and Ihsan lost his chance to speak with Zeheb alone. He tried again throughout the day. But Zeheb only smiled as if he'd been wandering in the desert and had just stumbled upon his favorite meal. Near nightfall Ihsan saw Cahil speaking softly with Husamettín. When they saw Ihsan watching, the conversation abruptly ended, and the two walked away from camp together.

"We want the Blue Journals," Husamettín said when they returned.

Ihsan stared at them both, knowing that this was the beginning of the end. If he refused, Cahil would likely torture him for the information before killing him. And if he told them, they might kill him anyway. At best he'd have until they had the journals in hand. After that, they would surely give him back to the desert.

In days past he might have given in to Husamettín's demand. He might have bided his time to find a way out of this. But he was certain that if they took the time to return to the journals' hiding place, they would fail in their mission. They'd lose their chance to find Nalamae, and then they'd lose Sharakhai itself.

"They're safe," Ihsan said carefully, hating how unintelligible he sounded. It made him feel small.

Yndris came to the fire and stood behind Ihsan. Nearby, Zeheb was babbling again.

"This has all been fruitless," Husamettín said plainly. "I need assurances that the path we're following is the one Yusam saw in his visions."

"And I've given you assurances." Ihsan couldn't help but cringe as he spoke. He paused to let the pain pass. When he spoke again, it was at a slower, more manageable pace. "Returning would take weeks of sailing. The return to Sharakhai even longer. I don't know that we have the time."

Husamettín's jaw worked. "You should have brought the journals with you, Ihsan."

"Well, I didn't. And now here we are." It was a challenge, plain and simple, a call of their bluff.

Husamettín stood and placed his hand on his sword. "Where are the journals?"

Beside them, Zeheb's whisperings were becoming stronger, as they sometimes did when trouble brewed around him. "On, on. Hurry now."

Cahil glanced at him, then stood, one hand on his god-given war hammer.

Ihsan lifted himself up, his hands in the air. "I only need time with Zeheb. A few more days."

In a flash of movement, Husamettín drew his shamshir. Cahil followed suit, as did Yndris.

"We've no more time to give you," Husamettín said. "As you say, there is much to tend to. Now give me the location of the journals, or I'll give you back to the desert here and now."

"I won't give them to you. Now stop this before—"

Husamettín advanced.

"Stop!" Ihsan said as he retreated. He tried to pour power into the command, but it had no effect. Husamettín drew his great shamshir back with both hands.

But the swing never came, for just then, Zeheb spoke. "Yes, yes, beyond the cutter. They're standing around the fire."

Husamettín turned and peered into the night. "Prepare yourselves!" he shouted, and sprinted away from the fire, into the darkness. "The enemy has found us!"

No sooner had he said it than a streak of orange light arced through the air toward them. The sound of breaking pottery came, followed by a burst of flame that spewed over the main deck of *The Wayward Miller*. Orange and yellow flames billowed upward, catching the mainmast boom and the sail tucked away on top of it. A moment later another firepot struck the foredeck.

Shapes resolved from the darkness. Warriors, many of them bearing the leaf-shaped shields of Kundhun, swept in like a murder of crows. A dozen of them, then two dozen.

"Stop!" Ihsan called, trying with all his soul to pour power into his voice.

But it barely rose above the ring of steel, above Husamettín and Cahil and Yndris pitting their weapons against wooden clubs and khopeshes of the Kundhuni warriors.

A wave of warriors swept past the others and ran toward Ihsan and the fire. They were the mercenaries, Ihsan realized, the same ones who'd been guarding Zeheb and his family.

Ihsan backed away, drawing his knife as if it would help him to fend off the tall warriors. "Stop!" he called again.

But they kept coming. He sprinted for the ship. The fire on the deck had spread, but if Ihsan could make the gangplank, he'd have some hope of reducing the number of warriors he had to face. They anticipated him, though, and cut him off with their long, loping strides.

The fire on the ship spread as Ihsan swiped at the nearest warrior. The warrior easily blocked him and brought his club down in a fearsome blow that Ihsan barely managed to fend off. The blow was blunted but still crashed against his head and sent him reeling. He fell to the ground and rolled, narrowly avoiding the head of the club as it thudded down in a spray of sand.

Above him, the warrior released a bone-chilling war cry and raised his club high. Hands raised, Ihsan made a pathetic attempt at shielding himself. There would be no stopping the blow. Not this time.

"Halt!" he shouted at the top of his lungs, putting all of himself into that single word, that single command.

And by the gods, he felt the dam burst. Raw power poured through him. The warrior stopped, still gripping the weapon tightly. He stared at Ihsan, terror coming on him, his breath ragged gasps. He watched as Ihsan stood. As Ihsan cut his throat.

The blood, nearly black in the darkness, flowed down his bare chest. The warrior's eyes dimmed and he fell with a thud to the sand. The warrior's three companions stood stock still as well and Ihsan dispatched them in the same way, then rushed to where Husamettín, Cahil, and Yndris were locked in battle. The three of them, just like the small host of Kundhuni warriors who surrounded them, were still as statues. Ihsan had been indiscriminate in his command, and they'd been caught up in it too.

The fire played over their faces as they watched him, Yndris with outright fear, Cahil with contempt, Husamettín with cold calculation, as if, even then, he wondered what Ihsan's choice would be, and what he, Husamettín, could do about it.

As if you have any choice in the matter.

Ihsan would be lying if he said he didn't consider ridding himself of all three of them—he could go to Sharakhai with Zeheb alone—but it was a fleeting thought, there and gone in a moment. He'd come here to save his home from the threat bearing down on it, and he would see that done. At least this episode had shown he could control the other Kings if need be, which might come in very handy one day.

With speed, he took his knife to the throats of the Kundhuni warriors, then said, "Return to yourselves," in a voice that felt utterly clumsy.

Slowly, Cahil, Husamettín, and Yndris began to move. They stretched their arms. They craned their necks and opened their jaws wide as waking jackals.

Then Cahil turned toward the fire.

"Where's Zeheb?"

Ihsan turned to look. He'd thought the warriors would kill them all before worrying about Zeheb, but they hadn't.

He was gone.

They rushed to put out the fires on the ship, scooping dousing agent out of wooden buckets, sending fistful after fistful against the flames until they had it under control, but by then the mainsail and two of the three foresails were badly burned.

Yndris, who'd been sent to track Zeheb, returned a short while later. "I spotted a lone ketch, sailing east," she said when they'd gathered around the dying campfire.

Cahil was beside himself with anger. "How in the bloody great desert could they have found us?"

And then it struck Ihsan. "I freed him," he said with his leaden tongue.

"What?" Cahil said.

"The other day"—Ihsan motioned to the carpet where Zeheb had been sitting—"I freed him. Zeheb himself called the mercenaries here."

"They couldn't have made it all this way in that time," Yndris said.

Husamettín's bearded face darkened. "They were already near, searching for us. Zeheb only had to guide them the rest of the way."

"Fucking gods!" Cahil kicked one of the burning logs, which spun into the night, spitting embers in a great, twisting gyre as it went. He looked like he was ready to kick another, but he suddenly stopped himself and placed one hand against his chest. For a moment there was fear on his face, a fear Ihsan had seen time and time again on those facing their own mortality. "Now what?" he asked in a strangely calm tone. "What are we going to do? Did your bloody journals tell you that?"

"Yes," Ihsan lied. The journals had told him no such thing, but there was really only one place for Zeheb to go. "There was a passage that saw both of you wandering the streets of Sharakhai in search of Nalamae."

Cahil stopped short. He hadn't expected this answer. His gaze slid to Husamettín. "Well?"

Husamettín shrugged. "We were going to head there eventually."

Cahil stalked off toward the ship. "Then let's bloody start making repairs to those sails before we rot out here in the desert."

Chapter 21

A BRILLIANT SUNSET laid siege to the western horizon, a clash of golds that faded to rust and cinnabar before giving way entirely to the deepening blue sky. Çeda, Sümeya, Kameyl, and Jenise had driven their wagon of manure north, to an estate owned by Osman, the one-time pit fighter turned businessman. He'd agreed to let them use the estate for a few days and had cleared his house of servants for the duration.

Çeda and the others had all but claimed the entire second floor, which was filled with large, richly appointed bed chambers. A thick layer of dust covered the floors and furniture. The beds were stripped. It looked like they hadn't been used in years. Within a freshly cleaned room, the one with the best view of the estate's gravel drive, Çeda sat in a ridiculously ornate chair next to a lavish bed that somehow clashed with every other piece of furniture and artwork in the room. Snoring softly under the covers was Lady Varal, the shipwright Çeda had abducted in the hope that she was a goddess in disguise. The powerful soporific Sümeya had forced on her had yet to wear off.

The door opened, and Sümeya stepped inside.

"Trouble?" Çeda asked.

Kameyl and Jenise were wandering the grounds, watching for signs that their cart had been followed to the estate, which was situated just north of the Fertile Fields and west of the city's reservoir.

"None yet." Sümeya dropped her weight heavily into a chair across from Çeda. She studied Varal for a time, then regarded Nalamae's gnarled staff, which was propped in the corner beside the window. Çeda had brought it all the way from the valley of the thirteenth tribe, where the last incarnation of Nalamae had died. "Do you really think she's the goddess reborn?"

It was a good question, the only question that mattered, really. After seeing Varal being attacked in the mere, Çeda had been certain she would find and rescue the goddess, but since leaving the harbor her certainty had slowly drained, leaving a gnawing feeling that they'd upended a woman's life for nothing.

"I certainly hope so," Çeda finally said.

Sümeya shifted in her chair, trying to find a comfortable position. "I understand why you might hedge, but this is no time for gambling, Çeda. We need to know."

Çeda shrugged. "She's certainly the woman from my vision."

"That doesn't mean she's the goddess reborn."

"I'd hoped she would recognize me, that my presence would trigger something inside her, but I saw nothing."

"What about *you*?" Sümeya motioned to the tattoos on Çeda's right hand. "You said you could feel the goddess as you feel the desert."

Çeda squeezed her right hand, deepening her awareness of her arcane senses, hoping she'd feel something of Nalamae in this plain woman. "I feel nothing, but that doesn't mean she *isn't* Nalamae, only that she might not have awoken yet."

Sümeya seemed disappointed. She worked her shoulders and stared at her chair with a cross expression. "Did a headsman carve these things or what?" She ended up leaning forward, her elbows propped against her knees. "And Goezhen? What of him? Do you think his attack has been averted?"

Çeda shrugged, feeling like a piece of flotsam borne on currents she had no ability to see much less control. Now that they had Varal, their plan was to make for the valley below Mount Arasal, where the bulk of the thirteenth tribe were hidden, but Çeda was starting to wonder whether they'd altered the course of time at all. Their actions might only have served to attract

Goezhen's attention. The god of misery might descend on Osman's estate that very day. Or Çeda and the others might reach the valley only to find Goezhen waiting for them.

Either way, the result would be the same: Goezhen would attack, and unless Nalamae had awoken by then, she would have no hope of standing against him. She would die, which was bad enough, but it wasn't even the worst possibility. If Nalamae wasn't fully aware of her own nature by the time Goezhen found her, Çeda worried she would be slain for good.

"It's maddening stuff," Çeda said, "trying to unravel the threads of fate. It's no wonder King Yusam always seemed a few arrows short of a full quiver."

"Yes, well, whatever the fates have in store for us, let's not wait for it like a nest of frightened pheasants. We should move on. Tonight." Sümeya took in the room with distrustful eyes. "I don't like it here."

Çeda snorted. "You sound like me three years ago."

Sümeya smiled. "That doesn't mean I'm not right."

"Have a bit more faith. If there was ever a man who had a reason to thumb his nose at the Kings, it's Osman."

"I don't doubt he has reasons, but I know broken men when I see them. He's liable to snap the moment the Silver Spears ride down the drive."

"No, he'll protect us."

"You're willing to bet everything on that?"

Years ago Çeda had trusted Osman implicitly, but the Osman from the pits and the Osman she'd met here at the estate were two different men. "In truth, no, but every other option has its dangers too."

Their original plan had been for Osman to supply nothing but a wagon and a horse, and to perhaps house them for an hour or two if need be after their mission to King's Harbor. They'd hoped to make for the desert immediately and return to the *Red Bride*, the swift yacht they'd sailed to Sharakhai two months ago. But the sands were crawling with ships. Varal's absence had been noted and Queen Meryam had clearly sensed something was amiss.

Kameyl had prepared two other safe houses, rooms and silence secured with a good deal of money paid up front, but when she returned to make sure all was safe, the neighbors said the Silver Spears had been sniffing around.

"We step foot into either of those houses," Kameyl had said on her return, "and we'll be up to our armpits in Silver Spears."

When he'd learned of it, Osman insisted they remain while he sent a half-dozen of his men to gather information. Çeda had been touched, seeing the same sort of protective nature he'd shown when she worked for him ferrying illicit packages all across Sharakhai. Yet Sümeya was worried that Osman, freshly freed from a prison camp, couldn't be trusted.

"How do we even know he's sent men to scout for us?" Sümeya asked. "They might have been sent straight to the Silver Spears."

"Osman wouldn't do that," Çeda replied.

Before Sümeya could reply, the door swung open and there Osman stood, looking as if he'd heard everything. Sümeya showed no embarrassment whatsoever. Çeda, meanwhile, felt her face burning red. Part of her maintained that Osman didn't deserve this sort of distrust, but another part, the part that had seen no end of cruelty in Sharakhai, knew that this was too important to leave to chance.

"Can we speak?" Osman asked Çeda.

"Of course," she said.

Osman led her to his study, an opulent room with ceiling-high shelves made of rich, deeply grained oak, filled with what looked to be very expensive books. The two of them sat in padded silk chairs, while the hulking, marble-topped desk separating them seemed ready to devour the chairs, the books, even the shelves.

Osman had been a ruggedly handsome man once. It had been that, along with the confidence that had once oozed from him, that had attracted her to him and led to their short but intense affair. He'd been a man full of vigor and verve, a man with an unquenchable thirst to expand the boundaries of his small empire, or to claw back the losses that went hand in hand with a life lived on the edge of lawlessness. Back then he'd carried much of the meaty weight of his fighting days on him.

That man was long gone.

He looked terrible. He'd been through a harrowing ordeal. Çeda could see it in his eyes. He was thin, shaking, fragile—words Çeda would never have thought could apply to him. Worse than the fragility of his body, though, was the fragility of his mind. He'd been sharp when she met him, keen, always ready to accept new challenges. Though that was before he'd been taken by the Kings. He'd been put to the question by Cahil himself and given up dozens of contacts, many of whom were part of the Moonless Host. Much of his testimony, Çeda was sure, had led to the near complete collapse of the Moonless Host here in Sharakhai.

She didn't blame him for it—a man could only endure so much—but it was clear Osman blamed himself. He'd made mention of it last night while they were preparing to go to the harbor. "I lasted a week with Cahil," he'd told her, though she hadn't brought it up. "A week, Çeda. How many men could say the same?"

It was a strange way to begin a conversation.

"Few," she'd told him. "Very few."

There in the study, a sudden shiver overcame him, and for a moment he had trouble meeting her eye. When their eyes finally did meet, Çeda had the distinct impression that every moment he was able to hold her gaze was a small victory for him. "I know you're thinking about leaving. I know Sümeya doesn't trust me. But I'm begging you to stay. Let me help you, Çeda. It's too dangerous out there."

"The Spears are everywhere," she said. "They might come here."

"They might," he said. "But I pay them, just like I used to."

"The city's changed."

"It hasn't changed that much."

Çeda paused. "Why is this so important to you?"

Osman swallowed several times, collecting his thoughts. "You've brought a woman into my home. A woman you stole from the House of Kings."

"Yes."

"She's someone important."

"Yes."

"Would you care to tell me who she is?"

Çeda brushed off a bit of dirt from the skirt of her dress. "I think that would do you more harm than good."

Osman stared at the veins in the marble desktop. "What you mean to say is you don't trust me."

What could she say? He'd already broken once. She couldn't risk telling him more and having him confess. "Osman, look, maybe it's best if we *do* leave."

She made to stand, but paused when Osman lunged across the desk and grabbed her wrist.

"Don't go," he pleaded.

"Let go of me, Osman."

He complied immediately, but there was terror in his eyes. "Just hear me out."

When she slowly sat back down, he looked to the shelves around him. "You'll remember I used to collect tales of war." He stood and moved to the shelves nearest the window, which gave a view of the horse barn and the expansive lawn. "Nasrallah. Safiyyullah. Zakariya the Bold. I even had one written by Husamettín two hundred years ago. I read them hoping to find the lessons that would teach me how to overcome my adversaries. And in this they worked. I built everything from the winnings I'd set aside from the pits." From a high shelf, he chose a book. "But I've thrown those books out. Now I read poetry, Çeda."

He sat back down and flipped through the pages. When he found what he wanted, he lay the book open on the desk and pushed it toward her. She read the page he pointed to.

Storm winds gather,
Full of bluster, full of pointless verve.
Toward the setting sun they blow, convinced of their worth,
And yet when the winds die, when all is calm once more,
Few remember their passage.
What they remember instead,
Is the forge of the sun they chased so poorly.

"Osman . . ."

"I don't care who she is. Not truly. I only care that it will help."

"Help what?"

"To change things." He paused. "It will, won't it?"

She realized what he was after. He'd risen about as high as anyone from the west end could hope to rise. And it had all been stripped from him. He'd been taken by the Silver Spears and tortured. He'd seen his once-sizable empire reduced to practically nothing. Even the pits, his pride and joy, had been lost. Tariq had refused to give back control when Osman returned, promising only a monthly allowance. Osman, a shadow of his former self, had simply accepted it. He'd had a glimpse of the land beyond, and like many men who'd stared into the face of his own death and lived to tell the tale, he'd reevaluated his life.

He saw Çeda's tale as one filled with glory, and he wanted a piece of it. If he could take that to the farther fields, well then he might be able to walk with his head held high, mightn't he?

Çeda nearly denied him. Nearly told him that she and the others would be leaving. But when she thought about it, this was perhaps the greatest motivator a man like Osman could have. He'd *had* money. He'd had the power it commanded. And it had all vanished like a mirage in the desert. But to help save a goddess? That was something the Kings could never take from him, a thing that would endure beyond his days.

"What we do here, Osman, with that woman. It could change the course of the entire desert." She couldn't tell him the truth. Not now. But she could give him this much.

Osman looked at her as if he was certain she was making it up. But the longer he stared, the more pride filled his watery eyes.

Before he could say another word, Çeda heard the sound of clopping hooves, faint but growing stronger. Looking through the curtains of the nearby window, she saw the gravel drive that ran toward the front of the estate. Along it, a dozen Silver Spears rode easily on akhalas. The light of the setting sun flung their shadows far across the dry earth. Among the soldiers were two women, one wearing the black battle dress of a Blade Maiden, the other the raiment of a queen.

Gods, Çeda had been such a fool. It was Queen Nayyan. She'd come to take Çeda and the others, come to take her prize: Nalamae. Had Çeda been wearing River's Daughter, she would have drawn the blade immediately. Instead she drew her knife. "Osman, what have you done?"

Osman backed away, hands raised. "Attack me and they'll hear, Çeda."

He wasn't lying. The front of the soldiers' line was already nearing the ornamented roundabout where the gravel drive split into three spurs, one going to the barn, another to the rear of the estate, the last to the front porch.

"Captain," Queen Nayyan called loudly, "your Spears will inspect the barn and the servant's quarters for Lady Varal. You'll leave the house to me."

"At once, my queen," replied the captain, and began issuing orders.

The queen, meanwhile, guided her horse toward the front of the house. Çeda recognized the Blade Maiden who accompanied her. She was one of those who'd been guarding Nayyan at the spice market, the one who'd told Sümeya and Çeda to return the following day to receive Nayyan's instructions.

Çeda shivered with rage. "You cur."

Osman stared at her. "This isn't how it looks, Çeda."

"You yellow-bellied cur."

"Çeda—" he started.

But Çeda refused to say another word to him. She couldn't *look* at him. She'd *defended* him and this was how he repaid her? She ran to the central stairway that led up to the second floor. Sümeya was already at the top of the carpeted stairs, holding Çeda's sword, River's Daughter, still in its scabbard. She tossed it to Çeda while rushing down along the steps. As Çeda caught her sword and buckled it around her waist, Jenise and Kameyl swept into the foyer from the rear. Before anyone could say a word, the front door swung open. "Stay here," Queen Nayyan said to someone outside, and stepped across the threshold, closing the door behind her.

Sümeya, Kameyl, Jenise, and Çeda all stared at Queen Nayyan, frozen.

Nayyan, meanwhile, approached them, her hands raised like a thief pleading innocence. "Remain calm," she said, barely loud enough to hear. "They'll be gone shortly, and then we can talk."

"What are you playing at?" Sümeya hissed, her hand on the hilt of her shamshir.

Osman stepped carefully into the foyer. He looked like a boneyard shambler, all awkward movements, eyes shifting nervously between the queen and the other women.

Nayyan glanced at him, then at Sümeya. "You knew the Spears would scour the Fertile Fields and every estate nearby for Varal. Better I came, to ensure they looked the other way, than trust to *him*." She waved toward Osman, who looked wounded, but said nothing in return.

"Why didn't you tell me?" Çeda asked him.

"I ordered him not to," Nayyan replied. "You would never have stayed until I got here."

"Why do you care?" Sümeya asked.

Nayyan's piercing eyes widened in surprise. "I care greatly what happens to you, Sümeya Husamettín'ava."

There were few things in the world that could make Sümeya look like a clumsy, adolescent girl, but apparently Nayyan's regard was one of them. In turn, Çeda felt her own gut twisting in knots—Sümeya and Nayyan were looking at each other in that way of theirs, as if with one small spark their romance would be rekindled. They'd been lovers once, back when Nayyan had been first warden of the Blade Maidens and Sümeya had reported to her. That had all changed the night Çeda's mother had killed Nayyan's father, King Azad, and Nayyan herself had taken his guise to hide his death from the public. More than ten years had passed since that night, but just then it felt like all it would take was a kind word between the two of them, and they'd fall into one another's arms.

"Just remain calm while the Spears search," Nayyan said. "We have much to talk about."

Not long after, the Silver Spears gathered at the front of the estate, their search complete. Nayyan stepped back outside and ordered them to continue searching the other estates then return to her palace when they were done.

"You as well," Çeda heard the queen say, surely to the Blade Maiden who had accompanied her.

"You're certain?" replied the Maiden.

There was deep caring in the way those two simple words were spoken, and Çeda wasn't the only one to notice. Sümeya's discomfort had returned, and she was avoiding Çeda's gaze.

By the time the Blade Maiden and the Silver Spears left, night had fallen over Sharakhai. They all gathered in the dining hall: Osman, Nayyan, and Jenise sitting on one side of the table, Çeda, Sümeya, and Kameyl on the other. They picked at cured meat and aged cheese and slightly stale bread, which they dunked into passably good wine to soften. Soon enough Osman was standing. "Well, I'll leave you to it."

Çeda felt terrible for having misjudged him. "Stay, Osman."

"No," he said. "This is for you to discuss alone."

And then it was down to the women. Nayyan, Çeda, Sümeya, Kameyl, and Jenise. *Quite a group*, Çeda mused. A queen, a traitor, a first warden, a storied Blade Maiden, and a tribeswoman, each with their own tale, each having found their way here, to discuss the future of a goddess reborn.

They told many tales over candlelight and brandy and wine. Sümeya told Nayyan of their mission in the harbor. Çeda added more about their plans to leave the city. Nayyan revealed some of the details around Lady Varal's disappearance from the perspective of the House of Kings. Queen Meryam had been preoccupied with many things in the weeks prior, but when she learned of Varal's abduction, she immediately understood its importance.

"How could she have known?" Çeda asked.

"I don't know," Nayyan said, using the stem of her wine glass to twist it slowly. "But the very fact that she became so animated about it shows that it's been a concern of hers for some time."

Çeda wasn't sure when it happened, or how, but they started trading stories. Of life in the palaces. Of life in the city. Of life in the desert. It was, Çeda thought, a *normal* conversation, the sort she missed so badly. And Nayyan, despite everything Çeda had thought about her, was charming. Her walls had dropped, perhaps because of the wine, perhaps because of the growing sense of sisterhood in the room. Whatever the reason, Çeda was starting to see why Sümeya had fallen in love with her.

Throughout, Nayyan's gaze lingered on Sümeya, and Sümeya's on her. Whenever it happened, Çeda would interject, taking control of the conversation, hoping to shift Sümeya's gaze to *her*. And it would work for a time, but then Sümeya's eyes would drift back to the queen, her former lover, the woman she'd missed so much she'd been driven into Çeda's arms, and soon Çeda gave up entirely.

They talked for hours, long into the night. Eventually, Jenise made excuses and went upstairs. Kameyl followed, leaving Çeda alone with Sümeya and Nayyan.

Çeda felt awkward as a newborn doe. She was just working up the courage to leave as well and give Sümeya over to the hands of the fates when Nayyan said, "There's one last thing I would share with you." From the purse at her belt she took out a bundle of fine linen. She lay it on the tablecloth before her. "Many have wondered how I killed the ehrekh in my younger days."

She unfolded the linen to reveal what looked like a perfectly preserved eye.

"The ehrekh are vulnerable to ebon steel, so you should of course have arrowheads and swords at the ready. But this"—she waved at the eye—"is how I stunned Drehthor, the terror of the southern wastes, before killing him."

Sümeya stared in naked wonder. "What in the name of the Great Mother who spawned us is *that*?"

"This is what remains of Navesh the All-Seeing. He was a prophet of the old gods who is said to have lived for eons after their death, wandering the world and protecting those whom the young gods had targeted in their anger over the departure of their creators."

"And you came by this how?" Sümeya asked.

Nayyan shrugged, a simple gesture made disgustingly winsome by the small, private smile she shared with Sümeya. "That's a story for another day."

It was clear that this was a mystery long kept from Sümeya. Çeda had spoken with her only once about the ehrekh Nayyan had killed, but even in that short conversation it became clear there was much that was unknown to her. What was more, Sümeya's hurt at being kept in the dark had been plain.

"You mean for us to use this if we meet Goezhen," Çeda said.

Nayyan swung her gaze to Çeda—reluctantly, it seemed. "It may help. It is said it has the ability to make one see truths they would rather not face."

"It is said?" Çeda echoed. "You're not sure?"

Nayyan shrugged again, this time without the smile. "I've never had the heart to try on myself." She slid it toward Çeda. "You may."

Çeda stared at it a moment, but found herself unwilling to do anything more than wrap it up in the linen and put it in the purse at her belt. That done, the mood of the room returned to one of intense awkwardness.

"Well," Çeda said, standing. "I'd better find some sleep."

Neither Nayyan nor Sümeya argued. As Çeda retired upstairs and lay down, she heard them talking, giggling, laughing. In Çeda's stomach, a snake nest turned over and over and over again, but then everything went quiet, which was hideously, infinitely worse.

Chapter 22

As the days passed in the silo, Meryam and Yasmine made water and passed soil in one particular spot, using dirt and the remains of the grain to cover it when they were done. The air still stank of it, though.

They were fed regularly, but were given a bit less each time.

"We're hungry," Yasmine would tell the men when they arrived with a fresh jug of water and more bread, sausage, or cheese.

"If you wanted more food, your father shouldn't have thought to cede our farmland away to some northern noble for his fecking winery. There would have been plenty to go around."

"That's what you want? Your land back?"

"That'd be a start. But what I really want is my brother back. The brother your father's men slew when he protested the annexation in Valdejas. I want his son back. He was hung when he brought his grievance to the *alcalde* of the city. But that's not going to happen, is it? *Gold's* what we want now, girl. Good, honest gold."

The following day, the skinny man returned. "Your father wants proof we have you. He's demanded your blood." He backhanded Yasmine across the face in a sharp, unavoidable blow. "I'm only too happy to oblige."

He held out a pair of clean white handkerchiefs to Yasmine, then jutted his chin toward Meryam. "Smear your blood on one without a fuss and I'll let you take your sister's share yourself. Don't, and I'll extract a good deal more from her than *you're* likely to take."

Meryam was aware that the plan was to deliver their kerchiefs to the royal magi, who would use the blood on them to verify that it was indeed theirs, but she'd been raised in a household that feared such things. Giving up one's blood was a dangerous thing in Qaimir. But what choice did they have? Yasmine took both handkerchiefs and wiped her mouth with one, smearing the cloth with blood. She turned to Meryam and held out the clean one. "Bite your lip, Meryam."

Seeing Yasmine's stern look and the man's grim face, Meryam did, wincing as she bit hard enough to draw blood. When she pulled her lip down, Yasmine pressed the kerchief to it, then handed both stained cloths to their captor.

"Thank you kindly," he said with a twisted grin, then left them alone.

When night fell, Yasmine stripped off her dress, petticoat, and shift. Before Meryam could think to ask her what she was doing, she slipped back into her dress and began to rip the satin petticoat into strips. When she was done, she did the same with her linen shift, then began braiding the strips into a rope, being sure to interlace the linen with the satin to make the rope as strong as it could be. "I'll need yours as well," she said to Meryam.

Understanding, Meryam complied, and with Yasmine's help tore her undergarments into strips. Her dress felt loose and itchy without them, and that in turn made her feel smaller and more useless than she already felt, like an ill-made doll that no one wanted and all would soon forget.

The work took a long while, during which Meryam was certain the men would return, discover what they were about, and beat them for it. They didn't, though, and Yasmine continued, braiding the strips together until she had a length that might bear her weight. Again and again she tried lofting it over the wooden supports of the conical roof. It wasn't easy, but she finally managed it. Gripping the lengths hanging down from the beam, she climbed, using her legs to pinch the makeshift rope as she went.

Meryam's heart soared as Yasmine stuck her head through the hole. Mighty Alu, she was going to escape. She was going to escape and then they'd be freed. But her heart plummeted as she saw that Yasmine's shoulders were too wide to fit through the hole. She tried for a good long while, but even Meryam could see it was never going to work.

"You're smaller," Yasmine said as she slipped back down. "You're going to have to do it."

Meryam shook her head so rapidly her cheeks wiggled. "I can't."

"You must."

Meryam didn't want to displease Yasmine, but she couldn't do it. She couldn't. She couldn't make it all the way up. Or she'd fall. Or she'd try to make it halfway through the hole and get stuck there. The entire thing was pure folly.

But then Yasmine's look registered. She'd been brave so far—braver than Meryam had given her credit for—but by the light of the moons filtering in through the hole above, Meryam could see the terror in her eyes. Yasmine was scared. Truly scared. "You can *do* this, Meryam."

"I won't know where to go!"

"Weren't you paying *any* attention on our way here? The horses took us south from Santrión to a road. It would have been the one that hugs the southern reaches of the royal forest and leads to Maracal. The center of Maracal has only two roads that split from it, one with a stone bridge, the other wooden. We went over the wooden one and rode for another two hours beside the river—we heard it the whole way here, remember? Then we struck north along a soft dirt road. We're right next to Oreño, Meryam. All you need to do is return to the river and follow it home."

As if it were all so simple.

Yasmine took Meryam's hands. "You must at least *try*. Here, take this for luck."

She took off her necklace and slipped it over Meryam's head. Meryam didn't feel any different—it was Yasmine's fear driving her—but she nodded anyway, took the rope, and began to climb. The trouble was she'd never climbed much. That had always been for Indio and Yasmine, not her, and she slipped several times. Her arms were aching and her breath was on her by the time she'd made it a quarter of the way up. And she was already petrified of falling.

"Squeeze the rope between your ankles, Meryam."

"I *am!*"

"No, you're not. Squeeze harder. Use your thighs, too."

She tried, but she felt as if she were losing half the height she'd just gained every time she stopped moving. "I can't do it!"

"Yes, you can! You're nearly there."

Meryam looked up. How very far away it seemed. But when she closed her eyes, she saw Yasmine's terrified look all over again. She stopped focusing on Yasmine. She stopped focusing on the height and her failing strength and fixed her gaze on that hole with the silver light shining through it. And tried again.

Her arms trembling, she made slow headway. She was halfway up, then three quarters. She came eye level with the hole and through it saw a forested landscape made of moonlight and silver shavings. Reaching one trembling hand out, she grasped the hole's rough bottom edge. She was halfway to escape, but the hole looked too bloody small. She was never going to fit—

Her hand slipped on the rope, which made her other hand loosen on the gritty stone lip. And suddenly she was falling, weightless, twisting in the air, screaming all the way down.

She struck the ground hard. The wind was knocked from her.

Yasmine dropped to her knees by Meryam's side. "Oh, gods. Oh, gods."

Through her panic, Meryam heard a door opening. Footsteps coming closer. A wavering, golden light reflected off the stones above.

As Meryam sucked in a long, noisy breath, Yasmine grabbed one side of the rope and pulled hard. It made a buzzing sound as the fabric rubbed against the beam high above. Then down it snaked to fall around Yasmine's head and shoulders. As a coughing fit overtook Meryam, Yasmine gathered the rope, shoved it behind her, and dragged Meryam's head onto her thigh.

"Cry, Meryam," she whispered harshly, mere moments before the door opened and the burly man stuck a lantern, then his head, inside.

The light swung toward the two of them. "What happened?"

"She cried out in her sleep," Yasmine said. "She's frightened."

Long, terrible sobs escaped Meryam, more from pain than fear. Her entire left side, especially her ribs, felt as if she'd been beaten with clubs, and her knee was throbbing so badly it was all she could do not to reach for it and hold it against the pain.

The lantern swung over the silo's interior. In the light, Meryam spotted a bit of the braided rope sticking out near Yasmine's knee. She cried harder, shifting as she did so, so that one hand covered the exposed braid. Moments passed, the light glaring at them, and Meryam was sure he'd seen it.

But then the man said, "Just keep her quiet," and slammed the door shut, locking it behind him.

Soon all was silence once more, and Yasmine was holding Meryam to her. "I'm sorry, Meryam."

Meryam wiped away her tears. "For what?"

"If I'd been quieter, you wouldn't have found me and they wouldn't have taken you. Just me."

"It's all right, Yasmine." She started taking off the necklace.

"No." Yasmine pushed her hands back down. "You keep it."

She took Meryam back in her arms and rocked her. It felt good being held. It made her fears and the aches from the fall feel muted. But the reprieve was short-lived. A moment later, as Yasmine began to cry, her fears came rushing back.

Meryam woke exhausted. She could hardly open her eyes, but every time she closed them, that dream of her and Yasmine in the silo haunted her. Taking a vial of elixir from the chest by her bed, one of only five remaining, she downed it quickly, willing it to work faster. It did as it always did—it revitalized her—but today it wasn't enough.

Her dreams had been of a young Yasmine, hardly more than a girl, but her mind kept wandering to the woman who'd sailed to the desert and been taken by an arrow. Her ship captured in the desert, Macide Ishaq'ava had forced the men to choose between themselves and their wives, and Ramahd had been ready to sacrifice himself when Yasmine threw herself at their captors and was shot through by one of Macide's filthy scarabs—she'd forced them to kill her that Ramahd and her daughter, Rehann, might live.

"I know you loved him," Meryam said as a tear slipped down her cheek, "but I wish you'd let him die instead."

She recognized the cycle she was about to slip into. She knew it would mean a day lost as she obsessed over what had happened. She hadn't even been there, but it didn't stop her from imagining Yasmine being shot through over and over and over again.

You have work to do, Meryam, and promises to keep.

She rose from her bed and somehow made her way down to the cavern and the glowing crystal. Near the scaffolding stood several tables with a small host of tomes and scrolls upon them. A few paces away were three chairs, two of which were occupied by a pair of men wearing simple, sweat-stained clothes. They were father and son, two scarabs of the Moonless Host who, as far as she'd been able to discover, had no other close family in Sharakhai.

They shivered from the cold that permeated the cavern. Or perhaps it was from their fear. Both were bound, gagged, and blindfolded. Most impor-tantly, their hearing had been taken from them, a necessary measure lest they learn what Meryam had planned for them. She couldn't have that. She needed to make sure it was the spell *forcing* the men to act, not them acting on their own.

Prayna, a blood mage and the de facto leader of the Enclave, was already there, standing beside a set of tables near the crystal. By the light of the crystal itself, she was reading over several ancient tomes she'd brought for the pur-pose. Beside the tomes lay sheets of vellum, which Prayna was using to mark new sigils, combinations she hoped would give Meryam what she wanted.

Meryam hated that she'd resorted to calling for the help of another mage, but there was no doubting Prayna was gifted in the red ways. More to the point, she knew more about sigils than anyone Meryam had ever known, including herself. Prayna was so engrossed in her work she didn't look up as Meryam approached.

"You've found something?" Meryam asked.

Prayna shivered and her head shot up. She blinked her elegant eyes at Meryam, then resumed the careful creation of her latest sigil. "I hope so, but we won't know until we try." With one last stroke of her pen, she was done. She spun the sheet of vellum, turning it toward Meryam.

There was a complex master sigil in the center that was surrounded by a dozen others, all of which were represented in the larger master. It was a dizzying spell combining a half-dozen sigils for *bonding* and *blood ties*, more for *attraction* and *find*, and several that added various shades of *compel*. Together they would put a compulsion on those related to the subject to cease what they were doing and search for them. Or so Meryam hoped. Their efforts so far had all been miserable failures.

Meryam noted the one major exclusion since their last iteration. "There's nothing for the trees."

"No," Prayna said. "The sigils have been too complex. Better if we can master the summoning first, then add more to combine it with the adichara."

Meryam couldn't argue with her logic. "Well enough. Have you tried any versions of it already?"

She held the sheet of vellum out to Meryam. "This will be the first."

Meryam accepted it and looked it over carefully. Then she sat in the empty chair across from the father and pricked the man's wrist with her blooding ring. The man flinched, but then sat quietly, unmoving. He knew that to do otherwise would invite punishment. He couldn't control his shivering, however. It grew ever stronger as Meryam used a vulture quill to draw the sigil upon his forehead. Meryam was exacting in her spell work, so it took time, but soon enough the sigil was complete.

Meryam stood and dragged the chair away, the legs thumping against the roots' gnarled landscape. Then she and Prayna waited, watching not the father, the one they'd drawn the sigil on, but his son. *He* was the one the spell should affect. If the sigil worked, the son would get up and try to reach his father. He would be drawn by their shared blood.

"We're sure they're father and son?" Meryam asked Prayna.

"As sure as we can be, yes."

They waited minutes longer. When nothing happened, Prayna tried the spell on the son instead, but this too failed.

Over the course of the day, they tried nine more combinations of the spell, but nothing worked.

"I'll develop more variations," Prayna said, an indication she was ready to leave. "And I still wish to speak with Nebahat. He might be able to help."

"No," Meryam said. "For now, this stays between us."

After a brief pause, Prayna said, "Very well," and made her way over the uneven floor toward the tunnel that led to other parts of the city.

When she was gone, Meryam left the two scarabs to the Silver Spears and returned to the Sun Palace. Within her apartments, tomes and tablets and scrolls lay over an expansive travertine table. It was late. She knew she should rest. She knew she should eat. But there was still so much to do, so she lit a lantern, sat at the table, and pulled one of the books closer. It was her most recent find. It described how one of the elder gods, Ashael, had been struck down by Iri after a terrible battle, how Ashael's presence soiled the land for centuries after, how demons had congregated there, feasting off his decaying soul.

Meryam wondered where that place might be, wondered if it might be used to further her goals. She had no idea where to begin, so turned to another book, one written by King Sukru's brother, Jasur, the Sparrow. In it, Jasur detailed the alchemycal experiments he'd started to conduct on the essence collected from the tendril in the crystal's cave.

An hour had passed, perhaps more, before Meryam realized she'd been staring at the same page, reading it over and over again without understanding the words. Stranger still, the page was wet, dotted with tears. The text itself had mentioned a rare flowering herb from Qaimir, named hartroot for the way the stalks looked like deer antlers. Yasmine used to pick them and pluck the smaller stems away, then weave them into Meryam's braids. It had always looked so pretty when she was done.

She'd managed to avoid thinking about Yasmine all day. She'd managed to avoid the black well of sorrow and misery that always accompanied the memories. But now it all came rushing back. She felt powerless again. Weak. She felt as if she were being blown around the Shangazi like any other of the countless grains of sand.

"No!" Meryam said aloud. The word sounded shrill and desperate in the harshness of the Sun Palace. She wiped away her tears, and said it again, louder this time, "No!" She dabbed the skirt of her night dress onto the page, blotting the tears away. "That isn't how you fix this. Blood is the way. Not with tears. Blood!"

"My queen?" came Basilio's voice from her sitting room.

Meryam tried to compose herself before Basilio came striding in, but she failed.

Basilio stopped in his tracks at the threshold. "My queen?"

She sniffed and blinked, trying ineffectually to clear her eyes. "You were to bring more elixirs," she snapped, more for something to say than anything else.

Basilio's reaction was not an encouraging one. "Yes," he replied, gripping his hands behind his back like a soldier on parade. "I'd hoped to have better news for you by now."

Meryam felt something tighten inside her. "What do you mean?"

"I'm sorry, my queen, but it seems the elixirs have . . ." He swallowed hard, then nodded, as if accepting his fate. "The elixirs are gone."

"Gone?" She needed those elixirs. She *needed* them.

"I thought perhaps it was a mixup, that in the move from Eventide they'd been misplaced. But I've come to the conclusion that they were likely stolen."

"Stolen? By *whom?*"

"We don't know as yet. My suspicion is that two of the servants moving your effects learned of their existence and arranged for them to be taken on the way down to the Sun Palace."

"You left their transport to someone else?"

Basilio looked beside himself. "There was so much to do. They were in a locked chest, which I ensured was loaded onto a guarded wagon. When the chest arrived here at the Sun Palace, I opened them myself and found the elixirs gone. And now Eventide, incensed over King Yavuz's death in the ritual the two of you performed with the golem, is saying we'll be allowed to interrogate no one until the question of succession has been resolved and the new King, whoever he might be, has had a chance to consider the matter."

Meryam dipped her head into her hands. It was likely that someone in Eventide had stolen them. Meryam wouldn't be surprised to hear that it had been Kiral's old vizira herself who'd arranged for it. She'd been beside herself with rage at news of Yavuz's death. Meryam had moved to the Sun Palace by then, but some of her effects were still in Eventide. When Yavuz had died, his vizira had practically thrown Meryam's things down the mountain.

Basilio looked uncomfortable. The look he'd had on his face when he entered, before he'd seen her state, had been cheerless at best. It meant foreboding news, something *other* than the elixirs.

"The reason you came," she said, "how bad is it?"

"Very."

Meryam pinched the bridge of her nose. "Go on."

After several moments in which Basilio seemed to be having trouble deciding where to begin, he steeled himself and launched into it. "It's the warfront, Your Excellence. It turns out, some of the Kundhuni warlords who've been helping to harass the Mirean supply lines have not, in fact, been harassing them at all."

Meryam reeled at the implications. "They've switched allegiance."

Basilio nodded. "We thought it only one at first, but now I suspect many have been bought off."

"Mighty Alu give me strength," Meryam breathed. They had some twenty Kundhuni warlords—each the king of some tiny grassland kingdom with a small fleet to call their own—sailing against the Mirean supply lines. If they didn't know which ones they could trust, they could trust none of them. *War can turn on the smallest of things,* Meryam thought. *This could be one of them.* "I want their heads on pikes, Basilio. All of them."

"That would be unwise. We'd lose them. Every single one of them."

"They'd balk at my killing a traitor?"

"They wouldn't see it like that. The rituals and rites of honor that surround their kings is complex."

"Then what's *your* suggestion?"

"You could dominate them."

She exhaled noisily while waving to the chest on her bed. "I've reached my limit, Basilio. I'm barely holding things together as it is. And with the elixirs almost gone, I can't afford to do more, not for long, and certainly not considering how far away they are from the city."

"Our magi from Qaimir, then."

"They're spread across the eastern desert. It would take months to round them up."

"Then the Enclave."

"I don't trust them, not for this."

Basilio eyed her warily. She could tell he was choosing his words with care. "My queen, perhaps if you spent less time in the cavern and more time here in the palace, things would go smoother—"

Meryam cut him off. "We're close to an answer. The riddles of the crystal have nearly been unlocked. I'm certain of it."

"You've been saying that for over a week."

"Because it's true!"

Basilio's look was mollifying, which made it all the more infuriating. "Then I'm afraid the only other option is to pay the warlords more than the Mireans."

Meryam stared, dumbstruck. "Only yesterday you said we could barely afford saddles for our horses."

"A slight exaggeration." Before Meryam could object, he went on. "We need the Kundhuni tribes for another six months at most. By then more of our fleet will have arrived from Qaimir, and more of the ships being built in King's Harbor will be ready. Then we'll take the war to the Mireans and the Malasani and we'll win it." He saw her hesitation. "This is an expense we cannot afford to skip, my queen."

Meryam flung her hand into the air. "Oh, very well!" She stalked away.

"My queen, where are you going?"

"Back to the bloody cavern."

"At this hour?"

"Well *someone* has to get answers, Basilio!"

But the answers didn't come that night, nor in the days that followed, and Meryam wondered if she was ever going to get what she wanted.

Chapter 23

DAVUD HAD BEEN SITTING in the chancellor's waiting room for over an hour before a serious looking woman wearing the wheat-colored robes of a collegia scholar entered and bowed her head to him. "The chancellor will see you now."

Davud nodded and followed her into a large office that looked much the same as it had when Davud had attended the collegia. Shelves adorned every wall. At the room's center was a large desk made of stout wooden legs with a brightly veined marble top holding stacks of books and papers, all impeccably ordered, all impeccably clean. Behind the desk sat Chancellor Abi, a bald man of middling years who looked every bit as clean and orderly as his desk.

Chancellor Abi's assistant, her mouth set in a grim line, waved Davud toward a chair, clearly ready to depart, but stopped with a sigh when the chancellor held up a finger while still writing on a piece of parchment. "Hold a moment." She waited impatiently while the chancellor finished his letter with a whirling scrape of a signature and held it out for her to take. "For Master Luwanga."

"Of course." She took it and rushed from the room.

Without so much as glancing at Davud, Chancellor Abi took out a wide, cloth-backed ledger and scribbled a few notes into it. He had a crooked nose, a dimpled chin, and a manner that Chancellor Abi himself once described to Davud's incoming class as *methodical*. Most would say it was *curt*, or even *dismissive*, but Davud knew him as a good man, an honest man who took his responsibilities as head of the collegia seriously, and as such tried to be as efficient with his time as possible, which made Davud think Abi didn't realize he was being used by the House of Kings.

But he was a meticulous man too. He wouldn't take on a project like the one his student, Cassandra, was spearheading without full knowledge of how the information would be used.

Which are you then, Davud mused, *puppet or accomplice?*

After closing the journal and squaring it against the edge of the desk, Abi stood and gathered several ledgers from the shelves behind him. When seven of them had been piled into his arms, he turned to face Davud. "Walk with me?"

"Chancellor Abi"—Davud stood, but made no move to follow—"I thought you'd been told, our discussion is of a rather sensitive nature."

"Yes, but I'm a busy man, and I deal with subjects of a sensitive nature every day."

With a tilt of his head, he beckoned for Davud to follow and whisked past him. Davud rushed to catch up, and the two left his office side by side. "You've been gone from the collegia a while now," Abi said as they wove around a group of laughing students and took a set of stairs down. "Two years, is it?"

"Just about, yes."

"And after the incident, you were in the employ of the Kings, as I recall."

Incident, Abi called it. Massacre was more like it. Several hundred had died on the collegia grounds, and dozens of graduates taken and later turned into shamblers, creatures straight out of a nightmare, which Hamzakiir had used in his plans to attack King's Harbor.

"I was not in the Kings' employ, no, but I spent some time in the palaces."

"Along with Anila Khabir'ava."

"Yes." They whipped around a landing and attacked the next flight of stairs. "Chancellor Abi, I've come to speak to you of a collegia student. A young man who's gone missing."

"You would be speaking of Altan, no doubt."

"I am, yes."

They reached ground level, at which point the chancellor made a beeline toward a tall archway on the opposite side of the crowded atrium. "I'm sure Altan will turn up." His pace developed a sudden hitch as he swiveled his head and fixed Davud with a goggle-eyed stare. "Did you know him? Personally, I mean?"

"No, chancellor."

"Because the collegia has already given all it can to the Silver Spears." Eyes firmly ahead once more, his dogged pace resumed. "And there *is* a war on, my boy. Perhaps you haven't noticed, but there are reports of people going missing every day."

"I'm glad you mentioned that. At the time of his disappearance, Altan was working on a research project."

"He was."

"At your direction?"

"Yes, yes, as I suspect you've already heard." Abi led them beneath the archway and onto the esplanade, a long, green space that abutted many of the collegia's halls of learning. Students were the most plentiful, but there were masters, scholars, and a handful of ordinary folk—likely the family members of attending students—roaming about as well.

"Chancellor, are you sure it's all right to—"

"Get *on* with it, scholar." Abi's tone was exasperated. "I have a meeting I'm already late for."

"Of course. Altan's project. Its stated purpose is to research the marriage and birth records of those who have blood of the thirteenth tribe, yes? Research driven by records obtained from the palace of King Sukru?"

Abi frowned. "Who told you that? Cassandra?"

"Never mind how I found out. Is it true?"

"Well, yes!" Abi seemed suddenly off-balance.

"Who told you to undertake the project, Chancellor Abi?"

"No one did. It was my own idea!"

"Why did you order a census of the thirteenth tribe?"

Chancellor Abi's footsteps came to a slow, unsteady halt. He was so near, Davud could smell the mint on his breath as he spoke. "As a scholar yourself, you're well aware how we in the collegia value truth. Unfortunately, many of the highborn, particularly those in the House of Kings, do not. They've been suppressing some rather momentous truths for"—he sent a glance toward the dark peak of Tauriyat—"well, a long while now." He spoke softer. "I recognize, even if the House of Kings does not, that the thirteenth tribe has become a power in the desert. We may hope to forge ties with them. What better way to do that than by locating those of their bloodline here in the city?"

"In order to do what, send them into the desert as ambassadors?"

"Or to host the tribe here in the city. There could be countless benefits."

Davud altered tack. "Chancellor, did Altan speak to you about his fears?"

"What fears?"

"I believe he and I have made the same discovery. That those found were being marked."

"Marked for what?"

"For abduction. For ransom or possibly murder."

The chancellor waited, clearly expecting more. "Don't be ridiculous."

"I've checked it myself," Davud countered, expressly avoiding Esmeray's name. "Many of those found in his research have gone missing."

Abi shook his head as if he didn't understand. "As I said, there *is* a war on."

"This isn't about the war. This is about Sharakhai and the darker histories you just alluded to." Davud paused. "Who do you give the names to, Chancellor Abi?"

His manner went suddenly stiff. "You're overstepping your bounds, scholar."

"Am I?" Davud handed him a piece of paper, a list of the names Esmeray had compiled after her many forays into the city. "The people on that list have all been reported as missing. They were recently identified in the course of Altan's and Cassandra's research. Some are from the Shallows. Others are from Roseridge or the Well or the Red Crescent. All are descendants of the thirteenth tribe."

Abi shook the paper. "I have no idea where these names came from."

"Check them against your own records if you wish, but I promise you, they're all there. You'll also find that they're all gone, presumed dead."

"Scholar, I've granted you an audience out of respect for your studies here. You've brought a serious matter to my attention, a matter that will be investigated with all haste. But those names have been given to no one, and if you imply again that I am somehow involved with the deaths of innocents in Sharakhai, I'll set down these books and punch you right in the nose."

Abi was so angry, so apoplectic, Davud found that he believed him, but they were dealing with blood magic—Abi could be a pawn and have no recollection of the things he'd been made to do. "Let me be frank, Chancellor. I fear that one of the Enclave, a blood mage, has ensorcelled you. I believe they're behind this project and are using you as their pawn."

Abi stammered, "I can assure you no such thing has happened."

"You wouldn't know if it had." Davud pulled his blooding ring from the bag at his belt and showed it to him. "They would have used a ring like this. They would have healed the wound after. They would have wiped your mind of the memory as well."

So confident moments ago, the chancellor looked completely out of his depth.

"Let me examine you," Davud pressed. "I know the signs. We'll find the truth of it. And if a compulsion *has* been laid upon you, I'll remove it."

"It seems impossible. What would they want with me?"

"That's what I'd like to find out."

"What about my family? My wife? My children?"

"I'll see to it that they're protected."

Abi took in the students enjoying the esplanade, regarded the tall, blocky buildings. He stared up at the bright sun, then down at the many books he held in his arms as if he'd just remembered they were there. "Come to my residence tonight," he said at last, "after the dinner hour. We'll find the truth of it then."

Davud nodded, feeling as though a great weight had been lifted from his shoulders. "Very well."

Abi left under a cloud, while Davud, after casting a spell of concealment, returned to his cellar room. That night, Davud did as the chancellor had bid him. He walked across the grounds to the chancellor's residence as the sun was setting, only to pull up short as a cold, sinking feeling was born inside him.

The front portico and lawn of Abi's expansive home was crawling with Silver Spears. There were so many that, despite Davud's spell, one of them, a burly woman wearing the white tabard of an inspector, bumped into him and looked straight at him.

"What's happened?" Davud asked her.

The inspector frowned. "It's the chancellor. He's been killed."

The sinking feeling yawned wider and wider. Davud felt sick from it. "How?" was all he could think to ask.

"No one knows as yet," said the inspector, "but it was grisly, I can tell you that much." The woman's eyes, dull, almost lifeless a moment ago, suddenly sharpened. "Did you know him, the chancellor?"

While intensifying the spell of concealment, Davud backed away. "No."

Oddly, the spell seemed to be ineffectual against her. Over and over, it shed from her like sand off a lizard's back. "Were you coming to see him?" the inspector asked.

"No," Davud repeated, and quickened his pace.

"Halt," the inspector said and took several loping strides toward him. "Halt!"

With a wave of his hand, Davud triggered a spell he'd cast that morning, a spell kept on the very edge of taking effect. A simulacrum of himself ran in one direction, while he, the real Davud, went in another. The Silver Spear lumbered after the illusion and Davud made it safely away, but he was unsettled now. Every shadow seemed dangerous.

Slow down, Davud. Think this through.

How could Abi's murderers have found out about Davud's conversation with Chancellor Abi so quickly? The only reasonable explanation was that Abi himself had confessed it to them. Sadly, it provided an answer to Davud's earlier question—Abi wouldn't have been killed had he been a willing accomplice, which meant he'd been a puppet all along. Had he been incensed and challenged those who were behind the request to identify more of the thirteenth tribe in Sharakhai?

Was it the lesser Kings? Queen Meryam? A mage from the Enclave? Or maybe it was Hamzakiir, or someone else with a grudge against the thirteenth tribe.

Standing there alone beneath the darkened buildings of the collegia, a terrible realization came to him. If they were searching for *him*, they'd be searching for Esmeray as well. He turned and rushed back to the cellar. Every moment that passed felt like the one that was going to make him too late to save her. The fates were kind, however, and he found Esmeray already there, waiting for him.

"The chancellor's dead," he said, and told her the story in a breathless rush.

"This isn't your fault," Esmeray reasoned when he was done.

"Yes, well, that isn't what's most important now." The whole way back to the cellar and all through the story, he'd felt like the door was about to crash in and Queen Meryam herself would storm in and kill them both. "You need to leave, Esmeray. You need to hide."

"*I* need to hide?"

"Yes. Someplace they'll never think to look. I'll find Undosu on my own."

Davud thought Esmeray would be angry with him for saying it. Instead, she smiled pityingly, as if Davud didn't understand a thing about what was going on. "There's no running from this, Davud, not for me, not for you. Not anymore. We're in this together, and there's nothing that's going to keep me from being by your side to see this through. I've seen too much, you understand? I've spoken to too many broken families, grieving loved ones, to stop now."

Davud felt impotent. This all felt hauntingly familiar. He'd escaped Ishmantep with Anila, only to see her body burned by coldfire when they returned to try to stop Hamzakiir from escaping with their friends. Anila had lived, though barely, but she'd suffered greatly, and it had all been Davud's fault. Now here was Esmeray, a woman he'd come to love. She'd already lost her magic because of him. He didn't want to see her lose her life, too.

Esmeray stepped forward and took his hands. "I know you think of me as fragile."

"Not fragile," Davud said. "Vulnerable."

"We're *both* vulnerable. You can run from me if you wish. You can go after Undosu on your own. There's nothing I can do to stop you. But know this, I'm still going to help. I'll comb the west end for more who've gone missing if you think to hide from me. This is too important not to." She squeezed his hands. "I'd rather it be with you, though. You ground me, Davud. You make this strange life bearable."

Davud stood there, dumbstruck. Esmeray's confessions of love were so rare that for a moment all he could think about was how she made *him* feel. She cherished life. She fought for it. She lived it to its fullest. It was a thing that had not only made him fall in love with her, but admire her. As scared as he was of the dangers that lay ahead, as much as he wanted her somewhere safe, he suddenly couldn't see himself taking another step without her.

Without a word more being spoken, the two of them fell into one another's arms. "You've found another place for us to hide?" he asked her.

She nodded, the movement subtle, the touch of her against his neck, cheek, and ear deeply intimate. "A seamstress I've known since I was a child."

He pulled away, still holding her hands. "We'd better get moving, then."

She drew him in and gave him one of the noisiest kisses she'd ever given him. "We're going to see this through."

He winked at her. "I almost believe you."

They packed up and moved immediately to a small home in a cramped neighborhood just inside the city's old walls. They spent hours laying down their spells of concealment and detection, their spells of confounding. Esmeray, exhausted from giving up so much blood and helping to cast the spells, soon dozed off in the tiny bed, but sleep proved elusive for Davud. He stared at the ceiling and listened to Esmeray's soft breathing as the night passed, feeling worse with each passing moment.

He couldn't shake the idea that he and Esmeray were being hunted or that he'd just betrayed those who'd been found by Cassandra and her efforts, and those who had *yet* to be found. Strangest of all, he felt like he'd abandoned whoever had left them the books. Whoever had done it had been trying to point him in the right direction. He still had no idea *why* they would have sent a message in such a cryptic manner, but it was clear they were trying to help—they'd posed Davud a riddle and, so far, Davud had been too thick to figure it out.

As his eyes fell on the topaz pendant he'd been using to watch Cassandra, a thought occurred to him. Whoever was spying on them clearly knew about the pendant—they'd used it to send Davud a message. So why couldn't Davud do the same?

Hope driving him, he lit a lamp and scoured the books their secret benefactor had given them. Eventually he found what he was looking for. After placing the lamp near the open book, he set the topaz crystal onto the page over one word in particular:

Help.

He waited, hoping, praying that whoever had aided him before would do so again. The hours crept by. Through the tiny window along one wall of the cellar he saw the crescent moons arc across the sky. Darkness reigned when they set once more. All too soon a pale pink light kissed the pre-dawn sky.

To come so close, Davud thought. He felt powerless, a minor piece in this grand game. On the bed, Esmeray rolled over. She'd wake soon. The peril they were in made him wonder what might have happened to their secret benefactor. Had he been found out? Had the one now hunting for Davud and Esmeray discovered the pendant?

I need to destroy it, Davud told himself. *It's too dangerous to keep. A gifted mage could use it to find us.*

He set the topaz pendant on the floor, then stood and retrieved the brick doorstop from the entrance and sat back down in his chair. He lifted the brick high, preparing to smash the pendant.

And then he saw it. Movement in the topaz's facets. In a mad, fumbling rush, he set the brick aside, took up the pendant, and lifted it to his eye. Within the large, central facet he saw a book. An unseen source of light illuminated the open pages in a golden glow.

The story was of Bahri Al'sir. He was searching for a fabled scroll that legend said was actually a page ripped from the original Al'Ambra. In the right hands, the story boldly proclaimed, the scroll could unlock the very secrets of the desert, and Bahri Al'sir was quite certain his own hands qualified. So it was that he entered the wizard's tower which, unbeknownst to the king he served, contained a vast library hidden deep beneath the earth.

Despite concealing himself with a magic cloak, Bahri Al'sir nearly lost his life that day, but was saved by use of his own blood. Guarding the library was a massive cobra that struck from the darkness. The poison filled Bahri Al'sir's veins, but he'd known of the danger and had inured himself to the poison by allowing other snakes to bite him, small ones at first, then larger and larger ones, until his body had become all but immune to it. He'd killed the cobra and stolen into the wizard's lair, only to be set upon moments later by the wizard himself. The wizard, not realizing Bahri Al'sir had been bitten, had drank of his blood, planning to kill Bahri Al'sir with the power thereby taken. The wizard succumbed to the poison moments later, but not before setting fire to his entire library.

Davud woke Esmeray, explained everything, then handed her the pendant before she could tell him what a fool he'd been.

Her tired, sour look showed how displeased she was, but she snatched the pendant from him anyway and used it to read the story. She was silent for a long while after, her eyes going distant, as if she were giving the story due consideration. "It's a message," she finally said. "There's a mage hiding in the collegia."

Davud nodded. "He's the one behind it all. The list. The disappearances. The chancellor's death."

Esmeray looked uncharacteristically worried—she knew it wasn't going to be easy to find the mage, nor defeat him—but then the look vanished and the fire in her eyes returned. "Let's go find him."

Chapter 24

IHSAN AND YNDRIS WALKED side by side along a wharf in Sharakhai's western harbor as the sounds of the city rose around them. Ahead, spanning the mouth of an alley, was an old stone archway with a briar rose at its peak, the sign of Naamdah, the Kundhuni goddess of good fortune. It wasn't common knowledge in Sharakhai that Naamdah was in truth the patron god of thieves. Her priest's efforts to rebrand their goddess had gone so well that they collected tithes from thousands of followers, even those of Kundhuni blood, which were sent back to the depths of Kundhun to the mother temple. Cahil said he'd chosen the temple with no more thought than it being a place unlikely to hide a bevy of Kings, but to Ihsan it felt like a sign. This caper of theirs amounted to nothing less than the theft of a god, so who better to receive a bit of good fortune from than the god of thieves herself?

By the time Ihsan and Yndris reached the small, walled-off courtyard behind the brothel, the sounds of the west end had become muted. The priestess, a half-Kundhunese woman with closely shorn hair and a pretty smile, looked up from her work in the small garden and winked at them. Ihsan wasn't truly sure which of the two she was winking at, but he smiled back anyway. Yndris ignored her entirely and stalked beyond the tiny temple to the building they'd called home these past few weeks.

They entered their room, shared between the four of them—Ihsan, Yndris, Husamettín, and Cahil—whereupon Yndris flopped onto the nearest of the criminally small beds. She wore a commoner's dress with a slit in the skirt and a low neckline. She hated it, but it was in line with what one would find in and around Sharakhai's western harbor, and that was the most important thing: to blend in while they searched for Zeheb.

Eyes closed, her arms folded across her forehead, Yndris said, "Didn't that bloody book say anything about *where* we were going to find him?"

"I told you"—Ihsan sat on his own bed—"it only mentioned Cahil and Husamettín walking through the city together."

"Then why do you assume it means *anything*? Maybe it was the two of them walking together a hundred fucking years ago."

"I assume so because Yusam assumed so. He wrote as much in the marginalia, and we both know his instincts were good when it came to such things."

"Yes, and we also know he was wrong as often as he was right."

"Well, it's something to go on," Ihsan said. "Unless you have some other brilliant plan?"

She glared at him. "Go fuck yourself."

"I'll pass," Ihsan said, and lay himself down. He wouldn't mind having a go at the priestess, though. He missed Nayyan, but he'd been parted from a woman's touch for too long, and there was no chance he'd be seeing his Queen any time soon.

A Queen, Ihsan thought. *Nayyan is a Queen now.*

It was but one of a thousand changes the city had undergone. The very tenor of life in Sharakhai felt altered, almost alien. Had he not known any better, he might have written off the feeling as stemming from his running around the west end like one of the lowborn, a thing that could easily convince someone of royal blood that the city had changed when really it hadn't.

But Ihsan *did* know better. The lesser Kings—a term that, counterintuitively, encompassed both the Kings *and* Queens of the new guard—had issued many new proclamations in his absence. Patrols of the Silver Spears were now common. As were their raids as they scoured the city for sympathizers of the Malasani or the Mireans. In a rather brilliant move, they'd managed to turn some of the Moonless Host to their side. Town criers called out news to all corners of the city, heaping praise upon the gains the Kings had made in the desert against their enemy, condemning the Mireans and the Malasani, and calling upon those who loved Sharakhai to help push the invaders out. They were demonizing all foreigners from the north or the east, even those who'd been living in Sharakhai for generations, even those with only a trickle of blood from those foreign lands running through their veins.

Blood runs thick in the desert, Ihsan mused.

The lesser Kings had reached out to the Moonless Host, freeing nearly everyone they had imprisoned, along with a message: join us, and together we shall save Sharakhai from her enemies. It seemed a simplistic gambit, but Ihsan had underestimated just how weary the scarabs of the Moonless Host and their sympathizers were of the war that had raged for generations. Many flocked to the Kings' cause, helping in the silent war where they could, seeing the offer as the Kings had hoped they would, as a way to turn over a new leaf and find a brighter day. It had Nayyan's fingerprints all over it. She wanted peace. She wanted to live in a city that was safe. Only then could she and Ihsan continue what they'd started and rule Sharakhai and the desert together.

It was a long game she played, which was precisely what was needed. And meanwhile, Ihsan was making moves in another long game. They'd had no word of Zeheb so far, but Ihsan had sent word to his own vizir, Tolovan. He hoped that Zeheb had reached out to the part of his family that had tried to kill him, and would come to an arrangement to share the power of his throne. Or that he'd reach out to the Kings for their help in pruning that particularly offensive branch from the family tree.

Tolovan had sent word only two days ago. *There is no contact yet, my lord King, but you will be informed the moment we learn of it.*

Cahil and Husamettín returned a short while later. Cahil flounced onto his bed in the corner. Husamettín, meanwhile, leaned against the wall near the door, crossed his arms over his chest, and stared down at Ihsan with his dour, disapproving stare.

"This can't go on, Ihsan. We need more clues."

"And we'll get them."

"When?"

"I wish I knew. But I trust in Yusam's vision."

Cahil took up a rag, wetted it from the ewer, and ran it over his forehead and the back of his neck. "You wave that vision around like a priest with an empty offering plate."

"Well, I'm sorry the fates haven't seen fit to grant us our wish immediately," Ihsan said evenly, "but I'm afraid I have no control over them."

Yndris, halfway to sleep, said, "What about Tolovan?"

"Well, I wouldn't know. We all agreed not to contact anyone from the House of Kings."

Yndris opened her eyes just long enough to roll them at the ceiling. "Let's pretend for a moment that you *had* contacted Tolovan. How might he have replied?"

Ihsan nearly smiled. Yndris had once been so brash—and make no mistake, she was still that—but life had filed off a few of the sharper burrs. "Well, I would wager that if I *had* reached out to Tolovan, he would have replied that there was no news of Zeheb so far and that he would notify his one-time King as soon as he learned anything different."

Cahil stared into the middle distance, then his gaze came to rest on Yndris. He actually smiled, the pride in him clear.

"And the other Kings?" Ihsan went on. "Supposing they reached out to their former houses, might *they* have found some hint of Zeheb's whereabouts?"

Cahil immediately said, "No."

Husamettín, normally so direct, was suddenly finding it difficult to meet Ihsan's eyes. With a brief guilty look, he shook his head like a surly adolescent who'd been caught stealing into the house early in the morning.

They'd all agreed not to contact their families, but of course they had. They each had their own designs on the city, after all. After months spent in the desert, the chance to see where each of them stood in the great game, and what moves they might make in response, had proved too tempting.

"Well, then," Ihsan said, "I propose we continue as we have been. Something will come up."

They ate a meal of dates, mild cheese with minced lemon zest, and some rosemary flatbread from the day before that was stale but when dipped in spiced olive oil was still quite tasty.

"I'm going out," Cahil said, and launched himself toward the door.

"To search?" Husamettín asked.

He stopped halfway through the doorway. "To *drink*!" And with that he closed the door behind him.

Yndris, all hints of her exhaustion now vanished, was up and following him in a flash. "Don't wait up!"

Husamettín stared at Ihsan, then the door, then at Ihsan again. Pushing himself off the wall, he said, "Coming?"

Ihsan shook his head. "A quiet night alone would be good."

Husamettín shrugged, then headed after the other two. Ihsan gave them a few minutes, then made his own way out and to the garden, looking for the pretty priestess. He ducked into the small temple, but found it empty. The refectory as well.

He was just going to head along the alley toward the wharf, thinking the clergy must have all left for some reason—some sort of celebration day in Kundhun?—when he noticed the door to the room Ihsan was sharing with the others was cracked open.

He approached warily, peering into the shadows of the courtyard, then into their room through the narrow crack left open in the door. But dusk had arrived, and it was simply too dark to see inside.

He drew his curved kenshar and stepped onto the stone porch along the front of the dormitory. He padded carefully toward the door. It creaked softly as he pressed it.

He'd only just taken a step inside when he heard footsteps pounding over the dusty courtyard behind him. He spun. Saw a shape outlined by the peaches and pinks still splashed across the western horizon.

"Halt!" he ordered.

But they kept coming.

"Halt!"

A tall man with wide shoulders barreled into him, drove him back into the room. Ihsan tripped over the corner of his own bed and fell hard to the floor. He'd no sooner turned over than the man fell on top of him.

"I command you to halt!" Ihsan grunted.

His power flowed—he could feel it—but it simply wasn't working.

The cool edge of a knife pressed against his throat. "Give me one more command," came a deep voice, "and I'll do more than take your tongue from you."

By the gods . . . "Zeheb?"

It was. It was Zeheb, dressed in the rich clothes of a Kundhuni caravan master. Taking a fistful of Ihsan's shabby khalat, and keeping the tip of his knife pressed beneath Ihsan's jaw, Zeheb drew Ihsan up and threw him onto his bed so hard that the back of his head cracked against the mudbrick wall, sending bits of brick and mortar raining onto the bed and the floor behind him.

Zeheb had been thin as a ghul when he'd escaped from their camp in the desert. He still looked haggard, but he'd clearly added weight since then.

"You're eating better," Ihsan said.

Zeheb slapped him hard. "For all you've done, I ought to kill you."

Ihsan's ears rang as he replied, "After long hours of torture, I suppose."

Zeheb slapped him again then gripped his throat. "Don't tempt me."

The ringing became worse. The pain over his cheek and ear stung badly and was long in clearing. "Zeheb, we've come a long way. We've been out to the desert and back. We've returned to a city that neither of us recognizes. There are strange games afoot, and I'd rather stop faffing about in the bloody west end and get to playing them in earnest so we can return to our thrones on the mount. So why don't you tell me why you've come so we can get on with it?"

Zeheb's breath came fast and heavy. He looked like he was having trouble ordering his thoughts. He blinked hard, a clear echo from his time of madness. If Ihsan were pressed, he'd guess that Zeheb was still prone to hearing the whispers, even when he didn't want to.

"Come, Zeheb. Get to the point."

"The Blue Journals," Zeheb replied, "is it true?"

"Is what true?"

"All of it. Nalamae. Sharakhai. The city being destroyed."

"If by true you mean, *Is it all truly in the Blue Journals?*, then yes. Just as I told the others."

Zeheb's hand tightened on Ihsan's throat. "Do *you* think it's true?"

"My good King," Ihsan rasped, "why *ever* would I have gone to all this trouble if I didn't?"

It took Zeheb some time to digest this. "What happens?"

"What do you mean?"

"To us? What do we do to help?"

"You find Nalamae using the whispers. We rescue her."

"From what?"

"I don't know."

Zeheb shook him harder still and kept shaking him. "From *what*?"

"In the account I read, the most lucid of Yusam's thoughts on the end, an angry god walks along the slopes of Tauriyat. I thought it was Goezhen but it might have been Thaash. The god nears a pillar of light and passes through it. A fog spreads from the rift, and all it touches is consumed. Men, women, children, all turn to dust. For many long years it spreads to the desert beyond, leaving all barren and lifeless and Sharakhai little more than a tomb."

Zeheb's gaze, distant as Ihsan had spoken, focused on Ihsan once more. "But Yusam was often—"

"I know what you're going to say. That Yusam was often wrong. And you're right, but this felt *true*, Zeheb. I felt it in my bones each time I read it. I swear to you, as surely as the Great Mother is merciless, *that* is where we're headed. That is what we have to stop."

Zeheb slowed his movements, then loosened his grip on Ihsan's neck. "And Nalamae helps?"

Ihsan nodded. "Nalamae helps. The journals weren't entirely clear, but this much is plain: after we find Nalamae, she regains her memories. She helps us save the city from the destruction that awaits it."

Zeheb's jaw worked. His eyes moved ceaselessly.

"Tell me your thoughts, Zeheb."

Slowly, his gaze returned to Ihsan. "Very well."

"Very well *what*?"

"I'll help you."

There was so much certainty in his eyes that it made Ihsan wonder. "You know something."

Zeheb nodded.

"You've found her, haven't you? You've found the goddess, Nalamae."

He nodded again. "I've found her, Ihsan."

"Where?"

"She's with Çedamihn."

Chapter 25

THE MORNING AFTER Queen Nayyan's unexpected arrival at Osman's estate, Kameyl burst into Çeda's room. "She's awake."

Çeda, who'd hardly had any sleep, was up in a flash, her grogginess vanishing as the weight of the moment began to settle on her. They found Lady Varal sitting in a chair in the far corner of her room with a wary look that almost, but not quite, hid the terror in her eyes.

Jenise was there, as was Sümeya. Queen Nayyan had apparently left some time during the night.

Çeda could already tell that this was going to go poorly if they were all in the room. Varal would only feel intimidated. "Leave us alone for a moment, won't you?" Çeda said to others.

They all seemed to understand and left, at which point Çeda closed the door and turned to Varal. "Would you like some tea? Some breakfast?"

Varal, her graying hair falling in her face, shook her head.

"You'll have many questions, I'm sure," Çeda ventured.

"You think you can ransom me?" Varal's chin quivered as she spoke. "Garner some favors from the Kings to secure my release? I tell you now, they'll not trade a thing for me."

Çeda felt horrible for having done this to her. The fear in Varal's eyes was once again making Çeda question herself and everything the mere had shown her. The vision hadn't been specific, after all. Varal might not be Nalamae herself, but the one to *lead* Çeda to her. But there had been no way to ensure they could find the truth of it other than to take her somewhere safe, to question her and see what came of it.

"I will explain all, but first I would ask you to hold this." She lifted Nalamae's staff from where it leaned against the wall, then held it out for Varal to take.

Varal stared at it, refusing to move a muscle.

"This will all go much faster if you just take the staff."

She looked as if she were going to decline, but then, hands shaking, she reached out and accepted it.

Çeda waited. She stared into Varal's eyes.

"What?" Varal asked.

There was no glimmer of recognition, nor any other change that Çeda could sense. Çeda even opened her senses and listened to her heart. She felt for something deeper. But there was nothing special about Varal. Nothing at all.

Varal twisted the staff in one hand, took in the gnarled head and the gemstones worked into the wood. "Am I supposed to do something with it?"

With a sigh, Çeda took it back, leaned it back against the wall, then scraped the other chair closer to Varal and sat down. "You know the goddess, Nalamae, of course."

"What child of Sharakhai doesn't?"

"Then prepare yourself for a wild tale."

Çeda proceeded to tell her all of it, how the goddess had chosen to remain away from Tauriyat on the night of Beht Ihman. The dark pact the Kings had made with the desert gods. The truth of the thirteenth tribe and the asirim. How the gods had chased Nalamae and killed her, over and over again.

When Çeda was done, Varal forged a smile of disbelief and genuine amusement. "And you think *I'm* Nalamae reborn?"

"Yes."

Varal's laugh was pure and bright and clear. "I can assure you that I'm not!"

"How would you know?"

She stared around the room with an expression of perfect impotence. "I grew up on the edges of the southern harbor. I've walked the decks of a thousand ships. I know every corner of every pier. I have a husband. I've had five children, two of whom died before their time. As our children grew, my husband, bless him, made time for me to apprentice with Yakinah herself, the finest shipwright the desert has ever seen." She pulled up the sleeve of her dusty workshirt and pointed to a long scar. "I got this when I slipped on freshly waxed skimwood and an iron bar caught my fall." She pointed to a host of small imperfections on the back of her hands. "These are from the endless war I wage to make the perfect ship." She pointed to a small puckered scar on her chin. "And I got this when Yakinah returned to the shipyard drunk and sent a chisel flying at my chin while trying to show me how her father used to beat her. I'm no goddess in disguise! I have my *own* life! I don't need another, certainly not a goddess's!"

Çeda replied in calm tones. "The mysteries of her rebirth cannot be explained. Not by me, anyway. Nalamae has been known to return as a babe. But she's also been known to come back as people who've already led full lives. She meant it to be so. It's how she avoids detection by other gods when she returns to this world. If she didn't, they would have killed her for good long ago."

Varal's whole demeanor had become one of sufferance, like a mother before a child who'd proclaimed that the sand in the desert came from the dried tears of the gods. "It's pretty convenient, don't you think?"

"What?"

"That all of my objections can be dismissed with the facile reply that it's Nalamae's will?"

"Isn't that always the way with the gods? Don't we always have to have faith?"

"You're expecting me to have *faith* in everything you're telling me?"

"Yes."

Varal threw her hands into the air. "Well I don't! I want to go back to my home. I want to see my husband again. I want to lose myself in his arms and forget this ever happened. I want to cook for my children and watch them grow."

"Let me explain something to you. By now the House of Kings knows why we took you. They were already hunting for Nalamae themselves. It's why she was shot through with an arrow by King Beşir. It's what led to her death in the mountains."

"So?"

"So what are the chances, knowing what you know of the situation, knowing what you know of the Kings, that they will let you live?"

Varal went perfectly still. The skin on her sun-weathered face went red. She hadn't even considered the notion, but now it was striking her like a charging akhala. She was a drowning woman, pleading to be saved, but Çeda couldn't. No one could. Now it was up to Varal herself and the goddess within.

"In her last incarnation as Saliah," Çeda said, "Nalamae kept an acacia tree with pieces of glass that granted visions. There is another such tree waiting for us near Mount Arasal. Let us go, let us visit the tree, and we'll see what happens then."

Tears had gathered at the corners of Varal's eyes. "I want to go home," she repeated.

"That is an option no longer available to you, Varal Andal'ava."

Varal blinked. Her tears fell, staining the wrinkled bodice of her gray dress. "Very well. I'll go to the mountains."

They prepared over the course of the day, planning to depart early the next morning just before dawn when the sky would be darkest. Osman offered to take them on his horses. He would escort them out to the *Red Bride*, then return home the following night after darkness had fallen.

"I don't know," Çeda had told him. "We've already asked so much of you."

"Let me do this for you." When she hesitated, he went on. "Think of it this way. If I'm with you, I can't tell anyone where you are."

Çeda laughed, and Osman laughed with her. It was the first time she'd seen him do so since they'd reached his estate.

"Thank you," she said, and kissed him on the cheek.

The following morning, he surprised her. He woke them while it was still dark and led them to the dining room, where he'd prepared a small feast. He'd prepared the horses as well. They weren't akhalas, but they all looked healthy, and would be fleet enough for their purposes. All six were fed, watered, saddled, and ready, each with a bag of provisions and skins of water, enough to last three or four days in the desert.

After breakfast, they stood in the barn by lamplight.

Kameyl, Sümeya, and especially Jenise went about their business quickly, saddling up, all eager to leave the city. Osman seemed pleased, almost proud. Varal, meanwhile, kept staring at the barn door, looking utterly unsure of herself.

"All will be well," Çeda said to her.

Varal nodded, and swung up to her saddle.

The rest were about to do the same when the sound of footsteps crunching over gravel came from beyond the open barn door. At first it sounded like a lone person approaching, but then it sounded like more.

Çeda drew her sword, as did the others, all except Varal, who bore no weapon.

"Those won't be necessary," came a voice from the edge of darkness. The words were slurred, as if the speaker were drunk. "Slide them back into their scabbards and remain still."

Çeda's right arm suddenly ached. The old adichara wound along the meat of her thumb flared to life, as it sometimes did when magic was being worked against her. She also felt an undeniable urge to do precisely what the voice had bid her.

By the light of the lamp hanging from a nearby beam, Çeda saw several silhouettes. Then from the darkness a man's form resolved. She recognized him immediately. Handsome King Ihsan, sleight of frame, wearing a light beard and a commoner's clothes. Behind him trailed three other men: tall King Husamettín, wearing a turban that almost, but did not quite, hide the scars on his forehead; King Cahil, whose face, as it had for four hundred years, seemed trapped between boyhood and manhood; and the last, a man with a broad frame who looked like he'd been starved of every meal for the past decade. He'd changed so much it took her a moment to recognize him. King Zeheb.

One more appeared. Yndris, Cahil's daughter. She wore a fighting dress and an expression that made Çeda want to slap it from her. "Well, well," Yndris said, "so the whispers spoke the truth."

Still trapped in Ihsan's command, Çeda was defenseless as Yndris walked up to her, gripped her shoulder, and punched her hard in the gut. Çeda's body curled around the blow, then fell to the barn's dirt floor.

King Ihsan sighed. "I told you to leave them alone."

"You told us not to kill them."

"Leave her be, Yndris," Ihsan commanded in a stronger voice, and this time Çeda felt power leeching into his words.

Çeda was facing away from the Kings and couldn't see what they were doing, but she heard one of them come nearer. "You said the vision spoke of the goddess and four other women." Cahil's voice.

"So?" Ihsan asked.

"It said nothing of a man."

A pause. "It didn't, but it wouldn't always—"

"You were in my care for a time," Cahil said. It took her a moment to realize he was no longer speaking to Ihsan, but to Osman.

No, Çeda tried to say. *No, no, no.*

She knew precisely what Cahil was about to do. He was just working himself up to it, as he often did. *Leave him!* she tried to scream, but she couldn't. She was prevented by the power of Ihsan's voice.

"Do you remember what I told you?" Cahil went on. "That if you ever defied the Kings again, I'd come back to deal with you?"

Please, don't do this!

"He *hasn't* defied the Kings," Ihsan interjected. "Not the rightful ones, in any case. We've all been gone."

Çeda heard the sound of metal sliding on metal. Çeda knew in her bones Cahil was drawing his hammer from the loop at his belt. "Close enough," Cahil said.

Words erupted from Ihsan's throat. "King Cahil, you will stop!"

Çeda felt the full power in that command, and yet a moment later there came a sickening crunch, followed by the sound of a body collapsing to the barn's earthen floor.

"No!" Çeda cried, breaking through Ihsan's spell at last. She fought. Tried to move her arms, tried to shift her legs. If she could move even a little bit, the rest would become easier. *He's alive,* she told herself. *He's still alive.* Though part of her already knew he wasn't.

"Gods *damn* you, Cahil," Ihsan said.

As if he'd just finished inspecting a horse and had decided not to buy it, Cahil sniffed. "I want you to understand me, Ihsan, and sometimes you must admit you have trouble focusing." A pause. "Do I have your attention now?"

"Yes."

"Good. Because I will do the same to you if you ever use your power on me or my daughter again."

With that Cahil's footsteps picked up, grew softer. A second set soon followed, Yndris trailing in her father's wake.

"Ihsan," came Husamettín's deep voice, "we have what we came for. It's time to go."

The horses were led away with Varal still on hers. The sounds dwindled, but one set of footsteps came nearer. Ihsan stepped over Çeda and crouched low, tilting his head so he could stare into her eyes. He wore an odd expression, a strange mixture of curiosity and regret.

"That was unfortunate," he said. "I know you were close." He glanced up toward the barn door. "I must know before I go. Is it true?" he spoke with an infuriating calm. "Is she the goddess reborn?"

Çeda refused to speak, but Ihsan repeated the question, and this time an ache developed inside her that was so acute she soon found herself answering in the only way she knew how. "I don't know."

"What do you mean?"

"*She* doesn't know," Çeda replied. "How could *I*?"

Ihsan nodded, as if that were a perfectly reasonable answer. Then his gaze drifted to her right hand, which had begun to twitch. His eyebrows pinched together, and she felt certain he was about to tell her to stop, to somehow reinforce his earlier command. But he didn't. He grunted, "Hmm," as if it were something he would dearly love to have studied further if prior commitments hadn't prevented it.

He stood and walked away, the sound of galloping horses came soon after, and Çeda was left alone with Sümeya, Kameyl, Jenise, and the body of a man she'd once loved.

A burning rage drove her. Her fingers had already begun to move, and the more she worked them, the more her arm and the rest of her body loosened. Soon she was pushing herself off the ground, jaw clenched, spittle flying from between her teeth as she released a long, seething moan.

She saw him at last: Osman, staring sightlessly through her, blood still oozing from a long cut in a deep depression in the crown of his head. "Oh, Osman," Çeda said, tears falling as she placed one hand on his stubbly cheek. "I'm so sorry I brought this upon you."

She left him there. She had to. There was no choice if she wanted to reach Varal in time. *Another thing Cahil and the others will pay for.* She reached her feet. She shifted on legs that felt heavy as lead until she was standing before Sümeya. "Wake, gods damn you. Fight him!"

She tried to extend her power to Sümeya. Tried to break the hold Ihsan's words still had on her. Whether it helped or whether it was Sümeya's will, or the simple fact that Ihsan was no longer near them, Çeda wasn't sure, but slowly she began to move. Çeda did the same with Kameyl and Jenise. Minutes passed. She was certain they were losing any chance they had of following the Kings. But she refused to give up.

As movement returned to the others in slow increments, Çeda rushed to the stalls, where only three horses remained. They would have to do. As Çeda saddled the first, Kameyl and Jenise did the same with the other two.

Sümeya, meanwhile, approached Çeda with a grim look in her eyes. "We'll go if you wish, but King Ihsan . . ." Her intent was plain. When they found the Kings, Ihsan could just command them to stop.

Çeda pointed to the bow and quiver of arrows at the back of her saddle. "Ihsan dies first, before we're close enough for him to use his voice. Now come," she said as she straddled the horse and held her hand out. "We owe the Kings a measure of justice."

Sümeya gripped forearms with Çeda and swung into the saddle behind her. Then the four of them were storming through the barn door, riding hard in the wake of the Kings.

Chapter 26

As THE DAYS PASSED for Brama and Mae, they continued to circumnavigate the blooming fields. Not once did Mae mention the grisly ritual Rümayesh had performed on the body they'd found. It wasn't for lack of courage. Mae was a brave woman, but some things were too dark to delve into, and she knew that discussing it wasn't going to change Rümayesh's dark urges.

At first, Mae kept her distance from Brama, remaining mostly silent, but as days passed into weeks, and they circled the entirety of the blooming fields, moving ever closer to the place they'd begun their circuitous journey, a sense of normalcy returned. Or what *passed* for normalcy—Mae trusted him only so far, and Brama fought daily to keep Rümayesh from regaining dominance.

"Near my home in Mirea, there are marshes," Mae said over a fire one night. "There are plants there, bodies shaping like bells. Bugs slip inside. Can't get out." She sipped jasmine tea as, nearby, her qirin, Angfua, snorted softly. "There are others, plants with leaves like ribbons that curl around spiders that try walking on them. Another with insides that moving like ants. It attract bright red beetles that can't escape once they go in. The dead help the plants live"—she waved toward the adichara trees—"so why these ones die, Brama? Why their food killing them?"

It was the very question Brama had been struggling with.

"Maybe the people attracted to them *because* the trees are dying," Mae submitted. "Their lure stronger in some way. Maybe trees *want* to die."

Brama poked the coals and watched the embers bloom. "Perhaps, though I think it more likely that they're being sent by someone to kill those specific trees, the diseased ones." They'd found no fresh tributes that *hadn't* been enveloped in a dead tree.

Staring into the fire, Mae nodded knowingly. She looked fierce like that, but wise as well, like one of the warrior poets her country was famed for. "Like pruning leafs to help sick plant."

"Maybe," Brama said, "but if so, it's not working. It's infecting the other trees around them. Whoever's doing it must know that by now."

"Why *must*?" Shadows played across Mae's round face and her bright green eyes as she considered Brama. "The Kings doing this for centuries, yes? With asirim gone, maybe they need keep it going. Appease the gods. Maybe they send them out and the cursed drawn to dying trees."

She had a point. The asirim *were* gone. Could it be that the tributes were still being sent from Sharakhai and simply left to the fates? Brama doubted it, but there was only one way to find out.

"Beht Zha'ir is nearly here again," he said. "We'll find another of the tributes, and get our answers."

"You free them?" Mae asked. "We question them together?"

"Yes," Brama said. He wasn't sure how he'd do it, but he would find a way.

Mae seemed both pleased and relieved. She was a dogged soldier. She wouldn't return to her queen without the answers she sought, but this mission was weighing on her—she wanted to be done with it and return to the Mirean camp.

As night fell on Beht Zha'ir, they waited near the blooming fields. The twin moons rose. Eventually they saw a lone figure weaving in and out of sight over the dunes, a boy of ten or eleven summers with a strange gait, trudging as if one ankle pained him. A clubfoot, Brama saw as he crested the dune ahead of them.

Suddenly, Brama felt a heat building inside him. A feeling like needles pricking his skin came soon after, the sensation rushing outward from his chest and down along his limbs.

He knew what was happening. It was Rümayesh. She was waging another assault against him.

He thought he'd been prepared. He tried to stand against her. He gripped the haft of his spear, calling upon the power of Raamajit, but he felt nothing. Somehow Rümayesh had walled him off from that well of power, precisely as *he'd* done to *her* over the months since they'd become one.

Gods, he'd been so confident. He often slipped when he was tired, but he'd been taking such care, and now he felt himself falling. He tried to touch the lump on his forehead but got no further than a swaying of his hand, a thing Rümayesh, overwhelming him entirely, turned into a beckoning motion.

"Come," Rümayesh called to Mae, and began walking toward the blooming fields.

No, Brama cried from within. *No, no, no!* His astonishment at how quickly it had happened was matched only by his terror about what would happen next.

Mae, clearly confused, waved to the boy. "Are you stopping him?" When Rümayesh made no reply, Mae followed. "Brama, are you stopping him?"

"The answers we seek are difficult ones," Rümayesh replied, "and it's doubtful the boy will have them on his own."

The boy limped between them, but Mae grabbed him by the scruff of his threadbare shirt. The boy fought, but not hard.

"Free his mind, Brama!" Mae shouted. "As we agree, free his mind!"

Rümayesh's response was to lift one hand and with a gust of sudden wind send Mae flying backward along the sand.

The boy fell too, but then he stood and moved on as if nothing had happened. Rümayesh followed. Mae, meanwhile, was slow in getting up. She coughed hard, then came lumbering forward as if it pained her to move. By the time she caught up to them, Rümayesh and the boy stood within a clearing. Nearby was a dying adichara, its blooms vastly weaker than those of the trees surrounding it. That was where the boy was headed. That was where he would die.

"You wanting to use him," Mae said, "like you use the other. You *letting* him die so you can hang his insides from the trees."

"You'd be surprised what answers you can get from the blood of the living and the light of the stars."

Brama was horrified that Rümayesh would do this, but he was also confused. They both knew that to kill the boy would make Brama all the more desperate. It would likely give him the resilience he needed to tip the balance back toward him, so why do it? Out of simple cruelty? It all became clear when Rümayesh turned to find Mae with her bow drawn, a diamond-tipped arrow nocked. The arrow's shaft, made of some lustrous white wood, shone in the night, almost luminous under the glow of the adichara blooms.

Rümayesh wanted Mae dead. That was what this gambit was all about. She couldn't attack Mae outright, though. Kill her and she risked ceding control of Brama's body, perhaps for a long while. But get Mae to attack *her* and part of Brama would want to defend himself. Rümayesh could accomplish two goals in one fell swoop: rid herself of Mae, a stabilizing influence in Brama's life, and the guilt resulting from her death would send Brama into a well of despair, a thing that might take him days, weeks to get himself out of. It would give Rümayesh more than enough time to gain dominance over him permanently.

The knowledge drove him to desperation. He railed against his bonds, but it did him no good. Rümayesh was too powerful. She had too great a hold on their shared form.

"Let him go," Mae said with conviction.

"If we want answers for your queen"—Rümayesh waved to the spellbound boy—"this is what is needed."

"I know who you are." Mae drew the string of her bow to her ear. "I know Brama gone."

"Then you know that to kill me is to kill Brama too."

"I think Brama doesn't mind."

When Brama saw Mae's face pinch, he knew what she was about to do. He tried to stop Rümayesh, tried to suppress the power she was gathering. But he was too late. Too weak.

Mae loosed the arrow. Rümayesh swept her arm up to ward the arrow away, but the arrow remained unaffected—the spell slipped from it like water on oiled canvas.

It punched into Brama's side, sent him spinning to the sand. One moment, the pain was oddly muted, but then Rümayesh's will retreated and it struck Brama full force.

"The boy," Brama growled through gritted teeth. "Get him away. Save him, Mae."

Had the adichara been healthy the boy would have been consumed by now, but as it was the desiccated branches were only just reaching around him. Mae sprinted forward, sand kicking up in tails behind her. She yanked him to the ground just before the branches encompassed him. The boy thrashed, somehow managed to regain his feet. He nearly dove into the adichara, but Mae tripped him and pinned him to the sand again.

By then Brama had made it to his knees. The arrow wound flared, forge-bright, but Brama was used to pain. With a snarl, he snapped the shaft and pulled the arrowhead free. Moving as quickly as he could, he shifted across the sand to the boy. Using his own blood, he drew symbols on his forehead, ancient runes that dispelled the compulsion laid upon him. He hadn't known them before, but it was easy to do now, with Rümayesh's mind so closely linked with his.

Slowly, the boy's thrashing subsided. His worried look became one of confusion. Instead of focusing on the adichara, he stared with terror-filled eyes at Mae and Brama.

"It's all right," Brama said softly. "You've had a bad dream is all."

Brama tried to delve into the boy's memories, but everything before that morning was fuzzy. After stacking a cartload of grain, he'd snuck behind the storehouse to pass water and had turned at the sound of footsteps scuffing along the alley behind the mill. He'd no more than spotted a shadow when his memories went dim.

As Brama helped him to stand, the boy took in the trees as if he feared they would attack him. He touched one closed fist to his forehead. "Forgive me, hajib, but why am I here?"

"A good question," Brama replied. "Would you like to know more?"

The look of fear on his face hadn't diminished, but he nodded just the same. *Braver than I would have been at his age*, Brama thought.

As soon as they left the adichara grove, Mae whistled a trilling note. Moments later, Angfua came trotting through a gap between two of the adichara groves, trumpeting as it came, throwing its coiled horns this way and that as if readying for battle. Kweilo, Brama's temperate mare, trotted calmly in Angfua's wake.

"I'll return when I'm able," Brama said to Mae.

Mae, however, had gone to Angfua's saddlebags. She'd taken out a piece of paper and was writing on it with a coal pencil.

"Mae?"

She finished her note, rolled it up, and stuffed it inside her saddle bag. "I know you not know me well," Mae said as she tied Kweilo's reins to the pommel of Angfua's saddle, "but if you think you going to Sharakhai without me, you have—how you say?—an other think coming."

"Mae—"

"I know you trying to get rid of me, Brama. But I don't go. You are my friend. I don't give you to her. Understand?"

Brama swallowed while the boy stared on, his confusion plain. Mae, meanwhile, pointed to the trail the boy had made in coming here and proceeded to remove her armor and change into simpler clothing.

"Well, we are going or not?" she asked.

Mae was taking a serious risk by coming with him, but the relief he felt was so great that he couldn't find it in himself to deny it. "We're going," he said.

Mae nodded, satisfied. "Good."

She whispered into Angfua's ear, and the qirin snorted loudly. It trumpeted, releasing a gout of flame, but then seemed to accept its fate and began cantering east into the desert, toward the Mirean fleet, with Kweilo in tow.

As their mounts were lost behind the line of trees, Brama and Mae set off, following the boy toward Sharakhai.

Chapter 27

EMRE WALKED WITH Shaikh Neylana over the dunes, their strides falling into a sympathetic rhythm. Behind them, Tribe Halarijan was preparing to depart. So were Emre's ships, but Neylana had agreed to grant Emre an audience first. The dunes were tall where they walked, the sand *slippery*, as they said among the southern tribes. It helped along the declines, the sand practically pouring one toward the trough, but made it doubly hard on the inclines as one's legs churned furiously to overcome the sand's give.

By the time they reached the fourth crest, Neylana was breathing hard. Emre was too, but worse, his head was pounding. Neylana, taking note, slowed her pace and navigated the top of the snaking dune instead of heading down the decline. "You're leaving," she said as she waved toward the *Amaranth* and the trio of frigates beyond, "but I wonder, will it be to return to your tribe or to find Hamid?"

"I suspect if I do the former I'll end up with the latter."

A smile seemed to want to break out over Neylana's stony face, but it was an incongruous thing, like a lizard trying to grin. "I was like you, at your age."

Emre started to laugh but choked it back, which sent him into a short coughing fit. Feeling the weight of Neylana's stare, he pretended to find the dunes in the distance terribly engrossing.

"I know what you must think," she said. "Many say there's no humor in me. That I'm too severe. I was once carefree, though. I made *jokes*, if you can believe it. But sadly, the mantle of shaikh is a millstone that grinds you down until all that remains is dust."

"It's a heavy weight to bear."

"You have no idea. Not yet. But you will."

Emre thought she was toying with him, but she looked serious as a hungry lioness. "I'm no shaikh," he said.

"No, but you've captained a ship. You've bargained with a foreign adversary, then played the grand game with him and won. You've convinced an aging shaikh to join an alliance against her better judgment. I see the care you have for others and the shrewdness that's needed to do anything about it. Just you wait. Unless I'm sorely mistaken, the title of shaikh is not far off."

"*Macide* is our shaikh."

The laugh from Neylana was like a tumble of bones. "You may not have noticed, but the Great Mother has a way of culling the herd. She's quite good at it."

"Well *you've* managed to keep her at bay."

As they crested a dune and headed along the leeward side, Neylana hawked and spat. "Let's see how funny you think that is when I bury you up to your neck in sand for the beetles to eat."

"I'm afraid I won't taste very good."

Neylana rolled her eyes. "Please don't tell me you're too sweet."

"No, too *bitter*. I'm becoming more like you already."

He said it with a wink. Neylana tried to hide her amusement, but then laughed. It felt honest and true, all the more so for how rare it was. Emre laughed with her while veil-thin clouds traveled in packs across the deep blue sky.

"So you'll return to your tribe, our final offer in hand. Will Macide accept?"

"It isn't a generous offer," Emre said truthfully, "but it's fair. I think Macide will agree to it."

"A desert united," Neylana said.

"A desert united."

"And in the meantime, Queen Meryam grows impatient. She'll want an answer from the tribes. What do you suppose Macide's position will be?"

"She didn't *make* that offer to the thirteenth tribe, only the other twelve."

"When she sees we're all united, she will."

"You're asking me what Macide will do with an offer from the woman whose sister he killed?" Emre shrugged. "It's difficult to say."

"Try," Neylana replied, making it clear she expected an answer before he left.

"I think he'll give it due consideration. Truly. I wasn't lying when I said Macide wants peace in the desert. He sees the presence of Mirea and Malasan as an offense that needs addressing, a rare bit of common ground between the tribes and the House of Kings. If Sharakhai and the tribes were to fight together to drive them away, it could lead to a lasting peace."

"And if, after all that, the lesser Kings and Queens take up their fathers' ways? If they resume their silent war against us once the invaders are gone?"

"Things can't go back to the way they were. Sharakhai is weaker than it once was. It will be weaker still by the time the war is over. The tribes will take what's rightfully ours. No more, no less."

"Spoken like a true shaikh." Neylana gave him a wry smile. It was like a window into the past, a rare glimpse of the woman she was *before* she'd taken up her father's sword.

"You know," Emre said, "I think we might have been friends if we'd met before you became shaikh."

"Might've been a lot more than that, Emre Aykan'ava."

The suggestive wink she gave him made his cheeks go red.

As he turned to see if anyone had witnessed it, Neylana's peals of laughter filled the dry desert air.

Emre was sailing toward Mount Arasal on the *Amaranth*, their three frigates trailing behind, when a ship was spotted along the horizon.

"A royal galleon," Sirendra said while peering through a spyglass.

She handed the glass to Emre, who lifted it to one eye. Indeed, the ship had the lines of a navy vessel but looked to be in poor shape. The canvas was patched and plagued with holes, and part of the stern was missing, gouged out in some battle, perhaps.

"What in the great wide desert could have inflicted that sort of damage?" Emre asked.

"I don't know," Sirendra answered, "but they're turning to match our course."

Nearby, Frail Lemi cracked his knuckles. "Time for a fight, Emre?"

"No. I don't like the look of it." Emre handed the spyglass back to Sirendra. "Let's see if we can't outrun it."

They tried. They put on more sail, they cut more carefully across the dunes, which rolled easily but could sap speed from the skis if the pilot wasn't careful, yet the strange galleon still gained on them.

By midday it loomed a quarter-league off the starboard quarter. The hair at the nape of Emre's neck was starting to rise. The galleon's hull and decks showed swaths of dry rot, making it look like it had been burned, the fire put out, and the ship put into service again. Stranger still was the crew. They wore the white tabards of the Silver Spears, but the fabric was torn and dirty. They limped from place to place, listless as plague men. Many had limbs missing. Others had gaping wounds in their necks, arms, or chests. One was missing half his face.

Dead, Emre said to himself, feeling suddenly cold. *They're all dead.* "Prepare fire pots," he ordered Sirendra, "quickly. And ready the asirim."

On the ship of the dead, the ship's captain, a woman, stood on the foredeck. She wore a violet dress and a black head scarf, the tails of which snapped in the wind. Her skin was dark like a Kundhuni tribeswoman, but it glinted under the sun as if she'd been dipped in crushed emeralds. Cupping her hands to her mouth, she bellowed across the distance, "Halt, that we may speak."

Beside the captain stood a man with a peg leg, the only crewman not dressed in the uniform of a Silver Spear. The first mate, perhaps? He wore trousers, a clean white kaftan, and a fashionable coat. "I really would listen to her if I were you," he shouted in a theatrical voice. "She is Anila, Dealer of Death, Destroyer of All Who Would Deny Her."

It was difficult to tell at this distance, but the woman seemed to take a moment to gather her patience. "I ask you to halt a second time! I won't ask again."

Four fire pots had been lit: one on the *Amaranth*, three more on the nearby frigates, all waiting for Emre's signal to launch. "I'll tell you only once," he shouted in return, "turn away while you still can."

The mate standing next to Anila cringed. "Might you consider telling us to *turn away before you light our ship like a beacon*?"

The strange, pregnant pause that followed was broken by Frail Lemi's booming laughter.

"That seems a bit on the nose, doesn't it?" Emre shouted, pointedly *not* looking at Frail Lemi.

The first mate waggled his head. "The audience wants what it wants!"

Frail Lemi's laughs rose even higher. "I like that one."

"That's *enough*, Fezek," Anila said.

Sirendra, meanwhile, came up beside Emre. "The asirim won't come. They're huddled in the holds, whimpering, refusing all commands."

Breath of the desert, this was spiraling out of control. "Speak to me now," Emre called. "I'll answer as I can, then you and your ship can be on your way."

"Not good enough."

Emre wished it hadn't come to this, but he refused to risk the safety of his ships and their crews. He nodded to Sirendra, who whistled a series of notes. A moment later, the first catapult launched, its arm striking the cross-member with a resounding thud. The fire pot arced through the air.

"You've made a very poor decision!" cried the first mate, Fezek.

The cold inside Emre grew deeper as the captain of the dead, Anila, traced a sign in the air before her. A white mist flowed from her hands. A blue glow trailed like a pennant behind her swiftly moving fingertip.

The fire pot shattered halfway to the galleon. Flaming oil and shards of pottery fluttered through the air, a swarm of orange and yellow moths that fell well short of the galleon to patter harmlessly against the sand. The black smoke lifting from the patchwork of flames was borne on eddying currents as the galleon, unharmed, sailed on.

The second firepot exploded while it was still in the catapult's cradle. The Shieldwife tending to it reared away in surprise, triggering the arm's release, causing the flames to spray over the frigate's quarterdeck. The crew set to immediately, throwing handful after handful of blue dousing agent to snuff the burgeoning fires.

By then Emre had taken up his bow and had three arrows pinched between his fingers. In a practiced move, he nocked the first, aimed at the captain while drawing the string to his ear, and let fly. Anila, meanwhile, had drawn another glowing blue symbol in the air. The arrow warped. Its path curved sharply. Instead of hitting Anila, it struck Fezek directly in the chest.

"Hey!" Fezek called with an annoyed expression, and pulled the arrow free with a mighty grunt.

Emre tried twice more but both arrows winged away like wounded doves. When he paused his fire—a terrible mistake in retrospect—Anila drew a third sigil. There was so much frost pouring from her hands it looked like smoke from a signal fire. She spread her hands. Arched her head back. Sirendra and two other Shieldwives tried to take Anila down with arrows of their own, but by then several of the crew were standing in front of her, holding shields to protect her. As the arrows thumped ineffectually into the shields, a cracking sound came, a rending.

Emre turned just in time to see a white crack forming on the nearest frigate's rudder strut, the thick support that ran from the turning mechanism inside the hull to the rudder's ski. Like Anila's hands, a white fog issued from that crack, then wood started to flake around it.

Emre ran to the starboard gunwales shouting, "Drop the rake! Drop the rake!"

But it was too late. The rudder gave way and the ship's stern dropped to the sand with a resounding boom that Emre felt in the gorge of his stomach.

The frigate's masts swayed menacingly. The sails thrummed. The ship slowed precipitously, and the crew were thrown to the deck. Two Shieldwives pinwheeled overboard and were lost in the spray and dust kicked up by the dragging hull.

"Drop rakes!" Emre bellowed. "All ships drop rakes!" Hearing the asirim howling within the frigates' holds, he turned to Sirendra. "I don't *care* if they've suddenly turned scared," he said to her, "order them up. Have them protect the fallen ship."

She nodded, clearly confused as to why the asirim had become so agitated. As she relayed the orders, the ship of the dead dropped its rake as well. It slowed, coming to a rest along the frigate's starboard side. A dozen ghulish soldiers dressed in white swarmed over the gunwales and onto the frigate's decks, coming to blows with the Shieldwives and the sandsmen who crewed her. The asirim, even with their ship under attack, remained inexplicably belowdecks.

When the *Amaranth* had come to a stop at last, Emre, Frail Lemi, and ten Shieldwives dropped to the sand and sprinted toward the wounded frigate. Only two asirim joined them: Huri and Imwe, the bloodthirsty twins bonded to Sirendra. They howled over the sand with their strange gaits. As they came near the ship of the dead, however, they stopped and would come no nearer.

"What is it?" Sirendra asked them.

The two of them only cringed, refusing to speak, forcing Emre and the others to go on without them.

By then the crew of dead soldiers had dragged the wounded frigate's Shieldwives and crew, twenty in all, down to the sand. Anila was there, standing in the shadow of her galleon, while her crew lined the prisoners up. From the galleon itself came the sound of rattling chains and a strange, rhythmic pounding. The entire ship trembled from it. A feeling of dread churned in Emre's gut. There was something terrible inside that ship.

Anila had her arms raised in a gesture of peace. Her mate, Fezek, stood beside her. Now that they were close it was clear that, though Fezek was a ghul too, he had the brightness of intelligence. Not so the ones in the tatty chainmail armor and threadbare tabards of the Silver Spears, who pressed their captives onto the sand and held bent, pitted swords to their necks.

"Order everyone to lower their weapons," Anila said to Emre, "especially that bloody great giant standing beside you."

Frail Lemi gripped the haft of Umber, his greatspear, and looked in no mood to let go of it, nor did Emre truly want him to, but there were lives at stake. The weight of the decision bore down on him, a thing made all the more difficult by the terrible headache he felt coming on. It grew so bad, so quickly, stars burst across his field of vision.

"Do as she says," he said through the growing pain. "Now," he added when they made no move to comply.

Finally they did. Their weapons thumped to the sand, all but Frail Lemi's.

Emre touched Frail Lemi's shoulder. "This isn't the fight we want, Lem. Save it for Hamid."

The muscles along Frail Lemi's jaw worked. A glimmer of understanding shone through his blood lust. He nodded, then let Umber fall to the sand with a thud.

Anila stepped closer with an intense look in her eyes that made Emre fear she was about to transform him into one of her ghuls. It made his headache feel all the worse.

Suddenly the pounding from inside the galleon came louder—*boom, boom, boom*. Everyone turned toward it, even the dead crewmen. All except Anila, who seemed transfixed by Emre. "You've known death," she said to him. "You've known it as I've known it."

Emre swallowed hard. "I doubt I know it half as well as you."

With another few steps, she came within arm's reach of him. "A shadow of it lays upon you still."

"Yes." For some reason, the admission intensified his pain. He couldn't so much as look at Frail Lemi or Sirendra for fear the stars would multiply and swallow him up.

Anila's night-black skin glinted in strange patterns as she lifted one finger toward his forehead. "Would you like me to remove it from you?"

"No!" he said, louder than he'd meant to. He had no idea what Anila could do to remove the pain, but he knew better than to bargain with a woman who'd been kissed by the lord of all things.

Anila lowered her hand, disappointed, and the wonder faded from her eyes. "So be it." Her look turned deadly serious. "I've a few simple questions for you. Things you'll not mind giving up but which are extraordinarily important to me."

Boom. Boom thoom.

"Ask what you will," Emre said, glancing warily at the galleon. "I'll answer as I can."

"Where have you just come from?"

"We sailed from the southwest."

Fezek stepped in. "She means, what were you doing and with whom were you doing it?"

"We met with Tribe Halarijan." He gave Anila the broad strokes of the Alliance and his reasons for meeting with Shaikh Neylana.

Anila's eyes narrowed as if she were peering into his mind. "But you went with another purpose in mind, did you not? A more personal purpose?"

Emre blinked. "How could you know that?"

Something inside the ship moaned, a thing that made Emre's skin crawl.

"Please just answer the question," Fezek said.

Emre ignored him, focusing only on Anila. "I went to right a wrong."

"A wrong committed by someone you knew," Anila said. "Someone you've known a long while."

"Yes, but—"

"Name him."

Before Emre could answer, the galleon was struck from within with so much force the hull boards cracked. Bits of wood sprayed outward then floated down, drifting on the breeze. A metallic clinking, a sound like chains being dragged over wood, accompanied it. Part of Emre wanted to know what was inside that ship, but another, much larger part just wanted to get out of there before the demon broke free and devoured them all.

"His name is Hamid," he said to Anila. "I tried to settle a score with him, but it didn't go as well as I'd hoped." He told her how he'd reached Tribe Halarijan, how the tribe's physic had healed him as well as she could, how he'd planned his revenge when he'd learned Hamid would be coming to treat with Neylana to convince her to join the Alliance.

"And where is he now?" Anila asked.

"Gone. Escaped on a skiff."

"Headed where?"

Emre shrugged. "I'm not certain, but I suspect he'll return to the tribe and try to poison Macide against me."

"And where are they now, the tribe? Where is Macide?"

"That information isn't mine to give."

Anila took a half step closer. "I need it."

"I won't give it to you."

She'd just reached up, her hand beginning to frost, when Fezek cleared his throat.

Anila stopped. Her lips were pulled back like a bone crusher ready to bite. "What *is* it, Fezek?"

"I rather think you have enough already, don't you?"

As the sun beat down, Anila looked unsure of herself. She glanced at her ship. Whatever was belowdecks had gone still. The pounding had ceased. Anila had a curious expression, as if she knew Fezek was right but didn't want to admit it. Her hand, which had been emitting a soft sizzling sound, went quiet, and the white fog trailing from it ceased. Without even bothering to look at Emre, she stalked away and up the gangplank to her ship.

"We sail!" she said. Her crew of ghuls followed, leaving only Fezek on the sand.

"I'm sorry about all this," Fezek said, his hands spread wide, "but I think you'll look back on this one day and count yourselves lucky. Perhaps it will lessen the sting to know that this will all be immortalized in the greatest epic poem the desert has ever seen, penned by none other than Fezek, the Warrior Poet of Sharakhai!" With that, he bowed like an actor at a curtain call, then headed up the plank after the others.

They were soon gone, leaving Emre, Frail Lemi, the Shieldwives, and crew to stare, bewildered, at its ponderous, dwindling shape.

Chapter 28

AS HER GALLEON GAINED SPEED, Anila went to the hatch at the center of the main deck and slid it aside with a shove of her foot. When she'd descended the ladder far enough, Fezek closed the hatch behind her—darkness, she'd found, was best when speaking to the creature below. The lack of airflow made the stink worse, though. She took a moment to become accustomed to it, knowing it would only grow worse.

As she descended further into darkness, the stench intensified to the point that she took out her sachet of dried rose petals and held it to her nose—the scent didn't help much, but it kept her from emptying her stomach all over the deck. She reached the ship's hold, where sunlight speared through gaps in the hull. The hold had been altered toward the ship's stern. The berth deck had been carved out, creating a large, open space, but the ehrekh chained to the deck still made it look small.

The ehrekh, Guhldrathen, was twice Anila's height—more if one counted the sweeping horns atop his head—and easily ten times as massive, what with his brawn and the twin tails that twitched lazily as she approached. Thick manacles of ebon steel bound his wrists and his taurine ankles. The chains attached to the manacles were anchored to the hull's exposed ribs, preventing him from moving far. The chains had been proof against his terrible strength so far. He was beholden to her necromantic powers as well, and yet Anila still feared what he would do were he to escape.

To remind him, she released a bit of her hold on his soul as she stepped closer. He slipped toward death, a thing that caused him pain and terror.

Guhldrathen moaned piteously. Dozens of wounds marring his black skin became clear, none so large as the ragged gash in his stomach that exposed his rotting innards. His head twisted lazily as if in a fever dream, while around him lay the strongest layer of protection: a halo of sigils drawn in Anila's own blood, their precise construction guided by Guhldrathen after she'd compelled him. "Show me how to create a prison," she'd bade him, "a prison that will keep you until my quest to find Hamzakiir is complete."

Like everyone in the desert, word had come to Anila of the Battle of Blackspear, the clash that had seen Kings pitted against tribes and where Guhldrathen had been killed by another ehrekh, Rümayesh. After leaving Davud at the Bay of Elders months ago, Anila had made for the site of the battle and eventually found the wrecks, a graveyard of broken ships. Soon after, she'd found Guhldrathen's half-buried remains.

It had taken her eight days to raise him from the dead, but she had patience, and her time with King Sukru had trained her well. She'd eventually done it.

The ehrekh were strange creatures, though. They were mystical and ancient, difficult to control. Keeping Guhldrathen alive was a constant drain, but it had all been worth it. She'd forced him to use his magic to guide her toward Hamzakiir, the blood mage who'd kidnapped her along with Davud and their entire graduating class, and learn how she might defeat him once she did. At Guhldrathen's instruction, she'd used her own blood and drawn sigils around his body where he lay in the hold. Guhldrathen became the focus of the spell. The sigils hemmed him in and granted him the second sight he needed to provide Anila the answers she sought.

Even with Guhldrathen's ability to peer into the future, though, finding Hamzakiir had been anything but simple. Hamzakiir's life was a thread complicated by dozens of equally powerful threads. Guhldrathen instructed her to sail to this place or that, to gather information for him, which he used to refine his scrying, his ability to perceive the path that would deliver

Hamzakiir to her. So they sailed. They searched and they scried. Days became weeks became months, and Anila felt no nearer to the man she had vowed to kill than when they'd begun their journey.

"Well?" Anila asked when she'd come near. "You heard Emre's answers."

Guhldrathen's head rolled toward her, and the tip of one horn clunked against the deck boards. "Blood," he said. His deep, rasping voice made Anila's skin feel as if worms were crawling beneath it.

"You've *enough* blood."

His milky eyes blinked. Death had robbed Guhldrathen of his mundane sight. All that remained was his farsight, his ability to see things beyond the ken of man. "The answers thou seekest art close." His throat convulsed, the rhythm like waves lapping against some dark, distant shore. "Give me thy blood, but a taste, and thou shalt have them."

When she said nothing, his head swayed. His twin tails thumped harder, and in stranger rhythms. Anila felt her eyes begin to roll up into her head, felt her grip on reality slipping.

"Stop it!" she snapped, and fixed her will on Guhldrathen.

Unlike mortal souls, the souls of ehrekh did not pass to the world beyond. They lingered about the body instead, slowly dissipating over time. Again she let his soul slip toward death.

"Have mercy!" His moaning made the deck boards shake. "Have mercy!" Only when he'd uttered his plea a third time did she draw his soul close and allow his pain to ease. For a time he was silent, but then he swung his sightless gaze toward her once more. "Thy blood," he insisted piteously. "I need but a taste."

She considered torturing him until he obeyed, but they were so close. Her curiosity won out. She came nearer to him while pricking her wrist with a blooding ring. She held the wound over his open maw, and his forked tongue lapped at the drizzle that flowed from it. When Anila sealed the wound, he licked his bloodstained teeth clean, then pulled his lips back in a beatific smile.

Gods, what a gruesome thing to behold. "Give me my answers, Guhldrathen. Tell me where to find Hamzakiir."

"Thy quest wends not so straight as that. But thou art closer. The man who died beneath the sand and was returned . . ."

"Emre?"

Guhldrathen nodded. "Follow the one who betrayed him, and thou wilt find Hamzakiir."

The one who betrayed him. He meant Hamid, who'd attacked Emre and nearly killed him. "And where is *he* going?"

"Mazandir," Guhldrathen said with a leering smile. "The winds of fate bear him toward Mazandir."

Chapter 29

BY THE TIME Ihsan and the other Kings reached *The Wayward Miller*, the sky was bright with the coming dawn. While the ship was being prepared, Ihsan led the woman, Varal, down to one of the cabins and tied her to the bunk with lengths of rope. He'd been trying since leaving Osman's estate to find hints that she was anything more than an aging shipwright, but had so far found none.

"Is it true?" he asked when the ropes were secured. "You have no memory of Nalamae?"

Strangely, the command he'd given her to obey had already worn off—which Ihsan would need to consider carefully when he had time—but the woman seemed all too eager to answer his questions. "No, Your Excellence. This has all been a terrible mistake. I swear to you, I don't know those women! They ambushed me in the harbor and spirited me away. They're *crazed* if they think I'm some goddess."

Ihsan had no doubt she believed those words, but the account he'd read, the one he'd been working to make reality for so long, spoke of him and three other Kings finding the goddess in a horse stall. In the vision, she lay there, weak, her hand pressed against a deep wound to her gut. It wasn't exactly how things had gone—Varal had no major wounds that Ihsan could see—but it was closer than most of Yusam's visions. The entry hadn't described her likeness other than to say a disk of golden light surrounded her head, a light that seemed to grow stronger the more she bled. It was a momentous vision, but it was the closing words that had stunned Ihsan. The vision recounted three women storming toward the woman's stall, swords drawn, followed by a voice that *seemed to shatter the heavens*.

It was Ihsan's own voice Yusam had been describing, and it had been the first piece of evidence that led Ihsan to believe he could find a way to regain his tongue. Yusam had made it abundantly clear the vision was one of the most important he'd ever seen. He'd not only stated it plainly, but the marginalia supported it—dozens of notes and ruminations had been scribbled in tiny script, most of which led Ihsan to other, related entries.

It was frustrating beyond measure to be this close and still have no idea how to proceed. It was still possible they had the wrong woman. Or it might have been the return of Ihsan's voice or the command he gave that was of primary importance in Yusam's vision. And there was one problem Ihsan had been wrestling with for months: the very nature of Nalamae's rebirths might obfuscate prophetic visions, thereby safeguarding her return. How else to explain why Yusam, despite trying many times, had never managed to locate the goddess in any of her previous incarnations?

"My lord King?" Varal said.

Ihsan was so lost in thought he lifted his hands, ready to sign to her. Remembering himself, he made a show of scratching his neck. "I'm afraid your nature has yet to be proven, one way or the other."

"You could command me!" She was practically breathless. "Ask me anything you wish. I'll prove I'm a simple woman of Sharakhai."

He smiled at her sadly. "I'll ask you only one question, and I won't even use my power to compel your answer."

She smiled as the ship lurched into motion. "Anything, my lord King."

"Nalamae has been hiding from her fellow gods for centuries. She has evaded them time and time again, falling only after decades of searching by her brethren. If she could avoid *them*, beings molded by the hands of the elder gods, how in the great wide desert would *you*, a simple shipwright by your own admission, know if the goddess had been reborn within you?"

She opened her mouth to speak several times, then said, "I just would." But the faint flame of hope was already fading. As she fell back onto the bed and stared at the ceiling, the flame flickered and went out.

Ihsan shut the door behind him and returned to deck. The sun was rising in the east, a bright, half-lidded eye. The harbor around them was just coming to life, a dozen crews working the ships of a caravan, preparing them to sail for the harbor's exit, which lay between two tall lighthouses. Ahead of *The Wayward Miller*, one sloop had beaten them to the sands and was slowing itself for inspection by two royal galleons.

The officials aboard the galleons would want to search the *Miller*, too, but Ihsan would command them to give a cursory inspection and allow them to move on, just as he had on their arrival. He was vastly more concerned about Çeda and her allies. He'd withheld a second watershed moment from the Blue Journals from his fellow Kings. In it, Çeda was riding across the sands on a horse, sword held high, as if she were ready to chop a man's head from his shoulders.

What followed, Yusam had written, *was dark, filled with blood and terror. I woke screaming from it. It wasn't what I saw that is important here, but what I felt. There was hunger and malicious intent. A jealousy so deep it would drive a man to commit any sin. It was one of the rare cases of seeing through another's eyes. I believe it was an ehrekh. It must be. The feelings were too inhuman for it to be otherwise.*

Ihsan felt certain the vision would take place here, today, but he hadn't mentioned it to anyone lest it upset the delicate tightrope act that was leading them toward Nalamae's awakening. *In the blink of an eye,* the entry had finished, *a spark is thrown, a light equal to the darkness is born, and that grand malignancy is driven back whence it came.*

A spark, Ihsan mused. *Some must burn before they truly shine.*

Ahead, the sloop had been cleared and was gliding past the checkpoint. The *Miller*'s crew slowed the ship, and the pilot steered them to a stop between the two galleons. A Silver Spear with a jutting jaw and a royal inspector's insignia on his tabard stepped aboard, holding a mug of steaming kahve, which he held up to Ihsan in salute.

"Submit for inspection?" he asked jovially.

Ihsan met him amidships. He was about to issue a command for him to conduct a cursory inspection, but paused. Something had gone wrong. Çeda was missing.

"My lord?" the inspector said.

"Yes, of course," Ihsan said, then put power into his words. "Inspect the ship. You'll find nothing of note."

"I'm sure of it, my lord," the inspector replied with a lift of his mug and an open-mouthed wink.

Ihsan followed him belowdecks, planning on telling him to find reasons to slow the inspection down, but unfortunately Cahil came as well, which prevented him from saying anything. When the inspector reached the cabin where Ihsan had left Varal, he opened the door, looked straight at her, then closed the door with a click. In that brief moment, Ihsan had seen Varal staring at the inspector beseechingly, but his gaze had passed over her as if he'd seen nothing more than an empty bunk. After checking the other cabins and glancing inside the hold, the inspector nodded to Ihsan and Cahil. "Well enough, my lords."

Ihsan wasn't sure what to do. He couldn't very well give the inspector a command in front of Cahil, and commanding Cahil himself was out of the question—Cahil would pay for what he'd done to Osman, but this wasn't the time.

When they returned to deck, Ihsan asked the inspector, "Do you ever find anything?"

"Oh, we do from time to time. Bricks of black lotus. Slaves hidden away. Why, one time—"

"Very well," Cahil said, "we've leagues to sail before the sun sets." He put a hand on the inspector's back and guided him toward his ship, but not without sending Ihsan a sharp look of disapproval.

"Yes, of course," the inspector said, lifting his mug in a final salute.

No sooner had he said the words than voices rose up from the crew of the portside galleon. There came a shout of alarm, soldiers pointing across the port bow. Ihsan, unable to see what they were pointing at, ran to the foredeck.

A hundred yards distant, a towering creature with bent legs, curving horns, and a pair of lashing tails was rounding a low line of rocks.

"Ehrekh!" one of the navy crewmen called. "Ehrekh!"

But it wasn't an ehrekh. It was Goezhen, god of chaos. *How strange to be filled with both terror and relief at the sight of him.*

The god loped over the sand, eating the distance at an alarming rate.

"Stop him!" Ihsan bellowed, putting power into the command. "Prepare the ballistae and crossbows. Lay bolts of ebon steel in the channels."

Ihsan had seen Goezhen only once before, on the night of Beht Ihman, and he'd never forgotten the sinking feeling in his gut when the dark god had regarded him with those jaundiced eyes. They'd taken him in from head to toe, hungrily yet patiently, as if Goezhen knew he would one day taste the flesh of Kings.

Those same feelings resurfaced as Goezhen lengthened his strides into a sprint. His crown of thorns, thick around his curving ram's horns, glistened in the morning light as the first ballista bolt flew. The bolt flew truly, but Goezhen merely lifted one hand and it shattered against his palm.

"I said bolts of ebon steel!" Ihsan cried.

A second bolt flew from the other ship, but missed, hurtling just above the dark god's horns. The ballistae's mechanisms clanked as the crews worked feverishly to reload them. Soldiers in white crowded the gunwales. A flock of crossbow bolts released with sharp *twangs*. With a flick of his twin tails, the sand lifted before Goezhen and fouled the bolts' aim. They flew high over-head, the dark streaks of their passage curving like pen strokes, and were lost in the desert beyond.

On Goezhen came, running in a half-crouch, arms spread wide, clawed fingers flexing. Ihsan found it almost impossible to look away, but he did, casting his gaze over the harbor's curving length instead.

He saw no riders. No Çeda with her sword held high.

He'd planned it all so carefully. He'd been sure that if he could lead them to this moment, it would give them the greatest chance of seeing Nalamae awaken. But now his certainty was fading faster than a guttering candle. Ihsan could feel the pounding of Goezhen's cloven hooves. He could hear the dark god's ragged breath. The hair on Ihsan's arms and neck stood high, not from fear, but the sheer potency of the god storming down on them.

Only one more ballista bolt managed to fly before Goezhen reached them. In a small miracle, it managed to clip his shoulder. Black blood flew.

Goezhen reared back with a long growl of pain, then leaned into his charge and sent one shoulder against the offending galleon. The blow was so thunderous the prow shattered and the entire ship pivoted on its skimwood skis. The crew tumbled to the deck. Some fell overboard. One was lost when Goezhen crushed him with a mighty stomp on his renewed charge toward *The Wayward Miller*.

Soldiers flooded from the nearby lighthouses. Some aimed with crossbows and let fly. Others engaged with swords and spears. But Goezhen was a terror. One tail wrapped around a man's neck and used him as a flail. After throwing the unfortunate man into a squad of Silver Spears, Goezhen swept an arm across their front line, sending many hurtling through the air. In a matter of moments, two dozen were reduced to a handful.

Goezhen laughed at their dread. He grabbed two fistfuls of the *Miller's* rigging and used them to pull himself up to the foredeck where Husamettín, with a roar and a mighty, two-handed swing of his shamshir, cut deep into Goezhen's thigh. Goezhen roared in pain. He tried to swipe at Husamettín, but the King of Swords dodged the powerful blow.

Cahil slipped in behind him, a shield and his bright war hammer in hand. As he delivered a pair of hammer blows, Husamettín leapt from the deck down to the sand, narrowly missing a smash from Goezhen's fists.

Zeheb, still much thinner than he once was, charged forward holding two shields with spikes in their center and steel-tipped horns to either side. Before he could engage, however, Goezhen crouched and placed one massive hand flat against the foredeck.

Cahil managed to strike one more blow with his hammer before the decking began to rip free. All around Goezhen, boards curled, snapped, broke in an expanding wave. Crewmen, equipment, and Kings alike were lifted and sent flying. The sound was calamitous. When the wave reached Ihsan near the ship's stern, he found himself tumbling through the air in an arc that revealed sky then sand then sky again.

He landed hard. The wind whooshed from his lungs as pain spread along his back and right hip. Stars filled his vision as he rolled over, spit grit from his mouth, and pushed himself up to his knees. By then Goezhen was standing amidships. The entire upper deck of their cutter had been torn away, as had much of the starboard hull, revealing the cabin where Varal was tied to a bunk. She screamed as Goezhen stepped down into the belly of the ship. The inspector, the one with the mug of kahve, was inexplicably there as well. He must have retreated into the ship for sanctuary.

Goezhen gripped the inspector's head and sent him pinwheeling—the inspector, his mug, and the kahve all flying in different directions.

As Goezhen returned his attention to Varal, Ihsan shouted, "Lord of Darkness, leave her be!" He poured as much of himself into that command as he ever had, but it seemed to have no effect whatsoever.

Goezhen was just reaching for Varal when an arrow flew in. It sunk into his forearm, tapping a flow of black blood that burst into the hot desert air.

As Goezhen ripped the arrow free, another punched into his shoulder. Ihsan turned, still dazed, to find four women on three horses riding at a breakneck pace toward the wounded god. Çeda rode the lead horse with Sümeya mounted behind her. Timing her moves with the rhythmic sway of the horse's movements, Sümeya lifted herself onto the horse's rump. Steadying herself using Çeda's shoulders, she launched herself high through the air toward *The Wayward Miller*'s stern.

Ihsan stared in wonder as she flew over the transom and landed on the quarterdeck. Losing none of her speed, she somersaulted down through the yawning chasm Goezhen's spell had created in the ship's deck and hull. Blocking a tail lash with her shamshir, she landed inside the cabin, beside Varal.

Despite the threat Sümeya represented, Goezhen focused his attention on Çeda. She'd slipped off the saddle in an easy move and come to rest before the god.

"Goezhen!" she cried.

She stood like a hero of old, her tattooed right hand held high, her fingers splayed wide. Goezhen dropped down to the sand and stared, transfixed. Ihsan felt it too, a well of power that was somehow, improbably, centered on Çeda's right hand.

Then, in a blur of movement, Çeda switched hands. Her right hand snapped down while her left hand, gripping something small and round, shot upward. Gods of blood and stone, it looked like an *eye*.

Goezhen seemed suddenly afraid. He roared and raised one arm while spinning away, as if acid had been sprayed into his face. He stomped one hoof, and a wave lifted up, rolling toward Çeda, the sand spraying high, the effect widening as it traveled.

The brawny Kameyl, riding a horse of her own, was galloping hard and fast toward Çeda. When she whistled a series of notes, Çeda spun, the two of them locked arms, and Kameyl swung Çeda up and into the saddle behind her.

Ihsan thought they might actually avoid the wave, but it was too fast. It hissed as it flew and crashed into Çeda, Kameyl, and their horse, sending them all flying. Ihsan saw others caught in the same powerful wave, and then it reached him. Sand scoured. Stones cut. A sound like a mountain tumbling down filled Ihsan's senses as he was thrown backward.

For many long breaths, the only thing Ihsan could hear was a high-pitched ringing. He had trouble remembering which way to face. But then the world began to settle, the dust started to clear, and the sounds of battle returned.

As Husamettín, Çeda, and Cahil engaged the god of chaos, Ihsan's attention was drawn to Varal. No longer on the ship, she lay on the sand. Sümeya was helping her to her feet, but something had caught Varal's attention: a small round object on the sand nearby. It was the eye Çeda had been holding. She must have dropped it when Goezhen's wall of sand struck her.

Varal picked it up and stared at it in pure, unadulterated wonder, as if the eye held the answers to all her questions and more. Suddenly her body tightened, her head tilted back, and she released a long, soul-rending howl that made Ihsan quiver just to hear it.

Beyond her, Goezhen backhanded Cahil, sending him and his hammer flying into the hull of the galleon. As Cahil fell limp to the sand, Goezhen rounded on Husamettín while one of his tails wrapped around Kameyl's ankle and flung her away. Husamettín staggered, his hand pressed to his throat from a noxious breath that issued from Goezhen's mouth.

As Husamettín fell to one knee, Goezhen rounded on Çeda, who'd just struck a deep blow to his calf. She retreated, but suddenly slowed, her legs sinking deep into the sand. She looked up fearfully as Goezhen lifted both hands high.

"No!" Ihsan cried, sprinting forward, but he was too late.

Goezhen brought his fists down onto Çeda's braced form. As his fists struck, Çeda's body turned to stone and shattered, the pieces spraying outward like a vase dropped onto hard tile.

A moment later, far beyond Goezhen, a swirling column of sand formed. From it, Çeda reappeared in the same position she'd been in when Goezhen struck, her arms still held high as if she were bracing for the blow. She stared about with a bewildered expression.

Goezhen, meanwhile, seemed to sense the battle had changed. He spun toward the woman who was once Varal. She was Varal no longer, though. Or not entirely so. Now she was Nalamae reborn.

For a moment, no one dared move. Nalamae, a hungry look on her face, strode toward the god of chaos. Goezhen roared and charged. Nalamae charged as well while holding up one hand. Cahil's hammer, which had fallen to the sand beside him, streaked golden through the air and flew into her waiting palm.

What happened next would be seared into Ihsan's memory until his dying day. Nalamae leapt toward Goezhen, while Goezhen swept a clawed hand to fend her off. He did it too slowly, though, and Nalamae brought the golden hammer across his prominent jaw. Light burst from the point of impact, and a boom shook the desert.

Back Goezhen flew, stumbling, dazed. Onto the wrecked cutter he fell, but he was not defenseless. One tail lashed out and cracked like a whip. From the point of impact, an arc of seething darkness sped toward Nalamae. The goddess lifted Cahil's hammer in both hands and held it against the darkness like a talisman. A brightness emanated from it, blinding to look upon. The arc spread to either side of her and tore swordlike cuts into the hull of the galleon's stern behind her. Where the light shone brightest, however, the darkness dissipated.

With a mighty shout, Nalamae spun and threw the hammer. It sped in a streak of golden light and struck Goezhen at the base of one great, sweeping horn. There came a brittle snapping sound, a thunderous impact, and the horn sheared away.

As the hammer flew back to Nalamae's waiting palm, Goezhen stared in shock and fear, and then, like ash giving way to a sudden, stiff wind, his skin began to crack, to flake away. Nalamae released a great cry and heaved the

hammer again. It struck true, flying swift as the sun into the center of Goezhen's chest.

His remains were blasted into a great cloud of dark ash, which fluttered
down toward the sand like leaves. Slowly it dissipated, fading to nothing, and
everyone understood.

Goezhen was gone.

Chapter 30

Ç EDA STARED AT THE WRECKAGE of the Kings' cutter. At the broken galleon near it. At the woman named Varal who had somehow, improbably, become the goddess reborn.

Nalamae, Çeda thought. *She's Nalamae now.*

The woman who was once Varal stared at her hands, turning them over, again and again, as if she couldn't understand what was happening.

"Keep the Kings away," Çeda said to Sümeya, then went to the goddess.

Nalamae lifted her head slowly. "How can it be?" she asked, for all the world a mortal woman, a child of Sharakhai who'd forged a life from that beautiful, sometimes cruel place.

Çeda felt for her—her life, her very identity, had been stolen by a goddess and she hadn't a clue how to get it back. "The goddess needed a new form."

"Well she can't have mine!"

She looked so lost and forlorn, Çeda stepped forward and embraced her. "I'm sorry that it's happened, but it *has* happened, and you have a purpose."

"What purpose?"

"We all want the freedom to live our lives as we see fit. We want to watch our children grow. We want to be with the ones we love. We want *peace*. But those things are not given. They're won by the edge of a blade. *That* is your fate now, to help us win these things for the people of the desert."

For a time, Nalamae was stiff in Çeda's arms, her own arms limp, but then she slipped her hands around Çeda, held her tight, and began to weep.

"Don't despair," Çeda whispered while rubbing her back. "You're not alone. And there's hope yet. The acacia waits. Let's go and find what it wishes to tell us. Then we'll see if we can't reunite you with your family."

"My family . . ." Nalamae sniffed and pulled away. She glanced around at the Silver Spears, to the waiting Kings, at the others who'd come to witness the battle with Goezhen. Then she stared in wonder at Sharakhai, that hive of humanity. "My family is a bit larger than I'd realized."

Çeda smiled. "If only more came to know that, the world would be a better place."

Nalamae suddenly laughed. It was such a pure, genuine moment that Çeda laughed with her.

Sümeya had her sword out and had so far managed to prevent the Kings from approaching, but Ihsan was clearly impatient.

"If you're quite done," Ihsan called, "I rather think we should be moving on."

Çeda ignored him, taking in the situation. Two ships ruined. Dozens dead or wounded. Scores more watching her exchange with the goddess. She pointed to their horses, which were, miraculously, still alive, and led Nalamae toward one of them. "Mount up." They would ride to the *Red Bride* and set sail as soon as they possibly could.

"I can't let you do that," Ihsan said, following them toward the horses.

"I won't let you stop me, Ihsan"—Çeda gripped her right hand, summoning the pain, and the power of the desert that came with it—"not this time."

Despite her words, Ihsan continued to close the distance, stopping only when Çeda had drawn River's Daughter and pointed it at his chest. "Please." He raised both hands, palms facing outward in a sign of peace. "We have common cause."

"Common *cause?*" She lifted the tip of her shamshir until it was inches from his face. "You dare say that to me after what you did to Osman? After what you've done to countless others?"

By then, Cahil was standing to Ihsan's right, his hammer gripped easily in one hand. Husamettín, Zeheb, and Yndris had moved in along Ihsan's left. Sümeya, Kameyl, and Jenise, meanwhile, stood behind Çeda with swords drawn.

"You all look ridiculous," Cahil bristled. "Put your swords away before I lose my temper."

Çeda had already taken a step forward when Ihsan placed himself between the two of them. "Lower your sword, Çeda. I know you're angry, but I beg you to listen to reason."

Çeda laughed. "The time for *reason* has passed, Ihsan. Now get out of my way before I cut you down."

"I can't let you do that." When she tried to move past him, he moved quickly, always sure to keep himself between Çeda and Cahil. "Çedamihn, it was *prophecy*."

Çeda couldn't believe her ears. "The Kings have used many excuses for their crimes. Now you would use *prophecy*?"

"This was all seen by Yusam, written in his journals. And he saw plenty more, things you need to know about. Things you need to act upon."

"Fuck you." Çeda swiped her sword in the air, forcing him to back up. "And fuck your prophecy!"

"This was preordained."

"No it wasn't! None of it was, don't you see? The mere. Yusam's visions." She glanced at Nalamae. "The visions from Nalamae's tree. They are but glimpses into *possible* futures. You had a choice to make, and whether you acknowledge it or not, you made one." She flicked River's Daughter toward Cahil. "As did he. Now it's time for him to pay."

"You speak of possible futures? Yusam saw many things, Çeda. He saw Sharakhai ruined. He saw every man, woman, and child dead. We must take the utmost care that it doesn't come to pass. All depends on it. Not just me and you." He waved to the others. "Not just them. But everyone you've ever known. Emre. Davud. His sister the bread baker. Seyhan the spice monger. Ibrahim the storyteller. Even that girl you used to train, Mala. Everyone, Çeda. They all depend on us." He took a step toward her and lowered his voice. "I found a path for us to follow. A path that saves everyone. Don't you see? We *must* follow it."

The concern in his voice was plain. Ihsan was a man who schemed, a man who hoped to rule Sharakhai alone. He'd been making moves to do so for generations at least, perhaps centuries. But in this she judged he was being earnest. He genuinely wanted to save Sharakhai and its people. That didn't mean he'd found the right path, though. He'd gone too far. Cahil had gone too far.

Ihsan, perhaps sensing her doubt, spoke low. "Don't make me compel you."

Çeda's right hand flared with pain and a heat like she'd plunged it in boiling water. The sensation traveled up her arm to her heart, and all the anger from moments ago returned. "Wrong choice of words, Ihsan." She pointed River's Daughter at his eye. "You don't threaten me. You hear me? You don't threaten me ever again."

Suddenly, Nalamae was beside her. She touched Çeda's shoulder. "I'm sorry for Osman. Truly I am. But perhaps he's right. We don't have to sail together. We have two sound ships. Let's take them to the valley, as you said. Let me receive whatever visions the acacia wishes to share. Then we'll see what future awaits the Kings of Sharakhai."

For a moment Çeda could only breathe, could only listen to the rush of blood in her ears. She knew the goddess was right. She knew it. Yet she wanted to forsake it all to wipe the smug smile from Cahil's face and see the light in his eyes fade. Shivering with rage, she threw River's Daughter to the sand. Then she screamed, which did nothing to quell the frustration that seethed within her chest.

"We'll go to the valley," she said slowly, each word like bile. Then, without warning, she stalked toward Cahil.

Cahil's eyes went wide. He lifted his hammer and, as she closed in, swung it at her in a strong yet mystifyingly incompetent manner.

Çeda was more than ready. She leaned away from the blow, then ducked below Cahil's clumsy recovery. As the hammer whirred above her head, Çeda rose, transferring all her power into an uppercut to Cahil's jaw.

His head snapped back. He reeled and tried to mount a new offensive, but it was over in moments. Çeda crossed with her elbow, landing it to the side of his head, then rotated her hips to send a deep punch to his gut that knocked the wind from him. When he bent over, she raised her knee to meet him, which sent him reeling backward, eyes glazed.

She stood over him as he curled into a ball. "That's for Osman, you piece of shit." Then spat on him where he lay.

Ihsan watched with a flat stare. Zeheb's eyes moved rapidly, and his lips were moving. Husamettín surprised her—during her fight with Cahil, he'd prevented Yndris from interfering.

"This isn't over," Çeda said to Husamettín, then took in Zeheb and Ihsan as well. "None of this is over."

With that she stalked back to River's Daughter, picked it up, and headed for their horses.

Chapter 31

WILLEM WATCHED IN HORROR as Cassandra began stuffing her things into one of several large, shapeless bags. She was leaving, and it looked like it was for good. But Willem needed her. She was his only connection to Davud, and Davud hadn't found Nebahat yet.

Davud had scoured the grounds after Willem's most recent message. He'd explored each of the collegia's halls, most of them several times. Willem wanted desperately to help him, but he couldn't. The binding that kept him from communicating with others had already been pushed to its limits. He'd given Davud the story of Bahri Al'sir and the fabled scroll. Davud had taken it to mean Nebahat might be hidden away in the largest of the collegia's many libraries. When he'd found nothing there, he'd searched the smaller ones, including the private collections kept by many of the faculty. But of course he hadn't found Nebahat's hidden archives there. He needed to go to the science building.

Willem made a mental list of the stories he might give to Davud through the use of the pendants—stories of alchemysts and astrologists, tales Davud might connect with the hall of science—but each time he thought of going to get one of the books, he was prevented. The will simply left him. No matter how tightly he held it, the notion would slip between his fingers—it was simply too close to the truth. He was even prevented from gathering loosely related stories that, when viewed as a mosaic, might give Davud the clues he needed.

So it was that he was forced to watch as Davud tried different tacks, the first of which was sneaking into the collegia's hall of records to look for clues of Nebahat's past. Nebahat had attended the collegia decades ago but had had the foresight to expunge his official records. Chancellor Abi had known him, but Nebahat had closed off that loose end in the same ruthless and efficient manner he used to deal with most problems.

To keep from being discovered after giving Davud the stack of books by the statue, Willem had returned Cassandra's pendant to the heart-shaped box where she kept her jewelry. So great was his desire to bask in Davud's light, he often returned to her room while she slept and stared into the pendant. Most nights Davud would watch from the other side, clearly hoping for more clues, but Willem could do no more than stare while cloaked in darkness. He even felt spells Davud had crafted in hopes of catching him, but as Willem had in the past, he forced them to slide past him. His binding not only prevented him from speaking; it forced him to avoid spells he knew would give him away as well.

Then one morning, as the sun resumed its unending battle against the night, something terrible happened. Cassandra was snoring softly in her bed when a knock came at her door. Willem had been so caught up with the pendant he hadn't heard anyone approaching. He should have made for the window immediately, but he didn't. He was too afraid of losing Davud forever. So when the knock came again, he slipped inside Cassandra's wardrobe.

Just as he was closing the door, he heard Cassandra stirring. "Coming!"

Again came the insistent knock.

"I'm coming!" The metallic rattle of the door being opened. "Why so *early*, memma?"

"I told you I'd be here at dawn. Are you ready?" A pause. "Cassandra, I told you to *pack*."

"I did!"

"One small chest? We need everything, Cassa. Or have you forgotten?"

Through the crack between the doors, Davud saw Cassandra stuffing her clothes into a large canvas bag, one of several her mother had brought to the room with her. "I haven't forgotten," Cassandra said, her movements slowing. "I just don't see why it's necessary to go home."

"Your father is *sick*."

"I have my studies."

"You're studies are going to have to wait." Cassandra's mother was out of sight, but there came the sound of ruffling, of cloth being snapped—Cassandra's clothes being picked up from the floor. "I need you at home with me."

Willem made himself small in one corner of the wardrobe. He was hidden beneath the ranks of dresses hung from above, but the moment they were pulled aside . . .

"Memma, I don't want to go."

The sound of footsteps came closer. Shadows passed over the gap where the slightly warped doors of the wardrobe met imperfectly. The leftmost door thumped hard, making him shiver with fright. Fabric was dragged across the stone floor.

"Honestly, Cassa, I thought I taught you better. Do you really have to dump your clothes everywhere?"

Gods, they were about to open the wardrobe. They were going to *see* him. All these years, never being found, never being seen, and he would be caught inside a bloody wardrobe because he'd been too dimwitted to leave when he should have. He'd been so taken by the pendant, though, and by Davud, and with trying to concoct some way to lead him to Nebahat.

He thought of running. He thought of bursting from the wardrobe and making for the window. But the same thing that kept him from speaking kept him from willfully revealing himself. He was so terrified tears gathered at the corners of his eyes. The wardrobe door flew wide. Willem cringed as light flooded the interior.

"By the gods who breathe, Cassa, how many dresses do you *have*."

Just then another knock came. "There's just the matter of a signature?" came a tiny voice. Willem knew that voice. It was the dorm mistress.

"Keep packing," the mother's voice said. "I'll be right back."

"Memma, I don't want to go!" Her voice had begun to dwindle. "Let me stay until the end of term at least."

A great wave of relief swept over Willem. They were heading for the dorm mistress's office! The moment the door clattered shut behind them, Willem rushed from the wardrobe. He'd already taken two long strides toward the window when he glanced at the table beside Cassandra's bed.

The heart-shaped box was there. The pendant.

He wept at the thought that he'd not be able to see Davud again, not be able to help him further.

Then a thought struck him like a thunderbolt. He refused to think about it lest it expand into something more fully fleshed. If he did, he would be compelled to leave. He was certain of it. So instead he reasoned with himself. Might it not be in Nebahat's best interests if the necklace were taken for safekeeping? Indeed, might he not want to examine it to see the sort of threat it represented?

Yes. Yes. Nebahat would like to see the pendant.

So he took it. He stuffed it into his shirt and flew through the window just as the voices of Cassandra and her mother grew stronger and the door opened behind him.

"I'll talk of it no further, Cassa. You're leaving, and that's that."

Cassandra's response was too faint to hear as Willem made his way over the angular landscape of the dormitory's roof. He returned to the hall of science and slipped through Nebahat's spells of hiding. He made his way to the hidden archive, nearly though not quite certain that he would wake Nebahat and show him the necklace.

No, he reasoned. Why wake him now?

He stuffed the necklace beneath his pillow instead, in the tiny alcove he called home. He'd show it to Nebahat later. Or tomorrow. Nebahat was a busy man, after all. He didn't need to be bothered with such inconsequential things.

Perhaps when his project was complete.

Yes, that was it. After Nebahat's project was complete, he would have time for such things.

Satisfied that he'd done the right thing by his master, Willem curled up and fell asleep.

Willem waited for days. He left the pendant where it lay. He avoided thinking about it lest the wrong sorts of thoughts begin to blossom. He couldn't
even bring himself to go looking for Davud lest he begin to have hope. Hope,
and his thoughts would surely give him away, and then what would be left
but to reveal everything to Nebahat?

So he went about his days as he had since he was old enough to remember. He collected books from shelves all around the collegia. He returned
those that Nebahat said he was finished with. He read stacks upon stacks of
others, often to occupy his mind but just as often to satisfy Nebahat, who
would quiz him about their contents, which would often lead to his asking
for additional texts. Of late Nebahat was quite curious about the desert gods,
the years leading up to Beht Ihman, and the early reign of the Sharakhani
Kings.

So it was that Willem read hundreds upon hundreds of books, scrolls,
and tablets that spoke of the desert gods. So it was that he began to see a
pattern. Most stories focused on the gods coming to Sharakhai and speaking
to the Kings on the mount, but there were a number that spoke of the gods
visiting the desert tribes. They'd *wanted* the war to happen, he realized. King
Kiral was mentioned in three separate accounts as having been visited in his
palace by Tulathan well before Beht Ihman. The gods had made sure that
Kiral knew he and his fellow Kings could turn to the gods if they wished.
And so they had. The tribes united. They sailed on Sharakhai. They assaulted
her walls. And the Kings, all too predictably, had begged the gods for help.

Of course the gods had granted it. It's what they'd wanted all along.
Willem could see it clear as day.

But *why*? That was the burning question Nebahat wanted to answer.

Now that he saw it, Willem became obsessed with the very same question. Why *would* the gods do that? They were the gods! Couldn't they get
anything they wanted with a snap of their fingers?

He reread all the texts Nebahat had given him, then read them again. He
found others that Nebahat had never mentioned. And in these texts, he
found a new pattern. There *was* something the gods wanted. There *was* something they couldn't get with a snap of their fingers.

It was the touch of the old gods. Those who had made them, who'd breathed life into them then, then left the world for the farther fields. The young gods *ached* for their touch but were forbidden from leaving this world for the next. As Willem was bound to the collegia, *they* were bound to this earth, unable to follow. So it had been from the beginning. So it would always be.

Then one day Nebahat brought three crates of old clay tablets to the hidden archive and said to him, "Read these."

This calls for silence, Willem thought. *Silence and darkness.*

He took them to his alcove and read them by the light that glittered off the angles in the cuneiform. The tablets were old. Very old. He wouldn't be surprised to learn they'd come from the time of Beht Ihman or before. Most of them were poems and simple parables, tales that had spawned countless offshoots over the centuries, but there was one near the end that made his fingers tingle. It had been written by a woman who'd witnessed Beht Ihman. She'd stood on the mount and watched the gods arrive, watched the Kings sacrifice Tribe Malakhed that the city might be saved, watched as the people of that poor, cursed tribe were transformed into the asirim.

That night, the gods spoke verses to the Kings. The Kings had been granted wondrous powers. They'd been given weaknesses as well. Both were shared with the Kings in the form of an epic poem, voiced by Tulathan herself. When the cursed asirim had been sent to deal death upon the tribes attacking the city, and the Kings and all the other witnesses had left, the woman lingered, transfixed by the gods who remained. There she spied the golden goddess, Rhia, who turned directly to her, where she hid behind an outcropping of rock.

It was in that moment Rhia spoke one last verse of the poem. The implications of that final verse kept the woman up night after night. She would wake, sweating, Rhia's voice haunting her. The only way she could think to be free of it was to write it down so that it was recorded for history.

Willem stared at those words: the final stanza of the poem, the one that revealed all.

Breath of the desert. Breath of the desert.

He was about to go to Nebahat and tell him when he noticed something shining beneath his pillow. He lifted it to find Cassandra's pendant. It was shining bright. Shining with Davud's light.

He was near. He'd come. Sand and stone, he'd found Nebahat's lair!

Willem's heart lifted in joy. He wanted to sing. To dance. Nebahat would pay for what he'd done to Altan and so many others. Davud would bring him to justice!

But then a horrific urge was born inside Willem's heart. Nay, a directive.

His hands shot beneath his chin. He swallowed. He shook his head so violently stars swam in his vision.

I can't. I can't. Please don't make me.

And yet the tablet that had so entranced him went practically forgotten in his left hand. In his right he took up the pendant. He carried it and the tablet down the dark, winding tunnel. He reached the maze of shelves, the spiraling stairs, the ground floor, where Nebahat was reading a massive tome that was laid out on the desktop before him.

Willem stood there before him, at which point Nebahat raised a finger, as he often did when finishing one last paragraph or page.

Go, a voice inside Willem screamed. *Take the pendant and run!*

But he couldn't, and soon Nebahat was lifting his head and staring at Willem in that way of his, asking him what he wanted without saying a word.

Willem watched in horror as his own arms extended before him. He tried to cry out, to warn Davud that he shouldn't come, but he was bound never to do such a thing.

Oh gods, he should have warned Davud away. He should have laid a false trail. Now Davud was going to die because of *him*.

Willem opened his hands so that Nebahat could see the pendant. He then pointed to the tunnel that led to the way up. He put on a worried face, making it clear that there was danger.

Nebahat immediately stood. He stared down the tunnel and disappeared in a waft of green smoke.

Willem turned toward the tunnel's mouth, where two shapes were resolving from the darkness. How he wished they would think better of this. How he wished they would flee.

But they didn't. Why would they? They stepped into the light, Davud wary, Esmeray wearing the sour look that seemed to define her.

"Hello," Davud said simply.

Run!

"Was it you who left us the clues?"

Run!

Davud stepped forward, his hands raised in a gesture of friendship. "I won't harm you."

Run! Run! Please run!

But it was too late. Nebahat materialized behind them. They'd no more turned than a nest of black cords flew from Nebahat's outstretched hands to wrap their necks, their mouths, their wrists and their ankles. As they fell to their knees, then to the hard stone floor, Willem watched, horrified, unmoving, tears streaming down his face.

Chapter 32

As DAWN BROKE over the darkened streets of the Shallows, Brama and Mae followed the boy they'd rescued from the adichara. His clubfoot caused the boy to limp, which slowed their journey, but he eventually led them to a dusty, stone-lined yard that sat between a small house and a squat building: the mill Brama had seen in the boy's memories. Using the power of Raamajit's bone, Brama had taken on the guise of a young street tough. His skin was smooth, the lump on his forehead gone. Mae had refused his spells, choosing instead to wear a simple shirt, a leather jerkin, breeches, and sandals.

Brama found the spot where the boy had gone to piss the day before. "Go on home," Brama told the boy, who wasted no time. He headed into the house as quickly as his deformed foot would allow.

As he called for his mother, Brama stepped carefully along the alley, with Mae following. Halfway along it, Brama crouched, placed his hands flat on the ground, and felt for the presence of those who'd trodden over that particular stretch of packed earth. Had it been along a busy street, he'd likely have been unable to detect the presence of the one who'd bewitched the boy and sent him into the desert to die, but the alley wasn't well traveled and he sensed it after a time.

Touching his fingers to his forehead, Brama called upon the power of the elder gods, willing the path to unwind. Before him, footsteps lit faintly in the early dawn light, footsteps he and Mae followed deeper into the Shallows.

As the city around them woke, Rümayesh fumed. She was angry she'd been beaten and was surely plotting a new path to ascendance, but she was curious as well, perhaps even more so than Brama. The riddle of the adichara, the very reason for their existence, was four hundred years old and had yet to be solved, and Rümayesh was as interested as anyone in the answers.

The glowing footsteps led toward the heart of the city—to the collegia, of all places—except, as they entered the grounds, the footsteps faded and were lost.

Brama stopped. Peered more closely at the gravel path.

"What wrong?" Mae asked.

He tried to pour more power into the spell, but it was no use. "They're gone," he said. "The trail just disappears."

Mae took in the sandstone buildings around them. Some were ancient, some quite new. Some were small, others large. A few were hulking monstrosities that dominated the space around them. "You think he live here?"

"It's possible he only passed through the collegia grounds, but yes, I suspect so." All around them, a light fog was lifting from the ground and dissipating in the cool desert morning. "There's something about this place."

"What?"

"Like it's alive."

"The students?" Mae asked. There were a few wandering the paths of the esplanade in the distance.

"No. The land. The buildings. It's a mystery, Mae."

Mae seemed doubtful. "Then what is the solution?"

Brama had no idea. But he would find out. For once, this was something both he and Rümayesh agreed upon. It chilled him to know that Rümayesh's dark soul was as curious about the tributes and the purpose behind their being sacrificed to the adichara as he was, but he had to admit he was glad she wasn't fighting him. What would happen when he found the answer, Brama didn't know, but for now she was content to let him search.

Brama *did* search, for weeks. He scoured the grounds, hiding his presence behind a spell lest the blood magi of the city take note of him. He cast spells of searching, spells of divination. Spells that would reveal sources of power, which should have been enough to uncover where the mage who'd ensorcelled the boy was hiding. None of them worked, a source of endless frustration for Brama.

One night he grew angry over it, and decided to take one of the collegia masters and perform a ritual on her to seek answers. He stalked behind her along a darkened gravel path, debating where to perform the ritual. It was the image of making that first cut along her belly that snapped him from his dark fugue.

It was Rümayesh's foul urges, not his own, that were driving him to chase this woman. Desperate not to let an innocent die for lack of trying, he pressed Rümayesh down, suffocating her twisted desires as the master, a woman with a round face, kinky hair, and clusters of moles beneath both eyes, sensed something. She peered into the night, searching for the source of her discontent. Failing, she rushed through the lantern-lit entrance to the residence hall, slamming the door behind her.

She might have provided answers, Rümayesh cooed.

"No," Brama said as he stared at the closed door. "You know she wouldn't have."

She didn't disagree, which was proof enough his words were true, and yet her absence made him feel her hunger all the more acutely. She fed on the fear of mortals, fed on their pain. She ached for it. Brama did too, which made him wonder how long it would be before Rümayesh had him, once and for all.

An echoing laugh seemed to follow him. Then it was beside him, the echo's resonance easier to discern than the laugh itself.

Mae contacted Queen Alansal's spies in the city. She found a safe house not far from the collegia and checked on Brama from time to time, but as the days passed and Brama found nothing, their meetings grew more sparse and his mood turned grim.

Perhaps I should abandon this, he thought, *return to the desert.*

No, Brama. This mystery runs deep. It touches the very heart of the desert's history.

He suspected she was right, but what did it matter? His search was starting to look like a lost cause.

Then one day he found something new. He was walking across the grounds in the light of day, students walking by him, many getting a chill when they came too near, when a glowing thread of gossamer appeared in the air before him. At first he thought it some random remnant of the sigils built into the walls of Sharakhai, or fading evidence of some clumsy blood ritual.

The longer he looked, though the more he saw its elegance. It was a spell of binding, of connection. He followed it, but when the thread trailed away to nothing—a victim, perhaps, of the same spell that concealed Brama's elusive quarry—he followed it the other way and discovered a wavering in the air, a less elegant spell of masking.

Taking care not to be detected, Brama pulled back the veil and, gods of the desert, saw Davud, the baker's son, the one who'd impressed the collegia masters so much they'd sponsored him. A woman walked beside him, somehow helping him cast the complex spell of finding. Brama didn't recognize her, but she looked like a typical west end girl—tattooed face, wild, braided hair, and a look like she'd cut you if you spoke to her the wrong way. Except that her eyes were bone white. He had no idea what could have happened to her, but he was intrigued. A refined collegia graduate with a rough-and-tumble west end mage, the two of them casting a spell to draw them closer to the place Brama suspected was the same one *he'd* been searching for these past weeks.

The two of them walked slowly, carefully, along the grounds. Brama followed, wrapped in a cloak of perfect silence. They entered a large, rectangular building, followed its high central hall to a room filled with an ordered mess of stone tables, shelves, and glass beakers held by metal contrivances of many sorts. They continued to a storeroom at the back. Brama had entered it several times and sensed nothing, yet when they pushed on a shelf that brimmed with brightly colored powders and liquids in glass jars and bottles, it swung wide.

They moved faster now, perhaps sensing the game was nearly won. They spun down a spiral staircase, then along a tunnel toward a room far ahead lit with lanterns. Brama sensed two souls inside that room. How they could have remained hidden from him for so long he had no idea, but just then he didn't care. He was transfixed by the unfolding story.

Suddenly, one of the two people in the room ahead vanished and reappeared near Brama. A mage. Perhaps the one who'd cast the spells to mask the catacombs from detection.

Davud and his companion reached the entrance to the subterranean room. Outlined in the light as they were, they looked like wights, souls traveling to the farther fields. In that moment the mage swept up behind them and touched their shoulders, at which point Davud and his companion fell instantly and unceremoniously to the floor.

Brama's instincts as a thief took over. He crept forward and watched as the mage dragged Davud further into the light. The mage's broad facial features marked him as a Malasani, as did his orange forehead with the bright yellow circle in the middle of it.

Using a blooding ring, the mage bent over Davud, pierced his wrist, and drank from the bleeding puncture. Then he traced a sigil in the air.

Davud woke, eyes glazed, then shivered. "Nebahat."

"Yes," the Malasani said. "Now stand."

Davud did, a marionette, his strings pulled by the mage standing before him.

"I'll admit," Nebahat said with an admiring smile, "you've avoided us so well until now I never thought to see you again. Why have you come?"

Davud's answer completely surprised Brama. "Because you killed Chancellor Abi," he said in an emotionless voice. "Because you're searching for the descendants of the thirteenth tribe. Because the people you identify keep going missing."

It was the last part—the very thing Brama had been searching for: the reason for the tributes being sent to the blooming fields. If what Davud said was true, it wasn't merely for their blood, but for their lineage. They were descended from the thirteenth tribe. Once again, those cursed people had been caught up in the plots of Sharakhai's most powerful.

"Is it true?" Brama asked as he stepped into the light.

Nebahat's entire body spasmed in fear. He stumbled backward and tripped over a pile of books, then scrabbled away like a crab.

"Is it true?" Brama pressed. "Are you sending tributes to feed the twisted trees?"

The man's eyes were locked on the ruin of Brama's face, on the strange lump on his forehead. He raised one hand, began describing a complex sigil in the air.

"No, no, no," Brama said, and stopped him with a wave of his hand. "Now tell me, is it you who's sending the tributes?"

Jowls quivering, his eyes wide as saucers, Nebahat nodded.

"Why?"

He swallowed hard, the apple in his neck bobbing furiously. "For Queen Meryam," he managed.

And then, most strangely, Brama's spell of command slipped off Nebahat like skimwood over sand. Brama thought Nebahat himself had done it, but realized a moment later it was the other occupant of the room, a young, clean-shaven man with thick eyebrows and an innocent face. Somehow he'd made Brama's spell *slide* off Nebahat.

Brama was completely and utterly bewildered. "Who *are* you?"

The young, bright-eyed man didn't move. Didn't speak. Brama was just about to force him when he realized there was a binding on him, *preventing* him from speaking. Brama tried to remove it, but the man eluded his spells with astonishing ease.

When he tried again, something bright flashed before Brama's eyes and the world swam before him. He felt nauseous.

In his disorientation, Rümayesh swept up from the depths like a leviathan. She traced a sigil in the air, banishing the spell that was causing the discomfort. By then Nebahat was casting another. Rümayesh tried to stop him, but fighting her way to full consciousness had cost her precious time, and Nebahat made his escape in a cloud of green smoke.

The young man stood there like a frightened lamb his eyes miserable. His lips moved, but no sound came out.

Rümayesh, seething in anger, stalked toward him. "You will give me the answers I seek." Gripping his neck, she drew upon the power of the bone in Brama's forehead to remove the chains that bound him.

"Tell me now," Rümayesh said. "Why does Queen Meryam search for those with blood of the thirteenth tribe? Why is she sending them to the blooming fields?"

In answer, the man lifted the clay tablet he held in one trembling hand. Rümayesh, filled with an awe that was unlike anything Brama had ever sensed in her, took it from him. The tablet was written in a centuries-old tongue. As Rümayesh read it, the thoughts of the young man, borne on the wings of her spell, drifted to her. Both the tablet and his thoughts spoke of the gods, of their deepest desires, of the ways they manipulated the people of the desert, not only the tribes and the people of Sharakhai, but the Sharakhani Kings themselves, to get what they wanted.

Understanding dawned, the purpose of the gods revealed at last, and the tablet slipped from Rümayesh's fingers, forgotten in the immensity of the moment.

The man gasped and reached for it, but he was too late. It shattered on the hard stone floor.

Rümayesh barely noticed. She could hardly contain herself. Her heart had opened its doors, and joy and excitement and fear were pouring forth. She felt as if she were standing at the dawning of a new world.

Without another word she left through the tunnel. She didn't return to the surface, however. She walked until she came to a place that was not hewn from the rock by the hand of man, but by time and erosion.

She wended her way, coming ever closer to a place she'd sensed many times but never visited, the place where the roots of the adichara met. This, she thought as she stared at the immense cavern and the violet crystal glowing in its center, is what it was all for. The Kings. The asirim. The tributes taken and fed to the twisted trees. The gods had built it all, step by painstaking step, for a purpose.

As she paced over the spongy floor toward the crystal, enthralled by its violet light, she saw how everything connected: the manipulation playing out over centuries, the unwillingness of the gods to interfere, the slow accretion of this crystal, fed by the blood of tributes collected generation after generation. The ruthlessness of the Kings had never been for their benefit alone. Its true purpose had been to serve the gods. To create this portal, a pathway to the lands beyond. It seemed impossible at first, until Rümayesh remembered that the first gods had granted mortal man their own blood, despite withholding it from the younger gods. That was what the young gods had wanted all along, what they'd *needed* to breach the impassable barrier that separate this world from the next.

The gods daren't interfere too much, though. Do that and they bound themselves to this earth, as Nalamae had done. They would be trapped. But trick man into feeding the trees? Trick man into creating this crystal? Trick man into forging a path to the farther fields, a path the gods themselves could follow? Well, then they would have what they most desired: to be reunited with the old gods, to feel their touch, to sit before them and bask in their glow, no matter that the cost would be dear to the world they left behind.

When at last the fields do wither,
When the stricken fade;
The Gods shall pass beyond the veil,
And land shall be remade.

So the verse in the tablet had read, the final pronouncement of the gods on the night of Beht Ihman. Sharakhai itself would be destroyed, of this Rümayesh was certain. But why should Rümayesh care? What happened to those who remained behind meant little to her. What mattered was that the gods had created a way to reach the farther fields. And if *they* could use it, then so could Rümayesh.

And she would.

She would ensure that the tributes continued. She would ensure the gods' plan worked.

And when it did, Rümayesh would follow them to paradise.

Chapter 33

WILLEM WATCHED IN FEAR as the scarred man strode away. Stone and sand, the sheer power in him. Nebahat was fearfully strong in magic, but he was a babe compared to the thing that had just prized the pages of Willem's mind open and stolen his memories.

Thank the fates that rule all, the darkness of the tunnel soon swallowed the scarred man. His footsteps faded and were lost. Only then did Willem crouch and try to piece the broken tablet back together. He remembered the words on it, but it felt like the desert was poorer for its breaking.

A twinkling caught his eye. Davud and Esmeray. Oh gods, he'd forgotten about Davud and Esmeray. He stood, breathless. He wanted to rush to their side. He wanted to slip Nebahat's spell from them. But how could he? He was still bound. No matter that the scarred man had lifted it momentarily. It was back, strong as ever, and there was nothing Willem could do to lift it.

Slowly, he backed away, stepping closer to the aisle between the nearby shelves. He would return to his alcove. He'd let Nebahat deal with them. It was the only way. He had no choice.

He wondered what Nebahat would do. Rip their stories from them, certainly, but what then? What would their punishment be?

The answer came as a whisper in his mind. *Death. Their reward for finding him will be death.*

He bumped into the book shelf behind him and turned, frightened, then spun slowly about, taking in all the other towering shelves holding hundreds upon hundreds of books and scrolls and tablets. He stood before one, touched his fingers to the bindings of an old tome made of cracked leather. Below it was a set of wooden trays containing ancient tablets, and beside that, the golden tracery on one of Nebahat's most prized possessions, an early copy of the Al'Ambra.

Willem had always been an observer. He'd always read stories, and wondered what it would feel like to be in one. *Like this*, the voice inside him whispered. *It feels precisely like this.*

What would the histories say about him? Would they recount him as a victim? A coward? Would they record him at all?

Not if you leave. Not if you abandon them to a man you know is evil.

Willem turned around. *I can't abandon them. I can find a way.*

Every step forward felt as if he were trying to lift the city onto his shoulders. Every moment that passed felt as if it would see the return of Nebahat. He could still turn around. He could still hide in his alcove and curl himself up into a ball and cover his ears until this was all over.

But he didn't. He took step after painful step until he stood over Davud. Except now that he'd arrived, he had no idea what to do. The chains that bound him were as strong as ever.

Davud stared up at him, unmoving, trapped. He looked confused, as if he didn't know what to make of Willem. But there was fear in him, too. Nebahat's return was a certainty. It was only a question of *when*.

The spell on Davud glowed fitfully, dulling his brilliance. *Such a travesty*, Willem thought. Davud deserved to *shine*.

What if . . .

Willem swallowed.

What if he could find answers *for* Nebahat, to give to him upon his return? What if he freed Davud and Esmeray that they might speak to him? Wouldn't that be helping his master in the end? He might even do a better job of it. They wouldn't be afraid of Willem. They'd be *glad* to give him his answers.

His stomach felt like it was curling in on itself, but Willem ignored it and crouched down. Sweat tickled his palms as he held one hand over Davud's face, then swept his hand down along Davud's body, drawing the spell from him like a snake shedding its skin.

His light shining brightly once more, Davud coughed and sat up.

Willem moved to Esmeray and did the same to her. She shone in her own way, though the raucous colors made Willem shy away.

Esmeray was immediately on her feet, and when Willem put his hands up, pleading with them to remain, she shoved him away. "Stay back!" she yelled, and took Davud by the arm, trying to lead him toward the tunnel.

But Davud, gods bless him, refused to go. He remained, staring at Willem with an expression of naked wonder. "Tell me your name," he said.

Willem shook his head violently.

"Then tell me what's happened."

But Willem couldn't. He hardly understood the story himself.

"Come on, Davud," Esmeray said, tugging on his sleeve. "It's time to go."

Please don't go! Willem needed them to tell their tale. That's the only way he could justify what he'd done. Fail in this and he'd . . . He wasn't sure what. He didn't want to consider it.

He held his hands up, forestalling Davud and Esmeray, and sprinted into the stacks, searching for one particular book. He remembered where he'd left it but couldn't find it. Nebahat must have taken it.

He checked all the tables, searching frantically.

"Davud, come *on*. He could return at any moment."

"Wait," Davud said softly, and remained where he was, calmly watching Willem.

A copy, Willem realized. *A copy of the same tale.* He ran up the spiral stairs to another shelf. And found it, a thick tome written a hundred years before. He brought it down, set it on the table closest to Davud and Esmeray, then opened it up to the story he needed.

Davud came closer. He read. Esmeray, her curiosity overriding her fear, stepped beside him and did the same.

It was the tale of a mariner who'd been imprisoned by an evil king in an oubliette for a hundred days and a hundred nights. He'd been freed, not by the king but by the king's daughter, who'd spent those many days telling him tales of her homeland. Never once had the mariner responded in kind, though she'd asked him many times to do so. The princess thought the mariner would simply leave, but before he did, he told her of his voyage, how he'd been looking for a fabled flower that could heal his dying wife. Quickly, before the king returned from his journey to the hinterlands, the princess spirited him to his ship, but not before giving him one of the fabled flowers.

Davud looked up from the tale. He stared at Willem, his eyes both gentle and kind. He understood what Willem needed from him. "I came here," he began, "because a student named Altan went missing. He's the cousin of a friend of mine, Tariq."

He went on, telling Willem more, how he'd gone to Tariq in the first place so that he could find Undosu, the man he hoped could negotiate a truce with the Enclave so that he and Esmeray and his friend, Anila, could find peace. He detailed his time at the collegia as he searched for Altan, finding the clues Willem had left him, finding Nebahat's archives through the link between the two pendants.

It was enough, Willem realized. It was enough that he could justify freeing them. But there was one last thing he needed to do.

He rummaged through Nebahat's things. He found it a moment later: a tiny brass compass. He took it and set it on the open pages of the book so that the needle pointed to the fabled flower the mariner had been searching for. He stepped back quickly as Davud stared down at the yellowed page, the faded ink.

"Undosu?" he said, picking up the compass. "This will lead me to Undosu?"

Willem averted his gaze, made himself as small as he could. It was simply too close to disobeying Nebahat to do anything else.

But please, please, please let him understand.

"Thank you," Davud said with a contented nod.

And then he and Esmeray were leaving. Their forms were soon swallowed by the darkness of the tunnel. Not their light, though. Willem saw that for a long while, twinkling, glimmering, until they were lost around a bend.

Only then did Willem allow himself to smile.

When Nebahat returned later that day, his anger was beyond measure.

He'd been attacked not once, but twice. And he blamed Davud and Esmeray and especially the scarred man—the Tattered Prince, Nebahat called him.

Willem didn't disabuse him of any of these notions. It would only make him angry if he learned of Willem's involvement, and what would be the good in that?

Part of him wished he'd told Davud about the tablet, the verse he'd found, the plan of the gods. But the more time passed, the more fanciful it seemed. Surely the woman who'd written it in the clay had merely been voicing her fears, fears she'd stoked and stoked until they'd felt like a raging inferno. From the distance of time, Willem could see it for what it really was, a fragile tale that would shatter when the least amount of scrutiny was applied to it.

Like an ancient clay tablet, Willem mused.

No, better that he told no one.

Chapter 34

ÇEDA SAILED EAST on the *Red Bride* with Sümeya, Kameyl, Jenise, and their goddess, Nalamae reawakened. The four Kings and their crew had claimed the lone, sandworthy galleon after the battle with Goezhen, and were sailing in the *Red Bride*'s wake. At Çeda's insistence, the galleon maintained a steady, half-league gap. She still didn't entirely trust them, particularly Cahil, but she'd admitted to herself if no one else that she believed Ihsan had told her the truth: that he had found a way for them to survive the coming conflict with the gods. Part of her wished she *didn't* believe him, but wants and wishes were like grains of sand, her mother used to say. Let them pile around you overlong and one day they'll bury you. It was simply too dangerous to ignore Ihsan's warnings.

As the days passed, Çeda grew terrified of Goezhen's return. Her every spare moment was spent scanning the horizon for signs of his approach, but eventually, when no sign of him appeared, she began to have hope that they'd escaped his wrath.

"Why would he follow?" Kameyl had reasoned. "He tried to attack the goddess once and nearly paid for it with his life."

Çeda shrugged. "He might be licking his wounds."

"Perhaps, but he also knows Nalamae's power has returned. He'll think twice about coming for us now."

Çeda wasn't so sure. He'd dared to attack them once; he might try again.

On their fourth day of sailing, Sümeya was sweeping her spyglass across the horizon. She paused as she came across the Kings' ship behind them. "Ihsan's asking to speak again."

Squinting, Çeda put her hand to her forehead, shielding the sun. Barely visible on the galleon's foremast was a white pennant flapping like the tail of a Mirean kite, a request for parley. It had been raised and lowered a half-dozen times, which made it clear just how keenly Ihsan wished to speak with them. Çeda had been too angry in days past to suffer the Kings' presence beside their fire, but the closer they came to the valley, the more important it was that they talk—she had to find out what Ihsan knew.

"Signal him back," Çeda said. "Tell him to come after we've made camp. Alone."

They stopped shortly after sunset. Jenise and Kameyl tended to the ship while Çeda built a fire and Sümeya set carpets around it. Nalamae, meanwhile, prepared plates of spiced flatbread, pickled vegetables, a cool, lemon-yogurt sauce, and smoked meat slathered in a spicy red paste, then set them, along with small cups and an ewer of water, onto the four carpets that had been laid out around the fire.

They were just getting ready to sit and eat when Ihsan appeared from the darkness holding a bottle of araq. He lifted it with an ingratiating smile. "I do not come empty-handed."

Kameyl, rolling her eyes, picked up her plate and walked away without saying a word.

Jenise headed up to the deck, leaving her food where it lay. "I'll take first watch."

Sümeya, being her usual, infuriatingly pragmatic self, sat down, motioned for Ihsan to join her, then did the same with Nalamae and Çeda.

Çeda sat across the fire from Sümeya so that Ihsan wouldn't be sitting near the goddess. Nalamae sat next, bearing her staff, which she set on the carpet beside her. Only then did Ihsan sit cross-legged on the patterned red carpet that had been laid out for him.

"May we one day meet under fairer skies," he said, and set the bottle of araq near Çeda.

Çeda drank from her cup of water, ignoring the araq. "Say whatever it is you wish to say."

Ihsan was content to take his time, however. He laid two strips of meat into the warm flatbread and dolloped the vegetables and yogurt on top. He took a large bite, savoring as he chewed. "It's good," he said to no one in particular.

"It's a family recipe," Nalamae replied.

Her words summoned a strange mood over the gathering. They were a reminder that a woman still lived within the body Nalamae now called her own, a woman with a family, a history in Sharakhai.

"Well," Ihsan said between bites, "I've never tasted finer."

He finished his water and lifted the bottle of araq. Pulling the stopper, he offered some to Sümeya. Sümeya glanced at Çeda, then downed her water and held out the cup. The bottle gurgled as Ihsan poured her a helping—in the firelight a stream of molten brass. Nalamae, shrugging, held her cup out as well. After filling it, Ihsan offered it to Çeda.

Çeda, closing her eyes and breathing out slowly, followed suit. "Just hurry up about it, will you?"

Ihsan poured, and the four of them lifted their glasses. Çeda took a swig. She didn't want it to be good, but gods, it was. Plum and tangerine with a hint of burning leaves. In fact, it was so good she downed the lot just so she wouldn't have to appreciate something Ihsan had brought as a gift.

"Tell us about the journals," Sümeya said.

"Yes, the journals." He swung his gaze across the fire to Nalamae. "If you'll permit me one small diversion first. I wonder, can you still call upon your power as you did with Goezhen?"

Nalamae seemed suddenly wary. "Why do you ask?"

"I'll take that as a no. And your prior lives. Have your memories of them returned?"

Nalamae glanced at Çeda and Sümeya before speaking, as if she didn't wish to disappoint them. "No."

"Do you currently feel any pull, a desire to go in a certain direction? Or have you felt such over the past few days?"

"No."

"Ihsan—" Çeda began.

But Ihsan cut her off with a raised hand. "Does the desert feel any different to you?"

At this Nalamae lifted her head and looked beyond the fire, which cast a strange, flickering light across her face. "Yes."

"Describe it."

"I feel . . ." She paused, searching for the right words. "I feel like I'm standing at the edge of a sea. That it will consume me the moment I step into it."

Ihsan nodded as if he'd expected it. "Some of the visions spoke of a goddess reluctant to take up her mantle. I would urge you, as difficult as it may be, to take that step. To let the sea swallow you."

"Why?" Nalamae asked, fearful. "What do you know?"

"I suspect that what happened at the harbor was but the first step of many. You must find your way, and you can only do that by embracing it and forgetting your former life. Do that, and I think you'll be able to hide yourself from Goezhen and the others." He meant that Nalamae should forget ever being the woman named Varal. "As for the visions," he went on, oblivious to the tears forming in her eyes, "I urge caution. Yusam saw many futures, and we don't yet know which will come to pass, but let me describe—"

He paused as Nalamae's emotions finally registered, then he fumbled like a child at a dinner party. "Forgive me. I know this must be hard."

Çeda squeezed Nalamae's hand.

Nalamae squeezed back while blinking away her tears. "Go on," she said to Ihsan.

Ihsan nodded. "Let me describe the visions I think are surest. We know the gods planned for Beht Ihman. We know they manipulated many in Sharakhai and the desert to ensure that the Kings felt hopeless in the face of the desert tribes who stood against us. We know they wanted something when they agreed to save us and sacrificed the thirteenth tribe."

"*You* sacrificed us," Çeda said.

The fire snapped as Ihsan chose his next words. "I don't deny it. The question now is: what did the creation of the asirim accomplish? Why did the gods insist that tributes be fed to the adichara? Why have their roots in turn been feeding a crystal beneath Sharakhai for the past four hundred years? A number of futures show Sharakhai destroyed, laid to waste. In some, the gods are present. In others, the city is nothing but a barren wasteland. In still more, Sharakhai is intact, but empty. A city of ghosts."

"If the gods wanted Sharakhai destroyed," Sümeya said, "why wouldn't they just destroy it?"

"Why indeed?" Ihsan replied. "There are two events that Yusam's visions foretell. Both will have great impact on the future." He turned to Nalamae. "In one, you again battle Goezhen. Whether or not you kill him will have a direct bearing on Sharakhai's fate."

"Tell me what Yusam saw," Nalamae said.

"I urge caution," Ihsan replied. "Often, the visions cannot be taken literally."

"I know." She said it with ease, as if intimately familiar with such visions.

Ihsan nodded. "You fight Goezhen. Some of Yusam's visions show it happening on the slopes of Tauriyat. Others in the tunnels beneath the city. Others still in the blooming fields. The question isn't *whether* you fight him, it's *why*. What might that battle lead to? What happens if you win, and conversely, what happens if you fail?"

"You've no thoughts on this?" Nalamae asked.

"I have some, but let me touch on Çeda's vision next. In Yusam's account, the lives of two who are close to you are threatened. You can choose one and only one to save."

A chill crawled down Çeda's back. She knew immediately Ihsan was referring to Emre and Macide—she'd seen both of them in Yusam's mere. Even so, she still asked, "Who?"

"Yusam wrote that one was a man with the bearing of a shaikh. The other had a scarab on his chest. The first vision originally came to him over a century ago, but a recent note identified one of the men as Macide. Likely seeing him in the flesh reminded him of the vision. The scarab, as described in the entry, matches Emre's description, which adds weight to Yusam's memories regarding the first."

The chill on Çeda's skin sunk deeper, to the point that she hugged herself and rubbed her arms. "And what threatens them?"

"It's unclear. You're standing at a fork in a road. Along one path, Macide lies dead with a bloody sigil on his chest while Emre kneels beside him holding the bloom of an adichara. Sharakhai looms in the distance, and a strange light is moving outward from Tauriyat, slowly consuming the city. The entry mentions words being spoken."

"What words?" Çeda asked. "Who's speaking them?"

"Yusam never said, but it was clear the words were powerful. They may have been a eulogy. Maybe Emre's. Maybe yours."

Çeda's dread deepened. "And along the other path?"

"Along the other, Emre is dead, strangled by the arms of a desiccated adichara. Macide is hacking at the branches. While he does, the healthy trees around Emre shrivel and the vision goes dark."

Çeda recalled her own visions, one of Macide hanging from a gibbet, a sigil drawn on his chest, the other of Emre staring into a bright light. They were not the same as the visions Ihsan had described, but that wasn't the important thing. The very fact that she'd seen anything remotely similar only added to the weight of their underlying message: that the two men were in grave danger.

"The acacia in the valley," Nalamae said softly, "may shed light on the two forks." Staring into the fire, all worry and doubt, she seemed more mortal than goddess.

"It might," Ihsan said, "and I agree that we should go, but we shouldn't tarry there. Remain in the valley too long and we may miss the crucial events that are sure to pass in Sharakhai. Malasan and Mirea are readying another assault on the city. What's worse, the crystal sits beneath the House of Kings, slowly growing in power."

Sümeya frowned. "With the asirim gone and Sukru dead, there will be no more tributes. The trees are no longer being fed."

The firelight intensified the sad, worrisome look on Ishan's face. "While we were in Sharakhai, Zeheb listened to the whispers. He picked up on a thread that spoke of people going missing. One of the whispers came from Tauriyat, and it spoke of how tributes were still being sent, arranged for by the Enclave."

"The Enclave . . ." Sümeya said. "Queen Meryam's had contact with them for years."

"Just so. No doubt Meryam is involved. The bigger question is why she would be, but I think we all know the answer to that. She is being manipulated, as the Kings were for centuries, by the desert gods."

Somewhere in the distance came a hissing sound, likely a sand drake emerging from its burrow to hunt for insects in the night. Further out, a song rose up from the crew of the royal galleon.

Nalamae had grown introspective. She was staring at the gemstones worked into the head of her staff while twisting it gently. "How jealous Goezhen felt," she said absently.

"Jealous?" Çeda asked.

"Of us." She grew suddenly self conscious. "Of you. Of mortals."

"But why?"

"I don't know, but there was a fear in him as well, a desperate desire to see his plans succeed." Suddenly Nalamae's back went straight.

Sümeya, Çeda, and Ihsan all shared a look.

"What is it?" Çeda asked.

"There was a *yearning* in him." Her voice was practically a whisper. "I felt his memories of touching the elder gods. *That's* what he and the others want." She looked at them all in turn. "They wish to pass beyond the veil. They want to reach the farther fields."

"But how?"

"Using the crystal, the power its built up for centuries using the blood of man."

"That makes no sense," Sümeya said. "Why couldn't they have built the crystal themselves?"

Çeda's mind was working madly, the pieces of the puzzle all fitting into place. "Because they were forbidden from reaching the farther fields while mortals were not. We were given the blood of the old gods. That's why the young gods need us. *We* create the portal and *they* pass through."

"Then why not just use our blood in some grand sacrifice?"

Çeda motioned eastward, into the darkness, "When I was in the fortress below Mount Arasal, I heard Nalamae speak to Yerinde. She said that there was something Yerinde had failed to consider, that she, Nalamae, had had time to reflect on her binding to this world, while Yerinde had not. She said she'd come to embrace it while Yerinde feared it above all else. Nalamae had somehow bound Yerinde to this world, to the mortal plane, and it enraged Yerinde, enough for me to approach. 'When I die,' Nalamae said, 'I will return. You, however, will simply cease to be.'"

Ihsan considered her words. "You're suggesting it's the *binding* she was worried about. That's why the gods step so carefully? Manipulate man too overtly, and they bind themselves to the mortal plane, thereby preventing themselves from stepping through the portal?"

"Just so," Çeda said. "The only question now is how it will be triggered, and what can be done to prevent it."

"Stop the tributes," Sümeya said, "and the crystal can gain no more power."

"Perhaps," Ihsan replied, "but try protecting league upon league of the blooming fields. Eventually some of the tributes will reach the twisted trees."

"Then we destroy the trees," Sümeya said.

"That's risky," Çeda said. "For all we know, the crystal is ready and awaiting a trigger. Burning or cutting the trees may provide just that." She told them how, after freeing the asir, Mavra, and her family from the blooming fields, she'd ordered them to tear up the trees they'd lived beneath, thinking it might free them from the hold the blooming fields had on them. But they'd no more begun than Çeda had felt a presence. "It was Yerinde. She felt expectant, almost hopeful, as if she *wanted* us to destroy the trees."

Nalamae held her staff in a white-knuckled grip, as if it were her only lifeline in a world of deadly currents. "So what do we do?"

"We continue as planned," Çeda said steadily. "We go to the valley. We see if your memories can be returned to you. With them might come your power."

Ihsan and Sümeya nodded. Nalamae, however, looked lost.

"You agree, I presume?" Ihsan asked her with a note of forced optimism.

When Nalamae spoke again, her voice was listless. "What else is there *to* do?"

As she stood and walked away, Çeda, Sümeya, and Ihsan shared worried looks. They were all thinking the same thing, Çeda was sure. Nalamae's awakening had come, but perhaps too late. There might be too much of Varal the shipwright and too little of the goddess of springtime's bounty for this to work.

Chapter 35

WHEN MERYAM WOKE on the silo's dirty, seed-strewn floor, Yasmine's arm was draped over her while Yasmine herself snored softly. The morning birds chirped. The cool air smelled of must and shit and piss.

The light from the hole high above, brightening with the new dawn, shed light on the heap of the cloth rope Yasmine had braided the night before. Their abductors weren't going to be fooled forever. Sooner or later they'd notice their petticoats were gone, or they'd spot the braided rope, and then it would all be over. They'd have lost their chance at escape. They'd likely be beaten for their trouble, and the gods only knew which of them would get it worse: Yasmine for having orchestrated the escape attempt, or Meryam, to teach them both a lesson.

Carefully lifting Yasmine's arm, Meryam slipped from her embrace. After a brief spell of searching for a comfortable position, Yasmine fell back to sleep.

Meryam immediately took the bundle of rope and began throwing it high into the air, hoping to send it over the support beam as Yasmine had done the night before. It didn't go nearly high enough, though, and came pattering back down to the dry earth. Each time, Meryam glanced at Yasmine, nervous that she would wake and tell her to stop.

Realizing she needed another approach, Meryam balled the rope up before launching it. It went much higher this time, unwinding itself as it went. It would have dropped nicely over the beam had it not bumped against it on the way up. She tried again, and this time it fell neatly across the beam and unfurled on either side like the unveiling of the new banners along the sides of Redhawk Tower.

Gripping the rope tightly, Meryam took a deep breath and began to climb. She was panting heavily by the time she was halfway up.

Below her, she heard Yasmine stir. "Meryam?" she said sleepily, then much louder, "Meryam, don't!"

"I have to," Meryam said without looking down. She'd started to realize how high up she was. Look down, and she would lose all hope.

"You'll fall!"

"I won't."

"They'll see you."

"Not if I'm quick."

She'd almost reached the hole. Her forearms were shaking from the vise-like grip she had on the rope, and she thought they might give out, but finally she made it to the top. The feeling of weightlessness and visions of her fall returned in a rush as she stared at that blasted opening in the stones.

Swallowing hard, she reached one arm out and grabbed its bottom lip, and this time she kept tight hold of the rope until she was sure she could transfer her weight over. Even still, she nearly slipped, only barely catching herself by shoving one arm through the hole and curling it over the lip like some long, makeshift hook. Her fears of falling were still strong, but she took heart from the simple fact that she could feel the chill morning air and smell the scent of decaying leaves from the forest.

With a great heave, she wiggled her head and shoulders through. Then pushed until she was out to her waist.

"The rope!" Yasmine called, muffled now that Meryam's body was blocking the way.

"I *know!*" Meryam called back, and used one leg to hook the rope. Wriggling one hand through the hole, she was able to grip it and pull both ends through, then she was out and slipping down until she'd reached the frost-covered ground.

She checked the silo door, but the rusty padlock was still there, secured. She wondered if she might sneak into the house and get the key.

"Go, Meryam!" Yasmine called from the opposite side. "You have to get help!"

Meryam knew Yasmine was right, but she found herself rooted to the spot.

"Meryam, so help me, if we're caught because you're too scared to run, I'm going to kill you."

Tears streamed down Meryam's face. "I'll be back, Yasmine. I swear I will."

"Just go!"

Meryam nodded, and then she was off, sprinting toward the forest, certain that she would be spotted at any moment. But she wasn't, and soon both farmhouse and silo were hidden by the trees. It was a terrible, harrowing day. One filled with fear that she'd made a horrible mistake in leaving Yasmine there.

She made it to the village of Oreño and thought of asking for help, but the fear that their abductors might have allies was strong and she skirted wide of it, found the river, and followed it to Maracal, then hiked through the forest beyond until she spotted the walls of Santrión. She'd been alternating between walking and jogging for hours, but when she saw Redhawk Tower, she ran until her muscles burned and her lungs ached. She kept running as she headed through the palace's private forest, past the hedge maze, past the pavilion that had yet to be taken down. She ran until she collapsed on the back steps leading up to the palace proper, where the palace guards spotted her.

As day gave way to darkness, she was whisked into her father's study and placed by a roaring fire to warm and tell her story. Her mother and father listened, until her mother said it was enough and that what Meryam needed now was rest. Her father, King Aldouan, relented and left them to see about guiding the search toward the farmhouse Meryam had described.

It was two days before Meryam saw Yasmine again. Two days filled with a gnawing certainty that the men would beat Yasmine once they realized the king's men were onto them, or that Yasmine would be killed in the rescue attempt. Meryam wondered what would become of the men. Had they been captured already? Would they be hung from Redhawk Tower as the Kings of old had punished those who challenged their rule? Meryam hoped so.

They deserved it. She'd watch and she'd spit on the earth below their feet when it was done.

Finally, while Meryam was sitting by the hearth in the great hall, Yasmine returned, bruised here and there but otherwise clean and wearing a dress Meryam didn't recognize, as if Mother had commissioned one for Yasmine's return.

Meryam sprinted into her sister's waiting arms. "They found you!" she said into the bodice of Yasmine's dress.

"Of course they did."

Meryam pulled away, sensing the haunted note in Yasmine's voice. "Are you well?"

"Yes, I'm well." Yasmine hugged Meryam, but only half-heartedly.

Late that night, after a strangely stiff meal with mother, father, and Yasmine, during which hardly anyone talked, Meryam went to bed, grateful for Yasmine's safe return but confused that such a pall had fallen over it. When the palace was finally quiet, Meryam got up and snuck into Yasmine's room.

Yasmine suddenly sat up in her bed, throwing her covers aside, a knife in one hand. When she realized who it was, she lay back down and faced the window. "Go back to bed, Meryam."

"What happened?"

"I said go back to bed."

"I *saved* you, Yasmine. I deserve to know."

Yasmine's breath came more and more rapidly. "You want to know what happened?" She sat bolt upright. "He *bargained* with them, Meryam."

"Bargained with whom?"

"Our *kidnappers*. They said they were ready to fight. That he had an insurrection on his hands. That if he didn't appease them, it would turn to civil war in the west."

"Will it?"

"I don't *care* if it will. He forgave them! He offered them gold in recompense for their lost land, more than it was worth. He *rewarded* their kidnapping."

"He didn't."

Yasmine stared at her, a dark, judgmental spirit in the night, then lay down and would say no more.

Meryam returned to bed, but she couldn't sleep. She got up again and wandered the palace, not really knowing where she was headed until she came to their father's study, where a low fire burned in the hearth. Father was sitting at the couch, the same couch she'd sat in when she'd returned to the palace. He was nursing a bell-shaped snifter of brandy.

"My darling daughter," he said when he spied her.

"Is it true?"

"Is what true, dear?"

"Is it true you gave them money?"

She could tell from his look that he understood, and yet it took long moments and several awkward expressions, as if he were trying out responses and discarding them in rapid succession, before he replied, "They'll pay for it in the end, sweet kitten."

"They *beat* us," Meryam said.

"A thing I regret. I truly do."

"We thought they were going to kill us."

"I know, but it would never have come to that."

"You can't know that," Meryam said. "You were supposed to protect us."

The smile he gave her was the sort he used when mother's family came to visit, fake in every way. "And yet here you are, safe and sound."

"And if they come for us again?" Meryam spat. "Will you give them more gold?"

"Meryam, don't be that way. This was all a terrible misunderstanding." He said it as if he were trying to convince himself. He tried to take her hands, but she backed away. He wasn't even man enough to try again. "It was an unfortunate mistake, but it's a mistake that's been fixed. No one is coming for you, and they never will. I promise."

Meryam had never thought of her father as weak. She'd ignored the whispers that he was a lamb in lion's raiment. She'd ignored the excuses her mother had made for his weak behavior when she thought Meryam wasn't listening. Meryam had always told herself they didn't know him as she did. They couldn't see the strength behind his mild manners.

That image was shattered as she stared at her father, the firelight flickering against his false smile. Hers had been the impressions of a juvenile mind, but now she saw him for what he truly was.

"You're a coward," she said.

He swallowed. Stared down into the depths of his golden brandy. The silence yawned between them.

Meryam left him there and took the stairs up to the royal apartments, but instead of going to her own room, she opened Yasmine's door and climbed into bed with her. She held Yasmine, as Yasmine had held her in that gruesome place. "I'll not let anyone harm you ever again."

A silence followed, like a smile shared between them. "Nor I you, Meryam."

Meryam squinted against the morning's light, blinking sleep from her eyes. Heavy curtains were pulled over the nearby windows, but a breeze blew them wide, allowing the light to sneak into the room in an irritating rhythm.

With a groan she got up and pulled the curtains tighter, then fell back into bed. Soon enough, she realized it was too late. She might be exhausted, but she would no longer sleep. Memories of her dream, of her shock over what her father had done, haunted her. It got her to thinking about Yasmine and the Bloody Passage and Macide and the Moonless Host, and suddenly her mind was alive with sigils. A flock of them flitted through her mind, each with their own magical properties. They complicated one another endlessly, one laying upon the next upon the next, the individual elements combining toward some grand effect.

It soon became clear she would need to return to the cavern to try some of the combinations before they drove her insane, but she was so very tired. She didn't know if she could take another day of it.

Spend one day away from the cavern. One day to restore your peace of mind.

It would probably help in the long run, but there was so much to do. She was a wartime queen. There were threats to her throne in the form of Ramahd and Duke Hektor II. And there were Mirea and Malasan who, despite her best efforts, were pressing the royal navy ever harder, moving closer toward Sharakhai. The civil unrest in Sharakhai was growing by the day.

And there was Macide . . .

It's him you need to concentrate on, Meryam. Sharakhai won't be safe until you rid the city of his taint.

Lifting the lid of the small chest on the bedside table, she took stock of her elixirs. Only three remained. Three. She'd had hundreds at one time, but she'd frittered them all away. *No*, she reminded herself, *not frittered*. They'd led her here, to one of the thrones of Sharakhai. And the three that remained might yet lead her to her greatest goal.

Taking one up, she unstoppered it and downed the contents in one go. Her limbs felt revitalized. Her chest swelled with warmth. Her exhaustion was driven away, as were the haunting echoes of her dream.

Let's make it worth it, she said as she prepared herself and headed down to the cavern. Despite her optimism, the day, like all those before it, proved fruitless. She and Prayna tried a dozen more combinations of sigils on the two scarabs, the father and his son. Then a dozen more after that.

Near the end of the day they found one that did something at last, a sigil Meryam had developed herself. It added a unique combination of *quest* and *desire*. As Prayna watched and the crystal shone its violet light, Meryam painted it on the father using his own blood. This time, she'd used a drop of adichara essence as well. In the chair some ten paces distant, the son, still blindfolded, his ruined ears bandaged, stirred.

Meryam's heart lifted as he stood. The hope in her soared as he spun in a circle, as if he'd heard his name being called. This was it. This was what would lead her to the final solution.

A moment later, however, the son began to wander away from his father. Where he was going and what was drawing him, Meryam had no idea, but it was clear the spell wasn't working as she'd hoped.

"Leave me," Meryam said.

Prayna looked ready to argue, but then she shrugged, stuffed several sheets of vellum into her leatherbound journal, and strode from the cavern without another word.

As Meryam sat in the chair before the largest of the tables, the son wandered into the darkness. She let him. She didn't care where he went. *This isn't going to work*, she realized. *It's too complex*. She'd focus on other efforts. The offer of peace she'd sent to the desert tribes had been answered only by Shaikh Neylana, and in the most nebulous of ways. She was *considering it*, and would forward her final decision soon. The gambit appeared to have failed, so she would order the Silver Spears' Lord Commander to step up his efforts to hunt the scarabs. She'd find some other way to bring the thirteenth tribe to her.

She touched her necklace, Yasmine's necklace, but it brought no solace. Touching it felt as if she were defacing her sister's memory.

Before Meryam knew it, she'd stood and flipped the table over, scattering the books, the scrolls, the ink, the quills, and the innumerable sheets of scribbled-on vellum. Her terrible, rage-filled scream felt small and inconsequential in the immensity of the cavern, which made her defeat taste all the more bitter.

Then she went stock still. She stared at the root-lined floor of the cavern, at the sheets of vellum that lay there. Some of the sigils stood out from the rest. Could it be? It seemed impossible, but the longer she stared at them, the more she saw how those particular sigils could be combined into a new master sigil to craft a spell she hadn't considered before. She gathered the sheets, laid them near the crystal, then knelt and stared at each in turn, running them through her mind. The more she stared, the more she realized how perfect it was, how precisely perfect.

With manic movements, she righted the table and readied an inkwell. On a fresh sheet of vellum she drew the new sigil, then stared at it while her world turned inside out. How peculiar was it that the fates would lead her to this only *after* she'd admitted defeat.

Her hands had started shaking—from the excitement, from fear, she knew not which. With all the care she could manage, she applied the sigil to the scarab who remained, the father. Long moments passed, but then she heard it: soft footsteps, the son returning. He walked unerringly to his father, felt around clumsily, found him, and immediately took him into a deep embrace. The father went stiff at first, then returned the hug.

Meryam unwound the bandages around their heads and pointed them toward the mouth of the large tunnel. The father and son, knowing the squad of Silver Spears stationed there would find them and lead them back to the Sun Palace, went hand in hand, both of them relieved, crying.

Meryam, meanwhile, cast her gaze about the cavern. It was a miracle, a triumph, but it made her skin crawl. Such things didn't just happen. She drew a sigil surreptitiously, a way to detect any who might be near, and for long moments she felt nothing, but then a chill sunk deep beneath her skin, and she sensed something on the very edge of her enhanced perceptions: a dark well of power beyond the crystal's light.

"You may as well come out," Meryam said.

A long silence followed. She prepared a number of spells, utterly unsure of what she'd stumbled across in the cavern. The more she was able to sense of it, the more ancient it felt, the more demonic. She was surprised, then, when it was no ehrekh that stepped into the light, but a man dressed in the Mirean style. His face was scarred badly, as were his hands. She knew this man. His name was Brama, and he'd been one of three men—Ramahd and the scarab, Emre, being the other two—who'd assaulted King Kiral's ship during the Battle of Blackspear. Brama had freed Rümayesh from the very sapphire Meryam had stolen from him.

"You've changed," Meryam said to him.

"You haven't. You're as single-minded as ever."

Meryam stared closer. There was a lump on his forehead, one with a straight scar running vertically over it. Meryam had no idea what it was, but she felt power there. He had a smell about him as well, the same scent as the ehrekh who'd been trapped within the sapphire. She had no idea how it had happened, but of one thing Meryam was certain: she was speaking not to Brama the backstreet thief, but to Rümayesh.

Meryam waved to the sheets of vellum. "Why did you give me these?"

"Because the way you've been flailing at it has been so very painful to watch."

"Why would you want to help me in the first place?"

Rümayesh smiled, a wicked thing on Brama's scarred face. "My reasons are my own."

"Were you sent by Tulathan? By Goezhen?"

"In a manner of speaking, yes."

Meryam's heart was beating faster and faster, partly from fear, but more so from the wild sense of hope building inside her. "If you know what I want," she ventured, "then you know I'm struggling with another problem."

"State your wish plainly, Meryam shan Aldouan."

The rules surrounding bargain-making with ehrekh were ancient and binding. Stories of those who had failed to navigate them properly abounded. Many seeking power had been left cursed or dead or, perhaps worst of all, beholden to the ehrekh. To ask Rümayesh for her help would be Meryam's entry into just such a bargain, which gave her pause, but she'd come too far to balk at it. She'd managed Guhldrathen. She could manage Rümayesh.

Pulling herself tall, Meryam spoke loudly and clearly. "I want Macide Ishaq'ava, the leader of the Moonless Host. I need him brought to me."

The smirk on Rümayesh's face made it clear she'd known what Meryam's answer would be. "A simpler matter than you may have guessed."

"And your price for sharing it?"

Rümayesh's eyes drifted down to Meryam's neck. "That will do."

Meryam felt her ears and cheeks go warm as she lifted one hand and touched the beads of her necklace, Yasmine's necklace. "This?"

Rümayesh nodded. "Just that."

"Why?"

"Because its story is a perfect morsel. I wish to taste it, savor it, *consume* it."

A morsel . . . Rümayesh wanted to revel in Meryam's pain. *You can't have it*, Meryam nearly said. *I'll never be parted from it. Never.* The very thought of having Rümayesh linger over Meryam's pain, *Yasmine's* pain, made her stomach twist in knots.

But what good was the necklace if she couldn't fulfill her promise to Yasmine? Keep the necklace and everything could fall apart. It would haunt her forever.

Rümayesh, apparently amused by Meryam's indecision, held her hand out. Choking back her contempt, Meryam slipped the necklace over her head and pooled it into Rümayesh's waiting hand. Her smile broadening, Rümayesh slipped it over *her* head, Brama's head. Mighty Alu, how foul it looked on her, how revolting to see her hands stroke the beads, to have her leer in that way of hers.

"Tell me now," Meryam said before she did something rash, "how will I get Macide?"

"By making a simple offer."

"An offer . . . ?"

"Of peace. You've sent one to the other twelve tribes. Send one to Macide Ishaq'ava as well and see what comes of it."

"I cannot. Not to *him*."

Rümayesh waved to the crystal, to the table with the vellum and the countless sigils. "You've done all this, but you won't send a simple offer to the man you hope to see hanged?"

"He'd never accept."

Rümayesh tilted her head, as if she couldn't believe Meryam was so dense. "The specter of war looms large in the desert, larger than you may think. To those who stand in its shadow, the lure of peace can be blinding."

"And if he still doesn't agree to meet me?"

The smile Rümayesh gave as she backed away was chilling. "I'm certain that he will."

She left, fading into the darkness of the cavern, but Meryam remained, wondering at all that had happened. After a long while, the chill of the cavern started seeping into her bones. As she breathed warmth into her hands and headed through the same tunnel the two men had taken, she considered how she could possibly offer peace to Macide Ishaq'ava, if it could ever work.

She felt naked without her necklace.

When Meryam left the cavern and the Silver Spears followed her up to the Sun Palace, Rümayesh returned to the crystal. She stared up at the lone tendril hanging down from above. She watched the slow drip of the adichara's essence, watched it patter against the crystal's surface and spread along the smooth sides.

She started at a sudden snap from within the crystal, a cracking sound. Within the crystal's depths, a bright line as long as her forearm had formed. It ran vertically, angular as a lightning strike.

Rümayesh smiled. For the first time since its creation, a fracture had formed within the crystal. The seal on a sacred door had just been broken. All that need happen now was to give that door a forceful shove.

Chapter 36

ALONG THE SEEDY EDGE of the Red Crescent district, Ramahd sat in the back room of a gambling den, studying the players while shisha smoke filled the air with a fragrant haze. Along with notes of old leather and loam, he could just detect the more floral scent of black lotus. Citing the growing epidemic of addictions, an edict had come down from the House of Kings preventing the smoking of pure black lotus, which had led to many drug dens being raided. In response, gambling dens like this one had sensed an opportunity and started offering tabbaq laced with lotus. Business was apparently thriving. The air was so thick with it Ramahd was starting to feel dreamy.

A few games of hollow head were being played with house dealers snapping cards over the red cloth tabletops with expert sweeps of their arms. Beyond them, near the rear door, a cluster of women and a few men threw dice in a heated game of barbudi. Ramahd had been to the den a handful of times, most often with Cicio and Tiron and the rest of the boys before all the troubles in Sharakhai began. It was run by a Qaimiri expatriate, which was precisely why he'd offered to meet Amaryllis here.

Ramahd was nursing a glass of brandy when she walked in. Amaryllis, who'd seen some thirty-two summers, had dark eyes and curly hair that fell halfway down her back. She wore a form-fitting dress of sky-blue cloth that had clearly seen better days. It lent her a confident air that made her seem all the more fetching, as if she was well aware she didn't need fine dresses to enhance her smoldering beauty.

She scanned the room while the room scanned her, then she caught Ramahd's eye and raised two fingers to the barkeep so that, by the time she was scraping away a chair at Ramahd's table, the burly barkeep was waddling over with a bottle of Qaimiri brandy and a pair of mismatched glasses.

"What's my girl been up to?" he asked in growling Qaimiran while pouring a generous measure of brandy into Amaryllis's glass.

She pulled the glass toward her and gave the golden liquor an energetic swirl. "The usual," she said, never taking her eyes from Ramahd's.

"Trouble then?" the barkeep said.

Amaryllis gave an alluring smirk. "Always."

The barkeep splashed a pittance of brandy into Ramahd's glass, slid it toward him, and shoved the cork back into the bottle. "If there's anything you need," he said to Amaryllis, "you have but to ask. You know that, right?"

Amaryllis lifted her glass to her nose and breathed in the scent. "I do." The barkeep left, but not without a sour look for Ramahd. Amaryllis, meanwhile, took a healthy swallow of the brandy. "I watched you come in, Ramahd."

"I thought you might."

She sent a glance over one shoulder, though not far enough to see the young man with straight chestnut hair sitting alone in the room's opposite corner. "And I saw young Duke Hektor come in an hour before that."

Duke Hektor looked up as the women playing barbudi cheered a good throw of the dice. He caught Ramahd's eye, looked embarrassed for having glanced his way, and returned to his own drink. He was Duke Hektor II, the eldest child of the man who'd been hanged on Meryam's orders shortly before the Malasani and their horde of golems swept through the city during the Battle for the Mount.

"I thought about summoning the Silver Spears," Amaryllis went on. "I thought about having you both brought to our queen in chains. We could have our chat then and be *sure* you're telling the truth."

Ramahd sipped his brandy. "So why didn't you?"

She pulled off a bracelet Ramahd had given her several years ago, during their short but passionate fling. "Because I think you believe you're doing the right thing." She tossed the bracelet onto the gouged wooden tabletop. It made a metallic *ting* as it slid into his glass. "This is your one chance to convince me of it, Ramahd."

He spun the bracelet around one finger, recalling how Amaryllis had smiled when he'd given it to her. It had been one of the rare times when she'd let her guard down. That smile had been a window into her soul, but like a break in the clouds showing a brief glimpse of the sun, it was there and gone in moments. "Do you know him," Ramahd asked, "Duke Hektor?"

She shrugged. "I knew his father. I'm sure I met him when he was a child."

"He's grown into a good man. He's wise for his age. Shrewd."

"And likely angry."

Ramahd waggled his head. "Of course, but he knows how the game is played."

"What does he want?"

"Let's hear it from the man himself." Ramahd raised his hand and beckoned Hektor to sit with them.

Hektor wove his way through the tables and joined them. A loud groan came from the entire hollow head table while Hektor regarded Amaryllis with a neutral expression.

"Well?" Amaryllis said. "I don't have all fucking day."

"I'm here to offer Queen Meryam an arrangement," Hektor began.

"An arrangement."

Hektor nodded. "An arrangement in which we divide the duties of running the Kingdom."

"You'll have to forgive me, but I have no idea what sort of *arrangement* our queen might make that could possibly accommodate that. She's already queen. There's no *sharing* to be done." Amaryllis sat back, her smile a charming combination of lush lips, perfect teeth, and beguiling dimples. "That's *literally* what it means to be queen."

Hektor's face went red, but Ramahd gave him credit. His voice was steady as he replied, "Some might argue that one who commits patricide to gain a throne is no rightful queen at all."

"A scurrilous, unjustified claim, Duke Hektor"—she waved to Ramahd— "with only a single witness to back it up."

"No," Hektor countered evenly. "Not *a single witness.* There is another who can testify to its truth."

Amaryllis paused. Her eyes slid to Ramahd. She knew who Hektor meant—Hamzakiir—and she was now wondering if they had him in their custody, ready to speak against Meryam.

"But that's a matter of little consequence for the moment," Hektor went on, just as he and Ramahd had agreed. "What I propose is not for Meryam to step down."

"It isn't?"

"No. I propose she remain queen in name, and to cede power in Qaimir to me."

"Cede power to *you*?"

"I will rule Qaimir, as is my right."

"And what, pray tell, would Queen Meryam be doing while you rule her country?"

"She would stay here in the desert. She's shown that she wants it more than her homeland, so let her have it. She can keep her title too. I'll even grant her leave to use our sandships to support her efforts, within reason of course."

Amaryllis laughed. "Enlighten me. Why in the great wide desert would she agree to all of this?"

"Because if she doesn't, it will mean civil war in Qaimir. Because I have lords committed to me, ready to raise an army. We will not bend. Should Meryam refuse and fight us, it will tear our country apart. We'll still win, but I would forego that. I would protect our people from the threats our kingdom would face should we weaken ourselves in some needless conflict."

"Come, Duke Hektor. How many could you possibly have beyond your own family? The Amansirs, certainly. Likely the Guerons as well, and if they've joined you, I'd wager the Remigios have as well. But beyond them?"

"I won't name names. We all know what Meryam does to those who stand up to her."

Amaryllis was a master at hiding her true emotions, but Ramahd knew her well and saw a brief glimpse of relief pass over her face. She thought they had nothing but a weak bargaining position with the might of a bare handful of lords to back them. "If this is all you have to offer Queen Meryam, then you have nothing." She downed the last of her brandy. "I see no reason to trouble her with it."

The moment Amaryllis stood, Ramahd saw the barkeep make a signal to a boy standing near the entrance to the front of the house. The boy dashed through the doorway and was gone.

Ramahd, heart racing, snatched Amaryllis's wrist, preventing her from leaving. She stared down in surprise, then anger, as if she were ready to draw the long, straight dirk from her belt and cut Ramahd for the offense. Her hard expression softened, however, when Ramahd picked up the bracelet.

"Just make her the offer."

"She'll laugh at it, Ramahd. She'll bite *my* head off for even meeting with you."

"You would risk war because you can't be bothered to talk to Meryam about an offer of peace?" He pried open her hand, placed the bracelet on her palm, and closed her fingers around it. "Present the offer, Amaryllis."

She stared at the bracelet but never got a chance to respond, for just then the back door was kicked in and a dozen Silver Spears poured into the room, swords and crossbows at the ready. "Down! Get down! All of you, on the floor!"

Ramahd stared at Amaryllis, his eyes wide with shock. "Mighty Alu, I *trusted* you!"

Amaryllis stared back with just as much surprise. "It wasn't me!" she cried as more soldiers burst through the front entrance.

"No talking!" said the captain, and shoved Amaryllis down to the floor.

"Easy!" Duke Hektor said, which earned him a punch across the jaw.

Hektor's face went purple with rage. He charged the captain, but three of his men swooped in, grabbed his hair and jerkin, and rained more punches down on him. Hektor gave a mighty roar and tried to fight his way free, but was tripped and fell hard against Amaryllis. A rather large soldier shoved Hektor's bleeding face into the bodice of Amaryllis's blue dress, pinning them both against the wall.

Ramahd tried to help Hektor, but he was intercepted and pressed into a nearby corner. While two men held him in place, a third aimed a loaded crossbow at his throat and grinned, showing off two rows of ragged, tabbaq-stained teeth. "I'd stay nice and quiet were I you."

"I am an agent of the queen!" Amaryllis shouted from beneath Duke Hektor.

The captain laughed. "If you're an agent of the queen, then I'm the fucking King of Kings." His men pulled Hektor up, while the captain grabbed a hunk of Amaryllis's hair, dragged her to her feet, and shoved her toward the back door. "Now get moving."

"You will release us!" Amaryllis cried. "You will release us immediately!"

But none of them listened. They were taken to a nearby garrison, where they were thrown into a pair of dirty underground cells, Amaryllis in one, Ramahd and Hektor in the other.

It didn't take long, however, before they came back for Amaryllis. Opening the door, the captain sucked his teeth. "You're free to go."

Ramahd gave her a look filled with disappointment and betrayal.

"It wasn't me," she said as she stepped out. With Hektor's blood all over the bodice of her blue dress, she looked like a murderer over a fresh kill. She seemed to fumble for the right words, then spoke softly. "I'll see to this."

And then she was gone.

Nearly an hour passed before the captain returned and fixed his grinning face on Ramahd. "It went just like you said. She headed straight for the House of Kings."

"Good," Ramahd said.

"Is that long enough in your cozy cell, my lord?"

Judging that it *had* been long enough for them to be unobserved, Ramahd nodded, and the captain unlocked the door with a clank, and led Ramahd and Hektor up to the garrison's main floor. They came to an office of sorts, a room once used for the lodging of citizens' complaints, and where the garrison's Spears received their daily assignments.

Waiting, his bulk leaning against a counter with several empty chairs behind it, was the drug den's potbellied barkeep. As Hektor neared, the big man held out his hand, sparing a cringe for Hektor's bloody face. "Hope the boys didn't rough you up too bad."

Hektor, whose lower lip was still bleeding, grasped forearms with him. "I've had worse," he said as the two of them shook.

The barkeep slapped Hektor's shoulder. "There's a good lad."

The barkeep had been an ardent supporter of Meryam's father, King Aldouan. He had blood ties to the throne, albeit distant ones, and his father had served under Duke Hektor I. When he'd heard Ramahd's and Hektor's tales, he'd grown angry enough to betray Amaryllis, a woman who'd treated him more or less like she'd treated everyone else in her life: as a useful lever in her manipulations of Sharakhai's seedier elements.

The barkeep's smile faded as he jutted his chin at Ramahd. "You think it worked?"

Ramahd shrugged. "We'll know soon enough."

"Indeed we will." This came from the back doorway of the grimy office, where Hamzakiir's rangy form was striding toward them. Behind him came Cicio, his compact swagger in stark contrast to the genteel sweep of Hamzakiir's long limbs.

The barkeep looked suddenly uncomfortable. "Well then, I'll leave you gentlemen to it, shall I?"

At this, Ramahd gave Cicio a sharp nod, and the small man sent a leather purse arcing through the air. The barkeep caught it, opened it, and smiled broadly. Their transaction complete, he left without another word, his boys, all wearing Silver Spears uniforms, filing after him like a pack of jackals after their leader.

It left only Ramahd, Hektor, Hamzakiir, and Cicio inside the garrison.

"How soon do you think she'll try?" Hektor asked. He was a brave young man, but Ramahd could see the fear brewing inside him. No one liked being the subject of blood magic, least of all the man who stood to inherit a kingdom.

"She'll do it tonight," Ramahd said, "perhaps as soon as Amaryllis returns."

"Agreed," Hamzakiir intoned. "Best we go and prepare our surprise."

The four of them left together, passing the ruins of the barracks, not visible from inside the office, as they went. The barracks had been damaged by the Malasani golems and had since been closed. It had made for a convenient location for their caper to play out, a way to lower Meryam's suspicions that Amaryllis had been part of a plan for her to use the blood that had been so conveniently smeared on her dress. Meryam would use that blood, either to kill or dominate Hektor, which would give Hamzakiir a conduit to Meryam herself.

They made their way north to the city's quarry and a set of tunnels that led to several small, manmade rooms once used by the Moonless Host. Several cots lay in one, which Hektor promptly availed himself of.

"Your wrist," Hamzakiir said.

Hektor hesitated, but they'd come too far for him to have reservations now. He held out his arm, and Hamzakiir used a blooding ring to pierce the skin of his wrist. He drank of Hektor's blood, the very same blood that Meryam, if all went according to plan, would drink as well, then closed the wound.

A nervous energy charged the room. The board was set. A very dangerous game was about to be played between Meryam and Hamzakiir, with Hektor, the rightful King of Qaimir, their battlefield.

Chapter 37

HALF A DAY'S SAIL from the foothills of the Taloran Mountains, the *Red Bride* signaled Ihsan's galleon to approach. Çeda told them of a small cove south of the valley.

"I know it," Husamettín called across the gap between their ships.

"If we're not finished at the acacia within a week," Çeda said, "I'll come in a skiff and let you know."

"You needn't bother," Ihsan called across the distance. "Zeheb will be listening to your whispers."

The very notion sent Çeda's worries over the Kings and their true purposes to swirling within her mind, but her thoughts were interrupted when two sharp whistles came from the top of the *Bride*'s mainmast.

"Ship ho!" Kameyl called.

Çeda groaned inwardly. She'd hoped to avoid being seen on the way to the valley. "Her shape?"

"A ketch, from the look of her! Might be Tribe Khiyanat's. Might not."

Well, there was nothing to do about it now—someone on the distant ship had surely already spotted them sailing next to a royal galleon. They parted soon after, the Kings' galleon sailing southeast while the *Bride* continued toward Mount Arasal. As the sun was setting, they reached one of three sandy bays where the tribe anchored their ships. The following morning, they made the trek up into the mountains and reached the valley.

To Çeda's disappointment, Macide was gone. He was tending to a harbor to the north where a dozen new ships were being built, but Leorah was there, and she welcomed Çeda and the others with open arms. She looked more bent than she once did, and was moving so slowly Çeda felt bad she'd had to come down from the old fortress to meet them.

"We would have come to you," Çeda told her.

"These bones aren't so old they can't make it down a hill, Çedamihn Ahyanesh'ala."

"It isn't the climbing down I'm worried about. It's the climbing up."

"Afraid I won't make it?"

"I'm afraid you'll topple down the mountain!"

Leorah smacked her lips, and waved to Kameyl with a mischievous smile. "Then why don't you strap me to that bloody great Maiden of yours? I could do with a ride."

Çeda laughed, then paused before asking her next question. "Has there been news of Emre?"

"I'm surprised it wasn't the first question out of your mouth."

"In truth, I was afraid to ask."

"Well, I'm sorry, child, there's been no news as yet, but don't you worry"—she patted Çeda's wrist while climbing doggedly along the trail—"that boy's a fighter. Sooner or later, he'll turn up."

Çeda certainly hoped so, but she couldn't shake the feeling something terrible had happened to him.

As they climbed the slopes of Mount Arasal, the heat of the desert gave way to a pleasant mountain breeze. Eventually they reached the valley, where Leorah, tired but still eager to trade tales, led Çeda beneath the shade of an ironwood. Jenise, Kameyl, and Sümeya came behind, speaking in low tones. Nalamae, meanwhile, gave the stone fortress above them a long piercing stare, as if she were reliving some memory, then moved toward the acacia near the banks of a clear green lake.

The acacia, planted by Leorah, Çeda, and Macide, had been a seedling when Çeda left the valley. Now, less than a year later, it was fully grown, ten paces tall with reaching arms and leaf-choked branches. Hundreds of glass chimes hung from the branches by thread-of-gold. Tied to the chimes were mementos—beads, charms, locks of hair, and bits of cloth. They were from the tribe, Çeda realized, small contributions from those who lived in the valley.

Nalamae, her staff in hand, stared up as the chimes played a subtle symphony. She stood unmoving for a long while, then raised her staff high and swung it in circles above her head. The wind picked up, making the boughs and branches sway. Sunlight speared through gaps in the canopy to glint off the myriad surfaces of the chimes. It made the tree look like a thing come alive, a creature from another world.

Word of Nalamae's arrival spread quickly. Dozens gathered to see. When Nalamae had been here last, she'd been tall and impressive. Even carried in on a stretcher, wounded by an arrow loosed from King Beşir's bow, there had been an undeniable gravitas about her. *This* Nalamae was a mousy woman who seemed tentative and unsure of herself. Some of those watching, maybe even most of them, must have thought Çeda had made a terrible mistake.

When Nalamae faced the tree and spread her arms wide in a gesture of welcoming, as if asking the tree to share its secrets, Leorah began ushering everyone away with broad sweeps of her arms. "Leave the goddess in peace."

And so they did.

In the days that followed, Nalamae spent every waking hour at the tree. She walked around it. She climbed it. She examined the chimes for hours on end, often forgoing food. She seemed content to keep her thoughts to herself, and Çeda didn't want to disturb her, but on the third day, with no indication of progress, Çeda could take the uncertainty no longer.

"Is it working?" she asked Nalamae.

The goddess was sitting with her back against the tree, eyes closed, but at this she opened them. "If you mean is it showing me visions, then yes, it's showing me many. But if you mean is it forming what one might call a memory of who I am and what I was before all this began, then no. It's a patchwork. I don't know what connects to what. It feels like a hundred people are telling me bits of their lives all at once. No context. Jumping from story to story."

Çeda cringed. "As bad as that?"

"As bad as that. It's maddening, Çeda." She smiled halfheartedly. "But I think it will come." She rubbed one of the gnarled roots beside her. "I've come to trust this tree. It *wants* to speak—it just doesn't know how. And *I* don't know how to talk to *it*. But it's like my ships. When I first start building them, it's a mountain of work, and all I have to show for it is a collection of individual, disconnected parts. But when it starts to take form, it does so quickly. We shipwrights say the ship is finding itself." She gave the root a gentle pat. "We're nearing that point, aren't we?"

Çeda was asked by many to tell her tale since leaving the valley months earlier. And she did, though she always left out her temporary alliance with the Kings. She thought about omitting the entire battle at the harbor, but she felt it important that everyone know about Nalamae's reawakening, so she said Goezhen had fallen on them on their way to the *Red Bride*.

The King of the asirim, Sehid-Alaz, seemed awestruck by the tale. He pressed her for details, particularly how the shriveled eye of Navesh the All-Seeing had helped Nalamae to find herself. She told him what she could and hid the rest. The deception made her nervous and sad—Sehid-Alaz wouldn't take kindly to her truce with the Kings, and he didn't deserve her lies—but there was nothing for it. The Kings' presence had to remain hidden.

Sehid-Alaz had changed greatly. He was once bent, nearly broken. Now he stood tall, though there seemed to be a different sort of weight on him. He was dour and taciturn. The blackened skin of his face was often pinched into an expression of worry or fear. He was free from the gods' curse, but chains of a different sort bound him.

"We deserve our time in the land beyond," he said to her one evening. The two of them were standing on the fortress's walls, staring down at the lake and the acacia beside it.

"You do," Çeda said, who had herself wondered when that day would come, and whether it would happen all at once, the asirim all going together to the land beyond. Might the answer lay with the adichara trees, the blooming fields, and the strange crystal in the cavern? Or would the asirim simply live on, fed by the magic that still infused them, until the fates took them at last? Çeda waved to Nalamae, who had just stepped out from beneath the cover of the acacia's branches. "The goddess may find the answer to that question as well."

"Or she may not." Sehid-Alaz turned and took to the stairs leading down to the courtyard. "The asirim are hardly the focus of her efforts, after all."

Çeda wanted to mollify him, but how could she? He was right and they both knew it. So she only watched him go.

Word came on the fourth day. Macide would return that night. A feast would be held in the fortress to celebrate Nalamae's return, though Nalamae herself had refused the invitation, preferring to remain near the tree.

"That many voices in one place," she'd told Çeda, "would be too much. It could set me back days."

That night, as the people of the tribe were beginning to gather, Çeda lingered in the fortress's courtyard. She looked down at the pair of graves that had been dug beneath the flagstones. The tribe had debated long and hard about what to do with Nalamae and Yerinde's remains. In the end they'd decided that neither should be removed from the keep—the site of their last battle was holy ground, and even though Yerinde had been there to do them harm, no one wanted to risk angering the other gods by desecrating it.

"And so our lost lamb has returned," someone called from behind her.

Çeda turned to find Macide, a bright smile on his handsome face, walking toward her. He looked much the same as she remembered, though there was more gray streaking his forked beard than before.

"You're back," she said.

"I'm back," he replied, and the two of them embraced.

He stared at the flagstones' engravings. One read, *Here lies Nalamae, lastborn and savior of the Thirteenth Tribe.* The other read, *Here lies Yerinde, goddess of love and ambitious thoughts.*

He motioned to Yerinde's. "Ambitious, perhaps, but I will admit I question the *love* part."

Beyond Macide, Sümeya was striding into the courtyard with Kameyl. "Yes, well"—Çeda waved to Sümeya with a smile—"love makes us do strange things."

Macide glanced over his shoulder. "It does indeed."

The feast was held in the keep's audience hall. A fire was lit in the hearth and dozens came, including Leorah, Dardzada the apothecary, Shal'alara of the Three Blades, and other tribal elders. Rasime, a severe young ship's captain and one of the Moonless Host's most ruthless agents, was there as well.

With her keen eyes and her hair pulled tight into a tail, she looked more than a little like a desert hawk. Even Sehid-Alaz came, though he did little more than sit in a distant corner near the hearth, speaking to few. With his dark, shriveled skin and his somber clothes, cut in their ancient style, he looked more memory than man.

They ate tangy bread dotted with pine nuts and slathered in goat's cheese. They had lentil soup topped with slices of grilled lemon and a sprinkling of a rare mountain herb that tasted like grapefruit and rosemary. They had wild rice, stewed tomatoes, and lamb marinated in yogurt and spices, spit-roasted for hours until the meat was deliciously crunchy on the outside and fell off the bone within.

Just before dessert was served, Macide was called away. Çeda was so stuffed she was tempted to leave the hall and walk off a bit of the meal, but the moment she learned kanafeh was being served, she sat right back down. Kanafeh was a soft cheese baked in delicate, flaky pastry dough then slathered in rosewater syrup and topped with toasted pistachios. It was gooey and crunchy, with the sort of salty-sweetness that made the mouth water with every bite, and it was paired with a Qaimiri port that stood up to the dessert's sweetness and brought its own flavors of wild berries, currant, and thyme.

It was as delicious a meal as Çeda had ever had, but halfway through something made it even better. Macide returned with two men in tow. Çeda's heart leapt as she recognized the first, Frail Lemi, who was greeted with a chorus of salutations. Waving to all with a toothy smile, he halted at the door, momentarily blocking Çeda's view of the man behind him. The moment Frail Lemi spotted an empty chair with a plate of kanafeh sitting before it, however, he immediately sat and began devouring the food, and the man who'd been hidden was revealed.

It was Emre.

A childish grin broke over Çeda's face. A host of butterflies took flight within her chest as all the worry that had been building inside her since learning of Emre's disappearance shed from her in a rush.

Frail Lemi had eaten his kanafeh in three massive bites and was already calling for more. Emre, meanwhile, made his way around the table, exchanging greetings along the way, always with one eye on Çeda. When he reached her end of the table, she stood and the two of them embraced tightly. Everyone was watching, including Sümeya, whose sober expression Çeda had no trouble interpreting. But in that moment Çeda could spare no thoughts for anyone else. Emre felt too good against her to do anything more than lose herself in the moment.

After a breath, maybe two, they were whistled at, and people began laughing and talking in low tones. Çeda finally broke away, grabbed an extra chair, and made room for Emre beside her.

"Try it," she said, and fed him a bite of her still-warm kanafeh. "Wait . . ." She handed him her glass of port as he chewed. "Chase it with this."

Emre put on a sour face as he finished the bite and sipped the port. "Horrible," he said. "Worst thing I've ever tasted."

She slapped his shoulder.

Emre laughed, but as he set down the glass, his brow furrowed, as if something pained him. When she gave him a questioning look, he made a miserable go of trying to smile. "It's only a headache."

"Should we call Dardzada?"

"He's already given me something."

Araq was poured into every cup. At the head of the table, Macide stood and raised his glass. The light from the oil lamps spaced about the room flickered off the viper tattoos snaking around his well muscled forearms. "I will admit I had my doubts that Çeda's mission would lead us to the goddess. But now Nalamae has been found, and so I ask all of you, what can it mean but that smoother sands lie ahead?" With a graceful swirl of his glass, he invited the room to share in his joy. "To brighter days."

"To brighter days!" the room replied as one.

All downed their araq, which tasted of oak and juniper and burning pine.

"And Emre's return," Macide went on, "has brought the news we'd been hoping for. Neylana and the southern tribes have agreed to join the Alliance."

The room roared and drank again, many calling out, "A desert united!"

"It clears the way for something the shaikhs and I have been discussing for some time. A path to peace." Macide paused, waiting for the hubbub to die. "Queen Meryam has sent us an offer." An immediate rumble of discontent swallowed Macide's next words, so he repeated them, louder this time. "An offer of peace!"

"Meryam is a *foreigner*," said Rasime. "She is but a stand-in for the Sharakhani Kings."

"The Sharakhani Kings are gone"—Macide stared directly at Çeda—"thanks to the sacrifices of many, some in this very room."

"Not all the Kings are accounted for," Rasime replied evenly, "and even if your words were true, who now sits their thrones? Their children, who are every bit as eager as their fathers to turn back the pages of time and make Sharakhai as it once was."

"That remains to be seen. And don't forget, the very fact that there *are* new Kings and Queens shows how far we've come. That they're willing to *bargain* with us shows they respect our power. They acknowledge our history. They acknowledge our right to exist. Who would have thought to see it only a few short years ago?"

"They're only doing so because the war is on."

"Yes, the desert is at war," Macide said, "but there's more to consider. The Kings are weakened. The thirteenth tribe has taken a stand. The asirim have joined our cause. And now there's the Alliance for them to reckon with. There are a dozen reasons besides, but the point is this: it is time for talks of lasting peace."

"The House of Kings is still intact," Rasime said, as if that disputed everything.

"The House of Kings is a house of *cards*," Macide shot back. "They tremble at the might of the foreign invaders."

"Let them! Let us back away and see what comes of Sharakhai and the fleets of Mirea and Malasan. When they're done, we'll go and knock whoever's left from their perch."

"That would cause untold misery in Sharakhai. And offers no guarantee we can face whoever's left, not if Qaimir or Kundhun retreat, or worse, turn traitor and join hands with the victors. This is the time to speak, while our leverage is greatest."

"So what do you propose?" This came from Sümeya, which pleased Rasime not at all.

"Meryam has offered to meet us in Mazandir," he said to the room. "I say we go and hear her out."

Rasime looked down her side of the table. "And the royal galleon that sailed with Çeda? Will they be joining us as well?"

Çeda realized it must have been Rasime's ketch Kameyl had spotted as they were sailing toward the mountains. "It wasn't a galleon," Çeda said easily. "It was a three-masted schooner, a merchant ship that wished to sail under mutual protection. By now it's halfway to Ishmantep."

Rasime stood. "The ship was a royal galleon," she said matter-of-factly. "The only question is who was on it?"

Çeda stared easily into Rasime's fiery eyes. "Believe whatever you wish. It makes no difference to me."

Suddenly Rasime's kenshar was in her hand. "Take that tone of voice with me again and—"

Rasime paused as the doors burst open. It was Jenise, her striking, emerald-and-amber eyes bright in the lamplight. "Come quickly," she said. "Something's happening to Nalamae."

The mood in the room immediately shifted. Suddenly everyone was rushing from the feasting hall and into the courtyard. The courtyard itself was surrounded on three sides by the fortress's stone walls. The large bonfire lit in celebration of Nalamae's return shed light on a dozen Shieldwives and guardsmen in thawbs and turbans. They were gathered around Nalamae, who was staring down at her own grave. She wore a gleaming set of armor— a mail shirt with shining pauldrons, greaves, and bracers. She had high leather boots tooled in the elegant designs of the thirteenth tribe. Charms and beads, surely taken from the tree, had been worked into her eggplant-colored turban. Dozens hung on it, shaking when she moved her head.

Where the armor came from Çeda had no idea, and in any case it was far from the most disturbing thing. For days Nalamae had been exploring the acacia's visions. She'd been persistent, but also inquisitive and accepting, a woman willing to take what the tree gave her. Now she had an intense look, as if the answers she'd found had done nothing to quiet her heart.

"What's happened?" Çeda asked as she stepped closer.

Ignoring her entirely, Nalamae knelt over Yerinde's grave, set her staff aside, and pressed both hands against the flagstones. The stones began to buckle. To lift. Some were thrown aside as the earth below surged upward with a sound like rolling thunder. From the dark, churning earth, the head of a bright, shining spear appeared. It was Yerinde's, buried with her after Çeda had taken Night's Kiss and cleaved her from neck to navel. Nalamae gripped it by its haft, lifted it against the night sky, and stared at it.

"What's happened, Nalamae?" Çeda asked again. "What have you seen?"

Still holding the adamantine spear, Nalamae took her staff up as well. "My eyes have been opened."

"I don't understand."

She turned to Çeda at last, her gaze chilling. "In my prior lives, I was blinded. I now know why. Had I allowed myself to see, it would have been too much, too soon. My brothers and sisters would have found me too easily. It was important that I hide from them, to have the time to learn who I truly was."

"And now?"

"The acacia granted me many things. Not enough to know all, but I saw the way I was hunted. I saw how my brothers and sisters sought to prevent me from returning, to ensure their grand plan would remain hidden. I remember how it felt. I remember their eyes upon me. I remember them closing in."

"That's good, isn't it? It will help you to avoid them now."

"You don't understand. They're no longer hunting me, not even Goezhen. They're content to let this play out, which means their grand plan is close to fruition. Very close." With that she threw her staff into the flames.

"No!" Leorah cried, and ran toward it.

But Nalamae stopped her. "Leave it, grandmother. It is a symbol of a different day, a different age. One I now leave behind."

"Please," Leorah cried, "don't let it burn."

But Nalamae would not relent. For long moments, the courtyard watched as the fire began to consume the staff. Çeda was terrified. She'd searched for Nalamae and against all odds had found her. And now the goddess was acting in ways she didn't understand.

Macide had come to stand by Çeda's side. "What do you propose we do, goddess?"

Nalamae considered him for a time before speaking. She looked like she regretted what she was about to say. "I don't know the right path for you." She gripped the spear tightly in both hands. "But I know *my* path. I'm leaving."

As a chorus of worried voices rose up, Çeda felt her own fear intensifying. "But why?" she asked the goddess. "Surely we have some time yet."

"No, we don't, but I might gain you some. My brothers and sisters have become comfortable. The very fact that they've gone quiet means that they think things are moving along their proper course. I bid you to return to Sharakhai. Treat with Queen Meryam if that is your wish."

"And you?" Çeda asked.

She began walking away. "It's time I took the hunt to them."

Çeda went after her. "Nalamae, please."

But she wouldn't listen. She kept walking, bits of her flaking away like so much sand, more and more borne on the wind until all that remained was a tight swirl, a dwindling gyre that lost itself in a threadlike stream that was drawn up and into the night sky. Soon that was gone too, and so was Nalamae.

Chapter 38

I N A HIGH MOUNTAIN VALE, Hamid followed a dry stream bed by starlight.
He was tired. His feet ached. He'd eaten little and drank naught but water
from mountain streams for days. He wanted to reach Darius. He wanted to
tell him the good news and then forget the terrible trouble he'd landed himself in for one night.

Thoughts of telling tales vanished, however, when he neared the copse of
pine he and Darius had been using as a shelter and heard voices from within.
Pulling his knife, he scanned the starlit landscape for signs of threat, then
stalked over the dry ground. A lamp was lit inside the copse, which he and
Darius had agreed not to do unless absolutely necessary.

As he came closer, he heard the voices more clearly. One was Darius. The
other, he soon realized, was Rasime, a one-time scarab and a woman who
detested the fact that the Moonless Host had all but vanished almost as
much as Hamid did.

His fears vanishing, Hamid slipped the knife back into its sheath and
approached the trees. The smell of pine struck him as he spread the prickling
branches wide and sidled into the shelter. Between the denuded tree trunks
was a hollowed-out space the size of a small tent. It was there that Darius sat

cross-legged with Rasime on a blue, horsehair blanket. Darius shifted, and Hamid plopped himself down, the three of them forming a rough triangle around the tiny oil lamp, which cast a soft golden glow over the needle-strewn ground.

Rasime stared at the bruises and cuts that still marked Hamid's face. "Frail Lemi really worked you over, didn't he?"

"Don't talk to me about Frail Lemi."

"He's in the valley. You want me to take a knife to his throat for you?"

"I'll save that pleasure for myself, thank you."

Rasime shrugged. "As you wish." With the space so tight, she lay to one side, legs folded while propping herself up on one elbow. "Macide is planning to treat with Queen Meryam."

"I know," Hamid said.

"He's got the tribe ready to pick up and go to Mazandir to meet her."

"I know."

Rasime's hawklike gaze became more intense. "How could you? It only happened today. And why do you look so fucking smug?"

There was no denying it. Hamid *was* smug. He felt like the fates were finally shining on him. Five days ago he'd been sitting in this very copse while Darius was out gathering berries when the branches parted and an intruder drove into the shelter. It had been Brama the thief, looking much as he had before the Battle of Blackspear save for the strange lump on his forehead.

"You're in a difficult situation, Hamid," Brama said to him.

Hamid stared, wary. "What would you know about it?"

"I know you're on the run. I know that when Emre reaches the tribe in five days' time, you'll be hunted down to account for your crimes. I know you're aware that Macide will believe *him* over *you*."

Hamid had no idea how Brama could be certain about everything he'd said, but Hamid knew things too. Like that the Brama of his youth couldn't know such things on his own. And that Brama had been caught up with the ehrekh, Rümayesh. He knew from the tales told in Sharakhai that Rümayesh liked to choose souls and inhabit them for a time before casting them aside like old clothes. "You're not Brama at all, are you?"

"Does it bother you to know that I'm not?"

"I suppose not." Hamid shrugged. "Unless I'm being used."

Brama laughed. "We are all being used in one way or another. What do you care, so long as you get what you want?"

"And what do you suppose I want?"

"A tribe free of Macide Ishaq'ava and his closest allies. A tribe whose reins you can take up to do with as you please."

Hamid tried to hide his surprise. That was *precisely* what he wanted. "And you can give that to me?"

"I can give you the tools to achieve it."

"Tools."

"Just so, Hamid."

"Such as?"

"Such as the location of four Kings of Sharakhai. Such as their recent dealings with one of your own, Çedamihn Ahyanesh'ala. Such as the offer that is even now on its way to the hands of Macide Ishaq'ava, sent by Queen Meryam herself."

Pulling himself back to the present, Hamid spied the bottle of araq Rasime had brought. Without bothering to ask for permission, he pulled the cork, but made sure to offer Rasime the first drink. When she declined, he took a long pull off it, then handed it to Darius, who took no more than a taste.

"The tale Rümayesh went on to tell me was wild," Hamid said, and told them what Rümayesh had told him: that Çeda had allied herself with Queen Nayyan to find Nalamae, that she'd allied herself with Ihsan and the other Kings to help fight off an attack by Goezhen, that they'd sailed together from Sharakhai so their Alliance could be blessed by Macide. He finished by telling them of his trek to the bay Rümayesh had told him about, where he'd found a royal galleon, and more. "Husamettín was there. As were Cahil, Ihsan, and a tall, skinny man who I swear to the gods was Zeheb."

"Sand and stone," Rasime said, "I *knew* Çeda was lying. I knew it was a royal galleon. Gods, you should have seen how she pranced about the valley, like she's our fucking savior. She'll die for this, Hamid. I swear to you she'll die."

"Calm down. This will take a bit of time. We can't go killing anyone until we've convinced others of what we've seen. Then and only then can we make a move on Macide."

Rasime's eyes narrowed. "He's well protected."

Hamid shrugged. "I can name a dozen who are grinding their teeth at the thought of treating with the Kings, even if it *is* through their mouth-piece, Meryam."

"So can I," Rasime said, "but there's still Sehid-Alaz. He won't stand for it. It would darken his honor, which is about all he ever talks about. That and being sent to the farther fields to take his final rest."

Hamid smiled. "Let *me* worry about Sehid-Alaz. You start talking to the others."

Three days after Nalamae left the fortress below Mount Arasal, Macide and the thirteenth tribe departed for Mazandir to speak with Queen Meryam. There were representatives from every tribe except Neylana's and the southern tribes, but a swift patrol ship had been sent ahead to warn them and have them send envoys of their own to attend.

Ten ships in all sailed the sand. Emre would captain the *Amaranth* with Macide, Frail Lemi, and Sehid-Alaz. The Shieldwives, several hundred of the tribe's warriors, and dozens of asirim would follow on other ships. In a bit of good fortune, young Shaikh Aríz of Tribe Kadri had arrived the day before they were to leave and asked to join them.

"My tribe is to be represented in these talks," Aríz had told Macide. "How can I report to them faithfully unless I'm there to witness it?"

Frail Lemi had nodded knowingly, proudly. Aríz had nodded back in the same manner, then the two of them had laughed.

Aríz's vizir, Ali-Budrek, however, objected strenuously. "Send *me*, my shaikh. I'll return as soon as it's over and tell you everything."

"And let you have all the fun?"

Ali-Budrek puffed up like a scared sand drake, but before he could say anything further, Frail Lemi chuckled and said, "Might be more fun than you can handle, Little Shaikh."

Aríz sneered. "If it turns out to be anything like the battle at the gorge, I'll need to be there to save your sorry tail. *Again.*"

Frail Lemi burst into laughter and the two of them clasped forearms, to the clear disappointment of Ali-Budrek. Ali-Budrek had always hated that Aríz and Frail Lemi had become like brothers, but Aríz didn't seem to care what Ali-Budrek thought, and Frail Lemi was often oblivious to the displeasure of others.

The *Amaranth* sailed at the head of their small fleet. The *Red Bride*, with Çeda, her Shieldwives, and the two ex-Blade Maidens, Sümeya and Kameyl, came next. Then came Aríz's caravel, the *Autumn Rose*, and five more. The irascible Rasime, who had fought for and been granted the right to join the fleet, brought up the rear on her ketch, the *Burning Sand*.

"I don't know why you let her come," Emre said to Macide as the ship heeled over a large dune. The two of them were sitting with Frail Lemi on the foredeck of the *Amaranth*. "Rasime spreads poison wherever she goes."

Macide was sitting cross-legged on the deck, one of his two shamshirs held in his hands as he ran the edge carefully over a sharpening stone. His other shamshir waited its turn on the sun-worn planks beside him. "What sort of leader would I be," he said without looking up, "if I allowed no one who spoke against me to bear witness to our talks? Let Rasime come. Let her see what we can gain, and then she'll tell the rest."

"If you think she's going to tell them the truth, I've got an oasis to sell you."

Frail Lemi, leaning against the bulwark, laughed like a hyena, then eased arms thick as most men's legs along the gunwales. "An oasis to sell you."

"Some people will *never* acknowledge the good you've done," Emre went on, "not if it conflicts with the lies they've told themselves. Rasime is lost in hatred, convinced the desert must be purified."

Frail Lemi rubbed his bald head with a lazy swipe of his hand. "Hamid once told me she thinks she's Suad reborn, the new Scourge of Sharakhai."

Emre waved at him. "You see?"

"Well she *is* pretty feisty," Macide said, sharing a wink with Frail Lemi. Frail Lemi laughed.

"I'm serious," Emre said.

"So am I," Macide shot back. "I can't control her thoughts, nor the thoughts of others. So we'll go. We'll meet with the Qaimiri queen."

"And then what?"

"We do what we've always done. Navigate the shifting sands as best we can. Some may willingly drink the poisoned broth Rasime brews, but many others will see the truth, that we did what was best for the people of the desert."

"Aren't you worried Queen Meryam has other purposes for you?"

"Because of the Bloody Passage?"

"No, because I heard she doesn't like men with tattoos." Emre's head was starting to hurt again. "Of *course* because of the Bloody Passage."

"And if I sent someone else to treat with her *for* me? What sort of message would that send?"

It was Frail Lemi who answered. "It would tell her you're rather attached to your head." Always proud when he thought he'd come up with something witty, he smiled that broad smile of his—the honest one, not the one he used when he was about to carve a man up.

Macide, sword raised, examined the edge against the sunlight. "I *do* like it attached." With a small frown, he lowered the blade and continued running it over the sharpening block.

Emre's head, the wound he'd taken when Darius had struck him with a spade, had never healed properly, and it was starting to flare up again. He rubbed his temples, hoping to prevent the pain from cascading into the sort that would leave him writhing on the deck. "That you're going to Mazandir should be enough. Let *me* meet with Queen Meryam's ambassador. *I'll* speak for you."

"I appreciate that, young falcon." Satisfied with the first shamshir, Macide started in on the second. "But it's the queen herself who will be speaking for Sharakhai, so you see, I *have* to go."

The brightness of the sun became suddenly brighter. The pain rose to new heights. "Queen Meryam is coming herself . . ."

"That's right," Macide said, "and she's—"

His words trailed away, for just then the pain at the back of Emre's head became too much and he slumped to the deck and curled into a ball.

Frail Lemi was right there beside him. "Get Dardzada!" he howled, then ran his big hand in circles over Emre's back.

"Was he like this on the journey back?" Macide asked softly.

Emre curled up tighter. Every sound, every utterance, felt like a nail being driven through his skull.

"Not so bad as this," Frail Lemi said, then swept Emre up in his great arms and bore him toward the rear of the ship. "You're going to be all right," he whispered like a father to his sick child. "Just hold on, Emre. Dardzada's on the way."

Soon Emre lay in his bunk and Dardzada was examining him. "I asked you to let me take a look at you in the valley," he said in that judgmental tone of his.

Frail Lemi immediately shushed him. "Soft as a sparrow's flight, Dardzada."

Emre thought Dardzada might ignore Lemi, refuse to take any sort of advice from another, especially a lunk of a man who'd never had any proper training in medicine, yet when Dardzada spoke again, it was in low, hushed tones. "It's been like this since Darius struck you with the shovel?"

He pulled Emre's eyes open and examined them. In that brief moment, Emre spied Dardzada's apprentice, a waif of a girl named Clara, standing nearby, watching everything with a keen-eyed gaze.

"No," Emre managed. "It's been getting worse."

When Dardzada probed the back of his head with his fingertips, Emre's world turned to stars. He tried to make himself small, but it didn't work. The pain became so intense that for a long while he could only moan, which made things worse.

Sometime later, the pain felt like it had ebbed. He couldn't be sure if he'd blacked out. All he knew was that he could think again, and Frail Lemi was gone and Dardzada was speaking to him.

"You fought Hamid like this?"

"I had to," Emre said.

"You bloody stupid fool, why?"

"Honor," Emre mumbled. "His word against mine."

"You actually think people in this tribe would take *Hamid's* word over yours?" Dardzada prized Emre's jaw open and stuffed a piece of bark between his cheek and gum. It was the size of an almond and tasted bitter, like a lemon rind gone bad. "You've underestimated your standing in the tribe, Emre, and you've *vastly* overestimated Hamid's."

He shoved another piece of bitter bark into his other cheek. "Leave them there. They'll help with the internal swelling."

Dardzada left with Clara. There was a hushed conversation outside the cabin door, but Emre couldn't make it out. *They're going to send me back*, he thought. *Macide's going to see how useless I am and he's going to send me back.*

He woke to someone rubbing his hair gently. It was Çeda. By then it was dark outside, the only source of light a small oil lantern on his desk. For a moment it felt like they were back in their place in Roseridge, and she was helping to heal him after some run-in with the Spears or a bout with yellow fever.

"What?" she asked, and he realized he'd been staring at her.

"Do we have any olives left?"

Çeda, bless her, knew exactly what he meant. "I think so. And a half a loaf from Tehla's I bought this morning."

"I'll get the bread and olives," he said.

"I'll get the wine."

They both laughed as she ran her fingernails through his hair. Gods it felt good. With her other hand, she grabbed a mug of water and handed it to him. "Dardzada's orders."

Emre rolled his eyes, but only because it's what he would have done back then—he had always been a terrible patient. He took the mug and downed half of it in one go, then lay back down. He was exhausted.

"Is this what you were hiding from me in the valley?"

Emre shrugged. He was too embarrassed to say it. He shouldn't have let the pain go on for so long.

"You stupid, stubborn ass," she said.

"Look who's talking."

"You can't go to Mazandir like this."

"Is that what Macide's saying?"

"Would you blame him if he did?"

"Çeda . . ."

"Dardzada said to give it some time, but he's not optimistic." She shook him gently until he was looking straight into her eyes. "You don't need to go. You can head back on a skiff and heal in the valley until this is all over."

"Stop trying to protect me."

"Stop being an idiot. You're *hurt*, Emre. Badly."

"No. My fight with Hamid just made it worse is all. I just need a bit of time to heal." Çeda opened her mouth to speak, but Emre talked over her.

"Everything's going to be decided soon. You know it and I know it. I'm *not* going to go back to some valley to lay there until it's all over. I won't."

"If this wound is going to heal as fast as you say it will, then you'll be back with us soon enough."

"If it heals as fast as I say then it can heal while we sail."

"Emre, if you're not going to say it, I will. You might become a liability. To yourself. To this mission. To the tribe."

He closed his eyes. It hurt to hear those words, particularly coming from Çeda, who'd been getting him out of trouble since they were kids. But he was man enough to admit that there was truth in her words—he very well *might* become a liability. Could he live with himself if his headaches came at the wrong time and jeopardized their negotiations with the queen?

"Look," he said. "We have a few weeks before we hit Mazandir. I can take a skiff at any time. Let Dardzada try to work his magic. If he can't, I'll take a skiff then."

She looked as if she were going to say no—he could see the words forming on her lips—but then she released her breath in a long, exasperated sigh. "The gods cursed me the day your path crossed mine."

"A curse for you, maybe"—he took her hand in his and stroked her fingers gently—"a blessing for me."

She looked as if she were about to say something biting, but then she leaned in, kissed him on the lips, and whispered, "Your charms won't work on me, Emre Aykan'ava."

"Won't they?" he asked with a smile.

"No," she said, and kissed him again. "They won't."

Then she lay behind him on the bunk and pulled him against her chest. The movement made the pain in his head flare, but it soon subsided. Their breaths fell into sync, became long together, and the warmth in Emre's heart did as much to bear him toward sleep as the feeling of Çeda cradling him in her arms.

Chapter 39

ON THE PATIO of an old tea house, Davud sat with Esmeray, sipping tea at a table so tiny it was likely to tip over at the first stiff wind. He looked up as the pot-bellied proprietor waddled over with a steel pot and sent fresh tea streaming down from the long, curving spout in an impressively long arc with hardly a drop spilt.

"Good aim," Davud said.

The proprietor smiled with a wink and waddled away. Esmeray, meanwhile, rolled her eyes. "Men and their streams of warm liquid."

"You're just jealous."

"Of being able to whip it out and piss wherever you please? Think again, Davud. That's vulgarity masquerading as sport."

Davud smiled an impish smile and sipped his tea noisily.

"Boys," Esmeray said under her breath, then glanced up and down the street. "They're not coming, you know."

Davud was tranquil about it. "Let's give them a bit more time."

The only other people on the patio were a trio of old women gabbing at the opposite end. The buildings on the near side of the street were tightly packed and tall. Their shadows angled down, slicing the battered cobblestone road neatly in two.

Across the street was an old, blocky mill with a mudbrick home crouched beside it. Davud could hear the mill grinding away within and a man barking out orders to his children, several of which occasionally ran to and from the nearby house. One of them, a boy of eleven, had a pronounced limp. He stopped in the yard, watching, waiting. When Davud shook his head, he kept going and lost himself inside the mill house.

The shadows grew longer. Esmeray and Davud finished their second cups of tea. The three old women at the other table laughed at some joke. When the women collected their things and left in a meandering cluster, an amberlark swooped in and began pecking beneath their abandoned table. The proprietor came out and collected the dishes and cups, trying and failing to shoo the amberlark away.

Esmeray, swirling the remains of her tea with a spoon, stood in a rush. "We're wasting our time."

Davud was just about to relent when he caught movement down the street. Leaning his chair back so he could see past Esmeray, he saw an old Kundhuni man with a strange, ambling gait walking toward the tea house with a much younger and delicate-looking Mirean woman by his side.

The Kundhuni man was the blood mage, Undosu, one of the Enclave's inner circle. The young woman was Meiying. She wore a dress of marigold silk with billowing sleeves, belted with a wide bolt of persimmon cloth. The overall effect was fetching and accented her jet-black hair, which was wrapped into a perfect bun. She had yet to turn sixteen, yet so impressive was her ability to control magic, so sharp was her mind, that she'd found her way to a seat in the Enclave's inner circle.

The two of them approached Davud and Esmeray's table. They were seated. Fresh tea was brought, the proprietor displaying his pouring skills once again until he came to Undosu, who immediately raised his hands. "This belly of mine is so full I'm likely to burst." He wore simple homespun clothes and a beaten leather cap with sea shells along the top. The cap's tassels hung alongside his clean-shaven cheeks, and his tuft of a beard somehow made him look both humorous and wise.

As Esmeray studied them warily, Davud took out the brass compass Willem had given him and set it beside Undosu's empty tea cup. Just as Willem had said, the compass had led him straight to Undosu. Undosu, completely unaware Nebahat had owned such a device, had made the compass itself a condition of this meeting. He scooped it off the tabletop with wrinkled, sun-damaged hands and stuffed it into the pouch at his belt.

"So?" he said, sucking on a long, unlit pipe.

"We asked you here," Davud began, "because we've uncovered concerning news about the Enclave's activities."

Meiying sipped her tea. "Concerning news," she said in perfect Sharakhan.

"Yes. For months Nebahat has been overseeing a project in the collegia's hall of records. Using the names of the scarabs they'd taken after the Night of Endless Swords—"

"The project is known to us," Meiying interrupted. "The House of Kings hopes to forge ties with Tribe Khiyanat and eventually sway them. They are, after all, spearheading the alliance that's forming in the desert."

"There's a deeper purpose, though," Davud went on. "A darker purpose. The names found were fed to Nebahat. In turn, Nebahat saw to it that many of those identified were sent as tributes to the blooming fields."

Undosu's teeth clacked against his pipe as he took a puff. "You're saying they were murdered."

"I am."

Davud told them how he'd followed Altan's trail to the collegia, which had led him to Cassandra, Altan's fellow collegia student who, along with Altan, had been researching lineage records for those with blood of the thirteenth tribe. Eventually he came to Nebahat and how he'd orchestrated the whole affair. "Those found in Altan and Cassandra's research were then compelled to go to the blooming fields and feed themselves to the adichara."

"Your proof?" Undosu asked.

At this, Davud beckoned toward the mill house, where the boy stood staring. He approached, limping badly, with naked fear on his face, and when he reached the table, one hand gripped the opposite elbow. He looked like he wanted to draw himself inward and keep doing it until he simply disappeared. He shot glances at them all but seemed especially fearful of Esmeray and her ivory eyes, which was ironic since she was probably the least dangerous person at the table.

"It's true?" Undosu asked in his thick accent. "You were sent to the blooming fields?"

Davud didn't think it was possible, but the boy suddenly seemed even *more* nervous. "I don't remember it, but since I woke up in one of the groves, I must've been."

"Do you remember *who* sent you?"

He shook his head, then glanced at Davud while waving toward the mill house. "Like I told him, I heard a sound behind the mill near nightfall on Beht Zha'ir. I went to look and before I could blink twice I was standing in the blooming fields, staring up at the Tattered Prince."

Undosu considered this, then swung his sallow gaze to Davud. "Forgive me, but the boy doesn't seem to know much."

"Tell them what you told me," Davud prompted. "About the smell."

The boy shrugged. "It was like—" He paused, and seemed to come to some decision. "Here now . . . I agreed to come and talk because he said it would make my family safe. If whoever did this will come back because I'm talking to you—"

"No one will come for you," Undosu said calmly.

The boy looked miserable. Davud felt for him. The fates had given him a bad shake, but he had courage and was doing his best to deal with it. "I need to know my family is safe," he finally said.

"If what you say is true"—Undosu paused, puffing on his pipe—"we'll talk to the man ourselves, and we'll have your house watched until we do. Is that sufficient?"

The boy's tight frame lost a bit of its tension. "The air smelled of chicken." Undosu smiled. "Chicken?"

"Well, not the chicken itself, but the lime and the spices they put on it."

"That who puts on it?"

"The Malasani. Who roast the kebabs in the bazaar near the spice market."

Undosu and Meiying exchanged a look. They knew as well as Davud did that the paste Nebahat applied to his forehead was made from similar peppers and spices.

"Thank you," Undosu said. "You can go home."

It looked like a weight had just been lifted from the boy's shoulders. "No one will come for us?"

"Not a soul," Undosu promised.

After a tremulous smile, he was running with his off-balance gait, momentarily scaring the persistent amberlark. As he headed into the mill house, a dog barked and the door clattered shut.

"So what is it you want?" Undosu asked. "For us to stop Nebahat?"

Esmeray's ivory eyes flashed. "That will be a start, yes, but Nebahat isn't doing this alone. The orders came from higher up."

Meiying tilted her head, a concerned look on her perfect face. "You're suggesting Prayna was involved."

"More than that," Davud replied. "I think it came from the House of Kings. I think Queen Meryam herself asked Prayna to do it."

"Prayna was born and raised in the Shallows," Meiying said calmly. "She protects the west end, even more than Esmeray does."

"That may be," Esmeray said, "but she's never had any great love for the thirteenth tribe."

"How would you know?" Meiying asked.

"I would know better than you! What Prayna cares about most is protecting *her* interests."

"The *Enclave's* interests," Meiying corrected.

"*Her* interests," Esmeray repeated. "The only question is, what did Meryam offer her in return?"

"This"—Undosu swept his pipe in a broad arc—"all of this. It puts the entire Enclave at risk."

"With Prayna and Nebahat's actions, the Enclave is *already* at risk," Davud countered. "The killings must be stopped, and Meryam's growing influence in the Enclave, in the city, must be put in check."

"And what do *you* get out of it?" Meiying asked with a polite smile.

"We want the Enclave to leave us alone," Esmeray said before Davud could reply. "No more hunting me or Davud, for anything we've done in the past."

"More than that," Davud added, "we want sanctuary."

He and Esmeray had fought over it for days. Davud wanted the Enclave to actively protect them, not to simply call off their hunt. Esmeray had been burned by them, her magic taken from her, and had refused over and over to even consider accepting their protection, but Davud didn't care. They needed this.

Undosu and Meiying stared at one another, silently deliberating.

"Give us two days," Undosu said as he stood. "We'll find you."

Meiying bowed lightly. "Thank you for the tea."

As they left, Davud prayed he hadn't made a mistake in trusting two of the most powerful magi in the city.

The amberlark beneath the tables continued to peck at crumbs, for all the world like any other lark in the city. The patrons of the tea house had failed to notice, however, that there were sigils painted in red beneath its wings.

Shortly after Davud and Esmeray left the tea house, it launched itself into the air in a flurry of wings. Westward it flew, over the nearby tenements, over the dry bed of the River Haddah, over the Shallows, the city's poorest neighborhood, until it neared the Red Crescent. It landed on a rooftop that was relatively clean save one corner, where several wire cages and covered pails of birdseed were stacked. Beside the cages stood a man who, upon seeing the amberlark land, crouched and crooked one finger toward it. With no hesitation, the bird hopped on.

The man, who bore a striking resemblance to Esmeray, stood and spoke in a low voice to the amberlark. "Now what did you hear, my pet?"

The amberlark gave its lonely call, a trill of rising notes followed by a long coo. Then it began to speak. The man listened—the city arrayed before him, a landscape of mudbrick and stone and clothes drying on lines strung between the buildings.

When the bird was silent at last, the man smiled.

Chapter 40

I N A CAVERN in the city's quarry, Duke Hektor lay on a threadbare cot. It may have been scorching above ground, but it made no difference in the caverns, where the chill was ever present. He shivered while Hamzakiir pulled up a stool and sat beside him. Ramahd and Cicio were guarding the entrance to the quarry's tunnels, leaving Hektor alone with Hamzakiir, whose long face seemed longer the closer they came to performing the ritual.

"You're ready?" Hamzakiir asked.

Hektor had had occasion to work with several blood magi in his eighteen years. In those times, he'd given his blood willingly, thinking little about it. But in the cavern, lying before a foreign-born mage who was trying to win Hektor's throne for him, he was terrified. Hamzakiir looked like a headsman ready to drop a bloody great axe across his throat.

"As ready as I'll ever be," Hektor finally said. He noted the fear in his own voice. *Not very regal, Hektor. You sound like a bloody jackdaw trying to chase away a hawk.*

"The fear helps," Hamzakiir said, putting to rest the question of whether he'd heard it as well. "It will play perfectly into the story we've concocted."

"Yes, but it's *Meryam* I'm afraid of. She'll surely sense the truth. She'll learn where we are."

Hamzakiir's pinched smile only made his long face look longer. "Emotions are difficult to fake, so play into them. Let *me* worry about thoughts and memories."

He doused the lantern, plunging the cavern into darkness.

Mere moments had passed when Hektor began to feel dizzy, as if he'd drank one too many brandies. Then his gut soured. He felt as if he were walking through a dark forest and the snatchers were coming to get him. He felt something dark swoop over him, a condor. It had a bald head, a black mantle of feathers around its neck, wings as broad as a house.

Hektor tried to retreat, but with two lazy flaps of its dark wings the condor landed hard on his chest. Its long, curving claws pierced his ribs and held him in place. Hektor cried out in agony, but the condor paid him little mind. Its head swiveled about, wary of danger, perhaps. Finding none, it peered down and used its hooked beak to peck at Hektor's eyes.

Hektor screamed, and the moment he did, he was laid bare. In his mind's eye he saw the condor rifling through his memories: his fleeing when his father, Duke Hektor I, was taken by the Silver Spears; his righteous anger when he'd learned his father had been hung without so much as a trial; Count Mateo counseling him to take up with Ramahd Amansir so that Meryam might be deposed.

The condor seemed especially hungry for more recent events. Hektor saw his own plotting with Ramahd, how they'd agreed that Amaryllis was the key, that if anyone could convince Meryam to share power, it was her. He saw their abduction by the men disguised as Silver Spears. He saw them being brought to the garrison, and later, once Amaryllis had been released, being blindfolded and brought to a new location where the Spears, men who'd turned crooked, were attempting to ransom Hektor and Ramahd away.

These last were planted memories, clues to a false trail placed by Hamzakiir. Unbeknownst to Meryam, she and Hamzakiir were sharing Hektor as the focus of their magic: Meryam plundering Hektor's memories using the blood from Amaryllis's dress, while Hamzakiir, mere steps ahead of her, sensed what she was looking for and supplied a fabricated version.

Hektor writhed where he lay on the frayed canvas cot. His neck craned from the sheer intensity of his fears. Hamzakiir had told him to play into his emotions—as if he had any choice in the matter. His mindless terror overwhelmed all logical thought, preventing Meryam from learning anything useful. She might have waited until he calmed down, or tried again another day, but either would be gambling with fate. Delay, and Ramahd might learn of her efforts and use his abilities to protect Hektor. Meryam reasoned that this was her one and only chance to use Hektor's blood to her benefit; if she couldn't get from him what she wanted now, she would ensure he could no longer threaten her claim to the throne.

So it was that after several unfruitful minutes, Meryam did exactly what Hamzakiir had predicted: she pressed on his mind, slowly suffocating him.

When Hektor was young, he'd gone swimming with his cousin and several of their friends. Hektor was not a strong swimmer, but his cousin, despite never having swum before, had jumped in when a girl called him a coward. When Hektor foolishly leapt in to save him, his cousin kept trying to raise himself above the water's surface by climbing onto Hektor's shoulders. Water bubbled into Hektor's nose and mouth. He gasped for breath in the rare times he was able to kick hard enough to get his head above water. He was convinced he was going to die in that smelly pond in front of all his friends.

As horrifying as that had been, the feeling of Meryam pressing him down was much, much worse. He tried to fight her. Tried to regain the surface. But her strength was irresistible. Down, down he went, the darkness pressing in as stars filled his vision. His breath bubbled from his nostrils in a gout. The sound of it mixed with the hollow sibilance of his own ineffective thrashing. The last of his breath came out in two short bursts of screaming. Knowing it would doom him, he tried to resist the drawing of another breath, but he couldn't help it. He sucked in a lungful of black water. It burned his nose, burned his throat, filled his desperate lungs.

Terror drove out all other thoughts, all other emotions. He could think of nothing but regaining the surface so that he might take in one final breath of sweet forest air. But he was as powerless in that as he'd been in denying Meryam. Ever lower he went, the water pressing like a vise against his ribs, until he was lost altogether.

When Hektor woke, his limbs were leaden. His head felt ponderously heavy. He couldn't so much as lift it off the cot. And how he *ached*. But sea and stone, it seemed a miracle that he was breathing at all, so for a time he simply lay there, reveling in that most basic function of life.

The subterranean air was as chill as ever, a balm against his hot skin. The lantern, relit, cast an orange glow against his closed eyelids. He blinked his eyes open, squinting against the sudden light, and found Hamzakiir sitting where he'd been before, staring at Hektor with the clinical expression of a physic who'd grown immune to his patients' feelings. Ramahd was there as well, smiling, his relief so plain that Hektor hardly had to ask how things had gone.

"So?" Hektor asked anyway. "It's done?"

It was Hamzakiir who answered. "It's done," he said in his baritone voice. "We have two weeks, perhaps three, in which I'll be able to listen to Meryam's thoughts. In that time, we should be able to find some moment and place that will leave her vulnerable."

When they did, they would attack and bring Meryam to justice. It was of paramount importance that they return her to Qaimir alive. Fail in that, and the likelihood of the country being plunged into a bitter civil war was all but guaranteed. Meryam had managed to rally many royal houses around her, some through use of blood but many through simple guile. She'd given promises and delivered on enough of them that they would fight to keep her on the throne, or work against Hektor if they discovered she'd been summarily killed in the desert.

As it turned out, finding Meryam at her weakest was easier said than done. Over the course of the following week, Hamzakiir did as he'd said he would. Through use of Hektor's blood, he listened to Meryam's thoughts.

"It's a dark day in Sharakhai," he said one night after Meryam had gone to bed.

"How do you mean?" Ramahd asked.

"Meryam is treating with the Enclave, promising them more power if they step from the shadows. In return, she's asking that they find tributes for her, so she can send them to the blooming fields to be taken by the trees."

He told them about the grisly experiments she was conducting in the cavern below the city using the strange glowing crystal. "She hopes to use it to gain power over the thirteenth tribe. She wants to see them all dead."

"You mean the Moonless Host," Ramahd said.

"She might have wanted that once, but not any more. She can't tell the difference between those who were once scarabs, those who were sympathizers, and those who had nothing whatsoever to do with the Host, so she's lumping them all together."

Hamzakiir was more unsettled by it than Hektor would have guessed, especially given how ruthless he'd been with the collegia graduates he'd taken before the Night of Endless Swords.

"Is it true she dominated your mind while you led the insurrection against Ishaq?" Hektor asked.

Hamzakiir had ingratiated himself with Ishaq and the Moonless Host early on, only to tear them apart from within later. Hamzakiir gave a reluctant nod, but Hektor still wondered. The man might have been manipulated, but who would believe that those terrible acts had been committed by Meryam, and Meryam alone? Certainly not Hektor. There must have been *some* part of him that wanted it.

Hamzakiir seemed suddenly uncomfortable. "I'm tired," he said, and left the cavern to find his cot.

When his footsteps faded, Ramahd turned to Hektor. "Let sleeping dogs lie, won't you?"

"What, forgive him for all he's done?"

Ramahd leaned against the rock wall and crossed his arms over his chest. "Our goal is to bring Meryam to justice. Let Sharakhai deal with Hamzakiir's crimes."

"His heart is every bit as dark as Meryam's. I felt it when he was rummaging through my mind."

"He's ruthless, I'll grant you that much, but that's why he's so effective."

"I don't know that I care to work with him any longer. It's distasteful."

"Then be prepared to give up your quest for the throne. The road to peace winds through many dark fields, Duke Hektor. You'll have no end of dealing with unsavory elements when you take the throne. Best you get used to it now."

"I swore when my father died that my reign would be just."

"And I understand why, but a great king looks beyond such things as *just* and *right* and *honor*. You think justice can be found by weighing good versus evil, but suffering can arise from the kindest of acts, and good can flow from the manipulations of evil men."

Hektor knew he was right, he just didn't like it. "Can we agree that we'll use him no longer than we have to?"

Ramahd smiled handsomely. "That much we can agree upon."

Days passed, and Hamzakiir continued his efforts, but they still had no clue as to where Meryam might go that would give them some sort of edge beyond the Sun Palace itself and the cavern where she was conducting her strange experiments.

"It's got to be the cavern," Hektor said one night.

He, Ramahd, and Count Mateo were sitting in their shared room in the quarry's catacombs, passing around a bottle of passable Qaimiri brandy. The husky Count Mateo, who'd drunk nearly half the bottle on his own, took another swig before handing it to Ramahd. "It's likely our best chance," he slurred.

Ramahd nodded, then took a swig. "Agreed."

No one was under the illusion that attacking her in the cavern would be easy. There were Silver Spears patrolling the tunnels, and within the cavern itself they would have to deal with Meryam and Prayna. But it would be a good deal easier than waging an assault on the Sun Palace.

Hektor wanted to wait, to find a time and place that could guarantee their success, but he supposed that had always been a foolish dream. "We'll begin preparations tomorrow."

"Not so fast." Hamzakiir strode in and dropped onto the free cot. His eyes were bleary, as they'd been more and more of late. He spent nearly every waking hour with Meryam, which was exhausting enough on its own, but it was compounded by its becoming progressively more difficult for him to remain in contact with her as Hektor's blood worked its way out of her system. "Meryam," he said, looking as though they'd already lost, "has managed to gain Rümayesh's services."

Count Mateo seemed displeased, though it was difficult to tell through the man's alcohol haze. Ramahd, on the other hand, stiffened, his eyes going distant.

"Who's Rümayesh?" Hektor asked.

"A powerful ehrekh," Hamzakiir replied, "one of the eldest in the desert."

Mateo, who'd taken up the brandy bottle again, swung it wildly toward Ramahd. "*He* fought her."

"I didn't *fight* her," Ramahd said. "I happened to be on the ship that she subdued with little more than a wave of her hand."

Mateo looked confused, but then his face brightened. "You discovered Rümayesh in the ruby!"

"It was a sapphire," Ramahd corrected.

"Yes, well, the point is . . ." Mateo frowned as if he'd forgotten what he was about to say. A moment later his head jerked back. "The point *is*, *you* know how to fight her."

Ramahd shook his head sadly, not so much at Mateo's words, but at their terrible misfortune. "I know nothing of the sort. I do know this, however. If Rümayesh truly is her ally, our chances of taking her in the cavern have just dropped considerably."

They agreed that the right course of action was to let Hamzakiir continue until there was no time left. If they found nothing new, they would try the cavern.

And so it went. Several more days passed with Hamzakiir growing progressively more exhausted and having more and more difficulty listening to Meryam's thoughts, until one day he said to them, "It's over. I'll get no more from her." At which point he left to sleep, a thing he hadn't done properly in weeks.

Ramahd, Mateo, and Hektor all agreed that it was time to prepare their assault in earnest. Ramahd summoned Cicio, who'd been combing the city for any signs that Amaryllis or the Kings' Spears had learned about their subterfuge. When Cicio arrived, Ramahd told him the news and bid him to head out to the desert, where the bulk of their knights and soldiers waited on several ships a half-day's sail from Sharakhai.

Cicio was just heading for the exit when Hamzakiir stumbled into the lantern-lit cavern. "Mazandir," he said, out of breath. "Meryam is going to Mazandir."

Ramahd stared at him with a look of disbelief. "You said you couldn't hear her anymore."

"I didn't think I could, but my inability to eavesdrop was due to my exhaustion. When I fell asleep, I dreamed, and it was filled with Meryam's thoughts."

"Why Mazandir?" Ramahd asked. "Why now?"

"She's reached out to Macide with an offer of peace. They're to meet in Mazandir." Hamzakiir stared at them soberly. "We'll never have a better chance to take her."

Ramahd looked to Mateo and Hektor. "Mazandir?"

Mateo, head lolling, shrugged his broad shoulders. "Why not?"

Hektor nodded. "Mazandir it is."

Chapter 41

A S THE DAYS PASSED and their small fleet sailed for Mazandir, Macide ordered that the Malasani and Mirean fleets, both of which had been spotted combing the sand east of Sharakhai, be given wide berth. Even so, the risk of coming across their ships was high. Indeed, at the end of their first week of sailing Çeda spotted a line of what looked to be Mirean dunebreakers in the distance, but the ponderous ships chose not to give chase and were soon lost beyond the horizon.

Frail Lemi continued to teach spearcraft to Aríz, who had become impressively good at it in the months since Emre last saw him. The two of them used wooden staves with padded ends. During their first several bouts, it was all Frail Lemi could do to force Aríz to yield. It soon became clear that, while Aríz couldn't hold a candle to Frail Lemi's strength, he'd inherited all his father's quickness and more. He would dodge, duck, or lean away from Frail Lemi's swings, often frustrating his opponent. By their fourth bout, Aríz was keeping up. And by their seventh, Aríz was anticipating all of Frail Lemi's moves, to the point that late in the day Frail Lemi got so frustrated he screamed and unleashed a blinding series of blows, all of which Aríz blocked or dodged, except for the last, which was so powerful it sent Aríz flying down the foredeck stairs.

Frail Lemi stood there, breathing hard, the hot sun shining off the sheen of sweat on his shaved head. He looked like he meant to leap down and strike Aríz where he lay, but then Aríz grinned and said, "Not bad, Lem."

Frail Lemi looked confused for a moment, then broke out into a toothy grin. "Not bad . . . Not bad like your sister's not bad."

"That's enough!" called Ali-Budrek.

But Aríz only grinned more. "Not bad like your mother's not bad." When he held out one hand, Frail Lemi clasped it and hauled Aríz to his feet. The two of them laughed, Frail Lemi quite a deal louder and longer than Aríz, all while thunderclouds passed over Ali-Budrek's face.

The bitter bark Dardzada had given to Emre seemed to dull his headaches, so Dardzada gave him more and told him to shove one in his mouth the moment he felt a headache coming on. Emre had done so three times since, and it had worked. It didn't happen quickly, and it didn't suppress the pain entirely, but it was a far sight better than it had been.

Çeda sailed aboard the *Red Bride* by day, but at night she would sing songs by the fire near Emre's side. More than once Emre caught Sümeya watching them, and he wondered what had gone on between her and Çeda. He wondered what they *still* felt for one another, too, but he cut those thoughts off before they'd had a chance to take root. Hadn't he asked the fates to bring Çeda back into his life? Well, now they had. What sort of fool would he be if he started questioning the manner in which they'd done it?

Çeda slept in Emre's cabin at night. The first night after his recovery, they kissed for a long while. Emre wanted to take it further, but Çeda was too worried about his headache to do anything more. "Dardzada said to take things easy."

"We will," Emre replied. "I'll just lie here. You can do all the work."

Which earned him a slap on the belly.

The second night, though, kissing had led to more. She straddled his hips and removed her dress slowly, taking her time, letting the lift of the fabric act like a veil being removed, showing her thighs, her tight stomach. When he tried to run his hands over her breasts, she threw the dress aside and set his hands easily but firmly onto the mattress.

She moved against him, her body tilting like a ship riding the edge of an easy dune. He'd already been stiff, now he felt like he had a bloody belaying pin squeezed between his legs.

When he tried to lay her down against the bunk's mattress, she made soft clucking noises. "No, no," she said, her lips pursed just next to his. "You were given orders."

He couldn't help but smile. "So I was," he said, and tried to kiss her.

She backed away before he could, then sat up and raked her fingernails along his chest. She played with the hair below his belly button, the path to the enchanted garden, she called it. Emre couldn't help it. He laughed out loud. Çeda, meanwhile, moved lower, toying with him, circling his ridge, stroking him, then she lifted herself and slid down on him in an easy motion that was so filled with pleasure it made his head arch back and his eyes flutter closed.

He tried to take her by the hips, but she wouldn't even let him do that. She pinned his wrists to the bed and rode him, softly at first, slowly, then with more and more verve, her breath coming faster, her gaze locked with his and her breasts swaying with her movement.

Only when he was close did she let his wrists go with an impish grin. "I suppose a *bit* of movement is good for the heart."

Her calm assurance that he was close was enough to send him over the edge. She smiled as she watched him, never slowing, a spectator to the throes of his pleasure, which only served to deepen them.

As it began to subside, a dark, smoldering look overcame her. Her nostrils flared and she rode him faster. He might have gone soft, but the way she was staring down, watching him enter her over and over, got him so excited he felt like he might tip over the edge again.

Suddenly a small squeal escaped her, and she shivered and dropped against him, the skin of their sweat-glistened bellies making a soft *smack*. She bit his ear hard as short, high-pitched moans of pleasure escaped her and her body writhed against his.

Emre couldn't get enough of her; his hands roamed from her shoulders to her back, over the perfectly round curves of her backside and along her well-muscled thighs. They glided down from the heights together. Emre kissed her skin where shoulder met arm, enjoying the taste of her sweat, enjoying the feel of her slick skin beneath his fingertips.

They lay there for a long while after, then talked in low voices about life in Sharakhai, about their childhood. It felt like one of those rare days in the city when you woke half asleep, cradled in dreams, and all you wanted to do was to continue to lay there and let the world come to you.

Eventually they fell asleep and this time it was Emre who cradled Çeda. He didn't sleep for long, though. Since waking in his desert grave, he'd been unable to sleep for more than a few hours at a time, the pain often returning as he slept. That night was no different, and soon he crept out the door wearing only a light shirt and a thin pair of knee-length trousers.

Within their circle of ships, the coals of the campfire were banked. He kicked them back to life and watched them burn, warming his hands against the chill of the desert night. For a time he wandered beyond the ships. Tulathan was low in the west, a tilted scythe, but Rhia was high, a near-perfect golden coin on a veil of onyx silk. The dunes around them were choppy and short, the kind that made for fast sailing but made the ships vibrate so much that by the end of the day one felt like an egg, beaten and frothy, ready to be thrown into a hot pan.

He was just headed back to the *Amaranth* when he heard voices. The wind played tricks in the desert sometimes, so he waited, trying to judge where it had come from. He heard it again and walked closer, wondering who else had had trouble sleeping, and saw two shapes, one tall, one stocky.

A rasping voice broke the silence. It was Sehid-Alaz, King of the Asirim. Who would he be speaking to at this hour?

As Emre crept closer, a muffle of low words came from the other, then Sehid-Alaz spoke once more, loud enough for Emre to hear. "My first duty is to the asirim."

"In doing this, you *will* be serving them."

That voice . . . The mere sound of it made the pain at the back of Emre's head flare back to life. It was *Hamid*. Somehow, he'd stumbled across their fleet.

No, Emre realized, *not stumbled. Rasime was to blame. If Hamid had shown his face, he would have had to stand trial for his crimes, so she'd smuggled him into the caravan on her ship instead.*

His mind could take the implications no further, for the pain in his head was building like a shooting star.

"Macide is blood of my blood," Sehid-Alaz rasped.

"*I* am blood of your blood," Hamid replied. "And once Macide is gone, there will still be hundreds for you to protect."

The gods as his witness, Emre tried to listen as they spoke, but the words had started to meld with one another. He couldn't make out one word from the next. Each felt like the stab of a needle to the backs of his eyes. He dropped his head into his hands and rubbed at his temples while stifling a groan. The fates curse him, he hadn't brought any of Dardzada's foul bark with him.

He tried to make it back to the ships. He had to warn someone. To tell them Hamid was planning to overthrow Macide.

He moved as quietly as he could over the sand—alerting Hamid would likely mean his death—but he was starting to panic, which drove him to move faster, which only served to intensify the pain. He felt himself fall, heard himself moan, but he could hardly pay attention to either of those things.

The tribesmen sometimes spoke of the meteor strikes in the Taloran Mountains that came late in autumn. The meteors would strike the slopes and the land would be lit, brightening the sky while mountain peaks loomed, black against the brilliant canvas of the meteor's dying fury. A great boom would follow, loud as the world's ending.

That was how the back of Emre's skull felt. A meteor strike. A brilliant thing, bright and blinding. And when the rush of sound came, it consumed him, and the world plummeted into darkness.

Hamid had waited until everyone in the camp was asleep. As there had been on the other nights, a pair of guards were posted on the *Amaranth*, but the guards never bothered with those who roused to make their night soil, nor those like Emre who didn't sleep well and took walks. Their concern was for threats from the outside, so it was child's play for Hamid to slip down from Rasime's ketch, wave to the guard, and wander the sand outside the circle of ships.

Hamid had been tempted to slip onto the *Amaranth* when the guard made his rounds and kill Emre where he slept, but Çeda had started sleeping in his cabin. That bloody bitch had been trained in the House of Maidens. She knew their sorcerous ways. So, tempting as it was to try and get rid of them both, it was safer to wait for Emre in the sand beyond the ships and kill him there. Çeda would eventually get hers.

Rasime had argued against doing even that. "You have a mission to complete," she'd insisted. "You must speak to Sehid-Alaz. Everything else can wait."

For days Hamid had stewed in silence, knowing she was right. But Sehid-Alaz had yet to venture from the *Amaranth*'s hold. He was well known for taking long walks in the valley, but so far on this journey he'd been content with staying on the ship, all day, all night. He didn't even go to the campfires at night.

Hamid was just thinking he'd have to steal onto the *Amaranth* when the ancient King of the asirim climbed up from the bowels of the ship, strode down the gangplank, and wandered beyond their circle of ships. Hamid followed from a distance, quiet as could be, but eventually realized he'd been discovered. Sehid-Alaz was waiting for him, staring with the twin pits of his eyes while the moons cast their glow against his blackened skin. "I have felt your heart and your mind laying heavily upon me these past many days. I'm weary of it. Tell me what you so desire."

"My name is Hamid Malahin'ava—"

"The one who attacked his fellow tribesman. And now you've come to me, searching for solace."

"Of a sort."

Sehid-Alaz drew his sword, Night's Kiss, the two-handed shamshir that had once belonged to Husamettín. It buzzed angrily, like hornets circling their prey, then settled into a low thrum. "Tell me what *sort* or begone."

Hamid held his hands high in a plea for patience. "I must first tell you of other things. Of the bargain to be made in Mazandir. Of the men they mean to make it with."

"No men, but the Queen of Qaimir."

"In the name of the Sharakhani Kings."

"Yes, but who now are named Kings but the whelps of their fathers?" He sounded weary, as if he prayed for the last storm to come and take him once and for all. He seemed almost sad that he couldn't wreak vengeance upon those who'd bound him and his people in chains.

"What if I told you the bargain he goes to make is not merely with Queen Meryam, but with the greater Kings as well?"

Sehid-Alaz paused. Night's Kiss thrummed. "You lie."

"I saw it with my own eyes."

"You *lie*."

"There were four," Hamid continued. "Husamettín, King of Swords, bearing a shamshir of ebon steel. I saw him working forms very similar to the ones you favor. Ihsan was there, and he was talking, the stories about him losing his tongue either lies or the elixirs have healed him once more. Cahil strutted about with his golden hammer. And lastly there was Zeheb, though he was only half the man I remember. They called him the Burbling King in Sharakhai, but he didn't seem that mad to me."

Sehid-Alaz's jaw jutted out like a black laugher's. His brow darkened, as if he didn't want to believe Hamid.

Hamid held out a length of yellow cloth that looked dark gray in the moonlight. "I took this from their ship, sliced from Cahil's turban while he bathed in a mountain stream."

Sehid-Alaz took it, held it to his nose, and breathed in its scent. The ancient King fell silent, brooding.

"Four Kings," Hamid said, knowing from Sehid-Alaz's silence that he believed his story, "sitting on a ship that Çeda herself sailed alongside. You know as well as I that she is Macide's favorite. I wouldn't be surprised if she'd brought him the King's terms to consider before he meets with Meryam. You said your role was to serve. The more important question is *whom* do you serve?"

"The shaikh of the thirteenth tribe," he said only half-heartedly.

"And if that title fell to another?"

"Only a fool would think I'd raise my hand against Macide, blood of my blood."

"You don't have to lift a finger," Hamid said. "I will. I only need your support once the new order is put into place."

"My first duty is to the asirim."

"In doing this, you *will* be serving them."

"Macide is blood of my blood," he rasped.

"*I* am blood of your blood. And once Macide is gone, there will still be hundreds for you to protect."

For long moments, Sehid-Alaz's raspy breath was the only sound he could hear. The chill night air seeped deep beneath Hamid's skin, and he wondered if he'd just made a terrible mistake.

But then the asirim King said, "Who would take his place?" And Hamid knew he had him. Whether forty years old or four hundred, the hearts of men were all the same—show them that their honor is threatened and they will fight to protect it.

"*I* would," Hamid declared. "I am ready to give the Kings all that they deserve, along with any who would take their thrones in Sharakhai."

Just then Hamid heard a groan from somewhere to his right. He saw a silhouette, someone staggering away, holding his head. The guard, maybe? When the man toppled over, though, he knew it was Emre—he'd done the same thing when they fought.

He drew his knife and approached, planning to slit his throat and be done with it, but Sehid-Alaz gripped his hand and pulled him back with surprising strength.

"You would no longer grant him his trial?"

"He *had* his trial, and he lost."

He waved to Emre's unmoving form. "It doesn't look like he lost."

"Only because a bull walking on its hind legs interfered."

"Hey!" someone called. And this time it *was* the guard. He was jogging over the sand with a torch. "Who goes there?"

The buzzing in Hamid's mind had been under control for days, but as the guard approached he felt it come rushing back. *The gods curse Emre and everything he's ever touched!* He couldn't very well murder Emre in front of the guard, nor could he stay.

"Think on what I've said," he said while backing into the darkness.

Sehid-Alaz gave no reply. A short while later, Hamid saw him gather Emre up in his arms and carry him back toward the ships while the guard held the torch high, lighting their way.

Chapter 42

ÇEDA WOKE TO THE SOUND of someone calling for Dardzada. She reached out for Emre, only then realizing he was gone. She knew immediately he'd had trouble sleeping and had gone off on one of his walks. Her first, terrified thought was that he'd succumbed to his injury and died, but if that was the case why would they be calling for Dardzada?

Relief flooded through her when she reached the deck and saw Emre lying there, still breathing. Dardzada waddled up from the berth deck moments later. Young Clara followed in his wake, bright-eyed as ever. Dardzada knelt beside Emre, then pressed his ear to Emre's chest and had Clara do the same. He felt Emre's pulse and had Clara mimic him. When he pried Emre's eyes open and showed Clara how wide his pupils were, Çeda felt a scream building inside her, ready to burst out.

"Can't you just hurry up?" Çeda shouted at him.

Dardzada stared up calmly. "As you can see, Emre is breathing perfectly well. His heartbeat is weak, but is not poor enough to cause me concern yet. His skin is clammy, which is within the range of symptoms for these sorts of fainting spells. And, unconscious like this, he is in no pain. What we need now, Çeda, is a cold examination of the facts, past and present, so that we might find the root of his problem and heal him if the gods allow."

"Fuck the gods," Çeda said. "Give him some of the bark."

"The bark has done little so far. I want to be certain I'm not missing something."

"He may be dying!"

"And you yammering at me isn't helping. Now either shut that fool mouth of yours or, if you can't, throw yourself off the side of the ship so I can concentrate."

Çeda wanted to shake him. She wanted to find the bark and give it to Emre herself. Instead, she forced herself to turn and pace away so Dardzada could examine Emre in peace.

The minutes stretched as he did just that, Clara attentive by his side. Finally he *did* give Emre some of the bark, but with the risk that Emre might swallow it, Dardzada ground it into a powder first and slathered it over Emre's gums. It wasn't a common medicinal, and she wondered how much of it he had with him. She was certain she wouldn't like the answer.

Satisfied, Dardzada ordered Emre brought back to the captain's cabin and announced that he and Clara would monitor him through the night. "Go back to your ship," he told Çeda. "Try to get some sleep."

She did, but got no sleep whatsoever.

Emre didn't wake the following morning, nor the following day, nor the day after that. Frail Lemi came to see him often, but he fretted over Emre so much it made Çeda's guts twist to see it, because it made *her* worry all the more. She felt bad about it, but she always sent him away after a few minutes.

"What's *wrong* with him?" Çeda asked Dardzada one night.

Clara dripped water into Emre's mouth with a wet cloth and ran her fingers over his throat to force it to convulse. Dardzada looked uncharacteristically serious, which made Çeda feel as if the world were about to be pulled out from underneath her. "I believe he suffered internal swelling from the injury he took. Over time it's been getting worse."

"And?"

Dardzada had an abashed look on his round, bearded face. "I'm surprised he's lasted this long. Injuries of this sort can cause dizziness, weakness, terrible headaches, sometimes memory loss and more. There are generally only

two ways it can go: either the swelling recedes on its own and the body re-
stores its natural function." He waved to Emre. "Or they slip into a coma.
Most of those who do never wake up."

"Dardzada, I swear to you, if you don't start giving me some good news
I'm going to go mad."

"You need to know the realities, Çeda."

"I need to know how to *save* him."

"There may *be* no saving him."

Çeda stomped her foot onto the floorboards. "Just stop it, you stupid
great goat! Stop it!" Seeing Dardzada's infuriatingly calm expression, she
took a deep breath, filled her lungs to bursting, then let it out slowly. "I *know*
there are risks, Zada. Now tell me how we're going to keep him from dying."

Clara's bright eyes were shooting from Çeda to Dardzada and back like
a hungry hummingbird.

Dardzada flexed his left hand, which didn't work well anymore after an
injury he'd taken helping Çeda escape from the blooming fields. It bothered
him when he got stressed. It prickled, pins and needles, he said, so he shook
it and regarded her soberly. "There was a cooper in Sharakhai. His son had
taken a beating from a few gutter wrens. He'd taken a barrel stave to the
back of the head, fallen unconscious, and never woke up again. He was still
breathing. I did much the same for him as I've done for Emre. But things
grew worse. I thought he'd simply slip away one night."

Dardzada scraped the captain's chair from around the other side of the
desk and dropped his bulk heavily onto it. "But then something miraculous
happened. With all the sense the gods gave him, which was not much at all,
let me tell you, the father got it into his head that what his son needed was
the coolness of their root cellar. He placed a cot there and tried to carry his
son, on his own, down the ladder that led to it. It was a small, awkward
space, the ladder in need of repair. The bottom rung came off and the father
stumbled, his son fell, and his son's head managed to hit the broken rung.
The nail had been pointing straight up and the weight of his fall was enough
to send it through his skull.

"By the time I arrived the nail was still there, the father petrified of removing it. There was no greater harm to be done, I thought, so I did, and
liquid was released, brown as wet dirt at first, but it ran progressively clearer

as time went on. I bled it more over the following days until it ran completely clear . . . and that boy fully recovered. Since then I've told the story to dozens of other physics and found similar stories having been reported over the centuries. In Mirea, they even developed a procedure for it."

"Dardzada, are you planning to drive a nail through Emre's head?"

"A drill. We're going to drill into his skull, just far enough to relieve the pressure."

Çeda was starting to feel lightheaded. "You're going to drill into his skull . . . ."

"Yes."

"It won't pass on its own?"

"He's had months for that to happen and things have only gotten worse."

Çeda swallowed hard. Dardzada was right. She knew he was right. But . . . "It could kill him, couldn't it?"

"Yes."

She went to Emre's side, then knelt on the floorboards and ran her fingers through his hair as she'd done the other night. He'd woken that time. He didn't now.

She thought back to all the tales they'd told one another about one day defeating the Kings. How they'd live in the halls of Tauriyat, or wander among the desert tribes, their only currency the stories they could tell.

She leaned close to Emre's ear and whispered, "You can't leave now. Our story's only just begun."

"If we're going to do it"—she heard the chair creak as Dardzada pushed himself to a stand—"we should get started."

Tears streamed down Çeda's face, but she didn't stop stroking Emre's scalp. "You hear that?" She leaned in close and kissed one cheek, then wiped away the tear that had fallen. "It'll all be over soon."

She offered to stay, but Dardzada said he needed both space and peace.

"But you'll need an assistant," Çeda said.

"I already have one," Dardzada replied, waving to Clara.

"But—"

"She's good, Çeda," Dardzada said seriously, "better than you ever were."

The comment stung, but really, what could she expect? She'd been an ungrateful ward to Dardzada. He wasn't free of blame, but there was no doubt she'd always been looking for ways to avoid doing work. Clara, meanwhile, had been constantly attentive, and when Dardzada threw questions at her, she'd been able to rattle off answers that needed only minor corrections.

Çeda nodded. "I'm staying, Zada. But I won't get in your way. I promise."

She could see the argument brewing within him, but then he deflated all at once. "Suit yourself."

It was more difficult to watch than Çeda had imagined.

Unable to sit, she stood and watched as Dardzada lay Emre on his side and positioned his head so that he was facing the hull. Under Dardzada's direction, Clara used scissors to cut his long hair, then a razor to shave the back of his head. Dardzada, meanwhile, gathered his instruments, laid them on the desktop, and cleaned each one carefully with alcohol and a clean cloth. The scalpels, needle, thread and compresses were expected. The basin, clearly meant to collect whatever came out of Emre's head, wasn't. And even though she knew Dardzada mean to drill into his skull, the carpenter's auger he'd found in the ship's stores made her guts feel as though a host of eels had been let loose among her innards.

Çeda had seen a lot of blood in her life. She'd treated a thousand wounds. She'd seen men and women die, many by her own hands. She'd seen enough misery to last her ten lifetimes. It had never been pleasant, but neither had she been squeamish about it. But there was something about watching Emre lying there, helpless, and having Dardzada press the tip of a gleaming scalpel to the shaved skin at the back of his head that made her want to vomit.

You have to be here for him, she told herself over and over again. So she pressed her hand to her stomach, set her ill ease aside, and forced herself to watch. *You'll be okay, Emre. You'll be okay.*

She paced as Dardzada lifted the auger, grimaced as he set the tip of the drill against the exposed bone. She could steal only the smallest of glances as he turned the crank and a sudden, incongruous squeaking filled the room. In all his preparation he hadn't thought to oil the drill. It shouldn't have mattered, but the sound kept going, on and on, and it was driving her mad.

When the drill suddenly pressed inward, and a thick, dark brown liquid began to pour from the wound, it was too much. Çeda ran from the room, rushed to the nearest gunwale, and loosed the contents of her stomach onto the sand below.

Throwing up didn't help. Her stomach felt just as queasy afterward. The look of it—the drill slipping into his head. *Oh, gods, Dardzada, what are you doing to him?*

She left the *Amaranth* after that and paced around their circle of ships several times. It still felt too close and so, just as the sun was beginning to rise, she headed directly away from camp and kept going until her stomach started to feel better. By the time it did their ring of ships looked like a collection of well-made toys.

She sat on the sand facing away from the ships and pulled her knees to her chest. The camp was waking. It wouldn't be long before they set sail, though it all felt distant and dreamlike now—sailing to Mazandir to speak to Queen Meryam. All her worries over it felt like she'd been worrying over nothing. The only thing that felt real, the only thing that *mattered*, was Emre.

When she heard the rhythmic crunch of footsteps approaching, she turned to see Macide. He sat cross-legged beside her, but *unlike* her faced the ships. "I'm sorry about Emre." Deeper in the desert, the asirim wailed. "Old injuries can haunt a man. Sometimes they can chase him to his grave."

"I trust Dardzada."

"As do I, though I never thought to hear it from you."

"Because of my childhood?" Her relationship with Dardzada had never been an easy one, and she still resented that he'd forced her first tattoo on her against her will. But time had healed some of those wounds. "I haven't forgotten," she finally said, "but I've forgiven."

"Well, he's in good hands, but I haven't come to speak of Emre." He picked at some dirt beneath his fingernails. "You mentioned trust. There are some who demand it, thinking it should be given whether it's earned or not." He looked at her, his expressive eyes searching hers. "And then there are those who've *earned* it. I think I've earned yours, Çeda. I've given you leave to do much because it was important to the tribe. Your journey to find the goddess took you to many places, led you to many people. Some of them may not have our best interests at heart. If that's true, if there are things that *threaten* the tribe, I need to know about them."

He knew, Çeda realized. He knew about the Kings. And yet she still couldn't bring herself to admit it. She was ashamed she'd agreed to endure their presence, to listen to Ihsan, to take his counsel even if it *was* in hopes of saving Sharakhai. Part of her wished she'd never agreed, but she believed in her heart that the best way forward was for them to work together. She needed Ihsan's insights from the Blue Journals, and he needed to know what they'd learned from the acacia and from Nalamae's reawakening.

"Were I to send a skiff eastward," Macide said, "would I find a galleon mirroring our path toward Mazandir?"

Çeda felt her ears go red. "You would."

"And who would I find on that ship?"

"Four Kings."

Macide's head jerked back. He'd likely thought them agents of the Kings, not Kings themselves. "Which?"

"Husamettín, Ihsan, Cahil, and Zeheb."

"Zeheb is mad."

"Not anymore."

Macide's eyes went distant. "He's been listening to our whispers. That's how they can follow us so easily."

"Yes."

"In truth, I thought Rasime was being paranoid. I thought her jealousy toward you was overriding her senses. I thought you would be the last person to do such a thing." He sat there awhile, the dawn's burgeoning light playing off the movements of his eyes, highlighting the specks of green among the brown. Suddenly he turned to her. "How could you have done this, Çeda? Help me to understand."

She told him all of it, how the Kings had found them in Osman's barn. How Cahil had killed Osman. How she and the others had followed the Kings to the harbor, the battle with Goezhen, Nalamae's awakening—all of it, especially the prophecies Ihsan had shared with her.

As Macide digested the story, his hardened expression turned to one of deep conflict. "This is bad, Çeda."

"I know, but I wouldn't have done it if I didn't feel like it was necessary. Sharakhai needs this. The desert needs it."

"How can you be certain Ihsan won't betray us?"

"He likely will in the end, but before that happens, I believe we can trust what he says: that he's working to stop the desert gods from achieving their aims."

"He wants to rule alone. You know this as well as I do."

"Yes, but he can't do that if Sharakhai is gone, can he? I truly believe he's made it his mission to save the city from the gods."

"I'll need assurances that they won't harm the tribe."

Çeda shook her head. "I can't give you any other than to say that the moment I feel we *are* threatened, I'll act. Up to and including killing the Kings."

"And if Ihsan compels you?"

"He may try"—she lifted her right hand, showing him the puckered scar where she'd been pricked by the adichara thorn—"but I've gained some resistance to the power of his commands. It's the twisted trees, the desert itself, working against him."

Macide nodded and stood, then offered her a hand up. "Speak of this to no one, least of all Rasime."

Çeda accepted his hand with a snort. "I'd sooner kiss a cobra."

As they headed back toward the calls of crewmen and the din of ships preparing to sail, Macide glanced at her with a wry expression. "Who could have seen this moment, Çeda, the two of us allying ourselves with the Kings?"

"The fates alone. I might have a word with them about it after I die."

"And what will you tell them?"

"That the world has never seen a more cruel collection of old hags."

A league from where Çeda and Macide walked, the man who was once a King knelt with one hand pressed against the sand. He heard the words spoken between an uncle and his niece, and became saddened by them. He wept when he heard the names of the Kings being spoken.

Husamettín, Ihsan, Cahil, and Zeheb.

I loved you as a daughter, once, he thought. But now she'd made a bargain with those who'd enslaved him, enslaved his people. Around him, his brother and sister asirim cried their anguish. How hated were the Kings. How reviled. The very notion that he and his would be forced to stand side by side with them, even if in name only, set a flame beneath his heart, made it burn with regret.

He'd thought Macide might see them through to the end. He thought Çeda a bright star among his people. That they could agree to betray him in this way proved how wrong he'd been. In truth, he was as disappointed with himself as he was with them. He should have seen it coming. He should have taken more of a hand in the running of the tribe.

But he was so very, very tired. He couldn't seem to concentrate on anything for long. He yearned for the days of his youth. He yearned for death. How dearly he wished to be reunited with those who'd died since the days of Beht Ihman. How dearly he wished to go hand in hand with those who still lived.

"That is not your lot," he whispered to the morning's wind. "Not yet."

Bones creaking, he came to a stand. *So be it*, he thought. *If the fates' will is that I have tasks ahead on this earth, then I will do them, but no longer will I stand aside and watch the thirteenth tribe slip into depravity.* It grieved him, what he was about to do, but the blame didn't fall on him. It fell on Çedamihn and Macide.

As the ships set sail, the asirim howled, and Sehid-Alaz howled with them.

Chapter 43

ERYAM STOOD ON THE DECK of a royal galleon, sailing far south of Sharakhai. Ahead lay her vanguard of three ships, and beyond them, Mazandir, little more than a wavering smudge of ochre in the distance. She'd dealt with the threat of Duke Hektor, smothering him through the blood he'd foolishly left on Amaryllis's dress, leaving Ramahd without a horse to bet on. It had made all the days since, including this one, feel filled with promise, not unlike the days when she'd first set sail on the *Blue Heron* with Ramahd, the two of them ready to scour the desert until they'd found her sister's murderer.

"Even after all you've done, Ramahd, I wish you were here to see Macide brought to justice."

As the galleon creaked over a dune, Meryam stared at her hands as they gripped the gunwales. *Mighty Alu, how thin you've become.* It reminded her of her awakening as a blood mage, which had begun only a few weeks after Yasmine's abductors had returned her. It was frowned upon for anyone of royal blood to become a mage. Her father, King Aldouan, forbade it, saying it would destabilize the tentative relationships he'd forged with the kingdom's dukes and duchesses.

"You'll be allowed to complete your transition," he told her one night, "and be taught enough to control it, but no more."

But when Meryam enlisted her mother, her father had relented.

"Well," he'd said in a bluster, "it cannot be open knowledge."

"Of course not, my love," her mother said, and promptly contacted five of the best magi in the kingdom.

Meryam took to her training horribly at first. She was obstinate and strong-willed, preferring to chart her own course. She frustrated her teachers. She thought to bend them to her will, but after two years of failed instruction, it was *Meryam* who finally gave in. She hated the idea that her fate was once again in the hands of others, but she knew that if she truly wanted to gain control over her life and protect the people she loved, she would need to listen.

Besides, she told herself. *Is this not a form of control, manipulating these stodgy men and women to get what I want?*

Reapplying herself, her knowledge and skill grew. It took years, but she became one of the most powerful magi the kingdom had ever seen, grooming herself to serve Yasmine when she took the throne, which in Meryam's eyes couldn't come soon enough. She never forgave her father for what he'd done, for the weakness he'd shown. When it was *Yasmine* on the throne, with Meryam standing at her side as high chancellor, nothing would stop them.

Shortly after, Yasmine was married to Lord Ramahd Amansir. They had a child, beautiful Rehann. As cynical as Meryam had become, she adored Rehann. She had visions of teaching her as she grew up, while Meryam helped guide her mother's hand in ruling the kingdom. But then the news came. Yasmine had been slain in the desert along with dozens of others. More had died of hunger and thirst in the days that followed, including Yasmine's daughter, Rehann. It was a massacre already being referred to as the Bloody Passage.

I'll not let anyone harm you ever again, Meryam had told Yasmine. "But I did," she whispered to the wind. "I let the desert take you."

She'd petitioned to lead the hunt for Yasmine's killer. Her father had balked, and as Ramahd was Yasmine's husband, *he'd* been given the right to lead the hunt, but Meryam had joined him, and gained more and more influence over Ramahd once she did. A half-dozen times she was sure they had

Macide, but he proved to be as wily as his legendary father, Ishaq Kirhan'ava. Time and time again he slipped the noose.

Then came her father's unforgivable act. He ordered Ramahd and Meryam to stand down when they had Macide cornered. And when they returned to Santrión with the blood mage, Hamzakiir, she'd told her father of her plans.

"The Moonless Host want him," she said to her father. "I'll break him and we'll insert him into their midst. We'll use him to tear the Host apart from within."

"Meryam," he replied in that way of his, when he was trying to appear oh so reasonable, "we have a kingdom to run. I need you here."

"I'll be back as soon as Macide Ishaq'ava is dead and the Host lies in ruins."

"We can't chase ghosts forever."

"Ghosts?" she said, incredulous. "You think I'm chasing ghosts?"

"Yasmine is dead and buried. So is Rehann. Let them rest."

How Meryam's blood had boiled. "How can they rest when their killer runs free?"

"You've killed dozens of scarabs and more besides, triple the number that were slain in the Bloody Passage."

"I don't *care*. Macide must die."

"You've had a dozen chances to kill him. That's enough, Meryam. You and Ramahd are home, and it's going to remain that way."

She'd left it there, vowing to try him again after he'd cooled. He didn't, though, and two weeks later she discovered why. The Host had made an offer through a wealthy Qaimiri caravan owner: gold from the Moonless Host, so long as King Aldouan called off the hunt for Macide. Infinitely worse, her father, the King, had already accepted.

Something broke in her that day. She'd already known her father to be a sniveling coward. Now she saw he was a dog, to be used or put down as she saw fit.

That very night, she went to him in his study. She carried a bottle of wine in one hand, already half drunk. He'd turned toward her, a stack of writs near to hand, a snifter of brandy even nearer. "Meryam," he said cheerily, then pulled a writ close and gave it a cursory read before signing it. "What keeps you up?"

Meryam took a long pull from the bottle. The wine was old, its taste so sour it was difficult to force down her throat, but the satisfaction that the wine's distinct note of copper brought on made it worth it.

She leaned close and spoke in her father's ear. "I know."

He signed another writ. "Know what, dearest?"

She smiled her widest smile. "I know about the chest of gold that is even now on its way to Santrión."

He stared up at her, his cheery expression vanishing in a way that wasn't half as satisfying as Meryam had thought it would be. "A chest?"

She nodded. "From Ishaq Kirhan'ava himself."

He blinked several times. His mouth worked like a fish. "Meryam . . ." Then his eyes fell on the bottle in her hand, and his face went white.

When she traveled to the desert, she always went with a bottle of wine laced with her father's blood—the very same bottle she now held in her hand. It was meant to allow her to communicate with him from hundreds of leagues away, but it could just as easily be used to control him, to dominate him.

"I won't let you to do it. Not again. You'll not sully Yasmine's memory, nor Rehann's, nor mine, by treating with the enemy."

The following morning, she'd left Santrión and the capital of Almadan and traveled to Ramahd's estate, Viaroza, with Ramahd and Hamzakiir. Each day that passed had seen Hamzakiir resist her attempts to break him. Her fury had risen with each failure. She wasn't angry with Hamzakiir, or even her father, but her own inability to seize the reins of the kingdom. No one—not her father, nor his brother, Duke Hektor, nor any other pretender to the throne—could steer the kingdom properly. Only she could.

So it was that she'd returned to Santrión with a broken Hamzakiir and done what needed to be done. She'd made it seem as though her father *wanted* to leave Santrión, but had done so in such a rush that they would all believe Hamzakiir had forced him. Then she'd fed her father to Guhldrathen and sent Hamzakiir to poison the Moonless Host. It had all worked beautifully, but it hadn't been enough. Not nearly enough.

Off the port bow, she saw a skiff in the distance, just as Rümayesh had said. She ordered the ship brought to a halt, and met with the one named Hamid. It was all she could do not to slit his throat as he sat with her in the captain's cabin. He'd been there. He'd watched Yasmine die. He might even have been the one who'd shot her before Macide cut her throat.

She let her anger simmer. She let him think he was doing her some favor by bargaining away Macide, the man he'd once called his leader. She finished their negotiations, and soon the skiff was sailing ahead toward Mazandir and their galleons were underway again.

Meryam returned to the bow as Mazandir approached. She touched her neck, feeling for Yasmine's necklace, only then remembering she'd given it to Rümayesh. Feeling foolish, she lowered her hand and retrieved a glass vial from the pouch at her belt.

"This is the very last one, Yasmine." She popped the cork and downed the lot, then tossed the empty vial over the side of the ship. "Macide is ours today, and the best thing about it is they're going to hand him to me themselves."

Chapter 44

Hamid sat in the captain's cabin of the *Burning Sand*. Across from him was Rasime, who leaned back in the chair with one sandaled foot on the desk, fixing him with the piercing stare she was famed for. "Well?" she asked.

Hamid had just returned from his clandestine meeting with Queen Meryam, a meeting that, despite his fears of betrayal by the queen, had gone surprisingly well.

"She's agreed," he told her.

Rasime stared at him doubtfully. "Just like that?"

"No, not just like that! She asked a thousand questions, but in the end she saw that I was speaking the truth. She'll get what she wants, and we'll get what *we* want. Now tell me about Emre."

Rasime seemed suddenly fascinated with her fingers. "I went to see him this morning"—she shifted positions in her chair—"told them I was coming to pay my respects." She paused, then lifted her gaze until she was staring directly into his eyes. "He's looking better."

In an instant, all the hope that had been building inside Hamid over the past many days vanished, replaced by fear and dismay. He'd prayed to Bakhi each night to lead Emre to the farther fields, but apparently his prayers had gone unanswered.

"Dardzada drilled a hole in the back of his head," Rasime went on. "You'd think his brains would leak out, but they didn't. He stabilized after the surgery. Dardzada said he's not out of the desert yet, but he's on the mend."

Hamid dropped his head into his hands. It was becoming clear that, just like everything else in his life, he was going to have to force the hands of the fates. It was easier said than done, though. There were people hovering around the *Amaranth* at all hours, particularly the captain's cabin where Emre lay bedridden.

"He's still in a coma," Rasime said hopefully. "Perhaps he'll stay there."

It was the lone saving grace of the entire situation. Had Emre awoken, even for a few minutes, he would surely have told everyone Hamid was hidden somewhere in the camp. And if *that* happened, the best Hamid could hope for was a fair hearing. In all likelihood, though, he and Darius would be dragged onto the sand, their heads lopped off for their treachery.

"Emre needs passage to the farther fields, and quick."

"No doubt," Rasime said.

Hamid paused. "*You* could do him."

Rasime's eyes shot wide open. "*I'm* not doing him!"

"Why not?"

"You started this fight. You can finish it."

"You sheltered me, conspired with me against Macide. You'll be in trouble if he wakes, too. We all will be."

"I'm not giving him back to the desert, Hamid, so you can get that out of your thick skull right now."

Her words were like a hive of buzzing bees. It made him want to do terrible things. To Emre. To Rasime. To himself. "What about the elders?" Rasime had agreed to talk to the tribal elders they thought most likely to join their cause.

"Better news there. Seven have agreed to join us, swords in hand if need be, but only if Sehid-Alaz gives his blessing."

"We'll have it."

"When?"

The way she'd asked it, as if *she* were the one in command, pushed him to the very edge of violence. "We'll *have* it," he growled.

Rasime might press him another time for an answer, but she knew what was good for her. She let the subject drop.

Soon after, Hamid left the ship under cover of darkness and headed in the direction where he'd heard the asirim yipping and barking at one another earlier.

He was nearing them when he saw a dark shape rise up, silent as death. As had always been true, his skin crawled just to be near one of the cursed asirim. He wished he didn't have to rely on them—he trusted them about as much as he trusted a hungry bone crusher—but they were his best hope for dealing with this mess.

"You've returned," said a stony voice. It was Sehid-Alaz, thank the gods.

"I've spoken with Queen Meryam, as I said I would, and she's agreed to my demands."

"She'll take Macide."

"Yes. And then you can deal with the elder Kings however you see fit."

Sehid-Alaz considered for a time, then turned and began walking back toward the huddled asirim. Just when Hamid thought he was going to say he needed time to consider, he called over his shoulder. "Very well. You have my blessing."

The buzzing in Hamid's skull immediately ebbed. He was so elated he nearly asked Sehid-Alaz if he would consider killing Emre for him, but it would likely only annoy the ancient King, so he kept his mouth shut.

This is a sign, Hamid told himself. *My fortunes are turning at last.* There was only one loose thread that could stop him—he *had* to take care of it lest everything unravel.

Filled with the certainty that the gods were looking over his shoulder, he returned to the fleet. So many things were falling into place. With the moons yet to rise and the camp quieter than it had been in days, it was child's play for him to reach the *Amaranth*, to climb the rudder, to scrabble over the ship's transom. Lo and behold, the rear shutters had even been left unlocked. He peered between them, ensuring Emre was alone. Another bit of good fortune: both Dardzada and the waif of a girl, Clara, were gone.

"Thank you, Bakhi, for your kindness," he whispered, and pulled one shutter open.

He was just inching the round of his gut over the sill when he heard footsteps approaching the cabin door. In a rush, he slipped back down, closed the shutter, and perched on the transom's lower lip.

The door flew open a moment later, and Clara, Dardzada's assistant, danced into the cabin and sat on the edge of Emre's bed. After checking the pulse at his wrist, she pried his eyelids open and peered into them while holding a lamp to aid in her inspection.

Hamid clenched his jaw so hard his teeth hurt. He'd just missed the best, cleanest opportunity he could have asked for. He could have pinched Emre's nose and clamped his mouth shut and been done in a few minutes. Now there was the girl to deal with too. He'd strangle her, suffocate Emre as planned, then carry the girl's body into the desert. It would raise questions, and would likely delay the caravan by a few days, but there was nothing for it. He couldn't chance Emre waking before they reached Mazandir.

He put a hand on the shutter and was just ready to pull it aside when the door flew open again and who should walk in but Frail fucking Lemi. He went to the captain's desk and sat, his back to Hamid. He took down a bag and a square aban board from a nearby shelf and proceeded to set up a game.

Hamid rolled his eyes, cursing his misfortune. Lemi, meanwhile, said to Clara, "Ready?"

"Almost!" Clara replied in the sort of cheery tone that made Hamid want to do foul things to her.

Soon she was done and the two of them had started their game. "You're not very good, you know," Clara said to him.

"I know," Frail Lemi replied. "I just like to try."

"No, you just like being near Emre."

"That too."

Fucking gods. They might be at it for hours, and only the fates knew who else might come in during that time. Dardzada. Çeda. Anyone. Hamid thought of sneaking in anyway, but the chances of Frail Lemi being alerted were too great. If that happened, even sticking that big, stupid ox with a knife would likely only anger him.

What the fates giveth in one breath, the saying went, they taketh away in the next. *Would it kill you to break your own rules once in a while?* Hamid thought angrily, then dropped to the sand and headed back to the *Burning Sand.*

The bed was comfortable at first, but Emre soon ached from inactivity, especially along his left side. Every once in a while, as he slipped in and out of sleep, he rolled to the other side.

No, he realized. He was *being rolled.* Others were shifting him in the bed to prevent bed sores. He felt this news should bother him, but it didn't, mostly because, for the first time in months, the pain that built at the back of his head at the smallest provocation was gone. It had vanished. All that was left was a dull ache. Well, that and the occasional prick of pain when his bandages were changed.

He didn't really understand it at first, and some visitors clearly didn't either: How had he survived? Over time, he pieced the story together well enough. Dardzada had cut him open and drained his skull of the bad blood that had built up.

It was a miracle, many said, though it didn't feel that way to Emre.

Time passed. Sometimes it was light when he woke. Sometimes it was dark. Sometimes people were there, speaking in low tones. Other times the room was still.

Dardzada and Clara were the voices he heard the most, but Çeda was often there too. He liked it best when they were alone and she told him stories like she used to in Sharakhai. And when she got bored with those, she would tell him news of the camp, such as it was—anything to keep him occupied, was his impression.

He couldn't really mark the passage of days, but he knew time was passing because every so often Çeda would mention how close they were to Mazandir. Every time she did, something about it bothered him. Maybe it was their task there, or those they were going to meet, neither of which he could recall. It felt as if the answer were floating in the air before him, just out of reach.

Often he tried to speak, especially when Çeda was in the room. He tried to squeeze her hands when she held his and gently stroked his fingers. But in all the days since he'd fallen under this spell he'd managed no more than a twitch or two.

"I felt him," Çeda said after one of those times.

"That's good," Dardzada said.

A pause. "That means he's getting better, right?"

Dardzada's reply had been measured at best. "It happens from time to time," he said. "It isn't a *bad* sign. But don't get your hopes up too high."

When Dardzada had left, he'd heard Çeda say under her breath, "Would it kill you to *hope* once in a while?" Then she'd leaned over him on the bed and whispered, "I swear to you, Emre, he could be dying of thirst in the desert, and he'd shake his fist at a rain shower, grousing that it got his clothes wet."

Emre wanted to laugh, but he could do no more than smile inside, and soon he fell back asleep.

Then one day things felt different. Çeda came to see him. "It's a big day," she said. "We're going to speak to Queen Meryam in the arena. We're taking no chances, though. We're leaving early to get the lay of the caravanserai and make sure the arena is truly empty. I'm nervous, Emre, but in a way I'm glad you're here. One of Ihsan's visions said I'd have to choose between you and Macide. I thought surely he'd meant here. Now."

He almost felt like he could talk to her. Almost. He stood on the very precipice of speech, but the words refused to come. After a kiss to his lips and a squeeze of his hand, Çeda was gone.

He drifted back down into darkness for a time, but when he came back he simply . . . opened his eyes. As if he could have done it the whole time but simply hadn't. He was worried his eyes might close of their own accord and not open again for days. But they didn't. He was awake and breathing and he felt as if he'd just been granted a new life.

He blinked several times, trying to clear away the crust. He stared for a long while at the ceiling boards above him, then turned his head and saw Clara reading a book. Sensing his movement, her head swiveled toward him and her eyes became two perfect circles.

"Dardzada!" she screamed, and ran from the cabin. "Dardzada!"

He came storming in moments later and loomed over Emre. "Emre?" His breath smelled of cumin. He had bits of what looked like cooked egg yolk in his beard. "Emre, can you hear me?"

"I—" His voice was a hinge in desperate need of oil. He swallowed and tried again. "I can hear you."

Dardzada poured him a mug of water and helped him sit. "Here," he said, lifting the mug to Emre's lips.

He drank. His throat hurt, but it went down well enough. Dardzada backed away, his look a perfectly forged alloy of befuddlement, surprise, and joy. Beside him, Clara stared in stunned silence.

"Well?" Dardzada asked. "How do you feel?"

Emre dared a touch of his fingers to the back of his head. Feeling the bandages, he slipped them off and felt the stubble skin of his scalp and the stitches Dardzada had applied. "I feel . . . magnificent!"

"Any pain?"

"Some," he said, "just here around the wound."

"Your headache?"

For months the pain had been a constant companion—its absence felt almost absurd. "Gone," he said, "all of it."

Dardzada was shaking his head in wonder. "Are you dizzy? Sick to your stomach?"

Emre shook his head. "I could do with a bit of rice. Or, come to think of it, a whole platter of it."

Dardzada smiled and fetched him a bowl of grapes. "The rice will have to wait," he said.

There was the sound of industry outside the ship. Emre had spent half his youth in and around the harbors of Sharakhai, especially the poor western harbor. It sounded just like that. Workmen calling. Winches lifting. The rattle of wagons along wooden piers and stone quays. There was even a desert heron singing its lonely call.

"Where *are* we?" Emre asked.

Dardzada was jotting down notes in a journal at the desk. "Mazandir," he said off-handedly.

And then it all came back in a rush. The purpose of the caravan. The queen they were set to meet. Hamid hiding himself away in Rasime's ship and planning to sabotage it all.

"Dardzada." Emre swung his legs over the side of the bed, a thing that was much more difficult than he'd given it credit for. "They're in danger."

"Who?"

"Macide. Çeda. All of them."

"What are you talking—hey now! None of that." He stood and slipped around the desk. "You're in no condition to walk much less leave the ship and try to save them or whatever other fool thing is running through that half-healed head of yours. Now lay back down."

"Dardzada. Hamid is here. He's been hiding on the *Burning Sand* with Rasime. He's planning to overthrow Macide."

Dardzada's eyes thinned, two shadowed slits in his pudgy face. "You're tired, Emre. You've just woken after nearly two weeks of being unconscious."

"No, Dardzada. I came across Hamid speaking with Sehid-Alaz."

"Next you're going to tell me that Sehid-Alaz is in on it."

"He is. He wants someone leading the thirteenth tribe who will punish the Kings as they deserve."

"Emre . . ."

Emre could see that Dardzada wasn't going to believe him. Not without proof. He'd want to hear from Macide. He'd want to hear from Sehid-Alaz. He'd want Rasime's ship searched.

Emre blinked and sat back down. He gripped the edge of the bed and took deep breaths. "This is important, Dardzada." He lay back down and put his hand over his stomach as if it were all he could do to keep himself from throwing up. "I'm feeling a little woozy."

"Well, of course you are. Didn't I just say you were in no condition to leave?"

Emre shut his eyes. Forced them to flutter open again. "Just promise me you'll speak to Macide."

"I will if you promise me you'll rest."

He nodded, then let his body go slack.

"Watch him, Clara," he heard Dardzada whisper. "Find me the moment he wakes again."

With that he left. Emre knew he didn't have much time, but he couldn't rush this. In his time in her care, he'd come to learn how sharp Clara was.

He opened his eyes again, made them look lazy. "Thank you for teaching Lemi how to play aban."

Clara looked at him warily. "You heard that?"

"Yes, though I got the impression he isn't the best student."

Clara smiled. "He isn't."

"Do you like aban?" He sat up again. "There's a place in Mazandir that sells ivory boards. I'll get one for you if you like."

Clara glanced at the door, and for a moment Emre thought she was going to alert Dardzada. "Are they really in trouble? Lemi and Çeda?"

A wave of relief rushed through Emre. "Yes, they are, and I'd very much like to help them."

Clara's bright eyes shifted between the door and Emre several times. Then she opened up the foot locker and began pulling out Emre's clothes. "Then you'd better hurry."

Emre could hardly believe his eyes. "You are a treasure, Clara." He kissed the crown of her head. "Has anyone ever told you that?"

"No. And certainly not Dardzada."

Emre winked at her. "As likely get a sonnet from a mule."

Clara covered her mouth as she laughed, as if Dardzada might see. Emre, meanwhile, donned his clothes and took up his bow and quiver full of arrows from the foot locker. He belted the quiver across his waist. The bow he slung over one shoulder so that it hung across his chest.

Clara, meanwhile, retrieved a glass vial from a cloth tray set on top of the desk. "Drink this."

Emre sniffed it. He didn't have to ask what it was. It was one of Dardzada's elixirs, a thing Çeda had forced him to drink many a time after one scuffle or another. It tasted terrible, but he couldn't deny it gave one a short burst of vitality. He downed the vial in one go.

"A treasure," he said as he handed the vial back.

And then he was off.

Chapter 45

THE DAY OF THE PARLEY in Mazandir started on an inauspicious note. Some of the asirim had gone missing in the night, including Sehid-Alaz, and none who remained would say more than, *"They will return when they return."*

"Do we delay?" Çeda asked Macide, a little nervous at this turn of events.

Macide stared at the overcast sky, his forked beard blowing in the breeze. "No," he said. "I don't want to be here any longer than necessary. We meet Meryam as planned."

They left shortly after, entering Mazandir from the east. Macide walked at the head of their group, with Shal'alara and Rasime by his side. Çeda, Sümeya, Kameyl, and Jenise followed. Behind them were twenty asirim in a loose group, and bringing up the rear were two dozen warriors and Shield-wives with shamshirs and bucklers hanging from their belts. Many held bows and some had been armed with rare arrows with ebon steel tips, which could pierce magical shields and armor.

They numbered fifty in all, and were a fine group of men and women, but Queen Meryam would have an equal number, comprised of her finest Blade

Maidens, Qaimiri knights, and Silver Spears. No doubt she'd have called on several blood magi from her country as well.

The streets were empty, making it eerily silent as they marched toward the center of the caravanserai. Queen Meryam had forbidden any from watching the proceedings, and indeed, they saw no one on their way in from the harbor save for a tow-headed boy who peeked at their passage from behind a goat shed.

Making matters more eerie, the asirim were strangely silent.

"What is it?" Çeda asked Sedef, the tallest of Mavra's children.

He kept walking with that odd shuffle of his, back hunched, gaze fixed on the walls of the sandstone arena in the distance. He'd lost his tongue and couldn't speak to her as the others could, but she heard his words through their shared bond. *The day weighs heavily on us, Çedamihn.*

How could it not? He likely hated what Macide was doing—who was Meryam, after all, but another ruler of Sharakhai, little different than the hated Kings themselves? Sehid-Alaz had probably found he couldn't face it and had gone to the desert until it was over. Whatever their reasons, it was adding to Çeda's sense of dread.

The arena rose over the center of Mazandir, rivaled only by the old caravanserai itself, the blocky structure that had once harbored ships but had long since been converted into an open air market and auction house. They reached the broad plaza at the arena's entrance, then filed through tall archways to enter the arena proper, at which point Macide ordered a dozen warriors and several asirim to head up the nearby stairs to watch from the highest boxes. The rest filed along a sloping passageway and exited into the lower seats.

The arena's interior was oval-shaped, and large—almost as big as those in Sharakhai. The rows of stone seats went twenty high and could seat five thousand.

As their cohort fanned out near the entrance, Çeda and Sümeya followed Macide down the steps toward the arena's earthen floor, which looked like a herd of akhalas had trampled it. On the arena's far side, a husky man wearing a thawb and turban exited from the shadows of the stairway. As he took the steps down with a leisurely pace, a low rumble of voices filled the air, and

Çeda knew precisely why. The newcomer's swagger was unmistakable. It was none other than Hamid, with a number of fresh scars gracing his lips and face.

Macide turned and looked at Çeda. "Did you know about this?"

"No," Çeda said, "of course not."

He turned to the others behind them. "Did any of you know?"

No one answered. Everyone seemed confused, even Rasime.

Ahead, Hamid arrived at the row nearest the arena proper and hopped down to the dry earth. "Afraid to talk now, Macide?"

"Don't trust him," Çeda said in a low voice. "Let *me* go."

But Macide ignored her and headed down the steps until he reached the stone lip dividing the seats from the central pit. There he stopped and stared at the man he'd once trusted above all others. "What are you doing here, Hamid?"

Hamid spread his arms theatrically and strode forward like a preening nobleman. "This is as good a place as any for your transgressions to be weighed."

"*My* transgressions?"

"Arenas are many things," Hamid replied, "but above all they're a place of judgment, and the gods know the time is long since passed when *you* should be judged, Macide Ishaq'ava."

"Do you expect me to leap down and fight you? You have no standing, Hamid, and much to answer for."

"My standing is beside the point." Hamid stopped at the center of the arena floor. "The real question is who is the larger traitor to the Moonless Host?"

"I'm no traitor."

Hamid laughed. "You took a *vow*, as did we all. You swore that you would see the Kings fall or die trying."

"The Host is no more, Hamid. There are larger things for us to worry about now."

Hamid stared at Macide with that emotionless, half-lidded stare of his. "This has been your problem since leaving Sharakhai. The Host is alive and well, Macide. You've only decided to ignore it."

"We were always going to move on. We've found our place in the desert at last. It's time we protect that, not step back into shadow."

"No one speaks of *shadows*. We want to fight in the daylight! We want to grind the memory of the Kings into the sand until there's nothing left but dust. And we will use the might of the allied tribes to do it."

We, Hamid had said, which made Çeda wonder who he meant. Macide must have been wondering the same thing, but before he could reply, a wail came from a tunnel that led to the lower levels. It was the mournful call of an asir, and was followed by another, this one higher-pitched, like the whine of a jackal pup. It made Çeda's skin crawl to hear them. She knew those calls like she knew her own heartbeat. They were the very ones the asirim had once used on Beht Zha'ir, the ones they used when bloodshed was near.

There came the sounds of a struggle, a shout and a grunt of pain. Along the ramp came a tall, dark form. Sehid-Alaz. He had Night's Kiss drawn, and he was hauling a body into the arena. By the gods, it was Husamettín. He was unconscious, head lolling, arms and legs scraping along the dusty earth as Sehid-Alaz heaved him toward Hamid.

Behind him came the others, the asirim who'd fled into the desert. Dragged between them were three more Kings: Cahil, Zeheb, and Ihsan. Where Yndris and the *Wayward Miller*'s crew might be Çeda had no idea. Dead, maybe.

They threw the Kings onto the ground in a heap. Çeda had thought them all unconscious, but now she saw that Ihsan's head was lolling from side to side. He, alone among them, was gagged.

"Here are the Kings of Sharakhai," Sehid-Alaz said in his haunting voice, "men Macide and Çeda sought to conspire with, men in league with the Qaimiri Queen."

In a great lifting of their voices, the asirim bayed and howled. They craned their necks and pawed at the ground. It was a wild thing, ritualistic, and it made Çeda's skin prickle just to hear it. The people of their tribe, of Çeda's tribe, looked to one another, their confusion and worry plain to see. There were some, however, who showed no signs of surprise, Rasime and her crew among them.

They'd orchestrated it together, Çeda realized. They were all in on it. This was a coup.

"Well?" Hamid called. "What of it, oh shaikh?"

"He's guilty," Rasime called from the seats. "You can see it on his face."

"No!" Çeda called. "It was necessary. There's so much you don't understand."

"Oh, but *you* understand?" Rasime said with a laugh. "You think us in-capable of it. You think yourself the only one who might comprehend this grand conspiracy of gods and men?" She stabbed a finger toward Husamettín and spoke to the tribe. "That is her *father* down there. She came to us claiming to be fighting for our cause, but I say she never left their service. Breath of the desert, she still has two *Blade Maidens* by her side!"

Hamid was the perfect image of smugness. "Step down, Macide. Step down and let those who know how to protect the tribe take the helm."

"The Kings mean nothing to me."

"No?" Hamid said. "Let's learn the truth of it, then."

He nodded to Sehid-Alaz, who dragged Zeheb away from the others. With one hand Sehid-Alaz grabbed Zeheb's thawb and lifted him up. He shook the King violently until Zeheb's head lolled. Zeheb's eyes opened. He took in his surroundings, then stared into Sehid-Alaz's face with a pitiful look that was half fear, half resignation.

"You have much to answer for," Sehid-Alaz moaned, and threw Zeheb to the dry, broken earth. "Let your makers be the judge."

"Leave him!" Çeda called.

But Sehid-Alaz didn't listen. Night's Kiss thrummed as he lifted it high into the air. Zeheb had managed no more than to roll onto his hands and knees before Sehid-Alaz brought the two-handed sword down in a vicious chop. It cut clean through Zeheb's neck. His head rolled away. Blood pulsed as his body fell and twitched, a freakish marionette, then blessedly went still.

Hamid pointed to Çeda with a broad grin. "Did you hear her? *Leave him*, she said! She's in league with them. She loves them. She's been working to feed them our plans since the day she joined us."

"I haven't! Everything I've done has been to protect the tribe and the asirim"—she waved to the Kings—"including this. Sharakhai is in danger. *We* are in danger. Please, you must listen."

"She spouts only lies," Hamid countered in a booming voice. "And her uncle, our self-proclaimed shaikh, sympathizes with her."

"You want to man the helm, Hamid?" Macide leapt down to the arena floor, drawing both his shamshirs as he went. "You'll have to take it from me."

Hamid drew his sword but made no move to engage Macide. "*Now* you wish to fight?" Hamid shook his head. "It's too late for that, Macide."

As he spoke, Çeda caught movement behind Macide. A war net with a tether, flung from one of the warriors who'd accompanied them to the arena, was flying through the air. "Watch out!" she cried.

But the net was already beyond the seats, over the arena floor. It enveloped Macide, and the moment it did, the one holding the tether, one of Rasime's crewmen, tugged hard on it, cinching the net's mouth and yanking Macide off his feet.

Çeda leapt down to the arena floor while whistling *free captive* to Sümeya, Kameyl, and Jenise. She'd hardly landed before the sounds of swordplay rang out behind her.

"For Macide!" Shal'alara yelled, and crossed swords with a burly man standing between her and Rasime. Others joined in, and soon the entire assemblage had devolved into madness. Swords clashed. Voices lifted in surprise and rage as the men and women of the thirteenth tribe fought one another. The asirim, meanwhile, backed away, apparently unwilling to interfere one way or another.

Çeda wanted to help defend those loyal to Macide, but King Ihsan was in danger. Sehid-Alaz had snatched his foot and was dragging him across the ground, away from the other Kings. As much as Çeda hated to admit it, he was too important to abandon. After catching a brief glimpse of Sümeya, Kameyl, and Jenise engaging several warriors who'd leapt down near Macide, she sprinted toward Ihsan.

Sehid-Alaz had released Ihsan's foot. He was lifting Night's Kiss high, preparing to bring it down across Ihsan's neck, when Çeda cried, "Sehid-Alaz!"

For just a moment he paused, his jaundiced eyes lifting to regard her as she sprinted toward him. It delayed him just long enough for Çeda to leap and snap a kick into his chest. Sehid-Alaz still managed to swing, but weakly, and Ihsan took only a nasty cut along one shoulder. He didn't wake, however, which made Çeda wonder if he ever would.

As the conflict in the seats grew fiercer, Çeda and Sehid-Alaz traded blows. He was fearfully strong, but his movements were neither quick nor precise, and she was able to dodge his blows or block them with sword or buckler. His eyes going wild, he lifted one hand, and the ground exploded beneath her feet, tilting the world as she was thrown skyward. She landed hard, her breath whooshing from her lungs as her head slammed against the ground.

As stars filled her vision, Çeda became vaguely aware that Sümeya and Kameyl had swooped in and were trading blows with Sehid-Alaz. She rolled onto her knees, coughing, and realized she'd lost both River's Daughter *and* her buckler.

Sehid-Alaz, roaring, bashed Sümeya with one hand and brought his sword against Kameyl's defenses in a move that sent her reeling. Freed from them, he turned and stalked toward Çeda. When she tried to stand up, he kicked her in the chest to knock her back down.

"Don't," Çeda called as he loomed over her. "Please listen!"

But he wouldn't. He'd given himself over to his rage. He was going to kill her just as he had Zeheb.

Chapter 46

SEHID-ALAZ LIFTED HIS BUZZING sword high into the air.

Çeda had felt the power of the desert keenly in the past, but never so strongly as she did just then. With a speed driven by her desperation, Çeda raised her right hand. Feeling in that moment not merely a part of the desert, but its master, its creator, she called upon that well of power. A dread wind pressed against Sehid-Alaz, and he was flung away so forcefully that his body spun and twisted until he struck the wall of the arena. As he fell to the ground, stunned, the other asirim backed away, shying from Çeda with fearful looks in their eyes.

"Raise no hand against the Kings," Çeda said to them. "None of you. They are under *my* protection now."

The asirim scrabbled and whined as they crawled away. What they might see in her that would scare them so she had no idea, but just then she didn't care.

As the battle continued to rage around her, she snatched River's Daughter from the rough earthen floor of the arena, then used it to cut the bonds at Ihsan's wrists and ankles. After removing his gag, she tried to wake him, but he didn't so much as move a muscle, so she shifted to where Husamettín lay and cut his bonds as well. She was just heading toward Cahil when she noticed a woman in the stands on the far side. She was wearing a red dress, and was watching the battle unfold with a wide grin, like a princess on her birthday.

By the gods, it was Queen Meryam.

Her gaze suddenly snapped toward Çeda. She'd been using a spell to conceal herself, Çeda realized—she'd been watching this entire time—but Çeda's gaze had alerted her to the fact that the veil of her spell had been lifted.

"Release me!" Cahil shouted.

Çeda stared down. She'd practically forgotten he was there.

After a fleeting thought of simply leaving him there, she knelt and cut his bonds while, in the stands, more soldiers were revealed: a dozen Blade Maidens, Qaimiri knights dressed in plate armor, forty Silver Spears wearing chainmail and white tabards bearing the King's sign, a shield with twelve shamshirs fanned around it.

Cahil retrieved his war hammer from the asir who'd dropped it. Nearby, Husamettín had picked up Night's Kiss. Ihsan had woken at last. He was standing on wobbly legs and gaping at the unfolding battle as if he was living through a nightmare. "Stop!" he yelled, but the battle raged on.

All too soon Çeda was lost in a storm of Silver Spears and swinging swords. Husamettín stood by her side, defending her, the two of them trading whistles to warn one another of threats and to position themselves more advantageously.

Cahil was there as well, swinging his golden hammer. Sümeya and Kameyl and Macide all joined in the fray.

Still in command of the desert's power, Çeda used it to send soldiers flying with gouts of wind and dirt, but the effort was weakening her, and the more that were felled, the more that seemed to rush in and take their place. Swords flashed. Steel rung on steel. Blood flowed in rivers. They fought, even Ihsan, who had taken up the sword and buckler of a fallen Spear, but gods, their enemies were so numerous.

One of Queen Meryam's Blade Maidens was a terror, full of fury and well-honed instincts. Çeda struggled to hold her ground against her, and then was stunned when the Maiden spun and bashed Çeda with her shield. The Maiden was readying a swing Çeda was woefully unprepared for when an arrow suddenly sprouted from her neck. More arrows sunk into the chests of the nearby Maidens. The Silver Spears as well. One of the Qaimiri knights caught an arrow in the hip. He stumbled along the arena floor, lost his sword while struggling to keep his feet, and was felled when Shal'alara ran her sword across his throat.

Çeda turned and saw, fates be praised, Emre—Emre!—sprinting down the stairs, bow in hand, releasing arrow after arrow in such rapid succession his bow string was a blur.

"Come on!" he said, waving Çeda and others toward the gladiator's ramp.

It was a wise move, but the entire arena was madness, what with the tribe fighting its own and both the Silver Spears and Blade Maidens entering the fray.

A small contingent of Meryam's forces had turned to meet another foe. Meryam herself was wielding a twisting cyclone of fire against a pair of men who stood high in the stands. One was, of all people, Ramahd Amansir, who seemed to be snuffing out the roiling column of fire before it reached him and his companion. The other was a man in robes who had his hands lifted high. They were surrounded by men who wore the same colors and style of armor as Queen Meryam's knights.

Çeda had no idea what was happening, only that Ramahd had somehow found his way here, and so must be continuing his quest to bring Meryam to justice.

Suddenly, all around the arena, the earth began to split. It ruptured, lifted in places, creating gaps through which hands could be seen, lifting, grasping, clawing, as if a company of soldiers had been buried alive just beneath the surface. Bodies were revealed—men in rusted, broken armor, the mail and tabards of the Silver Spears. They looked like poor simulacra of their live brethren.

Eyes vacant, skin torn and putrid, blood stains and wounds all over their bodies, they lifted from the ground—ghuls one and all. As they stood, Ramahd and his men slowed. Hamzakiir and Queen Meryam did as well, their spells sputtering then vanishing with the spitfire sound of forge-heated steel being doused in cold water. Strangely, the queen's soldiers were standing stock still, as if turned to stone. The same was true of the Blade Maidens, the warriors of the thirteenth tribe, the Kings, and the asirim all around.

Çeda, too, felt herself slowing. Becoming immobile. The air felt heavy as water, soft but unyielding. There was a strange counter-effect, however. The more the air pressed on her, the more her right arm burned. It suddenly felt as if she'd taken up a burning piece of coal, hoping to extinguish it in her grip.

Çeda's nostrils flared as a terrible stench wafted into the arena. It was caustic like lye and stank of rotting flesh. She thought it was due to the ghuls—the dead Silver Spears—but a memory nagged at her. She'd smelled the scent of ehrekh before. First from Rümayesh, then later on Goezhen himself. This peculiar scent reminded her of another.

But it cannot be. He's dead. Rümayesh killed him. I saw his body fallen on the sand.

Footsteps approached, a tympanic rumbling Çeda could feel through the soles of her feet. It rattled her bones. At the edge of her vision she saw something massive duck beneath the archway of the gladiators' entrance. It was nine feet tall, with massive horns that curled around its head.

Guhldrathen. It's the ehrekh, Guhldrathen.

He hunched low, sniffing the air like some grotesque bone crusher on the hunt. As he headed toward the center of the arena, Çeda realized he hadn't been healed. He wasn't even alive. With milky eyes he scanned those nearest him, then those in the seats. His chest still lay open. Other terrible wounds marked his skin, proof of the ruin Rümayesh had made of his flesh— evidence of the Battle of Blackspear, the clash between King Onur and the thirteenth tribe, where Rümayesh and Guhldrathen had fought a battle for the ages.

Behind his terrible, shambling form came a woman in a flowing jalabiya and a white hijab that made her blackened skin stand out in the sun. It was Anila, the necromancer, the one Davud had brought to the very threshold of death in Ishmantep while trying to douse a burning caravanserai.

As her undead soldiers fanned out, protecting her, Guhldrathen's corpse stepped aside. Anila strode across the arena floor, her eyes locked on Hamzakiir. "I'll admit," she declared, "I was beginning to think I'd never find you." She stepped on the back of a prostrate ghul to reach the stands, then waved one hand toward Guhldrathen. "But the ehrekh are wondrous creatures. Even dead, they can catch glimpses of the future."

Hamzakiir quavered.

Çeda's arm, meanwhile, burned. She willed it to greater heights. She felt her heart beat harder. Felt Guhldrathen's spell working against it. But her fear that everything—the future of the tribe, the future of Sharakhai, the very future of the Great Shangazi—might end here drove her on.

Like a flame melting ice, the spell's effect ebbed. Her arm, though leaden, began to move. She was able to shift her head, her torso, her legs, in the same deadened manner. She forced the same effect on those around her, concentrating on Sümeya and Kameyl, Macide and Emre, then the Kings. In dribs and drabs, they began to move as well, but so did the queen's nearby soldiers.

Surely sensing her efforts, Guhldrathen turned and roared. He pounded over the broken earth toward her. Çeda lifted River's Daughter, but too slowly. The spell's effect on her had only been diminished, not banished altogether. Breath of the Great Mother, how could she hope to stand against such a beast when she was trapped in honey?

Guhldrathen was so focused on her, he didn't see Husamettín. As the King of Swords brought Night's Kiss down in a blinding cut, a dark veil fluttered in the sword's wake. Night's Kiss buzzed angrily, and the blade cut deep into Guhldrathen's right calf. When the ehrekh turned, Cahil sprinted forward, leapt high into the air, and drove his hammer hard against the ehrekh's skull.

Guhldrathen stumbled and fell. Twisting his massive torso, he smashed Cahil with one flailing arm, then lifted one cloven hoof to stomp him where he lay, but Çeda, throwing off the effects of the spell at last, sliced his shoulder open.

His aim was thrown off enough that Cahil was able to scrabble away. By then a dozen asirim were swarming Guhldrathen, including Sehid-Alaz. Guhldrathen backed away, trying to throw them off, but there were simply too many, and his body was failing him. He'd suffered too many cuts, too many wounds. He fell roaring, snapping his jaws like a rabid dog.

The battle around Çeda had resumed, but most now seemed content to retreat, to escape what was now completely out of control.

"Where's Macide?" Çeda asked. She didn't see him anywhere.

The queen's contingent had started to move with her toward the far exit.

The faction of the thirteenth tribe loyal to Hamid were retreating, while those loyal to Macide gathered on the arena floor. Macide himself, however, was nowhere to be found.

"There!" Emre yelled.

He was pointing toward Queen Meryam and her cadre, where a burly Qaimiri knight was carrying Macide over one shoulder. Moments later, Queen Meryam herself swept through an archway and was lost to the darkened stairwell beyond. Her guard followed, including the one carrying Macide.

A terrible battle had broken out between Anila's undead soldiers and Ramahd's contingent of Qaimiri knights. Hamzakiir was on his knees, staring at Anila, one hand on his chest, powerless before her righteous anger.

Just then Ramahd caught her eye. Çeda wanted to speak to him, wanted to *help* him, but she couldn't—her tribe came first. "With me!" she shouted. "We must hurry if we're to save Macide!"

She and a dozen others ran through the gladiators' entrance. They wended their way through the arena's stone-lined halls then burst into an empty alley, hearing the clop of horse hooves on stone as they made for the stadium's northside plaza. When they reached it, a space bordered by squat, sandstone buildings, they found Meryam and her cohort. The first of them were already galloping out of the plaza.

Several of Çeda's fellow tribesmen launched a flurry of arrows, felling four Silver Spears who were just mounting their akhalas. Çeda leapt onto one of the abandoned horses and rode hard while, behind her, Emre, Sümeya, and Kameyl mounted more slowly.

"Follow me!" Sümeya shouted, and reined her brass-and-iron akhala into a narrow side street. "I know the way!"

The streets they followed were narrow but clear of debris and mostly straight. They flew toward the caravanserai's large, northern harbor, a handful of falcons chasing a host of fleeing crows. As they broke free of the caravanserai's squat buildings and filed onto the clear, dusty earth, they saw the queen's cohort break from the main thoroughfare and pound toward a small fleet of four royal galleons.

During their chase, Emre had gained steadily on Çeda, bow in hand.

"Go back, Emre!" she shouted to him.

"No!" he shouted. He still looked strange with his head shaved, like an ascetic who'd chosen to wander the desert in search of peace.

"Your head!"

"I know!" he said as he pulled even with her. "Isn't it wonderful? I feel great!" He whooped and pulled ahead, holding his bow high, sending arrow after arrow against the Silver Spears as their groups closed ranks.

"Emre!" she called.

But he wouldn't listen. He just kept riding.

Knowing he wouldn't relent, Çeda called upon the wind to drive against the queen's soldiers, to slow them down. The strength of it wasn't nearly as impressive as it had been in the arena. Even still, it spoiled the flight of the enemy's arrows, allowing Çeda and the others to close the distance between them and Macide, who lay across the saddle of the burly knight in the bright armor.

Their two groups clashed. Çeda lost track of Emre as she, Sümeya, and Kameyl drove into the queen's men, slashing with their shamshirs, using only their legs to guide their horses, which were clearly trained for war. Several enemy soldiers engaged with her, only to be felled by an arrow streaking in from behind—Emre, protecting her.

Cahil and Husamettín crashed into their opposite flank with a dozen more warriors from the thirteenth tribe who whooped and cried in high ululations as they met the enemy. Surprisingly, Yndris had joined them, though she was favoring her left side, and half of her face was covered in dried blood.

Çeda was close to Macide now, only a few horse-lengths away. Ahead, one of the queen's blood magi had turned in his saddle. His arms were raised high, and a thin tendril of blue light running from one hand to the other. He spread his arms wide, stretching the glowing thread into a tight line, which sped from his hands toward her.

In a blink, her horse was screaming, falling, suddenly, tragically limbless, and she was flying through the air. She fell to the ground and rolled away, trying to avoid being crushed by other horses, but something clubbed her head and made her ears ring painfully. All around, soldiers shouted in surprise and pain. Some of the horses, bloody along their front legs and shoulders, bolted upright and galloped away, riderless. Others did not.

Emre flew past, his bronze horse unharmed. He crouched in the stirrups, bow up, shooting as he went. He was slowly gaining on Meryam's cohort. Meryam had noticed, however, and had turned in her saddle.

Just then Emre released an arrow fletched in red—an arrow tipped with ebon steel, which struck Meryam's shoulder just as she was releasing a fan of green flames. Instead of spraying over Emre, the flames fell upon the Blade Maidens near her, knocking two from their horses.

By then Çeda was up and running alongside one of the healthy horses. "Hiyah!" she cried and used its building momentum to pull herself up and into the saddle. She whipped the horse's rump with the reins, moving faster and faster toward Emre, who was nearly even with the knight who bore Macide's limp form in the saddle behind him.

Emre, out of arrows, crouched on his horse's shoulders and leapt for the knight's horse. It was a bold and foolish move. He might even have made it had a Blade Maiden not lashed out with a whip and caught him around the neck.

The Maiden immediately reined in her horse and pulled on the whip, yanking Emre off the knight's horse and onto the packed earth. His hands reached up to the lash cinched around his neck, and just in time—the Maiden, having tied her end to the pommel, kicked her horse into motion, and Emre was dragged behind her toward one of the royal galleons; his grip on the lash had prevented her from snapping his neck outright.

The galleons' sails were already set, their crews ready on the decks with bows to hand. Çeda watched as Emre was pulled one direction, Macide the other.

Gods help her, for a moment she wasn't sure what to do. Ihsan's vision haunted her. *The lives of two who are close to you are threatened. You can choose one, and only one, to save.*

She knew it was a risk—a terrible, perhaps disastrous risk—but she couldn't abandon Emre. She couldn't.

She kicked her horse into a faster gallop over the dusty ground, then onto the open sand of the harbor. With Emre's weight slowing the Blade Maiden's horse, she gained on them easily. As Çeda pulled even with him, the Maiden drew a throwing knife from her sleeve and launched it at Çeda. Çeda ducked the throw, then blocked a second and a third with her shield. Before the

Maiden could launch another volley, Çeda swiped down with River's Daughter and cut the whip cleanly.

As Emre rolled to a halt, Çeda kept her pace to make sure the Maiden wouldn't suddenly turn and try to take Emre down. The Maiden did indeed slow, but instead of heading for Emre, she began trading blows with Çeda.

She was gifted and managed to fend Çeda off for a time, but when she saw she was outmatched, the Maiden kicked her horse into a full gallop and rode hard toward the nearest galleon, where more and more of the queen's knights were riding up the ship's rear ramp.

Çeda was just turning back toward Emre, who lay coughing on the sand, when a rider rode near and then past him, headed straight toward Çeda. It was King Ihsan, and he was staring at the galleon with a confused expression.

"What's wrong?" Çeda asked when he came near.

He reined his horse to a stop. His eyes shifted to regard her, but he seemed to be staring *through* her, not at her. "You must go with them, Çeda."

"What are you talking about?"

He looked confused, conflicted. "The Blue Journals. They showed you speaking with Queen Meryam"—he waved back toward the caravanserai—"after all this."

"What? Why didn't you *tell* me?"

"If I shared too much it would change, Çeda. You must know this much about prophecy by now."

Çeda was utterly confused. She didn't want to talk about this. She wanted to help Emre. "The vision was wrong," she said to him. "It must have been."

"No." Ihsan's eyes flashed, as if he'd just come to some realization. "It wasn't wrong. Too much that Yusam saw has happened. I'm certain we're on the right path." He was no longer staring *through* Çeda. He was staring *at* her with a guilty expression, as if he already regretted what he was about to do. "You *must* speak with her."

Suddenly, Ihsan's intent was perfectly, terrifyingly clear. "Don't do this, Ihsan. There are many paths to the same goal. You know that as well as I do."

"I'm sorry, Çeda. Truly. I don't want to do this. I have to."

She wanted to use the power of the desert to prevent him from compelling her, but the battle had all but sapped her strength. Instead, she kicked her horse toward him, drawing her sword as she went, desperate to reach him before he spoke.

But she was too late.

"Go," he said with an intense expression. "Give yourself to the queen's men. Do not resist them. Let them take you to Sharakhai."

She felt his compulsion on her. Part of her deep down wanted to deny him, but she *needed* to obey. Her right hand flared with pain, intensifying until it felt as if it were on fire. She grit her teeth and fought to resist. Moments later, the remains of her power guttered like a candle and was extinguished. Sheathing her sword, she reined her horse around and urged it toward the galleon where the Blade Maiden with the whip had gone.

"Çeda?" Emre called behind her. "Çeda, stop!"

His confusion and worry were plain, but she didn't so much as turn to look at him. She was focused solely on the queen's galleon. When she neared it, she raised her hands to show them she meant no harm.

"I must speak with the queen!" she called.

The ship was already on the move and gaining speed. The last few of the queen's soldiers were galloping up the ramp and into the shadows of the hold. They were ready to pull the ropes to secure the ramp, but Queen Meryam was there and she motioned them to wait.

"Why do you come?" Meryam shouted over the sound of the hissing skis.

"We must speak," was all Çeda said, an echo of Ihsan's words.

Queen Meryam's eyes stared out from her skeletal face. She was confused but clearly curious as well. After a moment's indecision, she waved toward the ramp. "Come aboard, then, and we'll talk."

With Emre's cries chasing her, Çeda's horse galloped onto the ramp and into the hold. The ramp immediately swung upward, landing home with a heavy thud, plunging all into shadow.

Chapter 47

IHSAN WATCHED AS THE GALLEON'S RAMP thumped closed. The queen's ships sailed on, having captured not only Macide, the quarry they'd come to Mazandir to secure, but Çeda as well.

"What did you do?" Emre, looking skinny, his head stubbly, stood a dozen paces away on the sand. His bow was at the ready. He had a fistful of scavenged arrows.

After taking careful note of the arrow that was already nocked, Ihsan replied in a calm voice, "I did what had to be done."

In a blink, Emre pulled the string of his bow back and let the arrow fly. It had already blurred past Ihsan's head by the time he felt the burning sensation along his left ear. He touched two fingers to the wound, found them glistening red when he pulled them away. As he rubbed his blood-slicked fingers, he realized the arrow could easily have pierced his heart.

"I asked you a question." Emre's voice was so loud it was practically a roar.

Ihsan raised his hands. "Let's remain calm." He put power into his words, but Emre seemed to shrug it off.

"Macide wasn't enough?" Emre's movements almost too fast to follow, he let a second arrow fly, and another bright line of pain appeared along Ihsan's opposite ear. "You had to give her Çeda as well?"

"Lower the bow, Emre." He poured more power still into his words, but again they seemed to have no effect.

"Did you make a deal with her?" Emre asked as the other Kings approached. "With Meryam?"

Ihsan didn't know what was happening to his power—it had been spotty at best since Cahil had healed him—but he had no time to worry about it just then. He put everything he had into his next words. "Lower. Your. *Bow*."

Emre's face went purple. He swallowed hard. The expression on his face was one of intense concentration. He had an arrow nocked, but made no move to draw the bowstring. Instead, he stood there, his body quivering as he wrestled with Ihsan's command. In years past he would have stood no chance, and yet as the seconds passed, Emre managed to lift his arm. He pulled the string halfway back.

The delay, however, had given Husamettín time to arrive and place Night's Kiss against Emre's throat. "Drop it," said the King of Swords.

Emre shifted his gaze to Husamettín, a look of pure exasperation on his face.

"You want Çeda back, I know"—Husamettín scraped the edge of his buzzing sword higher along Emre's neck—"but I fear you'll find that difficult with your head missing."

Finally Emre threw down the bow and arrow. "You saw it!" he shouted. "He *sacrificed* her!"

With the queen's ships gone, others were gathering: Cahil, Yndris, Sümeya, Kameyl, and more from the thirteenth tribe.

Husamettín looked at Ihsan. "What of it?"

"Yes, I sent her to Queen Meryam."

"Why?"

In truth Ihsan was still questioning whether he'd made the right move. "The journal . . . It said a choice would need to be made between two men in her life. I took it to mean Çeda would have to choose between Emre and Macide." He waved toward Emre. "She clearly chose him, but it was the wrong choice—"

"*That's* why you gave her to Meryam," Emre broke in, "because of a dead King's visions?"

"Yes," Ihsan said simply. "In the version of events where Macide dies and you live, Yusam noted words being spoken, words of power. I thought they were words of memory, Çeda's perhaps, but they weren't. They were *my* words. The choice was mine all along, not Çeda's."

One moment Emre looked as though he was trying to take it all in, to understand what Ihsan had done. The next he was shoving Husamettín away and sprinting for Ihsan.

Ihsan backed away. He raised his arms. But Emre still got in a strong right cross that sent him reeling.

Cahil tackled Emre before he could do more damage. He did little more than subdue Emre and haul him to his feet, though not before he'd offered a smug smile to Ihsan. In the past many weeks, he'd become as frustrated with the Blue Journals' visions as Emre was now.

Husamettín, meanwhile, looked like he was about to do something rash, but stopped when Ihsan raised his hands. "Leave Emre be." He worked his jaw. "I would have done the same in his place."

Sümeya, perhaps recognizing it as unwise to leave Emre so close to the Confessor King, separated him from Cahil. "Right or wrong," she said to the entire gathering, "the decision's been made. So what do we do about it?"

They had little time to discuss. Others were gathering. Some were from the thirteenth tribe, including the towering form of Frail Lemi, who held King Onur's greatspear easily in one hand. Others were Qaimiri knights, led by Ramahd Amansir and the gaunt form of Hamzakiir. Of the asirim they saw no sign—they'd apparently left with Hamid, who'd betrayed his shaikh and somehow brought Sehid-Alaz to his side.

"What happened to Anila and Guhldrathen?" Ihsan asked.

It was Hamzakiir, bloody and exhausted, who answered. "I managed to cast a spell that fooled them, sent them in the opposite direction. With any luck, it will continue to fool them until we can escape."

What a strange confluence of events, Ihsan thought. *It's no wonder King Yusam saw so many important threads leading to and from this day.*

"Can you hear Meryam's thoughts still?" Husamettín asked when

Ramahd told them how he, Hamzakiir, and Duke Hektor had arrived in Mazandir.

Hamzakiir shook his head while smoothing down his long, graying beard. "The power of the blood used to create that link has already faded."

"You said Meryam is preparing to use Macide in some ritual?" Ihsan asked.

Hamzakiir nodded. "I fear all is prepared in Sharakhai. Macide himself was the final necessary component."

"We have little time, then," Ihsan said. "She has the lesser Kings at her beck and call. She has the Enclave as well."

"True," replied Hamzakiir, "but there are those who would stand against Prayna and Nebahat. If we are to make an assault on the cavern, we must do so quickly. I would urge us all to find whatever allies we can before it's too late."

Ihsan took everyone in. "Are we agreed then? We return to Sharakhai to stop Meryam?"

It took a bit of time, but eventually everyone had agreed except for Emre. "I wouldn't trust you to sweep the sand from my porch," he said to Ihsan, then looked to the other Kings. "None of you."

With that he walked away, and those from the thirteenth tribe followed, nearly three dozen in all. Frail Lemi was the last to go. He'd started to follow the others, then stopped, stared straight into Ihsan's eyes, and said, "You shouldn't have given Çeda to them."

The impact of the big man's words were greater than any threat could have been. As Frail Lemi lumbered away, Ihsan felt shame burning inside him. He'd made Çeda trust him, then betrayed her.

It was necessary, he told himself. *I hope it was necessary.*

Husamettín, Cahil, and Yndris headed into the desert, making for *The Wayward Miller*, Ramahd, Hamzakiir, and his men toward the ship they'd sailed to Mazandir.

Ihsan held back. "Go on," he told the others. "There's something I need to address."

They gave him strange looks, but said nothing as he turned and jogged toward the retreating group from the thirteenth tribe.

"A word," Ihsan called, his hands raised high.

Emre slowed and turned, looking as if it was all he could do not to attack him again. Frail Lemi and the others watched, ready to do whatever Emre wished. Ihsan waved into the distance, where a fleet of nine ships could be seen sailing away, the ships of the thirteenth tribe. Only one ship was headed toward their position, the *Autumn Rose*, the Tribe Kadri ship.

"You've lost much this day, I know," Ihsan said, "and I bear much of the responsibility."

"Get to your point, Ihsan, or I'll let Lemi see if he can chop a King in half."

Frail Lemi grinned.

"I told you about the decision Çeda made," Ihsan said quickly, then amended, "That *I* made. What I didn't say was that *you* saved her."

"What are you talking about?"

"One of Yusam's visions showed you parting from the rest of us in Sharakhai and wandering through the blooming fields. Çeda finds you there after stepping from the mouth of a crystalline dragon."

There was a light in Emre's eyes that wasn't there a moment ago—a glimmer of hope? "Why didn't you say so before?"

"Because I feared that in knowing the vision you may not find the right path. But in this rare instance, I think you *need* to know."

Emre turned his head and stared beyond the *Autumn Rose*, toward the Khiyanat ships in the distance, then swung his gaze back to Ihsan, looking perfectly miserable. "I'm doing this for Çeda, you know, not you."

A wave of relief passed through Ihsan. "I don't care who you do it for. Just that you do it."

"Then let's get fucking moving."

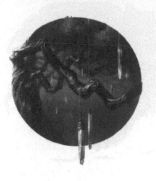

Chapter 48

NOT FAR FROM MAZANDIR, sand lifted and swirled along the top of a dune just as the sun was rising. It tightened, an eddy of sand and spindrift, before coalescing into a feminine form: Nalamae wearing her armor, bearing Yerinde's tall, adamantine spear.

After setting the spear beside her, she scooped up two handfuls of sand and threw them into the air. The sand lifted in a single, golden plume. As it settled, it reached outward, drifting like morning fog toward the wavering image of Mazandir. Oddly, it moved against the prevailing wind, then spread slowly, inexorably, through the whole of the caravanserai.

Satisfied it had reached the boundaries she required, Nalamae sat and lay her spear across her legs. Mazandir took shape within her mind—the buildings, the streets, the rooms within the many homes where the caravanserai's residents hid in silence by order of the queen. More and more became known to her. She felt the underground springs that fed the oasis's many wells and pools. She felt the horses, the goats, the bulls, and the oryx. She felt the scarabs that crawled, the midges that bit, the amberlarks that cooed their mournful morning song. There wasn't a thing that would escape her notice this day, not even her brothers and sisters, should they dare to come.

Nalamae sensed Çeda and the thirteenth tribe walking toward the arena, then entering it. She felt Queen Meryam and her Blade Maidens, Silver Spears, and Qaimiri knights all hidden from mundane sight. She felt the dead lying beneath the earth, each of them bound to the one named Anila. She felt the dead ehrekh, Guhldrathen, similarly bound, using his magic to mask himself, Anila, and the dead from detection of any sort. Approaching the arena from the east was the blood mage Hamzakiir, the Qaimiri lord, Ra-mahd Amansir, and his allies, ready to take revenge against their own queen.

It was a cavalcade of warring intent, a gnarled knot, a hundred thousand threads all leading to this time, this place. It was no stretch to say the out-come of the day's events would alter the course of the desert.

The visions the acacia shared had changed Nalamae irrevocably. She'd been hunted and killed in so many ways. The memories of those fearful days haunted her, not just for her own sake, but for the future of the desert's peo-ple as well. It was not always Goezhen who found her, but in the times he had, she'd been subjected to terrible torture. Goezhen had been trying to learn how she ensured her return, so that he might put a stop to it, but he'd never learned the trick of it. Whatever her former incarnation had done four centuries earlier, whatever ritual that particular Nalamae had performed, it had never failed to grant her new life.

She stared down at her hands, wondering at it all. Here she was in yet another form, a woman who'd had her own life before it had been stripped from her. It was a life that now felt distant, a dream that faded more with each passing day. Nalamae grieved for Varal's children and her husband—they still had no idea what had befallen her—but life sometimes brings ter-rible storms, giving no apologies for the pain and destruction it wreaks.

In the arena, the thirteenth tribe fought amongst themselves. Queen Meryam and her soldiers were revealed. Hamzakiir attacked, and Anila un-leashed her ghuls and the dead ehrekh soon after, which only added to the chaos.

Many died in the terrible battle that followed. Many mortal souls passed beyond the veil, their lives in this world snuffed out like so many guttering torches. Nalamae wanted to grieve for them, but she couldn't. Not now.

Instead, she wiped away her tears and waited, wary and watchful, at the top of the dune.

Just as the queen was making her escape toward her ships, Nalamae felt it: someone hunkered low near the caravanserai's northern edge. It was the very one who'd hunted *her* so many times: Goezhen, god of chaos and dark urges, one of his horns still missing, broken during their recent battle in Sharakhai's northern harbor.

With great patience, she stood and stepped forward, taking care to ensure that no swirls formed in the scintillant cloud of dust around her. She couldn't afford to have Goezhen sense her early.

A hot wind blew. The queen's ships set sails. Nalamae came closer and closer to the verdant pool of water where her quarry lay hidden.

Now came the most difficult part. Binding Goezhen to this place.

She began to work her spell while Goezhen was fixated on the events playing out in the harbor—the Silver Spears and Blade Maidens rushing toward the queen's galleons, the thirteenth tribe and Lord Amansir's men going after them, Queen Meryam throwing lashes of fire against her pursuers.

Nalamae's spell deepened, the spell of binding casting more and more threads around Goezhen. She was subtle as gossamer drifting on a breeze, but eventually, as she knew he would, Goezhen spun, his gaze wary. He'd sensed her spell but had yet to divine its nature, its source.

She worked faster now. Goezhen scanned the space where she lay hidden a dozen paces away, then waved a clawed hand before him. His eyes widened as Nalamae's spell of concealment was banished.

He roared and stumbled back, surely hoping to escape as he had in Sharakhai's northern harbor, but Nalamae was ready. She swore by the sun that bakes, the sand that shifts, and the water that grants life that Goezhen would never leave this place.

Goezhen sent dark, roiling clouds at her, spells she split with a swipe of her spear. Shifting to the attack, she landed a mighty blow to his jaw, then reversed her swing, cutting deep into his flesh while avoiding a lash of his tail.

For long moments they fought, Nalamae watching carefully for her opening and, when it came, moving like lightning, surging forward and thrusting Yerinde's spear into his chest with a mighty thrust.

Goezhen's eyes went wide as she drove him back. He clawed at her, swung at her with his tails. There was no avoiding his blows now, but she ignored the tearing of her flesh and pushed him further, faster, until he fell into the nearby pool.

Nalamae yanked her spear free as he plunged beneath the surface. The water churned and frothed. The waves became tinged with black, the blood of a fallen god. Goezhen's violent thrashing churned up mud from the pool's bed, but he failed to regain the surface. He stared up through the water. Realization dawning, his movements slowed, then stopped altogether.

When the waves had calmed, and the surface of the pool had settled into a mirror-like smoothness, Nalamae stepped onto the water, which was solid as stone. She strode forward until she stood above him, then crouched and stared down. Renewing his struggle, he clawed at the pool's unyielding surface, pounded his fists against it, but slowly he came to understand what Nalamae already knew: that he was trapped.

"How does it feel to be the hunted, *brother*?"

"Release me!" His words were muffled and muted. "Release me!"

Nalamae only smiled. "I know you hope to reach the world beyond. I know you all long for it. But I can't allow it. I won't. It would lay waste to the desert."

Goezhen stared with baleful eyes. His one remaining horn clunked and scraped against the underside of the pool's hardened surface. "Thou couldst still join us," Goezhen said. "The wish to feel the touch of our elders burns in thy heart, as it does in ours. I know that to be true."

He wasn't lying. The presence of the elder gods were distant memories now, but they were the deepest, sweetest, and richest Nalamae had ever felt. Even now she could feel the soft touch of Iri's hand on her cheek, the bliss it brought. She could hear the sound of Annam's voice as they walked among the newly made mountains to the west. She could recall perfectly the joy of pleasuring, and being pleasured by, Raamajit.

"That time is gone," Nalamae said, "never to return."

"Lies! Thou hast told thyself lies! Look within thy heart and see the truth. We may rejoin them, be reunited, and leave this foul world behind."

"That's just it. It *isn't* foul. It's grand, just as they meant it to be."

Goezhen stared up at her, his expression turning hard. He thrashed harder than before, and she felt the water's surface thump beneath her feet. He swam down and clawed at the pool's bed, hoping to escape another way.

But Nalamae lifted a hand and Goezhen rose with it. She rotated that same hand, and Goezhen's body twisted until he faced her.

Nalamae stood, her spear held easily in her right hand. "Tell me how to stop it."

Goezhen revealed the yellowed peaks of his teeth in a leering smile. "There *is* no way to stop it."

"There must be."

"There isn't," he replied.

And Nalamae found that she believed him. She'd hoped to get answers this day. She'd hoped that, even if Goezhen gave her none, she might get what she needed from one of their brother or sister gods, but she was starting to think she never would.

"So be it." Nalamae gripped the haft of her spear and pressed the tip against the water's surface, which gave ever so slightly. "Whether or not it can ever be stopped, you won't live to see it."

She put weight on the spear and pressed downward. Like a knife through cold butter, the water gave, the spear's honed point coming closer and closer to Goezhen's chest. Goezhen's eyes went wider than ever. He thrashed so hard the surface of the pool split, fracturing around the spear's point of entry. The surface buckled, lifting Nalamae where she stood. She thought it was going to shatter—such was the dark god's strength—but then the spear drove into his chest. Deeper and deeper it went, until it pierced his heart.

His screams shook the foundations of the earth. The buildings of the caravanserai rumbled. Stone cracked. A small roadside shrine nearby crumbled and fell. Even Nalamae stumbled back when, in a final burst of desperation, Goezhen struggled to break free. But then he went perfectly, utterly still.

Nalamae stared into his lifeless gaze for a long while, then used her spear to stab down, over and over, until the cuts had formed a rough circle around Goezhen's heart. Setting the spear aside, she reached into the hole she'd made in the thickened water, rooted through his ruin of flesh, and took up his heart.

"It may be unstoppable," she said to Goezhen's lifeless form, "but if so, none of you will benefit from it."

She walked across the pool until she trod upon sand once more, only then realizing how filthy her spear's blade was. She stabbed it into the sand over and over until it gleamed, then she became a column of sand, which collapsed and spread outward, settling until no one would know a goddess had once stood there.

Chapter 49

IT WAS NIGHT when Rümayesh walked among the blooming fields. Rhia waned gibbous in the east. Tulathan was a delicate, waxing crescent in the west. As distant as they were, they seemed displeased with one another, angry.

Generations ago, Rümayesh had become obsessed with the blooming fields. She'd spent weeks walking through the groves. She'd watched the blooms open and turn to face the moons. She'd watched them come alive on the holy night of Beht Zha'ir. She'd pricked her finger on the poisoned thorns, reveling not only in the pain but the faint taste of mortal blood, the redolence of lost souls.

She'd studied the asirim. She'd listened to their tortured screams, shared in their tortured dreams. She'd watched as they'd risen from their sandy graves and lumbered to the city to gather the tributes marked by the Reaping King. She'd stood by as the asirim threw the tributes, alive or dead, into the waiting trees and watched them die, strangled by the branches. She'd even saved some of the tributes and basked in the warmth of their gratitude before they fled back to the city.

In all those years, she'd only ever seen the branches move on the holy night of Beht Zha'ir. She thought it a rule inviolate, and yet here they were, over three weeks since Beht Ihman, just a bit over halfway until the next holy night, and the branches swayed ever so slightly, rubbing against one another. The thorns clicked, the branches clacked. It was a pleasant sound, like a leafless winter tree swaying in the wind.

The fact that they were swaying at all was an indication that things were changing. So few knew what was about to happen. The gods did. Rümayesh did. Brama did as well, a few of the Kings, a handful of others. A storm was about to fall upon the desert, to change the Great Mother forever.

How could you want that? Brama asked from deep inside her.

She railed against him, pressing him down, stifling his presence until her awareness of him faded.

He'd been trying to resurface more and more of late. She knew it would happen eventually—they shared the same form, after all, their souls commingled. As had been true when Brama was dominant, she could not be watchful at all times, and the longer she went without rest, the less strength she would have to prevent his ascension.

Well, she thought, *I'm not so tired that he'll gain dominance tonight.*

Since meeting Queen Meryam in the cavern, Rümayesh had been wandering the blooming fields again, considering them more deeply than she ever had before. Meryam needed one final component for her grand spell to work, an ancient and complex sigil, and the chances of her finding it on her own were slim at best.

Another twinge from Brama.

"Don't be afraid," she said while ducking beneath the gnarled bough of an adichara. "Once we reach the other side, this will all become a faint memory."

Brama said nothing, and she wasn't sure if it was because she'd treated him so ruthlessly or because he'd grown tired of the argument. She found she didn't care.

She came to a tree that looked sickly. Its blooms were not fully open, nor were they as bright as the surrounding trees. Its branches were stiff and unmoving. These were the key, Rümayesh knew. These were the ones that were ready to pass. It was imperative she find the sigils Meryam could use to draw tributes to these trees specifically, not to the healthy ones—the crystal needed their disease.

She sat crosslegged, pressed her sharpened thumbnail to her wrist, Brama's wrist, and drew blood. Using the blood, she painted sigils onto the adichara's bark, words written in the desert's mother tongue. She tried many variations using *bond, search, sympathize, unite,* and *strengthen.* To these she would eventually apply a very specific form of *summon,* a sigil she'd learned long ago when her mate, Behlosh, had used it on her.

Occasionally in these experiments she would draw too many sigils on a single tree and have to move to another and begin the process anew. It was painstaking work, but she could feel herself coming closer and closer to what she wanted.

Over and over she tried, and eventually moved on to the seventh tree of the night. *Seven by seven they came from the heavens,* went the old rhyme, referring to the number of elder gods who'd made the world, not realizing that there had been one more, the forgotten god who resided in the desert still.

This is no night to think of Ashael. Seven is a lucky number. The seventh tree will deliver that which I need.

And so it did. When she drew the symbol she'd been refining over the course of the night, she felt them, the diseased trees spread all throughout the blooming fields. They shone brightly, like stars ready to fall to the earth.

She reveled in the anticipation the discovery brought. These trees would deliver the gods from this plane of existence. They would deliver her as well. How she ached for it. It was so close she could taste it.

"Brama?"

Rümayesh spun, peering into a darkness that was ready to give way to dawn.

It had been a long, long while since she'd been surprised by anyone. "Who's there?" Rümayesh asked, wary of the gods, wary of the other strange creatures of the desert who might have come to stop her.

"It's me, Mae."

Rümayesh felt Brama's distress as Mae stepped out from the trees. She might have been wearing armor. Rümayesh couldn't tell. Mae was strangely difficult to look upon. She looked like an afterimage, the sort that remains on the eyes after staring at a thing for too long.

Magic. No doubt a gift from her queen. Rümayesh was forced to look away as she began to grow sick from it. "Why have you come?"

A pause. "I come for my friend." Mae had grown quite good at telling which of them was inhabiting Brama's form. "I have no wish to hurt you. I only wish you to leave him alone."

Only then did Rümayesh realize Mae was holding a drawn bow. Rümayesh peered close, barely able to perceive the glint of its diamond tip, but then she had to look away. Whatever magic Queen Alansal had given her was effective.

Rümayesh took a step across the rocky earth toward Mae.

As brave as she was, Mae took a step backward. "Brama? Can you hear me?" Nearby, an adichara branch clicked. "*Fight* her. *Fight* Rümayesh. You can win!"

"Shall I kill her?" Rümayesh asked aloud. "Shall I take her so that she'll be there, waiting for you on the other side?"

Brama's terror rose to new heights. *Leave her be. Let her go!*

Rümayesh took another step. "Why should I?"

Mae retreated and drew the bowstring to her ear. "Brama, hear me. I know you can find yourself again."

She's done nothing to you, Brama cried.

"She has a weapon trained on me."

She's only trying to save me. Let me speak to her. I'll tell her to leave.

Brama's and Mae's terror were playing off one another so deliciously Rümayesh didn't want it to end, but the diamond-tipped arrow *did* have some effectiveness against the skin of—

She felt the release of Mae's arrow. Saw it glint in the space between them, growing larger and brighter. She lifted one hand and cast a spell to block it, but the arrow wasn't where she thought it was. An illusion of some sort had been applied to it.

It punched through her magical shield and caught her along the ribs. Lightning quick, Mae released another arrow, which sank into her thigh.

As Mae released a third arrow, Rümayesh finally felt the edges of the spell that was obfuscating the arrows and flung her arm up. The arrow flew over her, lost in the adichara with a sound like snapping sticks. Catching the barest hint of Mae's sword being drawn, Rümayesh lunged backward, narrowly avoiding the swift cut. Crouching, Rümayesh gripped a fistful of sand and flung it toward Mae, infusing it with power as she did so.

As she dodged another swift swing of Mae's sword, Rümayesh heard the sizzle of the molten sand against Mae's armor. Mae screamed, flung herself backward with one arm across her face, hoping to put distance between them.

But Rümayesh was already on the move. She sprinted forward. Backhanded Mae's sword and sent it flying. It swirled away, a gyre of dizzying darkness.

"Brama!" Mae cried desperately.

Rümayesh, blinking fiercely from the vertigo threatening to overwhelm her, fell on Mae. She pinned her down, one hand on her throat. She used her other hand to paw at the neck of Mae's armor. And there she found it. An amulet.

She ripped it free and sent it flying away, and suddenly Mae was plain to see. A Mirean woman with a grinning demon helm and bright, lacquered armor.

One hand still around her throat, Rümayesh ripped away the mask and stared into Mae's bright, jade-green eyes. Spittle gathered around her mouth. She made choking sounds. Her light-colored skin turned dark, almost purple, as she fought for breath, and her eyes reddened. She looked desperate, but there was still hope—Brama might yet save her.

How perfectly rich, Rümayesh thought.

Brama could feel the sharp, stinging pain from the arrow wounds as well as Rümayesh could. He could feel the blood trickling over their shared skin. He sensed Rümayesh's anger at being tricked.

"She knew better than to come here," Rümayesh said to him.

It was then that Brama rose up like a creature from the depths of a dark, ancient lake and assaulted her. She was immediately on her heels, trying to fight him off. He was much, much stronger than she'd thought he would be. How he'd managed to store up so much energy she didn't know.

You've taught me many things, Rümayesh.

She knew it was so, but had thought him incapable of overwhelming her.

She knew that if she were to kill Mae, it would empower him even more, and if *that* were to happen, she might be powerless for too long.

She couldn't let that happen. All her efforts with Meryam would be put at risk—the very thought of missing the day the gods walked to the farther fields put a deep fear into her. But doubts were already beginning to surface in Brama's mind, doubts about what he wanted versus what would be best for his friend.

If he acted as she suspected he would, she'd be back in control soon enough. So she let him take control. She let him have his precious Mae.

She could hardly wait to taste his sorrow.

Brama was suddenly returned to himself. He trembled and tipped over, falling across Mae's legs. He tried to rise again and this time managed to keep his feet. His skin tingled. His fingers felt numb but were slowly regaining their feeling in waves of pins and needles. His world spun like a black lotus high and the pain from the arrow wounds was so bad he thought he might pass out from it, but slowly he regained control over himself, then the pain.

By then Mae stood before him, her bow drawn, the string pulled to her cheek, the diamond-tipped arrow pointed at his chest. Her whole body shook.

Brama didn't know what to say. Part of him wanted her to pierce his heart. Another part was just scared, so he stood there, his breath loud in his ears, hoping Mae would lower her aim.

"Brama?" Mae said.

"Mae, you have to go."

She glanced to her left, probably toward her hidden qirin, Angfua.

"Mae, you have to go! I won't be able to hold Rümayesh forever. And when she resurfaces, she'll finish what she started. She'll kill you."

The regret was plain in Mae's eyes. She'd come to the blooming fields hoping to free Brama, and gods, he loved her for it, but she was starting to see the truth—that she would never be able to free him, not truly—and so she did the thing she least wanted to do, the thing she'd kept as a last resort. As Brama took a step toward her, she let her arrow fly.

With perfect clarity, Brama reached up and grabbed it. The tip only a finger's breadth from his chest. As he snapped the arrow and threw it aside, Mae stood perfectly still, a shocked look on her face.

"I told you to *leave!*"

Brama put power into his voice, amplifying it, and finally it worked. Mae turned and fled and Brama watched as she was lost beyond the adichara grove. The full weight of what he'd done was starting to press in on him. The last person in the world who cared about him had just left him. He'd *needed* to frighten her—had he not, Rümayesh would eventually have resurfaced and killed her—but gods how it hurt.

He turned and walked to the pendant Rümayesh had torn from her neck. A pearl, pink and misshapen, in a gold setting. He wished he could slip the pendant over his head and disappear from the world as Mae had. He couldn't, though. His life wasn't his anymore.

"I'm sorry, Mae," he said, then let it slip from his hands.

He walked for a long while among the blooming fields. When he could take it no more, he found a tree as misshapen as any he'd ever seen and lay down near its base. There he wept, while above him, around him, the trees swayed with a sound like the world was breaking.

He felt Rümayesh rising up once more, and this time Brama did nothing to stop her.

Chapter 50

NIGHT HAD FALLEN over Sharakhai by the time Davud arrived at a stately home just north of the collegia grounds, the latest and most opulent of the many safe houses they'd hidden in over the course of the past several months. He entered through the front door without knocking. Inside, near the hearth and its dying fire, a man sat in a rocking chair knitting what looked to be a rather lumpy head scarf. As Davud added a few logs and coaxed the fire back to life, the old man, bald on top with white hair sticking out everywhere else like a horsehair brush, stared into the flames, ignoring Davud entirely. He was a wealthy caravan owner whose entire family had been killed during the Malasani invasion. The fates had spared him when they'd sent him to the western harbor to conduct a bit of business. Now he chose to live alone, keeping to himself, leaving room after room empty and unused.

Davud adjusted the shawl around his shoulders so he'd be more comfortable, then took the nearby stairs up to the third floor and entered the largest of the home's generous chambers. Esmeray lay in the bed, half covered by the rich sheets, reading a book of poetry by lamplight.

As Davud began to undress, Esmeray's gaze flicked up from the pages. "The fates were stingy, I take it."

He hopped naked into the bed. "They're always stingy."

"Oh, I don't know." She flipped a page. "They shone on you when they led you to that cemetery."

Davud tried to stifle a laugh, failing miserably. She was referring to the day they met, when she'd attacked him and the ghul, Fezek, had come to his rescue. "Some might consider it a curse."

"A curse on me!"

He took the bottle of scented oil from the table on his side of the bed and pulled back the covers. After pouring a drizzle over Esmeray's belly, he rubbed the oil into her skin using slowly expanding circles that centered on the well of her bellybutton. The air smelled of cloves. "Is this what you call a curse?"

She shrugged. "It's the one thing that isn't."

He felt how tight her muscles were as they rolled beneath his fingertips, then smiled as they relaxed. Esmeray seemed to enjoy these intimate moments, but they were a solace for Davud as well, a glimpse of normalcy in the madness that made up their lives.

Esmeray's eyes floated down the page as she read the poem. "And where did you go searching?" She asked as if she didn't care about the answer, but Davud could tell she did.

"The dormitories," he said. "I spent over an hour in Cassandra's old room."

"Nowhere else?"

Davud closed his eyes, knowing she already knew the answer. "Fine, I went to Nebahat's lair."

She lay her book down. "We *agreed*, Davud. You said you'd leave that place alone."

"I know, but I wanted to find Nebahat's assistant again. He knows Nebahat's secrets. I'm sure of it."

"I don't doubt that he does"—she'd begun reading again, but her face was so screwed up in anger he doubted a single word of it was sinking home—"but what good is that if you're dead?"

Davud's hand slowed over her stomach. He admitted it. He was entranced by the strange young man they'd stumbled across. He had the uncanny ability to counter and defeat magical spells, but more than that, Davud suspected he was a storehouse of information. The way he'd used the books to tell stories made it clear he'd read many of the ancient texts Nebahat had hidden away in his lair below the collegia.

"It wasn't worth it," Esmeray went on. "Not unless you're willing to give the rest of it up. The Enclave, Queen Meryam, the tributes she's sending to the blooming fields."

"You're right." It had been a stupid risk that jeopardized everything. "I won't do it again."

"Promise?"

"I promise."

She pulled the book aside and stared along the length of her body. "Promise me on my belly."

Davud's face suddenly felt very hot. "You're not . . . ?"

She paused, confused for a moment, then laughed long and hard—a genuine laugh, not the sort she used to mock. "Good gods, *no*, Davud. I know the right herbs to use. Now promise me on my belly!"

He leaned over and kissed her stomach. "I promise," he said to her bellybutton, then kept rubbing. "You said you were going to see someone who works in the Sun Palace?"

The woman he was referring to was the palace's primary archivist. At Esmeray's urging, the woman had made friends with Basilio, Queen Meryam's vizir. They were hoping to find someone, anyone, who might tell them what Meryam hoped to do with the tributes, and whether or not she still hoped to lead Davud and Esmeray to their graves.

"She's made inroads with Basilio," Esmeray said, "but he hasn't said much. He did let slip that Queen Meryam just returned from Mazandir."

They'd known that Meryam had left. It was the sort of secret one couldn't keep for long in a place the size of the Sun Palace. She'd been gone for nearly two weeks, but they'd never learned where.

"Mazandir," Davud mused while kissing her bare shoulder. "What's there?"

"Basilio wouldn't say. Something big, apparently."

"Well," he said, placing another kiss on her bared breast, "she'll just have to ply him for more secrets."

She set her book aside with a grin. "Perhaps you have thoughts on the best way for her to go about it? A way for her to ply, as it were."

"I do . . ." He was just running his hand down one hip and along her thigh, but froze when he felt a tingling sensation inside his chest.

Esmeray noticed. "What is it?"

He threw back the covers. "Someone's coming."

They both threw on their clothes. Esmeray rushed to the nearby window while Davud headed for the chamber door, planning to head downstairs. That's when they heard the entrance door open below.

"Davud!" barked a voice that sounded distressed, in pain, perhaps.

"It's Undosu," Esmeray said.

They rushed down the stairs but hadn't even reached the first landing before they heard a thud, as of something heavy falling. They found Undosu unconscious and curled up in a ball near the base of the stairs.

Esmeray crouched beside him. "Gods, what happened?"

His eyes fluttered open. His hat was gone, and he was bleeding from a bad cut to his scalp. A sheet of crimson stained his dark, wrinkled skin. Worse, he was holding his left arm tenderly. His forearm looked badly burned, but not from a fire. The skin had bubbled, revealing patches of raw flesh beneath.

"This old man wasn't careful enough," he said through gritted teeth. "They found me."

"Who?"

"Prayna and Nebahat." He tried to pull himself up. Esmeray pushed him back down, but paused when Undosu began shaking his head violently. "They're coming, girl! We have to warn Meiying."

Just then the front door creaked. It shook and rattled, then bent inward, straining against the hinges.

"Get down!" Esmeray yelled.

They ducked as the door exploded inward. Wood flew everywhere, shards embedding themselves in the furniture or the walls. A sound like sizzling meat filled the air as wood and plaster fell against the hardwood floor.

"The back door," Esmeray hissed, and pulled Undosu to his feet. But they hadn't even taken a step toward the hall leading to the rear of the house when they heard the back door explode as well.

"Upstairs!" Davud hissed. "I'll slow them down."

Esmeray helped Undosu up the stairs as rapidly as the old man's shaking legs would allow. Davud, meanwhile, called a shimmering blue shield into being. As he backed up the stairs, his eyes fixed on the entrance, he saw the old man, their benefactor, cringing behind the wood cradle. *Stay small,* Davud thought. *Stay silent.*

He reached the landing at the top of the first staircase and had started up the next flight when a blast of green fire streaked up the stairway, ricocheted off his shield, and plowed into the ceiling. More plaster rained down. By then Davud was sprinting up the stairs to the third level.

On the floor above he felt Esmeray constructing the framework for a spell. It was a spell she couldn't execute—her ability to use magic had been burned from her—but she and Davud had learned how to work together. She created the frameworks, he brought the spells to life. It allowed them to cast more spells than Davud could alone.

He was just infusing the spell with power when footsteps resounded on the stairs below. "Come quietly, Esmeray, and we'll spare you!"

It was Esmeray's brother, Esrin, which meant her sister Dilara was likely the one who'd blown the back door in.

"Come upstairs," Esmeray barked from above, "and you'll see what happens to those who break into my home."

Davud felt her spell spread along the stairs behind him. It cascaded like a waterfall, and where it touched, thin shoots grew. They thickened into switch-like branches, which grew thorns and began to wave wildly in the air. Soon the stairwell was choked with them, and Esrin was caught in it. He gave a sudden cry of pain, which was followed by the crackle of flames. Flickering light filtered through the branches, then a thick, black smoke roiled up the stairwell. Davud's nose burned from the noxious smell of it. His eyes itched and began to tear.

By the time Davud reached the third floor, Esmeray was guiding Undosu toward the small patio at the back of the house, creating the framework for another spell as she went. As they burst through the patio doors, Davud poured his reserves of raw power into her spell. The wooden table, the chairs around it, and the awning above shattered into a thousand pieces and rearranged themselves, forming a narrow walkway that bridged the distance over the alley behind the house to the building directly opposite.

They'd made it only halfway across when a great ball of flame lit the alley below and streaked upward, narrowly missing them. "You shouldn't have run!" Dilara called. "It's just going to go harder on you!"

Esmeray glanced down. "Eat shit, Dilara!" she cried, then dove as a spray of needles screamed up from the alley below, catching Davud across the calf of one leg.

Davud sucked air through his teeth against the pain. They paused only long enough to remove the barbed needles, then sprinted as quickly as Undosu's infirmity and Davud's wounded leg would allow. After crossing the roofs of several more buildings, they made their way down to street level and headed toward Tsitsian Village, the immigrant neighborhood where Meiying lived. They managed to stay ahead of Esrin and Dilara, but only just. Undosu could hardly walk, and the spells Davud used to hide their presence never seemed to work for long, the blood magi on their trail somehow managing to pierce them. By the time they came to the street where Meiying lived, Davud was flagging badly. He'd never cast so many spells in so short a time.

"She's just there," Esmeray said, pointing to a wooden archway lit brightly by the red lanterns hung along the street.

The three of them stopped short, however, when they saw someone walking down the center of the crowded street straight toward them. Gods, it was Nebahat, wearing a rich khalat of earthen tones, his forehead painted orange with a bright yellow circle at its center. The women and men outside the brothels watched, many with amusement. More and more, though, were backing away from a confrontation they were just starting to realize would be healthier to be as distant from as possible by the time it began.

As the street devolved into a panicked rush, Esmeray pointed to the nearby archway. "Through there, quickly."

Undosu groaned as they all but carried him through the arch. They were met with a rock garden with sculpted sand for a bed. In the center of it stood a woman, half of her lit in the ruddy light of the distant lanterns. It was Prayna, and at her feet, sprawled on the white sand, was a woman in a silver silk dress—Meiying, unconscious.

Moments later, Nebahat prevented their retreat when he stepped into the archway they'd just passed through. Dilara and Esrin were right behind him.

"Please," Davud said, his breath coming in great heaves, "we needn't be enemies—"

"Watch out!" Prayna called.

Davud hadn't realized it, but Undosu was drawing a sigil in the air. The next moment Dilara had her hands to her chest, her eyes and mouth wide in an expression of pure pain. And when Undosu jerked one hand back, the front of her jalabiya snapped outward with a brittle crunch.

She cried out, a sound of simple surprise, while staring down at the strange lump in her chest. Her hands pressed against the wound, as if she might hold it all in and in so doing save her own life. Then she simply collapsed.

"Dilara!" Esrin cried, and dropped to her side.

Nebahat, meanwhile, released a bellowing roar and sent a snaking line of green light toward Undosu, who had been trying to erect a shield. The shield, shimmering in the air ahead of him, burst into a cascade of golden light as Nebahat's spell pierced it. Undosu was struck along the top of his skull. Red shone, bits of white. A moment later, he collapsed to the ground.

"Esrin, don't!" Prayna shouted. "I wish to speak with them!"

Davud had been so preoccupied with Undosu he hadn't noticed Esrin coming to a stand. He stared at Davud with naked fury while a ball of flame roiled between his outstretched hands. Strangely, the flames shrunk and fizzled a moment later. He tried again, and this time only a spark was lit before the spell was snuffed out.

Prayna scanned the darkness, looking for the new threat. She sketched a sigil in the air before her, but nothing happened.

Davud had seen such things before, had felt them, in fact, when Ramahd Amansir, the Qaimiri lord, had sapped the energy from his spells. He'd felt like a child all over again, powerless to prevent the gutter wrens from stopping him and stealing his caramel sweets.

No sooner had Ramahd's name come to him than the man himself appeared in the street behind Nebahat and Esrin. Beside him came another. By the gods who breathe, it was Hamzakiir. Two more stood behind them. Davud knew them both, though it took him a moment to recognize them. One was a tall man in black armor with a bloody great two-handed shamshir in his hands. The other was shorter, and held a gleaming war hammer easily in his right hand. They were Husamettín, King of Swords, and Cahil the Confessor.

A third King joined them a moment later: King Ihsan, hands raised in a placating gesture. "Now why don't we discuss this like civilized people?"

There was a long, pregnant pause, and then the garden exploded into action.

When Esrin sent a quick but weak spell toward Husamettín, Husamettín lifted a shield and blocked it, then both he and King Cahil charged. Cahil threw his hammer, which smashed through a forming, scintillating spell and crashed into Esrin's face. Esrin cried out in pain as he was thrown backward over a lump of rock.

Hamzakiir, meanwhile, was gathering a ball of inky darkness. Nebahat managed to throw one spell at him, an orb of fire, cast with blinding quickness, but Hamzakiir lifted one hand away from his spell and blocked it with astounding ease. His other hand released the spell of darkness, which flew hungrily toward Nebahat, twisting and turning like a midnight bat, and struck him dead in the chest. The spell sunk into his ribs and flesh, devouring hungrily, gouging a hole so large it looked like a bone crusher had been at him for hours. Arms flailing for purchase, Nebahat fell backward and lay still as the sizzling darkness continued to devour him.

Things were happening so quickly Davud hadn't noticed the throwing star in Prayna's right hand. He couldn't have done anything about it if he had—he was too exhausted to cast another spell—but he saw who she was aiming for.

"Ramahd!" he called out, but too late.

Prayna's arm snapped forward. The star flew through the air, catching Ramahd in the shoulder. Two more followed and sunk into his flesh as he was stumbling backward from the first.

At the same time, Esrin stood from where he'd fallen and flung his arms high. The sand and rocks in the garden lifted and swirled, worse than a sandstorm. They stung and they bit, sometimes cutting deeply where skin was exposed. Davud, powerless to stop it, held Esmeray to his chest and waited for the storm to pass.

When the wind finally died and the air began to clear, Prayna and Esrin were gone.

Chapter 51

QUEEN MERYAM SAT AT THE CENTER of the table in the Sun Palace's grand council room, the seat once occupied by Kiral, King of Kings. A terrible sandstorm had swept through the city, and dust was kicking up in droves everywhere, even here in the palace. It made Meryam's eyes itch. Made her lips crack and bleed.

As they waited for Queen Nayyan to arrive, the lesser Kings and Queens chatted. Meryam ignored them entirely, cradling a brew of her own making between her hands, a combination of kahve, ginseng, and the finest Mirean schisandra her physic had been able to procure. With the fabled elixirs all gone, the last consumed before reaching Mazandir, the revitalizing mixture was necessary. Still, Meryam could hardly keep her eyes open. They stung, and not just from the dry air. Her body ached. Every time she sat still she felt as if a black hole were opening up inside her, threatening to drag her down into slumber. She was tempted to let it. She could just lay her head down on the table and sleep while the others prattled on.

King Alaşan, who'd risen to a place of prominence among the lesser Kings, sat to Meryam's left. As he droned on about how the ships being built in King's Harbor were delayed because of disruption in their shipping lanes,

Meryam saw Amaryllis enter the council chambers. She was Meryam's master spy and assassin, a beautiful woman with long curly hair and looks many women would kill for. She gave Meryam a pointed look before settling in next to Basilio.

Meryam dearly wanted to speak with her, but the council took precedence. Appearances must be maintained, for the time being, at least.

"They've begun to harass the caravans now," one of the Kings was saying. Mighty Alu, she could hardly keep track of which of them was speaking.

"No," Alaşan replied. "It isn't the Mireans, nor the Malasani, but the Kundhuni warlords. The very ones who were supposed to be guarding the convoys are taking the ships and claiming the Mireans ambushed them, when in truth they're stealing the wood and selling it to our enemies. And their boldness doesn't end there. Now they're saying that since the ships and cargoes have been lost, they need more coin for the shipments that *do* make it through. It's part of an intricate scam that began months ago, a thing that was hardly apparent at first but that is now rampant among the warlords."

Meryam sipped her drink, losing track of the conversation for a time, and was brought back to it in startling fashion when she realized they were all staring at her. "Pardon me?" she asked King Alaşan, the one who'd spoken to her.

Alaşan was a young man, handsome, with a gentle face, prone to kindly smiles. Just then, though, he looked ugly and dispassionate, a hangman grinding his axe. He spoke loudly and slowly, as if she were a child. "*When* did you *learn* that the Kundhuni warlords had started taking *bribes* from the *Mireans?*"

Meryam scanned the curving table. The other rulers of Sharakhai were waiting, but she wasn't sure how best to answer. She'd been caught flatfooted. Basilio had asked her what to do about the Kundhuni, but for the life of her she couldn't remember what she'd told him, nor the outcome. She certainly wasn't ready to spin a lie about it.

"She wasn't aware." With one hand raised in an admission of guilt, Basilio rose from his seat behind her. "The queen has had so much to worry about, I took this matter into my own hands."

"And your decision," Alaşan said, "was to bribe them *yet again* and to mention not a word of it to the rest of us?"

Basilio glanced at Meryam, then Amaryllis, as if either of them could help him now. "It was a temporary measure. Until we had more ships of our own."

"And now you see what's come of *that*," Alaşan said, his voice growing angrier. "Your *temporary measure* has delayed the very thing you hoped would rid us of the problem. And now things have grown much worse. It's not only skimwood we're short on, but oil, steel, medicinals, the components we need to make fire pots and dousing agent. We're even running low on skimwood wax! How do you suppose the war is going to go when our ships grind to a halt while our enemies circle them like vultures?"

"Poorly, I suspect."

"Poorly, indeed! Now we need to remedy the threat our Kundhuni *allies* represent."

"More Qaimiri ships will be arriving soon."

"As you've been saying for months. The war is poised to recommence. A dozen signs and more point to it. Ships that arrive in two months' time are useless to us when we must right the Kingdom now. And why are *you* speaking?" Alaşan's gaze slid to Meryam. "Why isn't your queen's voice being heard?"

"In this," Meryam said, "Basilio's voice is my own. I will take the blame, but I trust in his judgment. From what we knew at the time, I'm sure it seemed like the best course of action."

"And what has so occupied you, to the detriment of all else?"

"You know what I've been focused on." She took in the full assemblage. "You all do. Your ancient enemies. The Moonless Host. The tribal alliance."

Alaşan took a moment, his nostrils flaring with the breath he was slowly exhaling. "I've told you those are secondary concerns."

"I disagree. Your own Lord Captain of the Silver Spears came here not one month ago and told us how active the Host have become in the city again."

"Reports that by other accounts are overblown. And, disagreement or not, you do not rule Sharakhai alone, Queen Meryam."

"It seems to me she does not rule at all." This came from Queen Sunay, Sukru's sixty-year-old daughter who, Meryam swore by Mighty Alu, was the spitting image of her father, greasy hair and hunched back included. She flung a crooked finger at Meryam. "Never at council. Hidden away in darkness like a bloody vole. Content to let her vizir speak for her, as if a *vizir* is supposed to manage her throne. She hasn't even answered our questions about how King Yavuz died."

"I told you," Meryam said, biting back the bitterness that came to her, "that was an unfortunate accident."

Queen Sunay's face screwed up in anger. "He never should have participated in that ritual in the first place."

"He offered. I accepted. We nearly delivered King Emir's head to you on a platter."

"But you didn't, did you?"

"War never goes as planned," Meryam replied, slowly finding her footing once more. "We do not turn tail when we lose skirmishes. We regroup and move on."

Sunay stood in a rush. "We do not *move on* when one of our number is killed. And don't think we've forgotten how you attacked Cahil."

"I believe it was one of *your* number who attacked Cahil. Queen Nayyan held that crossbow, not me."

"Do you hear her?" Sunay asked smugly while scanning the other Kings. "One of *our* number. Our number is right. You're an outsider here, Queen Meryam. Never forget it."

King Alaşan rose, gesturing for calm. "Queen Meryam is one of us now."

Sunay stared at him, incredulous, her pale face splotchy with anger. She looked like she was about to say something rash, but choked back the words—she knew, as they all did, that if Meryam were to leave the city with her fleet, Sharakhai would fall. "Listen to her," Sunay finally spat. "She called the death of a King at her hands a *skirmish*."

"Her efforts were made at our behest," Alaşan countered, as if that settled the matter. Then, in a move as gracious as Meryam supposed she could expect, he flourished one hand toward Meryam. "Since, as you say, your days have been preoccupied with the Moonless Host, why don't you tell us where your efforts stand."

In truth, Meryam wasn't ready to share her progress with them. For weeks she'd had trouble completing the master sigil, the one that would see the end of the Moonless Host. Only last night, Rümayesh had returned from

her forays to the blooming fields and given her the last of the sigils she
needed. Finally she had all the components, but she hadn't had a chance to
test it yet, and she refused to unleash the power of that spell before she was
ready. To do so would ruin years of planning. She wanted, she *needed*, Macide to know precisely what was happening to him when the end came. He
had to know that *he* had been the cause of his tribe's ultimate destruction.

"I would ask for a day or two more, three at most, to refine what I have."

"What harm is there in reporting your progress?"

Meryam fumbled. "I wouldn't wish you to get the wrong impression
from a project that's incomplete."

The room was becoming ever more like a hornet's nest just whacked with
a stick. Alaşan, the closest thing she had to an ally, looked like he was about
to force the issue, but he was interrupted when Queen Nayyan strode stiffly
into the room, her boot heels clicking on the marble floor until she deposited
herself into her chair with an air of regal authority. Nayyan was a stark
beauty, but just then she looked haggard as a west end whore. "Our scouts
have returned. The Mireans and Malasani are on the move."

"As we knew they would be," King Alaşan replied evenly. "Our defenses
are ready, are they not?"

"You don't understand." Nayyan took them all in. "The Malasani are
sailing in from the east. But the bulk of Queen Alansal's dunebreakers somehow got behind our lines. They're sailing in from the west with a vanguard
of Kundhuni warships."

Meryam felt the blood drain from her face. Alansal was the centuries-old
Queen of Mirea, fearless and crafty. It took no collegia master to deduce that
the Kundhuni had been working to hide the movements of her fleet, likely
misreporting the enemy's numbers for months. Many looked to Meryam
accusingly. Others launched into conversations.

Standing, Alaşan rapped his goblet onto the table. He kept doing so, the
metallic ring filling the room, until order had been restored. "How far away
are they?" he asked Nayyan.

"With the storm it's difficult to know for certain. Less than a day's sail.
They may arrive tonight. They could attack the city as soon as tomorrow."

And likely will, Meryam thought.

The room devolved into a din of conversation, and this time it went on for a long while. Advisors came and went. Battle commanders from the Silver Spears and Blade Maidens arrived, though only for a short while. Various cliques of Kings and Queens and their advisors formed, spoke in low tones, then broke apart to form new combinations. *Like an inconsequential school of fish,* Meryam mused, *flitting about as if anything they did mattered.*

Amaryllis, with Basilio by her side, approached Meryam and spoke softly. "My queen, Prayna has returned. She reports that she's failed to quell the uprising within the Enclave."

Basilio looked nervously between the two of them. He'd been told only a fraction of Meryam's business with the Enclave, and it was now becoming clear to him how truly ill-informed he was.

"Can she still help us?" Meryam asked.

Amaryllis nodded. "But there is reason to make haste." Her eyes slid momentarily to the others in the room. "Last night they had Meiying, Undosu, and Davud cornered. It was Ramahd who saved them, aided by Hamzakiir and three Kings: Husamettín, Cahil, and Ihsan."

Meryam felt as if a noose were tightening around her neck. "If they've returned to the city," she said slowly, "it means they're making moves to win back their thrones. Hamzakiir likely wants *Alaşan's* throne for his own."

Amaryllis nodded. "My thought precisely."

Things were moving at a dizzying pace, but she'd always known they would. *Now is not the time for half-steps, Meryam. It's time to seize what you've always wanted.*

King Alaşan was calling the room back to order. "We'll take some time to consider this news. Let us convene a war council in this room in one hour."

Meryam held up her hand. "With respect, I will decline and let my fellow Kings and Queens deliberate."

Queen Sunay scoffed. Alaşan, meanwhile, looked genuinely surprised. "You're *declining?*"

"Basilio will represent me. In the meantime, I will prepare a demonstration of the crystal."

"You said you weren't ready."

Meryam waved to Queen Nayyan. "Given the recent news, I suspect it would be best if we did this tonight."

"We don't have time for this," Queen Sunay barked.

"Oh, I suspect you will all want to attend."

Sunay sneered. "And why is that?"

"Because I have Macide Ishaq'ava and Çedamihn Ahyanesh'ala in my care. They will be the focus of my spell. They will lead the Moonless Host to their own destruction."

A rumble rose up around the room. Surprised, even angry expressions abounded. Even the unflappable Alaşan looked affronted. "You never told us about them."

"I wanted to save the surprise," Meryam replied, "for the demonstration of the crystal's power."

Alaşan looked around the room, taking a silent tally. He received nods in reply, even from Sunay. "Very well," he said. "When the war council has finished, we'll come."

As the gathered council filed out shortly after, Basilio caught up with Meryam and strode with her toward her apartments. Amaryllis came just behind.

"My queen," Basilio said, "I beg you not to strike against the Kings and Queens while we're in the cavern."

"Why?"

He waved to the hallway behind them. "You've seen how they are. They're on edge. They may suspect something. They may take precautions before coming. If even one of them escapes, our ship may founder." Seeing her dismissive reaction, he rushed in front of her and blocked her way. "Our *kingdom* may founder." He lowered his voice until it was practically a hiss. "We would be expelled from the city, if we were allowed to live at all. It may end with Sharakhai declaring war on Qaimir, and even if it doesn't, it would take *generations* to recover from a mistake like that."

Meryam stared. Memories of Ramahd saying the very same thing danced before her eyes. *Yet another man*, Meryam mused, *trying to tell me what I can and cannot do.*

"We're resolved to the ritual," Basilio went on. "So be it. Bring them to the cavern. Take solace in the fact that Macide and his conspirators will be dead. It will only increase their awe for you. But I implore you, do *not* try to dominate them."

Amaryllis, ever the faithful servant, stood patiently at Meryam's side.

"And you?" Meryam asked her. "What do you think?"

Amaryllis smiled easily, a deflecting gesture. "There are risks whichever path we choose."

Meryam made a show of considering. "Perhaps you're right," she said to Basilio. "I have enough to worry about with Macide."

For a moment Basilio was speechless. He'd been prepared for her to put up more of a fight. "Good," he said simply, smoothing down the front of his jacket. "Good."

"Attend the council," she told him. "Amaryllis and I will prepare the cavern."

"Of course." He smiled, his relief plain. "I'll represent you faithfully and well, Your Grace."

His steps echoed as he strode away and was lost behind a corner. When the sound had faded, Meryam turned to Amaryllis. "You'll see to it that when the council finishes, Basilio never makes it to the cavern."

Amaryllis, such a pretty girl, gave a pleasant smile. "Of course, my queen."

Meryam strode away. "Make it so no one finds him."

Chapter 52

I N A STOREROOM below the collegia, King Ihsan met with his fellow conspirators. The room—filled with lanterns, picks, shovels, and a host of
other miscellany used by the collegia's geology students—was choked with
people, the hallway beyond a veritable thoroughfare for the comings and
goings of those helping to make plans for the coming assault on the Sun
Palace. They would have been discovered hours ago had it not been for the
spells of obfuscation and misdirection laid down by the two blood magi,
Meiying and Hamzakiir.

Ihsan sat in a simple wooden chair. On stools across from him were Emre,
Davud, Esmeray, and Ramahd's brash servant, Cicio. Looming in the corner
behind Emre, his impressive arms crossed over his barrel-like chest, was the
drolly named Frail Lemi, who more often than not simply glowered like an
old lion at everyone and everything. Closer to Ihsan, the final two members
of their unlikely council, were King Cahil, whose youthful appearance made
him look like the youngest among them, and Cahil's daughter, Yndris.

When they'd met an hour ago, Davud had relayed the news from Sharakhai, particularly where it applied to Queen Meryam and the tributes. Ihsan,

in turn, had shared the events from before and after the battle in Mazandir. Ihsan had nearly finished with the tale when Meiying entered the room.

Esmeray immediately sat up, the braids of her hair, barely kept in check with a red headband, splayed outward. "Thank the gods," she said, "there's far too much *man* in this room."

Meiying shot Esmeray a sympathetic look. "We've found five magi willing to join us," she said to both Esmeray and Davud, "but they've delivered ill news. Prayna, Esrin, and many of their closest allies are missing. Rumor says they've gone to the Sun Palace."

"Do we know why?" Esmeray asked.

"No," Meiying said shortly, and tipped her head toward the open doorway, "and Hamzakiir and I have more to do if we wish to remain undiscovered."

Meiying left, and Davud returned to a topic he'd raised just before Meiying had entered. "Help me to understand," he said to Ihsan. "You *ordered* Çeda into Meryam's hands?"

"I did," Ihsan replied.

"Because King Yusam saw it. Because it's in the journals."

"Now you're getting it."

"And yet the very thing we're trying to avoid, the destruction of the city, was *foreseen* by Yusam. How do you know that giving Çeda to Meryam won't precipitate that very thing?"

Ihsan smiled an easy smile. "I know it's difficult to swallow from where you're sitting—"

Cicio snorted. "Impossible, ah?"

Frail Lemi sucked his teeth.

Davud and Esmeray might well have done the same, given how unconvinced they looked.

"Believe me, I know it's much to ask," Ihsan said, "but I implore you to trust me. None of you have the benefit of Yusam's foresight. I do."

"You'll forgive me for saying this," Davud replied evenly, "but how do we know it's not another of your plots?" He waved to Cahil. "How do we know it isn't some grand scheme for you and your fellow Kings to regain your thrones?"

Frail Lemi nodded sagely. "How do we know?"

"Well, this is hardly how *I'd* go about it," Cahil said, spinning his golden war hammer easily in one hand.

Ihsan ignored Cahil. "I've said it as many ways as I can." Ihsan regarded each of them—Esmeray, Davud, Emre, Cicio, even Frail Lemi. "You either believe me or you don't when I say I want to save the city."

Emre crossed his arms over his chest. "Can we move on to the part where we save Çeda and Macide?"

"Yes, about that . . ." Ihsan had yet to bring up the most sensitive subject of all, particularly for Emre. Ihsan hadn't been sure how best to broach it, but before he could even try, the door opened again and in walked Husamettín, Sümeya, and the Shieldwife, Jenise. They were out of breath, their faces, armor, and clothes filthy with dust and sand.

"Malasan and Mirea have arrived," Husamettín said in his deep voice. "Their fleets have already anchored beyond the blooming fields." The storm that had settled over the city was unlike anything anyone, even Ihsan and his fellow, centuries-old Kings, had ever seen. Given Husamettín's news, Ihsan had few doubts it had somehow been summoned by Queen Alansal.

"Then let's go to the cavern *now*," Emre said. "All the planning in the world won't stop it from going to shit once we get there."

"It's all going to go to shit," echoed Frail Lemi.

"I don't disagree," Ihsan said. "But you should understand, we're not here to rescue Çeda or Macide, or even to fight Meryam. We are here to save the city."

"Mighty Alu, the way you talk"—Cicio motioned with one hand, like a mouth opening and closing rapidly—"it's like those fucking birds, the myna. Just out with it."

"Then stop interrupting me and *listen*. There are many threads that lead from this point. We might kill Meryam outright. We might burn the roots in that strange cavern. We might destroy the crystal itself. I haven't advised we do those things because it would only delay the inevitable—in the end, the gods would still have what they want."

Emre's look had grown harder as Ihsan talked. "Say it plainly, Ihsan."

"Very well. In the cavern, Macide will be put under a spell. Whatever

Meryam has planned will begin, and that, somehow, draws Çeda into it. We must allow it to take Çeda to its natural conclusion."

Emre sat bolt upright. His scalp turned red. "You're saying that for Sharakhai to be saved, Çeda and Macide have to *die*?"

"No. I don't know what becomes of Çeda or Macide. But the ritual precipitates other events, ones that could lead to our desired result: a desert that hasn't been laid to waste."

"Could, might," Cicio said. "What good are those fucking journals, ah?"

Emre ignored him. "We may be consigning them to death."

"That is a risk we have to take."

Emre stood in a rush. "Well, *I* don't."

King Cahil stood in a flash. "You'll do whatever we say, scarab."

When Yndris rose beside her father, her hand on the hilt of her shamshir, Frail Lemi pushed himself off the wall, looking like death himself. Davud rushed to intercept. He faced Frail Lemi, put two hands on his broad chest and said, "Stop it, Lemi! All of you, please calm down!" He turned to Ihsan. "*Why* must we let the ritual go on?"

"Your question presumes that Yusam's visions have cause and effect, that one thing leads logically to another. They don't. All I know is that Meryam's ritual leads to a vision of a man, always wounded, bloody, tortured. It's Macide. I'm certain of it. He has shackles on his wrists, from which he's freed by the swipe of an ebon blade."

"We're wasting time," Emre said, and headed for the door.

"Wasting time on bullshit," said Frail Lemi and started to follow him.

But before they'd taken two steps, the door opened and Ramahd walked into the room holding a portly man in Qaimiri finery by the arm. "We've got trouble," Ramahd said.

Ihsan recognized the man as Basilio Baijani, Queen Meryam's counselor, her *vizir* here in Sharakhai. He had a black eye and his neck was bruised in a straight horizontal line, as if someone had tried to strangle him. Blood-soaked bandages covered his chest and arms.

"Tell them," Ramahd said.

Basilio took a deep breath. "Meryam is planning to dominate the Kings and Queens of Sharakhai before the war can get underway."

"And upon learning this"—Ihsan waved vaguely to Basilio—"you had a disagreement with a black laugher?"

The apple in Basilio's throat bobbed as he swallowed. "When I warned her against it, she sent Amaryllis to kill me."

"She ordered your death for *advising* her?"

He glanced at Ramahd. "An unfortunate precedent was set when my predecessor struck against her. She was worried I might do the same."

"And would you have?"

"There's a good chance, yes."

"Tell them the rest," Ramahd said.

Basilio swallowed hard. "The preliminaries have already begun. The Kings and Queens have gathered. By now she's likely to have started the ritual with Macide."

Davud stared at Basilio as if he were working a difficult theorem in his head, then his gaze snapped to Ihsan. "You knew," he said with certainty. "You knew the ritual had already started. You didn't tell us because you didn't want us to interfere."

Everyone looked at Ihsan.

Ihsan shrugged. What could he say? "It had to be this way."

It was Emre who broke first. He reached for Ihsan's throat but, surprisingly, it was Frail Lemi who threw an arm across his chest and stopped him. Even so, Cahil was incensed at Emre's presumption. He lifted his war hammer while Yndris drew her sword.

"Stop!" Davud called. "All of you stop!" He drew a glowing sigil in the air and, just as had happened in Mazandir's arena before Anila's arrival, everyone slowed, then froze altogether. "We've trusted Ihsan this far. I believe he has the city's best interests at heart. I think the rest of you do too. If that's true, then let's go to the cavern. It's time we stopped Queen Meryam. It's time we stopped the gods."

Ihsan felt the spell relaxing. The room was tense. Ihsan wasn't convinced violence wouldn't still break out. But when Emre left, fuming, with Frail Lemi right behind him, the tension broke, and everyone dispersed to begin making plans.

Ihsan, knowing he couldn't let things rest here, rushed along the

stone-lined hallway outside the room and found his way to the tunnels beneath the city, where Emre had gathered with Shaikh Aríz and the warriors
of the thirteenth tribe. Seeing his look, Ihsan raised his hands in peace.

"Go away, Ihsan," Emre said, "I can't listen to another word from that
lying mouth of yours."

"I could use my power on you," Ihsan said calmly. "You know that I
could. But I won't. I want you to have your wits about you. I wasn't lying
about Yusam's vision that saw you with Çeda in the blooming fields."

Emre pointed beyond the open door, into the darkness of the natural
tunnel beyond. "Çeda's in the cavern."

"She may be. But the trees, Emre. The twisted trees are where you need
to be."

"Çeda's in the cavern," he repeated, "and I'm going to save her."

"Emre, please—"

But Emre wouldn't listen. He left with the others, leaving Ihsan to stand
there in silence, steeped in the feeling that the mountain was about to come
crumbling down on top of them.

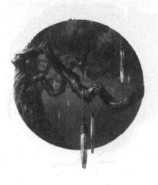

Chapter 53

NALAMAE CROUCHED WITHIN the blooming fields, her spear gripped
in one hand. The desert wind was up, shrieking through the branches
of the twisted trees, blowing dust and sand everywhere. But dust and sand
were no barrier for the goddess. Parting the branches of the adichara before
her, she peered into the distance and saw a monstrous hyena, its snout low as
it snuffled along the sand. Its coat was spotted along the legs and underbelly
but faded toward dark brown, the color of rotting meat, especially along its
shoulders and back, where long quills lifted like fur.

It hadn't yet picked up her scent, but it was close to the place she'd passed
only a short while ago. She'd known she might be followed and had left no
marks upon the sand, but this was no normal creature of the desert. It was
Tashaak, one of two mythical beasts Goezhen had crafted aeons ago as pets.
The other was Rühn. They'd been hunting for her since she'd killed their
master, likely sent by the other gods.

She could have avoided them, she could have fled and come another day,
but there was no time. If she didn't finish the ritual she'd begun two nights
ago to keep the gods from stepping foot beyond the blooming fields, she
would never finish it. She had to complete it now. All would be decided

before the sun rose, and the other gods *must* be prevented from reaching Sharakhai.

So she controlled her breathing. She calmed her heart. Even so, Tashaak, seeming to sense her, lifted her head and swiveled her saucer-like ears toward the adichara trees. Her black eyes glinted. For long moments the only sound was the scream of the wind. Then Tashaak smiled and stretched her mouth wide, revealing long, yellow teeth made for the rending of flesh. She yipped and cackled, a low sound that rose in pitch until Nalamae's skin crawled from it. From far away came a reply, the chilling laugh of Tashaak's brother, Rühn.

Tashaak padded closer, her massive head swaying as she sniffed along the sand. Nalamae took a pinch of sand and lifted it to her lips. She released it. Taken by the wind, it spread through the air like a luminous veil. Tashaak growled. She uttered a short whine, three sharp barks, then blessedly moved on. A reply came from Rühn in the distance, a long, rolling howl of anger and frustration.

When the sounds of their passage had been replaced by the wind, Nalamae left her place of hiding and went farther along the great ring of adichara trees. She came to a small clearing inside a grove, where she knelt and dug carefully into the rocky soil with a small spade, creating a hole that went down three spans of her hand. That done, she retrieved a kerchief from a pouch at her belt. Unfolding it revealed a shriveled hunk of flesh—the eighth and final piece of Goezhen's heart, the one that would complete her spell.

She placed the hunk of Goezhen's heart in the hole, covered it, and used her finger to draw a sigil in the loose soil. Wiping it away, she drew another, and another. Seven times did she do this, describing a different sigil each time, acts that connected this piece of Goezhen's heart to the seven others. It bound them together and would prevent her brother and sister gods from entering this place. It wouldn't last forever. The other gods would find her hiding places eventually and deconstruct her spell. But that would take time. Days. Weeks, perhaps. Enough that they wouldn't be able to interfere tonight.

It was essential, because she feared King Ihsan was right. He'd identified the right path in the Blue Journals. For there to be any hope at all, though, the other gods could not be allowed to interfere. If they did, all would be lost.

As Nalamae stood, a discomfort was born inside her. It grew by the moment, becoming painful. Soon it was so severe she was forced to move out of the adichara grove and into the desert. Her own spell was forcing her away, an unfortunate but necessary side effect. She had needed a way to keep the other gods outside of the blooming fields; the only way to be sure it would work on them was to affect *all* those of godly blood, and that meant her too.

She stared into the trees, stared *beyond* them, toward Sharakhai. "Fare well this night," she whispered to the howling wind.

Mere moments later, she heard footfalls approaching fast. She spun, lifting her bright spear, but Tashaak was already there, looming large with snapping jaws and maddened eyes. The beast bowled into her, knocked her to the sand. She lost her spear and was forced to scrabble away. Tashaak's teeth sunk through her bracer and into her forearm. And suddenly Rühn was there too, growling, scratching, clawing.

Nalamae kicked Rühn. Rolled away from Tashaak. She summoned her spear and it came to her, flying through the air like a burst of starlight. The black laughers fought viciously, Nalamae defending with her spear, never able to get in a good strike. The beasts were too fast, too powerful. She was constantly on the defensive, barely able to keep one step ahead of them.

She thought of casting a spell to escape, but she couldn't let the beasts get away. The chances that they would lead the other gods to the place where Nalamae had buried the final piece of Goezhen's heart were too high. So she fought on, sending the butt of her spear across Rühn's massive head. Stabbing Tashaak in the shoulder. She took a dozen wounds in the process. Bites to her hands, her arms, her legs. A gash along one shin tore her greave away. She suffered deep scrapes along one cheek when she stumbled and Rühn swiped her with one shovel-like paw.

Nalamae sent spell after spell against them, trying to debilitate, to slow them down, but their thick, needle-like fur was proof against it. When Rühn clamped his jaws on her ankle, she fell, and Tashaak came in growling, barking, the sounds causing sharp pain that disoriented Nalamae.

She held her spear across her guard, hoping to prevent Tashaak from ripping out her throat, but with a vicious clamp of jaws and a wrench of her great head, Tashaak tore it away.

Nalamae rolled as Rühn bit her shin. She scrabbled for her spear, her fingers narrowly missing the haft. Tashaak, meanwhile, clawed at her shoulder, went for her throat.

With one great lunge, Nalamae reached her spear. She sent the butt of it hard into the soft spot between Tashaak's hind legs. The black laugher yelped, repositioning herself to avoid another blow. It gave Nalamae the split second she needed. She swung the spear around, sent the point stabbing hard at Rühn's head. The tip caught him in the eye and sent him yipping away.

Tashaak lunged again, but Nalamae was ready. She dodged, then thrust the spear hard into Tashaak's exposed neck. There was a gurgling sound and the great beast tried to retreat, but Nalamae was already chasing after her. She drove the spear into Tashaak's chest, and when Rühn came barreling in, trying to protect his sister, Nalamae swung the butt around and caught him hard across the head. Rühn stumbled drunkenly, then collapsed onto the sand. He tried to get up but Nalamae was there, spear raised high. With a cry, she brought the spear down with both hands and pierced Rühn through his chest and into the ground below.

By then Tashaak was sprinting away. Her whines and gurgles mixed to form a wet, pitiful sound. Hefting the spear, Nalamae took five long strides and lofted the silver weapon with all her might. It flew through the air, a streaking comet, and pierced Tashaak through the back. The beast fell, the spear's momentum and Tashaak's own sent her scraping noisily over the rocky ground, where she lay, panting heavily for several long moments, before going still.

Nalamae was suddenly dizzy. It was their teeth, she realized. Their slaver was tainted with something that was spreading through her like poison. She turned to Rühn. Pressed her hand against the ground. The ground turned soft like quicksand, and Rühn's unmoving body was lost to it. She staggered to where Tashaak lay, pulled her spear free, and did the same with her.

Nalamae wished she could cast more spells to hide them from the other gods—their proximity to the buried piece of Goezhen's heart might allow her brothers and sisters to undo her work—but she was starting to lose consciousness. She had time for one last spell. With a final look toward Sharakhai, her body crumbled, turned to sand, and was gone.

Chapter 54

WHEN THE LOCK on her cell door clanked, Çeda sat up on the hard bench. The door creaked open.

"Come with me," said a captain of the Silver Spears, a portly fellow with a bulbous nose. Behind him stood a squad of Silver Spears and a full hand of Blade Maidens, all gripping their shamshirs, ready to draw their swords should Çeda make any untoward moves.

Çeda was in fetters, her wrists bound. "Where are we going? Where's Macide?"

The captain rolled his eyes, stepped inside the cell, and yanked on the short chain between her wrists, forcing her to move. "Ask the bloody queen. See where *that* gets you."

They led her down through Sun Palace into the lower catacombs. Soon they reached tunnels lined with roots, and came to a cavern with a massive crystal glowing at its center. When Çeda had been young, she'd gone to that very cavern. The crystal had been dim then, bright enough to illuminate the roots around the base and a bit of the fine tendril snaking down from the cavern's roof. All else had been lost to darkness. Now it was intensely bright, lighting the walls, the ceiling, the many tunnels. It felt as if they were trapped in the heart of a desert titan.

Beside the crystal, a scaffold had been erected. On its topmost platform stood a gibbet with a high, horizontal beam that stretched out toward the hanging tendril. Attached to the beam was a pulley with a rope running through it. Çeda thought the rope was meant for her until she spotted Macide being led from another tunnel across the root-lined floor.

In a blink, Çeda was whisked back to her time with the mere in King Yusam's palace, where she'd seen Macide hanging upside down, dead, a sigil drawn on his chest. The vision was echoed in an entry from Yusam's Blue Journals, a vision Ihsan had said was of supreme importance. Before she could think on what it meant or how she might stop it from happening, Çeda was yanked to a stop while a pair of Silver Spears led Macide into the cavern.

"Macide!" Çeda called, but he didn't so much as turn.

"Silence her!" called a Sharakhani woman Çeda didn't recognize. She had alluring eyes and full lips and what looked to be a fresh burn mark along one cheek.

"Yes, Mistress Prayna," the captain of Çeda's detail called from behind her.

A foul-tasting cotton gag was forced into Çeda's mouth and she was made to kneel, facing the crystal. Two Blade Maidens watched over her, their shamshirs drawn, while the captain went to speak with Queen Meryam, who'd just entered the cavern.

One of the Maidens, noticing the angle of Çeda's gaze, sent the flat of her blade against the side of Çeda's head, hard enough to make her ears ring. "Eyes ahead. You're to watch your thieving, murderous lord and nothing else."

Macide was being led toward the scaffold. It was clear he'd suffered in Meryam's care. His face was bloody. One eye was swollen shut. He could hardly walk. His fetters and manacles clanked in odd rhythms as he shambled over the uneven landscape of roots. At one point he fell, turning an ankle, and could hardly get up again.

His state turned Çeda's stomach, but it was no surprise—he'd orchestrated the Bloody Passage, after all, where Meryam's sister and niece had been killed. Meryam might simply have killed him, but instead she'd set up this elaborate event. The real question was, toward what purpose? To gloat?

That was surely one of her goals, but it failed to explain why she'd chosen the cavern or why a gibbet had been hung above the crystal. Nor did it explain why the servants were preparing tables with food and drink, as if this were some perverse celebration.

From the edges of her vision, Çeda saw people begin to arrive. They mingled and talked. They stared at the crystal in awe. They watched as Macide's ankles were bound and he was hoisted upside down above the crystal. Gods, Meryam was going to conduct some ritual. She was going to use his blood.

Çeda searched for a way to free herself, but the moment her eyes drifted too far, the Blade Maiden flicked the tip of her sword against Çeda's cheek.

As blood tickled along her jawline from a fresh, stinging wound, the Maiden leaned close. "Next time you lose an ear."

As it turned out, Çeda didn't need to move her eyes. Royal guests chatted, glasses of wine or brandy in one hand, canapés in the other. Çeda was starving and the food smelled delicious but it was so discordant with Macide hanging there it made her want to retch. Many wandered over to Çeda, still nibbling and drinking. The Maidens prevented them from getting too close, but otherwise let them be as they chatted, sizing Çeda up as if she were a statue about to go on auction.

Some wandered toward the crystal. They circled it, staring upward in awe. They studied Macide. Some even took up River's Daughter, Çeda's ebon blade, or her knife, or Macide's twin shamshirs, all four of which had been laid out on a table for anyone to handle. Çeda fumed as a woman her own age began swinging River's Daughter, pretending to be a Blade Maiden, to the entertainment of those nearby.

Çeda managed a muffled "No!" before the Blade Maiden was on her, her hand clamped over Çeda's mouth, her ebon blade held against Çeda's neck. She only released her at a wave from the young royal.

Tossing River's Daughter back onto the table, the woman approached, a stately woman by her side. The younger, who wore a fine, midnight blue abaya, pursed her lips, assessing Çeda as they came near. "Do you think she'll scream?"

The older woman sipped from a glass of sparkling white wine. "After all she's done, I should hope so! I heard she killed eleven Kings with the ebon blade she stole."

"And bewitched the women of her hand with her foul blood magic."

"Mmm," the elder agreed, "and she set the Malasani on us." She motioned to Macide, sending the wine in her glass swirling. "They're two of a kind. I hope she's forced to watch, then I hope the same befalls her."

The other looked to the milling crowd. "She's to become *proof*, some are saying."

"Proof of what?"

"That Queen Meryam's spell is working." She glanced back as two older men wearing skullcaps approached. "Good riddance," she said, giving Çeda a disgusted look.

The men arrived and the four of them chatted pleasantly, then left together as Sharakhai's Kings and Queens began to arrive. Çeda tried to reconcile how they could rejoice when a man was being tortured before their very eyes. Macide was a wanted criminal, but how could they revel in his pain so?

"Give us space," Çeda heard someone say.

It took her a moment to recognize the voice. It was Queen Nayyan. As the Blade Maidens retreated, Nayyan stood in front of Çeda, looked her up and down, then motioned to the cavern around them. "Well, did the mere show you *this*?" She paused, and the severe, judgmental look on her face faded. "That was base of me." She glanced over one shoulder at the gathered crowd. "In truth I wish this day hadn't arrived. I came to promise you this: if Meryam is unmerciful, I'll end it for you."

Just then, Queen Meryam moved to stand in front of the crystal. She tapped on her wine glass with her blooding ring, and all talk in the cavern ceased.

"Welcome," she called, over the coughs of a few. "I thank the Kings and Queens of Sharakhai for coming to witness this"—she waved up to Macide, whose body twitched, sending him slowly spinning—"the gift I've prepared for you. Come near, for what follows is a demonstration of the rule you can expect from the new Kings and Queens of Sharakhai."

Dozens approached, talking in low tones while Meryam set her glass on a nearby table and took to the scaffold stairs. When she reached the top, she stared down over all with the smile Çeda had come to associate with her, one that said all was proceeding as she wished and, whether you liked it or not, you'd not be able to do a thing about it. Except, tonight, the people she spent the most time looking at weren't her foes, but the Kings and Queens of Sharakhai.

Using the sharp point of her blooding ring, Meryam ripped open Macide's shirt, exposing his hairy chest, then pierced his neck near his collar bone.

Çeda was desperate to free him, to spare him the pain that was about to come. She pulled at the manacles on her wrists. She pumped her right hand, trying to summon the strength of the desert, but though she felt it coursing through her, it wasn't nearly enough to break the chains. She tried to stand, hoping to do something, anything, to make Meryam stop, but the Blade Maiden had returned and her grip was like iron.

Meryam, noticing her struggles, seemed to take them as some sort of cue. "You will note that Macide's niece is here, Çedamihn the White Wolf, the one responsible for many of the elder Kings' deaths."

Dark looks were leveled against Çeda. One by one, however, the eyes in the crowd slid back to the spectacle unfolding before them. The blood Meryam had drawn flowed in a thin stream. It wet Macide's beard, becoming an inkwell of sorts that Meryam used to draw a sigil on his chest.

"The spell I weave uses Macide's own blood, and *through* his blood his kin will be drawn. The roots you see all around made this crystal. They feed it their essence, as they've done since the days of Beht Ihman." The sigil became progressively more complex, covering his chest and a good amount of his stomach. "How fitting, then, that Macide's blood will be used to summon the hated Moonless Host to the trees above. How fitting that the trees should feast upon their souls, and their essence will feed the crystal."

With the next stroke of her finger, something was born deep inside Çeda. A yearning, a hunger. It was directionless at first, without shape, but as Meryam continued to paint in Macide's blood, that hunger gained form and her sense of the adichara trees grew. They glowed in the distance like torches in the night, marking a place of shelter against the coming storm. Indeed, as Çeda stood, the blooming fields seemed like the *only* safe place to be.

She sensed something amiss, something deeply wrong about the compulsion that had been laid upon her, but she couldn't put her finger on what it was. *The comfort you seek is a mirage,* some inner voice warned her, *and it will vanish the moment you come near.*

Not all visions were mirages, though. Some were oases that provided life, that cradled even as the desert sought to kill. Her gag still in place, Çeda's fetters and manacles were removed. She took her first step. She knew what she was doing was wrong, and yet the promised sense of solace was undeniable.

Around her, the audience watched, smiling as they realized Meryam's spell was drawing her toward the blooming fields where she would throw herself to the adichara trees, where the life would be squeezed from her, where the thorns would stick her skin and her blood would feed the trees.

And it wasn't only Çeda. There were others being drawn as she was—those of Çeda's tribe, the thirteenth. There were hundreds of them all across the city, standing, walking, some *sprinting* toward the distant fields, where they too would lose their lives. In one fell swoop, Meryam was doing what the Kings had never managed. She'd found a way to kill them all in a single night.

Her footsteps heavy, Çeda trudged toward the mouth of a dark tunnel. She thought it a random choice, but realized a moment later it was the very one Sehid-Alaz's wife had once used to lead Çeda from the dry bed of the River Haddah to speak with Sehid-Alaz. At the tunnel's mouth, two Silver Spears watched Çeda approach, one with dispassion, the other with a surprising amount of dismay. Neither made a move to stop her, and soon she was inside the tunnel, lost to the darkness.

Chapter 55

FRESH FROM LEAVING King Ihsan and the others in the collegia's sub-terranean chamber, Emre stood in a nearby cavern with Frail Lemi, three dozen warriors of the thirteenth tribe, and twenty more from Tribe Kadri. Jenise and her Shieldwives, their sandy veils pulled across their faces, swords and bucklers at the ready, were focused. Shal'alara bore a wicked scimitar. Shaikh Aríz of Tribe Kadri looked fierce, his bow strung, his quiver at the ready. His vizir, Ali-Budrek, stood nearby with a studded war club in his hands. The cuts and terrible bruising along his neck, evidence of the battle in Mazandir, only enhanced the wild look in his eyes. He looked like a wounded wolverine ready to protect his young.

"Things haven't changed much in the city while we've been gone," Emre said, pacing before them. "The thrones may have been passed down, but the sons and daughters rule as their fathers did."

A few grim smiles.

"They think to treat us like chattel. They think we'll cower when they do. They think everything in the city and in the desert beyond belongs to them. So, no, things haven't changed much in the city." Emre came to a halt. "But they have in the desert."

"Aye!"

"The thirteenth tribe stands united. Our allies have formed around us so that together we can oppose the power of Tauriyat."

Emre lifted his right hand, his fingers spread wide, as those in Tribe Kadri did on meeting an ally. Aríz raised his hand in salute, showing off the orange tattoos there. Ali-Budrek did the same. The others followed suit until all, be they Kadri or Khiyanat, had their hands lifted, palms facing out.

Holding his hand steady, Emre met the eyes of every single warrior standing before him. "They've taken Macide and Çeda."

"Aye," came the chorus.

"Should we abandon them? Should we let the Queens and Kings of this city have their way with our blood and kin?"

"Nay!"

"Nay, for they haven't counted on *us*."

Emre turned his hand until the palm faced his heart, then he tightened it into a fist. One by one, those gathered did the same. "Now is the time. Let's return our shaikh and the White Wolf to their rightful places."

Were they in the desert they might have roared, but in the caverns the need for quiet was paramount, so silence reigned, but that didn't mean they weren't ready. Every man and woman present stared back at Emre with grim smiles and fire in their eyes.

With the sort of hush that spoke of looming violence, they set off at a lope through the dark tunnels toward the cavern. Behind them came Ramahd, Duke Hektor, Cicio, and their contingent of Qaimiri knights. Hamzakiir, Meiying, and her blood magi allies had already gone ahead. Where the three Kings and their Blade Maidens were Emre wasn't sure, nor did he care—in all likelihood they'd let everyone do the fighting for them and step in once things were all but decided.

Emre was filled with as much purpose as anyone else, but he had to admit, Ihsan's words still lingered. *The trees,* he'd said. *The twisted trees are where you need to be.* Part of him wanted to do just that on the small chance Çeda would actually be there. He might even have gone had anyone but Ihsan said it.

Frail Lemi, carrying one of their lanterns, kept sending sidelong glances Emre's way as they ran. "You're troubled."

Emre wanted to laugh. "Lemi, why *wouldn't* I be?"

But Frail Lemi wouldn't be dissuaded. "You know how I get when I can't decide if I did the right thing?"

Emre shrugged. "I suppose so. Why?"

"Well, that's how you look now."

It was an invitation for Emre to confess his fears, an invitation Emre immediately chose to decline. Lemi wouldn't understand.

As they rounded a bend in the tunnel and began taking an easy slope down, however, Frail Lemi surprised him. "What if Ihsan was telling the truth?" he said. "What if that book *did* show you finding her in the blooming fields?"

They reached a winding path through natural stone columns, those at the front leading the way with bull's-eye lanterns. It was in that place that Emre's steps faltered and he came to a stop. *Gods, oh, gods. Have I made a terrible mistake? Should I have gone when Ihsan told me to?*

Frail Lemi, the lantern swinging in his hand, strode back toward Emre with the most compassionate expression Emre had ever seen on his face. "We're going to the cavern," he said solemnly. "If Çeda's there, she'll get the help she needs. But if she *does* end up in the blooming fields, who'll be there to save her?"

Emre felt dumbstruck, like he'd already condemned Çeda to death. Without realizing he'd already made the decision, he considered the vision Ihsan had described to him. "A crystalline dragon," he said as the other lanterns dimmed and the sounds of marching faded. "Ihsan said Çeda steps out of a crystalline dragon. I don't know what that means."

Frail Lemi handed Emre the lantern, then began walking toward the others, but backward. Facing Emre, he slapped his broad hand against his chest, replicating the cadence of a heartbeat. "Trust in your heart." Then he turned and jogged away, but not before calling over his shoulder, "Go get our girl, Emre!"

Emre watched Lemi's hulking shape dwindle as he caught up to the others. The sound of their passage soon faded, leaving Emre alone in a cavern that dripped softly, the sounds echoing in the darkness beyond the feeble light of his lantern.

A crystalline dragon. The mouth of a crystalline dragon.

Water dripped. Their echoes faded slowly. It reminded Emre of the Haddah, its riverbed dry for most of the year. That in turn reminded him of another time, when he and Macide had gone to find a blood mage in the catacombs of a desert palace, and his heart leapt.

With his lantern lighting the way, Emre sprinted in the opposite direction.

A quarter-league beyond the blooming fields, Emre ran along the right-hand side of the Haddah's dry riverbed. The wind howled. The sand was so thick that even *with* the lantern he could hardly see three paces ahead. Still, he tried. He kept the lantern's light along the river's edge, keeping an eye out for the natural opening that he, Macide, and other scarabs of the Moonless Host had used as they'd headed for King Külaşan's hidden desert palace.

A dozen times he thought he'd found it, only to discover that it was just another sandy alcove. "You've gone and fucked it up now, Emre."

Not only had he abandoned the others as they headed toward battle, he'd likely begun a chase that would end with his wandering the blooming fields forever. Çeda would be lost to some foul spell, his tribe would be slaughtered in the cavern below the Sun Palace, and he would have done nothing to help them.

But then he saw something along the riverbed, an opening that looked like a fresh sword wound. Crawling closer, he realized he'd found it, the place Macide had led him to years ago. He half expected Çeda to come crawling out of it at that very moment. But she didn't. And he was left feeling once more that he'd made a terrible mistake in coming here.

Over the wind he heard a sound, something rhythmic, metallic, accompanied by heavy thuds. Marching. It was the sound of soldiers marching.

He immediately doused the lantern, dropped to his belly, and sidled along the dry ground until he was in the mouth of the tunnel. The crystals protruding from the floor and ceiling tugged at his armor, bow, and quiver full of arrows. He knew how sharp they were, but he was in such a hurry he soon had a dozen small cuts along his hands and wrists.

He went deeper still as the sound of marching overtook the howl of the wind. He went perfectly still, however, when a lantern shone on the opening. He saw the outline of legs, a trio of soldiers standing just outside the low tunnel entrance. Words were exchanged in Mirean. Emre had no idea what they were saying, but their purpose was plain. They'd spotted his lantern. They were worried they'd been found by the Sharakhani forces and were deciding what to do about it.

The lantern dipped low and its light shone into the cavern. But the air was thick with dust, and Emre was partially hidden by the uneven landscape of the tunnel.

More words exchanged, sharp orders being given, and the lantern was lifted away. For minutes longer, Emre heard the steady crunch of infantry marching on the double, then rank after rank of cavalry. Some strange beast lowed, others trumpeted. At one point a sudden burst of blue flame lit the reptilian forelegs of some strange creature. At last the sounds faded, and Emre crawled back out from his hiding place.

He had no idea what to do. If he waited he might find Çeda, but chances were just as great she'd already come through and headed on toward the blooming fields. He might go to search the blooming fields, but he had no idea *where* to go—he might search all night and never find her.

Pressing away the fear that he'd be discovered for doing so, he relit the lantern and shone its light into the tunnel, praying Çeda's face would suddenly appear. Time slowed to a crawl, though it seemed to be passing quickly at the same time.

She's gone, a voice kept saying. *She's already gone.*

When the fear that she'd already passed through the crystalline passage became a certainty, he headed into the storm, trudging steadily toward the blooming fields. He hadn't been walking for long when he saw lights through the fog of sand. It was indistinct at first, an amber haze, but as he came closer, the light became individual pinpoints of white. The blue-white blooms of the adichara were glowing as he'd never seen them. And, Goezhen's sweet kiss, how the branches swayed! They shook and clattered. They rattled and clacked. It sounded as if an army of skeletons, the tributes who'd died in the arms of the adichara, had lifted from their graves to dance among the trees.

For a time Emre merely walked along the edge of the groves, afraid of venturing in. He was worried he'd miss Çeda if he did. He was also convinced that the branches would grab him and squeeze the life from him were he to go anywhere near them.

As he stood there, bathed in his own indecision, a sound rose above the wind, above the rattling. It was a long, pitiful wail. By the gods, an asir. As Emre walked toward the source, reckoning Çeda might be drawn there, too, he heard another, and another. Had the adichara called to them? Had they been drawn to the twisted trees?

Emre followed the sound of the nearest, still skirting the edge of the grove until he could come no closer unless he ventured inside.

After giving the sandswept area around him one last pass of his lantern, he steeled himself and walked through a gap between the trees. He crouched low, expecting the branches to reach for him. They didn't. They were still dangerous, but as long as Emre took care not to come too close he was safe from their poisonous thorns.

He reached a clearing. An asir, a man once, was on his knees before a tree that moved slower than those around it. Its blooms were dim. And the asir wore a *crown*. By the gods, it was Sehid-Alaz. Kneeling before that dim, diseased tree, he seemed to be working himself up to something. When Emre reached his side, Sehid-Alaz didn't turn, but his wailing ceased.

"What's happening, grandfather?" Emre asked him.

With rheumy eyes, Sehid-Alaz stared at the adichara. "They call to us, Emre Aykan'ava." His voice was hoary, little different than the chilling howl of the wind through the trees. "They call and we obey."

"But it isn't the adichara calling. It's Queen Meryam. She's cast a spell."

"I know, but what does it matter in the end? Our time is done. She's giving us a path to the land beyond. Why shouldn't we take it?"

He was bowed over his knees, rocking like a child on Beht Zha'ir trying to convince himself that the asirim *weren't* coming to get him, that he'd live to see the rising sun. He looked like he'd nearly given up hope.

Nearly, Emre echoed. *But he hasn't given himself over to the tree for a reason.*

"You're upset about what happened in Mazandir."

Sehid-Alaz's rocking movements grew in intensity.

"You're upset because you feel abandoned by the children of the tribe."

"You are no child of the thirteenth tribe," Sehid-Alaz said.

"You say that because you think blood means everything." Emre rubbed Sehid-Alaz's back. "But it doesn't. You are a part of me. All of the asirim are."

Sehid-Alaz turned his head. He regarded Emre with tears in his eyes. "How I've wronged you," he said. "I should never have looked away when Hamid tried to kill you." He waved to the adichara, his face screwed up in a look of pain and regret. "Now look at what's become of us."

"You must fight it," Emre said, pulling Sehid-Alaz against his chest. "*Fight it*, my King."

"Let him be," came a new voice.

Emre started and turned.

Breath of the desert. Standing there beneath the arc of the adicharas, like a goddess of bough and branch and bloom and thorn, was Çeda.

Chapter 56

ALONG A DARKENED TUNNEL beneath the city, Ramahd, Cicio, and Davud walked side by side. Behind them came Basilio, who'd decided to take up a sword and fight alongside them. Ramahd had nearly denied him when he offered, but he had good reason to want to fight Meryam, and Alu knew they were short on swords, so he'd let him come. Young Duke Hektor and Count Mateo brought up the rear along with the knights and soldiers who'd thrown their lot in with Ramahd.

Meiying had broken away earlier to help cover their approach. Hamzakiir had left as well, though in his case it was to deal with Meryam. "Wait for my signal," he'd said to Ramahd before parting. "She'll be prepared for resistance."

He gave the same message to the Kings and to Emre and his cadre. They needed a way to neutralize Meryam, he said, and that was precisely what he'd gone to the cavern to do.

Ahead, a faint light appeared. As they rounded the corner, they saw a half-dozen Silver Spears with lanterns—a patrol, there to ensure that no one could approach the cavern without being seen. Ramahd and the others stopped while Davud padded ahead. As he neared the Silver Spears, their lamps seemed to point anywhere but at Davud himself.

When he stepped behind one of the soldiers and whispered into his ear, the soldier collapsed, his fall broken by the spongy roots. Another soldier bent down to see what was wrong, and Davud whispered into his ear as well. And so it went, the patrol soldiers falling one by one until all of them were incapacitated. Ramahd heard their soft snores as he and the others walked past.

In the days leading up to this assault, Ramahd had worried that their numbers wouldn't be enough. They had Duke Hektor and over twenty battle-hardened men. But even with the warriors of the thirteenth tribe and Shaikh Aríz's crew adding fifty to that number, it had still seemed like too little to challenge Meryam. But when the Kings, several Blade Maidens, and a small cadre of Silver Spears joined their cause as well, he could no longer deny they were a respectable group. It brought them to well over a hundred swords—not as much as Ramahd would have liked, but with war having returned to Sharakhai's doorstep and the distraction it would cause, it gave him as good a chance as he was ever going to get at bringing Meryam to justice.

They snuffed the soldiers' lanterns, plunging the tunnel into darkness, and were guided by the faint silver outlines of Davud's pathfinding spell. Soon there came an eerie white light, which grew steadily until they arrived at the tunnel's mouth and the immense cavern beyond was revealed, the one Ramahd had heard so much about.

Another squad of Silver Spears stood guard at the cavern's entrance. This time when Davud whispered into their ears, they stood stock still. To anyone who might be watching they seemed attentive, on guard, and yet they made no move as Ramahd and the others approached, nor did they make a fuss when Ramahd stepped behind one of them and peered over his shoulder into the cavern.

The crystal was a sight to behold. After the darkness of the tunnels it was difficult to look upon. Macide, shirtless and bloodied, a rope around his ankles, hung above it. The crystal itself was pure white with tinges of violet, but Macide's blood was dripping onto it, staining it, making it look like a blunt instrument that had been used in some murderous act.

Beyond the crystal, nearly three hundred were gathered: the Kings and Queens of Sharakhai, their vizirs and viziras, and many lords and ladies, all come to witness the fall of Macide Ishaq'ava and the Moonless Host.

"Just look at them, ah?" Cicio whispered. "It's like a bloody fete."

Indeed, as strange as the scene before them was, the casual way in which everyone seemed to revel in Macide's pain was perverse. Ramahd had no love for Macide, but he'd lost his appetite for slow, painful revenge. Meryam clearly hadn't. Speaking to the gathered crowd, she would stop often and stare up at Macide as if this were the greatest achievement of her life.

Meryam looked healthy and radiant, the Meryam of old. It was all an illusion, though. Ramahd was able to see through it, and what *he* saw was a woman who stood at the edge of her own grave. He felt along the edges of the spell and found that it encompassed not just her, but eleven others as well: Prayna, Esrin, and nine more blood magi from the Enclave. It would take Ramahd a long time to unweave, time in which Meryam and the others would be able to sense it, which was precisely why Hamzakiir had said to wait.

"Where is he?" Ramahd asked Davud softly.

"I don't know"—Davud pointed up toward the cavern walls—"but our time grows short."

He wasn't sure what Davud meant at first, but then he saw it. Some of the roots were shrinking, shriveling, desiccating before their very eyes. The effect crept along the floor, heading ever closer to the crystal.

Meryam waved to one of the desiccating roots and spoke loudly. "You see? As we stand here, those who share Macide's blood, the filthy Moonless Host, have left Sharakhai. They've been drawn to the blooming fields and now the scarabs are giving themselves to the adichara. Their poisoned souls are killing the trees, even as the trees kill them. Soon the city will be free of its two greatest burdens."

"Sea and stone," Ramahd breathed.

The spell was staggeringly complex, staggeringly powerful. He'd try to dismantle it if he knew the first thing about where to begin, but he didn't. This was infinitely more complicated than anything Meryam had done before. What was more, it would be powerful enough to compel any of those in Emre's group of the thirteenth tribe as well.

"It's up to us now," Davud said softly, coming to the same conclusion.

"Us and the Kings," Ramahd said.

Their number had just been slashed by more than a third. At best they would have sixty valiant souls against the two hundred in the cavern who had swords and would be ready to fight. Part of him wanted to charge into the cavern anyway, to inflict what damage they could while they still had the element of surprise. Part of him wanted King Husamettín to storm into the room so the choice would be taken from him.

Cicio, grim-faced, asked the very question Ramahd was struggling with. "Do we go or not?"

Ramahd shook his head. "We wait. There's still a chance Hamzakiir can give us an edge."

It was torture watching the roots shrivel. Ramahd was certain each one meant another death. Or more than one. For all Ramahd knew dozens were dying, the deaths of many trees leading to the desiccation of a lone root in the cavern.

"Are we still hidden from them?" Ramahd asked Davud.

"Yes," he said, "but I won't be able to maintain it once you engage."

Ramahd nodded. He faced Duke Hektor, Count Mateo, and their gathered knights and soldiers, thirty stout fighting men who were no strangers to war. They all stared back, ready to heed Ramahd's call. Just then a sharp crack rent the cool air. He turned and saw a jagged white line running the vertical length of the crystal.

Meryam's guests gasped, pointing to it.

"Remain calm," Meryam said. "This is to be expected."

Meryam was good at hiding her emotions. No one else would notice, but Ramahd could sense the tightness in her voice. She hadn't expected the crystal to crack.

Then something miraculous happened. Meryam—the *real* Meryam—stepped back while an illusion of herself strode *toward* the crystal. The false Meryam beckoned others closer, and they came, their expressions and movements a mixture of curiosity and fear. A similar effect happened to Prayna and Esrin and the other magi, their false selves following the others toward the crystal while their real selves moved behind the Kings and Queens.

Prayna touched Queen Sunay's neck. Esrin did the same with King

Umay. A third mage touched Queen Nayyan. Each time, new illusions were born. The Kings and Queens appeared to be walking toward the crystal along with the rest, while in reality they were standing stone-faced near the magi.

"It's happening," Ramahd said to Cicio. "Meryam and the other magi are dominating the Kings and Queens."

There was one magi for each of the Kings and Queens. Using their blooding rings, the magi pierced the wrist of their chosen monarch, then sucked the blood from the wound. Meryam herself moved behind King Alaşan, the man who'd risen to one of the central seats in Sharakhai, a King of Kings in the making.

The crystal cracked again, much louder than before, and several stepped back in fright.

Meryam, meanwhile, pierced King Alaşan's wrist. She bent forward and drew his hand to her lips. The moment she sucked on the wound, however, she went rigid. Her body convulsed. She fell to the ground, and the illusion around them simply disappeared.

This was it. This was the surprise Hamzakiir had arranged. "Now!" Ramahd called, and charged into the cavern, heading straight toward Meryam. His men followed, roaring as they went.

From another tunnel came Kings Husamettín, Cahil, and Ihsan. Behind them ran Sümeya, Yndris, and Kameyl. They were joined by a group of twenty Silver Spears. The patrols, Ramahd realized. Husamettín had said he would try to win them to his side, and it had clearly worked.

"To me, Maidens!" Husamettín raised Night's Kiss and pointed it toward Meryam. "Join the true Kings of Sharakhai against the traitor queen!"

The Maidens nearest him hesitated. The gambit might have worked on the Silver Spears, but Ramahd thought surely it would fail against the Maidens, but then, lo and behold, one of them obeyed, peeling away from the others. A second came, and another, until the full hand stood by Husamettín's side.

Queen Sunay, who still stood with glazed eyes before the blood mage, Prayna, bellowed to the Maidens, "You will protect your Kings and Queens!"

It seemed to wake the soldiers clustered around the crystal. They didn't attack, but they closed ranks as Ramahd and his men approached.

"Lay down your weapons and you won't be harmed," Ramahd shouted.

Husamettín led his cadre of Kings and Blade Maidens and Silver Spears closer. "Do as he says. All of you."

In a flash, Prayna spread her hands wide and sent a blinding ball of lightning streaking toward Husamettín.

Ramahd was ready, though, and the spell dimmed to nothing before it reached him. A man behind Prayna touched her neck, very much as she'd touched Queen Nayyan moments ago, and Prayna collapsed. The man who'd touched her strode easily toward Ramahd, his appearance changing as he came. He grew taller. His beard turned pepper gray as it lengthened. His face narrowed while wrinkles and sunspots appeared on his skin. Hamzakiir once more, he turned and faced the crowd.

"I said lay down your weapons!" Ramahd repeated.

Many looked to one another. Some stared at Meryam where she lay, shaking. Others seemed to be having some intense internal debate.

Then, by Mighty Alu's grace, they obeyed. The Silver Spears dropped their swords and shields. The Blade Maidens laid down their ebon blades.

They'd done it. They'd actually done it.

In the silence, another great crack rent the air, and all eyes turned toward the crystal, where an angular rift could be seen.

King Ihsan pointed his knife up at Macide. "Cut him down."

Kameyl, shamshir in hand, climbed the scaffold stairs and, instead of lowering Macide to the platform, swung her blade and cut the rope that held him. Macide crashed onto the crystal, then slipped off its slick surface and fell tumbling to its base, landing with a muffled thud against the roots.

As Ramahd strode toward him, Macide stared up, blinking slowly, his face bloody and cut and bruised. For long moments he said nothing, but then he croaked, "Here we are at last."

Ramahd had been so certain this moment would feel cathartic, that it would release him from all the pain and misery and the self doubts he'd had for so long. But it didn't. It felt completely, utterly hollow. Yasmine and Rehann deserved their revenge, but just then all he could think about was the hollowness that had been created in his life with their passing.

In that awkward silence, Ramahd became aware of a pounding, a rhythmic beat growing louder. There came shouts from one of the tunnels beyond the crystal. Then terrible screams of pain. A dozen Silver Spears burst from the tunnel. They scattered upon reaching the cavern, throwing desperate looks over their shoulders as they went.

The smell of rot and decay wafted through the cavern and Ramahd felt a twisting sensation in his gut, then a deeper, soul-rending wrench, as if a demon had woken inside him. He recognized the feeling—he knew the creature that instilled it.

"Mighty Alu, no," Duke Hektor breathed beside him.

A moment later, the towering, undead form of the ehrekh, Guhldrathen, ducked low beneath the mouth of the tunnel and entered the cavern. His tails curled and twisted. His ribs were splayed wide, reducing his chest to a grotesque display of rotting organs. His skin was the mottled, putrefied shade of sand after dusk. And his eyes were filmy and white with only a hint of their former, acidic yellow remaining.

Standing tall, the ehrekh swung his baleful gaze toward Ramahd.

And charged.

Chapter 57

ÇEDA STOOD WITHIN THE ADICHARA GROVE, watching Emre stand from his crouch beside Sehid-Alaz. She'd known that her people were also being drawn to the groves. She hadn't realized it had caught the asirim up as well, but of course it would have. Were she and the others not descendants of those cursed souls, after all?

"Çeda?"

The look on Emre's face was one of deep concern. He alternated glances between her and Sehid-Alaz, whose voice called her when she'd stepped from the mouth of the cavern onto the Haddah's dry bed. She'd wandered toward the sound and had been surprised to find Emre, but now she thought it a gift from the fates. Emre should be here at the end. She would hold him one last time. She would say goodbye before she was taken.

"Çeda, can you hear me?"

She stared at the adichara that Sehid-Alaz knelt before. Like so many of the twisted trees, it was diseased, dying. It was ready for its release, ready for this grand tale of kinship and pain and blood to be over. Just as Sehid-Alaz was. Just as all the asirim were.

"Çeda!"

Her body felt leaden, but she managed to draw her eyes to his. "You can't stop this, Emre," she said as she took a step forward.

"Listen to me." He placed himself between her and the tree. "*Listen*, Çeda. This is *Meryam's* doing."

"Meryam is but a cog in the machine. This day was long in the making. The gods have been working toward this for centuries. You think *you* can stop them from seeing it done?"

"Yes! And you would too, were you not wrapped in Meryam's spell. She's using Macide. She's using his blood, your kinship to him. It's drawn you here." Emre waved beyond the nearby trees where, somewhere in the distance, the wailing of an asir lifted impossibly high. "It's drawn *all* of you here."

Çeda felt the asir who cried, a woman once, a mother of three. She'd just stepped into an adichara's embrace.

Much nearer, another cry rose up. This was no asir, but a man of sixty summers, a distant cousin of Macide's, a distant cousin of Çeda's, answering the same call. She felt more such calls all along the great ring of the blooming fields. Souls succumbing to the desire, the need, to give themselves to the trees and find peace at last.

They all felt what Çeda felt: the ache inside the trees, which echoed in the asirim. So much misery had run through these groves that even the trees yearned to see the end of it.

Before she knew it, she'd taken a step forward.

Emre was there, his hands on her shoulders, forestalling her. "Çeda, you must *fight* it." He looked down at Sehid-Alaz, who was on his knees. "Both of you must!"

But he didn't understand how strong the call was. All around the blooming fields, more and more trees were dying, and the more that did, the more their deaths weighed on the living. It was a process that fed on itself, slowly accelerating.

"Don't give in to her!" Emre shouted, though he might as well have been shouting at the trees. "Don't let Meryam win!"

"I'm sorry, Emre," Çeda said to him, "you're too late."

"Çeda, listen to me." He gripped her shoulders, keeping her in place. He shook her until she was staring into his eyes. "Do you remember when your mother used to leave for the blooming fields? Do you remember staring at the stars?"

Çeda's eyes were drawn to the blooms, to the way they glowed. They reminded her of the night Emre was referring to. He had come to her home near nightfall, only minutes after Çeda's mother, Ahya, had left. She was sure Emre had been watching, waiting for Ahya to leave.

Emre had been nine years old at the time, Çeda eight. It was mere months from Ahya's death at the hands of the Kings. They'd lain together in the bed Çeda shared with her mother, holding each other, terrified at first because the asirim had for whatever reason flocked to the squalid neighborhood where her mother had moved them only weeks before. But the asirim came and left early, taking their tributes back to the blooming fields well before the moons had set. When silence reigned and their fears abated, Çeda led Emre to the roof of her tenement. There she'd thrown down a blanket, and the two of them lay side by side, shoulders touching, staring at the twin moons and the myriad stars.

"Do you think Sukru ever marks people from the desert?" Emre had asked.

"Why would he?" Çeda replied.

She felt Emre shrug beside her. "It doesn't seem right that the only ones who die come from Sharakhai."

"I suppose," she'd replied, "but the tributes are payment, aren't they? Many more would have died if Suad and his gathered tribes had attacked Sharakhai."

In the blooming fields, Çeda shrugged off the memory, returning to herself. "That was years ago, Emre."

"Çeda, it was *yesterday*. Do you hear me? *Yesterday*."

In many ways it was. How she'd loved the feel of his shoulder touching hers. How thrilled she'd been when he'd pointed out the stars and told her about the constellations.

"Do you remember what you said to me," Emre asked, "when I told you about the stars?"

Çeda felt tears slipping down along her cheeks. They'd been the stories Emre's mother had told him before she'd died. They weren't the same ones Çeda's mother had told her, nor the ones she'd read about in her mother's books, but she loved hearing them all the same. "I said it made me feel powerful."

"Yes, but *why*? What did you tell me?"

"I said it felt like *we* could write history. We could write it as we saw fit. We could bring justice upon those who deserved it. We could free those who were oppressed."

"Yes!" Emre squeezed her hands. "We still *can*, Çeda. We can write our own future still." He motioned to Sehid-Alaz, who was doubled over, his forehead pressed against the sand as the nails of his hands gouged the sandstone near the base of the tree. "All of us can."

But Emre didn't understand. He didn't understand the call of the adichara. He didn't understand the sheer weight of the centuries of pain. Çeda did. So did Sehid-Alaz. They recognized the simple truth: that giving themselves to the trees would erase the past, as if it never was.

"Çeda." When she didn't reply, when she couldn't take her eyes from the tree, Emre placed her hands against his chest, just over his heart. "Çeda!"

The call of the tree was so strong, and yet, how warm Emre's skin felt. He'd always been that way, even when they were young. How she'd yearned for his touch these past few years. How she'd yearned to rekindle the flame between them.

Behind Emre, Sehid-Alaz stood. Took one step toward the tree.

"Don't!" Emre called. "Sehid-Alaz, don't!"

She saw the terrible conflict in Emre's eyes. He wanted to go to Sehid-Alaz, wanted to protect him, prevent him from reaching the tree, but he refused to let go of her.

As Sehid-Alaz stood before the tree and the branches began to curl around him, Emre stared deeply into Çeda's eyes. "On that rooftop, we thought Beht Zha'ir was about repaying the gods for their favor. We didn't *like* it, but we'd accepted the lie. We didn't know any better then, but we do now! We *know* the lie. We see the shame of that day, of the Kings sacrificing their brothers and sisters for their own gain."

The adichara embraced Sehid-Alaz. The branches squeezed, ever tighter. Çeda wanted to help him, but she couldn't. *This is how it must feel*, Çeda realized. *This is how the asirim have felt for generations beyond count. They know the truth, they've always known, and yet they're still beholden to another's will.*

There were tears in Emre's eyes. He looked so kind, so caring. She wanted to rub the stubble along his head. She wanted to hold him in her arms and tell him it would be all right after she was gone.

"You may not know it," he said, "but I heard you on the ship. You said I can't leave now, that our story's only just begun." Emre rubbed the backs of her knuckles with his thumbs. "It's time to write the end of that story. Let's do it, Çeda. Let's do it together."

Çeda shivered from head to toe. She'd had no idea. She'd imagined he could hear her, she'd *hoped* he could, but she'd never truly thought it possible. Her tears flowed freely now. Gods, she wanted to do just as he'd said— she wanted to write their story together—but sand and stone . . . "It's so very strong, Emre, the call of the trees."

"I know." He pulled her close. "But stay with me. Stay here."

She felt his heartbeat pumping madly. She remembered the training she'd received from Zaïde. *Feel for the heart of your enemy,* she'd said many times, *that you may use it against them.*

What about those you love? Çeda had wondered. *What good is such power if we don't use it on those we love?*

As she held Emre, her sense of his heartbeat grew stronger. It expanded, moving beyond the two of them. She felt Sehid-Alaz's, beating more strongly in fear. She felt other asirim, some succumbing to the dreadful embrace of the trees, others barely resisting the call. She felt other tributes, those of the thirteenth tribe, called upon by the blood they shared with Macide.

Together, they made a grand ring around the city, an echo of the blooming fields themselves, which made Çeda realize just how attuned to the trees she was. She felt it in her right hand first, where the thorn had pierced her skin. She felt it in her left hand next. Then her arms, her chest and shoulders, all along her back.

It was the tattoos, she realized, the first one inked by Dardzada, the others by Zaïde, Sümeya, and Sehid-Alaz himself. They told her story, but they also told the story of the asirim, the adichara, Beht Ihman, and the lies the Kings of Sharakhai had been telling from the very beginning.

On her back was the tattoo of the acacia tree Sehid-Alaz had inked. In it, the names of the asirim had been subsumed. It was not the names themselves but Sehid-Alaz's connection to each that sobered her to everything that was happening.

As Sehid-Alaz's cries became unbearable, she squeezed Emre's hands and pulled him aside. He sensed something had changed or he never would have allowed it. Çeda approached the tree. Touched its branches. The tree shivered. It didn't want to give Sehid-Alaz up, but when Çeda started to pull the branches aside, heedless of the thorns piercing her skin, it relented.

Slowly it spread its arms wide, and Sehid-Alaz collapsed at its base.

"Help me, my King," Çeda said.

Sehid-Alaz knew precisely what she meant. The two of them were weakened, but together they reached out to the other asirim, lending them their strength. Slowly, they began to resist too, and as their bond strengthened, so too did their sense of the mortal souls being drawn toward the trees.

At the center of it all was Macide, at the heart of Meryam's foul spell.

"Hold them off," Çeda said. "Support the rest."

"I will," Sehid-Alaz said, his voice weary. "But hurry. We cannot last forever."

Çeda turned to Emre, who'd already unslung his bow from around his shoulders. With tears streaming down his dusty face, he nodded. Then they were off, sprinting together toward the Haddah.

Chapter 58

THE EHREKH, GUHLDRATHEN, pounded over the cavern floor like a rampaging bull. Everyone scattered, shouting, the noise only adding to the mayhem. Many backed away, including the Silver Spears. The Blade Maidens, however, several dozen of them all told, picked up their swords and prepared a defense of their Kings and Queens, including Husamettín, Cahil, and Ihsan. Some few who had crossbows let their bolts fly, including Ramahd's own soldiers. Ramahd stood ready, sword in hand, preparing to dart behind the crystal and use it as cover. Davud fought beside Meiying, the two of them sending bright spells against a thickset man, one of the Enclave.

A great ball of flame streaked over Ramahd's shoulder. He felt the heat of its passage as it sped toward Guhldrathen. The ehrekh would not be taken so easily, however. It slowed, crouched, and backhanded the flame as it came near, sending a burst of orange fire in a wide fan that fell across the soldiers and the crowd of royal guests.

Screams of pain mixed with the bellow of commands and the sharp whistles of the Blade Maidens as they prepared their defense. From several tunnels came more Silver Spears, more Blade Maidens. They looked about wildly, their confusion plain.

As Guhldrathen paused, bashing another ball of flame from the air, Ramahd sensed Hamzakiir forming a second spell, one that imbued life into the roots. They grew wildly around Guhldrathen's hooves, around the coarse fur of his fetlocks. Before Guhldrathen could charge again, the roots snaked up along his legs, wrapping them tightly. Guhldrathen tried to free himself, but the roots were strong as rigging and difficult to break, and he would no more than snap one than two more took its place.

As factions began to fight one another behind Ramahd, Guhldrathen moved his massive hands in arcane ways. Ramahd tried to sap the power he was gathering, to break the spell before it took effect, but this was magic of a different sort and his efforts had little effect. The roots around Guhldrathen turned brittle, making it child's play to snap free of them and stalk forward once more.

"Ramahd," came a weak voice.

Ramahd looked down. Macide was there, his wrists and ankles still bound. He had his hands clasped, lifted before him, in the manner of prayer in the desert. His face was anguished. Ramahd felt certain he was about to ask for forgiveness, but then he spoke two breathless words.

"Kill me."

Ramahd blinked. "What?"

As the battle raged around them, Macide motioned to the roots, which were still dying. "Meryam's spell is part of me now. I'm being used to kill hundreds. Take my life, Ramahd, and save many innocents." He looked up to the crystal, his eyes red, watering. "Take my life and stop the gods. Take my life and *save this city*."

Ramahd blinked, disbelieving. They'd arrived at the end of a tale which began when he visited Sharakhai with his family, and his caravan was stopped by the Moonless Host. Ramahd had killed many in his pursuit of Macide since then. Here and now was his wish granted at last. Why, then, did he hesitate?

"Kill me." Macide's eyes were red, his chin quivered. "For your wife. Your child."

Ramahd hesitated to kill in cold blood, but to hear Macide speak his daughter's name nearly wiped those reservations clean. His vow to kill Macide spurred him to grip his sword tight and approach, but he'd regained his love for life since coming to Sharakhai in his search for vengeance. Meryam had shown him what giving oneself wholly over to one's vengeance looked like. It was an ugly, voracious thing, a thing he wanted nothing to do with anymore.

For a moment, the battle was forgotten as Ramahd and Macide stared at one another, Macide accepting responsibility for what he'd done, Ramahd not forgiving, but moving beyond it.

"Now, damn you!" Macide cried, his agony rising to new heights.

Ramahd knelt beside him. He put one hand over Macide's eyes, swallowed hard, and drew his sword across Macide's neck. Blood flowed, seeping into the roots. Macide quivered, quieted, and finally went still.

Mere moments later, the desiccation of the roots slowed, then stopped altogether. But the crystal . . . As Ramahd stood and looked down at Macide's dead form, another crack appeared. The sound it made was much louder than before. He would swear he'd seen fine bits of glowing crystal spray outward as it formed.

He stared at it with renewed horror, and the sound of the battle returned in a rush. Something struck him from behind. He fell, not knowing which way was up. The sound of clashing steel came just above him. He rolled over to find Cicio, red-faced, raging, trading wild blows with a Silver Spear. Basilio, Count Mateo, and young Duke Hektor were there as well. The rest of their men had joined forces with the elder Kings of Sharakhai in a scene that had devolved into a wild, vicious brawl.

Meiying stood beside him. She had a crimson cut along the porcelain skin of one cheek. She moved lithely, ducking beneath the swing of a sword in a display of such perfect timing that she was lunging toward the man before he'd even finished his overly aggressive swing. She touched the soldier and he went down. Then she turned and pulled Ramahd to his feet.

"You're hurt," she said, words Ramahd could barely hear over the ringing in his ears, the shouting, and the clash of steel all around.

"I'll be all right," Ramahd said, glancing down at Macide's lifeless form.

Then he spun and scanned frantically for Meryam. She was nowhere near where she'd fallen earlier, nor could she be seen along the edges of the battle.

"Dear gods," he said as the battle raged, "she's gone." As Guhldrathen bellowed and renewed his charge toward Hamzakiir, who disappeared in a cloud of black smoke, Ramahd pulled Cicio close. "Carry on the fight. We're going to find Meryam."

When Cicio nodded, Ramahd signaled Duke Hektor to join him. Soon Ramahd, Hektor, and Meiying were running along the tunnel that would lead them to the Sun Palace. The sounds of battle faded behind them and Ramahd stretched his senses wide, wary of Meryam and any spells she might have cast to cover her trail. He found none, and pushed hard to catch her before she could reach the palace proper.

In this he failed. They'd seen no signs of her thus far, only a few of the royal guests fleeing as they reached the palace's lowermost stairs. It was eerily silent. The sounds of battle had long since ended. They stood in a tall corridor at the foot of a wide set of stairs. Ramahd thought to continue up to search Meryam's apartments when he heard a voice coming from the corridor to his right. He waved to Hektor and Meiying, and together they walked along the passage.

For a time there was silence, then the voice came again. "Hear me, oh goddess!" It was Meryam, and she sounded desperate. "Have I not done as you asked? Have I not fed the tributes to your trees? I was promised the power to defeat Macide and the Moonless Host! I was promised his head!"

At the end of the hall, Ramahd could see a chamber with a brazier lit in one corner. As he came closer, he could see a marble slab. On it were the dried remains of a Malasani golem, its chest cut open, revealing a place at the center where something was missing, as if the golem had once had a heart.

Meryam stood on the opposite side, draped over the golem's chest. She had her hands clasped, praying much as Macide had done only a short while ago. She wasn't praying to Alu, though. She was pleading with a desert god—which one, Ramahd wasn't certain.

What does it matter? Ramahd thought. *They're all scheming together.*

Meryam's head lifted and she shivered in fright. "Ramahd," she said. She noted Meiying as well, but when her gaze landed on Hektor, her eyes narrowed with confusion. "Duke Hektor."

Ramahd strode into the room. "Who were you talking to, Meryam? Who promised you Macide?"

Meryam stood crookedly. She was frail and impossibly thin, a scarecrow made of twigs and twine. Her eyes shifted from Hektor to Meiying then back to Ramahd again. "How *dare* you speak to me after sparing your wife's killer."

"Macide is dead, Meryam." He let the words sink in. "Now *who* made that promise to you, and what did you promise in return?"

Her face turned sour and spiteful. "You're as weak as my father ever was. You think with Macide dead the score has been settled?"

"The debt has been paid, by Macide and the Moonless Host both."

"I used to think it was that girl, Çeda, who'd made you go soft, but now I see it was the city itself." She straightened herself, stood taller. Her hands shook. "Every step you took led you farther from Qaimir, each a betrayal to the memory of your wife and daughter."

"Don't speak of my wife and daughter ever again. We're done here in the desert. We're going home, and you're going to answer for your crimes."

"Crimes . . . ? My father *deserved* what he got."

"Whatever failings you saw in King Aldouan, and there were many, he didn't deserve death. Now come quietly, Meryam."

"No, Ramahd." She raised her hands and was suddenly holding a slim knife. She held the point to her chest and gripped it with both hands. "I'll not stay for your *trial*, nor to be judged by those who think themselves my betters."

She pulled the knife toward her chest, but Meiying was as swift a spell caster as Ramahd had ever seen. She drew a sigil, and the steel blade crumbled, the remains pattering against the floor like ash.

Meryam stared at the handle, at the ash on the front of her dress. She lifted her gaze and stared into Ramahd's eyes with a look that said it wouldn't matter in the end. Ramahd didn't much care what she thought. She would be brought back to Qaimir. She would be tried. Her patricide would be proven and the throne would pass to Duke Hektor the Second. But there was something that needed doing first.

"Hold her," Ramahd said to Duke Hektor.

Hektor stalked toward her, and when Meryam tried to retreat, rushed forward and grabbed her arms, forcing her to face Ramahd and Meiying.

"What are you doing?" For the first time, she looked worried.

"No longer will you be allowed to walk the red ways." Ramahd motioned to Meiying.

"No," Meryam said, understanding dawning on her. "No!"

She struggled, but she was no match for Hektor, who held her firmly in place as Meiying approached. Meryam screamed, but it did her no good. Meiying blooded her, then began drawing complex sigils over her forehead and face. It took a powerful wizard to cast such a spell, and few knew the sigils needed to cast them. Meiying was one of them, as part of the Enclave's inner circle.

After collecting more of Meryam's blood into the reservoir of her blooding ring, Meiying cast one last spell on the blood itself. "Now," she said when she was done.

Ramahd forced Meryam's mouth open, and Meiying fed Meryam her own blood, blood that had become like poison. Ramahd forced her mouth closed lest she spit it out.

Meryam fought wildly, but she was simply too weak. Her rapid breathing eased, her wild movements slowed, and when she opened her eyes again, her irises were bone white. Meryam's magic had been burned from her.

Chapter 59

FAR BELOW THE HOUSE OF KINGS, Anila paced along a subterranean tunnel with the ghul, Fezek, limping by her side. Fezek had been making a show of rubbing his arms for warmth for some time. "It's awfully cold down here, isn't it?"

Anila might have been annoyed if she weren't so preoccupied with what was about to happen. "Can you even *feel* cold?" she asked.

"Well, my skin's a bit numb, but yes!" He stumbled, catching his balance with several wild swings of his arms.

"I told you to be more careful."

"Well it isn't *my* fault." Fezek glared at her from beneath his wide-brimmed hat. "*I* didn't fix the end of a rake to my leg and call it a day."

"You could have replaced it a thousand times by now."

"I have more important things to do. Work on my latest epic goes apace. I'm preparing it for a first reading at a very special place, an institution, really." Anila saw the way Fezek was watching her as they took a fork in the tunnel, but she kept silent. "Don't you want to know where?"

"The Four Arrows."

His eyes lit up. "How did you know?"

"Isn't it *the most famous of all venues for the serious, avant-garde poet?*"

"You're quite right! Have you been?"

"Not even once."

"Then clearly you've heard of its renown!"

"No."

"Then how—"

"Fezek, your *triumphant return* is all you ever talk about."

"Oh . . . Yes, well, I may have mentioned it once or twice."

Fezek's memory was becoming progressively worse. She had half a mind to let his soul go, to let him return to the farther fields, but there was something about the sheer wonder in him. His poetry was about as pleasant as chewing a mouthful of sand, but she couldn't deny he had a certain lust for life that, while she might not admit as much to Fezek, she knew she needed from time to time.

"Well," Fezek went on breathlessly, "it will be a grand night. A grand night, indeed. You'll have to come. You can hear your *own tale* as viewed by a master poet!"

"And how would I do that, Fezek?"

"Why, after . . ." He looked startled, then stared at her with naked sadness. "Oh, right . . ."

He'd forgotten, again, what would happen after she'd dealt with Hamzakiir—Anila would lose her hold on life, and when that happened, Fezek would surely die too. He fell into silence, and Anila was glad, for her memories of this place were flooding back, particularly memories of her mother's death—her *second* death—the moment she'd touched the strange, glowing crystal. Part of Anila felt that if she just kept walking these tunnels, she'd eventually come across her mother. She'd be there waiting, her arms spread wide, and Anila would rush to embrace her.

But that was nothing more than a childish dream. Her mother was gone. They would be reunited, just not in this world. *Find Hamzakiir,* Anila told herself. *Make him suffer and then snuff the life from him. Then you can slip to the land beyond.*

Guhldrathen's roar reverberated through the tunnel. It was followed by screams of terror and calls to battle. It was distant and dreamlike, so much so that it felt inconsequential, but it wasn't. It meant everything. What

Guhldrathen was doing now would flush Hamzakiir from the cavern and into the tunnels. In his final vision for her, Guhldrathen had revealed that she would find him in the tunnels. In that same vision, the ehrekh had seen his *own* death—he would be slain, he'd told her in the stuffy confines of her ship, while trying to kill the King of Swords, who lay wounded on a bed of intertwined roots.

She reached a small cavern littered with smooth, mounded rocks. Two tunnels leading from it stood like gaping mouths. Elsewhere, glowing, mustard-colored moss grew on the exposed rock, lighting the space in ghostly relief, including the silhouette of a man crouched in the gloom.

She felt her heartbeat quicken. *At last I have you, Hamzakiir.* Each careful step she took forward felt heavier than the last, as if the others were watching from the land beyond. Jasur, Raji, Collum, Aphir . . . The rest of her fellow collegia graduates as well. The weight of their expectations pressed in on her.

She drew a sigil in the air, a spell that cast light over the small cavern. The man stood and faced her, and Anila drew a sharp breath. He wasn't Hamzakiir at all, but a man of middling height with a mop of curly brown hair hanging around his head. He looked to be thirty summers, perhaps less—it was difficult to tell with the scars that crisscrossed his face and hands.

Anila tried to reach out with her senses but found them to be deadened, all but useless here. It cemented her fears that the man must be Hamzakiir in disguise, but then she noticed what he'd been crouching beside: the naked body of a tall, bearded man. She rounded the rock to get a better look, knowing that it must be Hamzakiir, and indeed it was. He lay on the root-lined floor, so still Anila wasn't certain if he was alive or dead.

She tried to reach out with her senses again, but it was no use. The scarred man was blocking her attempts, which made the hair on the back of her neck stand on end. She was in much greater danger than she'd realized at first.

"Hello," Fezek ventured. "I'm Fezek. And you are?"

The man waved a hand in a simple gesture—nothing more than a roll of his fingers—and Fezek collapsed to his knees.

"Oh my," Fezek said, and fell flat on his face.

As he lay there motionless, Anila peered more closely at her unexpected adversary, who had a large lump in the center of his forehead. "Who *are* you?"

His smile was the sort one gives to a child who'd just asked why the sun hides at night. "Call me Brama." He flourished toward the light she was creating through her link to the land beyond. "There's no need for me to ask who *you* are, Anila." He studied her as if he were an ornithologist who'd just stumbled upon a phoenix. "You're a curious one, aren't you? A woman who walks in the land beyond. It almost makes me wish I could stay."

Anila's instincts screamed for her to run—there was something terribly *wrong* about Brama—but she'd come too far to run away now, so instead she pushed beyond the walls Brama had erected around her and spread her senses toward Hamzakiir. Finally it worked. She sensed a faint heartbeat. He was alive, then . . . But that did nothing to unlock the mystery of Brama's presence here.

As if he'd heard her thoughts, Brama waved to Hamzakiir's body. "Please," he said, "be my guest."

With one eye on Brama, she stepped closer and intensified the light. Since entering the tunnels, many of the roots threading through them had begun to shrivel, turning hard and brittle. Not all of them, though. Some were as they'd always been: supple and delicate. From a handful of those fuller roots, small tendrils had grown over Hamzakiir's shoulders, his hips. They moved between his thighs and over his manhood. They pressed between his lips and crawled into his eyes and nostrils and ears.

It made Anila's heart race. Hamzakiir was one of the most powerful wizards the desert had ever seen, and he'd been rendered powerless by Brama. Anila had been the hunter moments ago. Now she felt like prey, as if at any moment Brama would focus his foul intentions on *her*.

In her fear, Anila pushed as she had with Hamzakiir and examined *Brama's* soul. She'd grown accustomed to examining the fabric of a soul's making, and Brama's was unlike anything she'd ever seen. It was a whole made of two parts—one recognizably that of a mortal man, the other like Guhldrathen's, the soul of an ehrekh. It shouldn't be possible, but it was staring right at her, the halves of two souls stitched imperfectly together.

A story drifted up from her memories, the story of a thief who'd broken a fabled sapphire in the Battle of Blackspear. There had been an ehrekh trapped inside the sapphire, and the thief had freed it. "You're not just Brama," Anila said, "you're Rümayesh as well."

It would explain how he could have overwhelmed Hamzakiir. It would explain how he was able to stop her from using her own abilities.

The smile on Brama's face deepened. "How very perceptive, but that's hardly the most important question at hand. A better one is: what are you going to do with Hamzakiir now that you've found him?"

Anila's heart beat madly. "That depends on what you've done with him."

"After all he's done to you . . ." Brama smiled a condescending smile, then pulled a kenshar from his belt, a nicked weapon with a wicked, gleaming edge. "After all he's done to your friends"—he held the blade out, hilt first—"you would put preconditions on taking your rightful revenge?"

Anila didn't know how Brama had come to be here. She didn't know his purposes. But she couldn't deny that this was a gift from the gods.

She moved to stand near Hamzakiir's feet, realizing only then that his tendril-choked eyes had opened and he was staring straight at her. He had a sleepy, emotionless expression, and on seeing it Anila's anger returned in a rush. Memories of the chaos of her graduation day resurfaced. She heard the screaming in the collegia forum again. She smelled the gas after they'd taken shelter in the nearby basilica. She felt the sting in her eyes as she'd woken in that forgotten, subterranean temple in Ishmantep.

The anguished pleading of her friends was the worst—that and their endless screams. They echoed in her mind, making her relive the terror of wondering what they were going through, a terror that was somehow accentuated when their screams were silenced. Their days of captivity had taught them that when silence came, it meant Hamzakiir had finished with one, and would soon come for another. Every time it had happened, Anila prayed she wouldn't be taken. And then, when someone else *had* been chosen, a ceaseless guilt scraped at her insides, a thing made all the worse when the screams started up again. Her own cries had nearly suffocated her.

Brama smiled, still holding the knife.

Anila stared at it, feeling her own heart beat, then she snatched it up and crouched over Hamzakiir's naked body.

Hamzakiir's lips trembled and he said, "Please," the sound like the wings of a wounded dove.

"Please?" Anila asked, incredulous.

His eyes closed languidly, then opened again. "Please don't do this."

Anila laughed. "After all you've done you would ask for *mercy*?" She straddled his chest, as she had with King Sukru before leaving him to die in the cavern not far from here. She paused, however, when she noticed the web of roots. They were burrowing deeper into Hamzakiir's skin.

A noise came from one of the tunnels leading to the cavern, and a woman's voice rang out. "Brama?"

Brama turned toward the sound. Anila did too, just in time to see something metallic spin through the air and lodge in Brama's chest. Suddenly a shining length of steel, a pin of some sort, shone brightly against Brama's dark clothes. Brama grunted. One hand reached for the pin as a second came flying in to land just beside the first.

Releasing a long groan, Brama staggered backward, struck the cavern wall, and slid down until he was curled up like a drunk in the corner of an oud parlor.

Chapter 60

BRAMA WATCHED IN HORROR, trapped within his own body, as Anila crouched over Hamzakiir. It was all his fault. He'd let Rümayesh get to this point. After nearly killing Mae in the blooming fields, he'd spiraled into a well of despair. His doubts and failures had left him vulnerable, more so than he'd realized, and Rümayesh had regained dominance once more.

For months the bone of Raamajit had given him the illusion that he might be able to expel her from his body, but it had been a mirage. All he'd managed to do was delay her plans. She was sure to get what she wanted now—passage to the farther fields, the cost to Sharakhai and the desert be damned.

Worse, there was a part of Brama that *wanted* her to succeed if only this could all be over. He hardly challenged her as the days progressed. She spent time with Queen Meryam, instructing her in the final sigils needed for her dark spell. She wandered the halls of the Kings, enflaming tensions here, quelling them there, applying the small flourishes that would set the pieces on the board just so.

As the ritual in the cavern had begun, she'd watched with a smile on her face as more and more had been drawn to the blooming fields. In a grand arc beyond the city, the candle-flame lives of mortal men, women, even children, were snuffed. Many asirim died alongside them. Meryam came closer and closer to achieving her goal, and so did Rümayesh.

But then Çeda and Sehid-Alaz had somehow countered the spell. Rümayesh had nearly raced to the blooming fields to kill them, but she was terrified of interfering too much—do that, and her nature as a child of Goezhen, even with the soul of a mortal fused to her own, might bind her too tightly to this world.

Shortly after, Macide, the focus of Meryam's spell, had been slain, banishing the spell entirely. The blood of the dead still fed the adichara, but Sehid-Alaz and the asirim were slowing its effect. She was no longer sure whether the crystal would break and to come so close only to be stopped now was tearing her apart.

But the crystal was close to the tipping point. It would take only one more, someone powerful, to push it over the edge. It was in that moment that she'd sensed the arrival of Guhldrathen, and through him, the necromancer, Anila. She'd watched them closely, studied the lines of fate that linked the two of them. Those same lines had led Rümayesh to Hamzakiir, and a plan that would tip the balance for good began to form.

It had been a simple matter to lure Anila to the proper place. From there it had been child's play to enflame her hatred. She'd been ready to kill Hamzakiir and have his blood feed the crystal when a steel pin had blurred through the air.

Pain exploded in Rümayesh's chest, in *Brama's* chest. It was terrible, and grew infinitely worse when the second pin came streaking in, sinking deeper than the first and piercing her heart. Rümayesh stumbled. She fell against the rough cavern wall, her hands reaching up to grip the pins. The barest touch made the pain soar to new heights, a thing that Brama felt every bit as much as Rümayesh.

Brama fought for dominance, but Rümayesh had felt the touch of the elder gods in those pain-filled moments. The pins, remnants of a distant age, had been forged by Annam, and it made her yearn for their touch all the more. *No,* she said to Brama. *Not with the end so near.*

Brama fought her with everything he had left, but nothing seemed to work. Even with all her pain and fear and worry, she was the stronger of the two.

Along the tunnel, two forms approached. First was Mae, wearing her lacquered armor and her grinning demon mask. Just behind her was Queen Alansal in an elaborate silk dress, her shining black hair flowing like a waterfall past her shoulders and down her back. As the queen stared grimly, Mae let her demon mask fall aside. She spoke, though her words were lost to Brama. Rümayesh was too fixated on Anila—*she* was what mattered, *she* was the one who would tip the scales one way or the other.

Alansal paced carefully toward Anila, her hands raised as if she considered Anila a threat. "We've heard your tale," the queen said. "And we know Rümayesh's quite well. Believe me when I tell you she cares nothing for you. She only cares that you're willing to kill Hamzakiir."

But Anila was so very vulnerable. With the smallest of urges from Rümayesh, her anger was rekindled, and it pushed her beyond all reason. "He must die!" she shouted at the Mirean queen.

"No." Alansal took careful steps closer. "Don't you see? The crystal threatens the city we now stand beneath. We are on the very edge. Rümayesh needs it to be pushed over, and she wants *you* to do it. I beg of you, stay your hand until we can find a way to—"

Her words caught in her throat with a sound like choking. The queen's war pins made it nearly impossible for Rümayesh to work her magic, even with the bone of Raamajit, but she still managed to turn the air thick. Brama felt it pressing down on his chest like a hundredweight. Mae and Alansal slowed, their movements becoming glacial.

Anila was slowed as well, but not nearly so much. Rümayesh was granting her near free movement. Anila stared into Hamzakiir's eyes and gripped the knife in both hands, its point facing down.

Queen Alansal, coughing, cried out for Anila to stop. Then, abandoning her pleas, began speaking in a language Rümayesh didn't know. A spell, perhaps.

Mae shouted, "Hear me, Brama! Fight Rümayesh! Fight her!"

Rümayesh, meanwhile, was speaking through Hamzakiir's mouth. "Collum," Hamzakiir intoned. "Jasur. Raji. Aphir."

They were the names of Anila's classmates, the collegia scholars Hamzakiir had performed his grisly experiments on, transforming them into instruments of death. It enraged Anila, but at the same time reminded Brama of those he loved: his family, his lost friends from the west end, the people from the Knot with whom he'd worked to rid the black lotus's taint from the city. If Rümayesh had her way, they would all be lost.

Mae, still caught in Rümayesh's spell, stood over Brama, her pretty round face revealing how much she cared for him. He was lucky to know her. She was a true friend, and she would be lost too if the crystal shattered.

So Brama *did* fight. He used Rümayesh's own spell against her. As Anila raised the knife high, ready to drive it into Hamzakiir's chest, Brama forced the spell to work on her as well. And it did. Anila slowed, then froze altogether, the muscles along her arms and neck standing out in the ghostly light.

No! Rümayesh screamed in his mind. *No!*

But it was too late. Brama ascended like a desert storm, fighting, scratching, sending Rümayesh down, down, deeper than she'd ever been.

The fates' ways were as cruel as they were inventive, though. Brama hadn't anticipated the ghul, Fezek. With Brama's ascendance, Fezek was freed as well. He stood on quivering legs only a few paces away. Seeing Anila trapped, he thought her under attack and lunged for Brama. With an animal roar, he clubbed him on the crown of his head.

Brama was stunned, and his spell of holding was released. Mae and Queen Alansal were suddenly, unexpectedly freed, but so was Anila. As Mae and her queen darted toward her, Anila gave a shout of pure red rage and drove the knife in her hands deep into Hamzakiir's chest. Hamzakiir went rigid and blood pooled from the entry wound, then flowed freely as Anila yanked the blade free.

The blood spread like a plague across his chest.

Alansal tried to mop it up with her silk dress, but it was everywhere, already seeping into the meshlike roots spread over Hamzakiir's body. "The roots!" she cried. "Tear up the roots!"

With a wave of Brama's hand, a spell was cast, and all around them roots were ripped free. But they'd already begun to shrivel. The effect flowed outward along all three tunnels as if Hamzakiir were some newborn fount of power. Alansal yanked her pins free from Brama's chest and used them like machetes to hack at the roots.

As Brama groaned in pain, Mae dropped to her knees and pressed a bandage to his chest. "I know you there, Brama. I see it in your eyes." She waved to the roots. "Please stop them dying. Stop them dying before there no time left."

Brama tried, but he didn't know how to stop what was happening. Seeing his despair, Mae joined her queen, hacking the roots with her sword, a single-edged dao. A moment later, Brama took the knife from Anila's quivering hands and joined them, but there were simply too many.

Soon it was beyond their reach. The effect rushed along the three tunnels, and everyone stopped trying. They looked at one another, stunned, afraid to speak. Silence or not, they all knew the truth. In moments Hamzakiir's blood would find its way to the cavern and the crystal.

They'd failed.

Brama had failed.

Queen Alansal was furious. She stared at Brama, Anila, and Fezek in turn, gripping her pins as if she were considering killing them all. Then she gave a rapid sequence of orders in Mirean and strode away, her hair and her stained dress flowing in her wake.

Mae looked heartbroken. "I must leave. My queen order it." She buckled her demon mask back into place. "She will take Sharakhai, Brama. Better you not be here when she do."

Then Mae followed her queen. Alansal had come to try to stop Rümayesh and prevent the devastation the crystal was sure to cause to the city she coveted. Having failed, she would try another way, though Brama had no idea what she thought she could do to prevent it.

Anila was on her knees, leaning against a large rock. She looked stunned, and more and more it seemed as though she might close her eyes and cross the threshold into death.

Which sparked an idea. A wild idea. A *magnificent* idea. An idea as mad as it was vast.

Rümayesh's voice drifted up from somewhere deep inside him. *It will never work.*

Brama ignored her. "Quickly," he said to Fezek, "help me with Anila."

"Why? Where are we going?"

"We're going to the cavern"—Brama grit his teeth against the pain in his chest and helped Anila to her feet—"and we need to reach it before Queen Alansal does."

Chapter 61

ÇEDA'S LEGS ACHED, her lungs burned, but she pushed herself hard as she and Emre made their way along the root-covered tunnels toward the cavern with crystal. She could still feel the adichara beckoning to her. *Come*, the trees whispered. *Lay beneath our branches. Find your final rest.* Even with help of her tattoos and her connection to the desert, even with Sehid-Alaz shoring up her will, it was all Çeda could do not to turn around and go back.

Then, of a sudden, it stopped.

Çeda's footsteps slowed. She set her hand against the tunnel wall, holding herself up as she caught her breath.

"What is it?" Emre asked between heaving breaths.

"The spell," Çeda said. "It's gone. It just vanished." Which implied more. She'd felt the focus of the spell itself vanish as well. "Macide is dead."

Emre, outlined in the faint light from the glowing moss along the tunnel's ceiling, took in her words with a look of confusion, as if he wasn't sure what they meant. "It's over, then? You're free?"

"Yes, I'm free, but the trees . . ." The adichara's lure had faded, but her sense of the adichara had not. All around the city, more were succumbing to Meryam's spell—like a poison, it spread among the trees. "They're still dying."

From the blooming fields came Sehid-Alaz's faint voice. *We can support them for a time.* Indeed, she felt the asirim shift their focus from supporting one another to supporting the trees themselves. *But hurry, Çedamihn. We cannot last long.*

"Come on," Çeda said, "let's keep moving."

They resumed their mad dash though the dark tunnels. Çeda left it unsaid that she didn't know what to do. She had no idea how to stop this. What was there to do, though, but reach the cavern and see?

Soon, the clash of steel grew louder, as did the wails of pain and full-throated rally cries. More alarming was the fact that the roots beneath their feet were growing ever more brittle. They cracked and gave as she and Emre traversed them. Even with Sehid-Alaz's efforts, more of the trees were dying.

Somewhere ahead she could sense the crystal. It felt like it was going to give at any moment. *And then what? Will we all die in a burning white fire? Will everything simply cease to be?*

Refusing to give in to the fear, she focused on the way ahead. The light in the tunnel increased. The sounds of battle became markedly sharper. She was filled with a singular purpose—find the others, learn what they knew of the situation—yet when they reached the cavern itself, Çeda stopped in her tracks and stared at the searing brightness at the cavern's center.

"Breath of the desert."

As she stared at the blinding white light that was the crystal, a cold certainty ran through her. *We're too late. We've come too late.*

It was painful to look upon. Hundreds of hairline cracks ran through and beneath the crystal's surface. Worse was the way her skin prickled. Deep inside her, it felt as if a thread were strung through the center of her soul and was trying to draw her toward the crystal.

"Çeda," Emre said, pointing to one of the many pockets of fighting throughout the cavern.

She forced herself to focus and saw what Emre was referring to. The forces of Sharakhai, Silver Spears in white, Blade Maidens in black, were squared off against scores of Mirean regulars dressed in banded leather armor, some—their commanders, surely—with blue horse tails flowing from the top of their steel helms.

The most intense fighting was near the crystal itself. On one side stood rank upon rank of the Damned, the elite Mirean warriors who wore lacquered armor and grinning demon masks, led by none other than Juvaan Xin-Lei, dressed in similar armor painted white. Juvaan was a terror. His white hair flew as he fought a cadre of Silver Spears and Blade Maidens. Sümeya, Kameyl, and, strangest of all, Queen Nayyan, were among them, the three moving with catlike reflexes, trading ringing blows with the Damned even as they protected one another. Cahil, bloody and screaming, brought his hammer down onto the helm of a fallen Mirean warrior. Husamettín fought behind him, Night's Kiss a buzzing blur in his hands. Ihsan lay on the ground near them, bloody and unmoving.

Beyond the crystal and the scaffolding beside it was a sight that made Çeda's knees go weak. A creature ten feet tall if it was one stormed about madly. It was a scene straight from a nightmare. The ehrekh, Guhldrathen, roared, swiping his terrible claws against any soldier, Sharakhani or Mirean, who stood before him. He rushed from group to group, decimating one before moving to the next as if his only goal was to deal death.

No soldier could stand against him, but in his mindlessness he took cut after cut from spears and swords. Dozens of arrows, some broken some not, pierced his gangrenous flesh. Just when it seemed the beast could hardly take more punishment, it locked its cloudy gaze on Husamettín. Çeda's eyes watered and her mouth filled with spit, the taste a foul mixture of copper, sulfur, and ash.

As Guhldrathen pounded over the dry roots, many sprinted away, their eyes wild with fear, but not Çeda and Emre. They ran toward it. Emre, short bow at the ready, drew arrows from his quiver. Three flew in rapid sequence, each drawing a sharp line in the air before sinking into the flesh of Guhldrathen's face or neck.

Husamettín and Cahil called for an ordered retreat toward the crystal, and used it to halt Guhldrathen's advance. Ignoring the damage being inflicted against him, Guhldrathen swiped at Husamettín, but the King of Swords was always quicker, using swings of his buzzing sword or dashes over the uneven landscape to keep his distance.

When the ehrekh stomped one foot hard, however, a wave traveled outward from the point of impact. Roots were sundered and everyone nearby,
Çeda included, lost their footing.

Husamettín fell backward, but rolled over one shoulder and was up again
in a flash. Guhldrathen, fearfully quick for his size, stormed forward and
backhanded Husamettín, sending the King and Night's Kiss flying in two
different directions. The King ducked the next blow, and Guhldrathen's fist
crashed into the side of the crystal instead, striking home with a great boom.
One of his tails lashed out behind him, catching Sümeya's sword and sending it flying. As Husamettín wove and dodged like a fluttering swallow,
Cahil charged. Kameyl did as well.

In that moment there came a splintering sound. Another hairline fracture
appeared in the crystal, a jagged white line that was hard to discern among
the cracked-glass pattern of the rest. Even in the sound of battle Çeda could
hear the high-pitched tone that accompanied a piece of the crystal breaking
free. It was like a shard of light, as big as Çeda's forearm, tipping end over
end to land near Davud's feet.

Davud immediately picked up the shard and lifted it high above
his head. While his free hand described sigils in the air, he called,
"Guhldrathen!"

The ehrekh had been rounding on Husamettín, but stopped and stared,
transfixed by the shard held in Davud's hand.

Çeda, meanwhile, sprinted toward Guhldrathen's back and whistled
sharply: *warden* then *crouch*. Sümeya, understanding, stepped into Çeda's
path and crouched low. Kameyl, meanwhile, having retrieved Night's Kiss,
sent it soaring through the air toward Çeda. Çeda leapt onto Sümeya's back
and launched herself high into the air, catching Night's Kiss as she flew.

She landed on Guhldrathen's back, steadying herself by grabbing the
curve of one horn. Whatever spell Davud had used on Guhldrathen was
broken. The ehrekh roared, trying to dislodge her, but Çeda's hold was strong
and sure. Slipping Night's Kiss across his throat, she used her opposite hand
to grip the blade. Guhldrathen reeled. His bough-like arms flailed as he tried
to knock her free. His horns swept this way and that, bludgeoning her, but
none of it worked. Çeda had him like a wolf bitch clamping her jaws around
her latest kill. With a cry built of fury and fear, Night's Kiss buzzing louder

than she'd ever heard it, she sawed the blade back and forth, cutting Guhldrathen's neck to the bone.

The resistance against the blade suddenly vanished, and Çeda was sent tumbling down Guhldrathen's back and onto the dried roots. Guhldrathen's head, meanwhile, rolled down his hulking frame like a melon off a cart. As it thumped away, his headless body tipped and crashed against the roots, which gave like the brittle bones of a long-dead acacia.

Only then did Çeda realize how quiet it had become in the cavern. In the madness of fighting Guhldrathen, the Mireans had chosen to retreat and regroup. Husamettín, finding his feet slowly after having been struck a glancing blow, regarded Çeda and the sword in her hand, *his* sword for over four centuries. After a moment's pause, Çeda handed it to him—now was not the time to fight over the ownership of a weapon. Husamettín in turn slid the blade into its sheath, then went to one of the tables that had been knocked over. Near it, half hidden in a bolt of black velvet, were River's Daughter, Çeda's knife, and her sword belt. He took all three up and handed them to Çeda.

She accepted them with a nod, then buckled the belt around her waist. Gods it felt good to have her weapons back. By then a group was gathering around them. There was a large contingent of Silver Spears and several hands of Blade Maidens who'd decided to throw in their lot with Queen Nayyan and the elder Kings. A group of Qaimiri soldiers and knights had remained as well. Around them was a bloody battlefield. Dead bodies lay everywhere, clustered where the fighting was strongest. Fallen weapons and shields were scattered about. Ihsan, conscious now but limping badly, and Queen Nayyan, supporting him, wove their way among them, occasionally slipping on the uneven landscape of the roots.

Many of those gathered stared up at the crystal, at the place where the shard had broken free. Others stared at the shard itself, which Davud had dropped near the crystal's base. It lay half buried in the roots, still glowing, though faintly, like an ember dying in the night.

Yndris burst from a nearby tunnel, speaking in a breathless rush. "The Mirean have taken the city. They're sweeping through the Sun Palace and will be here in minutes."

Ihsan, always so composed, had a look of naked worry on his face. "That doesn't matter if we can't do something about the crystal."

A long silence followed, a silence in which everyone looked perfectly helpless, including Ihsan.

"Please tell me Yusam's journals told you something about this," Çeda said.

Ihsan shook his head. "Yusam never saw this far. We have arrived in uncharted territory."

The feeling that Çeda was losing her soul to the crystal was strong and growing stronger. Others must have felt it too, their looks of unease plain to see. More than one had their hands over their stomachs. Already the cry of soldiers engaging in battle was nearing. The Mirean forces were returning, and they wouldn't be able to hold them off again.

"Gods," Çeda said, "we can't have come so far only to fail in the end."

The others seemed to agree, but had no idea what to do. And soon enough, any choice would be taken from them.

"Any ideas?" Çeda asked Davud, who'd always been clever and well read and who now had the power of a blood mage running through his veins.

He stared back with a helpless expression. "I wish I did."

"We have to destroy it," came a voice from beyond their circle.

The Blade Maidens and Silver Spears parted, creating a path and revealing Brama and a strange looking ghul, a shambling man with a peg leg. They supported a woman between them, Anila the necromancer, who looked so weak Çeda doubted she could stand on her own.

"The crystal," Brama repeated, "must be destroyed."

"Why?" Çeda asked.

"Because if it reaches its breaking point on its own, it will be too late. But if we can break it now, on our terms, then Anila and I can step through and halt it."

"Halt it . . ." Ihsan said.

"For a time, yes," Brama replied.

Çeda shook her head, confused. "How?"

Anila, with the ghul and Brama still supporting her, took them all in. "It must be done from the other side," she said in heavy tones. Her black, patterned skin was radiant, chromatic. Her eyes were heavy and her head hung low. She looked close to death. There were no obvious wounds on her, but Çeda knew some wounds left no marks.

The sounds of orders being called, of soldiers marching, grew louder, particularly from two of the cavern's many tunnels. Fighting erupted along one of them.

Brama swung his gaze over the assemblage. "All of you, go, quickly. Get as far away from the cavern as you can."

Cahil ignored him and turned to Ihsan instead. "Will it work?"

"I don't know." Ihsan looked at Çeda. "Will it?"

Çeda wanted to laugh. How absurd of him to ask *her*. Her eyes drifted to the lump on Brama's forehead. He had a piece of an elder god inside him, the bone of Raamajit the Exalted. It made him seem otherworldly, a demigod himself. It was power she could only dream of, but just as important was the determination in his eyes.

"I trust Brama," she said, "and it's our best chance."

Ihsan, Nayyan, Husamettín, and Cahil all shared a look. One by one, they nodded, then broke away. The Spears, the Maidens, and the soldiers from Qaimir all followed, moving ever quicker toward a tunnel far from the approaching soldiers.

Davud went to Anila and embraced her tightly. He gave her a long, tender kiss, as heartfelt a thing as Çeda had seen in a long while. "Go well," he said as tears streamed down his face.

In return, Anila whispered something into his ear, then broke away with a melancholy smile. Brama spoke to Davud as well, something about a young man trapped in the collegia.

Emre, meanwhile, took Çeda's hand. "Let's *go*."

"A moment," she said.

Standing before Brama, she took in his round cheeks, his curly hair, the vulnerable look in his eyes. He had so much power at his command, but she saw the handsome young thief she'd met so long ago in the Shallows, a man who made his living by stealing into homes and taking what he wanted. She'd asked him to join her on her mission to tame Rümayesh, the ehrekh who'd eventually mastered him, precisely because he'd been so good at it. It had changed him entirely—the thief transforming into someone prepared to give everything that Sharakhai might live.

He was scared. Petrified. He didn't know if he could do it.

Çeda took his hands in hers. She rubbed the skin along the backs of his hands, ignoring the many scars. As she stared into his fearful eyes and smiled, words of reassurance came to mind—*you can do this; everything will be okay*—but they felt false, so instead she pulled him into an embrace. Shivering terribly, he slipped his arms around her and they held one another.

Behind Çeda, a trumpet blared, a call to battle. Brama pulled away and stared into her eyes, he was not calm, but there was strength there. And gratitude.

"You're brave," Çeda said to him.

"I'm a thief."

"You're about to steal a treasure unlike any other, something the gods themselves conspired to make."

He smiled. "I think what you're trying to say is that this will be the greatest heist the world has ever seen."

"The greatest by far."

Brama actually laughed, and the mischievous twinkle in his eyes, a twinkle he was once so well known for, made a sudden and unexpected reappearance.

Çeda stepped away, then she, Emre, and Davud left, retreating as war spilled into the cavern.

Chapter 62

BRAMA HELD ANILA'S HAND. The crystal was now blindingly bright. A steady thrum suffused the chill air of the cavern and resonated deep within his chest.

I know what you wish to do, Rümayesh repeated, *but it won't work. You cannot part from me. You cannot leave me behind. We are linked.*

Brama heard panic in her words. She wasn't certain her words were true. She was terrified of dying, her soul fading until she was forgotten. But she was right about one thing. Brama *couldn't* leave her behind.

"I'm not parting from you," he said aloud. "I'm bringing you with me."

A silence followed as Anila stepped toward the crystal.

After all I've done to you, Rümayesh said, *all I've done to those you love, you would bring me with you?*

I would. I release my hate, Rümayesh. I release my pain. Hold my hand on the other side. Join me in saving this city.

Shouts came. Crisp orders were called. Men and women died in the bloody clash that followed. Anila, meanwhile, raised one hand, fingers splayed, and pressed it against the crystal's surface. Brama felt something prickle over his skin. She was reaching through the crystal to the land beyond.

She was weakening it on purpose, opening the gateway just enough that the two of them might pass through and hold it closed from the opposite side.

The crystal emitted a sharp *ting*. Several new cracks formed. It seemed brighter than only moments ago.

You have moments to decide, Brama said.

He felt a moment of confusion, of indecision. Even now she didn't trust that he would bring her through. But then Anila, so intent, so powerful a moment ago, collapsed to the cavern floor. She'd died in that moment. Brama had felt her passage through the crystal.

So had Rümayesh. *Very well, Brama.*

As the cracks in the crystal widened, and a pure golden light shone through, Brama pressed his hands against its surface. He felt Anila calling to him from the other side, her hand reaching to pull him across.

For the first time in many years, a feeling of deep and pervading peace spread through Brama. Reaching out for Anila's hand, he stepped into the light.

Chapter 63

ÇEDA GLANCED OVER her shoulder while running for the tunnel. Anila had already crumpled near the crystal's foot. Brama, a strange, beatific smile on his face, fell next, while beyond, hundreds of Silver Spears were being driven back by a company of Mirean regulars who outnumbered them many, many times over. More came from a second tunnel.

Queen Nayyan and King Husamettín shouted for them to retreat. Some obeyed. Many others, locked in combat, never heard the orders and fought on.

The crystal was bright as a newborn star. As the soldiers streamed past it, King Ihsan stared into the light, transfixed. As a keen ringing filled the air, the battle first eased, then ceased altogether. Everywhere, soldiers, be they foreign or native, were turning toward it, squinting, hands raised against the light.

Nearby, Davud stopped running. With frantic movements he drew a symbol in the air. An azure blue shield went up mere moments before the crystal exploded in a grand display of light and flying shards. Near Çeda, the shards sparked off Davud's shield with a sound like shearing steel and fanned toward the cavern's roof. The soldiers near the crystal weren't so lucky. Like a scythe through wheat, hundreds were felled in the blink of an eye.

As their anguished cries filled the cavern, Davud's shield faltered, then winked out of existence. Where the crystal once stood, a condensed point of light glowed fitfully. It hovered in the air, expanding slowly outward. First it consumed Brama's and Anila's unmoving forms, then Macide and the scaffold, then more and more fallen soldiers. Its outer edge shimmered like Davud's shield, but in a gentler manner, like the surface of a sunlit pond. Everything within it was lit strangely, as if dusted in gold.

It expanded ever outward, hungry, a wall of cold coming with it. The chill felt like a harbinger of the lord of all things coming for them. All around, the soldiers, regardless of nation, began to recover. They pointed and shouted. They helped fallen comrades to their feet while casting their gazes about as if the cavern itself were coming alive. All sense of enmity, of opposing sides, had drained away, leaving them all mere mortals—delicate, breakable things—who hoped that the light wouldn't swallow them.

Everyone in Çeda's group had headed into the tunnel, all save Ihsan, who remained even when Çeda tugged on his arm. He glanced at her, giving her an unreadable expression. "Go on," he said, and returned his attention to the center of the expanding light.

Only then did Çeda realize what he was looking at. She hadn't noticed, but within that magnificent brightness, a man and a woman stood holding hands. It was Anila and Brama.

"You can't help them," she said to him.

"I know," Ihsan replied.

Çeda left him standing there—he could remain there until the end of days if he wished—and ran to catch up with the others. With nearly a hundred soldiers as their escort, they wove their way through the tunnels. Terrified of the light, Çeda threw glances over one shoulder while navigating the uneven terrain—as sure as rain was rare, she was certain she would pass to the land beyond if the light touched her.

On they went in silent desperation, Cahil leading them steadily upward. The light was lost behind them for a time. Çeda prayed they'd escaped it, or that Anila and Brama had managed to contain it in some way. As they reached the marble-tiled halls of the Sun Palace, however, her hopes were dashed. The expanding, glimmering shield lifted through the floors, passed beyond walls, growing ever larger, ever faster.

We're too late, Çeda thought. *It's going to consume the entire city. It's going to consume the desert.*

She and countless others fled the palace—soldiers, servants, children, the elderly, the injured, the sick—as dawn arrived, bathing the landscape in a soft, beautiful glow that seemed wrong with so much pain and terror around them. All across the palace's manicured grounds lay soldiers, both alive and dead, and evidence of a greater battle, a battle that would surely still be raging had everyone not stopped to stare at the shimmering dome expanding through the palace walls, colonnades, and porticos. Many screamed. All gave ground to the light save for some few who, like Ihsan, seemed transfixed by it and stood there staring, awaiting their fate.

Çeda took Emre's hand. They sprinted over the dry palace lawn, their breath coming in great, heaving gasps.

She felt Emre's hand tighten as it swept over them. A deeper cold caressed Çeda's skin. It was tender but awful and ghulish at the same time, like the kiss of a dead lover. It was hardly the worst part, though. Now that she was within the light, it felt as though a great chasm had opened up beneath her. She now existed in both worlds, and she was no longer certain she could return to the land of the living. She was no longer sure she *wanted* to.

The lure of the land beyond was so strong her steps slowed. Then she stopped and turned. Near the palace's grand entrance stood a wavering form with long black hair in a flowing blue dress. Her features were cloaked in white light, but Çeda knew her from her shape, her stance, from the way she favored one hip over the other.

Memma, came a whisper in her mind.

How she wanted to go to her. To speak to her. To embrace her and walk among the field of blazing blues once more. She'd already taken a step toward her when she realized Emre was doing the very same thing.

She turned to find him staring at a wavering form not ten paces distant. "Rafa?" he breathed.

She suddenly remembered the vision from Yusam's mere of Emre walking toward Rafa, ignoring her pleas. It so unnerved her that she spun away from her mother, turned her back to the palace's entrance, and sidestepped toward

Emre. Grabbing the neck of his leather armor, she yanked him into motion. He stumbled, his movements leaden.

"Look away, Emre!"

She snatched his hand and pulled on it and kept pulling until they were running once more. She stared doggedly ahead, fixating on the war-torn landscape, the walls, the city beyond. *Another few paces,* she prayed. *Just another few paces.*

High above, a white haze streaked the sky. A cold wind blew. It toyed with their hair and clothes. The smell of burnt honey carried on the wind— that and something acerbic, like a smithy, as if the first gods had returned, ready to forge the world anew.

All around lay evidence of a larger battle. Dead bodies littered the grounds, the walkways, the gardens and patios. They hailed from all five kingdoms: Sharakhai, Qaimir, Kundhun, Mirea, and Malasan. Many had terrible, bloody, mortal wounds—lost limbs, crushed skulls, arrows through throats—and yet some now moved, becoming animated, their souls return- ing to them through some artifact of this strange place caught between two worlds. They pushed themselves up from the dry ground, then stood, looking about with vacant expressions.

Davud was suddenly beside her. "Çeda!"

The panic in his voice made her turn. Some of the Silver Spears accom- panying them had stopped. By turns they were terrified or inexplicably calm. Without fail, though, they all took on a look of peace and acceptance, then simply fell to the ground, lifeless, their souls shedding their mortal coils like burdensome cloaks.

King Cahil had stopped, much as Emre and Çeda had moments ago. His right hand was pressed to his chest. His left was pumping into a fist over and over. He stared about, but it was only as Çeda neared him that she saw what he was looking at. Standing in a circle around him, barely discernible, were the faint outlines of many, many souls. Some were hunched and aggressive, others curled inward over their bodies as if in pain. Many had arms lifted, fingers pointing at him accusingly.

Cahil turned slowly, taking them all in. They were those he'd tor- tured, Çeda realized. Hundreds of them, standing, waiting, judging. In that moment the centuries of Cahil's brutal reign as the Confessor King were stripped away, exposing him as the young, petulant man who'd risen to become King in the days before Beht Ihman. He was fragile, scared. He knew what was about to happen.

"Father?" Yndris called to him.

Cahil turned, but he didn't look at his daughter. He looked at Çeda. His brashness gone, he seemed vulnerable. He wanted her help, though what he thought she might do, Çeda had no idea, nor would she have lifted a finger to help him even if she *did* know. *That which is sown shall be reaped,* promised the Al'Ambra.

As the forms closed in around him, Cahil's eyes went wide. His right hand pressed against his chest, directly over his heart. His mouth worked soundlessly and he collapsed to the dry ground. A white outline rose from his prone form, a wight where the man had once stood. Cahil spun about, his fear plain. The wights around him wasted no time. They descended on him, tearing, while Cahil's attenuated scream filled the chill air.

"Father!" Yndris screamed. She sprinted toward him, only stopping when Husamettín grabbed her wrist.

Çeda, Davud, and Emre, meanwhile, skirted the thrashing mob, watching in wonder and horror as the grand, golden vault ballooned beyond the walls of the Sun Palace, beyond the House of Kings, beyond Tauriyat itself and into the city proper. Nearby was an empty war chariot with two Malasani horses still harnessed to it. The driver was slumped over the front, an arrow stuck through his chest. Emre leapt up, dragged the driver off with a grunt, then took up the reins.

When Çeda and Davud had crammed in behind him, Emre snapped the reins, and called, "Hiyah!"

They rode hard and caught up to the soldiers who'd escaped with them from the cavern, some of whom had taken horses or chariots or war wagons of their own. Emre steered wide of the remaining pockets of conflict and eventually they passed through the House of Maidens, beyond its broken front gates, and into the city. All was madness along the cramped road known as the Spear, soldiers retreating, the people of Sharakhai braving the streets, drawn by the unexpected silence. On seeing the shimmering dome, some raised their hands to the sky and cried tears of joy, viewing it as deliverance from their enemies, a gift from the desert gods, proof that Shara-khai and her people were favored above all others.

As they headed for the Wheel, the city's busiest intersection where the Spear met the Trough, they caught up with the expanding edge of the glittering dome and passed beyond it. When they did, the feelings of cold, of being stretched, of being drawn toward the cavern, all eased sharply but did not abate entirely. When they reached the Wheel's central fountain, Emre pulled on the reins and spun the chariot about. Others had done the same, creating a strange patchwork of soldiers and citizens all about the Wheel's broad, cobblestoned surface.

From the Wheel, the whole of the House of Kings was laid bare—the palaces dotting the slopes, King's Road running its winding path, the stout barracks, the blocky archives of the House of Maidens. Outside the walls stood the Temple District with its hulking testaments to the gods. More buildings, both ancient and new, plagued the landscape, becoming smaller and more ordinary as they cascaded down the slope away from the House of Kings.

Everything trapped inside the great, glittering dome was limned in gold, an effect that encompassed Tauriyat, the House of Kings, and a quarter of the city beyond. It was so large it encompassed King's Harbor, the fertile fields, and surely a great, curving swath of the desert as well.

For a long time no one spoke.

"Did they succeed or didn't they?" Emre asked absently.

"They did and they didn't," Davud replied. "I suspect we arrived too late. Or it was too powerful to stop entirely. Maybe it was both. But somehow, they've managed to stall it."

"For how long?" Çeda asked.

No one answered, for just then something new happened. Something utterly unexpected. Something the desert hadn't seen in who knew how long?

The white haze hanging over the city had grown thicker, darker, and from it, tiny flakes of snow were falling. They floated gently, sometimes circling playfully in vortexes before breaking suddenly. Where they fell upon the ground, they melted, leaving a small dark spot like rain that evaporated almost instantly.

Çeda blinked and stared up at it, disbelieving.

Davud stared in wonder as the snow fell upon his outstretched hand. Then, a child all over again, he tipped his head back, opened his mouth, and let some fall upon his tongue. Others stared in wonder as the snow thickened. A dusting accumulated on the ground and soon Tauriyat and its curtain wall and other distant buildings were swallowed by a storm of swirling white.

"Where do we go now?" Emre asked.

"To the desert," Çeda said, seeing the snowfall for the boon it was. "We can't be caught inside the city."

Emre nodded, snapped the reins, and they rode north through the city, toward the harbor and open sand.

Chapter 64

AS DAWN BROKE OVER THE DESERT, four gods stood on the outer edge of the blooming fields. There was lithe Tulathan, winsome Rhia, clever Bakhi, and mighty Thaash. Between them lay the sand-ridden corpses of Goezhen's pets, Tashaak and Rühn, the massive bone crushers he'd crafted in the desert's early days. Nalamae had hidden their remains so well it had taken them three days to find them.

Rhia, pacing along the edge of an adichara grove, stopped suddenly and stared intently into the trees. "There," she said in desert's eldest tongue, "a piece of Goezhen's heart."

The four of them approached the indicated patch of sand and found it buried there, just as Rhia had said. A small, dried piece of their brother's heart. Working together, they found the others: seven more pieces, hidden all about the grand circle of the blooming fields like points on a compass rose. They realized Nalamae had killed him, taken his heart and cut it into eight pieces, then used them to form a spell that prevented them from stepping within the blooming fields.

It had been a long time since Bakhi had been frightened. Truly frightened. Not since the elder gods had fled this world, abandoning them, had he felt what he'd felt the night they'd been unable to step inside the grand circle of trees. *After all we've done,* he'd thought as Thaash threw himself impotently at the barrier, *we'll be stopped by our youngest sister.*

Nalamae had truly returned to herself. She was the Nalamae of old now—young but proud, and powerful too. She'd not only killed their brother, but used his remains for her own ends. *First Yerinde,* Bakhi mused, *now Goezhen.* A fair turn of events, he supposed, given how many times they'd killed her. But where did it leave them?

The four of them had stood in abject horror the night the crystal broke. They couldn't see it, but all of them felt it—an awakening, a doorway—but in a strange twist of fate, the effect had been blunted. The doorway to the farther fields wasn't as large as it should have been. It had been stopped, by what, none of them knew. But Bakhi was certain it wasn't enough for them to step from this world into the next. For mortals, certainly—for days he'd been feeling the flutter of their passage like beats of a butterfly's wings—but not for gods.

Through a gap in the trees, the four of them stared at the grand, glittering dome in the distance. When it had appeared over the city, none of them had been sure if it would linger or if it would eventually shrink and be gone, taking their last chance to reach the land beyond with it. In a strange twist of fate, it had grown large enough to encompass all of Tauriyat and then simply stopped, reaching some obscure equilibrium.

It was Nalamae's doing, certainly. She'd somehow managed to halt the crystal's destruction, but all was not lost. There was time yet to undo their sister's work.

The question was how? What were the four of them going to do about it?

"We could begin by tearing down her spell," Tulathan said, but she spoke in a way that made it clear there could be consequences.

"It might leave us vulnerable," Rhia said, finishing the thought.

None of them knew what might happen if they tried. Nalamae might have found a way to bind them more tightly to this world if they dismantled her spell, and breaking down the barrier she'd made by use of Goezhen's heart wasn't the most important thing in any case.

"We must force things back into motion," Thaash said, his bronze skin shimmering in the sunlight.

"Of course," Bakhi said, "but how?"

He stared at Tulathan as he said this. After Yerinde's death, she'd done the most to ensure their grand machine was well oiled and moving. She paused, perhaps balancing the risks, as they all did with every action they took, every move they made. Make one move too many and they would be trapped while the others left for the land beyond. But make no moves at all and they would all surely lose.

"You *know* how," Tulathan replied.

"Yes, but were I to step in, there would be questions. Doubts might take root. The path to the buried elder is a precarious one."

Tulathan knew he was right, but still she hesitated. He thought she would deny him, that she would demand the others help.

"A subtle wind is all you need," Bakhi said. "With but a shift in the breeze, she'll do as you wish."

Tulathan took them all in, one by one, then nodded. "Very well. Leave it to me."

Chapter 65

NIGHT REIGNED AS WILLEM sat atop the collegia's library. The moons were rising and the stars were bright, but they had a new adversary for dominance over the nighttime sky. Draping over Tauriyat like some grand veil woven by the gods was a great, glittering dome—the vault, as it had come to be known—a thing that had simply appeared the night of the Mirean invasion. The light the vault gave off was chilling, and Willem didn't like looking upon it, so he focused instead on the students returning in dribs and drabs from their excursions to the Trough.

On the wings of a terrible sandstorm, the forces of Mirea had swept into the city and taken control. The following days had been tense. Martial law had been imposed. Pockets of resistance had broken out spontaneously. The sounds of screaming and killing were terrible, enough to make Willem weep, but thankfully with each day the clashes had grown fewer in frequency and less intense. While the Malasani continued to fight the remains of the Shara-khani fleet, it was the Mireans who occupied the city, hoping to shore up its defenses before the city's former rulers, the Kings and Queens of Sharakhai, could mount an insurrection and take it back.

While things were tense in every quarter of the city, including at the collegia, the Mirean queen seemed to hold respect for the halls of learning. As a result the collegia was a relative calm in the storm. An edict had been handed down, however. Should protests be waged by anyone in the collegia, be they student, scholar, or faculty, the entire collegia would suffer. So far the order had held, but more and more students were gathering and talking about ways to resist the occupation.

Willem wished he could join them. He hated the occupation too.

Come now, Willem. Be truthful. That isn't the reason why.

No, he admitted to himself. He had felt empty since Nebahat's death. It was a strange reality to be faced with. He should be dancing with joy from sunup to sundown at being freed, but he'd been enslaved for as long as he could remember—to Nebahat, and to someone else before him. (Just who the other might have been Willem was unsure. Unlike the countless stories he'd read, any one of which he could rattle off by heart, the days of his youth were strangely muddled.)

By the gods, he was *free*, so why hadn't the great weight on his shoulders been lifted? *You know why,* said that voice as he walked along the roof's peak to its opposite edge. He crouched and watched as a dozen students talked in low tones on the library steps. Given that one was waxing on about the percentage of alcohol required for a mixture to burn, clearly trying to impress the prettiest of the girls, he guessed they were the fresh recruits to the alchemycal studies program. They were young, but oh how they shone. Their lights were bright, and flitted like starlings among the group, one thought leading to another leading to another.

Suddenly their conversation ceased and their gazes swung toward the forum. A patrol of eight Mirean soldiers wearing bright, jade-colored half cloaks were marching in two by two. Unlike the students, the light the soldiers gave off was dull as ebon steel. It made Willem wonder what they would look like in their homeland, far from the war, far from the desert. Most in Sharakhai considered the Mireans their enemies, but Willem wanted to visit them, to see them shine as they were meant to shine.

Without a word being spoken, the students broke apart and went their separate ways. Queen Alansal had decreed that groups larger than three were unlawful and would be punished with public floggings. Many had already taken place. By the time the patrol had passed, only two still lingered on the steps, a pair of young men whose attraction for one another was plain, though neither seemed ready to admit it. The way the light played between them was like an explosion of autumn butterflies. It made Willem so happy he put one hand over his mouth to stifle his giggling.

When they left and the square at the foot of the library was empty once more, Willem sat cross-legged and wondered where he should go, what he should do. When he was beholden to Nebahat there'd always been things to research, histories to read, solutions to find. And if there wasn't reading to be done, there were forays to gather medicinals or various alchemycal agents for Nebahat and the other magi in the Enclave. But Nebahat was gone and so was the Enclave, or enough of it that Willem had no hope that one of them would come looking for him to do the things he'd done for Nebahat.

In reading the private letters sent to the new chancellor, Willem had learned that some great confrontation had taken place below the Sun Palace. Many of the Enclave's highest ranking members had died, including Prayna and Esrin. Dilara, Undosu, and Nebahat had been killed a few days before that. Who did that leave? Meiying? Davud? *Please let Davud be alive.* Even if both of them were, even if the Enclave was formed again, there was no telling whether they'd have a use for him. He was a forgotten soul, a bit of detritus fallen from the Enclave's decomposing form.

Find something else, said the voice inside of Willem. *Find another purpose.*

But how could he? He knew nothing beyond the collegia and its books. He hadn't a voice, and even if he did, what would he say? *Hello, you don't know me, but I can read forty-seven different languages and I know you didn't ask me but may I please work in the library sorting your books?* No, they had students for that. And the moment they found out he'd been in the collegia for so long, rooting about, they'd give him over to the green cloaks, as they'd started calling the Mirean patrols. If he ever revealed his existence, he'd be lucky to keep his head.

He was just about to leave when he saw a glimmering across the way. The person making it was hidden behind the corner of the basilica, but the patterns of light they cast . . . Willem dared not hope. He nearly turned and ran, unsure what he would do if it *was* him.

And then, there he was, Davud, striding in that way of his, confident yet unassuming, between two tall pillars in the forum. He had a small sack slung over one shoulder, and he made his way toward the tall bronze statue at the center of the square.

Willem's heart tripped as Davud turned a full circle and scanned the area as if looking for someone. Davud had come to the collegia many times after Nebahat's death, but he'd stopped the night before the invasion, and Willem had thought surely he was dead. Willem had pleaded with Bakhi for his mercy. He'd told himself a thousand times that if Davud came again, he would gather his courage and go to him, even if it was only to bask in his light.

Yet here he was, his prayers answered, and Willem merely stared, shaking his head gently, his throat constricting over and over while his skin prickled with goosebumps. *He's going to leave. He's going to leave at any moment. Go to him. See why he's come.* But he didn't, and each moment that passed made him more certain he would *never* go, which made him feel like going to his small bed in Nebahat's lair and staying there forever.

But then Davud did something new. From his cloth sack he took out a blanket, the sort students used on the mall when they shared meals with one another in the sun, and proceeded to lay it out on the ground near the foot of the statue. After seating himself on one side of the blanket, he reached into the sack again and retrieved two glasses and a blue bottle of what looked to be water. He poured a helping in each glass, then pulled a cloth bundle from the sack and unfurled it to reveal two sandwiches, two apples, and two wedges of cheese. He set one of each—water, sandwich, apple, and cheese— on a small kerchief near the far side of the blanket. The others he set before him, then proceeded to take a bite of his apple. "You're welcome to join me," he said between crunches.

Willem shivered and ducked low. Had Davud spotted him? *What does it matter, you imbecile? He already knows you live here.* For a long while, Willem rested on the very edge of a decision.

What did it in the end was the cheese. It was a rarity for Willem, but every time he'd had it, it had made him dream of the animal that had given up its milk to make it, where it had come from, and how different it must be from Sharakhai. In many respects, the taste of food was very much like the light he saw in people. It was varied and deep and beautiful.

He climbed down and approached while Davud, realizing he was no longer alone, smiled and waved to the space across from him. "Please," he said.

Willem smoothed down his rumpled clothes, feeling a perfect fool for doing so, then sat across from Davud.

"Go on," Davud said. "Eat. I've a story to tell you when we're done."

They ate together in silence. It was hardly a sophisticated meal but it was as grand as anything Willem could ever remember. The apple was more tart than sweet, a perfect counter to the cured ham. The bread was crusty with a pillowy crumb. And the cheese . . . The rind had just the right amount of bite while the flesh was soft and tasted of rich cream, honey, lemon rind, and almonds.

When they were done, Davud poured them each some more water. "You'll recall the one named Rümayesh, the ehrekh who came to you in the form of Brama."

Willem nodded as he sipped at the water, which was deliciously cool—a spell, Willem saw from the way the bottle glittered.

"The two of them, Brama and Rümayesh, are working together even now to prevent *that*"—he waved vaguely toward Tauriyat and the glimmering dome above it—"from getting worse. Before he left for the farther fields, however, Brama and I had a chance to talk. He told me some truths about you, truths that were revealed when Rümayesh spoke to you."

Willem's hand had begun shaking so badly he set the glass back down.

"He told me about the bindings that had been placed on you. And he told me what Rümayesh did to them so that she could pry your secrets from you." Davud paused, staring deeply into Willem's eyes. "Do you realize they're gone? That in that moment Rümayesh took them away?"

Willem wanted to get up. He wanted to run away and hide. He was certain his world was about to change forever, and he was petrified of it. Fearing he would do just that, he pulled his knees to his chest and hugged his legs, then shook his head slowly.

"They *are* gone," Davud said. "Stripped away. You're no longer prevented from doing things that might have displeased Nebahat, and you're no longer prevented from speaking." He paused, a look of encouragement on his face. "You have a voice. You have only to use it."

He could hardly look at Davud for how he shone. His light made Willem's eyes water. It was no longer pretty and mesmerizing, but confusing and worrying. He remembered a time when he was young, before being taken to the collegia, when he spoke words, but it was all a haze. He'd hardly realized he wanted it back, but in that moment, with Davud staring at him so kindly, he did. He wanted it very much. But where to begin?

Davud, perhaps sensing his uncertainty, said, "Can you tell me your name?"

"Wi—" Willem coughed and cleared his throat. He took a sip of water. "Willem." It came out in a terrible croak. He might have been embarrassed over it had the moment not been composed of such pure and unfiltered joy. He laughed. "My name is Willem!"

In the distance, a woman, a collegia master in simple robes carrying an armload of books, glanced toward him, then hurried on her way. It made Willem laugh all the harder.

"Willem," Davud said when his laughter had died down at last, "you're no longer bound to the collegia, either. You can go where you will. Would you like to? Would you walk with me around the city?" When Willem didn't answer, he went on. "I promise you it will be safe. I'll ensure it."

Willem shook his head. "Too much, too soon."

Davud smiled. "That's fine, Willem. You'll let me know."

"We'll—" He almost daren't ask. "We'll see one another again?"

"I hope so. It's why I came." He motioned to the library. "The collegia is filled with knowledge. There's more stockpiled around the city, collected by the Enclave. I have several hidden stores that need to be read and sorted." Davud gathered himself. "I need *help*, Willem. I need it badly, and I think you can provide it."

Willem blinked. Part of him swelled with joy at the thought of helping Davud, but another part feared it would be just like Nebahat. Too much like Nebahat.

"Help for what?" he finally asked.

"Four days ago, Sharakhai changed hands. There are those who hope to take it back, and I would lay money that they'll succeed. Even if they do, though, this city must face facts: a vacuum has been left by the passing of the Sharakhani Kings. As sad as it is to say, the desert doesn't know what to do without them, and I do not wish to leave nature to its course. I want to *choose* what fills that vacuum. That's what I want your help with. I want to be ready when the question is asked: 'What do we do now?' Will you help me answer it?"

Suddenly Willem couldn't see. He was crying so hard that everything was a wavering mixture of light. Part of him was thrilled he would get to see Davud again, but it went so much deeper than that. He would get to read stories he'd never read before. He'd get to share them with Davud. They would talk of culture and shifting politics and injustices that bred more injustice. They'd strategize. They'd mine the past for tools to build a better world. They could make the desert anew.

"You don't have to, Willem. You're free to go your own way. I can help you with whatever you need."

"No!" he cried. "I mean yes."

Davud laughed, a beautiful sound that played with the light around him. "Does that mean you'll join me?"

Willem nodded. "Yes."

Chapter 66

IN THE LIGHT OF DAY, enveloped in the buzz of the rattlewings, Çeda walked side-by-side through the blooming fields with Emre. Both were armed, Emre with his bow and a long fighting knife, Çeda with River's Daughter, returned to her by Husamettín on the Night of Northern Winds, as the battle for Sharakhai had come to be known.

A full week had passed since the battle. She and Emre had been searching the groves for Sehid-Alaz ever since, but they hadn't found him. They hadn't found *any* of the asirim, nor had Çeda been able to sense them.

"Maybe they're dead," Emre said as they passed a particularly thick grove, "taken by the trees."

Maybe, but Çeda didn't think so. They were hiding from her, and the reason was plain enough—they were ashamed. They'd become so enraged that Macide and Çeda had been willing to fight alongside the Kings of Sharakhai, they'd betrayed them both, and many others loyal to them.

"It's more likely they returned to the valley," Çeda replied.

"Then we should go. We've spent enough time here."

They agreed that they needed to set the thirteenth tribe aright. Hamid had betrayed them. Worse, he'd led an insurrection that threatened to upend the Alliance Macide and Emre had worked so hard to build. They couldn't let that go on. The tribes needed to remain united, and to do that, they had to squash Hamid's militant dogma before it took root.

Men like Hamid would never admit it, but Sharakhai was a melting pot. So was the desert. The tribes were built on trade with other nations. Their culture was not *pure*, as some would claim, nor had it ever been. Purity had always been a fantasy, a way to exert power over others. There wasn't a tribe in the desert that didn't count amongst its people those who hailed from the grasslands of Kundhun or the mountains of Mirea or the temperate lands of Malasan or even the shores of the Austral Sea. But it went far beyond that. Whether it was recipes, customs, sailing ships, or the simple joy of being entertained, the lives of the desert's people had been enriched by neighboring lands, and those lands in turn had been enriched by the desert.

The time when nations could remain of themselves and only of themselves had long since passed. A new day was dawning in the desert. It was only a matter of how soon it was going to arrive.

Çeda had a secondary purpose in the valley. Nalamae was missing. Neither the Blue Journals nor Yusam's mere were available to her, but they needed guidance. Perhaps the tree and the visions it could grant could help. It was the only thing she could think of.

"One more day," Çeda said. "If we don't find them by nightfall, we'll set sail tomorrow."

Among the groves, tree after tree was gray and ashen, either dying or already dead. It was evidence of all that had happened: the trees slowly dying over time, the Enclave's magi sending tributes to their deaths after the asirim were freed, Queen Meryam's spell summoning hundreds more on the Night of Northern Winds. The grand web of trees around Sharakhai, a thing crafted through guile and trickery to allow the gods to pass to the land beyond, had once seemed as much a part of Sharakhai as Tauriyat, or the harbors, or its many neighborhoods. Now it was fragile and likely to fail.

"Do you think the trees are helping them in some way?" Emre asked, referring to Anila and Brama.

"I've no idea," Çeda said.

Through a gap between the groves, above the wavering black peak of Tauriyat, she could see the glimmering vault, which now stood between both worlds. They were surely still on the other side, working to save Sharakhai. But time was running short. Even with the power of the bone of Raamajit, they couldn't last forever, and the gods would not remain idle. They would already be working to undo the spell Anila and Brama had woven together.

They skirted wide of a grove when they heard the drone of a rattlewing nest inside it, then headed for another. After long days of hiking from sunup to sundown, they'd finally returned to the place where they'd left Sehid-Alaz on the night the crystal broke.

The adichara branches were still and unmoving. The blooms were closed. They stopped before the very tree that had wrapped its branches around Sehid-Alaz. Çeda knelt before it and pressed her right hand against the sand. She called on the power of the desert, the power of the trees, which had felt deadened since the night of the battle, and pushed as hard as she could, reaching outward, searching the nearby desert, but felt nothing.

She was reminded of the time she went to the blooming fields to learn once and for all whether she was the daughter of a King. She'd poisoned herself that night, a thing that had nearly killed her, but the Matron Zaïde had inked tattoos onto her hand and wrist, thereby hemming the poison in. She'd always been able to feel the trees to a degree, but the adichara's poison had made it blossom. She wondered, with the crystal gone, had the trees changed in some fundamental way? Was that why her senses had felt deadened since that night?

Knowing it was a risk, but feeling it was right all the same, Çeda held her left hand out to the tree.

Emre's eyes went wide and he snatched her wrist away. "Çeda, what are you doing?"

She calmly pried his hand from her wrist. "The poison can't hurt me anymore."

"You don't know that."

"Yes, I do."

And with that she focused on the tree. It was diseased, dying, and the branch beside her hand didn't move. She pressed the exact center of her palm against a large thorn, and only then felt the sting, felt the burn of the poison.

When she was young, after finding her mother hanging upside down at the foot of Tauriyat, she'd cut her hand, taken up a fistful of sand, and spoken a vow for the desert itself to hear. She did so again, but this time she spoke no vow. She whispered a plea instead.

"Come to me, Sehid-Alaz. Come, for we have need of you."

The bloody sand sifted through her fingers to fall against the gnarled roots of the tree.

She heard the wind gust through the adichara. Heard the sand as it sprayed against the leaves. She waited a long while, but the desert did not speak to her.

Çeda stood, saddened, and faced Emre. "It's done."

Emre put a hand on her shoulder and squeezed. "You did all you could."

Just as they'd taken their first steps toward the gap that would lead them from the grove, however, Çeda felt an awakening. She turned to see the sand churning, a head wearing a crown lifting up, Sehid-Alaz climbing from his sandy grave.

Çeda had always felt in awe when she'd been in his presence. No longer. He'd done a grave disservice to the tribe, and it showed in the way he looked at her. As she held his gaze, it was Sehid-Alaz who blinked first. His eyes dropped to River's Daughter.

"That you made it out alive," he said in his hoary voice, "brings joy to my heart."

"I made it," Çeda said, "but many others did not, including Macide."

"I know," was all he said in return, and it made Çeda angry.

"Have you no regrets?"

"I have too many regrets to count."

"You betrayed him."

"Because I thought he betrayed us."

"You were the King of our people in Sharakhai once. You thought to shelter us then, and in your own way, you thought you were doing so when you gave Hamid leave to kill Macide. But you must see, now, it isn't only the tribe that's threatened, but the desert. We must work to protect it. You, me, our tribe, and all the asirim."

For some reason unwilling to voice the words, he spoke within her mind, *I will always work to protect our tribe.*

"No," she said, then waved to the trees. "You will speak it to the adichara. You will speak your vow to the desert itself."

His gaze shifted from her to Emre and back. She knew why the ancient King was conflicted. He'd been forced to uphold the vows of others for four hundred years. He was worried that this would be more of the same—him becoming beholden to powers that would not negotiate, that did not see him as an equal—but she needed this from him, and she was certain he sensed it.

"I will work to protect our tribe," he said in his hoary voice, "for in doing so, I will be protecting all the people of the desert."

Çeda, judging him sincere, nodded once. "Emre and I are going to the valley to take our tribe back."

"The asirim cannot follow." He reached out and touched the tree that had nearly killed him. He did so lovingly, as if envisioning its final embrace and the peace he would find. "If we leave, the adichara will die."

Whether it was the poison working its way through her or some act on Sehid-Alaz's part, she wasn't sure, but Çeda realized she could sense more of the asirim now. She felt them all around the blooming fields, lying beneath the sand, sharing their strength with the trees.

When Sehid-Alaz turned back to her, there was grim determination in his eyes. "Go to the valley, Çedamihn Ahyanesh'ala." He turned to Emre. "Go, Emre Aykan'ava. Take the tribe for your own, for I've come to see it is now yours more than it is mine. But return quickly, for I fear the end is near."

The sand churned at his feet, and he was drawn down into the sand once more.

Epilogue

IN THE CABIN OF A YACHT, Meryam, once queen of two kingdoms, lay in her bunk as the ship sailed on. Where the ship was exactly, she had no idea. Somewhere south of Sharakhai, to be sure. Ramahd was intent on seeing her returned to Qaimir to host some sham of a trial. They would no doubt find her guilty, and in all likelihood she would be executed for trying to protect her country.

What did it matter, though, really? The world had changed. Once vibrant and full of color, it was now gray and lifeless. As she stared at the wooden beams above her, she recalled a spell she might use to make its surface rough. Modify that spell to a minor degree and it would make the wood brittle. Change it again, deepen it, and the wood would turn to ash in a matter of heartbeats.

She could once have traded guises with one of the crew, forcing them to remain here in her place while she escaped. She could once have cast an illusion and slipped from their notice, leaving them to search fruitlessly for her. She could once have commanded all of them to slit their own throats.

No longer.

Her magic had been burned from her.

You deserve it, a voice inside her whispered. *You deserve it for killing our father.*

"No, I don't," Meryam said. "We were so close to having everything."

That doesn't make it worth it.

"It would be worth it for Qaimir."

A gentle laugh. *You didn't do any of this for the kingdom, Meryam. You did it for you, for you, for you . . .*

The echoing voice faded slowly. It was Yasmine's voice, and she'd been coming to Meryam more often now that she'd lost her magic.

It isn't Yasmine at all, you fool. It's you.

She knew that too, but she didn't care. The ship slowed for the night and Ramahd came to unchain her himself while Cicio brought in a tray of food. Ramahd set it on the small table before her. "Eat, Meryam."

Her eyes drifted down to the bowl of thin, sugary gruel. To the almond milk in the clay mug. It made her want to vomit just to smell them.

"Is there nothing you'd like?" Ramahd asked. "I could make fekkas for you, sweet or savory, any flavor you'd like."

Meryam stared into his eyes. "If you mention fekkas one more time, I'll gouge your eyes out with my bare hands."

Ramahd's eyes went hard, then he and Cicio did what they'd done every other time she'd refused to eat. Cicio held her while Ramahd forced a brass funnel into her mouth. They gave her the milk and gruel while she tried to scream.

When they were done, her eyes were red, her throat was raw, and her belly was full. Cicio left while Ramahd chained Meryam back to the bed and followed him out. Meryam lay there for long hours, feeling nothing.

No, that wasn't true. She *did* feel something. She felt betrayed—not by Ramahd, he was just doing what he felt was right, nor by young Duke Hektor, now *King* Hektor, who was as ambitious as his father ever was. No, she felt betrayed by the goddess, Tulathan. She'd promised Meryam much.

"You promised me the Moonless Host."

Macide lies dead. Many others died with him. When will the ocean of blood be enough?

"I don't know," Meryam replied. "My will for it refuses to die."

Then stop using me as your excuse. Let me rest, Meryam. It's time you let me rest.

Meryam said no more, and neither did Yasmine.

Days passed, and the ship sailed ever southward. She found that she was putting on a bit of weight. She'd eaten little in Sharakhai over the months of her rule. By the end she was so thin she looked like a beggar—*any* amount of regular food was bound to put some meat on her frame.

She hated every dram of it. It felt like a betrayal to all she'd wanted, all she'd accomplished.

In the end, though, it didn't matter. Sooner or later Ramahd's vigilance would fade. Or she'd reach Almadan and her gaolers' attention would slip. One way or another she would find a way to kill herself. She refused to allow them to parade her before the court as they fawned over their precious new king, who would hardly know what to do with the throne that had been handed to him.

Then one day the yacht reached a caravanserai, Mazandir, most likely. It was too noisy to be one of the other, smaller caravanserais. Once they were docked, there came the sound of the crew, their boots thudding over the deck, of vendors hawking wares, and fierce haggling besides. Somewhere, a winch squealed endlessly, threatening to drive Meryam mad.

The day waned, and the sunlight slanting in through her small cabin window slid slowly across the far wall. Night arrived, and the hustle and bustle of the docks and the market was replaced with the sound of music and revelry. How odd, Meryam thought, that they could be so calm when Sharakhai is gripped in the throes of war. Soon enough those sounds faded too. Meryam was checked on one last time by Cicio. And then the ship fell into an easy silence.

Sometime later, Meryam woke to the sound of her cabin door clicking softly open. A dark form stole into the room and came to her bedside. A woman with long, curly hair. It was her scent that gave her away.

"Amaryllis," Meryam whispered.

"Not now, my queen," Amaryllis whispered back.

"You're risking much for a dead woman."

"You don't look very dead to me." She worked the locks on Meryam's manacles and had her freed in moments. "Now come."

They moved swiftly along the passage and upstairs to the deck, where two crewman lay face down. Alive or dead, Meryam wasn't sure, and she didn't have time to check. They made their way through the caravanserai to a small house on its outskirts where an old woman let them in—Qaimiran from the look of her. "My queen" she said, and closed the door quickly behind them.

Meryam and Amaryllis were led to a room on the second floor, where Amaryllis shared a most unexpected gift. Yasmine's necklace.

"I went to the cavern to see it for myself and found this around Brama's neck."

Meryam held it for long moments, rubbed the beads, long since worn from the nervous attentions she'd given it. It felt like a missing part of her had been returned. For several, wonderful moments she felt whole, but then the hollow of her lost magic returned and tears of bitterness came to her eyes.

"Thank you," was all she could manage as she slipped the necklace over her head.

For a week they remained with the old Qaimiri woman, though for Meryam it was much like being in the cabin of the ship. She remained in a lone room on the second floor. She ate, though this time it was of her own free will. Guards dressed in the livery of the caravanserai's master came twice, surely at Ramahd's behest, but the owner of the house knew the master well, and the guards confined themselves to the ground floor. Their search bearing no fruit, Ramahd's ship eventually departed along with two other Qaimiri ships he'd commandeered—to search for her in the desert, she supposed, or in another caravanserai.

"I think we're free," Amaryllis said to Meryam the next day.

"Free . . . I'll never be free again."

"You can be as free as you wish to be. I've gold and jewels enough to last a lifetime, enough to buy a ship. We can go wherever you will, my queen. You can retake your throne."

And what if I no longer want it? Meryam mused. *What then?*

The following day a wild tale reached them. Some in the caravanserai had witnessed a battle, a battle waged on the very same day she'd fought the elder Kings and the remnants of the thirteenth tribe. A woman with a shining white spear had fought with an ehrekh and won. The ehrekh had been trapped within a pool, and the pool itself had been transformed to glass.

Meryam went alone that night to investigate. With Tulathan shining high overhead, Meryam stared at the surface of the pool. It reflected the stars, mirror-like, and when she touched its surface, she found it to be solid, unmoving, and strangely warm . . . and within its depths was no ehrekh, but Goezhen himself, god of chaos, misery, and all creatures dark and foul. His chest had been pierced. Dark blood spread outward from the wide, open wound, as unmoving as Goezhen himself.

Meryam walked out onto the surface of the pool where she crouched and stared down into Goezhen's pained eyes. "A god trapped like a fly in amber." She half expected Goezhen to wake, for him to free himself from his prison and tear her limb from limb. When he didn't, she wondered aloud, "What happened?"

His boldness became too great, spoke a voice inside her head.

She knew immediately who it was, yet still she shivered when she turned and saw Tulathan in all her glory standing on the pool's lush, green verge. As she'd been on their first meeting in the Sun Palace, she was naked, her skin and her hair glowing softly silver. There was a different look in her eye, though. The last time she'd seemed almost amused by their encounter. Now she seemed intense, a fury burning inside her, perhaps because her brother god had been slain.

"It was Nalamae who slew him, was it not?" Meryam asked.

Tulathan nodded, then stepped onto the pool's surface. The scent that came with her was like autumn's first chill. *Thou bearest anger towards me.*

"I do not," Meryam lied.

Tulathan smiled and gestured to the desert around her. *I have heard it on the wind, heard thee fouling my name.*

Meryam paused. It wouldn't do to lie again to the goddess. "I was promised the thirteenth tribe."

The promise made was to grant thee the power to destroy them, and it was.

"No. In the end, it was *Rümayesh* who gave me what I needed."

Tulathan laughed, a sound like distant wind chimes. *And who dost thou think delivered her to thy doorstep?*

Meryam paused, thinking over all that had happened, how close she'd been.

Thy road is not ended, Meryam shan Aldouan. There are choices yet to be made.

"My road *is* ended."

Because thy power was taken from thee?

"Yes! My throne is gone. My magic burned from me. What's left?"

Whilst thou still draws breath, there is time to reach the end. There are wonders still hidden in the desert that one might use. One has but to find them.

"What power could give me what I want?"

Tulathan ambled around Meryam, slowly circling her. *In all thy searching, didst thou find no mentions of such? A creator abandoned as thou hast been abandoned? A soul lost as thou art lost?*

Meryam thought back. She'd read hundreds of accounts of strange artifacts and creatures of the desert. But none were powerful enough to alter the winds of fate, and even if they were, she had no idea where to find them.

Lost as thou art lost, Tulathan had said. An abandoned soul. What could she be referring to?

But then she stared down, and went perfectly still. Tulathan had used another word. *Creator.* Who was it that had created the desert gods? The elders. The elder gods had made them.

Seven by seven they came from the heavens. So the legend went. But there were whispers in the old texts of another, one who'd been cast down and left behind, just as the young gods had been left behind. In all that she had read, a lone name had been written in a single text. Ashael. He'd been struck down by Iri and abandoned as too dangerous, too malignant, to bring to a bright new world.

Tulathan's smile showed perfect teeth. *Very good.*

Spit formed in Meryam's mouth. It was all she could do to clear it. Those two simple words were as close to an acknowledgment as she was going to get.

Tulathan came to a stop and crouched, staring at Meryam like a child examining her first dragonfly. *Though I wonder if thou possess the will.*

"I do," Meryam said, feeling her old fount of anger and ambition returning. "I do."

Tulathan's silver eyes dropped to Meryam's neck. *If what thou sayest is true, thou must look ahead. Thou must leave thy past behind.*

Meryam reached up and touched the necklace that rested there. Yasmine's necklace. "Leave it behind?"

And admit the truth. Admit thy heart's desire.

Tulathan seemed to be waiting for something. Meryam was almost certain what it was, but she couldn't take that step. She needed Yasmine's memory now more than ever. The goddess seemed to sense her doubts. Her smile faded, and she stood and walked away. She'd reached the verge when Meryam cried, "Stop!" When Tulathan turned around, Meryam took off the necklace. "I can do it. I can leave the past behind."

And the rest?

Admit the truth. Admit her heart's desire. She felt Yasmine's cold, judgmental stare. *Stop using me as your excuse,* she'd said. *Let me rest.*

Staring into Tulathan's eyes, Meryam swallowed and nodded. "I did it for myself," she said. "Everything. It was for me all along. I wanted the power for myself. I want it still."

Tulathan's smile returned. *If thou speakest from thy heart, thou hast but to offer a token in sacrifice.* Her eyes drifted down to where Goezhen lay trapped. *The rest will follow.*

With that she turned and strode away, leaving Meryam feeling more vulnerable than she'd felt in a long while. She might not understand all that lay ahead, but she knew what Tulathan meant her to do.

She stared down at the necklace, gave it one last kiss. "Goodbye, Yasmine." Then tossed it onto the pool's unyielding surface.

There was a sound like breaking glass followed by a stomach-lurching sensation, and Meryam plunged into warm, fetid water. She coughed and spluttered and saw the necklace sink, growing dimmer and dimmer until it was lost to the pool altogether. Goezhen's yellow eyes, meanwhile, stared up at her.

She swam to the edge of the pool and stood where Tulathan had just been. The body of a god. Tulathan had just given her the body of a god. It was far from everything she would need, but it was a start. The rest lay in Sharakhai, in the countless tomes filled with knowledge. Between those two things she would have all she wanted, all the power she would ever need.

Walking away, Meryam smiled for the first time in a long while. They had thought to take the desert from her, but they didn't realize: the desert was hers now. Hers. And nothing was going to stop her from taking it back.

Appendix

aba: a loose, sleeveless outer garment woven of camel's or goat's hair

aban: a board game

abaya: long-sleeved robe worn by women, often with a headscarf or veil

açal: rattlewings, poisonous beetles

adichara: thorned trees that only spread their flowers in moonlight; their petals grant heightened awareness and strength

Adzin: a soothsayer, a "mouse of a man"

agal: circlet of black cord used to keep a ghutrah in place

Ahya (full name: Ahyanesh Ishaq'ava or Ahyanesh Allad'ava): Çeda's mother

akhala: rare breed of very large horse, "widely considered the finest in the desert"; "giants of the desert"

Al'afwa Khadar: a/k/a the Moonless Host; men and women from Sharakhai or the desert wastes, sworn to fight the Kings

Alamante: Ramahd's second after Dana'il

Al'Ambra: old set of laws the desert tribes had used for thousands of years; precedes the Kannan

alangual: half of a whole (couple), meant to "hold hands in the farther fields"

Alansal: Queen of Mirea

alchemyst: one who works in the ways of chemicals, agents, and reagents to produce magical elixirs

Aldouan shan Kalamir: king of Qaimir, Ramahd's father-in-law

Alize: one of Okan's riders in the Traverse

Almadan: capital city of Qaimir

Altan: a collegia student collecting the names of the thirteenth tribe, sent to his death by the blood magi, Nebahat

Amal: Çeda's best dirt dog student

Amalos: a master of the collegium

the Amber City, Amber Jewel: where Çeda lives, a/k/a Sharakhai

amberlark: a pretty bird with a lonesome call

amphora/amphorae: narrow-necked bottle/bottles

Anila: a necromancer who gained her powers when Davud used her as the source of a spell that went out of control

Annam's Crook: a peak in the Shangazi

Annam's Traverse: legendary horse race, held once every three years

araba: a horse-drawn carriage

araq: an intoxicating beverage with a strong smoky flavor

Aríz: shaikh of Tribe Kadri, cousin of Mihir

Armesh: husband of Şelal Ymine'ala al Rafik; "the man who'd done the most to shelter Leorah and Devorah after their parents had been killed"

ashwagandha: a healing herb

Ashwandi: beautiful, dark-skinned woman, sister of Kesaea

asir: individual asirim

the asirim: the cursed, undying warriors of the Kings of Sharakhai, members of the thirteenth tribe

Athel: carpetmonger, father of Havasham

Austral Sea: a large sea to the south of Qaimir

Avam: a cook with a food stall near the spice market

Bagra: physic of Tribe Rafik

Bakhi: god of harvest and death

Bahri Al'sir: a legendary adventurer, musician, and poet; a common figure in mythic tales of the desert

ballista/ballistae: a large crossbow for firing a spear

Behlosh: a male ehrekh, one of the first made by Goezhen

Beht Ihman: the night the Kings saved Sharakhai from the gathered tribes

Beht Revahl: the night the Kings defeated the last of the wandering tribes

Beht Tahlell: the holy day to commemorate when Nalamae created the River Haddah

Beht Zha'ir: the night of the asirim, a holy night that comes every six weeks. "The night the twin moons, Tulathan and her sister, Rhia, rose together and lit the desert floor."

Benan: son of Shaikh Şelal

Bent Man Bridge: the oldest and bulkiest of Sharakhai's bridges; crosses the dry remains of the River Haddah

Beyaz: a former King of Qaimir

Biting Shields: a nickname for the people of Tribe Rafik

Black Lion of Kundhun: Djaga Akoyo

black lotus: an addictive & debilitating narcotic

the Black Veils: of Tribe Salmük

the Black Wings: of Tribe Okan

Blackfire Gate: one of the largest gates into the old city; also the name of one of the wealthiest neighborhoods in the city

Blackthorn: Lord Blackthorn: pseudonym for Rümayesh as an opponent of Çeda's in the pit

Blade Maidens: the Kings' personal bodyguards

blazing blues: migratory birds that travel in great flocks, considered good luck

Blood of the Desert: bright red mites no larger than a speck of dust

Bloody Manes: a nickname for the people of Tribe Narazid

Bloody Passage: a massacre in the desert in which Ramahd Amansir's wife and child were killed

the Blue Heron: Ramahd's family yacht

bone crushers: the large, rangy hyenas of the desert

Brama Junayd'ava: a thief, Osman's "second story man"

breathstone: one of the three types of diaphanous stones; it needs blood. When forced down the throat of the dead, they are brought back to life for a short time.

Brushing Wing: name of Kameyl's sword

Burhan: a caravan master

the Burning Hands: a nickname for the people of Tribe Kadri

burnoose: a hooded mantle or cloak

burqa: loose garment covering the entire body, with a veiled opening for the eyes

caravanserai: a small village or trading post built on caravan routes; provides food, water, and rest for ships and their crews

caravel: sailing ship

Cassandra: a collegia student collecting the names of the thirteenth tribe in various records

Çeda (full name: Çedamihn Ahyanesh'ala): daughter of Ahyanesh, a fighter in the pits of Sharakhai, a member of the thirteenth tribe

Coffer Street: See: The Wheel

Corum: one of Ramahd's men

cressetwing: beautiful moth; also known as irindai (See also, gallows moth)

Dana'il: first mate of Ramahd's Blue Heron

Dardzada: Çeda's foster father, an apothecary

Darius: one of the Moonless Host

dasheen: edible roots

Davud Mahzun'ava: one of Tehla's (the baker's) brothers

Dayan: shaikh of Tribe Halarijan

Derya Redknife: female rider for Tribe Rafik; "thrice Devorah's age but also thrice the rider"

Desert's Amber Jewel: a common name for Sharakhai

Devahndi: the fourth day of the week in the desert calendar

Devorah: Leorah's sister

dhow: sailing vessel, generally lateen-rigged on two or three masts

Dilara: a blood mage and member of the Enclave, sister to Esmeray

dirt dog: someone who fights in the pits

Djaga Akoyo: Çeda's mentor in the pits; known as the Lion of Kundhun

doudouk: musical instrument

Duke Hektor I: the brother of King Aldouan, slain by Queen Meryam for treason

Duke Hektor II: the son of Duke Hektor I and the rightful king of Qaimir

Duyal: the shaikh of Tribe Okan

Ebros: one of the tribes; a/k/a the Standing Stones

Ehmel: was to have competed in Annam's Traverse but broke his leg

ehrekh: bestial creations of the god Goezhen

Emir: the king of Malasan, son of Surrahdi the Mad King

Emre Aykan'ava: Çeda's roommate, her closest friend since childhood

Enasia: see: Lady Enasia

Esmeray: a blood mage who lost her ability to use magic when the Enclave's inner circle burned it from her

Esrin: a blood mage and member of the Enclave, brother to Esmeray

falchion: short medieval sword

fekkas: a hard biscuit, can be sweet or savory

fetters: a length of tough, braided leather wrapped tightly around one of each fighter's wrists, keeping them in close proximity

the Five Kingdoms: a name used to indicate Sharakhai and the four kingdoms that surround the desert

The Flame of Iri: a/k/a the Sunset Stone; a giant amethyst

Floret Row: Where Dardzada's apothecary shop is

the Four Arrows: one of the oldest and most famous inns along the Trough

Frail Lemi: a giant of a man; suffered a bad head injury when he was young; is sometimes aggressive, sometimes childlike

Galadan: stone mason Emre sometimes works for

galangal: aromatic, medicinal rhizome of the ginger plant

gallows moth: beautiful moth; sign of imminent death but also, to those who know it as cressetwing or irindai, it is considered a sign of luck

Ganahil: capital city of Kundhun

Gelasira: Savior of Ishmantep; former wearer of Çeda's sword

ghee: clarified liquid butter

Ghiza: elderly neighbor of Çeda & Emre

ghutrah: a veil-like headpiece worn by men; an agal keeps it in place

Goezhen the Wicked: god of chaos and vengeance, creator of the ehrekh and other dark creatures of the desert

golden chalice of Bahri Al'sir: from Tribe Narazid to the winner of Annam's Traverse

Goldenhill: an affluent district of Sharakhai

Gravemaker: the name of King Külaşan's morning star

greaves: plate armor for the leg, set between the knee and the ankle

Guhldrathen: name of the ehrekh Meryam consults

Haddad: a caravan owner from Malasan

Haddah: the river that runs through Sharakhai, dry for most of the year

Hajesh: Melis's oldest sister

hajib: term of respect (not to be confused with hijab)

Halarijan: the tribe of Sim and Verda; a/k/a the White Trees

Halim: Lord of the Burning Hands (of Tribe Kadri); the tribe's shaikh

Hall of Swords: where the Blade Maidens learn and train

Hallowsgate: one of the twelve towers spaced along the city's outer wall; is "due west of Tauriyat and the House of Kings, at the terminus of the street known as the Spear"

Halond: a craftsman, wanders the desert looking for lightning strikes

Haluk Emet'ava: a captain of the Silver Spears, "a tower of a man" a/k/a "the Oak of the Guard"

Hamid Malahin'ava: one of Macide's men and a childhood friend of Çeda & Emre

Hamzakiir: son of Külaşan, the Wandering King

a hand: a unit of five Blade Maidens

hangman's vine: a distillation that can make one lose one's memories

Hasenn: a Blade Maiden

Hathahn: Djaga's final opponent in the fighting pits before she retired

hauberk: chainmail tunic

Havasham: handsome son of Athel the carpetmonger

Hazghad Road: See: The Wheel

Hefaz: a cobbler

Hefhi: carpet maker

Hidi: one twin fathered by the trickster god, Onondu; brother is Makuo. Hidi is "the angry one"

hijab: Islamic headscarf (not to be confused with hajib)

the Hill: where the Kings live; a/k/a Tauriyat

Hoav: driver who takes Ramahd to the inner docks

House of Kings: a collective name for the House of Maidens and the thirteen palaces on Tauriyat, the home of the Kings of Sharakhai

Hundi: the fifth day of the week in the desert calendar

Ibrahim: old storyteller

Ib'Saim: a stall owner from the bazaar

ifin: an eyeless, bat-like creature with two sets of wings, a creation of Goezhen

Irem: a spy for Hamid

Irhüd's Finger: a desert landmark; a tall standing stone

Iri: an elder god, called three times before the sun awoke in the heavens

Iri's Four Sacred Stones: a/k/a the Tears of Tulathan (Result of the breaking of the Sunset Stone)

irindai: beautiful moth; also known as a cressetwing, considered a sign of luck (But see also: gallows moth)

Ishaq Kirhan'ava: Macide's father and Çeda's grandfather, one-time leader of the Moonless Host, Shaikh of the newly formed thirteenth tribe

Ishmantep: a large caravanserai on the eastern route from Sharakhai to Malasan

Iyesa Külaşan'ava al Masal: Külaşan's dead daughter

The Jackal's Tail: smokehouse known as a seedy place

jalabiya: a loose-fitting hooded gown or robe

Jalize: a Blade Maiden and one of Sümeya's hand

Jein: Mala's sister

Jenise: a Shieldwife

Jewel of the Desert: Sharakhai

Jherrok: shaikh of Tribe Narazid, a tall man

Juvaan Xin-Lei: albino from Mirea and Mirea's ambassador to Sharakhai

Kadir: works for "a powerful woman," i.e., Rümayesh

Kadri: See "Tribe Kadri"

kaftan: alternate spelling

kahve: a bean, a stimulant when ground and brewed to make a hot drink

Kameyl: a Blade Maiden and one of Sümeya's hand

Kannan: laws written by the Kings and based on the much older Al'Ambra, the laws of the desert tribes

Kavi: a jeweler

keffiyeh: a cotton headdress

kefir: a milk drink

Kenan: one of the tribes

kenshar: a curved knife

Kesaea: a princess of the thousand tribes, sister of Ashwandi

ketch: small sailing ship

khalat: a long-sleeved Mirean silk outer robe

khet: a copper coin

Khyrn: see "Old Khyrn"

kiai: a percussive sound used when striking an opponent

King Azad: King of Thorns; makes mysterious draughts, never sleeps

King Beşir: King of Shadows, can move between shadows

King Cahil: the Confessor King, the King of Truth; known to be cruel

King Husamettín: the King of Swords and Lord of the Blade Maidens

King Ihsan: the Honey-tongued King, serves as Sharakhai's chief ambassador, known to be plotting and conniving

King Kiral: supreme among the Twelve Kings; "with burning eyes and pock-marked skin"

King Külaşan: the Wandering King, the The Lost King

King Mesut: the Jackal King, Lord of the Asirim

King Onur: once known as the King of Spears, more often referred to as the Feasting King or the King of Sloth

King Sukru: the Reaping King, controls the asirim through use of a magical whip

King Yusam: the Jade-Eyed King; sees visions in a magical mere granted by the gods

King Zeheb: the King of Whispers, rumored he can hear speech from far away, particularly when it relates to the Kings' business

King of Glittering Stone: appears in the poem; a cipher

King's Harbor: where Sharakhai's warships dock

Kirhan: Macide's grandfather

the Knot: a district in Sharakhai; a "veritable maze of mudbrick"

kufi: a hat

Kundhun: a kingdom west of Sharakhai and the Shangazi Desert, a vast grassland

Kundhunese: a people, a language

Kundhuni: adjectival form

Kydze: (f) one of the best fighters to come out of Kundhun since Çeda's own mentor, Djaga

Lady Enasia: Matron Zohra's companion

Lady Kialiss of Almadan: a dirt dog, one of Djaga's opponents

Lasdi: the sixth day of the week in the desert calendar

lassi: a yogurt drink

lateen: a rig with a triangular sail (lateen sail) bent to a yard hoisted to the head of a low mast

Leorah Mikel'ava al Rafik: Devorah's sister, Ihsaq's mother, Çeda's great-grandmother

Lina: a girl in one of Çeda's childhood memories

Lord Veşdi: King Külaşan's eldest living son; Master of Coin

Macide Ishaq'ava: leader of the Moonless Host

Mae: a qirin warrior in service to Queen Alansal of Mirea

Makuo: one twin fathered by the trickster god, Onondu; brother is Hidi

Malahndi: the second day of the week in the desert calendar

Malasan: a kingdom east of Sharakhai and the Shangazi Desert

Malasani: inhabitant of Malasan

Masal: one of the tribes; a/k/a the Shining Spears

Master Nezahum: a woman on the faculty of the collegium

Matrons: healers and trainers from the House of Maidens

Matron Zohra: an aging woman, owner of an estate in Sharakhai

Mazandir: a large caravanserai on the southern route from Sharakhai to Qaimir

Meiying: a powerful Mirean blood mage, one of the Enclave's inner circle

Melis: a Blade Maiden and one of Sümeya's hand, daughter of King Yusam

Meliz: former dirt dog, Djaga's mentor

Memma: like "mommy"

Meryam: Queen of Qaimir; sister of the murdered Yasmine, aunt of the murdered Rehann; a powerful blood mage

merlon: on a battlement, the solid part between two crenels

Mihir Halim'ava al Kadri: son of the desert shaikh of the Kadri, Halim

mind's flight: one of the 3 types of diaphanous stones; is said to bestow the gift of mind-reading when swallowed, though the imbiber dies rather quickly

Mirea: a kingdom north of Sharakhai and the Shangazi Desert

Mirean: adjectival form

the Moonless Host: a/k/a Al'afwa Khadar; men and women of the twelve tribes that once ruled the entirety of the Shangazi Desert; sworn to fight the Kings

Mykal: Ramahd's nephew and pageboy

nahcolite: a carbonate mineral, naturally occurring sodium bicarbonate

Nalamae: the goddess who created the River Haddah in the Great Shangazi desert, the youngest of the desert gods

Narazid: a desert tribe; a/k/a the Bloody Manes

Navakahm: captain of the Silver Spears, Lord of the Guard

Nayyan: First Warden before Sümeya, daughter of King Azad, Sümeya's one-time lover

Nebahat: a powerful Malasani blood mage, one of the Enclave's inner circle

Neylana: shaikh of Tribe Kenan

nigella seeds: a spice used in desert cuisine

Night Lily: a sleeping draught

Night's Kiss: the blade the dark god, Goezhen, had granted to Husamettín on Beht Ihman

Nijin: a desert harbor

niqab: veil made of lightweight opaque fabric; leaves only the eyes uncovered

Nirendra: a slumlord lady, rents space in rooms

Old Khyrn Rellana'ala: judge from Tribe Rafik

Old Nur: a shipmate of Emre's

Onondu: the trickster god, "God of the Endless Hills," god of vengeance in Kundhun; father of the godling twins Hidi & Makuo

Ophir's: the oldest standing brewery in Sharakhai

Ornük: Urdman's son

oryx: large antelope

Osman: owner of the pits, a retired pit fighter and a one-time lover of Çeda's

oud: a kind of lute

pauldrons: shoulder guards

Pelam: the master of games, the announcer for the gladiatorial bouts held in the pits

pennon: flag, pennant

Phelia: one of Melis's sisters

physic: a medical doctor

prat: an incompetent or ineffectual person

Prayna: a powerful Sharakhani blood mage, one of the Enclave's inner circle

Qaimir: a kingdom south of Sharakhai and the Shangazi Desert

Qaimiri: adjectival form

qanun: musical instrument, a large zither

Quanlang: a province in Mirea

Queen Alansal: of Mirea

Quezada: one of Ramahd's men

Rafa: Emre's brother

Rafik: one of the tribes; a/k/a the Biting Shields

Rafiro: one of Ramahd's men

rahl: a unit of currency, gold coins stamped with the mark of the Kings

ral shahnad: "summer's fire," the distilled essence of a rare flower found only in the furthest reaches of Kundhun

Ramahd shan Amansir: of House Amansir; one of only 4 survivors of the Bloody Passage

Rasel: Scourge of the Black Veils; former wearer of River's Daughter

rattlewings: see "açal"

The Reaping King: a/k/a King Sukru, one of the twelve; commands the asirim by use of a magical whip

rebab: a bowed string musical instrument

Red Crescent: a neighborhood near the quays of the western harbor

Rehann: Ramahd's murdered daughter, Meryam's niece

Rengin: footman on Matron Zohra's estate

Rhia: goddess of dreams and ambition, the sister moon of the goddess Tulathan

River Haddah: created by the goddess Nalamae in the Great Shangazi desert

River's Daughter: the name of Çeda's sword

Roseridge: Çeda's neighborhood

Ruan: half-Sharakhani man who works for Juvaan Xin-Lei

Rümayesh: a female ehrekh, one of the first made by Goezhen

Saadet ibn Sim: killer of Emre's brother, Rafa; a Malasani bravo

Sahra: Seyhan's daughter

Salahndi: the first day of the week in the desert calendar

Saliah Riverborn: a witch of the desert, the goddess Nalamae in disguise

Salmük: one of the tribes; a/k/a the Black Veils

saltstone: one of the 3 types of diaphanous stones; can be swallowed, but is more often
    sewn beneath the skin of the forehead. It slowly dissolves, bleeding away memories
    until none are left. The victim becomes completely and utterly docile

Samael: an alchemyst

Samaril: capital city of Malasan

Savadi: the seventh day of the week in the desert calendar, the busiest along the Trough

Sayabim: an old crone, a Matron at the House of the Blade Maidens, a sword trainer

scarab: a name for a member of the Moonless Host

schisandra: a woody vine harvested for its berries

the scriptorium: a kind of library

Sehid-Alaz: a King of Sharakhai sacrificed on Beht Ihman, cursed to become an asir

Şelal Ymine'ala al Rafik: shaikh of Tribe Rafik

selhesh: a term for dirt dog

Serpentine: a winding street in Sharakhai

Seyhan: a spice seller in the Roseridge spice market

a shade: a mission to ferry goods or messages from place to place in Sharakhai

shaikh: the leader of a desert tribe

Shal'alara of the Three Blades: one of the elders of the thirteenth tribe, a storied
    swordswoman and adventurer

the Shallows: slums

shamshir: curved saber having one edge on the convex side

the Shangazi: the desert, a/k/a Great Shangazi, Great Desert, Great Mother

Sharakhai: a large desert metropolis, a/k/a the Amber Jewel

Sharakhan: the language spoken in Sharakhai and much of the desert

Sharakhani: adjectival form

shinai: a slatted bamboo practice sword

Shining Spears: a nickname for the people of Tribe Masal

shisha: hookah

Sidehill: a neighborhood in Sharakhai, a nickname for Goldenhill

Silver Spears: the Kings' guard, the city police

Sim: works for Osman

Sirina Jalih'ala al Kenan: Mala's mother, a lover of King Mesut

sirwal trousers: loose trousers that hang to just below the knee

siyaf: term of respect for a master swordsman

song of blades: tahl selheshal; a/k/a sword dance

the Spear: a large street running from the western harbor to the gates of the House of
    Kings, "one of the busiest streets in Sharakhai"

the Standing Stones: a nickname for the people of Tribe Ebros

Sümeya: First Warden, commander of the Blade Maidens, daughter of King
  Husamettín
Sun Palace: the lowest of the thirteen palaces on Tauriyat, once belonged to Sehid-Alaz
The Sunset Stone: a/k/a The Flame of Iri; a giant amethyst
Sunshearer: King Kiral's sword
Surrahdi: the dead king of Malasan; a/k/a the Mad King of Malasan
Sweet Anna: a fragrant plant
Sword of the Willow: from Tribe Okan to the winner of Annam's Traverse
Syahla: Mihir's mother, Halim's wife
sylval: unit of currency
tabbaq: a cured leaf, commonly smoked in a shisha
tahl selheshal: song of blades, a/k/a sword dance
tamarisk: a tree
tanbur: a stringed instrument
Tariq Esad'ava: one of Osman's street toughs, grew up with Çeda & Emre
Tauriyat: Mount Tauriyat, home to the House of Kings, Sharakhai's thirteen palaces,
  and the House of Maidens
Tavahndi: the third day of the week in the desert calendar
the Tears of Tulathan: a/k/a Iri's Four Sacred Stones (result of the breaking of the
  Sunset Stone)
Tehla: a baker, friend of Çeda; Davud's sister
tessera, tesserae: tiles of a mosaic
Thaash: god of war
Thalagir: Rümayesh's new name, given by Brama
thawb: a common outer garment in the desert, consisting of a length of cloth that is
  sewn into a long loose skirt or draped around the body and fastened over one
  shoulder
Thebi: character in a tale of the god Bakhi
the Thousand Territories of Kundhun: another name for Kundhun, one of the four
  kingdoms surrounding Sharakhai
Tiller's Row: a street in the Shallows, "one of the few with any businesses to speak of"
thwart: a seat in a rowboat
Tolovan: vizir of King Ihsan
Tribe Ebros: one of the twelve desert tribes; a/k/a the Standing Stones
Tribe Halarijan: one of the twelve desert tribes; a/k/a the White Trees
Tribe Kadri: one of the twelve desert tribes; a/k/a the Burning Hands
Tribe Kenan: one of the twelve desert tribes; a/k/a the Rushing Waters
Tribe Khiyanat: the name the thirteenth tribe chooses when they form anew; khiyanat
  means "betrayed" in the old tongue of the desert
Tribe Malakhed: the ancient name for the thirteenth tribe, abandoned when the tribe is
  reborn
Tribe Masal: one of the twelve desert tribes; a/k/a the Red Wind
Tribe Narazid: one of the twelve desert tribes; a/k/a the Bloody Manes
Tribe Okan: one of the twelve desert tribes; a/k/a the Black Wings
Tribe Rafik: one of the twelve desert tribes; a/k/a the Biting Shields
Tribe Salmük: one of the twelve desert tribes; a/k/a the Black Veils
Tribe Sema: one of the twelve desert tribes; a/k/a the Children of the Crescent Moons
Tribe Tulogal: Devorah and Leorah's childhood tribe; a/k/a the Raining Stars
Tribe Ulmahir: one of the twelve desert tribes; a/k/a the Amber Blades

the Trough: the central and largest thoroughfare in Sharakhai, runs from the northern
    harbor, through the center of the city, and terminating at the southern harbor
Tsitsian: capital city of Mirea
Tsitsian Village: an immigrant neighborhood in Sharakhai
Tulathan: goddess of law and order, sister moon of the goddess Rhia
Undosu: a powerful Kundhuni blood mage, one of the Enclave's inner circle
Urdman: one of Narazid's riders in the Traverse
Vadram: Osman's predecessor in the shading business
Vandraama Mountains: a mountain range bordering the desert
Verda: works for Osman
Lord Veşdi: Külaşan's eldest living son; Master of Coin
vetiver: the root of a grass that yields fragrant oil used in perfumery and as a medicinal
vizir/vizira: a high official, minister of state
Wadi: Devorah's borrowed stallion
Way of Jewels: location in the city
the Well: a neighborhood near the Shallows; Osman's pits are there
western harbor: the smallest and seediest of the city's four sandy harbors
the Wheel: the massive circle where four thoroughfares meet: the Spear, the Trough,
    Coffer Street, and Hazghad Road
White Wolf: Çeda's moniker in the fighting pits of Sharakhai
Willem: a brilliant young man with strange magical abilities bound to the blood magi,
    Nebahat, in Sharakhai's collegia
wyrm: worm
Yael: mother of Devorah and Leorah
Yanca: Çeda and Emre's neighbor in Roseridge
Yasmine: Meryam's murdered sister, Ramahd's wife and mother of Rehann
Yerinde: goddess of love and ambition; once stole Tulathan away "for love"
Yerinde's Kiss: a honey collected from the rare stone bees' nests; used as an aphrodisiac
Yerinde's Snare: the convergence of a twisting, misshapen web of streets & the most
    populous district in Sharakhai
Yndris: a Blade Maiden with a hot temper, the daughter of King Cahil and an enemy of
    Çeda
Yosan Mahzun'ava: one of Tehla's brothers
Zaïde: a Matron in service to the Kings; heals and takes Çeda into the House of
    Maidens
zilij: a board Çeda fashioned from skimwood, used as a conveyance to glide easily over
    sand
Zohra: i.e., Matron Zohra, resident of an estate in Sharakhai

Acknowledgments

As always in the undertaking of such a large, painstaking endeavor, there are many people to thank for their help. First, a big thank you goes out to Paul Genesse. Thank you once again, my friend, for providing your keen insights into this book and the story overall. This series wouldn't be what it is without your help.

My publishers, DAW and Gollancz, provide tireless work and expertise to get these books onto shelves (both physical and virtual). To Betsy Wollheim, thank you for your continued guidance. I will always be grateful for your belief in this series. To Gillian Redfearn, thank you for your many insights into writing in general and on this particular book. To Marylou Capes-Platt, as ever, I appreciate your skill and insight into writing, not only in the art of brevity, but also the larger issues of continuity, character, clarity, and so much more. And to the DAW and Gollancz production, marketing, sales, and back office support teams, I thank you for everything you do. You are the unsung heroes of publishing.

I am indebted to my agent, Russ Galen, not only for this book, but for helping to ensure that the full series will see the light of day. Many thanks to Danny Baror and Heather Baror-Shapiro as well for your dogged efforts in bringing this series to readers all over the world.

Lastly, I'd like to thank you, the Shattered Sands fans. I continue to be blown away by your enthusiasm and your kind words. Thank you for coming on this journey with me.